Harmony Hill

Harmony Hill

by John S. Hall

Burlington, Vermont

Onion River Press
191 Bank Street
Burlington, VT 05401

ISBN: 978-1-949066-87-6
Library of Congress Control Number: 2021911862

Book design by Doni Hoffman
Cover art by Linda Hall

Dedicated to all the farmers I have known.

The town of Hayesville and its characters are a work of total fiction, with the exception of some actual Vermont locations and mention of the Ayrshire and Jersey farms. Any grain of truth comes from the author's life experiences as a farmer and his observations of human nature.

Chapter One

Jubilant Brown. Yeah, that was his name, but everybody called him Jubal. A young guy of sixteen, he was waiting on a hot summer afternoon in his folks' junky '34 Ford pickup. His ma, Rose, had stopped to buy Jubal's dad, Clyde, his supply of booze. Lately, the trip into town happened several times a week—a "beer run" as Vermonters called it.

They were parked right out front. A red sign with bold letters, *Hayesville Country IGA Store,* was nailed just under the eaves over the entrance. The store had a porch with a long bench regularly inhabited by old-timers, mostly men, who liked to gossip and swap lies about the glory days of their youth. Rose, originally from downcountry, was a snappy dresser with a nice figure and a likable personality that no woman in town could match.

As she passed, Clem Gochy, one of the bench sitters, yelled, "Here comes Rose Brown makin' her beer run."

Clem wore an old felt hat full of holes and a worn flannel shirt buttoned up at the neck. His bib overalls were frayed at the knees. He lived outside of town in an old rebuilt chicken coop with his common-law woman, Millie, whom he'd met in grade school. In his early sixties, Clem had worked on the roads for the town after prohibition and bootlegging ended. During prohibition days, he ran liquor from Canada. Most in town knew about it, but he never got caught.

Two other men seated with Clem, Oscar Smith and Charlie Jones, had walked to the store from the Hayesville Town Farm, a home for the poor and less fortunate. Clem and his buddies could usually be found sitting outside the store on any given afternoon when the weather was good.

As Rose climbed the wooden front steps, she certainly pumped new life into the tattered crew. She laughed as she saw their looks. "I'll slip you fellows a bottle or two of *Rheingold* on my way out."

They hooted in appreciation. But when she was out of earshot, through the open truck window, Jubal heard Clem's comment.

"Clyde Brown's a worthless bastard."

"I guess," Oscar said. A humped-up guy in a checked wool hat worn even in the heat of summer, he pointed a finger at his buddies. "Why is it that the nicest women always tie on to a loser for a husband?"

Clem was thoughtful. "Well, now Clyde and Rose were an okay couple years back, but my guess is Clyde couldn't handle a downcountry gal."

Charlie leaned forward and tapped the porch floor with his cane. "Baloney! Clyde can't handle the bottle!"

Jubal knew the bench sitters weren't the only ones that enjoyed seeing Rose Brown. The cashier inside the store, Bert Sausville, was in his forties and balding with a round face and a broad smile. Jubal suspected that his ma added a glint of joy to Bert's otherwise humdrum existence. Until recently Bert had been the owner of the IGA, and though the store had changed hands, Bert still appreciated the *Rheingold* profits. However, selling beer was in direct conflict with the beliefs of his wife, Bernice, who proudly headed up the Temperance League sponsored by the Hayesville Baptist Church. The conflicted Sausville household was fodder for a lot of gossip. Clem reported that Bernice and Bert slept in separate bedrooms. Clem should know since he had often caught threads of conversation between the Sausvilles that filtered through the store's screen door.

Bernice routinely claimed that the Catholic church down the street was loaded with drunkards and the Baptists' pristine purity up the street had the right ticket to heaven. They served grape juice for Holy Communion, while the Irish Catholics used wine.

Just that past winter, Clem had been privy to an especially heated conversation—a dispute regarding young Lizzy LaFlam—which took place when Bert still owned the store.

Bernice had whined, "What were you thinking, hiring that trash? Just trash! Mark my words, the good Lord will smite you and throw you into the fires of Hell. She's not a Christian! If you for one moment feel the sin of lust, you'll be damned."

Behind the checkout counter, Bert had roared back, "Bernice, in the name of Heaven calm down! She's a good kid trying to make it on her own."

"A good kid, huh! She's over-sexed. I know the type! You're probably enjoying seeing her bounce around, with her . . . her things freely jiggling."

"Oh stop it, Bernice! She can't afford fancy clothes like you and your Temperance friends."

"Well if that's the case, I'm sewing her a loose-fitting smock. She can wear it when she works here in public."

"Do it then. If that satisfies you."

Clem laughed, now holding court with retelling the story just outside the door. "Bernice can't stand seeing Bert gettin' his jollies up over Lizzy, but she's a good kid. As ya know, Millie and I helped raise her. And just look now at all the girl has done fer herself. She's a real go-getter!"

Lizzy LaFlam was Jubal's classmate. She had sharp features, pretty dark brown eyes, straight black hair, and a devilish smile for him.

Lizzy came from a notorious clan of outlaws who lived back in the hills outside of Hayesville. When Jubal and Lizzy were younger, at school she had been seated right behind him where she'd pestered him with spitballs and bits of eraser stuffed down the neck of his shirt. When the bell rang, on leaving class she sometimes bumped him with her hip and laughed, which immediately caused his face to turn red. One day she had even passed him a note, asking him to meet in back of the school to share a Camel cigarette she'd stolen from one of the guys. Jubal had crumpled the paper up in his hand and stuffed the note deep in his pocket. He had not answered the offer and instead took great pains to avoid her. He smiled to himself now, remembering. Recently Lizzy had matured in a hurry. He supposed she really had no choice considering her circumstances.

Jubal hated hearing the talk about his folks, though, and seeing his ma's joking manner, because at home the situation was no joke. However, Jubal admired the way his ma could bring the place alive, something he could never do. She amazed him. His dad had served them up a plate of burning nettles and she had the ability to sugarcoat the heap of pain. Jubal knew his ma was in misery over her husband.

Life had changed for Jubal when he was twelve—the time his ma came on a cold February morning to take him out of school.

She had told him, "You left early for school, and I left shortly after for work at Lady Lamont's. Benny was asked to help cut ice at the reservoir this morning. So no one was home but your father."

Benny was his ma's brother. He lived with the Browns and had significant intellectual disabilities, but he had unbelievable strength. When it was time to cut ice, the town called for Benny. Folks claimed he could spike ice with tongs and pull blocks out of the water like Hercules and, furthermore, Benny could keep it up all day.

As they drove, Jubal's ma fretted, "With everyone gone, your dad never milked the cows or fed the cattle and horses at chore time."

"No fooling!" Jubal had been stunned. "That's awful. I've noticed lately Dad hasn't been starting chores until seven or eight—he's lucky to get the cows milked in time for the can truck that comes around eleven."

"Right," his ma agreed. "But when I returned around ten this morning to do our weekly washing, I found your father dead drunk, lying on our bedspread with his manure-caked boots on."

As they sped across town, she mused, "This can't happen again! As of right now you're taking charge of the barn chores. I'll bring you late to school."

Jubal turned to her. "Why not sell the herd and horses?"

She kept her fierce brown eyes trained on the road ahead. "We can't sell. It's in the agreement with Lady Lamont that your dad signed when he bought the place."

Jubal felt conflicted and somewhat ill over his dad's neglect of the barn and farm. In spite of his father's flaws, he loved his dad. But leaving hungry animals unfed and chores undone, that was terrible.

His mother had torn up Harmony Hill and into the farmyard. As they got out of the truck, the barn sounded ready to explode with bellowing cows and the hoof stamping of hungry horses.

The scene was a bitter memory that Jubal didn't care to recall. He hoped his ma would come soon from the IGA. As he waited, he heard a car making its way up the gravel street. He turned to see the Styles' black Chevy. Noticing that his friend Maria was in the passenger's seat, he brightened. In June when Maria had been away at camp, he hadn't seen much of her, and no one had seen her since the July 5th parade two days earlier.

She and Jubal had been friends since way back in the first grade. Earlier that spring they'd worked together at the Avery Ketchum Farm. He always chuckled at her spitfire ways. She had stunning blue eyes with a look of determination when she faced a job like pitching hay. She could throw a forkful bigger and further than he could, and he was no wimp. Full of confidence, Maria often had a winning smile. Some guys called her a "knockout," even at fifteen, but he never thought of her as being sexy. Well, he agreed she was beautiful, though she went about in flannel shirts and baggy bib overalls, often having hayseed in her hair.

Her ma, Kathleen Styles, pulled in and parked right next to their truck in the only spot left in front of the store. The older Irish woman left the car in her usual loose print dress that fully covered her figure and a kerchief tied to cover her hair. She was tall and big boned, with a purposeful stride. As she climbed the store steps, the welcoming committee of town characters simply looked down at their boots with no comment. They knew not to joke with a woman like Kathleen.

After Kathleen was inside the store, Jubal quickly rolled down the window. "Hi, Maria!" He grinned, waving to get her attention.

Maria slowly turned his way. Her normally shining eyes were dull with little expression as she stared out the window at him as if he were nothing. The delicate skin around her eyes was purple and her lower lip was swollen.

Jubal whispered, "Maria!"

His normally vibrant friend sat pale and stiff in her family's car. This wasn't Maria. Not the Maria he knew. Yet it *was* Maria, changed from a warm summer day to winter.

When she wasn't working on the farm, she'd always worn her hair neatly combed and held in place with a barrette. Now her long black hair looked like it hadn't seen a brush; it hung in snarls. She turned away and rolled up her window, shutting him out, not even speaking. Then she sat like a stone. Gosh, he was sorry. Maria's strange behavior chilled him. He wished she would speak to him. Say hello or something?

He looked back at the store and saw his ma in the doorway clutching a brown paper bag full of beer. As Jubal and his ma headed towards home, he noticed a car with New York plates parked down the street at the Catholic rectory. He didn't often see the unusual color of orange and black in town among the Vermont license plates, dark blue with white numbers. He wondered who might be visiting the priest.

Chapter Two

In early April 1941, some months before Jubal saw Maria looking like death in her folks' car, his dad was plunked in front of his Philco radio listening to the morning news. The story came in a far-off voice, sounding like the commentator was talking into an empty box:

Possible World War II worries Americans. A tyrannical Hitler and his hunger to conquer has taken most of Europe. Will the United States be next?

"Crazy Hitler!" In his drinking corner, Clyde looked as if Joe Louis had just landed him a sucker punch.

Jubal wasn't worried about Hitler. He was worried about what was going on in the barn. "Dad, we're close to running out of hay. The cows and horses will be hungry. What are we going to do?"

Clyde fumbled for the volume knob to turn down the radio. Then he reached for the phone crowded in among the magazines and books on the table next to his chair. "Operator, get me Avery . . . Avery Ketchum."

Jubal waited in silence, watching the phone receiver shake as his dad pressed it to his ear. His dad sucked in a breath, trying to act sober, already on his second bottle of *Rheingold* laced with a generous amount of Jim Beam.

"Avery, ya there? My boy says we're . . . we're almost plum out of hay, feedin' chaff off the haymow floor." Clyde raised his free hand to steady the phone. "Okay . . . okay, it's a deal."

He hung up and gave Jubal his instructions. "I just bargained a week of yer work for all the hay ya can get on our wagon." He gulped more drink and smacked his lips. "Now, build a big load."

Jubal, with his slender six-foot frame and long blond hair, had adequate muscle to do a man's job and didn't mind working up a sweat. "Avery puts up good hay. I can't wait to get some home," he told his dad.

He knew his cash-strapped father had no choice but to use his labor to buy hay. A case of Jim Beam out of Rutland had taken a chunk out of the last milk check; the remainder went to pay overdue bills. For Jubal, the need for hay overshadowed any feeling that he was being used. Besides, he took pride in knowing he was holding the farm together, even as it teetered on the verge of failure.

After breakfast, Jubal went to the barn where he harnessed the team and backed them to the hay wagon. The wagon was substantial: twelve-foot long with an eight-foot headboard and a backboard built shorter to accommodate a hay loader. Just lately, he'd grown enough to have the strength to hook the last tug chain onto the whiffletree in the second link of the trace chain. In doing so, the taut four tugs raised the weight of the wagon's pole and neck yokes from the horses' collars—something his dad had taught him. Previously, Jubal had needed to call on Benny to connect the last tug.

To go along with his newfound adolescent strength, Jubal was wrestling with a weird dream he'd had recently involving Lizzy LaFlam. In it, he and Lizzy were rolling naked in an open-ended wooden barrel, her bare breasts pressed to his chest. He had awakened with a start. God, he thought, was there something wrong with him? Lizzy LaFlam, of all girls!

The team, Dick and Dan, were a medium-sized pair of Belgians, thin with rough coats. Currently they were fed only hay, with no oats or grain since there wasn't enough money to buy extra feed. His folks owned a third horse, Trueboy, a big strapping Belgian, so big he didn't match up well with the smaller horses. But Trueboy's size never bothered Jubal because the horse was as gentle as a purring kitten. Sadly, Trueboy was in the same shape as the team—thin and in need of some good feed. The big guy loved the attention he was seldom given, and he whinnied when the team left the barn.

When Jubal was just a kid, while on their way to hunt for beechnuts, he and his childhood buddies—Eugene, Polly, and Maria—would come across Trueboy in the pasture. All four would climb up to sit and "ride" while the horse grazed the field. After catching Trueboy by his halter, Jubal would boost Maria up first because she wanted to pretend to guide the horse. Little Polly was second, wrapping her arms around Maria's waist. Eugene with his long legs could grip the horse's broad midsection. Jubal would then lead Trueboy to a big rock, high enough for him to jump aboard to sit on the horse's rump. As the workhorse ambled around munching on grass, Jubal held tightly to Trueboy's tailhead to keep from falling off. When he was young, the ground was a long way down.

Those were fun times; however, as they grew older, the four kids became too big for Trueboy. They also didn't have much time to be together. Eugene had responsibilities at the mansion to help his mother, Lady Lamont. Maria worked for Avery Ketchum at his farm. And Jubal had more than enough to do on his family farm. Polly no longer wanted to be stunk up by a sweating horse and besides, when not in school, she and her mom listened to the afternoon soaps.

Feeling guilty about Trueboy's mournful whinny, Jubal quickly climbed up to stand in the empty wagon. He gathered the reins and clucked to the team. As the wagon lurched forward, he planted his feet so as not to lose his balance and drove the wagon the half-mile down the road to Avery's place. He hoped one big load of hay would be enough to make it to spring turnout time for the cows and horses. He left Benny behind to clean up the barn, since shoveling the gutters and sweeping the aisles was something Benny could easily do and he did it well.

The higher spring sun shone brightly in a cloudless sky. Melting snow left patches of bare ground in the pastures and meadows, seeming like holes in nature's winter blanket. Snowbanks beside the road were still substantial, especially where wind had drifted the snow that winter. An overnight rain had drawn the frost, and Dick and Dan's hooves kicked up thick clumps of mud inches deep on the gravel road. The wagon creaked on its axles, rolling on the downhill slope.

On ahead, a whitetail doe leapt across the road, plunging into the roadside snowbank and scrambling for solid footing. Her shedding winter hair revealed new chestnut growth as a coat for the summer ahead. Jubal slowed the team to allow the deer, trembling from winter weakness, to gather herself. She eventually made it onto the meadow to graze the sparse grass that had survived the long winter. He saw a robin bobbing on high ground and heard its song, a series of low whistling phrases—a sure sign of spring.

Turning into the farm, he could see Avery, a wiry old guy with a friendly personality, leaning on a new set of crutches. Maria stood at Avery's side waiting. Maria's dad, Chester Styles, was Avery's hired man, and she and her folks lived in the tenant house at the farm. From a distance he could see that Maria had tucked her jet-black hair under a red bandana. His feelings were mixed towards her. While he admired her no-nonsense style, he didn't exactly warm to her personality that seemed to always take charge. As a young guy, he wasn't sure just where he stood, though his ma had a similar take-charge way. Just the same, he liked Maria.

Polly O'Mara was his girl. Polly was into romance, feeling it important to have a boyfriend. Jubal and Polly liked kidding around and he felt protectively drawn to her innocence. They often took long walks in the evening and as the night turned to dusk, they'd sneak up his folks' high drive to the haymow where they'd end their night with some heavy smooching.

Polly often fussed, "I don't like this place" while picking strands of hay from her clothes and hair. "This awful hay!"

Jubal, embarrassed over the inside of his house compared to Polly's newer, more expensive home, was at a loss as to where to go for privacy. The junky truck was out, but he realized Benny's '36 Packard was perfect. When Lady Lamont bought a new Packard in 1940, she gave the '36 to his ma for her total commitment to the heiress in not only modeling for her paintings, but keeping house and preparing meals. As a special gift,

Rose then gave it to her brother, a reward for all his hard work done with no pay. Benny couldn't drive the Packard but kept it spotless inside and out. The car was almost never used. It sat parked and unregistered next to the barn. On their next date, Jubal planned to bring Polly to the car instead of the barn. Certainly, the interior of the classy Packard would live up to Polly's standards.

As the team trudged down Avery's driveway, Jubal couldn't help but notice the contrast of their neighbor's neat, well-kept farm compared to his family's place. Avery's bright red barn and two-story white farmhouse were in top condition. The house faced the road with the farm drive going between the house and barn. A line of century-old maples framed the yard, giving shade to the driveway and lawn. Avery owned the most prosperous-looking farm around. He was also known for his outstanding Jersey herd.

When Jubal and the team drew near, Maria smiled. In the early light, the freckles on her fair complexion stood out like sprinkles of brown sugar on white frosting.

"Hi, Jubal!" Maria pulled her hand out of the pocket of her overalls and waved.

Nodding hello, he gently pulled on the reins. "*Whoa. . . .*" The team eased to a stop.

She stepped closer to the horses and wagon. "So you've come for a load of hay?"

"Yeah, Dad sent me."

Avery raised a crutch, directing him. "Pull up next ta the barn right under the haymow door. It'll be easy loadin' with Maria's help." Avery paused. "Your horses stand okay?"

"Sure thing."

Driving past Avery to the barn, Jubal noticed the older man wore his usual Blue Seal feed cap pulled over his scruffy white hair. Avery, about sixty he guessed, was a talker, especially since he lived alone after his wife died. It looked like he hadn't used a razor for several days. Jubal expected it was because of a nasty scrape on the side of his face.

He parked the wagon and jumped off. "What's up with the crutches?" he asked.

"Oh, thrown from my new buggy." Avery reached for his leg and side. "Broke my leg and a rib or two."

"Wow, that's too bad! What happened?"

Avery motioned, "Come ta the barn and I'll tell ya 'bout my accident." As he hobbled along, he instead told Jubal excitedly of his plan to grow a large amount of corn, claiming, "Those yellow kernels mixed with chopped stalks will make lotsa milk." A crew of men were already at his farm, putting up two new silos.

As Avery rattled on about the corn, Jubal caught himself staring at Maria as she strode ahead of them into the cow barn. The way she walked in her muddy barn boots, she certainly was not "girly" like Polly.

Once inside, Jubal saw a row of Jersey cows with glossy hides—most were lying contented, chewing their cuds. He didn't see them standing, but they looked equal to the claim that Avery Ketchum kept an outstanding herd of cattle.

Avery proudly looked over his cows. "These gals will be milkin' first rate once I git my corn harvested."

From what Jubal could see, his cows were already treated first rate, stabled in the fresh smell of pine sawdust. The barn walls were chalky-white, recently sprayed and whitewashed with limewater. Light brown calves rested in the aisle in back of the cows, comforted by two cats curled against them for warmth.

"Come on with me," Avery said. Jubal followed him and Maria from the cow barn to the horse barn. As they walked, Avery began his tale. "Ya remember last summer, I lost a dandy pair a' horses? They was standin' head to head under a tree up on the ridge when a bolt of lightnin' struck—killed 'em both. Come early this spring I was lookin' ta buy a team. I left Chester, my hired boy Ned, and Maria to take care of the place while I was gone on a bus ta Lancaster, Pennsylvania.

"Seems I rode fer hours on a Greyhound ta reach the horse auction at New Holland—biggest I'd ever seen. Hundreds a' horses went on the auction block. That's Amish Country, ya know. Them folks farm with lotsa mules and horses."

Once inside the horse barn, Maria picked up a brush and entered the stall of what looked to be a well-bred mare. Another horse like it was in the next stall. She gently drew the brush down the mare's side while listening to Avery.

Avery pointed to the mares. "I always fancied ownin' a flashy pair a' Morgans. The granddaddy of the breed was Vermont born. And by golly, Morgans are some handy—fast, strong horses that can shine in a parade and then pull a plow all day.

"Well now, when I come to the auction yard, the place was crammed with Amish buggies. At the sales barn I was told they'd already sold a bunch. Amish men with beards, straw hats, and dark blue frocks all looked like birds perched on a telephone wire. They leaned shoulder ta shoulder on a rail, watchin' harnessed teams with a young kid on foot, runnin' and holdin' tight ta the reins." Avery paused to see if his audience was still listening.

Jubal was amazed to hear that such a place in Pennsylvania existed where everybody dressed alike and drove a horse for transportation.

"Seated high over the crowd, the auctioneer announced a startin' price fer the next team of mares. 'These girls have plenty of snap,' he sang out. An auction-house fella stood at each end of the passway with a whip. As the kid turned the team, one guy would *crack* his whip and off the horses charged ta the other end ta meet the second fella. *Crack!* Back and forth the team charged. Folks biddin' with the lift of a finger or tip of a hat. In minutes the team sold and the next entry was ready ta go. I tell ya, Jubal, I was dizzy tryin' to follow the doin's."

Avery winced a little, adjusting his crutches. "After an hour or so, this pair a' black Morgan mares, three-year-olds, pranced in. They was sired by General Gates, the famous 'Government' sire over at the US Morgan Horse Farm at Weybridge, right here in Vermont. They're a direct breedin' line right to Justin Morgan's horse Figure. Fancy harnesses came with this pair—all polished black, with bright red collar pads and brass knobs on the hames shinin' like mirrors. Their heads were up, ears pokin' forward, nostrils flared, and manes and tails flyin'. Them Amish never say much, but they all bent forward lookin' at this pair a' beauties.

"Them horses tore down the runway with that young kid holdin' the reins, his heels dug in, his backend near draggin'. He turned the pair and that guy snapped his whip . . . *crack.* Mister man, them black beauties flew lightnin' fast."

Jubal thought about the load of hay and edged towards the barn door. However, Avery pinched the elbow of his shirt.

"Biddin' started at two thousand. I couldn't step ta the rail . . . too crowded, but I was taller, seein' over a sea a' Amish straw hats. I went ta three grand ta brush off the competition. There wan't another bid. After a second of silence, the gavel went down. *Bang.* Sold!"

Avery hobbled over to the stall were Maria was now combing the forelock of the pretty black mare. "I named the new gals Sally and Di. When the trucker from New Holland come ta the farm, I puffed up some, seein' them Morgans walk off inta the yard. He also delivered a fancy two-seater buggy I'd seen ta buy.

"Maria's taken to 'em all natural-like, passin' treats and talkin' in a calm voice. She works 'round them horses as if they was newborn babies. Ned, my hired boy, polished the carriage."

As Avery talked, Ned stood in the background. Jubal had hardly noticed him. Ned lived in a room at the farmhouse. About sixteen, he had a hollow chest and uncombed hair. It was common knowledge that Ned left school in eighth grade.

Avery continued, "I commenced ta thinkin' folks would see me dressed in my Sunday best, drivin' them mares and that shiny black buggy in the parade this summer. Miss Curry at the library says she'll ride with me.

"July's a long way off, but I wanted them horses calm and trained good. So I thought I'd take a short ride." He paused and grinned at Maria. "Ya know, the parade's goin' ta be special this year 'cause Maria'll be ridin' in the back of a pickup all decked out, holdin' a bunch of red roses. Did ya know, she's been chosen as St. Anne's Catholic Rose Queen?"

"Really!" Jubal tried to imagine Maria dressed as a queen.

"I'm not nuts about it." Maria shrugged, holding some grain in the palm of her hand to feed Sally. The mare collected the treat with her lips and flicked her ears forward, expecting more. Maria ran her hand over the horse's back and rump. Then she went to the next stall to do the same for Di. She glanced back towards Jubal, changing the subject from Rose Queen to horses. "They weren't so calm when Avery took his first ride."

Avery interrupted. "I guess not. I sat in my carriage while Chester and Maria hooked the traces. The mares was actin' a little nervous—snortin' and treadin' in place.

"Ned was watchin' at the barn door, leanin' on the handle of a barn shovel. I was ready ta go, holdin' the reins when Ned spotted a mouse enterin' the barn. He slammed the flat of the shovel on the floor just inside the door, missin' the dang mouse. Hearin' that *bang,* the team reared free and off they charged. The reins slipped from my hands. All I could do was hold on! Them horses headed fer the open field in back of the barn, plowin' through a foot of spring sugar snow as if it was nothin'. Hooves and buggy wheels were kickin' up meltin' snow as I held tight in a storm of spittin' slush. I was livin' a ride I feared would be my last."

Maria chimed in, "I ran as fast as I could, hoping the horses would tire and stop when reaching the deep snow next to the hedgerow."

Avery continued, "I was soaked—cold and wet, holdin' tight ta my seat. Through the watery glaze, I spotted bare land where wind had cleared the ground. Not havin' ta traipse through snow, the team picked up speed, runnin' flat out. My hat flew off while the ride was practically bouncin' me outta my seat. Suddenly I caught sight of a big stone up ahead. Sure as shootin', the left buggy wheel hit that boulder straight on and I shot outta that rig like a jumpin'-jack outta a can. When I landed face first on the frozen ground, I heard all kinds of bones snap—then my lights blinked off. Out cold."

Maria shook her head. "When I reached him, I thought he was dead . . . face bleeding, his eyes rolled back. Finally, he came to and groaned. 'I'm busted real bad,' he said."

Avery wiped his mouth. "Hurtin' like never before when I come to, all I could think on was the fact I'd spent near four grand on them horses and rig."

"Then what happened?" Jubal asked.

"As expected," Maria explained, "the horses ran out of steam when they hit the deep snow at the far end of the field." She patted Di's rump. "I yelled to Dad, 'Come with the Percherons. Have Ma call the funeral home for the hearse to double for an emergency vehicle. Slide my mattress onto the work sled. Bring plenty of blankets. And quick!'

"It seemed to take forever for my Dad to come with the work-sled. Avery was shaking, lying on frozen ground. All I could do was cover him with my barn jacket until the mattress and blankets came."

Avery took the weight off his right side and leaned on one crutch. "Of course, Ned ran and hid when the team broke free, knowin' he'd caused the whole mess."

Jubal watched Ned turn red and slip out of the barn, as insignificant as the mouse that got away.

Avery turned to Maria with a smile. "Maria was my life saver. She practically runs this place . . . a real smart gal."

"Well, someone had to help." Maria ran her hand down the full length of the mare's silky tail, but quickly stepped to Avery's side when he suddenly wobbled on his crutch.

Avery grabbed her arm for balance. "Yup, my legs were numb and it felt like I had an arrow stuck in my side. But Maria was amazin', gettin' me onta that mattress with her dad helpin' ta slide me onta the work sled. She's a capable young gal and by golly, the church made a real good choice, havin' her ride in the Catholic youth float as Rose Queen."

She scowled. "I don't want to do it, but my dad and mom are making me. Me, in a dress?"

"We're all proud of ya!" Avery nodded. "Maria's ma has already bought the stuff to sew a gown."

Jubal looked at Maria, thinking she was like a hard-shelled egg—once hatched, she'd be a beautiful Rose Queen. "I can't wait to see you in a fancy gown. I'll bet you'll be the star of the parade."

"Yeah, okay!" She winced and abruptly turned in disgust. "Let's get your wagon loaded."

When they entered the dark mow, the sweet-smelling hay, mostly the previous June's grass and clover, was far better than any hay Jubal was feeding. The hay at his own barn was late-cut and smelled like stale bread—when he handled it, dust and chaff stirred in the air, sending him into a coughing spell.

He and Maria climbed a ladder to a higher level in the mow, forked the hay down onto the bare floor near the hay barn door, and then jumped onto the pile. Maria gripped the end of the hayfork handle and pushed the three tines into the hay, using her strong arms and legs to move the pile. Jubal pushed as well, but had to scramble some to keep up. He felt like a slack horse in a team's effort to move a heavy load. Although they had a large mound in front of them, the pile easily slid over the worn, polished floor. They continued shoving the hay out the door and into the wagon, building a big load.

The two worked without saying much. As they labored, Jubal tried to imagine Maria acting the part of a regal queen. "So, how did you get to be Rose Queen?"

She continued throwing forkfuls of hay. "I don't know. I guess because I didn't miss any catechism classes and always knew the answers when Father MacMurray called on me. We all call him Father Mac."

"I don't suppose your good looks had a thing to do with this guy, Father Mac, choosing you."

Maria offered no comment, staying focused on the work at hand.

Jubal imagined that Maria could easily pass for twenty all dressed up, even though she was only fifteen. At school, he and his friends sometimes kidded her that she had the looks of actress Gloria Swanson with the determination of Eleanor Roosevelt.

Maria stayed quiet as they worked, and the wagon seemed to fill in no time, until the load rose several feet above the headboard. When he drove the team home, he'd have to sit high with feet braced on the top crosspiece.

"We're loaded," he announced.

Hay chaff had landed on the rumps of Dick and Dan while they patiently stood in place. He climbed down off the load and swiped the chaff off the horses, giving them a handful of the sweet-smelling hay—like candy to them.

Maria motioned. "Let's go to the milk house and get a drink."

In the milk house, forty-quart cans, milking machine pails, and buckets were tipped upside down on pipe racks. Jubal noticed the familiar smell of chlorine used as a disinfectant. The small room included a boiler for hot water and an eight-can milk cooler that hummed as it cooled the morning's milk. Maria drew water from a faucet connected to the wash sinks and passed Jubal a cup. As the cool water soothed his dry throat, it seemed even Avery's water tasted better than the water at his house. After the drink, he slapped his Red Sox cap on his knee to rid it of hayseed, and then he took off his flannel shirt, removing bits of hay.

Maria slipped off her red bandana, shaking it free of stems and seeds. Her long black hair lay over her shoulder. While buttoning his shirt, Jubal watched her roll her hair into a knot, cover it again, and tie the bandana.

"I've got some hay scratching my neck." She moved her shoulders as if uncomfortable. "Something back there is bothering me."

"Sure, let me look." He found a dried stem down the neck of her shirt. He'd never been that close to Maria in a helping way. She didn't object to his hand as he removed the short stem. "There . . . feel better?"

She rubbed her neck. "Yeah, it does. Thanks."

They left the milk house and Jubal climbed the headboard of the wagon. Reins in hand, he gently nudged Dick and Dan with a cluck of his tongue and a light tap on their rumps. The team dug in and moved the load towards the road and home. He waved. "I'll be down week after next to help with the plowing to pay Avery for the hay."

She waved back. "I'll see you later."

It was a hard pull for the horses going home up the steep muddy road, but he rested them several times. They made it to the farm by noon.

⁂

Maria watched Jubal leave the yard, thinking that his poor horses looked rough, skinny, and in need of some good feed. When and if he came again with his team, she would get her dad to trim their hooves. She could at least do that so the horses wouldn't be working in what she thought of as oversized boots while having to pull a heavy load.

As the wagon moved slowly up Harmony Hill, Avery hobbled from the barn. "It's a big jag you kids put on."

"Jubal said he'll need it to go until turnout time."

"'Spect so. I got the best of the deal, though. A week of his work. Golly, he's growed since I last seen him. I've sorta lost track of what goes on up at the Brown place."

"Yeah, well he works the farm on his own. His ma's hired by Lady Lamont at the mansion, and he has the care of his ma's brother, Benny. You know, Benny isn't quite all there."

"Yup, seen Benny a couple times in town. And I did hear tell that Jubal's dad is drinkin' that place clear inta the ground."

The wagon grew smaller and smaller, leaving deep tracks as it neared the top of Harmony Hill.

"Watchin' those wagon wheels sink, it's mud season all right," Avery commented. "First best day of sugarin' season. Warm sun'll make the sap run plenty." He scanned the sugar bush at the edge of the field. "My dad was inta sugarin'. I'll tell ya, I sure wan't! Snowshoein' through the woods tappin' maples with a hand drill, drivin' spouts and hangin' buckets."

Maria looked at the maples that lined the farm drive. "Did you tap these old trees too?"

"Sure did." Avery looked fondly at the big maples. "These were easy ta get ta. Those in the woods wan't so much fun. My dad had ta tap every maple in sight. Ya know, he was an old Yankee—leavin' an untapped maple was a squander. He said a thousand times, 'Waste not, want not.'"

"Sugaring sounds like fun," Maria said. "We ought to do it."

"Maria, ya ain't listenin'. After ya tap, ya got ta wallow through the snow collectin' sap. Then stay up most nights boilin'. If it's a big run, ya might go days on two or three hours sleep."

Sleepless nights didn't phase her. Sugaring still sounded like something she'd enjoy.

Avery studied the melting snow under the noonday sun. "Yup, sap would sure run today. I'd like ta be young again."

As Avery hobbled away, Maria noted what a tough old bird he was, as well as having a heart of gold. She made a mental note to wander to the old sugarhouse down in the woods after evening chores to investigate more fully.

Chapter Three

While in school during the following week, Jubal dreamed of driving Avery's Percherons pulling a plow. He marveled at the old farmer's wealth to own two quality teams. Whereas, his dad hadn't turned a furrow since his early days in farming.

After Lady Lamont's father and mother had passed away, she'd divided up the estate. She sold one parcel of land to Polly's folks, Andrew and Trudy O'Mara, where they built a modern single-story home. She sold the dairy farm to Jubal's dad when he was his early twenties. As a faithful worker for the Lamont estate, Clyde was able to buy the land, barns, and cattle through a promissory note held by the heiress.

Lady Lamont's father had built the farmstead as a wealthy man's hobby, using only the best available materials. The red barn had a high-drive haymow over the stable. The stable was made of masonry walls with glass blocks between the windows to allow for plenty of light. The white farmhouse had a boxy appearance and a long front porch. However, in the past twenty years his dad had done nothing for upkeep. The buildings were peeling paint and the porch sagged, having begun to pull away from the main house. The whole place looked like it needed a friend.

At the time of the farm purchase in the early 1920s, Clyde had enjoyed high milk prices—agriculture was booming. But the good times were short-lived. On October 24, 1929, the stock market crashed and milk prices fell like a rock. A forty-quart can of milk was next to worthless, bringing less than fifty cents.

After that, farming was too much for Clyde. His milk income was scant, so he was not able to keep up with his bills, even though Lady Lamont had waived his payments. Clyde started drinking bootleg liquor, provided by Clem Gochy, to ease the pain of a measly income and relentless hard work. Though Jubal's dad drank heavily, he never spoke a mean word to anyone. When drunk, he acted like a sun-drenched mushroom, melting into his easy chair.

The O'Mara family lived within easy walking distance from the farm but had never been neighborly. They were among the rich upper class in Hayesville, and Jubal's family was, so to speak, in the mud, sucking swamp water. When Jubal mentioned to Polly he'd be helping Avery with spring plowing, she thought he was nuts to be so excited about doing work on Avery's farm, especially with no pay. With a high degree of disgust, she told him he was going nowhere if he worked for nothing. He kept the fact to himself that his working for Avery was pay for a load of hay. In no way did he want to tell his gal that his dad was dead broke and their livestock were hungry.

The first morning of Jubal's April vacation, he rode his bike down Harmony Hill to Avery's place. The warm mid-April days had finally melted all the snow. Maria and her dad already had the Percherons hooked up to a two-way sulky plow with a seat. A second identical plow, one Avery had just bought, was planned for his new team. Sally and Di were prancing in place, nervous to be hooked to the strange-looking contraption. Though the two horses were lightweight compared to the stocky Percherons, Morgans were known for the endurance to work all day.

"Plow the whole thirty acres," Avery instructed. "There ain't one stone I know of in the whole piece 'cept fer the one on the hummock my buggy wheel struck." He looked down at his crutches and back at the field. "And after plowin', I want ya kids ta yank that confounded stone and put it on the hedgerow."

Jubal led the way to the field, which was almost a perfect rectangle. Maria and he would be plowing the longest distance from the farmstead to the end that bordered a field road leading onto Harmony Hill. With a handle, Jubal set the right-hand plow for medium depth and the Percherons pulled, rolling the furrow towards the hedgerow.

Maria tried to make the Morgans follow, but Di, the right-hand mare, wouldn't walk in the deep furrow. She jumped in and out, laying fresh earth in the shape of a snake. By the time the team reached the end of the field, Sally and Di had settled down, mostly due to Maria's ability as teamster. Her gentle voice relaxed the mares and her hands were steady on the reins, telegraphing the message that they could trust her. On Jubal's next pass back to where he'd begun, he was able to somewhat straighten the crooked furrow.

The work was fairly easy for the teams, turning the sod and soil of a fine sandy loam. They plowed all morning, leaving long, neat furrows like a dark blanket of ripples. At noon, they drove back to the horse barn to water the horses and then tied them in the shade for a rest. Jubal and Maria went to the tack room where they sat to eat their lunch on a grain box big enough to hold several hundred pounds of grain. Large hooks lining the walls held various harness parts. Harness soaps, a leather punch, copper rivets, and strips of leather were stacked on a small bench against one wall. Above the bench, a window faced the yard. As they ate, the distinctive smell of horses and leather blended with their sandwiches.

Maria shared her lunch since Jubal hadn't brought much other than a jar of tea and a peanut butter and jelly sandwich. Her mother, Kathleen, was a good cook. He especially enjoyed a piece of yellow cake with chocolate frosting. He placed the empty tea jar in his paper bag and leaned back against the wall.

"I've been looking at that stone each time we pass by. Moving it like Avery wants might be impossible." He pushed a lock of long hair from his forehead.

Maria chuckled.

"What's so funny?" he asked. What was she looking at? Did he have dirt on his face? Peanut butter?

"Your hair . . . you wear it like a girl."

"I don't! I've always had long hair." He took off his Red Sox cap and pushed the blond strands further towards the top of his head. "There, is that better?"

"Well, if you like it hanging below your collar. Let me cut it sometime. I give Dad his haircuts."

Jubal shrugged. "I don't know. I'm used to it this way."

"If you cut it," she teased, "I could claim you as a guy friend instead of my girlfriend."

Jubal was surprised to feel Maria's words get under his skin. Nobody had ever mentioned his hair before, especially a girl. His folks hadn't. Polly hadn't. He adjusted his cap again, trying to cover any long hair that showed. "My hair shouldn't matter." He looked grumpily out the window and wanted to leave the little room to get back out on the plow.

She poked him in the ribs. "Aw, I'm just kidding."

He softened. Was she flirting with him? He couldn't be sure, and anyway, Polly was his girl.

Through the dusty window they could see Avery leave his house and hobble towards them on his crutches. When he made it to the horse barn, he leaned into the room where they were still sitting on the grain box.

"From the looks, ya kids are doin' a corkin' good job."

Just then a car sped into the yard, slinging gravel and dust as it came to an abrupt stop. It was Hayesville's part-time sheriff, Tatum O'Mara, who happened to be Polly's uncle. A man about town, Tatum also worked as a chauffeur for Father Mac and as a handyman for the local St. Anne's Catholic Church. What did he want? Jubal narrowed his eyes. Polly's uncle was a jerk.

Tatum got out and slammed the car door. Then he leaned against the vehicle and looked towards the barn. Jubal and Maria watched through the grain room window.

Avery gimped towards him. "What's up Tatum?" Next to the sheriff, who was impressively tall, Avery looked even older than his years curled over his crutches. "Thought you'd be fishin' out at the reservoir on a nice day like this," Avery said.

"Went this mornin' before work. Fish ain't bitin'." Tatum tipped back his felt fedora to reveal a square jaw and pockmarked face. "That Brown kid around?" He drawled "around" and the word hung in the air between the two men like a challenge.

Avery glanced towards the barn window. "What's the problem?"

"Someone's been drivin' Benny's Packard."

"So?"

Jubal jumped quietly off the grain box, sneaking into an unlit horse stall where he crouched down in the hay. Maria saw his reaction and slid off the grain box also, listening silently by the door, poised like a cat smelling a rat.

Avery spit on the driveway not too far from Tatum's shiny shoes. "It's pro'bly Benny been drivin' his own car!"

"Benny ain't got the smarts to drive," Tatum scuffed some dirt over the spot where Avery spit. "My niece told me Jubal is workin' down here."

"Yup. But he rides a bike. He ain't drivin' yet," Avery said.

Tatum shook his head. "Yeah, well them Browns are trouble. Clyde's drunk most days, and we all know about the kid's ma, Rose. As the sayin' goes, apples don't fall far from the tree."

Avery chuckled. "Heard tell years back, ya was acquainted with Rose better than most in town."

"That's cheap talk!" Tatum squinted at the barn as if trying see through its walls.

Jubal shrank further into the stall corner as the sheriff's voice boomed. He could still see all that was going on through the open stall door.

"I wanna see the kid. Anyway, this ain't no place for him, bein' around our CYO Rose Queen. I know you got her workin' here."

Tatum's last comment must have set a fire under Maria. She sprang through the horse barn door. "You're awful!" she shouted across the drive. "Jubal's my friend."

Tatum stepped back in surprise at the girl bursting from the barn. He growled, "He comes from a lousy family and he ain't Catholic!"

"That doesn't matter!" Maria walked up to the sheriff and stood with her hands on her hips.

Tatum looked her up and down. "It matters to Father Mac. He don't want a heathen kid hangin' around his Rose Queen."

"Oh, really!" She stepped closer. Jubal could picture her fiery glare. He was surprised by her fierce defense of him. "You go back and tell Father Mac that the church can't pick my friends!"

"But—" Tatum was speechless in the face of the fuming Irish girl.

"But nothin'," Avery chimed in, "Ya'd better go back ta fishin' 'cause ya ain't catchin' nothin' here."

Avery and Maria stood side by side, a united front. Jubal was glad he wasn't out there under the angry look Tatum cast upon them both before he hitched up his gun belt and turned on his heels. Once in his car, the sheriff backed out and spun off as rapidly as he'd arrived.

After Tatum left, Jubal came from the stall, brushing sawdust and bits of hay from his knees, thankful to have escaped the law's examination. One night recently, just for the fun of it, he'd driven Benny's Packard without a license to give Polly a ride through town. She was scared to death they'd get caught, so he turned around and drove back home. However, Jubal really didn't think the sheriff cared about him driving Benny's car. For one, Tatum just liked hassling the Brown family. And he figured Father Mac had sent Tatum to deliver the priest's message: "Stay away from our CYO Rose Queen."

That night after Tatum's visit, Maria was getting ready for chores in Avery's milk room. She yanked a can off the pipe rack and banged it on the cement floor, slamming a strainer on top of the can. She pulled two milker pails from the rack and slammed on the covers.

Avery came checking on all the racket. "What's goin' on in here, Maria?

She whirled around. "I'm mad!"

"Well now . . . calm yourself. What's the big trouble?" Avery inched into the milk room on his crutches.

"I *don't* want to be Rose Queen! It's the dumbest idea Father Mac could ever dream up! If he thinks he can control my life, forget it!" She yanked a wash pail off the rack.

Avery balanced with one crutch as he rubbed his chin.

Maria figured Avery thought she should be grateful for the honor of being selected as Rose Queen. Well, to her it wasn't an honor but rather one big embarrassing pain in the neck.

"Father Mac is using me," she continued, "wanting me as his example of purity, the perfect Catholic girl who has never committed a mortal sin! I'll tell you, next Friday at confession I'll give him an earful. I'll make up a bunch of stuff about how I've been raising holy hell with Lizzy LaFlam!"

Avery put up his hands as if calming his spirited Morgans. "Easy . . . slow down. It ain't all that bad."

Maria continued her rant. "That big shot sheriff—what a jerk! Our Holy Father, huh! He just wants to put on a show for the parade. As Rose Queen, I would be the main attraction."

Avery sat on a milk can and rested his hands on his knees. "All fancied up in a gown, I 'spect ya might be. Ta tell ya the truth, Tatum irked me too, him comin' onto my farm on some kinda tear. No offense, but I could never warm ta the Catholic church and all their rules. 'Course, I'm a home Baptist. Never got all wrapped up in the hereafter."

Maria pulled the milk hoses from the sink, connecting them and the teat cups onto the machines. "I'd like to tell Father Mac I'm not going to be his stupid queen. He can find someone else. Polly O'Mara would love it, even though she's got her hooks into Jubal and isn't as pure as she seems."

"Polly O'Mara. . . ." Avery paused. "Ya mean Andrew and Trudy's girl? Lives in that new fancy house up on Harmony Hill?"

"Yeah, she's the girl. She's been selected junior counselor for CYO camp as the nurse's helper. Since her folks are big shots in the church, Father Mac had to find something for her to do."

"She's just a kid. She ain't no queen material. Now mister—ya get dressed up all fancy and ya'll look the part of a queen."

"Thanks, Avery, but no thanks. I still don't like the idea."

"Now, yer folks are countin' on this. Ya're their pride and joy. Mine too."

"Thanks again for saying so, Avery. But that's no help."

"Ya go, when the time comes, and be Rose Queen for us old folks. It'll be good fer ya ta do somethin' ya ain't ever done.

"I 'member when Daisy and I got married. She wanted a fancy church weddin'. Well, now, I didn't. Finally, it come down ta the fact that if I was havin' Daisy fer a wife, I'd have ta do as she wished. Me in fancy duds, in *church* of all places; that wan't Avery Ketchum. But I caved ta her wishes and ya know it didn't hurt me none. Ya go and wear that fancy dress and when it's over, I'll bet ya'll admit it wan't half bad."

"Avery, the parade is only part of it. I've got to spend the summer as a counselor at CYO camp. Me at a Catholic youth camp, a place I've never been! Working with kids—what am I going to do with them? I'd rather brush a horse."

"Oh." Avery looked down at his barn boots, lost in thought. Then he frowned. "All summer. Ya ain't helpin' all summer?"

"Yeah." Maria's heart sank at the thought of being away from the farm for so long. Who would keep the Morgans in line before the parade? She also pictured a rundown, musty cabin in a dark mass of pines, and little girls jumping up and down on cots, ignoring her orders to go to sleep. She sighed. "Now you'll have to find some extra help."

Avery pushed up the bill of his cap and scratched his head. "I 'spect so. Geez, we'll sure miss yer help." He was silent, and then he looked her straight in the eyes. "Just the same, ya go and do the Rose Queen thing. It'll stretch ya. Find out what yer made off."

"I guess. . . ." She clamped a filter into the milk strainer. "It's time to start milking."

She carried the two machines into the barn thinking it was a mistake to spill her feelings to Avery. The old guy didn't have a clue about this.

She'd like to see him faced with a cabin full of whiny brats. He'd probably run and hide in the woods.

The next day, Maria forgot her woes temporarily as she embraced the challenge of plowing the big meadow with the Morgan team. She loved holding all that power in her hands, controlling the leather straps that told them what to do with only her thumbs and index fingers. The mares with their heads held high were ready to bust loose at any moment, but they didn't. They trusted her with the reins. To boost their trust, she frequently stopped to let them have a breather. As they stood puffing and stomping, she climbed down from the plow to stroke their heads, giving the peppermint candy they loved to crunch with their powerful jaws.

Jubal led with the Percherons. The big team plodded along with no effort, pulling the plow while turning the single furrow. When Maria stopped for a break, Jubal did as well so he never got too far ahead. His team stood, never offering to move until the reins were lifted and Jubal clucked for them to go.

On one break he walked back and stood next to Maria, surveying their work. "Gosh, we've turned a lot of ground."

She looked over the field. "Sure have. Jubal, don't you like the smell of freshly plowed land and to see the earthworms crawl into hiding?"

"Yeah . . . and bugs. The soil's alive with all sorts of critters."

She smiled, liking how tall and lean he was, standing there by her side. "Jubal, do you think we're different, liking farm work so much?" She glanced at him. "Do you suppose Polly would like being here all dressed in her latest fashion with her polished nails and red lipstick?"

He laughed. "God, no! And she'd never be caught dead wearing anything like your bib-overalls and flannel shirt."

Maria stroked Di's neck as the mare nudged her for another candy. "Polly comes from another world." She reached into her pocket, passing more treats to both mares. "I don't see her that much anymore, only in passing on Sunday at Mass. She's usually dressed in a new outfit her mother's just bought on a trip to Rutland."

"Yeah, her folks give her most anything she wants."

"Well, I wouldn't trade places. You . . . you see her much?"

Jubal hesitated. "Well, she comes for her folks' milk every morning."

"Oh. That's all?" Maria wondered if they were still dating, but he didn't say. However, his cheeks reddened as he quickly turned and walked back to the plow. She had learned with Jubal that sometimes words weren't necessary.

Chapter Four

Jubal's school vacation passed quickly. It was fun plowing, sitting on the sulky and watching the muscular Percherons plod along. The effort for the strong pair was as if pulling an empty cart, turning a furrow with a bold scent rising from the damp earth. Occasionally a horseshoe clicked against a pebble, reminding him how at home their horses were never shod. His dad couldn't afford it. What a contrast to the way Avery's animals were kept. Here there were new ideas and new ways of doing things, like growing a large field of corn for improved milk production.

While Jubal admired Avery, he also liked working with Maria. She was a no-nonsense girl—his equal in knowing her way around a farm. She would never admit it, but she was already the queen at Avery's place.

After they finally finished plowing, it was time for Jubal to uncover the one stone that had caused Avery's accident.

Since Maria would be working the land alone, she asked to harrow and smooth the soil using a four-horse hitch. "You know, Avery," she said, as the two of them studied the freshly plowed field, "pulling the two-gang cutaway harrows and spike-tooth drag on behind will take a lot more horsepower than plowing."

"I know." Avery looked doubtful. "But I ain't got the hookup to handle four horses. I always put the big team on the harrows and the smaller horses pullin' the smoothin' drag."

"Well, I'd like to try four horses," she persisted.

"Jest how do ya plan ta do this?"

Maria pointed to the cultivation equipment. "Hook the Percherons to the two-wheel rig and have the Morgans pull in front of the big team. The two-wheel rig can haul the harrows with the smoothing drag on behind."

"Shucks, Maria. Ya've got this all figured. We'll have ta lengthen the Morgans' reins." Avery nodded. "Let's try it."

Her plan worked well. The spirited Morgans led the way with the Percherons pulling more than their share. Jubal could see that Maria was tickled to be handling all four horses. And it was saving time—one pass with the tillage tools left the soil smooth, ready for planting.

Jubal's job wasn't much fun, digging around the stone. The rock seen above ground was only a small part of what lay below. It was a lot like his home—what folks saw from the outside gave not a clue of what went on behind the four walls, and Jubal intended to keep it that way. He would never tell how his dad sat all day in his drinking corner, sometimes to the point of passing out. Lately, he and his ma had to help his father to bed. His ma had tried a number of times to get his dad to cut back but it never worked, and she was at a loss as to what to do. The days and months slipped past with no solution in sight.

While working on the stone, Jubal got thinking about how his family's bony cows sure loved Avery's hay. The big load was disappearing much faster than expected. Since that was the case, he had promised to continue work on the stone and to cultivate Avery's corn when necessary in exchange for another load. Cultivating had to be done twice before the weeds took over. Avery had gladly accepted his offer.

On Friday morning Jubal drove his team and wagon to work, planning to leave that night with another load of hay. Maria met him in Avery's yard with a plan.

"Jubal, I asked Dad to trim your horses' hooves. Would you like that done?"

He jumped off the wagon and walked to the heads of his horses. Patting their broad foreheads, he studied their ragged, chipped hooves. "Sure, they need it. I forgot that your dad's a blacksmith."

"Yeah, he does all of our horseshoeing. Avery sent him to farrier school."

Jubal left his team in the shade of a big maple and went out to the field to continue shoveling out the confounded stone. It was tremendous—gray, oblong, and as big as a bull, with a vein of soft sandstone about two inches wide running lengthwise through it. The more he dug, the more soreness spread through his shoulders and arms, his hands forming blisters from the shovel handle, but he didn't complain. His cows were paying him back for his labor for the hayload by producing nearly two full cans of milk a day, an increase of nearly a full can.

About mid-morning, Maria drove the four-horse hitch over to check on his progress. With reins in hand and a satisfied smile, she was a picture of total contentment, her freckled face slightly tanned from the late spring sun. She scanned his handiwork, her blue eyes sharp. "Gosh, Jubal, our horses will never move that thing."

He nodded. The stone was looking to be even bigger than a bull.

Maria inspected it, running her hand along the sandstone vein. "If you go to Avery's woodshed, you'll find several steel wedges on a chopping block. Let's see if you can drive them into that soft line dividing the stone."

He chuckled. "You've got a lot of good ideas for me on the end of this shovel while you sun yourself driving those horses." He opened his hands. "See the blisters?"

"Oh, Jubal, your hands! You don't have gloves. I wish we could trade places. I'd love to give you a break."

"Thanks for the offer, but I can keep at it." Jubal turned back towards the stone. "The wedge idea sounds like a good one." He struck the narrow layer of soft rock with the point of his shovel. "You think with a chain around the wedges, the horses can pull enough to split this thing?"

"It's worth a try. And my dad will help tomorrow. He had a lot of experience using horses to move stones when he lived in Ireland."

"Good, because it looks to me like we'll need all the help we can get."

Maria turned the teams around with ease and headed back to work the land. He heard her talking to the two pairs of horses as they leaned into their task. At fifteen, she had such a knack for solving problems. Avery was lucky to have her.

He walked to the back of Avery's house to the woodshed and quickly spotted the wedges on a chopping block right where Maria said they would be. While picking them up, he heard the *thump* of Avery's crutches. The back screen door creaked on its hinges as Avery pushed it open.

"By golly," Avery exclaimed. "That field's lookin' great!"

"Thanks." Jubal held the wedges and reached for a sledgehammer. "We're going to try and split that stone. Maria's idea."

"Seein' it's hers, it'll pro'bly work. By gosh, boy, ya're handlin' that load real gingerly. How 'bout a pair of gloves?"

"Gee, I'd like that. My hands *are* kind of sore."

"Don't wonder." Avery left and returned with a pair of worn leather gloves. "Here, you can have these. I ain't usin' 'em again. I 'bout wore 'em out diggin' a ditch ta run a lead pipe from a spring up on the hill ta the place here. Damn good spring, but layin' that line took most a' the summer. That's the second pair I near wore out."

Jubal slipped them on. "These will help. That stone's taking a lot of digging."

"I'll look at it tomorrow. Hope them wedges work."

Back at the stone, Jubal spent the rest of the day finding the right places for the wedges and driving them into the seam. The wedges didn't sink deep enough so it was necessary to chip away at the rock. This labor would have blistered his hands even more if it weren't for Avery's gloves.

By chore time, Maria had finished working the corn land, and they decided to wait until morning to see if Avery's teams could move the stone. It was time to load up the hay for his cows.

The Belgians stood under the maple where he'd left them that morning. They appeared content in the shade while stamping away flies.

Maria's dad had trimmed their hooves nicely and smoothed the ragged edges with a hoof rasp. It must have felt good to the horses, just as anyone would feel with a new pair of shoes. He saw that her dad had also watered the team while they waited.

After they built another load of hay from Avery's mow, he drove out of the yard. "See you tomorrow morning," he yelled from the top of the wagon. "Thank your dad for fixing up our horses."

"I'll be sure to tell him," Maria called.

It was amazing how the road mud had dried up. Dick and Dan's hooves struck hard ground and the wagon wheels rolled easily on the gravel surface. Roadside tree buds had shed their winter shells, unfolding leaflets. The fields had changed from drab brown to a tender green. On their trimmed hooves, the team moved easier, and he only had to stop them once for a rest. Upon arriving at the farm, he parked the load on the haymow floor for easy feeding, and took the horses for water and on to their stalls.

As he did the evening chores he was no longer thinking of Avery's stone. Polly and he were going to meet at Benny's blue Packard. He knew Polly was already impressed with the flashy car. It had generous chrome trim, a covered spare tire on the left front fender, and twelve cylinders under the hood. The shiny headlights each had a lens the circumference of a basketball.

Despite the fact that he was enjoying working at Avery's, he couldn't wait to see his sweetheart and find out what she'd been doing all during spring vacation. This meeting at the car was their secret. They hadn't told anyone, not even their folks, who were unlikely to find out. Polly's parents were leaving for their weekly bridge game. His ma was working and Benny would be in bed by seven o'clock. His dad would be dead drunk. This was their first date in the car other than the joyride through town.

Up to this point, he and Polly had enjoyed their long walks while Polly talked about being a nun and he told her of his dream to be a farmer. Recently, however, she'd changed her mind on the nun idea. During the past year their friendship had turned to romance, so her new Catholic mission was to eventually have lots of kids—the church's tenet to increase the faith. It seemed odd to Jubal, who had no church connections. However, he wasn't going to make a big deal over it. His worries about family size were years away as he was only just about to turn sixteen. Still, he had heard the guys at school remark, "If you screw a Catholic, you can't use a rubber." He'd passed that remark off because Polly and he hadn't, as yet, reached that point. But the thought of having her in his arms was exciting.

Polly, who lived just a short way past Lady Lamont's mansion, came right on time. When they met at the car, she reminded him right away how Father Mac had told his girls to conduct themselves on a date: no French kissing, stay in an upright position, and skirts should remain well below the knees.

"I'll get in," she said. "But don't you dare let your hands travel into forbidden territory." She held her blue cotton flared skirt so that it wouldn't brush against the car.

"Don't worry." He was suddenly a little nervous. He hoped he had washed away the smell of the barn, knowing how she didn't like it.

They stood outside of the car in the cool April evening. The Packard's side-by-side shiny chrome door handles—one for the front and one for the back seat—were easy to see in the dim light. Jubal hesitated as to which one to open. Regardless, he knew opening either and climbing in would start a new chapter in their friendship.

He admired Polly's nice skirt and matching short-sleeved top that showed her exceptionally prominent figure. All of a sudden it seemed she had developed into womanhood. A gold cross lay beneath her open collar. She seemed stiff, probably thinking of Father Mac and the confessional booth.

"It's cold out here." She shivered.

"Let's get in and use the car blanket." Jubal looked in the rear window. "It's hanging on the back of the front seat."

"Yeah, anything. I'm freezing."

Jubal opened the back door and they slid onto the cold leather seat. He leaned over the front seat to turn on the radio, a special novelty in this particular '36 Packard. Then he settled in next to his girl. With Polly nestled in his arms, they snuggled under the heavy blanket, cuddling for warmth. Songs like "In Apple Blossom Time" and "Stardust" were favorites played on the *Hit Parade*, as were the big-band sounds of Glenn Miller and Artie Shaw. The popular radio show aired on WGY, coming from the New York metropolitan area.

Jubal, and most of the folks who worked the farms, listened every morning over the barn radio to "The Chanticleer," a local celebrity throughout the region. The sound of a rooster crowing to start the broadcast, followed by the gravelly voice of the old Chanticleer was the background to morning chores. Farm real estate prices were announced, and the Extension Service out of Albany also gave poultry, cattle, hog, and sheep prices recorded at the local sales barns.

As Jubal held Polly, a familiar song began: "You Are My Sunshine." He whispered, "This is the perfect song for us."

She squeezed his hand and he held her tighter.

As the night progressed, they sang along with the tunes that came clearly over the radio, until the programming was interrupted with news of Hitler's aggression and torpedoes sinking United States supply ships headed for England. They didn't react. Hitler and Germany seemed worlds away from Hayesville.

Since there were no songs to listen to for the time being, Polly instead told him what had been happening on her soap opera, *One True Love.* She'd been following the drama all during vacation. While she rattled on about characters he knew nothing about that were tied up in crazy situations, she bored him to distraction. But as she talked, their closeness under the blanket generated steam that collected on the windows. Teenage hormones quickly outran any church rules of proper dating behavior. Their wet kisses were filled with passion. Polly, a gum chewer, loved *Juicy Fruit* and so they swapped the taste in the curl of their tongues. The heat intensified under the blanket when Jubal felt the softness of Polly's breasts against his chest. He had flashes of his dream about Lizzy LaFlam. But this moment was real. His excitement increased to the point where he began exploring. He slid his left hand up under her top.

Her breath blew hot as her tummy rose and fell with the speed of a galloping horse. She panted, "You're close to forbidden territory!"

"Just a little more," he said. He was fascinated by her sudden development.

"Stop!" She warned, grabbing his hand.

He sat back. "Sorry. I . . . I'm just curious."

"Curious!" she gasped. "About what?"

"Well you've . . . you know . . . you've grown so big." He threw the blanket off and looked at her. "Is it something you ate? A new diet? Pills?"

She sniffed. "So you've noticed?"

"Well, yeah. All of a sudden you're big as, big as . . . well, almost as big as . . ." He hesitated. "Lizzy LaFlam."

"Oh my God!" She grabbed the blanket and pulled it to her chin to cover herself. "That big?"

"Did I say something wrong?"

"I surely don't want to look like Lizzy LaFlam. That's too much. She's too big!"

"Well, you are who you are. That tight top shows more than I ever realized."

"They . . . they aren't real." Her eyes watered.

"What? You mean—"

"Mail order boobs. I bought them from an ad in the back of a magazine." She wiped her eyes with the back of her hand. "The advertisement promised, *Guaranteed to please*."

"Oh, so that's it! I wondered." Jubal laughed heartily. "Well, you sure had me fooled."

"It just isn't fair! I . . . I haven't grown like most girls. When I check myself in the mirror, I just don't change. Recently my bra has been padded, but it still isn't much, so during vacation I . . . ordered bigger ones."

Jubal put his arm around her. "Your breast size doesn't matter to me. That isn't the reason I love being with you."

"But, I'm worried. Will I ever change?"

"Just relax about it." He squeezed her hand.

"As a guy, you don't understand," she said, brushing his hand away. "My breasts are only the size of eggs."

"Well, Polly, eggs are fine with me. You're making too much of this."

"But . . . even if they're fried . . . sunny-side up?"

Gosh, she was serious! He'd thought she was making a joke. "Oh, the size of eggs as in *fried*?" He wanted to laugh again. "Let's change the subject."

"Now you know all about me." She folded her arms to cover the falsies.

"Don't worry, I'm good at keeping secrets." He certainly felt sorry for her.

Around ten o'clock they left the car and wrapped their arms in a tight hug, giving each other sweet lovers' kisses. They said goodnight with plans to meet at the car the following week—same time, same place.

Chapter Five

On Saturday morning Maria looked up Harmony Hill to see if Jubal was coming down the road on his bike. Sure enough, at a distance she saw him coasting as he gripped the handlebars, his shirttails and long hair flying in the breeze. Her dad and Avery had hooked both teams to the two-wheel rig that pulled a stoneboat—a structure of elm planks bolted to a steel skid, used to transfer stones from the field to the hedgerow. Maria was glad Jubal had arrived just in time.

Avery sat in a rocking chair on the stoneboat holding both crutches in one hand. "Well, well," he said to Jubal. "We're about ta see if we can move that stone ya been workin' on."

"It's not going to be easy," Jubal said as he leaned his bike up against one of the old maple trees.

Maria climbed up in the seat of the rig and waited until Jubal stepped onto the boat where he took hold of the back of Avery's rocker. She gently slapped the reins on the backs of the horses and the two teams jerked forward. As the stoneboat lurched, Jubal tipped the rocker backwards.

"Ahh!" Avery hollered as he grabbed tight to the arms of the chair. "Don't dump me, boy!"

"Don't worry, I won't. But, Avery, why a rocker? Seems awfully unsteady."

"I ain't bringin' no good furniture outta the house."

"Well, geez." Jubal tried to steady himself as the stoneboat bumped along. "It would be quite the scene with the two of us landing in a heap. You should be sitting in a sturdy armchair."

"This rocker's one Gertrude, my mother-in-law, give us years ago as a weddin' present. I never did like the confounded thing. Reminds me too much of her. She was crazy. As the sayin' goes, she was a little off her rocker." He laughed at his own joke.

"Well, I'll try not to dump you off *your* rocker," Jubal said.

As she drove the four horses on ahead, Maria smiled at their banter. She also heard her dad, usually a quiet man, chuckle at Avery's odd behavior. Maria turned to see her father raise an eyebrow at his boss who sat like a countryman riding in an open-air chariot.

She thought about her dad and his thick brogue that was not always easily understood. He was a clean-cut, closely-shaven Irishman with black hair and deep-set blue eyes. He'd come to Hayesville in 1925 right off the boat from Ireland, and her folks first met on the voyage across the ocean. They'd married in a small ceremony at St. Anne's church when they first settled in Hayesville. Father Henry had found Chester the job at the Ketchum farm, and her dad had been there now for sixteen years. Maria was glad that her father was with them to try and move the stone, because in Ireland he'd worked on many stonewalls in the country around Galway Bay.

Once on the corn land, the stoneboat glided along with its edge nearly level with the soil. After they went several hundred feet, Maria stopped the teams by the stone.

Avery stood with the help of his crutches. "Holy jumped up . . . that's big!" He turned to Jubal. "Set my rocker so's I can watch."

Jubal placed the rocker out of harm's way and Avery settled himself into the chair as if it were on his front porch.

"What do you think, Dad?" Maria glanced over at her father who walked around the giant gray stone, examining it from all sides.

"Goldarn, that's big! One thing's fer sure—we kin only move it if it splits."

Maria knew from her dad's expression that he had an idea forming.

"Hook the Percherons' whiffletrees ta the stone by wrappin' a chain 'round the heads of the wedges," he said.

Maria listened intently as she held Sally by her bridle. Her dad could make a good plan to move the stone if anyone could.

Chester further instructed, "Then hook the Morgans ta the wedges wi' a second chain. Jubal kin drive the Percherons. When I gi' the word, we'll see if all four horses'll pull together." He picked up a crowbar from the stoneboat. "If that stone separates, I'll slide this bar inta the separation."

When both teams were hooked to the stone on their separate chains, her dad gave the command to pull. "*Git*!"

Both teams jumped forward. The Percherons dug into the soft ground and pulled for seconds with no results. The Morgans jumped back and forth, never giving a united effort, their seesaw action worthless. Her dad gave the command and they tried again. "*Git*!" And a third time. Maria could not get the flighty Morgans to fall in line, while the Percherons pulled with all their strength. The stone didn't separate.

"Them showcase Morgans ain't worth nothin'." Lifting the bill of his cap, Avery looked disgusted. "Jubal, I had ya wastin' yer time, uncoverin' that monster."

Maria turned to her dad. "Can we have both teams pull from one chain?"

Chester nodded. "Let's try. Hope the whiffletrees don't break."

Avery sat at the edge of his rocker. "Let's hope not! Them oak whiffletrees cost plenty." He shook his head. "Confounded rock! Shoulda left it."

Her dad slipped a grab hook onto the single chain from which the Percherons were pulling and ran it along the ground to the Morgan team's whiffletrees.

Maria and Jubal held Sally and Di tight by their bridles.

"Okay," Chester said. "Let's see if all four'll pull together."

Maria picked up the reins and backed the teams to slacken the chain. Standing behind the dappled grays, she slapped their rumps, commanding loudly, "*Get!*"

The four horses lurched ahead as their hooves again dug into the soft soil. The harnesses lifted off their rumps and the leather tugs tightened. Luckily, the oak whiffletrees and eveners didn't break from the strain, but something had to give. Avery leaned forward intently, eyes wide, his mouth open. Everyone held their breath.

The driven wedges held and the stone gradually separated, moving inches before the teams stopped. Standing up on his good leg, Avery raised his crutches. "Hooray!"

Everybody laughed, surprised the horses had done the impossible. With Chester's directions, they left half the stone in place. It took the next hour to edge the huge split slab onto the stoneboat. Even at that, a good part of it rode off to the sides of the planks.

With the stone in place, Maria and Jubal hitched the two teams to the rig and the horses stood ready to drag the stoneboat. Avery clapped his hands.

"Let me sit on that thing." He pointed across the field. "We're puttin' it on the side of the openin' leadin' ta Harmony Hill Road." He grinned, triumphant like he'd just slain his mortal enemy. "This stone damn near kilt me!"

As Maria drove the rig to the field's edge, the weight of the load over the soft ground left a deep pathway, allowing for easy walking. Jubal and her dad followed behind in the stoneboat's path. Maria noticed in the hedgerow a flowering shrub with bursting buds and leaves the size of mouse ears. She pointed it out, calling back to her dad.

"That's the shad bush," he said. "We had similar ones in Ireland. First white flowers in the spring after the cold, wet winter."

Just then Avery told her to stop the horses near the field opening. She awaited his direction.

He got off from the rock with his chair. "See how the ground rises ta the left of that big maple?"

Maria looked at the slope by the tree and nodded.

"Drive them horses so as the stone hangin' over rides high on that hump 'gainst the tree roots. The stone'll nearly tip on its edge."

She started the horses. When reaching the mound of maple roots, she drove the teams perfectly so that the rock slowly lifted and leaned against the ancient tree. The stoneboat slid free. After crossing the road, she stopped the horses where the road met Harmony Hill and turned them around.

Avery yelled, "Whoa!" as he hobbled over to the tree. "Just the way I wanted it." He gestured to some low bushes near the base of his stone. "And these wild roses we ain't trampled will grow lookin' like a real grave. But guess what, I ain't 'neath them flowers!"

Maria climbed down to join Jubal and her dad beneath the maple. They watched as Avery leaned on the upright stone, took a nail from his pocket, and scratched out AKL in big letters as if written on a schoolroom blackboard.

"Now, Maria, I want ya ta take some of that leftover red paint we used on the front of the barn and paint over them marks. Use two coats so's I can see it from my place and folks can see it from the road."

"Why?"

"This AKL stone says to me that Avery Ketchum Lives. Folks'll know I won, cheatin' the grim reaper."

She nodded. "Okay, sure." Sometimes Avery was a bit odd, but she didn't mind a little paint job.

The next morning before church, she went into the farm shop and located the red paint for the stone. First she practiced her lettering on an old board to see if the size brush she'd selected would work to make the AKL lettering look neat and professional. She was amused, still thinking that Avery's request was a little strange. But that was Avery; he was always known to be eccentric. Folks told how as a young man he'd advertised for his wife, Daisy, by putting a sign on his front lawn: *Eligible girl Wanted.*

The sign had worked. In a short time a gal from town, Daisy Green, came calling. They were married for nearly forty years before she died of a fatal heart attack. Folks said she was overexcited while giving a speech on the evils of drinking beer and hard liquor.

By the time Maria reached the stone, the sun was high—perfect light for her lettering. The red oil paint spread easily, which made it possible to paint within the bounds of sharp lines. In a short time, the job was complete. With the high-gloss red paint, the AKL stood out boldly. The next day, she returned to put on a second coat. When she was done, Avery reported he was pleased since he could easily see the bright red letters from his house.

Chapter Six

After several Friday nights in the back seat of the Packard, Jubal and Polly had broken nearly all of the church's rules regarding dating behavior: plenty of wet kisses and cuddling while they lay together on the seat, arms wrapped around each other in a ball of passion. Her skirt was often way above her knees as Jubal explored every inch of her figure. While he explored, she would whisper her dream.

"When we're married we'll have lots of kids, with the priest blessing each child at its Holy Baptism. We'll stand so proud, Mr. and Mrs. Jubal Brown, the perfect Catholic family. Our children will all be towheads, each about a year apart, lining up in height like steps on a stairway."

Her talk about their future kids fired his imagination. "Golly, getting you pregnant sounds like fun." Jokingly he said, "Let's start right now."

"Jubal, I . . . sometimes imagine it but . . . I sure don't want to get pregnant yet. I'm still in school and—"

He leaned in for a long passionate kiss and she responded. The steam from their heavy breathing filled the car. They were a gal and guy under a blanket, cocooned in their own world with no one to bring them to their senses. The freedom was just too overwhelming.

He whispered, "Our first time will be right now."

"Oh! Okay," she said. "We'll just . . . try a little."

As he slid her panties off, fumbling to lower his own, his heart pounded and his mouth went dry.

She whispered, "Jubal . . ." and wrapped her arms around him even tighter.

He hesitantly entered her, dizzy out of his mind. Nothing in the world mattered as she pressed her hips against him.

Suddenly she screamed and pulled back. "JUBAL!"

He yanked away. "Did . . . did it hurt?"

She sat up, hurriedly smoothing her hair and pulling her skirt down. "What did you do! I'm scared!"

He was dismayed that she started crying uncontrollably.

"I'm going to get pregnant! PREGNANT! Do you hear?" She put her hands over her face.

"No you won't!" He sat up also.

She dropped her hands and frowned. "Oh, and I suppose you're some kind of authority!"

"I didn't . . . have it. Don't be scared!"

"Well, I am— *It?* What do you mean by 'it'?"

"You know. . . ."

"I don't know."

"The stuff that makes babies." He put his hand on her arm, trying to comfort her. "So just calm down." He certainly didn't want her to get pregnant. "We lost our heads."

"You sure I won't get pregnant?" She wiped her tears.

"I'm sure," he said, nodding. He knew that their split-second of "going all the way" had not ended like some of his wild dreams at night. At school he and his friends once looked in a health book in the library and had learned that such dreams were called *nocturnal emissions,* which they'd all thought was pretty funny.

Just when he thought he had her calmed down, she erupted again into tears.

"I . . . I just remembered. Father Mac warned us, 'Sex is like playing with fire; you're bound to get burned.'" She gasped, her eyes widening in realization. "Next week at confession, I'll have to tell!"

A bolt of fear shot through him. "Tell what?"

"That I've . . . I've committed a mortal sin!"

"Oh, Polly, you've got to tell? I mean . . . everything?"

"Yes, Father Mac will ask for details!"

"No way!"

"That's the reason for going to confession."

"Oh, great!" He looked out the window at his rundown house and barn, envisioning the gossip that would run through town: *That young Jubal—irresponsible kid. Just like his father who never grew up.* He turned back to Polly. "You don't have to say anything. We just lost our heads, only for a minute!"

"That doesn't matter. I still have to tell."

He struggled for what to say to change her mind but couldn't think fast enough. "Well I sure wouldn't!" he declared. Suddenly, an even bigger concern struck him. "Polly, it sounds fun to have lots of kids, but . . . I want to be a farmer. You know that. Farmers don't have much money. We could never have a big family."

"Gosh, what a life!" she said. She pulled a compact mirror from her purse to fix her makeup. "Stinking like a cow barn and living in poverty!"

"Geez, I hope I could do better than poverty." He wanted to say *And I'll never be a Catholic!* But he held his tongue. Polly had often teased him that he was a heathen, but that was just fine with him.

There seemed to be little more to say, so they climbed out of the car and kissed goodbye. From her guarded peck on his lips, he could tell she had come down to earth from their passion. He supposed his passion had calmed too. The fear of an unwanted pregnancy had reined them in. Still, they made plans to meet at the car sometime in the future. Polly said she wasn't sure when exactly, since Father Mac had started a Friday night youth group that she was expected to attend.

When he was away from her and the car, the whole subject of marriage brought up certain details of his mother's experiences as a young gal, reminding him that he and Polly probably shouldn't ever have kids. But he vowed to never tell her why. As he walked towards his house, finding his way easily in the dark, the stark facts of the story that his mother had shared just a few years earlier were hard to ignore.

⁂

Ever since Jubal had learned about the birds and the bees, which a youngster discovers early on a farm, he'd known his mother had lived her life on the wild side when she first came to Hayesville. But he figured many townsfolk had stepped over the line in their younger days.

Still, Eugene once told him, "Word is that your ma was with a bunch of guys before she married your dad. Their marriage was a shotgun affair."

If this were true, Jubal began to wonder if his dad was his real father, a question that had nagged at him until one morning three years prior at breakfast, right out of the blue, he'd asked his parents who his real father was.

His question had jarred his ma. She shifted in her chair, raising her brow in surprise. His dad paused dumbstruck, forkful of eggs halfway to his mouth. Neither of his parents said a word. The silence was painful, but he really wanted to know.

Finally his ma spoke. "Your father's your dad."

"But I mean my *real* dad."

His ma always wore three silver bangle bracelets, which clicked faintly as she rubbed her brow.

"Jubal, you deserve an answer," she said.

His father gave his ma a warning glance and dug into his eggs. Jubal could see pain in his ma's eyes. He wondered what terrible thing she was about to reveal.

"Well, yeah, I do." He seldom had the upper hand with his ma, but he did at that moment.

His folks sat stone-faced for an unbearable amount of time. He waited, unable to even take a bite of his food, the heavy smell of fried bacon now making him queasy in wondering if he'd made a mistake. Nothing more was said. The subject seemed closed.

After breakfast, he escaped to the bathroom, listening as his parents began clearing breakfast plates.

"I knew this day would come!" his ma said.

His dad sighed. "I know."

Plates clanked. Water ran in the farmhouse sink.

"A big help you were!" his ma exclaimed.

"Rose! What could I say? Ya ran with a bunch."

"Yeah." Her tone was regretful. "My foolish days."

"I remember seein' Tatum, Clinker, Kreb, and Quinn pull inta Lady Lamont's one night. Oh, and Harlow, he was with 'em."

His ma groaned, "Clyde! Okay, okay. Don't remind me."

That night after chores, Benny had gone to bed and his father was in the front room listening to the tail end of a Red Sox game on the radio.

Jubal could tell by his ma's mood that she'd come home early from work with a lot on her mind. He sat at the kitchen table waiting, wondering what was coming. In the background he could hear the announcer, "*Foul ball! One ball, two strikes.*" His mother took a sip of her coffee and set the cup in the saucer.

"Jubal, we're going to have a talk."

With her smile gone, he knew it was serious. She went into her bedroom and came back with a folded piece of paper, pulling up a chair next to him.

"I want to tell you my story. It's a story I'm not proud of, but you have the right to know, and must know as a friend of Polly's.

"I never knew my parents. They died of influenza, as you already know, when just arriving in our country as immigrants from Sweden. My earliest memory was of growing up in a girls' home. At a young age I realized I could influence other kids—I was a rebel leading the rest of the girls into trouble, convincing them to pull pranks. Later on, my wild attitude wasn't so innocent. I started smoking, and I egged the other girls into starting riots to demand better food and more freedom.

"Benny was already in a reform school for delinquents. With his temper, he'd beaten up kids who called him 'dummy' and 'half-brain.' He'd grown to be downright dangerous with the strength of an ox. Not too long after, due to my shenanigans at the home, I was sent to the same reform school for a few months until I was placed in a foster home."

He sat wide-eyed, hearing of his ma as a ringleader who started trouble. He did wonder why he should learn about all this because of Polly.

His mother continued her tale. "As I got older, I not only had the ability to persuade, but I also had the looks that drew attention. After leaving reform school, I picked up a few odd modeling jobs in New York's garment district. At that same time, I lived with a family headed by a strict grandma-type—Mrs. Clough. Her rules kept me out of trouble, even though I was in a perfect place to join the street girls. She told me that peddling sex was a fatal path to follow. So, I surprised myself and actually finished high school, as few girls in my neighborhood did. Most got pregnant or left school to hang out on the streets."

"How did you make it to Hayesville?" he asked.

"An ad in a New York paper. When calling the telephone number, I talked to Lady Lamont and she asked for an interview. Taking the chance I'd be hired, Benny and I packed up our things and made the trip up to Vermont. Lady Lamont and I seemed a perfect match. She loved the lines of my figure and knew her daring art, with me as her subject, would sell well on the New York market. For me, I thought that finally I might have found a good home for Benny, a huge improvement from reform school.

"Sure enough, she promised me a job and afterward showed me around. We visited the neighboring farm and it was here that I first met your dad." His mother smiled at the memory. "He was sitting on a stool milking a cow, hayseed in his hair and his blue coveralls stained with what looked like cow manure. Now remember, I was a New York City girl back then. I hadn't been exposed to cows and barns. Never thought about all the hard work that went into the milk I drank. I stood with my mouth hanging open when Lady Lamont introduced us. As I took in the long row of cows and the *smell*, Lady Lamont laughed at the look on my face.

"But I immediately liked your dad—tall, handsome, and a ready smile. Your dad seemed serious about managing the farm for a profit. He was dedicated to hard work and not afraid to get dirty doing it. He seemed the first rock solid guy I'd ever met. Fortunately, he was willing to have Benny as a helper and gave him a place to live. Benny, being Benny, was worried about a different home, as was his way when facing a new situation. However, he quickly adjusted while working for your dad and learned to love the farm."

Though it was neat hearing how his ma had met his dad, Jubal kept wondering what was coming that would affect him having Polly as a girlfriend.

"After Lady Lamont hired me, I spent long hours posing naked for her, draped in a see-through shawl. As my new employer suspected, her paintings of me sold quite well. Each painting was unique. She had me pose in different positions, using light from her studio windows to reflect her shading of my figure."

"Gosh Ma, you posed naked?" He'd not seen any of these paintings and wasn't sure he'd want to. He knew Bernice Sausville and the ladies at the Baptist church likely had plenty to chat about knowing the type of paintings Lady Lamont turned out. He could just hear them, "Lord save us, Rose Ringquest poses without clothes for Lady Lamont!"

"Yes, Jubal, I posed nude. In the art world such paintings are not unusual. Having success in selling her work, Lady Lamont made frequent trips down to New York City during the time I was working for her.

"When I was posing, she'd tell me of nightlife in the big city. I was too busy and too broke to enjoy that party scene when I lived there. But Lady Lamont made connections with all kinds of artists and jazz musicians black or white, didn't matter to her. It was the middle of the 1920s with the Harlem Renaissance in full swing, the jazz age. New York City was hopping. She used to tell me how she danced until the early morning hours in the speakeasies. Back then she had cut her hair in a bob and dressed like all the other flappers, skirts above the knee. Daring at the time."

"Flappers?" he asked. He pictured a line of crows on a roof peak.

His ma laughed. "It's not what you think. Flappers were rebellious women wanting freedom and respect. Lady Lamont also drank gin and smoked cigarettes in long, fancy holders."

"I guess I can picture that," he said. "She still seems pretty rebellious."

"That she is. She sure did enjoy shocking people back then. She loved her image as the 'crazy artist' here in Hayesville.

"But the biggest shock of all was when she came home with Eugene after one of those trips." His ma shook her head, remembering. "It was the year I got pregnant with you. She'd been gone down there to the city for quite a while, a few months I think. She left me to take care of the mansion in her absence. I didn't mind. I was young and full of oats myself, liking the independence.

"Well, there were quite the rumors burning through town about just where Eugene came from, and she never said. I did the math though, back to a story she'd told me about a trumpet player she'd been head over heels for. Eugene was such a beautiful baby with his tight curls, brown eyes, and light brown skin. Along with his angelic features, he developed a joyful personality, winning the hearts of almost all who met him."

Jubal nodded. "He hasn't changed. The girls especially all think he's the living end. So that's where Eugene came from. I never knew."

"Soon everyone in town just piped down and seemed to accept Eugene. Never asked another question. Lady Lamont was a force. Folks didn't like crossing her. At town meetings she was outspoken about the horrible conditions of the Town Farm. She was so upset at the Board of Selectmen for their not funding the farm nearly enough, that she ran for an opening on the board and won. She's held that position and has been re-elected ever since. And she's been very generous in funding town projects.

"Even though I was thrilled with my job and happy for Benny that he had a place with your dad, I missed the city life—the sounds of the street, all the people, the latest fashions. So I visited your dad often, but he was always busy doing barn chores, fixing fences, haying. He never did fun stuff away from the farm."

Jubal sat thinking about how much his father had changed, now sitting in his chair all day long, hardly ever leaving the house to do farm work.

"Jubal, it just occurred to me," his ma said, raising her coffee cup for a sip, her bracelets clinking. "I don't think you've ever seen this." She set the cup down and slid three silver bracelets over her hand. "When I align these just right, the inside reads, *Mi Madre.* It means My Mother."

"That's neat." He bent for a closer look. "Why does it say that?"

"Well, while I was modeling, a photographer gave me these sterling bracelets as an accessory. After my modeling session that day, not thinking, I walked home with them still on my wrist. I discovered this inscription when I took them off. Never having had a mother, now *Mi Madre* is always with me." She slowly slid them back on, lost in thought.

He didn't know what to say. He'd always had his ma and his dad, and couldn't imagine growing up the way she did with no parents.

"Anyway," his ma looked at him as if shaking off a dream. "Living in Hayesville was quite the change for me—the nightlife doesn't exist and never has. Almost everything closes down at six.

"So, beginning in early summer, the Saturday night grange dance was one place I could go to have a good time. I drove Lady Lamont's Packard that's now Benny's. That car and I sure turned a lot of heads when I pulled into the grange yard and parked.

"From eight to twelve, I danced every number. I was the new gal in town. Young guys came from farms, sawmills, lumber camps, you name it. They brought their bootleg liquor and lined up for a turn on the dance floor with Rose Ringquest, the talk of the town. They were raring to go, lacking in metropolitan ways. While in the city, I'd handled a bunch of street-smart ragtags. So it was easy to tempt a bunch of country boys. I'll admit, it was fun—drinking hard and teasing the guys."

He was all ears, sitting up straight in his chair. "Wow, I can't imagine all this!"

"Well, after the dance, I had the Packard and they had their booze. A whole bunch piled in for a ride. They told of a deserted farmhouse a few miles from town. We traveled a road with grass growing down the middle to the old house.

"The place was in shambles. It had no front door. Junk and trash littered the floor. There were piles of gnawed wood in an old pantry—porcupine damage, 'searching for salt' the guys told me. Those fat critters with their quills ambled into hiding when we all took over and started a fire in the stone fireplace.

"The guys sat in a circle while I entertained them with my latest rendition of the Charleston. I wanted to look pretty and wore a tight skirt, a swooping neckline, and flashy necklaces. I put plenty of pizzazz into my dance steps. They all loved it, especially Tatum O'Mara. He tried to match me as a dancer, looking like an overgrown kid for the first time on ice skates. I teased him a lot with my dancing, but that was as far as it went. We stayed until four in the morning, making drunken fools of ourselves. That was the beginning of frequent parties. I guess I loved the attention, knowing that most of Hayesville's pious adults frowned on the new rebel gal in town."

"That sounds pretty daring."

"Yeah, but it only got worse. Local girls started to get in on the parties, just kids in their early teens. The scene got out of control and there was talk of *mickey-drops*. The guys were hinting they could use them to get their way with the girls. I'd heard of the drug before but ignored the thought. I was pretty sure these country clods could never get the stuff."

"What are *mickey-drops*?" The whole scene was hard to imagine in Hayesville. And his *mother* at the center of it!

"Chloral hydrate." His ma's expression was pained. "A little, put with alcohol, knocks you out."

"Seems dangerous." Suddenly he was worried for his ma, for what came next.

"It was dangerous. As summer wore on, the deserted house was crawling with young folks. I was tagged as the instigator, the party girl, which I'll admit was true. But I held off the guys, remembering Mrs. Clough and her warning against ending up as trash."

"Well, what happened?" He realized he was gripping the chair seat and relaxed his fingers.

"One night Tatum brought a jug of sweet grappa, a brandy he bought from the Quinn family—eighty percent alcohol. He offered me some in a cup. I loved the sweetness of grappa but soon felt dizzy. As I look back, I'm sure it was all planned beforehand. . . . Tatum's chance to have what I'd denied him and all the guys."

Jubal swallowed hard, not sure he wanted to hear the rest. "Gosh, that's a nasty trick."

"Yes, it was. I woke in the morning with a monstrous headache, nearly naked, and stinking. I got dressed as best I could and staggered to the car, feeling like a truck had driven over me. I was furious with Tatum. Since he handed me the grappa, I figured he drugged me, but I had no proof. I was disgusted with myself. Playing the big catch in town, I'd fallen as a victim. In that moment, I grew up. With Mrs. Clough's warning echoing in my ears, I vowed to change.

"At first I blamed myself. I supposed I deserved it—teasing the boys, dressing the way I had. But over the years, I knew better. They took advantage. They raped me. And I suspected Tatum was the leader."

Anger welled up in him. "Tatum is bad news!"

"Yeah, if it was him and he participated. I was never able to find out for sure. Funny thing is, in Tatum's way, I know he liked me. I took advantage. He was a striking guy like the kind you might see in the men's clothing section of a Montgomery Ward catalog."

She stared blankly across the kitchen. He could tell she was seeing another guy in another time.

"Yet his shifty eyes and brute strength always made me uneasy. Tempting a man like that, it was playing with fire.

"Towards fall of that year, an awful thing happened. The old place burned. I wasn't there since I'd stopped going to the parties. During the fire, fifteen-year-old Kelly O'Mara came up missing. She was in a back room passed out. Some suspected she was slipped a *mickey*. Tatum was so drunk he didn't realize he'd left his sister behind to die."

"Wow, really!" As he observed his ma's tortured look, he could hardly believe his ears. He had no idea his innocent little country town was so messed up with tragedy.

"I was the lightning rod for the whole disaster. Many thought Rose Ringquest should leave town, but influential folks like Lady Lamont felt differently. The town divided down lines of Irish Catholics against the Yankees—morality versus good old common sense. My defenders said that Rose Ringquest wasn't even at the scene of the fire.

"The well-respected O'Mara family mourned the loss of their daughter, but no investigation followed. Since their son was there on that awful night, it was assumed that foul play was unlikely, and Kelly's death was deemed an unfortunate accident."

"Gee, all this went on and Kelly's folks didn't know?"

"They were at a Saturday night party themselves and had trusted Tatum to look after his sister."

The thought of the young girl—who would have been Polly's aunt had she grown up—drugged out of her mind and burning in a fire sickened him. He got up from the table for a glass of water, drawing it from a hand pump at the edge of the cast-iron sink. It was all a bit much to take in: his ma's rape and then Kelly's death, all due to out-of-control partying. Maybe Bernice Sausville wasn't off base with her temperance work. The bottle sure as heck wasn't a friend to his dad.

As he looked at the clear glass he noticed grains of sand settling to the bottom. "Ma," he groaned, "we've got a problem with our water. I'm going to have to check our cistern downstairs."

"Oh dear." His ma stood with a start. "We haven't done a thing with that well house since your dad—"

"Yeah, took up his new occupation."

With a light in hand, he stomped down the cellar stairs. The cellar smelled damp as he opened the small porthole to check on the water. "Damn!" he muttered.

The two-hundred-gallon cistern was loading with sand. A pyramid-shaped sandpile had formed under the inlet pipe from the spring.

Within hours the water would stop as the line to the spring clogged. Already the overflow pipe, directed to the outside of the house's foundation, had stopped. The cistern would empty soon and the barn would be out of water. He had to go to the spring, even though it was almost dark, to make sure that the water kept running. He remembered once seeing his dad try to force water through a clogged pipe with the sand set tighter than cement. His dad had spent days digging up the line trying to find the blockage, and meanwhile he had to lug water from the country store in an old sap tank.

He charged back up the cellar stairs. "Ma, we've got to go to the spring."

His ma turned from the window where she'd been looking out. "Really! Tonight? Is it that urgent?"

"I don't want the water to stop!"

"What about Benny? I haven't been to that well house since . . . I can't remember."

"Ma, this is an emergency. Benny's no good at something like this. Be sure to wear your boots."

"Okay, okay. I'll change and be ready soon. I do wish your dad could do this."

"Yeah, tipsy Clyde would be a great help!" he said under his breath as she left the room. He no sooner spoke than he regretted his words. Regardless of the story he'd just heard and the possibilities it raised, Clyde Brown had always been his dad. In spite of all the pain and struggle the man had heaped on his ma, he was a good and decent guy.

While collecting supplies for the trip to the well house, Jubal's head filled with unpleasant images. His ma out cold and stripped naked, lying flat out with a bunch of guys looking on. Tatum on top of his ma, his pants thrown in a heap. "Eech— God, he's an animal!" Maybe Tatum was the only one who took advantage and the rest just stood watching. He hoped not all guys could do such a lowly act.

Still . . . his ma's story made him think. Was one of those guys his real dad? Was it Tatum? Suddenly he understood how Polly fit in the picture.

He put on his dad's hip boots that curled at the toes, and found the hand-operated force pump, a half-gallon of Clorox, and a shovel and pail. He checked his flashlight and headed for the truck where he waited for his ma. Their water had been taken too much for granted. He bit his lip. Cattle with no water and a cistern sucked dry could be their ruin.

When he was a kid, his dad had sometimes taken him to check on the well house located in the pasture high above the farmstead in back of the barn. Mister Lamont had built the well house as a double-door shed on top of a cement structure that was six or eight feet deep with iron steps leading to the water. His dad would climb down in hip boots to the spring's bottom. Knee deep in water, he'd scoop heavy wet sand, along with a brown frog or salamander, as there were always a few that made their way to the spring. He remembered kneeling on boards while his dad passed him the tin pail. His job was to carry it outside to dump the sand.

In years past, the cool well house was a perfect place for Clem Gochy to store the extra liquor he hadn't distributed in town. It was in part thanks to Clem's bootlegging days that his dad was dead to the world tonight in his living room chair.

When his ma finally got in the truck, he was glad to get going. She allowed him to drive around the farm since he was big enough to reach the brake and clutch. He drove through the pasture gate and the old truck climbed the hill in first gear. Leaving the lights on and the motor running, he parked close to the little building. The truck had no emergency brake that worked, so his ma got out and blocked a rear wheel with a good-sized stone. She then swung open the well house doors.

Pail in hand, he lowered himself into the spring and scooped the sandy water into the bucket while his ma grabbed the bail and threw it out the doors. The watery sand kept coming, heavier and heavier with each pail. His ma eyed a salamander swimming around in one pailful.

"I'm not sure I like the idea of sharing my drink with these things," she commented.

"Dad told me salamanders are supposed to purify water." He smiled as he watched her dump the pail while trying not to splash her pants. In many ways, his ma was still a New York City gal.

"Maybe your dad was right." She placed the empty pail on the ledge. "I guess I can live with a salamander or two."

"The water's clear now," he announced after considerable bailing. "I'm going to start pumping to drive the sand into the cistern."

Shifting on her board, his ma sighed. "I hope you are aware that I don't particularly enjoy kneeling here waiting for your next move."

"Sorry," he laughed. "This may take a while. When the pumping eases up, I'll know the line is clear. You can pretend you're at St. Anne's. Polly said they kneel a lot in her church."

She again shifted her weight on her knees. "I guess she's preparing the way for the life hereafter."

He continued to pump, pushing the handle down harder and harder. "Maybe this is like the Heaven that Polly talks about. When the pushing gets easy, I'll know we're in Heaven."

"Oh, aren't you clever. Some people like Bernice Sausville would tell you that it takes a lot more than pushing water to get to Heaven." She stood and stretched. "Who really knows? Your dad doesn't believe in Heaven. He accuses the church of trying to scare folks so they'll support ministers and priests with what he thinks of as a plush living."

"Yeah, Father Mac riding in that big black Cadillac doesn't look like he's headed for the poor farm." Moments later he yelled, "Hey, I've reached Heaven. We've pushed all the sand into the cistern. See how easy this pumps?"

"Great, Jubal!"

"Before Dad left he'd always pour Clorox in the water."

"Sounds like we're almost done, thank god." His ma hurried to the truck for the Clorox.

It was obvious she wanted to get back to the house, not particularly liking night work at the spring. But in her story he'd found out one reason she'd ended up a farmer's wife—to give him a dad.

Chapter Seven

The next night after the trip to the well house, his ma stood at the sink washing supper dishes. The smell of stewed beef hung in the air. Having eaten his fill of his ma's delicious stew, Jubal remained at the long wooden table. The mysterious paper she'd brought out the night before still lay there and he was curious to see if she'd explain it.

"Well Ma," he said. "Benny and I cleaned up the cistern and the chlorine smell is gone. We're all set." He held up a glass of clear water.

"Good. I don't know if I could stand another night on my knees." His mother went to the laundry rack by the wood stove and began folding dishtowels and sheets.

She was quiet for so long that Jubal wondered if her story was over. He almost headed for his room, but she spoke again, so quietly he could barely hear her.

"Months after the fire, about the time Lady Lamont brought Eugene to town in early fall of 1924, my modeling career was interrupted. The curves of my figure began to change. My body grew puffy, and Lady Lamont and I knew the reason. I was pregnant."

"So it's true—one of those guys, or *Tatum*, could really be my . . . my *dad*?"

His ma remained focused on her folding task. "Yes . . . I'm afraid so." She shook out a pillowcase before creasing it neatly into thirds. "But with a bunch taking turns, who knows?"

"Gosh, since Tatum and Andrew O'Mara are brothers, then . . . Polly and I could be . . . first cousins."

"That's right."

Jubal felt sick. He liked Polly, dreamed about her. She was cute. But he knew first cousins shouldn't marry. Suddenly his dad yelled out in the other room. They hurried to the living room where he sat in his drinking corner with the radio blaring.

The Roosevelt administration continues to push for a preparedness program to improve American defenses, finding the activities of German Chancellor Adolf Hitler and the Nazi state deeply troubling. Congress is considering one billion dollars to build up our naval forces.

His dad snapped off the radio. "Bastard Hitler'll have us inta another war. Mark my words!"

His ma rested her hand on her husband's shoulder. "We can't do much about what happens in Europe." She pulled on his arm and Jubal grabbed the other, helping him to the table for supper. "Time to eat, Clyde," she said.

His dad scuffed along between them. "Help me forget the bad news."

His ma filled a bowl of stew and passed it to his dad. Jubal took a chair and she joined them, reaching for the folded paper. Clyde huddled over his bowl, slurping spoonfuls of carrots and meat.

"When I got the word I was pregnant," his ma said, "desperation hit. In the 1920s, in Hayesville, a fatherless child was unacceptable. I wanted what was best for you, Jubal, and right next door was an eligible, lonely guy."

"Yeah," His dad gestured with his dripping spoon. "Weren't much of a life, tendin' cows all day with no one keepin' the home fires."

His ma fondly looked Clyde's way. "Having tea with Lady Lamont up in her stone turret, I'd watch from the lookout window to see you working the fields. I looked forward to visiting when I could, following that worn path from the mansion."

"Yer pretty ma was always welcome, 'specially when she brought me somethin' good ta eat."

"Over time, I grew to love your dad. He wasn't wild and crude like most I'd met. So one day, I asked him to marry me and if he'd be willing to help raise my baby."

"Ya can bet I jumped at the offer." His dad grinned and dropped his spoon in the empty bowl. "Been eatin' good ever since."

"Gosh, Dad, that was easy. You never had to date Ma or stuff like that? She just fell in your arms?"

"Yup," his dad nodded. "What a catch."

His ma reached for Clyde's hand. "It was so cold that day. December 10, 1924. Your dad and I stood in front of a blazing fire at the mansion. Benny and Lady Lamont, holding baby Eugene in her arms, were my witnesses as we were married before a justice of the peace."

His father stood and gripped the back of his chair to steady himself. Jubal wished he'd known the strong, young guy dedicated to his farm and his new wife.

"Gotta get back ta the radio."

His ma sighed as she cleared her husband's place at the table. Jubal could bet she was thinking the same as him—Clyde Brown had to change his ways.

She continued her tale. "Thank God for Lady Lamont. She not only shielded me from the uproar in the village over the death of Kelly O'Mara, she did most of the shopping and other errands in town. Not easy, since she had a newborn herself. But I enjoyed watching Eugene. He was an easy baby and it made me excited for you. So during those months I was pregnant, the only time I left the house was to walk from the farmhouse to the mansion." At the sink, his ma pumped some dish-water into the kettle. Clear spring water poured from the spout. "We did good work last night at the well house," she said. When the kettle was full, she brought it over to the wood stove to warm and sat back down next to him.

"Tatum was devastated by the loss of his sister. I suspect he was haunted by guilt. One day he came to the mansion to visit and I had mixed feelings about this. Though I felt sorry for him and his family, I was angry and confused. Yet, something in him seemed to have changed. When I answered the door, he stood holding a box of Russell Stover candy. He simply said, 'Here, I thought ya might like this.'"

"Gosh, he came to the mansion?"

"Right, what a surprise. I thanked him and invited him in. With Lady Lamont and Eugene nearby, I had no reason not to, though candy was the last thing I needed.

"I was very pregnant, wearing a smock and feeling as though my bottom half was under a tent. We sat in the living room, he at the end of the couch and I in a rocker. You could hear the patter of rain on the window.

"The yellow candy box was on a tea table between us. Not knowing what else to do, I untied the ribbon and opened it to the sweet smell of chocolate. He leaned over, reminding me of a hungry dog drooling, and popped a candy in his mouth, chewing it open-mouthed with bread-mixer brown teeth. 'This one's my favorite,' he mumbled.

"I noticed a chocolate nutty one and took it from the brown paper cup, thinking it was all I wanted. Being pregnant, food didn't always taste quite right, and the candy being from him made it stick in my throat. In minutes, he had the box at the edge of the table and downed five or six more. The first layer of chocolates was nearly gone. 'Well, I gotta leave,' he said. That was all.

"He didn't say a thing about any wrongdoing. I sat dumbfounded. What a clod! I guess the remaining half box of candy was his peace offering."

"So if Tatum felt guilty and brought you chocolates," Jubal reasoned, "it probably means he *is* my real father?"

"Well, maybe." She studied him. "You do have Tatum's height and coloring. And sometimes your expressions remind me of Tatum at a young age." She shook her head as if to clear away the memories. "Anyway, after I married Clyde, on occasions when he went to town he noticed the reactions from guys at the store. They would change directions to avoid him.

"He wondered, was this guy or that guy there when I was attacked? Did they take part or just stand and watch? Of course no one was volunteering any information."

"Why didn't he just come right out and ask? He'd known them all his life."

"That's not your dad. He talks about weather, milk prices, or politics. He's not much for confronting people."

"Yeah, Dad's too nice a guy."

"You're right. Well one day he came home after meeting up with Tatum. Said Tatum was acting edgy and told him, 'Ya know, ya got a helluva woman. Now, she'll be able to raise her kid with a decent name.' Your dad didn't know what to say."

Reality sank in and Jubal fell into a sort of daze. Tatum was *not* who he wanted for a dad.

"Sometime after you were born, Tatum left town for a few years. Went south. Some said he worked on a shrimp boat out of Georgia. Meanwhile, Father Henry at St. Anne's was growing old and feeble, so when Tatum returned, he brought Father MacMurray to town with him. It was a two-for-one deal. Andrew O'Mara, with his influence in the church, made the arrangements. The priest had the credentials, and the deal gave Tatum work as an all-around handyman and chauffeur for the church, as well as a chance to be elected county sheriff."

Jubal put his hands to his face. "Do you really think I look like Tatum?"

She ruffled his hair. "Don't worry about it. I always thought that you look a lot like me."

"How could I ever find out if Polly and I are first cousins?"

"Why do you want to know that?"

"Oh, no reason." He didn't want his mother to know he was sweet on Polly. Up until lately girls had been, well . . . not interesting. If Polly really was his first cousin, his crush could go nowhere. "So, what happened to you then?" he asked.

"I had months to think about my situation and get used to facing folks in town. But I had a good job and a perfect place for myself and Benny. And I'd just gotten married. Down deep I knew I couldn't fall victim to the guys who took advantage. I couldn't let them win."

He realized how strong his ma was to face all this, shut out and blamed by almost everyone in town. Anger rose like a burst of fire—*she* was the one who was wronged.

She smiled. "On May 1, 1925, you came into our lives, a beautiful baby boy. Your dad and I couldn't have been happier. However, there were complications. The doctor said I would never have children again. Just the same, I felt okay because we had you."

"A good ending to a bad situation," he said.

"Yes, you certainly were." His ma picked up the mysterious paper. "Even though I felt content after you were born, I wanted to set the record straight with that bunch of guys." She looked down at the paper. "So I wrote up this birth announcement and sent it to all the guys who were at the party." She handed it to him and he read aloud.

> *May 1, 1925. A horn has blown. Shout for joy! A beautiful baby boy has arrived. His name shall be Jubilant Brown, a standout among many. He'll be known as Jubal.*
>
> *From the night you gave me the miracle to conceive, God knitted in me a baby, born of the sturdy men from Hayesville. I make no demands, but if I ever have cause, I'll ask payment from you guys that left behind my gift.*
>
> *Signed: Rose Ringquest Brown*

He looked at her in surprise. "Wow! So what happened after you sent this?"

"Nothing. The cards circulated through town. Some thought it was hilarious while others howled in disgust, particularly Andrew O'Mara. I suspect that as a church leader and a member of the selectman's board, he didn't want reminders of what his family had suffered, nor any more tarnish on the O'Mara name."

Chapter Eight

The morning after Jubal and Polly's lovemaking in the Packard almost came to a risky end, he was on his way out to the barn to do chores after a restless night. The early light was beginning to show towards the east over Hayesville Mountain. House sparrows perching on the electric wire leading to the barn began their constant chatter, while the night's chorus of spring peepers in a nearby pond had quieted to an occasional "peep."

He was thinking about how, three years earlier, he'd very much wanted to meet the guys who were with his ma the night she was given the *mickey*. He'd wanted to see who might have done it, to size each one up and get a good look.

Coincidently at the time, Eugene had offered him his paper route because he had too many responsibilities at the mansion and didn't want the bother of the once-a-week Saturday delivery. Jubal jumped to take the job since money was tight at home and the route provided the chance to meet the guys in question. All he needed was a dollar and sixty cents to pay Howard Perkins, the editor, for the twenty papers to start his route. He would charge a dime and make two cents for each paper sold. He asked his ma and she loaned him the money.

Howard Perkins wore a flat cap pushed back with a yellow stub pencil behind his ear and cranked out the town paper in a dilapidated office on Main Street. Folks in town joked that Howard's face, with his droopy eyes and sagging jowls, matched that of his hound dog. They also complained that *The Hayesville Weekly* was loaded with errors, but it sold because folks were eager to see their names in print, especially if it was good news.

The first week delivering papers on his bike Saturday morning, Jubal had fun earning money, collecting a dime at each stop, while some folks gave him a nickel tip. Most customers were happy with his service, so he came home with coins loading down his pockets.

He did have one problem at Clinker's Plumbing and Heating. When he walked into the dusty store, with its shelves sagging under a jumble of pipes, wires, and bolts, Howard Clinker was looking at a magazine with a naked lady on the cover. Jubal cleared his throat and put the newspaper on the counter, but the burly guy didn't look up.

"*Mr. Clinker!*"

Mr. Clinker dropped the magazine in surprise and sprang from his seat with a guilty expression. He scowled at Jubal. "So, the orphan's our new paperboy I see."

"I'm not an orphan!"

"Oh, no?" Clinker said. "Well, your old lady whored plenty. You might's well be."

Jubal stood speechless, anger boiling, and he wanted to smack the guy. But Clinker could likely take him down with one cuff to the head. So instead he ran out the door, picked up his bike, and pedaled furiously to his next stop, deciding he'd be happy with one less customer.

When he biked into Mike Harlow's place, Mike and his wife had just come home and were sitting in the front seat of a beat-up Model A Ford. When Mike saw him, he swung open his door and stepped out onto the gravel drive. He was young and slim, dressed in a mechanic's work clothes.

"So, you're Jubal," Mike said. "Gosh, it's great to see you're our paperboy."

"Gee, thanks." He studied Mike's face, wondering if he himself had similar features. The wide cheekbones? The calm expression? But the brown eyes, dark hair, and dark complexion were not like his. Unfortunately, this nice guy probably wasn't his dad. Lost in thought, he jumped when a rooster, hearing the voices, came running.

"Meet Reddy, my rooster." Mike pulled a cracker from his shirt pocket. The rooster stretched his long neck and took the treat.

"He's smart!"

"Yeah, if he gets any smarter he can run up to the mansion and have his picture painted. I heard Lady Lamont paints animals as well as people like your ma."

"You know Ma?"

"Of course. Everyone knows Rose Ringquest . . . er, Brown." Mike reached in his pants pocket to the tumbling of change and handed Jubal a dime. He reached into his pocket again. "Here's a nickel for extra measure." He opened the door to the Model A and pulled out a grocery bag.

"Thanks." Jubal didn't want the conversation to end just yet. "Um, I was wondering . . . do you know my real dad?"

Mike paused, clutching the bag to his chest. "Son, that's between you and your ma."

Jubal noted that Mike's wife, now waiting on the porch to help with the groceries, looked tensely at her husband, her lips drawn in a tight line. Thinking their reactions a little strange, he said goodbye and pedaled on to the next stop, Kreb's place.

Mr. Kreb, bent over with white hair and a wrinkled face, held his leather money pouch close to his chest and plucked out a dime, handing it to Jubal as if it were his last cent. His grandson, Zig, lived with him. Jubal guessed Zig was about thirty-five. He was tall with blond hair and had scads of pimples. When Zig smiled, it looked like black bullet holes had been shot between his front teeth.

"Hi, Jubilant." Zig stood on his tiptoes in back of his grandfather before the old man slammed the door.

Zig Kreb, who gave him the creeps, could be his dad he realized. He sure hoped that wasn't the case.

At the Quinn place, a weathered board hanging cockeyed at the foot of the drive declared the property *God's Little Acre.* Jubal guessed he could have put up a better sign in first grade.

The Quinn family was an "odd lot," as his ma described them. Henry, the family leader, claimed they made more money selling manure than milk, since day-old milk usually turned sour before it left their place. Tarpaper huts housed farm animals of all sorts. As Jubal steered down the trash-strewn path to their door, a coonhound with three legs leapt to the end of his chain and was within inches of grabbing his leg. Startled, he lost direction and almost ran into a pen of half-starved heifers pushing and shoving each other over a pile of rotten hay. He righted himself and sped past several weathered haystacks that looked like giant haunted teepees, continuing towards the largest tar-paper shack where the family lived.

After parking his bike, he stood on a rotted wooden step, getting up the nerve to knock. He peered through the dirty window next to the door. Three people—he could barely see their outline—were huddled around a small table lit by a kerosene lamp. It was so dark inside the shack that even in daylight, they needed a lamp. Jubal decided that the old man with a forest of scruffy gray hair mostly covered by a wool cap, and what looked like a hunting license pinned on the visor, must be Henry, the name listed on his paper route.

Henry looked up towards the window, slid back his chair, and limped on bowlegs to open the door. To compliment the cap, he wore red wool hunting pants and a faded flannel shirt. Through the open door, the smell of kerosene was overpowering.

"Well, well, our paperboy. I'm Henry Quinn—just call me Quinn."

The old man scuffed towards a leather-covered steamer trunk at his left. Jubal followed him into the stuffy room as Henry lifted the cover of the trunk and reached inside. He slowly rolled out a cloth money bag and slid his hand to the bottom of the pouch. With the top edge of the bag halfway up his arm, Henry's tired eyes sparked an expression of fake surprise.

"This is where I keep all my millions."

"I only need a dime," Jubal said. He watched the old man pull his arm from the bag.

"Yup, might upset yer ma if I don't pay what's due Jubilant." He gave a raspy smoker's laugh.

A younger guy at the table yelled, "Quinn, shut yer mouth!"

Jubal took his dime and backed out of the shack, closing the door. He figured the younger guy was probably in on the *mickey.* He jumped on his bike and left, weaving around the ghostly haystacks and lifting his feet off the pedals when he zoomed by the three-legged dog.

Delivering down Main Street, he spent extra time visiting retired English teacher Miss Curry at her library. He hadn't seen her in a while, and when he found her seated behind a cherry desk, he noticed she still wore her white hair in a bun. Upon recognizing him, she broke into a welcoming smile that deepened the crow-tracks at the edges of her eyes.

"Hello, Jubal. How are you?"

"I'm okay, Miss Curry. I've started delivering the weekly paper."

"I heard that. Good for you. Remember when you were just learning to ride your bike? You came here often to read the *Mother West Wind* stories. They were your favorite."

"Yeah, Miss Curry, I sure do miss coming. But I've really been busy on the farm with chores and also going to school." He walked beyond the desk where there were openly displayed books and articles about Germany's Adolf Hitler on a shelf. Some people in town called her a Nazi for having such reading available, but she fiercely defended it. "After all, it's my library!"

Jubal liked that Miss Curry was a tough-minded lady. "I wish I had the time to come here and learn about things that I never knew."

"You do that. The world awaits you from the pages of a book." She pulled a desk drawer open and passed him a dime and nickel for the newspaper he handed her. "Thank you, dear. I hope to see you come in more often." Miss Curry took the paper and scanned the front page. "Oh, no!"

"What's the matter?"

"Trouble is brewing," she said, shaking her head. She put on her reading glasses, placing her index finger on the paper.

"What kind of trouble?" He peered over her shoulder and she pointed to a small square at the bottom left of the page. It was a picture of a soccer team with their arms raised straight in front of them in a salute.

"A Nazi salute," she told him. "The English team, along with the German players, did the Nazi salute at the World Cup, for the sake of friendly relations with Hitler." She squinted at the caption. "Some fans threw tomatoes and eggs."

He laughed. "That must have been something!"

Miss Curry frowned. "This is no laughing matter. War is coming, mark my words."

He nodded. "My father says the same thing."

They both stood in silence, staring down at the picture.

"Well," he said, backing away, "so long, Miss Curry. I'll try to come when I can." But he wondered with all the farm work he had to do when he'd ever have another chance to come to sit and read at Miss Curry's library.

The next few stops on his route were a row of houses on Main Street that belonged to old couples and single ladies. They all made of him as if he were the living end, saying stuff like, "Handsome young man. Rose must be proud of you." And, "I'll bet all the girls love you. . . ." Most gave him the dime and nickel tip.

One stop on Main Street was important. Mary White was Hayesville's town clerk, treasurer, and tax collector. Her office was on the backend of her house and all the town's business took place there. He remembered that his folks never paid their taxes on time, hearing them discuss the issue sometimes at meals. Consequently, he was nervous when going to the back door to collect his dime. Miss White was busy writing in a big book at her desk. Her hair was neatly styled and she wore just a light touch of makeup. She wasn't interested in him when he entered the little office, which he did without knocking because there was a *Welcome: Please Enter* sign at the back door.

She was all business. "Let's see. You're Clyde and Rose Brown's son?"

"Yes." Since owing back taxes, he figured his family's name must be significant. But, if so he couldn't tell.

She opened a drawer at her desk. "Here's a dime."

"Thanks." That was it, the end of their conversation. He was a little surprised he didn't get a tip, but he guessed that in town business every cent had to be accounted for and therefore no tips were allowed.

Leaving the town clerk's office, he rode past the Hiram Garfield Hayes statue. Hayesville had gotten its name as a memorial to this small-town hero. Jubal had once read at the library that in 1775, Hayes and a band of pioneers forged their way up a large river into fertile bottomland. They named the river the Walloomsac in honor of their heritage—Walloom Celtics from Belgium. The three letters, *sac*, were added to the name in recognition of the Indians who, at the time, shared the river with the pioneers.

Hayes, a fearless patriot, had joined in the fight against England and was eventually killed during the War of 1812. In a military uniform, the likeness of Hayes featured a cocked hat and a musket held at his side. The statue, carved of granite from the Barre quarries, was a focal point in the center of town.

He pedaled on.

O'Mara's Drugstore already sold the paper, so there was no need to stop. He was glad he didn't have to face Andrew O'Mara, a big shot at St. Anne's, and feel like a country clod. To Mr. O'Mara he guessed he was a heathen, a lowly farm kid. However, even after his mom's story, he still fantasized about Polly. No doubt, her dad would not approve.

Down at the end of the street, Jubal passed by Sean O'Grady's service station and figured Mr. O'Grady probably got his paper at the pharmacy since Eugene had told him not to leave one there.

Near the end of the village, the Catholic rectory sat next to the church. Jubal knocked on the side door and Mipsy Green's mom, Mabel, answered.

"Oh!" She looked surprised to see him instead of Eugene holding the rolled-up paper. "Come in, Jubal."

The rectory was in great shape with polished floors, beautiful rugs, and shiny wood trim. "I have your paper," he said, holding it out to her.

Mabel reached in her pocket and handed him a dime.

As he was about to thank her, Father Mac came out from a side room that appeared to be his office. He wore a black suit and a collar that resembled a neck strap for a dog, only it was white. Father Mac seemed young for a priest. His smile, which took up most of his round face, struck Jubal as weird—like a smiley face pasted on the moon. Father Mac pulled a comb from his vest pocket and ran it through his short black hair, apparently a nervous habit since his hair was already neatly in place. Jubal backed up a couple of steps as Father Mac came towards him.

"You're Jubal Brown, Rose Brown's son."

As Father Mac looked him up and down, he felt as though the priest could see right through to his sinful notions about Polly. "Yeah." He cleared his throat. "Clyde Brown's my dad."

Father Mac's expression didn't change. Though the man wasn't Hayesville's priest in 1924, Jubal wondered if he knew something about his real dad since Father Mac regularly heard confessions from the townsfolk.

"Polly O'Mara, delightful young girl, is your neighbor I think?" Father Mac asked.

"She lives next door. Eugene and I see her once in awhile." He continued to feel that the priest could sense his attraction to the girl who might be his cousin.

Father Mac's strange smile changed ever so slightly at the mention of Eugene.

"Oh, of course, Eugene." He stuck two fingers inside his white collar and ran them back and forth, as if the cloth was choking him. "He's, well . . . he's— "

"You know Eugene? He's Lady Lamont's son."

Father Mac wrinkled his forehead as if smelling a bad odor. "Yes, of course."

"Eugene lives nearby and we're good friends."

He wanted Father Mac to know skin color didn't matter to him. Eugene was Catholic but almost never went to Mass, so the priest probably didn't know him well, or maybe thought Eugene would never get to heaven if he didn't mend his ways and come to church. Jubal realized that Father Mac probably considered that he was also bound for hell, since he had no church at all. However, a couple of years back, his dad had straightened him out on the subject.

"Hell is something we never see," he told Jubal. "A belief that can't be proven. Father Mac scares folks so they'll come to Mass and fork over money so he can buy his big cars."

Jubal thought his dad's take on the matter was likely right. He felt the urge to escape the shine and polish of the rectory and get back to his paper route. But he stood as if under the spell of the black-clad priest, still wondering about the guy's reaction to Eugene. Polly said that Father Mac was a "man of God," yet he now wondered if God saw color. He, himself, never thought much about Eugene being Black. That's what friendship does—people are just people.

Father Mac edged closer and Jubal caught a whiff of the guy's breath: peppermint. A Life Savers candy rode on his tongue, looking like a white pebble. Jubal took another step back.

He remembered Polly saying that Father Mac came from the South and he knew from history class in school that many southerners felt differently about color than his family.

Father Mac's shoulders relaxed and the smile returned. The vapors of mint were strong.

"If you'd like," Father Mac said, "you could join us for catechism."

The offer caught him off guard. Thinking quickly, he replied, "Oh, I'm in the barn doing chores when Polly leaves for catechism." What he really wanted to say was that he was quite happy not being Catholic.

The priest nodded. "Be that as it may, let me show you where we meet with our parish's young people, in case you change your mind." Father Mac moved towards a doorway, gesturing for him to follow.

Jubal looked at the flight of stairs carpeted with a thick red runner. "Uh, thanks but . . . I've got to go."

"Oh. Okay." The priest looked genuinely disappointed.

"Maybe some other day," he lied.

Outside he grabbed his bike and jumped on, happy to be away from the place and the creepy priest. After leaving the rectory he passed the town hall and rode out to Hammer Brown's house. Hammer was his dad's brother. He lived at a run-down farm deserted since the Civilian Conservation Corps left. A smooth, flat field in back of the barn had been used as a campground for the workers while the dam was built. At the time, Hammer had lined his pockets with easy rent, spending the money on booze and gambling. He'd also been a boxer in the Saturday night fights among the CCC workers, but he'd taken too many blows to the head and hadn't been right since. "Punch Drunk" they called it.

For some years after the dam was finished and the workers had left, his dad cut hay at Hammer's, but didn't anymore. The only item of value at the place was a shiny black '39 Chevy. Hammer, who did odd jobs around town, probably poured his last cent into the fancy rig.

He never came to visit, so Jubal didn't know him well. His ma claimed Hammer as her brother-in-law just to be nice, for he didn't act in a brotherly fashion, much less like an uncle. The few times that Jubal did meet him, Hammer had turned him off as being just a big bag of wind.

He knocked on the weather-beaten door and Hammer's wife, Gloria, answered. She was haggard with a long, thin face and black bags under her eyes. She wore a faded print dress draped over her skinny frame. Clem Gochy had been heard to say that Hammer beat the crap out of his wife whenever he got the chance. Although Clem was known to exaggerate every story he told, Jubal believed the claim when meeting her. Hammer came striding over to the door in his undershirt to stand behind her.

"Our new paperboy, Jubilant Brown."

"Folks just call me Jubal."

"Yeah, well, I hope ya do better deliverin' my paper than the nigger kid. Can't have him showin' up a Yankee fathered by the horny boys of Hayesville." He tipped his head back and laughed, an ugly, mean sound.

The hair rose on the back of Jubal's neck. "Eugene and I are friends!" He wanted to dive into the jerk right then and there, but knew better than to tackle a boxer. The guy probably wore the undershirt to show off his bulging muscles.

Hammer reached for a dime. Jubal wasn't expecting a tip. Gloria had long since left the doorway, and without a doubt she didn't have a cent to her name. He turned and left quickly.

As he rode his bike, the morning was moving on and the warmth of the day made him glad he was almost done his route for the week. He didn't think much of the guys he'd met so far, except for Mike Harlow. Jubal decided that Mike would be an okay dad.

Jazz Crow's junkyard was his last stop. A sign by the road squeaked on its hinges as it swung back and forth in the breeze:

Crow's Garage
Elderly Parts on Sale

Crow's twenty-acre field ran along the Walloomsac River. Jubal wove his bike in and around a bunch of wrecked cars, heading for the office. Looking more like a huge shed, the "office" was a flat, one-story building, unpainted with few windows. He entered to find Jazz playing his clarinet and Slag Perkins, his helper, tap-dancing with the *clickity-clack* ringing off the floor. The large room, lit by three bare bulbs hanging from wires, was full of engine blocks, radiators, transmissions, generators, and carburetors. Smaller auto parts lined the path to Jazz's desk. Jazz stopped playing and laid his clarinet down when he saw Jubal.

"Meet Jubal Brown," Jazz said to Slag. "My neighbors' boy from up on Harmony Hill." Jazz, wearing greasy coveralls, had a twinkle in his eye. "Let's see that paper. We'll find out who got caught doing somethin' I already know about."

Reaching to give him the paper, Jubal noticed a German shepherd stretched out in front of Jazz's desk.

Jazz looked down. "Babe's my guard dog, takes over for the night shift when we leave." The dog slapped her tail on the floor at the sound of her name.

Slag said, “Yeah, when no one’s around Babe’ll bite yer ass if she catches ya stealin’ parts.”

Jubal noted Babe’s sharp teeth as she caught the biscuit Jazz tossed her way. “I’ll bet she could.”

Jazz handed him two dimes. “Here, have some extra.”

“Gee, thanks.” It was the best tip he’d gotten all day.

“Sure thing, Jubal.” Jazz opened the paper and began scanning the headlines.

Riding his bike towards home, Jubal wished everyone on his route was like Jazz Crow. Jazz and Mike Harlow were the best guys he’d met, but neither man matched his looks. He came to realize, based on looks and build, that Tatum O’ Mara was most likely his real dad and this caused a rush of regret.

Part way up the long hill, he had to get off and push his bike up the steep grade. His pockets being heavy with change gave him a good feeling—tip money he could call his own.

When he got home he put every cent he’d earned into a glass Esso bank he kept on top of his bureau, slipping the dimes and nickels through the narrow slot. When he had eventually saved enough from his route, he had a plan to swap out the change for dollar bills. With a long, flat knife, he figured he could retrieve the change, but once he slipped the paper money through the slot, he knew he’d have to smash the glass to get it back—his idea of forced saving.

Chapter Nine

At the start of her summer vacation early that June of 1941, Maria left home for the Catholic Youth Organization camp. It was Saturday. She was jealous because Polly didn't have to go early—only when camp opened the next day on Sunday. Maria had seldom been away from Avery's farm and felt pangs of homesickness already. Even as a kid, she had poured over farm magazines, especially *The American Agriculturalist* where she learned things like proper care for draft horses and methods of harness repair. Avery often called her, "The idea girl who grow'd up fast."

She preferred to clean out horse stalls and help her dad work on farm equipment, yet she'd gained the attention of Father Mac to become his Rose Queen. It was probably because she was grown up for her age and serious about Catholicism. Father Mac wanted a proud showing of St. Anne's Catholic youth. This year, the new bishop, Father Shea, was invited to attend the 5th of July parade. A viewing stand in front of the rectory was to be built for Father Shea and other Catholic big shots coming from the Rutland and Burlington dioceses. She continued to feel that Polly would have been the better choice for queen with her ladylike ways and her father's standing in the church.

Maria's spirits were low as she left the yard riding in the back seat next to Father Mac in St. Anne's black Cadillac with Tatum as chauffeur.

There was one thought, however, that made leaving Avery's for the summer almost bearable. Lately, she had fantasies of having a boyfriend, someone new, different from Hayesville boys. She often imagined, before she fell asleep, being in some worldly, handsome guy's arms, though she didn't have a clue what an exciting lover would be like. Just maybe, she could meet such a guy at camp.

Yet, it was often Jubal who walked, big as life, right into her imaginings. This surprised her as Jubal in no way measured up to her fantasy guy—he was too young and too ordinary. She did admire how upbeat he was despite the sorry state of his family's farm. But really, he was just a friend.

On their way to camp in the classy car, they passed many farms through the Champlain Valley with herds of cows grazing on fields that went for acres and acres down towards the shore. The New York side of the lake had a ridge of deep green mountains abutting a road that followed the shoreline. When leaving the Lake Champlain countryside, they soon came to a smaller body of water. The highway wound close to a cluster of camps near the road, only feet from the water. There she saw sailboats, rowboats, and a number of swimmers. It seemed strange to her that there were folks who took vacations and didn't have to work all the time.

Within minutes the view opened up to more farmland where teams of horses pulled mowers through hayfields. She saw her first tractor, a Farmall pulling a rake. She wondered how long it would be before Avery would have tractors instead of horses, since he was always in the lead to modernize his farm.

Father Mac had been quiet for most of the ride. But he now announced that they were nearing Camp Saint Mary. He began to explain what was expected of her as a camp counselor, how she would sleep in a cabin with ten girls, assist in the daily program, and help at mealtimes. Right away, Maria felt under the priest's thumb.

"I know nothing about CYO camp," she protested. "Never been there in my life. I won't know where to start!"

She stopped, worried her outburst would anger the priest. Father Mac leaned against the passenger door in his pressed black suit with his knees drawn up.

When he didn't react, she finished, "I know all about farm stuff, but a bunch of girls?"

He turned and gave her a jerky smile. "Look, don't worry. Mother Superior, Sister Naomi, is in charge. She rules the place with an iron fist. Try your best, stay on her good side, and you'll do fine."

Her stomach turned sour as if hit by a rotten tomato as she realized she'd be under the orders of both the priest *and* the nun. She preferred to be in charge of her own decisions.

Tatum muttered, "You'll see. Empress Superior struts around all important, like she has a cob up her ass."

Father Mac let out a high-pitched giggle. "Tatum, don't talk like that! We have a young lady with us!" He took a comb from his shirt pocket and ran it through his closely-trimmed hair. He giggled again. Then he turned to her. "You didn't hear that!"

She had no comment. She continued to feel sour as the big car exited the highway onto a gravel road that traveled through dense woods. Within less than a mile, they came to a stop in the camp yard where she saw low, weathered buildings surrounded by spruce and fir trees. Father Mac explained that the place was once the home of the Civilian Conservation Corps.

On arrival they saw a nun in her black habit walking slightly bent with a cane. As the old woman hobbled towards a door with a placard, *Office,* over the entrance, Maria saw what Tatum was talking about—the cob thing. But in her present mood, she didn't think it was funny.

Tatum grumbled, "There's the old bag!"

Father Mac giggled again and then told Maria to report to the office.

With her suitcase, she left the car feeling a pang of dread and proceeded slowly across the gravel yard to the drab office building, her feet feeling heavy as workhorse hooves.

She found Mother Superior sitting behind a makeshift wooden desk. A large crucifix hung above the nun between the vertical studs of the rough-board wall. No other pictures decorated the small room. Mother Superior, in her robe designating her service to God, barely smiled as Maria stood before her.

She peered over the top of her steel-rim glasses. "So you're the Styles girl that has come with a glowing recommendation," she said. "I hope you'll find your time here to be pleasant."

"Yes, I hope so." Maria decided to try her best to live up to the glowing report, though she felt like an unwilling prisoner.

Mother Superior pointed a gnarled finger at Maria's faded jeans. "I'm sure you will present yourself as a proper example for our girls. You will wear skirts and dresses at all times while camp is in session."

Maria nodded. "I've come prepared with proper clothes in my suitcase."

Truth be told, her mother had made plans for a special trip to Rutland to buy her the needed clothing from a department store, but at the last minute Maria refused her ma, claiming she had nearly enough to wear. What she needed could be purchased from the general store in town. She already had a couple of dresses for church, enough to stay clean and ladylike.

"Good." The nun gestured to the window and the campgrounds. "I've asked Father MacMurray to bring you today so you can familiarize yourself with Camp Saint Mary before the children arrive, since you've never been here before. We'll have nearly one hundred boys and girls for the week. Saturday will be cleanup, and by Sunday afternoon, a new group of children will arrive. I'm assigning you to Cabin Ten. After breakfast, I'll inspect for general orderliness with all beds made and clothes neatly put away. The other cabins throughout the grounds will be the responsibility of older counselors here from the Burlington and Rutland dioceses."

Maria nodded again. Of course the nun had made no mention of a Mr. Right. Still, she hoped some guy might walk out of the woods and take the sting out of her unwelcome daily duties. Looking at the sour old woman, she found it hard to imagine that the nun was ever young. Had she been pretty? Had she ever been kissed?

Mother Superior continued, "A cabin of ten-year-old girls will be your nighttime responsibility. We are strict at Camp Saint Mary. Lights out at nine o'clock with no talking. I insist on complete quiet. You and your girls will sit together for meals—set, serve, and clear your own table. You can also help in the dining hall. During the day you'll be under the direction of Father Hebert who is in charge of recreation. Do you have any questions?"

Maria felt as if about to cry. "I don't know if I can do all this."

"You'll learn quickly."

"That's it? All the help I get?"

Mother Superior answered sharply, "I'm here around the clock. Come to me with questions or any problems you might have."

"I'm sure I'll be coming to you a lot."

"You'll find Cabin Ten a short walk to your right and up the hill."

Apparently dismissed, Maria picked up her suitcase and turned on her heel. She already hated the cold, all-business nun and dreary Saint Mary's.

Cabin Ten was a simple structure, painted green and perched on a knoll with no shade. It was the only cabin that wasn't tucked back into the woods. By the time she hefted her suitcase onto her narrow bunk, the day had grown hot. She immediately opened a window for fresh air. The cabin was stuffy, smelling of pine pitch that oozed from knotty boards.

There were five other bunk beds, enough for ten campers. She dragged her single bed to place it near the door. After she unpacked some of her things, she looked around for something to do to quiet her irritation. The campers wouldn't begin arriving until the following afternoon, and she had seen Tatum and Father Mac leave. It seemed like a good time to check out the grounds.

She changed into shorts and followed a path that climbed to the top of a steep slope where she could see the lake through a stand of hardwood saplings. The forest floor gave off an earthy scent. A red squirrel scampered across the matted leaves and up a tree where it rested on a limb, flicking its tail as a warning of danger. She huffed, "What danger! You little scuff."

Next to the pathway, she passed several cabins shaded by evergreens. Maybe it was a seniority thing, being assigned the least desirable cabin, the only one in direct sun—she was the youngest with no experience. She had also noted that Cabin Ten was situated where she could be watched like a little kid.

She took a deep breath, refusing to wallow in a negative outlook. On chilly mornings, she and her campers would wake up to a warm room, while the shaded cabins would be cold. And the woods around her were beautiful with occasional ground cover of velvet mosses and blankets of bluets. At the end of the path, she spied the lake's sandy shore. The noonday sun glimmered off the calm water, alive with various hues of yellow and orange. There wasn't a soul in sight.

Then came a guy about her age, or a bit older, walking from a beach house tucked at the wood's edge. He carried an armload of tangled rope. She watched from the pathway while he tried to untangle what she quickly assessed might be the boundary line to be placed in the water for safe swimming. The rope looked like a nest of coiled snakes.

His voice rose in anger, "Son-of-a-bitch! What a goddamned heap!" He threw the rope on the ground and looked at it in a sulk.

Though his reaction struck her as that of a spoiled kid, she also noticed that he was handsome and shirtless, wearing only a pair of khaki shorts. He had short blonde hair, a square chin, and a pug nose. He hadn't noticed her yet.

She walked into view. "Want some help?" she called.

In the midst of his anger fit, he jumped to attention. As she walked towards him, his demeanor changed quickly as a wide grin spread across his face. "I'm Freddie, Freddie Coleman. Swimming instructor and life-guard. Your name?"

"Maria Styles, counselor in Cabin Ten." She took in his hard-muscled chest the color of a new penny.

"Some no-brain left this rope in terrible shape," he said, pointing down at the tangled mess.

She nodded. Close up, Freddie looked much older, showing creases at the edges of his eyes. Maybe he was thirty or more. He exuded a strong, sweet smell. She was puzzled, never realizing such a smell was a manly thing. Then again, she'd never before been up close to a Mister Atlas.

"You . . . you've seen lots of sun?"

"Yeah, Key West."

"Key West?" She frowned, suddenly feeling like a country bumpkin.

"Florida. It's the furthest key."

"Key?" She pictured a large gold key.

He laughed. "Yeah, a key's like an island."

"Oh." To hide her red face, she bent and easily located an end of the rope, beginning to follow it through the snare. In a couple of minutes she had untangled the whole pile.

He stared down at the neatly coiled rope. "How . . . how did you know to . . ."

"Trip rope on a hay fork."

Now it was his turn to look confused.

She smiled. "The small rope you pull to open the jaws of a hay fork, dumping the loose hay where you want it in the mow. Gets tangled all the time." While she rather liked his muscular presence, the flowery smell put her on guard.

"Oh." His gaze dropped to her breasts then roamed down to her bare legs.

She edged a little closer to the shore. "That pile of wooden floats need to be threaded on to this thing?"

"Yeah, sure. Want to help?"

She shrugged. "I've got nothing better to do."

She started the process while he placed the floats at intervals on the hundred-foot rope. When the last slid on, she knotted the end.

He pointed at two steel rims. "We'll carry an anchor out about three feet deep and drop it."

She kicked off her sneakers, picked up the anchor and rope, and waded into water up to her thighs. "Right here?"

"Perfect!"

When they emerged from the shallows, Freddie looked back at the floating white markers. "I dreaded this job, doing it alone. Thanks . . . you made it easy."

"Glad to help." She sat in the sand putting on her sneakers.

"Would you have time to help me with the benches and chairs? Oh, and the rowboat? I need to bring them out from the beach shed." He reached down and grabbed her hand to help her stand.

His forceful pull caused her to nearly fall into his arms. She put out her hands at the last minute, catching herself, palms to his chest, avoiding a full body collision. She dropped her hands and stood back.

"Wow! Thanks for the lift up. I'm pretty strong, just so you know," she joked. "I'll be glad to help."

He reached out for her midsection and she took another step back.

"Sorry," he said, dropping his arm.

"It's fine. Let's get that stuff out."

They walked side by side to the small building at the edge of the woods. Before long they had all the beach furniture in place, along with a rowboat. She wondered if she'd be able to spend time on the beach or go out on the water, more things that might make her summer bearable. If the other guys were as good-looking as Mr. Atlas, perhaps CYO camp wouldn't be so bad after all.

"Well, Maria," Freddie said, turning to her, "you've been a great help. Care for a soda?"

"Sure, that would hit the spot."

He pulled a couple of Sun Crest bottles from his knapsack, opened them, and sat on a bench they'd just pulled from the shed. He patted a spot on the seat and held out an orange soda. The cold, fizzy drink looked thirst-quenching after having dragged the heavy items around in the hot sun. She took the glass bottle from his hand and sat at the far end of the bench. Freddie slid to the middle, stretched out his long legs, and kicked off his sandals.

As much as Freddie seemed decent, possibly even kind, she felt in uncertain territory. She really had little experience with guys, being mostly on the farm. She didn't feel the boys at school counted. Freddie was at least fifteen years older and worldly with having lived down in Key West, which sounded like a fancy place. He probably had plenty of women in his past. The way he acted—his hands almost in a tease to touch her, closing the space between them—he seemed to be testing her reactions.

"You in school?" he asked.

"Yeah." She took a swallow of the orange soda, the sweet bubbles a delightful taste. "Friday was my last day."

"You teach? What subject?"

She paused. How easy to lead him on in a white lie.

"What do you teach?" he repeated.

"Oh, it's not important. I'd just as soon forget about school." She looked out across the water as a sailboat made its way from the far shore.

"Well, sorry."

She had a host of wild thoughts. Here was a chance to be someone other than a pure and innocent Rose Queen, just an ordinary gal wanting a guy. Maybe she was much different than Father Mac thought. "Romance languages."

"Romance languages?"

"French . . . and Spanish." She'd taken French in school, but was far from bilingual.

He raised an eyebrow.

"Oui, Monsieur." She hoped he couldn't tell that, other than French basics, she didn't have a lick of knowledge concerning either language.

He cleared his throat. "I'm impressed—you know farm work *and* foreign languages. A girl of all trades. So being here at camp, staying at number Ten is . . . your summer mission?"

"Right, something like that. I like helping out wherever I can." She smiled.

He raked his fingers through his blond crew cut. "I pegged you as being in your early twenties when I saw you from the woods, when you came with Tatum and his sidekick."

So, he'd been watching her then. "Sidekick? You mean Father Mac?" This was a first, speaking of a priest without respect.

"Yeah, he's a priest, but he's a Key West kinda guy."

"What do you mean 'Key West kind of guy'? Father Mac is our priest at St. Anne's."

"He and I are Key West friends from way back. Bumming around on the beach. We bar-hopped on Duval Street and stuff like that."

Maria tried hard to picture Father Mac on a beach and drinking in a bar. "Father Mac? That's impossible!"

"Hate to tell you, it's true. No matter. Forget I even mentioned it." He took a last swallow of his soda and tossed the bottle in the sand by his knapsack. "By the way, if you don't mind my asking, how old *are* you?"

This was her chance to string the guy along and have some fun. "Just turned thirty," she said.

"Oh, wow! Older than you look." He studied her. "Well, I've still got you beat by a couple of years. I bet you're already taken by a handsome guy waiting in the wings."

She laughed. "Gee, you want my whole story on first meeting?"

"Right, we'll be together a lot this summer. You know, there are night parties and things like that. We manage to pull 'em off without Mother Superior snooping around."

"At cabin Ten, I'll be under the eagle eye of Mother Superior."

He grinned. "Maybe, but not tonight. Camp hasn't even started yet. What do you say we graze the kitchen cooler for a bite to eat and then change into our suits to take a dip in the lake? We can sit in the beach house, have a nip of wine—we'll make a night out of it."

"That sounds fun. Better than sitting in my cabin by myself."

He winked. "It's a date. Meet me at six at the dining hall."

She slipped through the trees, out of sight of the beach, and headed for the path back to her cabin. The brilliant green of the trees cast a thousand shafts of afternoon light through the low hanging branches as she flew with the feel of wings on her feet. A date! Already! She didn't know when she'd been so excited. Maybe even more excited than when Avery brought home his new, spirited Morgan team. Getting to know Freddie might be interesting, that is, if she could maneuver her way around the lies she'd just left behind. Then she recalled one of her English teachers quoting a poem by Sir Walter Scott: *Oh! What a tangled web we weave when first we practice to deceive!*

When she reached the parking lot, Mother Superior was just coming from Cabin Ten. The old nun proceeded slowly, intent on placing her cane in just the right spots on the path. Seeing the Mother Superior, Maria felt her white lies were hanging visibly in the air.

"So there you are," the nun said, looking up.

"I've just taken a walk to familiarize myself with the grounds."

"Good idea. Did you meet anyone on your walk?"

"No. Should I have?"

"Well, no. But I am expecting our swimming instructor to arrive soon. He comes and goes as he wishes when not on duty."

"I didn't see anyone. But . . . the lake is pretty," Maria said.

"It is. Since you're first to arrive, I'd like to take you to hear Bishop Shea's message in Burlington, followed by a Saturday evening Mass. Father Hebert will be here soon to give us a ride. I don't want you alone here at camp. Father Mac and Tatum have gone to play bingo, it being their night off."

A long ride to Burlington in the car with Father Hebert and the stern old woman sounded positively like torture. She had to think fast. "Uh, thank you for the offer," she said. "But, I'd really like to stay here to . . . continue my study of the saints. Since I'll be so busy after tonight, I'd just like to stay in my cabin and read. It's been a long day."

Mother Superior narrowed her eyes. "Just what saint particularly interests you?"

The lies were piling up like dead cluster flies on the window sills of her bedroom at Avery's farm. "Saint Christopher, patron saint of travelers. You see, my folks always had his medallion in our car."

"Interesting. Saint Christopher is one of my favorites." Mother Superior smiled thinly. "Okay, as long as you won't be scared here in your cabin all by yourself. I certainly want to encourage your studies."

"Thank you, Mother Superior."

"I'll return later tonight. You can easily find food for a snack in the kitchen's refrigerator." Mother Superior planted her cane to continue on her way.

Maria's heart leapt. Tonight the good girl Rose Queen would be swimming and sipping wine with Mr. Atlas. At the same time, she felt uneasy. She was definitely stepping outside of her comfort zone. As Clem Gochy was known to say when telling one of his tall tales, "One big lie always deserves another."

⨯

Back in his apartment at the beach house, Freddie was thinking he was mighty lucky to have snagged a gorgeous doll for some night action. It was always a long summer at CYO camp, but it was money at a time of year when the tourists had left the Keys, so he came. And what a catch she was! She had class, and a body to die for. He thought her possibly his age or maybe younger, didn't matter. She was self-assured, like she probably had a lot of experience on the pad. Unlike his fat stepsister that diddled him as a kid, pulling him onto herself. He'd felt helpless with his face in the folds of her bosom, his groin responding. He had tried hard not to give in to feeling scared and kept quiet about it after.

Always at CYO camp, he'd been monitored by the nuns with eyes of God watching him like a hawk. He was goddamned sick of it, so today he'd made it in the back way from town to camp without anyone discovering he was there. He was free for a while, out from under the supervision of Mother Superior, the old bitch. She didn't have a ghost of an idea about what he'd suffered.

He stood in the shower, soaping himself into a good lather, slowly running his hands over his body and dreaming of the night to come. His beach house bungalow had only a bed, a table, two chairs, and a cupboard where he kept snacks and a few bottles of his favorite red wine, *Valley of the Moon.*

He'd had many glasses of the stuff as an altar boy. The priest in his church had used that brand of wine for the Eucharist. After Mass, the guy drank generous amounts of the bottle and shared it with him, turning

Freddie in his drunkenness into an easy victim. Rather than recalling those moments when the priest had taken advantage, *Valley of the Moon* now reminded Freddie of how he'd had the last laugh. Revenge was so very satisfying.

But no need dwelling on such memories now. The wine made being out in East Puckerbrush, Vermont for days on end tolerable. Tonight would be different.

He played out the scenario: It would start at the dining hall. They'd eat a snack and walk back to his place, possibly holding hands. He'd get her to think he was romantic. They'd maybe sit at his little table. He'd stare into her eyes, and tell some jokes to get her laughing. He bet he could convince her to drink a glass or two, possibly more. After the wine, he'd lead her to the beach where he'd spread a blanket on the sand. They'd sit side by side and watch the sun go down.

When night fell, the drink would have made her real sociable. He'd suggest the thrill of skinny-dipping. It would be daring and sexy. This gal wanted to shed her good girl image—she wore that desire like a neon sign. If she was agreeable, they'd splash around and get playful. She'd be trusting him then. The perfect time for a long kiss in the water. She'd feel like she was in a beach movie with a tan, muscular blond guy. She'd feel the cool water on her skin, notice the first stars coming out. When they headed back to the blanket, the action would begin. A slam dunk, easy as pie.

He was so excited over his plan while slathering cologne over his chest, it felt like he was about to bust out of his undershorts. He cautioned, "Play it slow and easy. No hurry—we have all night." He'd never had a chance at such a nice, sexy babe, ever.

Chapter Ten

On the run, Maria reached Cabin Ten in a puzzle over her upcoming date with Freddie Coleman. Once through the door and into the cabin, she picked up a small hand mirror she'd packed in her luggage, wondering what she must have looked like to attract Freddie's interest. On Avery's farm she hardly ever gave a care about her looks. She set the mirror on a narrow pine ledge that ran the length of the wall above her bed.

First, she collected the wild, loose strands of her hair, pinning them in place with bobby pins. Next, she studied her blue eyes and freckled face . . . not bad. She angled the mirror downward. Tentatively, she raised her shirt. God, her breasts were awful. Two grapefruits with nipples the shape and color of decapitated earthworms. Continuing on, she was okay with her slender waist, but then lower, that patch of black hair was the doorway to trouble. She could protect her secret self with clothing—her entrance was her temple and she wouldn't let any fellow through the door until after marriage. She'd been warned at school that some enter without knocking, which put her especially on guard. Moving down, she rather liked her long, shapely legs. She was also satisfied with her feet; they were slender with perfect toes and curved arches. But she couldn't imagine that a guy would get passionate over feet.

Her mother had insisted she buy a bra for working at the camp. Since Maria refused to go to Rutland, there had been no choice but to shop for her first bra at the Hayesville Store where the selection was small. Up to that point, she'd been wearing a tight jersey under a loose-fitting shirt, on the farm and at school, to solve the problem.

Dressing for her date, she tried on the new bra and found that the cups fit but were sewn to a point, making her look like some Hollywood sex queen. That wouldn't do. She took the thing off and tossed it on her bed.

Freddie had mentioned swimming, so she thought she should try on the one-piece suit that she'd also bought at the store, selected from Bert's sparse inventory. It was navy blue, all wool with a very short skirt. Since the IGA had no dressing room, she'd never tried it on.

With the cabin door shut, she stripped down to put her first foot through a leg-hole in the scratchy suit, and then the second. Grabbing each strap, she pulled the suit up and slipped a strap over each shoulder. She tried to tuck in her breasts only to discover that the cup size was way too small and her waist was too long. The suit had no elasticity. Consequently, she couldn't stand up straight as the bottom of the thing cut terribly into her crotch. She scuffed around the cabin, bent like an old woman, hoping somehow the fabric would stretch. It didn't. She tore the suit off, threw it across the room, and flopped on her bed in tears. She'd been stupid, lying to Freddie. Since when does a thirty year old *not* have a swimsuit that fits?

And what about the wine? Certainly a woman of her fictional age would have had a drink or two, but of course at fifteen, living in an alcohol-free home, she'd never had a drop. She tried to picture herself downing her first glass. She needed to act casual or pretty quickly he'd realize she had lied. When he discovered that fact, what would he do? He'd been nearly in a rage over a bunch of tangled rope. A terrific pang of homesickness and an urge to leave camp took hold. She wanted to start walking home. A crazy thought, since she hadn't a clue which road to take.

After a short cry, she got up, slipped on her panties, and put on a sky-blue t-shirt that flattened her chest. The pocket watch on the shelf by her bed was one her mother had given her as a going away gift. She tipped up the silver timepiece. Five-thirty. In a hurry, she chose a navy blue skirt and a dark blue V-neck sweater to accent the t-shirt. Checking in the mirror, she decided she looked okay and applied a little lipstick she'd also bought though her ma had been reluctant feeling that a plain but proper appearance was best. Having never worn the stuff, it took several tries and a few blots with a tissue before Maria was ready to go.

She walked out of the cabin into a beautiful evening with a warm breeze and a cloudless sky. But she couldn't enjoy her surroundings for long, or the evening call of a white-throated sparrow, because soon her sights were on Freddie headed towards the dining hall off in the distance. She stopped abruptly on sight of him, standing hidden behind a tall spruce.

His appearance caught her breath. His unbuttoned shirt flapped in the breeze, showing his magnificent muscles and the bronze tan she'd noted earlier. His idea of a swimsuit—tight-fit like underwear briefs—was like nothing she'd ever seen on Hayesville guys when they swam at the reservoir on hot afternoons. She decided it must be a Key West thing. If it weren't for the shirt, the briefs, and a pair of sandals, she could have pictured him stark naked like a statue of a Greek god.

After he opened the door and went inside, she continued on, clutching a small bag under her arm with a change of shorts and an extra shirt in case she went swimming. The weathered dining hall had stood the test of time, minus a sag here and there, and easily had the size to seat over a hundred. She climbed the few stairs to an open porch outside the entrance. Then she stood with her back to the door, looking out over the deserted parking lot. With Mother Superior gone for the evening to the Saturday night Mass, she realized how very alone she was here at the camp. Alone except for Freddie. She paused before making her grand entrance, promising herself to avoid his advances. She had to play it calm and cool and keep the upper hand.

She entered to find a long row of tables stretching the length of the hall. On the first table, Freddie had placed two paper plates side by side with a setting of wooden forks, knives, and spoons—throwaway utensils for just such an occasion. She met him coming from the kitchen carrying a tray of peanut butter and jelly jars, a loaf of white bread, and two cups of what looked like lemonade. Closeup, his much-older face sent an odd shiver through her. Now he struck her as not particularly attractive, seeming less the perfect Mr. Right of her dreams. Perhaps she was not one to fall into his arms.

He placed the tray on the table in front of the two place settings and turned to greet her. "How's it going?" He scanned her from head to toe. "Looks like you planned on a movie or something, not swimming."

It was not a great start that he was judging her outfit. She pushed the food tray aside to pull one of the place settings around to the opposite side of the table. He gave her a questioning look.

"I like that for better visiting," she explained.

"Okay," he shrugged. "Let's take a seat."

Pulling up her chair, she motioned towards the bread and peanut butter. "You go first. I'll watch to see if I can measure up to how a Key West guy makes a sandwich."

As his hand gripped the knife to slather a big gob of peanut butter in the center of a piece of white bread, she couldn't help notice he was wearing a gaudy, plastic ring she hadn't seen earlier in the day.

"That's quite a ring!"

"Yeah." He flexed his finger. "It's my girlfriend. I take her out on special occasions."

He closed his fingers and held his fist close to her face so she could get the full effect. The ring was imitation gold with a picture the size of a dime for the setting. A slight turn of his wrist and she saw the faint silhouette of a voluptuous gal in a two-piece bathing suit. Then he slightly tipped his hand to reveal the same gal as a nude pin-up.

He chuckled. "Pretty neat, huh? Quick way to undress my girl."

She blinked. This guy was an absolute jerk. She thought quickly to come up with a zinger. "How interesting. In physics class, I remember learning about the refraction of light rays. I also remember the image was that of a hen laying a golden egg—it appeared, then it vanished."

She had actually seen the picture of a hen laying a golden egg in an ad for baby chicks. It was there that she saw the words *light refraction*. She was delighted to have put one over on the dodo bird sitting across the table from her.

Freddie took a bite of his sandwich with no remark. But as he chewed, he slipped off the ring and dropped it into his shirt pocket.

She dipped with the wooden knife into the peanut butter jar and pulled out a big gob, placing it in the center of the white bread. Pressing to free the knife, she tore a hole in the bread's center, bringing with the knife a large swatch of bread. She'd always made sandwiches with her mother's homemade bread that was more durable than this white stuff. She glanced up to see him smile in amusement.

Not to be outdone by Mr. Freddie Refraction and annoyed that she seemed unable to make a simple sandwich, she quickly returned the peanut butter and bread swatch back onto the slice, rolled the corners and edges of the flimsy bread around the knife, and pressed the whole concoction to the plate. With the bread firmly stuck to the blade, she held the handle of the knife, creating what looked like a bread ball mixed with peanut butter stuck to a stick, sort of like a sausage link in appearance.

Freddie looked puzzled.

"This is how my science professor taught us to make a perfect germ-free Peanut-Switch," she explained.

"Looks like a mess to me." Freddie munched on the first half of his perfectly constructed sandwich.

She smiled. "Looks can be deceiving. Normally, I never touch my food without wearing gloves. You'd be surprised what you can catch."

Boy was she getting in deeper and deeper. The lies rolled off her tongue like rain off a tin roof.

He scowled. "That's a little weird."

To prove her point, she held the stick and nibbled on the end of the bread ball. "I bet you never washed your hands before wiping all sorts of bacteria onto the spongy pores of that bread. You might be sucking in loads of germs with each mouthful that will grow in your warm digestive system."

"Really?" Freddie looked doubtfully at his half-eaten sandwich. "I had no idea." He set the sandwich down and wiped his hands on his shirt.

She was on a roll with him snagging her line in total belief. "It's true! They've done autopsies on the dead and found oozing pus from boils clinging to the stomach wall."

"Really!" He pushed his plate away. "Don't we have natural things that control diseases?"

"Sometimes, but not always." She purposely looked at his hands. "Why take a chance and wipe your fingers all over your food when you can use my nifty Peanut-Switch method?" She realized as she fibbed that she actually had touched the bread while taking it from the wrapper. But he seemed not to notice this flaw in her logic. She leaned forward. "Lately, have you gripped anything that's not very clean?"

He closely examined his hands. "I just never thought about it."

"That's why a college degree is important. Did you know the death rate is much lower among the more highly educated?" She was rather enjoying laying it on thick. She crossed her arms and sat back, triumphant.

His stomach growled. "I don't feel quite right." He supported his head with the palm of his hand, elbow on the table.

"Oh, nonsense!" What a baby. From rage over a tangled rope to this? He was a strange fellow. "It will take at least two days before what you just ate to take hold in your body."

"Two days? What happens in two days?" He looked worried.

"If your stomach growls tonight, you'll know that the bacteria are trying to take hold. It becomes a battle of the good germs against the bad as they fight it out down below."

"Oh." He looked down at his stomach. "Oh, I see."

"Listen, go home and drink a bottle of wine. The alcohol will burn out the bacteria, and you'll sleep like a baby."

He brightened. "Now that's an idea I like!"

"Great! Let's go." She stood up, wanting to get away from this strange older guy who now seemed a little creepy.

She realized as they took their trays to the kitchen that she hadn't eaten but one bite of her sandwich. At least she'd found a way to get out of drinking the wine.

When they were out on the porch, she touched his arm. "Do you feel strong enough to get back to your cabin to start your defense against disaster?"

"I'm fine." He shrugged away her hand.

"This cool night air will help," she said, as they walked down the steps. She turned to go.

"Aren't you coming?" he asked.

"Not if you're not feeling well. How about if I check on you in the morning?"

"Yeah, whatever." His stomach growled again and he frowned. "That wasn't much of a date." He walked off into the night.

She watched him, in his ridiculous tight swim trunks, disappear up the path. Then she hurried back towards number ten. Part of her was disappointed that he was so far from her Mr. Right, yet she also felt smug upon realizing that he was dumber than she'd thought. She would have to proceed with caution around him—if he found she'd lied, who knew what he might do. She did win the night, however. She didn't have to reveal her true self.

On the way to her cabin, she stopped by the office to check a list that Mother Superior had told her she would post before leaving for Mass. Maria wanted familiarize herself with the names of the kids that were assigned to number ten, since they'd be arriving the following afternoon. Her name jumped off the paper.

Maria Styles, Junior Counselor at #10, from Hayesville High, 11th grade.

Her knees went weak. Freddie Coleman would learn the truth quicker than expected. At least the nun had noted the grade she would be in come fall, rather than the tenth grade she'd been in the past year.

Chapter Eleven

Dead tired, Rose had come home early Saturday evening from working at Lady Lamont's. It being the first weekend of June, it was still light out. However, her kitchen was dreary, lit by one forty-watt bulb hanging in the center of the room on the end of a twisted wire. She sighed while noticing, as if for the first time, the plaster that had broken loose in patches on the walls, showing the lath boards. The cupboards were old with doors that didn't fully close, hanging on the wall next to an icebox that she knew needed a block of ice. The contents in the lead-lined box were room temperature, which wasn't good as the weather had been warmer than normal. The weatherman on the Philco had recently said that 1941 was off to a strong start for crops—some positive news at least.

She hadn't left anything for the guys for supper. The milk check hadn't come and she didn't want to ask for any more advances on her pay. Consequently, she hadn't been shopping except to buy Clyde's daily supply—a situation she needed to change and soon, but it would mean taking time from work to help him dry out. Currently, it was easier to supply the beer and liquor because getting him to stop completely would be hell. Since he wasn't in his living room chair and the radio was silent, she knew she'd find him on their bed dead to the world and passed out in his clothes.

She searched the cupboards for something to cook for a meal. The guys liked tuna-pea-wiggle and biscuits. She found a can of tuna, a half loaf of bread, some canned peas, and felt relieved. But her heart sank when going to the flour bin. She'd forgotten it was empty. The recipe needed flour to make the white sauce and baking powder biscuits.

Just then Jubal and Benny came in from chores. She panicked, having come to the end of her rope. The truck needed its battery charged at Jazz's. She'd been coast-starting it when taking it to work, making sure to park it on a slope. In minutes, Bert would be closing his store, and anyway, she couldn't drive there in the truck because it often stalled when starting in first gear. If it did stall, she wouldn't be able to coast and jumpstart it on Main Street. Anyway, she only had pennies in her pocketbook. She didn't know when she had ever come to such a desperate end. She sank into a chair and put her hands over her face, fighting back tears.

"Gosh, what's wrong, Ma?" Jubal stared at her in surprise. Then he turned to Benny. "Why don't you go wash up in the bathroom?"

As Benny lumbered off, she said, "Everything's wrong. I need a bag of flour, the truck needs a charged battery, and I need money to buy the flour to make you fellows something to eat."

"Did you spend all your money on Dad's booze?" Jubal asked.

"Yes, but he's all set." She heard the judgment in his tone. "The milk check should be in the morning's mail."

He sat in a chair across from her. "Ma, this is stupid! You've let Dad run us right into the ground. You're spending too much on booze. And if Clem Gochy, gossiping out there on that bench, knows that Dad's a hopeless drunk, then everybody in town knows."

Hearing his words, it struck her that her son was becoming a man. She'd been so busy working she hadn't marked the passage. In fact, his sixteenth birthday had come and gone the previous month with little fanfare. Not all that unusual in their household but still, she should have done something, even a little celebration. A cake would have been nice. Her spirits sank further. "Look, it's not like I can control your father. What he chooses to put down his gullet is his affair."

"Well, you help him, you know . . . by buying the stuff."

"I know, I haven't handled your dad's problem as well as I could."

Clyde had slid so far. He'd been different in the days when they were first married. They'd taken romantic drives together after night chores. And he was once a great lover, holding her tenderly. But that was all in the past. He'd traded her for the bottle.

She looked Jubal in the eye. "I promise you, I'll come up with a plan to dry him out. But it's something I dread."

"I know, Ma. You've tried before. At this point, I'll help all I can to make a change."

The withdrawals were terrible—Clyde would moan and retch and shake. When he couldn't handle it anymore he'd take off for the bar downtown. If there was no money to snatch from the kitchen jar, in desperation he'd call the cattle dealer while she begged him not to. He didn't care which cow went in order to get drinking money.

Jubal glanced at the clock and she followed his gaze: twenty of seven.

"Look," he said. "I'll go to town now and buy the flour before Bert closes."

She brightened, but confessed, "I have only pennies."

"I'll take care of this; I'll get some flour."

"Oh dear, money from your bank?"

"It's okay. But while I'm gone, can you put on the coffee pot and give Benny a bowl of Vermont Crackers with milk? That ought to hold him until I get back."

After Jubal left the kitchen, she sat quietly, ashamed. In seconds, he returned from his room with his glass Esso bank. She watched him go to the silverware drawer and pull out a dinner knife. Sitting at the table, he held the bank at eye level, running the flat of the knife through the slot to retrieve the change needed—nickels and dimes saved from his paper route, in and among the dollar bills. Tilting the slot level, he slid the knife back and forth, shaking the bank until the change settled flat on the blade. He then tipped the bank and pulled the knife. The change fell in a clatter onto the table. He repeated the knife action until the change totaled a dollar's worth, enough to buy the flour. He pocketed the coins.

"I'll be back soon." The screen door slammed behind him.

Getting water for coffee from the hand pump at the sink, she wondered at her son's determination, both proud and sad for the situation. When she heard Benny's Packard start up, she rushed to the window to see Jubal leave the yard, and a sudden surge of anxiety filled her. She hadn't even seen to it that he get his license to drive when he'd turned sixteen on the first of May. There just wasn't the time or money to travel to Rutland to take the driver's test. Jubal hadn't said a word about the oversight. Now he was on the road with no license, driving an unregistered vehicle to boot. She'd driven her son to break the law in order to put food on the table.

She wished she could feel on top of her household responsibilites even for a day. She stared out the window at the gathering twilight, shrugging off her gloomy thoughts as she prepared the crackers and milk for Benny. She had no choice but to keep plugging along. Luckily her son was tough. He'd be okay without a birthday cake.

Jubal knew he likely wouldn't be arrested since Tatum had gone with Father Mac to take Maria to CYO camp. He pulled the Packard up in front of the store, noting that Clem and the gossip hounds of Hayesville had left the bench for the night. He'd be free of any backlash for having broken the law.

He found the store still open, but Bert was already counting change at his cash drawer located above a glass case that displayed a variety of candy bars and brands of cigarettes and cigars.

"Evening, Jubal," Bert said, nodding in his direction. "This is a surprise. Haven't seen you in here for some time. How can I help you?"

"I need a bag of flour," he said, walking up to the glass case. He tried not to look at the sweets as he knew he had no money for them.

"Sure thing, young man. Bags are out back." Bert left and returned carrying a big sack that puffed white powder when he set it down. "Ten pounds of King Arthur will be seventy-five cents."

Jubal carefully counted his change and passed it to Bert who added it to the pile he was counting. "I also have enough for a gallon of gas. I'm running on empty."

"Well now, you've come just in time. I'll turn on the pump."

As Bert turned to flick the pump switch, the store's overhead lights showed a sheen on the man's bald crown. Jubal wondered how such a nice guy could tolerate a battle-ax of a wife like Bernice. He was just about to leave when Lizzy LaFlam appeared right behind him, seemingly out of nowhere, and plunked a scratch feed bag full of groceries onto the counter. He could see the bag once held a hundred pounds of cracked corn. When she saw him she broke into a devilish grin.

"Hello there, Jubal Brown."

He tried not to focus on her slightly crooked, yellow-brown teeth. She needed a trip to the dentist. Being poor himself, he didn't judge a person in less fortunate circumstances. But when he looked down from her face, his gaze instead fell on her breasts, recalling his dream of the wooden barrel! The t-shirt she wore was a couple sizes too small and she held some sort of work smock under one arm. He looked quickly to the sack on the counter.

"Hi . . . uh, Lizzy," he stammered. "Looks like you're gonna feed an army."

"Almost! Spent my week's pay on what's in this bag."

Bert stopped counting his coins and looked at Lizzy, concerned. "You can't carry that much food all the way home. It weighs a ton."

"Well, no. I was sorta hopin' ya might drive me after closin'."

Bert shook his head. "Sorry, Bernice is expecting me home. Maybe Jubal would run you up the mountain."

"Me?" Jubal shifted the bag of flour under his arm. "I . . . I can't. I've got to get this flour home so Ma can make us supper. Anyway, I don't have the gas to go very far—"

Bert interjected, "Jubal, I'll gladly pump you an extra gallon to get Lizzy home." The storekeeper turned to his employee. "I know you usually walk. Tonight I assumed someone must be due here to get you with all these groceries."

Lizzy hung her head. "Nobody in my family has a car. Tatum gives me a ride sometimes but he ain't here in town tanight, and he's never taken me all the way home."

Bert closed the cash drawer. "It's near dark and a long way. I don't like the idea of you walking, but Bernice would be fit to be tied."

Jubal was caught. If Bert was willing to give him extra gas, there was no excuse why he couldn't take his flour home, leave it, and then drive Lizzy while his ma was cooking. But he didn't want Lizzy getting the wrong idea, thinking because he was doing her a favor that he liked her. He could place the burlap feed bag of groceries squarely between them on the front seat. He'd offer no friendly chitchat. From past experiences, he feared she'd try to use the ride to strike up a romance. Besides, the LaFlam family was a notorious clan. He'd be smart to keep his distance.

He couldn't help but glance again at her tiny t-shirt revealing her breasts the size of grapefruits. Again he looked away. She probably didn't have anything better to wear.

"Okay then," he said to her. "Get in the car and I'll take you home after I leave off this bag of flour."

In minutes, he and Lizzy sat in the front seat of the Packard with the bag of groceries riding between them. The car climbed Harmony Hill easily with the roar of the twelve cylinders under the hood. Neither of them said a word until they reached his yard.

"I'll be back in a minute," he said, grabbing the flour.

"Okay, I ain't leavin'."

As he walked away, the strangeness of the evening struck him. Necessity had him drive with no license and spend his own cash to help his family, and now charity had Lizzy LaFlam sitting in the front seat of the Packard. His ma was at the kitchen table going over farm bills.

Seeing him, she brightened. "You're a lifesaver."

He emptied the ten-pound flour bag into the bin under the counter. "Uh, Ma?" He hesitated, unsure how she'd react to his helping Lizzy.

She looked up from her receipts. "Yes?"

"Um, I'm taking . . . Lizzy LaFlam home. She has a big bag of groceries to carry." He spoke this last part quickly and made for the door.

She jumped up from the table. "What?"

He paused with his hand on the doorknob and turned to face her. She looked as fierce as only Rose Brown could.

"You're taking a terrible chance bringing her home! Almost no one in town has been up to that place. I hear horror stories about Big Daddy LaFlam. Lady Lamont told me that one time the truant officer, sent to enroll the LaFlam children in school, was driven off the mountain with a shotgun. Lizzy's the only one of his kids that insisted on going to school. They're a bad lot!"

"Gosh, Ma, I'm only taking her home. It can't be all that bad."

"Well, I'll worry! Why can't she walk?"

"Her bag's heavy—a hundred-pound scratch feed sack full of groceries."

His ma didn't reply as she went to the bin for a scoop of flour, which she added to a bowl on the counter. After stirring in the other ingredients for the white sauce, she poured them into a pot on the woodstove and placed a lid on the pot. She sat again at the table, seeming defeated.

"Okay. I'm too tired to argue tonight. You did me the favor. Now, for God's sake, be careful not to get caught driving the Packard! And just watch that girl. I'm not sure I trust her entirely."

As he opened the door to leave, she called, "And hurry back for supper!"

In the twilight outside the house, a mourning dove cooed as the feathered flock that perched on the wire watched him go off on his fool's errand.

Inside the car, he was dismayed to see that Lizzy had rearranged the front seat. The big bag was next to the passenger door and she sat in the middle. He hesitated, standing beside the open car door. This was a bit too chummy.

"You didn't like where you sat?" he asked, sliding into the driver's seat.

"Well, no. I'd have ta look over and around that bag ta talk ta ya. Are ya scared a' me?" She grinned.

She met his eyes with a lively spark. She seemed to be enjoying his discomfort. Strong-minded, just like Maria, and like his mother. Upon noticing Lizzy's full red lips, his face and ears grew warm.

"No, not scared, but I didn't realize we'd be squeezed in so tight." He put the car in gear.

"I'll pack in next ta the bag much as I can . . . get outta the way of the shiftin' lever and the big bossy driver." She chuckled and shimmied sideways across the seat, opening up a slightly bigger space between them.

He felt he could breathe again. They left the yard and he soon idled through town so as not to attract attention. Once past Main Street, he picked up speed, anxious to get the detail completed as soon as possible. After several minutes of silence, Lizzy sighed.

"Ya gonna talk or ya gonna sit there like a dummy with a cork in yer mouth?"

"No, I'll talk." He concentrated on the road that twisted and turned after leaving the village.

"Shoot then." Lizzy relaxed and inched closer.

"I know one thing," he said. "I've got a feeling it won't be easy getting you all the way home."

She brushed her long, tangled hair from her face. "Who ya been talkin' ta?" Alert cat eyes gave the impression she was ready to pounce.

"Oh . . . word travels. I heard the road is rough or something."

"Well, it ain't the road. It's Big Daddy. Folks are scared a' my old man. He rules LaFlam Mountain. He and the boys walk the boundaries checkin' on poachers that might be sniffin' around."

He shrugged. "I'll just be leaving you off."

"Sure, but he don't want nobody on his mountain. Ya see, we live off the land huntin' deer, bear, coon, gray squirrels, and alike. Big Daddy and the boys trap 'n sell furs." She slid closer as they went around a curve.

"Where's the turn? I don't want to miss it." Jubal drew in his shoulders. "You're crowding me."

"Ain't ya in for a little fun?" She gave him her vintage smile. "Hey, here's the turn!"

"Here?" He brought the Packard to a halt and peered into the darkness.

"Yeah. I live up the mountain a piece."

He sighed in disgust. "This is like two cow paths for a road—tall grass in the middle, bushes hanging from the sides. Can you carry that bag the rest of the way? Benny's Packard will get all scratched and we might lose the whole exhaust system."

"If ya help me heft it. It's heavy ya know."

"That will take too long. I'm supposed to be home for supper."

"My mimy will fetch ya some grub—some squirrel stew."

His stomach turned at the thought. "I just want to get home."

"Ya're strong ain't ya? All that work for them cows? Quit yer belly achin'. Park the car. Won't take too awful long."

He groaned.

Lizzy let out a laugh as she wrestled the bag from the seat. "Just makin' yer night ain't I? Grab an end 'n gimme a hand."

In the fading light he could see up ahead, but soon it would be pitch black. Heavy clouds skated across the sky as they climbed the mountain step by step.

After a few hundred feet, Lizzy puffed, "Let's rest awhile on that stone. Afterwards, we'll change sides. My hand's 'bout to fall off grippin' that burlap."

They sat on a flat ledge at the edge of the path. He knew his ma was no doubt pulling her hair over his long absence. He began to wonder if he'd get out alive after facing Big Daddy, and then walking back down to the car alone in complete darkness.

"Let's go," he urged, impatient.

"Hold on will ya?" She gripped his arm. "Look, I know ya ain't likin' me 'cause I ain't class. Just another minute. Don't ya like listenin' ta the night?"

"Lizzy, I've got to get home!" He shrugged her hand off. "Anyway, who did your lugging before I came along?" His mood was darkening like the clouds building overhead.

"No one." Lizzy looked down at the holey sneakers she wore. "Ya see, Big Daddy ain't likin' outside vittles comin' onta his mountain. Couple times a year, in trade fer furs, Clem brings the fixin's for liquor, salt, sugar, kerosene, and smokes fer Big Daddy . . . that's all."

Jubal could see her sneakers were too big, probably hand-me-downs. He wondered if Lizzy had ever enjoyed something new from a store. "How come this Big Daddy of yours lets you slip away to go to school and get a job?"

"'Cause Clem Gochy talked right up ta my old man—told him ta let me leave the mountain and go ta school. Tanight I wanted ta bring my mimy somethin' ta cook with. I'm sick a' livin' on wild stuff—rabbit, coon, deer. Like a goddamned cave girl."

"I can't wait to meet your Big Daddy. He'll probably shoot me, skin me, and sell my hide."

She laughed. "We'll see. I'll bet yer hide would bring a big price." She nudged his arm. "All right, let's go."

Shortly, the steep mountain path leveled as it neared a shallow brook.

"This is where I wash," she told him as they sloshed through the inches-deep water. "This here mountain brook is Christly cold at six in the mornin' before school."

It was hard for him to believe that this was her wash water. "I'll bet it *is* cold!"

From that point, the climb was steep, with the added nuisance of hanging branches slapping them in the face. They kept trudging, fighting off the twigs and leaves with their free hands, the heavy bag between them. Up ahead, Jubal spotted a makeshift log cabin just as a pack of dogs, five total, noticed him and Lizzy. The dogs tore down the slope, making a terrible racket of howling and barking. As they leapt around him, he noted a mixture of breeds, from beagles to bloodhounds.

Lizzy hollered, "Calm down! It's only me and a friend."

Five noses sniffed Jubal and especially the bag. He heard a door slam. In the darkness, the shadow of a figure well over six-foot tall stepped out onto the front porch. "Who's there?"

"It's Lizzy. I brung along Jubal Brown ta give me a hand." Then she said in a low voice, "Switch sides. My arm's achin' like a bastard."

The dogs wouldn't leave him alone. Amid the barking, one or the other drove its nose into his crotch while he tried to hang on to the bag and keep his balance. One hound bayed and shook his head, flinging saliva in every direction. A big stringy gob landed on his wrist. Grimacing, he wiped the goo on his pants.

Lizzy yelled up to the shadow. "Call them hounds off!"

The shadow raised a double barrel shotgun and fired—*bang*! Jubal jumped and almost dropped the bag. The sound resonated. The air smelled of gunpowder. All five dogs dropped to the ground and cowered towards the house.

He and Lizzy lugged the groceries closer to the cabin, passing what looked like a large garden. Within feet of the log cabin he looked up to the shadow, now a man—the infamous Big Daddy.

The giant had a dirty gray beard long enough to lay on the barrel of his chest. He wore a bearskin robe over what looked like deerskin trousers. With his coonskin hat pulled low over his forehead, his whole get-up reminded Jubal of the half-man, half-animal creatures in myths he'd read in school. Big Daddy was as if created from the mountain he claimed.

"What the hell are ya doin' here showin' your puny white ass?" His deep voice thundered as though from the lungs of the bear whose hide he wore.

Three scraggly-looking boys of varying heights came from the house to crowd around Big Daddy. To Jubal they looked maybe part Indian.

Lizzy spoke before he could answer the question. "Big Daddy, watch yer mouth! This here fella helped me heft this heavy bag fer Mimy's cookin'.

"Fer Mimy's cookin'?" he growled, "I ain't lettin' any outside grub onta this here mountain!"

"Well, ya're lettin' this bag of cookin' stuff. Mimy's been scratchin', tryin' ta put meals together fer us all. She deserves what's in this here bag!"

Big Daddy paused. His boys stood staring, fascinated by a stranger. Jubal wondered if Lizzy's father liked the idea of some tasty meals but didn't want to admit it.

"Grab yer end—we're takin' this inta the house," Lizzy said.

He bent to pick up his end and followed her, edging by Big Daddy. He half expected the mountain of a guy to kick him in the seat of the pants. A rancid stink like a hunk of rotten cheese hit him. He thought maybe it was the bearskin.

Big Daddy huffed. "By holy thunder, ya ain't doin' this regular, ya little hussy, breakin' all a' Big Daddy's rules."

Lizzy stopped short. "Rules! What rules? Ya trade furs with Clem fer yer smokes and kerosene. And liquor for yer gut. I guess Mimy can have somethin' ta cook with."

"Look, ya wise ass. Ya won't be talkin' ta me like that!" He grabbed for Lizzy, but she slipped away.

She pulled Jubal through the door.

The cabin's inside smelled of kerosene and body sweat mixed with wood smoke. He couldn't believe the surrounding cabin walls. The logs were covered with animal hides and heads—fox, bear, and lynx, a few skunks and weasels. Open jaws showed white fangs at eye level. The surroundings had all the makings of a bad dream. In the center of the room a huge rectangle of connected logs made up a tabletop. Long split logs with smaller sticks for legs served as benches.

Big Daddy followed behind and roared, "Ya won't be comin' onta my mountain, actin' like ya can do as ya might!"

Jubal dropped his end of the bag and turned to see that the boys, with their long black hair, brown eyes and narrow faces, stood tight around their father, forming a wall between him and Lizzy and the door. They looked to be in disbelief that their sister was standing up to Big Daddy.

Lizzy's mimy was in front of a huge stone fireplace, stirring the contents of an iron kettle that hung over the fire. She wore a sleeveless dress that looked like it was woven of reeds collected in a swamp. She showed no reaction on seeing her daughter. Jubal knew his own ma would be happy to see him. If emotion flowed in Mimy's veins, she sure didn't show it.

She looked like a full-blooded squaw, with high cheekbones and her coal-black hair in a long braid. She seemed oddly relaxed, as though she were at peace in another world. Maybe that was how she survived living with the fur-covered tyrant that ruled the place.

"Mimy, look what I fetched ya!" Lizzy said. She turned to Jubal. "Here. Heft that sack up onta the table."

She removed the items: several cans of Campbell's soup, a ten-pound bag of King Arthur flour, two ten-pound bags of Domino sugar, several cans of tuna fish and corned beef, canisters of baking powder, a big box of Arm & Hammer baking soda, several cans of Hershey's chocolate, and a bag of salt.

"And see Mimy, I bought ya a cookbook made up by the Baptist church ladies. See the pictures of all the stuff we can cook? I'll read ta ya things we can make. There's cakes, pies, breads, 'n stuff like that."

Mimy turned her back and continued stirring her dinner creation which, to Jubal, had a distinct oily, gamey smell.

He turned to see the three boys bug-eyed over Lizzy's offerings, reminding him of the way the five hounds might drool over being offered a bone.

Big Daddy's mouth dropped open and his eyes bulged at the bounty on the table. His breath rattled in his throat. He seemed conflicted. The contents of the bag obviously violated his long-held belief that his mountain should do the providing, but the store-bought food looked mighty good. He appeared to be deciding what to do about the fact that Lizzy had sprung from his control. To Jubal's surprise, Big Daddy inched over and glanced down at the pictures in the cookbook. His eyes darted to his daughter and back to the pictures. Jubal held his breath, feet glued to the floor.

Mimy continued to be in her own world. She reached up on the mantel for jars of twigs and flowers, garden herbs maybe. She sprinkled some in the iron kettle and took a sip from her ladle.

"Mimy, don't ya like what I brung ya?" Lizzy asked.

Her mother returned a blank look as if she didn't hear.

"Mimy, what's wrong with ya?"

As if on cue from his woman, Big Daddy bellowed, "This ain't ta be in my house!"

He dove at the table and heaved the sugar, salt, and flour across the room, smashing the bags against the walls, sending sugar and salt crystals like freezing rain all over the hides. Especially, the flour bag erupted into a white powdered cloud. The cans of food came next. With a hatchet that leaned against the stone fireplace, one of the older boys swung the blade at the cans, spraying soup everywhere. Next, his ax fell on the corned beef and tuna fish. As meat and juice squished from the torn tins, the boys fell on their knees. They dug their fingers like hungry rats into the split cans and drank what was left of the soups, making their own recipe of corned beef, soup, and sugar. They laughed. Lizzy's hopes of cooking meals together with Mimy were dashed, the ingredients now plastered on their faces.

Big Daddy threw the Baptist church cookbook, a sacrilege to be sure, into the fire. In the confusion, Jubal backed into a corner, amazed at the boys' behavior and their father's triumph over his daughter. Quick as lightning, Lizzy grabbed two cattails with brown heads soaking in a kerosene pot and stuck them into the fireplace. She held nature's torches aloft as they burst into flames.

"Come on, Jubal; we're leavin' this crazy place!" She thrust a stalk in his hand.

Each holding a blazing cattail, the two of them charged out the door, their torches lighting the way. They ran across the garden and started on a dead run down the mountain path, the dogs howling after them. All Jubal could think of was putting distance between himself and Big Daddy.

Chapter Twelve

When Lizzy reached the road, she could barely see the outline of the Packard in the pitch-black night, her cattail torch having burned to an ember. She tossed the cattail on the gravel road and felt her way along to the passenger-side door. On the other side of the car, Jubal threw his fading sparks also and the two of them climbed in. Both were gasping to catch their breath.

"Whew, we escaped," she said. "Whatta nut house! I ain't ever goin' back." She owed Jubal some sort of reckoning for him having basically risked his life to carry a bag of groceries. "My folks are a bunch a' crazy bastards. My poor mimy. Big Daddy has plum sent her over the hill ta another world." She rolled down her window. "Damn, I stink like a week-old dead chicken. Sorry, I ain't washed fer a few days and after runnin' down the mountain . . ."

Jubal scrunched up his nose and lightly coughed on the exhale as he started the Packard and left the woods road.

"So what's next?" she asked.

"I don't know."

His face was hard to read. She worried she'd come to be a burden on him. "Do ya 'spose the Town Farm would take me in wearin' rags and stinkin' this way?"

Jubal stayed silent, focused on the rough mountain road, so she sat wondering where she might end up now.

The first time she'd gotten free of the mess up on the mountain she'd had Clem Gochy to thank. On one of his trips trading furs for supplies with Big Daddy, Clem had taken her aside.

"Lizzy," he'd said. "Why don't ya leave this crazy place and come with me? Millie and I ain't never had a little one so ya can be our girl. If ya don't come with me, you'll end up havin' a kid by your dummy brothers."

She didn't know how he knew. Maybe Big Daddy told him that she'd already had to fight those bastards off, especially at night when they slept on the floor in the same room.

That very day, Clem had taken her with him down into town. On the way to the chicken house that he called home, they stopped at the Baptist church rummage basement to set her up with some clothes. Clem and Millie took her in as one of their own and helped her with her schooling. Night after night she read to them and learned her numbers. Lizzy recalled how she felt then that life was maybe looking up for her.

The dim shadows of roadside trees passed in a blur as the Packard bumped along. She had no idea where this night's turn of events might lead and figured not to think on it much. Instead she drifted in memories of her time at Clem's, the closest thing she'd known to a real home.

Bert had arrived home from the store to tell Bernice how Lizzy had spent her week's earnings on food for her family, and that Jubal, who'd come for flour just before closing, was driving Lizzy home. While Bernice didn't like one bit that the girl was working for her husband, it did spur her to wonder, not for the first time, just how bad things were up on that mountain. She turned in her twin bed, hearing Bert's snores down the hall. Lord only knew—no one, and certainly not she, dared set a foot on Big Daddy's property. But this brought to mind another time when she had felt it her Christian duty to check up on Lizzy LaFlam, and she had figured a way to do so.

It was when Lizzy was just a child. Word around town was that Clem—likely due to his connection with Big Daddy with both of the men being on the wrong side of the law—had brought the girl down to live with him and Millie. While folks had mostly been of the opinion that this was a charitable act, Bernice just knew that Clem Gochy, having been a bootlegger, was a bad influence on young Lizzy. He was probably getting her hooked on his hard liquor. Most other people in town didn't seem to care about Lizzy's living situation. They figured now, at least, she was in school, even though her personal hygiene was a problem and her clothing, or lack of it, was a disaster.

Bernice had figured that the annual Thanksgiving dinner at the Baptist Church, put on for the needy in town, would be a good chance for her to investigate Clem, Millie, and Lizzy living in that awful old hen house. Since they never came to the dinner, she had an excuse to pay them a visit.

Clem always openly scoffed at the meal, declaring, "It ain't worth nothin'. Ya have ta eat three hundred and sixty-five days a year. Them church folks don't care most days 'bout the poor 'til Thanksgiving. Ta ease the guilt of the well heeled, they put on a feed so big most can't eat what's put in front of 'em."

Bernice and Clem had also had a falling-out, since her Temperance League had put plenty of heat on him for his bootlegging. But that bad history didn't hinder her plan. She would bear witness and report on the welfare of Lizzy.

On Thanksgiving Day, she went to the Gochy shack to deliver meals for the family. Since Clem had no driveway, she had to leave her car beside the road and then struggle to carry the steaming hot food on a tray. She followed a path bordered by dead weeds, mostly Queen Anne's lace with their dried flowers weighed down by wet November snow. She brushed by them, knocking clumps of snow onto the path as she trudged on. She had to admit that she and the ladies of the church were good cooks. Delicious smells of generous cuts of turkey, bread-crumb dressing, gravy, cranberry sauce, and pumpkin pie seeped out from under the plate covers.

As she got closer, she observed that Clem had tacked up black tar paper to cover the clapboards, excluding the windows. He'd also banked the foundation with mounds of pine needles and boughs. She knew the decrepit structure had once been part of a much larger farmstead, but most of the buildings had burned, leaving this one remaining shack. The owner had left Vermont in the thirties, common for hardscrabble, bankrupt farmers. Clem, Millie, and now Lizzy occupied the property with no one caring that they weren't the lawful owners.

When she reached the side door, she placed the tray of goodies on the steps and reached up to knock. The door flew open. Standing on a lower level, Bernice looked up at Clem's figure filling the open space. Tremendous heat equal to that of a blast furnace poured out the door. Clem's booming voice startled her.

"What in all hell are ya doin' here, wantin' ta snoop 'round my place?" He wore only undershorts and an open shirt showing his hairy belly.

She knew from Clem's character that he wanted his half-dressed appearance to shock her. Her face burned hot as she unwillingly looked up at his knobby knees, hairy legs, and his bunched up scrotum and penis the size of a big baking potato cradled in his ratty underwear. She'd never seen a man up close with only a flimsy layer of fabric between his nakedness and the outside world—not even, in quite some time, her husband who slept in his own room. When she was in school, the anatomy of a man's reproductive organs were intentionally and rightly left blank.

Was it seeing Clem in his indecent get-up or the heat blasting out the door that made her suddenly light-headed, weak in the knees, and close to a faint? Modesty was next to Godliness and what stood no more than a foot away was a violation of her image of purity. She stepped back to gain her bearings. Her mission, as president of the Temperance League in service to God, took precedence. She would not allow him to intimidate her.

"Well, you old fool," she scolded. "I've brought some good eating for you!" She raised the tray with its delicious scents wafting upwards.

"Huh, well I think ya jest want ta check us out and gossip 'bout what ya saw at Clem Gochy's!" Hands on his hips, he did not budge an inch from his proximity to her face.

"No, I've come in the name of the Temperance League and our church." She didn't waver, holding out the tray, which was growing quite heavy in her grasp. "If you would let me in, I'll just leave this food and take the dishes back." She knew she hadn't fooled Clem as to her purpose, but that didn't matter.

"Well, if ya ain't laced the eats with poison, I'll let ya in." He reached for the tray. "Millie! Here, take this."

Millie was a mystery to most in town—seldom seen, living her days in the confines of their little shack. Bernice noted she was slight with white hair in a long braid down her back. Her face showed deep age lines giving her a shriveled, pinched look. Her full-length dress hung off her figure.

The heaping tray was quite obviously too much for Millie to hold, so Lizzy, who appeared to have had her nose in a book, jumped off the bed to help. Bernice squinted to see the book's title, but couldn't make it out.

"Here let me take that." Lizzy plucked the tray from Millie's hands and turned for a place to set down the Thanksgiving offering. Seeing no other option, she set the tray on the bed which sagged in the middle. A quantity of books and papers were scattered all over the faded quilt, indicating this was Lizzy's study space. Lizzy wore undershorts that looked like Clem's and a robe that appeared to have been made from scraps of a sheet.

The one-griddle stove cranked out an unbelievable amount of heat, and Bernice, sweating under her heavy coat, noticed a steady stream of water that came into the house from a pipe, emptying into a small tub and overflowing through the outside wall near a door in the corner. The room smelled like three coons living in a den.

The small eating table was loaded with pots, pans, and dishes of all sorts, so Lizzy raised a leaf in the table before pulling three plates from a shelf. The wooden leaf that could be raised and lowered was apparently their regular eating space. With quick hands, Lizzy neatly divided the food into three equal parts on their plates. Then she dunked the now empty church dishes in a pail of water that sat next to the stove.

"It's ready ta go," Lizzy said to Clem and Millie. Before she sat down, Lizzy placed the rinsed dishes back on the tray and passed the tray to Bernice. "Thanks fer the eats."

Clem edged closer to Bernice where she stood by the door. She abruptly closed her mouth which had been hanging open as she surveyed the scene.

Clem laughed. "Well Bernice, ya got a good look at our classy livin'."

He leaned close. His hot breath smelled of coffee maybe mixed with a little red-eye gin.

"But ya know what, no one's died yet livin' here, and Lizzy's makin' it just great in her schoolin'. She's learnt a lot, readin' ta Millie and me. Also doin' her numbers."

"Well," Bernice sighed. "I guess better here than up on LaFlam mountain from what I hear tell." She just had to concede that, gruff and outside the law as he was, Clem must have some good in him, as it looked like Lizzy might even gain a bit of love from her makeshift parents.

Bernice reached for the door, her thumb holding the pot and dishes in place on the tray. "Enjoy your meal that we Temperance League ladies cooked for you all." She didn't want to leave without giving a plug for her crusade.

Clem didn't answer. But before the door closed, Lizzy called out, "Thanks a lot, Miz Sausville."

Outside again on the step, Bernice's heart lifted knowing that three of Hayesville's less fortunate were gathered around the table leaf to the good eats she had brought from the church. She could now report to the Temperance ladies that Lizzy LaFlam, from what she saw, was not in moral danger living in that old hen house.

※

As she rode along with Jubal, Lizzy recalled how, after four years of her living with Clem and Millie, Clem had talked to Bert that past winter about giving her an after-school job at the Hayesville IGA. Though he'd had heated conversations with Bernice, Bert had finally agreed, and Lizzy had begun her first job, walking there every day after school.

Lizzy liked working the store—stocking goods, cleaning, and running the register. Socializing with the townsfolk made her feel like she belonged, even just a little, to the Hayesville community instead of being an outcast from the boonies. However, Bernice had immediately swooped in to "dress her decently." The smock she had to wear was ugly, so she stashed it on a shelf when Bernice was off on her good deeds. Otherwise, she tried to stay out of the bossy woman's way.

At the point she'd started working the store, she'd also outgrown Clem's tiny house.

"It's time ya made it on yer own," Clem told her. "My shack ain't no longer a place for a growin' girl the likes of ya."

Due to lack of space, she slept in their bed, and three in one bed wasn't much room to roll over, especially since she'd grown to be a young woman.

So she had left Clem's place and gone back to live under Big Daddy's rule, but now she knew that was a mistake. She'd forgotten just how bad home life was up on LaFlam Mountain. Because she'd gotten out once, she knew she'd find a way do it again on her own.

The Packard clipped off the miles and they drew closer to Jubal's house. Jubal was at a loss over what to do with Lizzy. The Town Farm was no place for her. She'd be living with old men the likes of Oscar Smith and Charlie Jones, the bench sitters down at the store.

He was realizing his dream had come true. Like it or not, he and Lizzy LaFlam had been thrown together as if rolling along in a wooden barrel. Of course, not naked and not really in a barrel, but as the saying went, he felt 'over a barrel' as to what to do next. He had to help out this girl, while all this time he had wanted to stay clear of her. Of course, he could kick her out of the car and leave her to wander somewhere in the night, but he wasn't one to be cruel. And she'd showed him in the hours just passed with her courage that she was nearly a miracle, coming from a home that was hell on earth. It was late besides, at least past ten o'clock.

"You're coming with me for the night," he said. Even as he told her this, he knew walking in through the door of his house with Lizzy Laflam would be no simple matter.

He'd left his poor ma probably in knots, worrying over him as to where in the world he'd been. Surely she'd been imagining him shot by Big Daddy and tossed in the woods, which wasn't too wild a thought considering the events at the cabin. The tuna-pea-wiggle had likely dried to a crust and the biscuits were no doubt hard as rocks. What would his ma say, him several hours late and bringing home this bedraggled outcast girl from the LaFlam clan? He drove up Harmony Hill and parked the Packard beside the barn, bracing himself for the confrontation.

When he turned off the car, Lizzy spoke up. "Well, much as I 'preciate ya givin' me a place fer the night, ya got any other ideas in that head of yers? Now, I know ya ain't likin' me much, and are prob'ly not wantin' ta take me inta yer house 'cause I'm from trash and stink like a hog."

He opened his door. "I like you enough to give you a place to lay your head."

"Well, I guess at this hour, I ain't in any mood ta be fussy."

In the entryway, Lizzy hung back in a dark corner among the hanging coats and overalls reeking of cow barn. The smell blended with her own, though the Brown family work clothes couldn't entirely cover up her stink. At the doorway into the main house, Jubal kicked off his shoes. He gestured for her to follow. But she figured Rose Brown, a lady with city living in her past, wouldn't greet her with open arms. More likely, she'd look bug-eyed in horrified disgust.

When Jubal entered the kitchen, his ma flew at him.

"Where on earth have you been, Jubal Brown! I've been worried sick. Imagining all sorts of things! Like maybe you crashed the car or got stuck on the mountain. I was sure Big Daddy had captured you because *that* girl led you up to that awful place!"

Lizzy saw Jubal freeze.

"Ma, believe me, I worried for you. I'm sorry! I just had to help Lizzy out and had no way to let you know what was going on."

Lizzy inched further into the barn clothes.

His ma let out an exasperated sigh. "What was so important that you *had* to help this LaFlam girl?"

"Well . . . uh . . ." He turned towards the entry door. "Aw, Lizzy come on out and meet my ma."

From her dark corner, Lizzy peered into the dim kitchen lit by one bare bulb. Rose stiffened and put her hand to her mouth.

"She . . . she's here?"

Lizzy noted the table had been scrubbed clean with not a scrap of food in sight. Now she felt even worse. She knew Jubal was starving. Neither of them had eaten.

"Yes she is, Ma," Jubal replied. "Hey Lizzy, it's okay, really."

She left the security of her hiding place and walked into the kitchen. Somewhere in her past, she'd come to know being polite was important to most people. That idea hadn't come from Big Daddy or Clem—both handled most situations with the crudeness of a swinging hammer. But she knew it best to use good manners and had the sense to tread softly. Rose Brown needed a better impression than *that LaFlam girl from that awful place.* She was sure challenged, though, not having much to offer other than baggy trousers worn out at the knees, a t-shirt showing plenty of skin, hair that looked to be scattered to the four winds, and a backwoods twang that made her sound stupid, to say nothing about her unwashed condition that would drive anyone away.

She gave Rose all she had—a big smile. "Thanks, Miz Brown, fer takin' me in tanight." She reached with her outstretched arm and grasping hand while Rose backed away, bumping into the sink. "Sorry ma'am. I'm sure I stink like hell. Ya see, we were runnin' through the woods and—"

Rose's eyes widened as she gripped the counter to steady herself.

Jubal shot Lizzy a look of warning and shook his head. Lizzy tried again. "Ya see up on the mountain the brook ain't warmed much yet. It's cold as ice." She stopped. This likely made no sense at all to Jubal's ma.

Rose rolled her eyes towards the ceiling, crossed her arms, and fixed Lizzy with a stern look. "Do you plan to sleep in one of my clean beds with *those* clothes?"

"If it fits yer fancy?" Seeing the look on Rose's face, Lizzy continued, "Or, I . . . could sleep on the floor?"

"Goodness, the floor!" Rose looked skyward again and shook her head. "Lizzy, I've seen lots of girls come off the street in New York City, but I don't ever remember seeing anyone as needy as you. Let's start with a warm bath and some decent clothes."

Lizzy took issue with Jubal's ma calling her "needy." She accepted her lot in life with no self-pity. "Thanks, Miz Brown, but I ain't thinkin' all that's necessary. I'll take the floor." She drew herself up and looked Rose in the eye.

Jubal backed away and busied himself on the far end of the kitchen.

"No guest of mine will go out to Hayesville folks saying that they slept on the floor in my house," Rose declared. Then she smiled, softening. "Look, Lizzy, we'd all feel better if you'd take us up on some hospitality. I'm happy to offer you warm water, a towel, and some of my clothes."

"A bath! Ain't it kinda late?" She couldn't imagine, of all things, sitting in a pool of warm water. Still, it would be nice to get cleaned up and maybe do something with her hair. It was wild enough to scare the devil. She noticed Jubal lugging water to what she thought must be the bathroom.

Rose explained, "Since I've been cooking, the Glenwood stove's reservoir water should be nice and warm. I think I have a bra and panties that would fit you, a blouse, and a pair of slacks."

Lizzy wasn't sure what "slacks" were, but they sounded nice.

"And your sneakers—" Rose looked down, frowning. "If you don't mind, I'll burn the ones you have."

She'd forgotten to remove her soggy, holey footwear in the entryway. "Yes . . . they're what stinks most, them and my rotten socks."

Rose wrinkled her nose. "We'll take care of that, and after you clean yourself up, I'll wash your hair with warm water from the kettle on the stove."

Speechless as tears filled her eyes, Lizzy was thankful to have ended up in this odd, wonderful place, if only for the night.

After she undressed in the bathroom, she stepped into the warm water and laid flat-out where the water seeped into all parts of her body. The warmth was like heaven—a feeling she'd never before experienced. Washing in the mountain stream had always sent a chill through her. Now she could lather and fill a washcloth with soap and suds, covering her body with a scented smell that made her almost dizzy with pleasure. Rose knocked on the door and placed some clean clothes, as promised, on a bathroom chair.

"Since it's getting close to bedtime, I brought you a nightgown and an old robe of mine," Rose said. "I'll give you an outfit in the morning." She picked up the sneakers and the heap of stinking garments with her thumb and forefinger, and closed the door.

Lizzy heard the clatter of stove griddles that meant the burning of her clothes. She smiled into the water. The noise marked a new beginning for Lizzy LaFlam.

Rose returned with the kettle of warm water and a bottle of shampoo, kneeling by the tub to wash Lizzy's tangled mass of hair. It took some time to wash, rinse, and wash again.

"Miz Brown," Lizzy hummed. "Yer fingers workin' my head is the nicest feelin' anyone's ever give me."

"Wait until you see the plan I have for your hair, if you'll agree. But first we'll sit down to a serving of tuna-pea-wiggle and biscuits that Jubal's been working on. Our very own midnight meal."

Rose held out a clean towel and glanced away as Lizzy stood in the tub.

"Sounds good. I'm sure hungry!" She looked down at her naked pink body towards her clean feet where her past self was swirling down the drain in grimy bubbles.

After Rose left, Lizzy pulled the soft, cotton nightgown over her head and slid into the light-green robe. With her hair damp and fabric swishing around her calves, she stepped out of the bathroom feeling like a beautiful Indian maiden. Still, she hated to admit it—Big Daddy would always be a part of her.

Chapter Thirteen

Lizzy woke to the familiar sound of songbirds, but she was in an unfamiliar place. She lay on a cot in a little room under the eaves of the Brown's farmhouse. The room was just big enough for a single bed, nightstand, small bureau, and chair. The flowered wallpaper was torn in places with the plaster lath showing, and the bed was level with the single window, allowing her to look out towards the barn. Although her surroundings were common for most, only she with her horrible past could feel like a princess in a palace waking from a wonderful dream.

She'd never slept between two white sheets that smelled fresh like the early summer breeze that whistled around her window. She peered out, seeing a robin bouncing along the lawn searching for worms. She could hear a motor hum coming from the barn. Other than the sights and sounds outside, the house was quiet until she heard the clock downstairs strike seven. Suddenly, something caught her attention. To her left was the only fixture on the wall: a small work of art stitched with blue and red thread for a border of tiny blue forget-me-nots. It was the message that caught her attention:

For those who have little
much will be given.

She grinned. That saying was about her! But then Clem's often-repeated words came to her also: "In life, help comes to those who help themselves." She had taken his words to heart, and still he had given her a lot. It was only because of him that she entered fifth grade and was able to do school work equal to the other kids.

Lying with a cozy feeling on the cot in the Brown household, she was also thankful for Jubal and Rose Brown, especially when she sat up to notice a pretty jumper and a pair of panties laid out for her to wear. There was also an extra pair of dungarees and a plain cotton blouse neatly folded and placed on the chair by her bed. Although grateful for the gift, she wasn't going to stake her future on the Brown family. It was known all over town that they were hanging on by the pinch of their teeth and their jaws were getting mighty tired. She saw no future in adding to their load of care.

She'd leave the house and walk to the store. She had an idea that perhaps Bert Sausville would let her stay nights at the store, especially when he saw her all dressed up, a smart-looking gal. He was the kind to give her the world if he could; that is, if Bernice wasn't standing in his way.

In her time at the Hayesville store, Lizzy had learned a number of ways she could help Bert's business by filling his empty shelves. She thought he ought to take on a line of *Blue Seal* feeds, the grain advertised by a handsome trademark with a cow, horse, and chickens in the blue seal. She would nail the sign where folks could see it and they'd know that Bert had pumped new life into his store. She saw signs in the back rooms that he used to sell the feed, but apparently he didn't have money to restock. While lying in her bed, she made up more big dreams for Bert Sausville and a thriving country store. She'd make a real solid place for herself at the Hayesville Country IGA Store, but he didn't know it yet.

Suddenly she heard the clatter of cookware coming from the kitchen. She jumped out of bed, slipped on her fresh clothes, and hurried to meet the first day of what just might prove to be an exciting new life.

After breakfast, Lizzy left the Brown farm on foot, feeling as bright and perky as she could ever remember—the new Lizzy LaFlam. Rose had fed her a generous meal of bacon, eggs, and toast, all topped off with a big glass of milk. As promised, Rose had also cut Lizzy's mop of tangled hair, pinning a bright red satin ribbon to hold it back from her face. She felt like a beautiful butterfly recently changed from a lowly caterpillar.

As she walked, Lizzy basked in the sunny morning with the roadside bushes and trees lush and green in early summer bloom. She strode down Harmony Hill, overjoyed in thinking that the people she passed wouldn't have a clue as to who this beautiful Indian maiden was.

When she reached the store at about nine o'clock, Clem Gochy and his bench buddies hadn't yet arrived, though Bert had been open since seven. She came up behind her boss in the canned goods aisle where he was taking inventory and probably wondering how he would pay for the small restocking order.

"Mornin' Bert."

He spun around. "Holy jumped-up! Is that you, Lizzy?" He put his clipboard and paperwork aside on a shelf. "What happened to you? If it wasn't for your voice, it would've taken me a minute to realize who you are wearing that nice blue jumper and red ribbon in your hair all cut and styled."

She smoothed her hair and patted the ribbon. "I'm the new Lizzy LaFlam."

"Oh?"

She wasn't sure how to gently break the news about her recent homeless state, so she blurted, "I wanna live here so I can help ya make yer store a roarin' success."

His mouth dropped open. "Why . . . whatever gave you an idea like that?"

"'Cause I know yer store is dyin'. Besides, Bernice is marchin' in here takin' cash outta the drawer fer her Temperance trips."

Bert ran his hand over his bald head, frowning. "Wherever did you hear such a thing?"

"Oh . . . just talk out around." She picked up a can of tomatoes and set it down, rubbing the dust between her fingers. She needed to clean the shelves. "Ya prob'ly don't wanna hear that. Or that folks are complainin' ya don't have much on the shelves they want. Years ago ya sold Blue Seal feed, but no longer."

Bert picked up his clipboard and stared at it, as if it could confirm or deny what she was saying. "Well," he nodded. "The feed business is something else. Farmers run up big grain bills."

"Ya're too easy. Like yer wife treatin' all her lady friends ta a free ride and free lunch so as ta make a big showin' at her rallies. I know I can help ya if ya let me stay here and gimme a few more hours in the store."

He walked over and sat down heavily in his chair near the potbelly stove that he fired up during cold weather. He tapped his pencil on his clipboard. "Where are you going to sleep, and wash, and get meals? There's only a sink and toilet here in the building. No tub."

"I'll sleep in what ya call the grain room—all protected with mesh wire ta keep the varmints out. I can cook my meals on a hotplate." She took a seat next to him on a wooden straight-back chair. "It probably seems rough ta ya, but a makeshift washroom is better than anythin' I ever had."

He continued to sit with a thoughtful expression. She sensed he knew what she'd said about his dying store was true. She felt confident she could help him.

Bert sighed. "Bernice won't take kindly to you having some say in this store."

"Well, she's suckin' the life outta this place with her Temperance League." Lizzy knew she was rather bold for repeating this, but she'd always spoken her mind. It was the only way to survive up on LaFlam Mountain with the likes of Big Daddy. Sometimes her smart tongue had earned her a lashing, but it was worth it to be on the right side of truth.

He hung his head. "I know. Bernice has been taking funds from the cash drawer for a few years. It's gotten so she doesn't even ask anymore, just helps herself as if I had a counterfeit cash printer in the back room."

She leaned forward, intent. "Let me prove myself—I can price out an order ta get ya back on track. Show ya what I can do."

"Oh, I can't let you do that." He shook his head. "You're just a kid."

"I'm just about sixteen," she said helpfully.

"Right . . . a kid who knows her numbers with a big plan," he muttered. He sat in thought awhile longer. He sighed again. "Okay. Tell me your plan."

"Well, I'll make up a decent order of the best goods that folks'll want. I know what they're hankerin' fer as I've been listenin' and payin' attention. I'll come up with an amount needed and take it from there."

"And where does the money come from?" His expression was doubtful.

Just then, a customer in bib overalls, barn boots, and a red-checkered hunting coat came through the door. He went directly to the shelf where the laundry soap was kept. "Geez, Bert, ya goin' out of business? No Duz on the shelf!"

"I . . . I have some ordered. It should come in soon," Bert said.

The old codger groaned, "My old lady will be mad. Monday is her wash day!"

Lizzy jumped up. "I can let ya have an opened box ta hold ya over 'til the order arrives." She went to the back room and came back to the counter in seconds. She handed over the opened box of Duz powdered soap. "Here ya go."

"Well, I'll be." The ruddy-faced farmer stroked his whiskers, and then he took the box. "I ain't knowin' who ya are, but this'll be mighty helpful. Bert's smart in hirin' ya." He looked at Lizzy closely. "Who are ya anyway?"

"I'm Lizzy LaFlam, sir." She was especially pleased with herself as she watched the old guy leave with a smile. She turned to Bert who had watched from his chair. "Now, ain't it nice ta have a satisfied customer leave yer store?"

His face turned red. "I wish I'd thought of what you just did. That was Elmer Grant. He'll have it all over town that I've got quite the gal working for me that knows her business." He stood. "Bernice is out of town today, and God knows she'll want to know your plan, but here you go. It's my store." He handed her his clipboard. "Fill out an order and restock my shelves. Let's see how your plan works."

Having made his decision, he took up his usual station behind the checkout counter. "I don't know how we'll pay when your big order comes in. I hope whatever you've got in mind is legal."

She nodded. "It will be."

Clipboard in hand, she spent the morning studying the shelves, counting items, and entering them on her list. Bert read the morning paper from his perch behind the register. Things were slow with only two customers stopping in. She still wasn't sure where Bert stood on her request to live at the store. And she didn't want to share how she planned to get the money for the order she was making up. The plan was bold, and there was a good chance it wasn't going to work. If it happened that she was not able to get the money, she figured to simply charge the amount when the delivery came and pay at a later date.

Clem Gochy was actually the one who had given her the idea that hatched her plan. Clem had one time recalled how in March of 1933 President Roosevelt had declared a bank holiday, and hundreds of banks across the country had to close for a week. The little Hayesville National Bank, however, had never reopened, a bitter disappointment for Lady Lamont. Her father was the bank founder, known as an easy lender to farmers and businesses in town. Clem said that Mister Lamont's dream had been to help build a thriving village through his lending practices, but the '29 crash came, making it impossible to meet his goal before his death.

In the mid '30s, Andrew O'Mara, then a young upstart pharmacist in town, began offering a courier service out of his drugstore. Folks could make deposits to the Rutland National Bank through a locked portfolio delivered by an auto stage that Andrew also owned and operated. Clem had complained that the president of the Rutland Bank and O'Mara served on state banking boards as well as committees of the Catholic Dioceses of Burlington and Rutland. Few in town could get a loan from the Rutland Bank because the directors, as Clem told it, "were tighter than a bolt on a rusty nut."

Meanwhile, Lady Lamont was furious when her request for a new bank charter in Hayesville was rejected by the Vermont Department of Banking on the grounds of inadequate start-up funds. Consequently, she became the person to borrow from, as folks in town preferred not to deal with the Rutland Bank. Of course Clem was never one to borrow money, but Lizzy remembered him saying some years back that Lady Lamont was the one to go to if there ever was a need for cash.

Well, Lizzy needed cash. She figured the big order she was putting together for Bert would come to about a thousand dollars; however, to also cover future store needs, she'd ask Lady Lamont for a loan of two thousand. She knew, when she started out on her walk to the mansion, that her request would be a long shot. But Clem had taught her to have confidence.

He'd said, "Lizzy, ya're goin' ta make it in this world 'cause ya've got more grit than a bobcat with kittens."

She was going to conquer the day like the she-cat that Clem saw in her. She had reached the entrance to Jazz Crow's junkyard when an old truck pulled out into the road. It was Jubal.

He stopped and rolled down the passenger side window. "Hi Lizzy, want a ride?"

"Sure, but what are ya doin' on the road again with no license?"

Jubal looked sheepish. "Just going home after getting the battery charged. The turn for Harmony Hill's right close-by."

"Oh. Well sure, thanks." She climbed in and slammed the door. "Can ya take me fer a short bit more, up the road ta the mansion's drive?"

"I think I can do that."

With hands on the steering wheel, he made no move to go. Instead he stared, as if puzzled by yet another chance to be with her.

"I dunno if ya've got all day, but I sure don't," she said. "Are we goin' or ain't we?"

"Sure, yeah." Jubal put the truck in gear and it lurched forward.

As they bounced along the gravel road, she remarked, "Ain't it strange when a guy don't like a gal, but he keeps poppin' up in her life?"

"Never said I didn't like you." Jubal looked straight ahead, concentrating on his driving.

"Well, I figured ya thought of me as a pain."

He pushed his cap back, scratching his forehead, and was quiet for a few minutes. Lizzy was getting used to his silences—they meant he was thinking hard on something.

"Last night, well, you . . ." He shifted the truck into second gear for the climb up Harmony Hill. The old truck blew a cloud of black smoke while the engine labored into the task. "You've showed me a different gal than when you were plugging spit wads at me in school."

She laughed and struck the dusty dashboard. "But that sure was fun watchin' ya duck fer cover."

He frowned. "It wasn't *that* funny." He pulled the shifting lever down into first gear while entering the steep grade for the Lamont mansion. "Say, why are you headed here?" He glanced her way. "You look to be on a mission to meet the queen."

"Well, sort of." She reached up to see if her ribbon was still in place. "How do I look?"

"You're— Wow, you look *different* . . . *nice*. All this just to meet Eugene?"

She chuckled. "'Course not. Lady Lamont. She's the queen of the town, wouldn't ya say?"

"You're right on that. So really, why do you need to see her?"

"I'll give ya three guesses."

"Um . . . a modeling job?"

"God no! I hear she does nudies and I like wearin' clothes too much." She didn't want to tell him of her need for money. Not that he'd blab the reason for her visit, but what if Lady Lamont turned her down? "Next?"

"A cleaning job? My ma already does that stuff for her you know."

"Cleanin'! I already got a full-time job, workin' at the store. I just got a promoshun."

"Sorry, I . . . Well, congratulations."

His embarrassment was obvious. Compared to her hoodlum brothers, Jubal really seemed an okay guy. "Thanks. Didn't mean ta jump on ya. One more guess."

"I give! Are you taking a special grocery order for Lady Lamont?"

Gosh, he'd come up with the perfect excuse. "Ya guessed! And just in time. Here we are."

They pulled to a stop in front of the magnificent stone house.

"Thanks fer the ride. Come down ta Bert's store and see me once in a while."

"I'm sure we'll be needing something, like another bag of flour," he said.

"Right. And then ya can have me up fer that tuna-biscuit thing. Yer ma cooks better than my mimy—" She stopped as a heavy feeling of missing came over her.

He tilted his head. "Sorry you had that happen last night, with the bag of food and all."

She shrugged. "Just another night of crazy. I'm used ta it."

"Yeah, well . . . see you soon."

She slammed the door and stood watching the truck rattle down the hill. When it was gone, she followed the neatly-edged walkway to the mansion and looked up at the stone structure, in awe at its size. Not sure at which door to knock or ring a bell, she noticed a well-traveled path and followed it to a solid oak door. Such a stately entrance left her with doubts that she'd find a friendly face inside. She pressed on the black button of a doorbell and stood back. No one answered right away so she rang a second time.

Then the big door swung open until she was face to face with Eugene. She knew Lady Lamont's son from school—a tall, lanky guy without an ounce of extra flesh, all muscle and bone and a perfect face. The girls turned to jelly when seeing him, but he'd never given her a second look. He drove his mother's latest Packard and was a friend to many but to no particular one, except for Polly.

"Hi, Eugene. I've come ta see yer ma."

He looked at her blankly and then recognition sparked in his eyes. "Oh my gosh! You're Lizzy LaFlam!"

"Yup, the new Lizzy LaFlam. Miz Brown fixed me up real pretty."

"Wow. You look so different, and really in a nice way."

"Aw, thanks." Well he noticed her now.

Eugene motioned. "Come on in. Mother doesn't like to see visitors in the morning as that's her studio time to paint, but she'll be glad for your visit." He shook his head in wonderment. "Lizzy from the LaFlam clan. You know you're famous in town and probably never knew it."

"Oh, I knew it, but I plan ta leave the famous part behind."

She followed Eugene through a dim hallway that led to a bright room with a lot of glass. The space was full of all sorts of paintings in different stages—one was of a bowl of fruit, another a single red apple hanging from a tree, and then there were some of Jubal's ma scantily dressed which Lizzy tried hard not to stare at. Lady Lamont stood in front of a half-completed country scene. She seemed not to notice them as she added broad splashes of color with the brush, looking at every angle of her work.

Lizzy was surprised at how old Lady Lamont seemed. She was smoking from a cigarette holder, with the long gray ash about to land on the floor. She wore a faded blue robe spattered with paint, and her nearly white hair was held in a loose single braid that hung over her back.

Eugene went to her. "Mother, we have company."

She didn't look up or towards him, but the lines on her face deepened in irritation. "Dear, you know that I don't wish to be disturbed in the morning hours."

Lizzy knew from Lady Lamont's classy tone that the woman was certainly not from the hick town of Hayesville. She wished she sounded more like Lady Lamont when she spoke.

"But we have a guest," Eugene insisted. "I know you'll want to meet her."

Still studying her painting, Lady Lamont drew on her cigarette and flicked the ash into a white porcelain bowl on a nearby shelf. "Now, who might that be?"

"It's Lizzy LaFlam from LaFlam Mountain!"

"Oh, my goodness!" Lady Lamont just about dropped the cigarette and holder into the bowl. She whirled to face Lizzy. "I *sure do* want to meet her."

Lizzy stepped forward and stuck out her hand. "Please ta meet ya, Lady Lamont."

The heiress reached out her paint-speckled white hand. A large diamond ring dwarfed one finger—jewelry rarely, if ever, seen in Hayesville.

"Well, for goodness sake," Lady Lamont said. "The efforts I've made over the years to get you and your brothers into suitable homes and now here you are, a very attractive young lady." She placed a chair next to the one she obviously used that was covered with blotches of paint. "Let's have a seat."

Lizzy settled herself, crossing her legs like she imagined a young lady should do.

"What brings you here, Lizzy?" Lady Lamont asked.

She took a deep breath. She just had to win Lady Lamont over. If she didn't prove her worth to Bert, she'd likely be bunking at the town poor farm. "Ya know how I've been workin' at Bert's country store?"

"Yes, Rose told me." Lady Lamont narrowed her eyes. "She also said that you appeared at her house with Jubal late last night looking in tough shape with terrible clothes and well . . . well needing, shall I say . . . a bath."

"Yes ma'am, I sure did need one, and Jubal's ma took care of that. She also gave me some badly needed clothes."

"That's my Rose. Such a lovely person."

Lady Lamont reached forward to pat her hand. Her touch was light and cool.

The heiress continued, "Rose would be here now but she's gone to Rutland to do some grocery shopping." She turned. "Eugene, would you mind bringing us some of that leftover rhubarb pie and a pot of tea?"

Eugene nodded and dutifully left the studio for the kitchen on his mother's errand.

Lady Lamont lowered her voice as if sharing a secret. "You know, I had but one shredded wheat biscuit soaked in milk and boiled for my breakfast. Yesterday Rose went down to the store and returned to say that Bert didn't even have one single box of Shredded Wheat cereal on his shelf."

Since Lady Lamont had brought up the particular subject of Bert's problem, Lizzy jumped in. "That's exactly why I'm here this mornin'." She shifted her chair to speak intently to the older woman. "Bert is always low on stock and to make matters worse, Bernice is killin' his business takin' money from his cash drawer fer the Temperance League. I want ta run Bert's store. I know my numbers, and I know I can do it."

Her potential benefactress sighed. "Yes, everyone but Bert knows about Bernice." She put her hand to her chin and stared in the direction of the big windows, her ring glinting in the light. She turned back to Lizzy. "That store sure could use a makeover. But how do *you* plan to turn that business around? You're only what, fourteen?"

Lizzy drew herself up, smoothing the skirt of her jumper. "I'm fifteen. Be sixteen 'fore long. I've growed up fast dealing with the likes of my brothers and Big Daddy."

Lady Lamont smiled thinly. "Yes, I suppose you have."

Lizzy continued. "I've been workin' the store and studyin' the folk that come in. I see what they're needin' and wantin' that he don't have. Bert just put his faith in me today. I've made up a big order of just the right products ta make his store a success in no time."

"Better selections would make a good start, you're right," Lady Lamont nodded. "But how will Bert pay for this big order of yours? I hear the store funds are pretty low these days."

It was time for the big sell. "Well, ma'am, that's what I come ta ask ya. If ya could help with a loan, say 'bout, a thousand or even two thousand? Enough ta get this order and have a bit of extra to fancy the place up some. I got ideas I know folks'll like. I know I can turn things around quick-like and get it back ta ya."

Lady Lamont's eyes widened. She raised her arms skyward as if celebrating good news. "Young lady, you're amazing. I most certainly want to help you. For starters, we'll need to go to the Rutland Bank and open an account for you. While we're there we'll do some shopping and . . . I think I can get you in to see a dentist.

"A dentist! I ain't never seen one of them." Lizzy put her hand over her mouth. "Will it hurt?"

"Not much if you go now," Lady Lamont said as she stood. "Eugene will drive us."

Lizzy was trying to process all of the good fortune she'd just encountered in the meeting. "Why, thank you, Miz Lamont. My order will most definitely include Nabisco Shredded Wheat."

Lady Lamont laughed. "Lizzy, you are an exciting young lady. I'll loan you the money, but you must be willing to accept a lot of guidance from me."

"Oh, I'm most willin' fer sure."

Just then Eugene returned with a silver tray containing a fancy teapot, three cups and saucers, and three plates with thick slices of rhubarb pie. As Lizzy sipped her tea and enjoyed heavenly bites of pie, she felt she was in a dream. How her life had changed overnight.

Chapter Fourteen

Maria had slept terribly. She was nervous about the arrival of the kids for their first day of camp, but mostly she had been expecting that Freddie Coleman would come barging through her cabin door at any moment in the night.

However, as of Sunday afternoon there was still no sign of him about the camp's grounds, and her cabin of ten new girls had settled in with little problem. She was Miss Styles to them. Gee, they were young—kids eight to ten years old. Regarding the five bunk beds, who had ended up sleeping on the top was an issue. Suzy White, the last to arrive, of course had to take the last top bunk. She'd balked, with immediate tears.

"Way up there scares me."

Everyone lay on their beds, looking with big eyes over their headboards like bunnies in hiding. Maria raised her voice, "Okay. Who's willing to give their bottom bunk to Suzy?"

Not a word from anyone. Maria stood waiting by the open door. Finally, a little redhead, Gloria, rolled off her bed. "I will."

Maria exhaled a deep breath, having solved her first crisis. "Thank you, Gloria. If I had a big candy bar, I'd give it to you!"

"My mother doesn't let me eat candy."

Maria made a funny face and most kids laughed. She was off to a good start.

The supper meal had opened with Mother Superior giving all the campers a welcome. She'd listed the rules for the week and ended by saying grace. The dinner continued with no problem—even the beef stew disappeared without a single comment. After they had dessert, chocolate pudding in paper cups, Father Hebert, a young theology school graduate, taught them a few camp songs.

Partway through the meal, Maria spied Freddie from a distance. She ducked her head, taking care not to give him eye contact. She hadn't ventured back to his cabin that morning to check on him as she had promised. So far it looked like her lies and broken promise were of no consequence. Still, she seemed to have exposed his anxieties with her joke about the peanut-switch. He was a guy that thought much of himself, and she'd likely made him angry.

After the songs were over, she worked alongside her kids to clean up the dining hall. Her girls turned out to be great little helpers. When the tables and floor met Mother Superior's standards for cleanliness, they all headed across the yard in summer evening twilight for games and dancing in the recreation hall, a long building with a huge dance floor. They were about to start the activities, but realized there was no piano. It had yet to be moved from winter storage. Father Hebert spoke with Tatum who was there for the opening night from Hayesville with Father Mac.

"Why hasn't the piano been moved?" Father Hebert asked. "That was on the list for maintenance director. I trust you knew camp was to begin today?"

Mother Superior, in a high, crackly voice, had her say. "Really, Tatum!"

Tatum growled. "The movers never came!" He looked out the door at the storage shed. "Let's see where the piano is. Maybe we can do the job without movers."

Maria could see Father Hebert was not happy about having to teach kids the dance steps without music, but he made the best of the circumstance. After first helping her campers with the routine, she then asked Father Mac to take her place so she could go and try to help with the piano. Seeing as Freddie was on the dance floor, she figured it would be a good way to avoid him.

In the shed, she and Tatum easily found the piano amid a jumble of chairs. Though likely out of tune, the upright looked in okay condition.

"This thing's a heavy bastard," Tatum warned. He tried to heft one end, managing to raise it only a couple of inches from the dusty floor. He lowered it, cursing softly. "We'll never get it to the rec hall."

Meanwhile, Maria's strategy to avoid Freddie failed. Mister Muscles suddenly appeared in the early evening gloom.

"Let me at that thing," Freddie said, grabbing one end. "Awk! Damn, this weighs a ton." He dropped it, causing a terrible chord, and scowled at the piano.

Earlier that morning before the cars streamed in to deposit campers, Maria had helped unload a big government surplus order that included heavy boxes of peanut butter, bags of flour, and other items which they had placed on carts to push into storage.

Standing by, it occurred to her, "Why not try the carts that are used to bring heavy items to the kitchen?"

Tatum looked at Maria in surprise as if seeing her for the first time. "Good idea. Let's try it."

She and Tatum went to the kitchen's cold storage at one end of the dining hall where two heavy-duty flatbed carts with hard rubber wheels sat waiting. She grabbed one cart, while Tatum took the other, and they wheeled them easily across the uneven ground back to the shed where Freddie was waiting.

"If I hurt my back lifting this goddamned thing," Freddie said, "the church will pay."

Tatum ignored him. "We'll lift one end together while you slide a cart underneath," he told Maria.

The two men grunted and groaned, and when they finally hefted one end, she deftly moved a cart under the piano. In a flash she flipped the wheel locks down to hold it in place.

"See? Easy as pie," she said, glad her plan had worked.

Tatum went to the other end of the piano with the second cart as Freddie joined him for the lift.

"Now, let's see if our smartass counselor can position this one 'easy as pie,'" Freddie smirked.

Her throat constricted. Tatum was too intent on moving the piano to react to Freddie's sarcasm. Once they had the other end of the piano elevated, she slid the second cart under. It worked beautifully. The ride for the instrument across the yard didn't jar it much and within minutes they were unloading the old black upright right where Father Hebert wanted it.

"You guys did the undoable," Father Hebert said.

Tatum pointed to Maria. "The brains—the way to moving this heavy thing was all her idea."

"It took a French teacher to figure how to move it," Freddie mumbled.

"What's he talking about?" Tatum asked.

She shrugged, hoping Tatum wouldn't expose her lies. Thankfully, he didn't.

The program quickly resumed as Father Hebert asked all the counselors and kids to stand in a circle around the dance floor. He began to teach basic square dance moves: *Bow to your right and bow to your left. Take the partner to your right and promenade around the hall.* Soon Father Hebert, lively at the piano, had them all enjoying the moment—it was *allemande left,* and *do si do,* and *swing your partner* until bedtime. As the circle formations changed, Maria was worried she would end up partners with Freddie, but with so many kids in the dance, that luckily did not come to pass. When the fun was over, she headed for her cabin with her girls for the night.

The following days flew by. Maria was always busy and on the run. The camp staff had learned that she was willing help, more so than most, and that she usually had a smart solution to get things done faster.

Her girls were valiant little campers and she was surprised to find that she actually enjoyed their company. For the first couple of nights

Suzy and a friend ended up sleeping with her because of homesickness. While in a crowded bed, Maria didn't get much sleep, but she didn't make a big deal over it and chose not to report the minor problem to Mother Superior.

At week's end, all of the kids and most of the staff left late Friday afternoon. Maria was looking forward to going home for a short break before the next round of campers came on Sunday. But she was asked by Mother Superior to help Tatum rearrange bunks because a lot more girls than boys were enrolled for the second week. Tatum planned to bring Maria home to Hayesville in his sheriff's car after they finished their job.

Moving bunk beds among the ten cabins, following a plan Mother Superior had given them, was not that hard but it was hot. The late afternoon sun beat down through a haze, making it muggy along with the heat. Maria's Cabin Ten with no shade was like an oven.

Tatum was out of sorts because Mother Superior also wanted him to go into town nearby to buy some needed camp supplies. As they worked, he grumbled that he was anxious to get back to Hayesville as soon as possible for his sheriff's duties. When it was time for him to run Mother Superior's errand, Maria chose to stay at camp until he returned so that she had some time to tidy up her cabin for the coming week and pack for home.

Because of the heat, and since Mother Superior was nowhere around and the campers were all gone, she gratefully changed out of her camp dress into a t-shirt, shorts, and sneakers. Still, the sweat just poured off of her. It didn't take her long to clean the cabin or pack, leaving her time for a dip in the lake to get cooled off. Freddie had also left the grounds in his car, so the beach would be empty. She grabbed a towel and a dry change of clothes to put on after. Then she ran over the path through the woods to the lake.

With everyone gone, the place was strangely quiet. The woods were also silent without a bird or creature stirring in the steamy afternoon.

She left her change of clothes and towel on the beach and splashed into the lake, immediately loving the coolness. She was glad she kept on her white cloth sneakers due to stones farther out from shore. Even though basking in the refreshing water, she couldn't linger long. When Tatum returned, he'd be wanting to get on the road. She ducked her head, liking the feel of the chill as the soft water cleaned the sweat from her face. She surfaced and gained her footing on the rocks with her back turned to the beach.

The sound of a car halted her swim, and she turned with a rush of fear. It was Freddie. Without slowing at all, he maneuvered his Ford convertible around the beach furniture, driving right to the water's edge for an abrupt halt. He cut the engine and jumped out barefoot. All he had on were his skimpy swim briefs, and even from a distance she could see sweat creating a sheen on his coppery body. He looked out across the water, a cunning smile spreading across his face.

"Oh! This has worked out better than I'd planned," he called out. In a shockingly lewd gesture he grabbed his groin.

Maria froze in place. She stood in water up to her thighs with her wet t-shirt and shorts sticking to her skin, revealing every curve she had. Her change of clothes and towel on the sand next to his rear tire seemed impossibly far away. She lowered herself down into the water.

"You're disgusting!" she yelled.

"And you're a lying son-of-a-bitch, Miss French teacher."

Whether from heat or excitement, his face was red and his pug nose flared in anticipation like she'd seen in a bull after a cow. God, this guy was an animal!

"Guess what? It's payback time for that sorry excuse of a date!" he said.

On pure instinct, she lunged through the water, reaching the shore in seconds. As she dove at him, his sweet cologne smell hit her. He couldn't react as she made contact, flopping backwards onto his butt. Before he could rise, she snatched her clothes and towel and charged towards the path in her soggy sneakers.

Freddie jumped to his feet, swearing and stumbling after her in pursuit.

Her athletic ability allowed her to gain on him as he winced over the ground barefooted. She whizzed over the path and entered the camp parking lot with number Ten in sight. Freddie was now tiptoeing over the painful gravel surface, giving her just enough time to rush into her cabin. She slammed the door and snapped the hook into the eye.

When Freddie reached the cabin, he pounded on the door. "Let me in, you lying bitch! Make a fool of me? Huh? Thirty years old? A teacher with a big fancy degree spewing a bunch of garbage about germs. What bullshit! I saw Mother Superior's list of counselors and you're still in high school! But don't you worry, I especially like them young."

Hearing his words, Maria hoped she was safe inside the cabin but wasn't sure what was next. He kept pounding and pulling at the door. The hook eye was bending and about to pull from the soft wood that held it. The entire door and casing was squawking, never properly nailed, and looked like it would come completely separate from the cabin.

"Freddie, stop! I was just having a little fun. Can't you take a joke?" She grabbed the door handle and held the two-by-four frame that was soon to give way. She continued pulling to delay the screw of the eye popping from the wood. "Look, I'm sorry!"

"Yeah, now you're sorry! Wait until I get this goddamn door open. I'll screw your eyes out, just as you deserve!"

Her heart pounded seemingly in her ears. "Leave me alone! Get out of here," she warned. She just had to stay calm, and hold on. For a moment there was silence, only the tension of the two of them pulling on the cabin door. She squeezed her fingers tighter around the handle.

Just then she heard a car. She leaned back and craned her neck so she could see out the cabin window. Sure enough, in the distance dust rose from the gravel road near the camp's entrance. It had to be Tatum. Her only hope was to get help from the sheriff.

Freddie seemed not to notice that someone was coming. He continued to swear and yank on the door, so she kept pulling. She leaned back and turned again to see the car pull into the parking lot. It was Tatum. She let go of the handle and frame and screamed, "Help! Help!"

As the two-by-four frame and door started to break free from the building, she saw her chance to totally disable the monster until Tatum arrived. With the whole end of her cabin about to separate, she ran at the door with her shoulder down. Her weight and force finally separated the cabin parts from the building, no doubt surprising Freddie who was just on the other side. Suddenly it all ripped free and slammed down on top of him, the dismembered cabin parts clattering across the steps. He let out a wail.

She stood in what had been the doorway looking down on the pile of debris, her attacker underneath.

Meanwhile, Tatum had gunned the car across the yard and up the knoll to number Ten. He jumped out hollering, "Freddie, what in hell are ya doin' there hiding under a bunch of lumber practically bare-ass?"

Freddie wiggled like a snake, freeing himself from the door and casing, emerging with red marks on his forehead and arms.

"I was just wanting to talk to Maria about next week's water activities for the kids. Spooked her I guess. Don't know what's wrong with her. She got all panicked. The door got stuck." He turned and glared at her. His look said, you dare contradict me and I'll kill you.

"Looks to me like she didn't want to talk to you." Tatum said. He turned to her. "Maria, what's going on here?"

Freddie continued his look of warning.

"Nothing." She lowered her eyes. It was her word against Freddie's and her instinct told her to keep mum. "Everything will be okay if we can just get this door back in place." She attempted a laugh. "They sure didn't build this very well."

Freddie nodded. "Nope."

Tatum scratched his head, looking from her to Freddie and back again. "How come you screamed?"

"I was . . . afraid the door was going to come off, just like it did," she said.

Freddie bent to pick up the door. "It's okay. We can fix this."

"I'll get a hammer and nails in the tool room," she said. All she wanted was to get away from the two men. Once inside the tool room, she sat on a bench and burst into tears, crying quietly into her hands. Then she dried her face on her still-damp t-shirt and gathered the needed tools.

Freddie and Tatum put the cabin back together in short order, and the whole time Freddie acted like nothing had happened.

Riding home in the back seat of Tatum's car, a terrible blackness came over Maria—a horrible pounding headache. All she could think about was a nearly naked Freddie chasing after her. Someday he'd catch her. She'd been so stupid to get herself into this situation.

Chapter Fifteen

Chester Styles had planted Avery Ketchum's thirty-acre cornfield on Memorial Day, and now the time had come for Jubal to cultivate. Avery wanted it to start just as the weed seeds sprouted and showed their faces. "I want them little kale, lamb's quarters, and pigweed seedlin's uprooted before they take hold and crowd out the corn," he declared.

Meanwhile, Jubal's own hayfields needed cutting with the grass maturing coarse and over-ripe under the summer sun. Their cows also needed fencing for fresh pasture. The fence repair was coming slowly, and the small jag of hay had gotten wet a couple of times so that by the time he and Benny put the one load up, it wasn't worth much. The beautiful hay that Jubal had taken from Avery was nearly fed out. The cows loved it, but now he had to pay the price. He was torn. When at Avery's, he couldn't get his work done at home. It wasn't Avery's fault—the deal was fair. There was no avoiding it; Jubal had to keep his end of the bargain.

After chores in the early evening's long summer light, the cultivating job at Avery's was endless and difficult. The two-horse rig would only do one row at a time. Besides, Avery wanted him to use the Morgans.

"Ya know," Avery said, "that parade's comin' real soon. I want the piss and vinegar worked outta them jumpy beasts."

Avery also asked to adjust the cultivator shoes to nearly touch the corn that was just poking through the ground. Jubal didn't have the knack with the team that Maria had. She handled them calmly, while he held tight on the reins, tight as newly strung fence wire. He couldn't relax. The mares reacted likewise, prancing down the corn rows, throwing their heads with their ears back, hooves landing every place except in the middle of the row. Thus, the cultivator shoes were ripping up plenty of corn.

Now free of crutches, Avery limped to the field to see how the cultivating was going. He didn't say much.

Jubal complained, "I'd rather drive the Percherons. They'll do a better job and I won't ruin as much corn."

"Jubal, just relax. A few trips up and down this field will calm the pair a might. Besides, we're in the midst of hayin', needin' the stronger team."

"Okay, I hope you're right. Better yet, give me more space. Adjust the shoes so I don't rip up so much corn."

"No. Them weeds is bad. I ain't wantin' ya ta change a thing." And with that Avery left the field.

Jostling along in his seat, Jubal tried to make sure the team straddled the row. It was far from easy, but Avery was right. After a few trips up and down the field, the Morgans calmed down. Still, the job was taking way too much time. At the end of the row, he'd lift the cultivator with the lever and lower it onto the next row. He headed in view of the farmstead, studying the back of Avery's barn that hadn't been painted in years. He smiled, realizing the Yankee way—paint what shows. In the distance, the glossy red paint of the AKL stone shone in the late setting sun.

He tried best he could to fit in Avery's job with his own farm work. Benny, in his absence, could only shovel the stable gutters, which he did daily, pushing the wheelbarrow full of slop out the back door and up the plank ramp to dump onto the gigantic pile of manure that hadn't been spread in years. Benny also swept the aisles and brushed the horses. And while his ma worked up at Lady Lamont's all day, his dad sat drinking in his easy chair. At least the longer days meant that Jubal could cultivate down at Avery's after supper.

From his high vantage point, he looked down to watch and listen to the click of the steel cultivator shoes digging the soil as they covered the weed seedlings on both sides of the row. When he turned the horses onto the next row to head back towards the farm, he glanced behind to admire his work of newly disturbed black soil. Rows of germinated corn plants appeared to reach nearly to the back door of Avery's tenant house. The two-leaf seedlings looked similar to columns of toy soldiers dressed in green with arms extended. Chester must have planted with the Percherons because the rows were perfectly straight.

The Morgans continued to step lively when reaching the end of the row in back of the Styles' home. To his surprise, he saw Maria walk out of her house across the lawn to meet him. It had been weeks since they'd worked together. Seeing her gave him a thrill. He'd missed her.

"Maria, you're home!"

She came to the edge of the lawn, standing in front of the Morgans, who had stopped at the end of the row. The pair nickered in greeting.

"Yeah, I'm having my gown fitted for the parade." She reached in her skirt pocket and pulled out two small carrots.

He realized with a start how weird it was to see Maria in a skirt. Come to think of it, she looked different in more ways than that. She seemed sort of *grown up,* he decided.

The horses nibbled the carrots from the palm of her hand. "Are you two girls behaving for Jubal?" she murmured. She stroked their faces and patted their necks. "So, how are you doing?" she asked, looking up.

"Well, you can see," he said. He pointed back towards the field. "It isn't fast work. Just row by row."

She looked wistful. "Well, it sure beats my job—dressed in skirts and stuck at a summer camp."

He chuckled. "I was kind of surprised to see you wearing one."

"It's the honor of being a counselor at a Catholic camp. Lucky me."

"Well . . ." He wasn't sure what to say to make her feel better. "You *look* great."

"Thanks." She glanced down at her skirt, smoothing the fabric. "Of course, I'd rather be wearing overalls and barn boots," she grinned.

It was the smile he loved to see, but it vanished quickly.

"Can I drive the team down and back just once?" she asked.

He glanced down at her saddle shoes. "Sure. I'll turn the team onto the next row so you won't have to walk in the freshly turned soil with those shoes." He clucked to the horses.

When he had pulled the team back around, she climbed up onto the single seat and he edged to the side of the machine, finding a place to sit and hold on. She took up the reins and as she gently released the tension, the team eased ahead at a moderate walk. Sally and Di seemed to know Maria was in control.

"I love this," she said. "I could do it all day."

"Be my guest. When the Morgans behave, it can be real boring."

"Maybe for you."

He settled in on the frame of his makeshift seat. "So how is it riding in that fancy black car of Father Mac's?"

"Oh, not too exciting, and Father Mac is rather strange. My mother says that he's not at all like our former priest—she and my dad really miss Father Henry."

"I hear from Polly that most folks feel the same."

She stopped the team at the end of the row while he lifted the cultivator for the next pass down the field.

When the horses were moving again, she turned to him. "On my way home from camp this afternoon, Father Mac fell asleep in the back seat next to me in his shirtsleeves with his arms and legs sprawled. If I hadn't hugged the door, his arm would have dropped right in my lap. Just above his wrist on his forearm, I saw in blazing red ink the words *Connelly's Mary Lou*. They were tattooed across the side of a little boat."

"A priest with a tattoo. How odd." He lifted his cap to scratch his head. "Connelly's Mary Lou. Huh. What does that mean?"

"I don't know, but when Father Mac woke and saw me looking at his arm, he buttoned up his sleeve in a hurry."

"He sounds like a creepy guy." He hated to think of her under Father Mac's thumb all summer.

When they reached the end of the field near her house, she brought the team to a halt. To his surprise, her eyes welled up with tears.

"Jubal, I'm . . . I'm really scared."

"About what? Father Mac?" This was not like Maria. In fact, he'd never seen her cry.

"No, not Father Mac. It's this guy . . . Freddie." She wiped her eyes.

"Who's Freddie?"

"A swim instructor. He's . . . I'm . . . I'm afraid of what he might do!"

"What? Why?"

"He's, well, he's . . . *older*," she said.

"Older? And . . .?" He waited for some further explanation that made sense.

She shook her head and handed him the reins. Then she stood and climbed down off of the cultivator. "Never mind."

"Hey, if you think there's a problem with this Freddie fellow, then tell Father Mac, or someone else who's in charge." Gosh, Maria usually had control of most situations. Whoever this Freddie guy was, she could easily run circles around him.

She began walking away, stepping carefully over the rows in her nice shoes.

"Wait!" he called. "Better yet, why don't you quit and come home to work at Avery's with me?"

She turned, hands in her skirt pockets. "I can't come home. My mother wouldn't hear of it. Look, you're the only one that knows about this. Don't tell anyone. I'll work it out best I can."

"Maria, I . . ."

She put up a hand. "It's okay. Thanks for letting me drive. It felt good."

He sat on the cultivator as she went to the house. The horses watched her, ears pricked forward. Reluctantly, he picked up the reins and turned the team to the next row, glancing back as she climbed the front steps. She seemed far from the fiery farm girl he'd worked with in the spring. The first evening star was visible above the house, and he silently made a wish that it would look after her until she returned home at summer's end.

⁜

Midway through June, Jubal finally finished his first cultivation and wanted to celebrate. He had just completed the last row when Avery came to check his work and nodded his approval. Jubal then stabled and fed the horses before walking back to meet Avery who was bent over in the cornfield, examining the soil.

"What do you think?" Jubal asked.

"You might's well start right in again. With the bit of rain last week, little weed seeds are sproutin' plenty."

Jubal was crestfallen. "So soon?"

"Yup, this is the best time ta kill the weeds. And I want ya ta keep workin' the Morgans. The parade's 'round the corner. It's been moved ahead ta Saturday 'cause the kids have gotta march and they're still at CYO camp on July fourth. If yer willin', would ya also drive them mares with the two-seater buggy?"

"In the parade?" Jubal sighed. Sally and Di in a parade was a bad idea in his estimation.

"Yup. The horses know ya now. Miss Curry and I will ride in the back seat all dressed in our duds."

"Well, I guess I can, but I sure hope they don't spook."

"So do I. Why don't ya take them on a ride through town tomorrow night and see how they act?"

"Okay, but I'll go alone in case they act up."

"Darned good idea! You'll be fine, boy." Avery shaded his eyes, looking across the field. "Yup, we're gonna have us a good harvest come late summer." He looked pleased. "See ya tomorrow then."

Jubal nodded and went to pick up his bike to ride for home. He wasn't looking forward to more cultivating, or to seeing how Sally and Di would act when hearing strange noises on a trip through town. However, at certain times of the day, there was almost no traffic in Hayesville and he hoped that would be the case the following evening.

When he arrived at Avery's the next night, he saw that Avery's hired boy, Ned, had spent a great deal of time grooming the team and polishing the buggy. Avery had the pair harnessed, having put on their bright red-lined collar pads and their fancy black driving harnesses; it was to be the first showing of his new team in the village, and apparently he wanted it to be impressive. Jubal wished he'd put on a clean shirt and pants before leaving his farm after chores.

With some apprehension Jubal took his seat and picked up the reins. Their team at home wasn't car-shy, but of course he didn't know about the Morgans. Expecting the worst, he hoped for the best. He drove Sally and Di at a reasonable pace down Harmony Hill to meet upper Main Street. They passed Jazz Crow's junkyard and the ballpark before coming to the houses in the village where folks sitting on their front porches waved as he passed.

Miss Curry left her house and library to stand on her front steps. "They're gorgeous, Jubal."

"Thanks, Miss Curry."

He had to admit the team was looking snappy traveling at a moderate trot with their heads high. He felt more at ease, slack reins in hand. The leaves on the maples lining the street rustled in the soft breeze, but the team didn't react to the familiar sound. Up ahead, two women were decorating the Hiram Hayes memorial, and a few men had begun construction of a viewing stand in front of St. Anne's. Polly had told him Father Mac was expecting the bishop and other church officials to come to the parade.

Main Street divided at the statue with traffic heading south traveling at the right side of the mound. Northbound traffic passed on the other side of the life-size likeness of Hayesville's hero.

As Jubal continued on, he noted that the county jail had no sign of life. The empty Ford police car was parked beside it, so he figured Tatum must be out chauffeuring Father Mac. He passed the Baptist church and several businesses that were closed for the night, including O'Mara's Drugstore and Sean O'Grady's garage. The Catholic church and rectory, several hundred feet ahead, had no cars and no activity. Town was quiet just as he had hoped. The horses moved along with an easy gait, handling the scene much better than expected.

Suddenly, he heard the roar of an oncoming car. Instantly uptight, he pulled the slack from the reins. Sally and Di's ears dropped and they threw their heads high.

"Easy, now! It's all right," he said, quickly easing back the rein tension.

The roar became louder, the car sounding like it wasn't slowing at all. When the vehicle was beside the horses, its horn blew a long blast. It was Tatum in the Cadillac with Father Mac.

In tandem the horses jumped to the side as Jubal struggled to keep control of the pair. Through the window he saw Tatum bent in laughter, clutching the wheel of the big car.

"You jerk!" Jubal yelled.

But his attention was immediately drawn back as the team picked up speed on a dead run. Di and the right side of the buggy traveled in the ditch, which thankfully wasn't terribly deep. As the car moved past, he glanced up to see Maria's horrified face in the rear window. With all his strength on the reins, he managed to wrestle the team back onto the road and slow them some. The Cadillac pulled into the rectory drive and Maria scrambled out of the car to meet him.

Fearlessly she grabbed Sally's bridle while he continued to pull tight on the reins. The team finally stopped and stood with nostrils flaring.

"How awful!" Maria said. "Tatum's an idiot. Just a rude dummy! Poor horses."

Jubal was just thankful she happened to be there to catch Sally. "What are you doing here?" he asked. "I thought you were back at camp."

"I came home again to have the final fitting for my gown. Such a fuss for a dress I'm going to wear one time."

He smiled. "I wouldn't know about that."

She laughed. "No, I guess not."

"Hey, want to get in and drive with us to the reservoir?"

"I'd love to." Without hesitation or even a backward glance at Father Mac and Tatum, who were unloading a couple of boxes into the rectory, she climbed into the buggy and took up the reins.

As they were about to take off, Father Mac, in his black suit and white collar, hustled to the edge of the road. "Maria! Where are you going?"

"I'll be back in a few minutes."

"You can't leave," Father Mac ordered. "I'm just picking up a couple of things here, and then we're heading out. We'll be late for camp."

"Camp can wait! I need to settle these horses." She clucked her tongue and, before Father Mac could do or say a thing, the team took off at a fast pace. Her blue eyes were in a squint as she declared, "I hate working for him!"

"No kidding." Jubal looked back at the rectory. "And I wouldn't enjoy being around Tatum much either. He's full of himself."

"Right. But most people at camp are okay . . . except—"

"Except what?"

Maria rolled her eyes. "Freddie. Don't you remember?"

"Oh, right. Freddie. I'm sorry. How is that going?"

"So far, I've been able to avoid him because he teaches swimming and I help with recreation. We're in different parts of camp most of the day."

"Why do you need to be in different parts of the camp?"

Avery's buggy rocked along the road as the now peaceful Morgans slowed to a walk.

"I just wish I could be back on the farm," she said, "doing stuff like cultivating."

"Well, unfortunately I guess you can't be. You'll need to figure out how to face this guy." He was still puzzled over her fear. What had riled the guy? Something was missing. She wasn't telling all.

They rode along in silence until they pulled up at the reservoir. As they climbed down from the buggy, he adjusted the reins to hold the team so he and Maria could sit on a nearby bench and let the horses graze the white clover at the reservoir's edge. Shafts of light reflected off the water and a warm breeze stirred up ripples that turned into waves rolling onto the beach sand. A mother mallard with her clutch swam towards them, probably expecting some goodies.

Maria smiled at the sight. "Aren't those ducklings the cutest?"

"So innocent. Most newborns are, don't you think?"

She sighed, her dark hair moving prettily in the breeze. "And then we grow up. Scary, unless you're confident like Lizzy LaFlam."

"Why Lizzy?" Jubal was befuddled on hearing her name out of the blue. He chose not to share his recent wild time with Lizzy.

"Have you noticed her in the store? She started working there not long ago."

"Yes, I know." He looked out over the water, not caring to add to the conversation.

"She helped me shop for a few items I needed for camp. I'd made assumptions about her like everyone else, but this was the first time I actually talked to her. She was very pleasant while trying hard to help me."

"That sounds like Lizzy." He leaned forward, clucking to the ducks, hoping to draw Maria's attention back to them.

"You won't believe it," she continued, "but I was surprised that afterwards Lizzy sent me a postcard, a picture of the Hayesville Country IGA Store. You want to know what she wrote?"

"I guess." The mallard turned in the water and he could see her webbed feet paddling. The clutch circled around, too, in perfect formation.

"I don't get postcards ever," Maria said. "Lizzy wrote:"

Hi Maria,
Have a great summer. Watch out for the guys (just fooling)!
See Ya, Lizzy

"She has good penmanship and punctuation. Better than me. I guess maybe it was her way of trying to make friends."

He kept silent. Lizzy LaFlam was a whole other can of worms. Maria had her Freddie issues it seemed, and he had Lizzie, a larger-than-life gal that he just didn't know how to handle.

Maria stood up from the bench, seeming brighter. "Well, I guess it's time we go. I'm sure Father Mac is madder than an old setting hen."

He climbed back up to his seat on the buggy, while Maria sat beside him and started the team at a brisk trot towards town. After leaving her off at the rectory, he knew he would be seeing her again soon at the parade. He wondered what was going on with this Freddie guy, and also puzzled over his strange connection to Lizzy.

Despite Maria's enjoyment of the little campers under her charge, the weeks at camp were living hell. Her cabin was beastly hot, especially with an additional bunk often squeezed into the tiny space to accommodate an extra camper. The kids were cranky, due to the high summer heat, and she spent her precious few moments alone lying on her bed crying. Except for what she'd shared with Jubal, she had told no one about Freddie's wanting to force himself on her. The secret inside wanted to yell out from fear. Since the day the cabin door had fallen on Freddie, he had ignored her, but she knew if given a chance he'd come after her again. That possibility weighed her down like Avery's big stone, as if its mass had been set upon her chest, crushing her.

Mother Superior was continually on her case, questioning the cause of her gloom, but she wouldn't confide in the nun. If she were to confess, she envisioned a lecture from the old woman on proper behavior for young ladies and the perils of sin.

One bright spot was the two times when she'd been home and had run into Jubal. When she talked with Jubal, her nerves stopped humming in fear. He had a way about him like a comfortable blanket. She'd told him some, but not all about Freddie. What would he think of her? Flirting as she had and spinning such big lies?

So, feeling alone with her secret, she simply dragged through the days as the Fifth of July Parade drew near. She made sure she was always with other counselors, or Mother Superior, or the kids. That way Freddie dared not approach her. He kept his distance, but she could still feel him watching.

Chapter Sixteen

Bert Sausville was stocking shelves at the Hayesville Country IGA, pricing the huge order that had arrived like a miraculous windfall that morning. He kept checking his sheet to be sure that the shelf price included the markup. He'd been in the store business for over thirty years with most of those years under the guidance of his dad. Since his dad had run the business end and Bert had done most of the grunt work, Bert had never learned much as to what a profit and loss statement looked like. Consequently, he never got the hang of how to properly price the items he sold and he had no clear accounting of his gains or losses. But he was good at greeting folks and helping customers with their groceries, despite his struggle with the financial part.

When his father passed away, Bert had inherited the store debt-free. Since his dad never believed in debt, Bert operated on a strictly cash basis and had never had a checking account. In order to pay for the stock he purchased, he depended on cash from sales. But since he didn't price items high enough or do many promotions, the items stocked on his shelves had dwindled because of a lack of money to buy more. This drove folks to instead do their grocery shopping some twenty-odd miles away in Rutland.

Bert did set aside a little each week in a coffee can for the electric bill and a big amount in a second can for his property taxes. Both containers were in a secret hiding place in back of the tobacco and the condoms, out of the public view. The sale of condoms was, in fact, lucrative because Andrew O'Mara, a strict Catholic, didn't believe in birth control at his pharmacy. And Bernice was so disgusted that Bert would stock such sinful items that he knew she would never go near his hiding place.

Lately, his store sales had plummeted to a pathetic amount and he was at the end of his rope. He'd said nothing while Bernice had robbed the store nearly out of existence with him having no idea of how much she was taking out of the cash drawer for her Temperance cause. Now a fifteen-year-old girl had virtually taken over and was living in the back room. He had let himself fall into a trap.

At six that morning before the store opened, Lizzy and he had discussed the store's future. He suspected that most of Lizzy's ideas, which were impressive, came from Lady Lamont. Everybody in town knew the heiress was a shrewd businesswoman, and while Lizzy was only a teenager, she had gumption. Enough gumption, apparently, to seek out the elderly heiress for advice and financial backing.

According to the deal struck with Lady Lamont for financial help, Bert had little to say concerning the constraints he'd be working under with Lizzy in charge. Lizzy, in turn, would answer to Lady Lamont. Before the store had opened at 7 a.m., he had been asked to accept conditions which Lizzy had laid out with Lady Lamont's help:

— rental of the store to Lizzy for $50 per month.
— sale of all present stock he owned for $1000.
— a salary for him of $30 per week.
— no loans allowed to the Sausvilles.
— all sales counted, recorded, and deposited at the end of each day in a locked deposit pouch.
— the pouch to be taken to O'Mara's Drugstore to be delivered promptly to the Rutland National Bank.
— all draws on the store account to be done by a bank check co-signed by Lois Lamont.

After reading the agreement, with Lizzy waiting, he set his copy on the counter.

"This is so sudden," he said. "Why do I have only an hour to agree?"

"Bert, ya know that most of the stuff on the shelves don't belong ta ya," Lizzy reminded him. "I paid fer it with borrowed money. Lady Lamont took me ta open an account." She came around the counter and reached into a drawer, holding up the pouch. "Each night we'll make a deposit and the daily auto stage travelin' from O'Mara's will leave it off at the Rutland National Bank."

He threw up his hands. "What can I say? You caught me at a weak moment."

"Bert, I'm doin' ya a favor. Be honest, ya were within weeks of closin' this place."

"I suppose—things were sliding downhill fast. I wasn't wanting to face it. But how do I know you can do any better?"

"Ya don't, but I know I can, 'specially with Lady Lamont's help. She's askin' me ta report ta her twice a week and is already teachin' me lots about bookkeepin' and dealin' with the bank."

He picked up the agreement, rereading it as he leaned on the counter. Then he looked up at her. "You can't deal with the bank. You aren't old enough."

"All my dealin' with the bank will be under Lady Lamont's name."

Lizzy then explained how his weekly salary would no doubt quickly increase as the business grew.

Now he would never admit it to a soul, but in the time they had worked together, he'd grown to love Lizzy as a father loves his daughter. He'd given her a job when certainly no one else in town would. Initially, he thought he was just giving one of Hayesville's downtrodden a helping hand—she'd struck him as a grubby, wild young thing, and he'd assumed she might even be a bit simple as a result of her upbringing. But she'd quickly shown her true colors. She'd turned into a powerhouse of a gal with a kind heart that he'd never thought to be humanly possible. He looked forward to her plucky company. Despite her age, she could be his savior in more ways than one. He was lucky to have her by his side.

He signed the agreement. It was seven o'clock on the nose when he went to the door and unlocked it, opening the Hayesville Country IGA Store under new management.

His big problem was Bernice. As he stocked the shelves, part of his difficulty with pricing was due to poor concentration. He kept playing out the scenario of telling her the news.

She usually came into the store around ten. He mopped his round face with a counter-cleaning rag as sweat poured from his bald head due to heightened blood pressure—a chronic health issue. Confronting Bernice felt like waiting to be shot, the anticipation probably worse than the main event.

Lizzy was deep into her work far down one of the three main aisles, washing shelves that hadn't been stocked for quite some time. She was as far away from the cash drawer as she could get. He knew why the distance. In minutes, Bernice would be in, headed for her almost daily draw, wanting to get her righteous hands on money to pay for her day's activities in the name of the Lord. Bert was going to have to hold his hand on the cash drawer and that wasn't going to be pretty. He repositioned himself at the front of the store to be ready.

Customers started coming in at a steady stream, commenting on the volume of new stock. He wasn't sure how the word had gotten out, but it had. He reassured customers that in the future he would have all the items to meet their needs, and it would no longer be necessary to grocery shop in Rutland.

"My new partner has big plans for the future of this store," he told them.

He became so caught up in his conversations with customers, which brightened his day with hope that the Hayesville store might not go under after all, that he didn't notice Bernice at the door dressed formally and wearing a fox fur as a comforter. She had heard his comments.

"New partner?" She approached him in back of the counter. The redness of the fox stole clashed with her red lipstick and pink powder that failed to cover the age lines on her face. "What is the meaning of *that* comment?"

Bert stood with his back to the cash drawer. "I have a new partner."

"You mean, *we* have a new partner? I don't know what you're talking about, but get out of my way!" she ordered. "I need some cash. The Temperance League meets this afternoon in Burlington!" She continued to press him to step aside.

He didn't move.

Worry lines creased her forehead. "Did you hear me?"

"Yes." He stared her down, unsure how she'd react. She was used to doing as she pleased.

Her lips quivered in repressed frustration. "Get out of my way!" she repeated.

Customers gathered and stared. From his seat just outside on the bench, Clem Gochy walked into the store and pushed his way to the front of the crowd.

Bert turned to face those gathered and cleared his throat. "Folks, I have an important announcement." Silence settled and he drew a deep breath, figuring he might as well get it over with. "Um . . . I . . . no longer own the stock in this store."

Bernice looked at him sharply. "That's nonsense. Of course you do."

He shook his head. "No. I don't. As of seven o'clock this morning, Lizzy LaFlam became the new owner. I leased the store and now I'm working for her."

The crowd gasped and spoke in hushed tones.

He turned to his wife. "Bernice, I'm afraid this cash drawer is now off limits. The money belongs to the store and to Lizzy."

Color drained from Bernice's powdered face. She paused like a pressure cooker building up a head of stem.

He continued, "So . . . so we can be a business we're proud of and . . . one that can better serve our customers."

The crowd was silent, waiting to see what would happen next.

Bernice's color flooded back. "Bert Sausville!" she exploded. "You are the most milky-toast excuse for a man I've ever met! Your father worked himself to the bone for this store. Built it from nothing to be a proud business in our town. Now look what his weak-kneed son has gone and done!"

"I'm doing what I can to save—"

"How could you? How could you allow a smart-mouthed floozy from the backwoods to get the upper hand? A little . . . little . . . well, I'll come right out and say it—a whore!"

As she yelled out the awful word, he saw Lizzy quietly standing in back of the store, partially behind a shelf as if to be invisible.

"Did you let her take this store out from under you without a peep?" Bernice shook her finger at him. "Yes, not even a peep to allow me to know what was going on. I won't stand for this. You're a . . . a disgrace to the Sausville name!"

She yanked off the fox fur, with it's gaping mouth and beady eyes, and slapped it on the counter. As she did so, the fur's tail brushed the face of Clem Gochy who stood directly across from her.

Almost as one the crowd took a step back. Bert was speechless, but firm with his back to the register.

Clem had plenty to say. "Bernice, ya're speakin' ill of my Lizzy, and I won't stand fer it! She's a girl I helped raise from practically nothin', a girl that's straight, honest, and pure of heart! Now, speakin' of bein' a floozy, I know from a good source that you were quite the run-around in yer day 'fore comin' ta town, and it was Bert who saved ya from what ya often call the 'Fires of Hell'." He swept the fox fur to the floor. "And likely ya bought this fancy dead animal wrap with store money, keepin' yer husband from runnin' things proper."

Bernice gasped. Bert knew Clem had just dredged up a past that she apparently thought was forever hidden, right in front of the assembly of townsfolk. She reeled back and fell onto the stool. A look of defeat came over her as her eyes welled up with tears. Her mouth turned down in a look of remorse.

Bert quickly stepped to her side and took her arm. "Before this gets out of hand, we'd better go back to the house." He leaned down and, with thumb and forefinger, picked up the decorative specimen by its morbid, dried head. Then he headed towards the door with Bernice on his arm and the bushy, red fox tail dragging on the floor.

He saw Clem turn to face the crowd. "Ya folks go now about yer business. Ya can bet this store will be in good hands with Lady Lamont guiding my girl Lizzy."

That said, folks dispersed throughout the store to complete their shopping, muttering to each other and nodding, while Bert took his wife home to try to make amends.

On June 28, 1941, after breakfast, Clyde Brown sat in his overstuffed chair in his drinking corner reading *Successful Farming.* The clock on the stroke of seven diverted his attention to his Philco radio as he listened to the morning news:

German forces have directed Lithuanian militias to go on a shooting spree, killing scores of Jews in the city streets while spectators cheer them on. It's estimated that over three thousand Jews have been massacred in Kaunas alone.

The announcer's voice was shaky, obviously appalled by what he had just read. However, true to the custom of news radio, he was not free to editorialize the facts.

Clyde gripped his half glass of *Rheingold.* "That goddamned Hitler!" he grumbled aloud. "Poor bastards gunned down just because they're Jews. Jacob Levine, our cattle dealer, always treated me right. He's a Jew. And that old guy that goes around buyin' rags, newspapers, and scrap metal, he seems to be okay. What the hell's wrong over there in Europe?"

He drained his drink and poured himself another, adding a generous shot of *Jim Beam.* Tipping his glass for a big gulp and smacking his lips, he whispered, "Son-of-a-bitch, that feels good goin' down."

Now, Hitler might be a rotten apple, but Clyde had his own problems to contend with. He'd tell anyone that his Rose Brown was no pushover. Damn, did she ever lace into him that morning, telling him that he wasn't worth a red cent and wasn't the man he used to be. That last bit stung just a little. Of course she claimed he'd have to stop his drinking and had given him until the parade to cut back. Ridiculous. Just over a week away!

And what the hell for? He wasn't bothering anybody. Yet, he had to admit the booze was costing him, costing them all. Speaking of money, Jubal, he knew, had a big stash of cash sitting on his bureau in a glass bank. He noticed it every time he passed Jubal's room on his way to the bathroom to take a leak. Why Rose didn't just spend a little of that, he didn't know; it might ease the pinch until the next milk check.

His boy was a smart kid and all, but he was getting big for his britches. He'd heard the boy pressuring his ma to stop spending from the milk check for liquor. Who did Jubal think he was, crowding into his drinking business?

He swirled his glass and studied the gold color in the morning light. He'd worked damned hard in his early life, with nothing to show for it but a rundown barn and some bony cattle. The whiskey and the beer gave him a break, and god knows he deserved a break. With the world going to hell over there across the sea, nothing seemed to matter much anymore. The way things were going, it would not surprise him one bit if all of humanity went up in smoke under a steady rain of bombs. He took a long, slow sip, letting the drink linger, feeling the bite of the bourbon. The news on his Philco faded in his mind as his head flopped back on the chair.

The morning of July 5th, the day of the parade, Jubal put on a new suit, a light blue seersucker. His ma had bought it for him by stashing some of her earnings from Lady Lamont in a safe place at the back of her lingerie drawer. The new suit fit perfectly, and his dad with shaky hands attempted to help Jubal with his tie.

"Well, Rose," his dad said, wrestling the slippery cloth of the tie into a knot just below Jubal's Adam's apple, "seems we're short on cash for just about everythin' and now a new suit?" His father shot his ma a questioning look.

His ma shrugged. "It's none of your mind where the money came from. It's some you haven't drank away yet." She smiled at Jubal. "Our boy will make us proud today driving that fine pair of Morgans for Avery Ketchum."

His tie tight around his neck and feeling like a noose, Jubal gratefully left his folks bickering in the house and headed for the Ketchum place. When he got there, Avery was all decked out in a stovepipe hat, stiff white-collared shirt, a red vest, and deep blue jacket and pants. The old farmer had even cut his shaggy white hair and shaved. Jubal had to admit, as they stood together by the buggy, that the two of them looked real sharp.

The Morgans' harnesses had been decorated with white Bakelite rings and silver button-like rivets on the leather strapping. A red felt-covered heart hung from small straps snapped to rings on the hames. The bright red collar pads had been washed, with edges showing to look especially vivid. Ned had also done a good job polishing the two-seater carriage.

By ten o'clock, the sky was clearing with spotty clouds remaining. Jubal figured everyone in town was crossing fingers that the weather would hold.

Chester jumped up into the front buggy seat, stating that he was coming along just in case he was needed. Picking up the reins to start the team, Jubal was sure Chester did not want to miss his daughter as CYO Rose Queen. Maria's mother, Kathleen, had already made plans to travel into town to watch the parade. As the three men rode in the carriage down the hill to the village, Jubal was aware this was a special day for both of the Styles to leave home for the big event.

He drove the team the short distance beyond Jazz Crow's junkyard towards the ball field where the parade entries were lining up. Miss Curry walked out from her house to meet Avery's carriage. They stopped and Chester helped her step up into the carriage to join Avery in the seat of honor. She, too, was dressed for the occasion, wearing an old-fashioned gown decorated with white lace and a matching hat with a big red rose above the brim.

As they arrived at the field, Jubal saw that Andrew O'Mara was heading up the parade, giving directions to Tatum.

"The color guard first. Stand right at the edge of the road and hold your position," Mister O'Mara said. "We'll end the parade at the reservoir."

He listed the order of at least fifteen entries. The CYO kids, led by Father Mac, were to be followed by a new '41 Chevy pickup carrying Maria as Rose Queen. Jubal could not help but stare at Maria all decked out in a beautiful white floor-length gown with sequins that sparkled when the sun wasn't hidden behind the clouds. Snug through the midsection, her gown revealed her beautiful figure. In fact, he hardly recognized her with bright red lipstick, red rouge, and a powdered face. Her hair, in shoulder-length ringlets, had been cut to include bangs. Far from the country girl he knew, Maria had a starlet quality, holding a huge bouquet of red roses and wearing a rhinestone crown.

Jubal was instructed to line up Avery's buggy after the Chevy pickup since Avery had asked that his team follow the Rose Queen, thinking that Maria's presence could somehow keep the Morgans calmer. Jubal didn't know if it ever occurred to Avery that he should scrap the whole idea of using his flighty team, because it sure had occurred to Jubal. Following Avery's buggy, completing the parade, was a pack of kids on decorated bikes. Jubal hoped they would behave and keep their distance behind the buggy.

The horses acted plenty bothered by Andrew O'Mara hollering out orders to get folks in place. Nipsy Pearl's mom was putting the finishing touches on Maria as Jubal pulled the horses into position in back of the pickup. Chester stood holding Di's bridle, and Jubal jumped to be at Sally's side as they tried to keep the pair still by handing them treats.

As they waited, Jubal spied Polly up ahead with the CYO group lined up in marching columns. He hadn't seen her for a while since she was also at camp for the summer. He waved and she waved back, jumping excitedly in place. He caught his breath at her beauty. She had a new shingle haircut and wore red lipstick. All of the girls in the line were dressed like Polly—white short-sleeved terry-cloth tops with a modest V-neck, and pleated skirts. He and Polly had planned a special date for after the parade and he couldn't wait. She continued looking around eagerly as if to see who else she could recognize.

Meanwhile, Maria sat on a bench in the truck with her back to the cab, facing him. In contrast to Polly's sunny smiles, her lips were tightly drawn in a pained expression, and when he tried to gain eye contact, she simply stared down at the truck floor. Gosh, she acted miserable as Rose Queen. She looked so beautiful, but sad as well.

Jubal and Chester kept the horses quiet for nearly half an hour until they were all finally ready to go at about eleven. The team could sense that the parade was poised to move, so Jubal had to hold the reins firmly when getting in the buggy. The long line of odd entries—new shiny cars, two horse-drawn wagons decorated with ribbons and balloons, a couple of teenagers on stilts, and even a large yellow cat on a leash—started in a crawl. Mister O'Mara had instructed the participants to keep a good fifty feet from the entry in front of them. Jubal found that if he held the reins too tight, the horses put their ears back as if ready to bolt, but if he slackened the reins, the horses pranced forward, getting too close to the pickup. Maria ignored the crowd, concentrating instead on the team. For safety, Chester got out and walked beside Di, which encouraged the team to step along more slowly. All the while, Avery was in his glory, tipping his stovepipe hat to nearly everyone along the route. Miss Curry also enjoyed herself, waving like royalty.

While waiting in line, Jubal had heard someone remark that Lizzy was giving a free ice cream cone to anyone who came into her store during the parade. She'd hired Clem to help Bert scoop the cones and hand out the gift. Apparently, Lizzy had gotten Clem to clean up with a new shirt, bib overalls, and an engineer's cap. The gossip also noted that Lady Lamont had taken Lizzy to the dentist. He was glad to hear that and couldn't believe how in such a short time Lizzy LaFlam had become the talk of the town.

As they traveled down Main Street, Maria sat frozen in place, not looking left or right but rather looking straight back at the horses as if they were the only thing keeping her together. But for her pinched expression, she could have doubled as a mannequin modeling a beautiful gown in a store window.

Luckily, the rain held off with the sky remaining partly cloudy. A big crowd lined the street. It seemed to Jubal that everybody in town and the entire countryside had come to watch. Mothers stood with baby carriages, while fathers held the hands of children waving small American flags. Older kids crowded at the side of the road, waiting to grab the penny candy thrown by Mike Harlow who was dressed as a clown and riding a mule. Jubal wondered if Mike still had Reddy, the rooster.

The viewing stand, as anticipated, was filled with Catholic clerics. Jubal picked out a guy that he figured must be Bishop Shea. The man was surrounded by a number of priests seated in back of him. A sharp-looking fellow wearing a cream linen suit stood at the entrance of the stand to help those advanced in years to manage the steep stairs. The handsome guy was muscular, with broad shoulders and a slim waist. He also sported a striking tan. Jubal wondered if this was Freddie Coleman, the one he'd heard about from Maria. There was something phony about the guy—his cocky manner and fake smile. Jubal turned to look back over his shoulder and Freddie eyed him briefly before returning to his work and offering his hand to an elderly priest in a black robe. Up in the pickup he saw Maria watching Freddie also. Her already troubled face was like a black thundercloud.

Up ahead, red, white, and blue crepe paper fluttered in the breeze, draping the statue of Hiram Hayes on his pedestal. The mares flicked their ears forward, alert. A group of kids crowded around the monument. The LaFlam boys, with their shaggy black hair and ragged clothes, were yelling rude comments as each entry passed. Other kids joined in. Town citizens scowled their disapproval at the rowdies. However, no one stepped forward to shut them up. The horses reacted by lowering their ears and double-stepping on the road. Jubal held tight to the reins, talking in a low voice. "Easy, now . . . easy."

The parade was passing only feet from the edge of the statue's grassed mound. Maria saw the reaction of the horses and jumped to stand in the truck. "Shut up, you guys!" she yelled at the kids. "Shut up!"

One boy yelled, "Come're and kiss my ass, Queeny. Come're!" Whistles and catcalls added to the commotion.

In a flash, Maria threw the giant rose bouquet with such powerful force at the brazen bunch that it hit Hiram Hayes' feet and burst apart. Roses, petals, and leaves sprayed in all directions, raining down over road, boys, and mound. The dignitaries, their mouths dropping open, stood as one from their seats. The roses, sacred symbol of the Virgin Mary, had just been used as a weapon in clear view for all to see.

Without missing a beat, the hooting rowdies dove for the flowers—not caring a whit about the oncoming Morgans. Within feet of the scramble, the team reared up in unison on their hind legs, ready to charge. Chester lost his grip on Di's bridal in the abrupt yank. As if having springs in his shoes, Chester jumped and caught the bridle again before the mare could charge unrestrained.

At the same time, Maria dove from the truck with her crown flying, tearing the hem of her sparkling dress. As the team came down on all fours, she grabbed Sally's bridle while her dad struggled to hold Di. The boys scattered in all directions with most having a long-stem rose in hand, and one had a prize—the Rose Queen's crown. It took all of Chester and Maria's strength to hold the team standing in place as the wide-eyed mares snorted and shook their manes like wild mustangs.

The columns of CYO kids stopped abruptly, some bumping into each other. Father Mac hustled back to the empty pickup, his pale, round face now puffed red with anger.

"How dare you throw those roses in view of Bishop Shea!" he railed. "How dare you, young lady!"

Maria stood stock still, holding Sally's bridle with her back to the priest, not answering.

"Get back in that truck, this instant!" Father Mac ordered.

Avery rose to his feet. "Maria needs ta hold that horse or them critters will take off!"

The flustered priest glanced up at Bishop Shea who sat with attention riveted on the scene. Father Mac pointed at Maria and Avery. "This is a travesty! The CYO Queen is totally out of order!"

Maria whirled around. "Really! Well, I quit!"

The bystanders gasped. All eyes were on the priest.

Father Mac's face deepened to the shade of a beet. As the sun broke from behind the clouds, a sheen of sweat glistened on his brow. "Quit? Quit? You can't quit! We're in the middle of the parade."

Maria glared. "I quit as your Rose Queen. I'm helping lead this team to safety."

The confrontation was at an impasse. Jubal saw that Freddie had edged towards them and was listening intently to the exchange.

The priest rocked back on his feet and folded his arms. After a long silence in front of the hushed crowd, Father Mac said, "You will see me this afternoon at the rectory, right after my meeting with Bishop Shea. We will talk about your camp obligations."

"I'll do that." Maria did not look at the priest again, or Freddie, or the crowd.

With Maria and Chester's help, Jubal carefully maneuvered the team and buggy out of the parade line. Behind his buggy seat, he heard Avery and Miss Curry both sigh in relief. Maria walked at the head of the team with her dad while their section of the parade continued on without them.

The kids on decorated bikes slowly peddled past the idle CYO entry. The campers were milling about as Father Mac spoke up into the viewing stand to Bishop Shea, no doubt apologizing for the spectacle. Jimmy Reed, the driver of the now empty pickup, backed the vehicle slowly out of the line and parked it in the church lot.

Away from the noise of the parade, Chester and Maria led the horses for some distance until the team settled down. Eventually they stopped and a humiliated Chester walked back towards the center of town to find Maria's mother.

Fancy dress and all, Maria jumped into the front seat, tucking the trails of her gown safely inside the buggy. "I'm so glad to be done with this stupid Rose Queen stuff!"

Avery stood, holding on to the seat in front. "Thanks for savin' the day, Maria."

Miss Curry added, "I was terribly frightened."

"Right so," Avery said. "No tellin' where we'd end up with them beasts on a charge. Don't need to be dumped on my bad leg again." He sat and nodded for Jubal and Maria to drive on.

Jubal let Maria hold the reins as they clip-clopped back up Main Street. No one spoke a word in the buggy, each lost in their own thoughts. So much for impressing the town. Now they would all be the 5th of July parade's laughing stock. Jubal could just hear the bench sitters now. The day it rained angry roses on Hiram Hayes, and the Rose Queen quit. The day Avery's Morgans reared high with flames in their manes, nearly trampling the town's youth. The day the residents of Harmony Hill upended the parade in front of the bishop.

When they drew near the rectory, Maria stopped and passed the reins to Jubal. She got out and left to wait for the return of Father Mac who no doubt had a severe scolding in store for his Rose Queen. Jubal was sure Maria would not back down one bit regarding her decision.

Chapter Seventeen

Waiting for Father Mac, Maria sat inside the rectory in the room where the weekly catechism was held. She looked down to see her gown was not only torn at the hem, but dirty from the horses. The priest didn't come for quite awhile. He was probably still with the bishop trying to explain her behavior or was seeing to the CYO kids. She figured he was going to demand that she stay on as a counselor at camp but she had news for him. She was finished with CYO camp as well as being Rose Queen. She wanted nothing more than to be back on the farm.

She considered telling Father Mac about Freddie, wondering if this might excuse her behavior in the Father's mind, but her gut told her this would be a bad idea. She didn't trust Father Mac as she had trusted their former priest. It would be her word against Freddie's, and she had no evidence except Tatum's witnessing the scene at her cabin where she and Freddie had both lied to Tatum. Besides, Tatum was just an underling to Father Mac and likely would not risk his chauffeur's job to take her side.

As she sat, she noted the plush carpeted floor, the heavy drapes, and the elaborate furnishings. The rectory was eerie and silent. Outside, she knew everyone was getting organized to head home after the parade. Finally she heard Father Mac's light step on the carpeted stairs. She didn't look up as she heard him approach, not caring to face him, but instead stared in the direction of the room's nearest window.

Suddenly a strong, stiff arm hooked around her neck from behind, pressing hard into her throat. Her air abruptly cut off, she frantically squirmed to free herself, to no avail. Instinctively, she threw herself to the floor with all her force and tried to roll free, dragging her assailant, who somehow managed to keep his chokehold, on top of her while she landed on her back. As she continued to fight for air, she heard a voice snarl:

"That's perfect, Queenie."

Maria came to in a haze with Father Mac calling her name and slapping her cheeks. She lay terribly sore all over. Her eyes and lips felt swollen and her mouth dry as she ran her tongue over a deep cut on her lip. A sickening, sweet smell made her want to retch.

"Who did this to you?" The priest repeated his urgent question.

Maria tried but couldn't talk. Instead she felt down her body, with hands heavy as horse hooves, to find that her gown had been ripped to shreds. The skirt was torn from her bodice and her top had been wrenched open showing her breasts. She moaned as Father Mac covered her with a blanket.

The priest called on Tatum and both men lifted her up. She had trouble finding her footing, her legs being weak, arms now pinned by the wrapped blanket. Father Mac looked to be shaken as they practically carried her down the stairs where she saw through an open door the long, black car backed to the rectory with its rear door open.

Was she dead? Were they loading her into a hearse? She twisted to the side, almost causing Father Mac to lose his grasp.

"Easy," he said quietly, tightening his grip. "It's okay." His fingers dug into her flesh even through the blanket.

No, she was alive.

Just as they maneuvered her into the back seat of the car, Lizzy LaFlam appeared. Maria turned her head to see that Lizzy held a container of ice cream.

"Someone has brutally beaten and possibly raped Maria Styles," Father Mac said to Lizzy.

His voice was high-pitched, cutting through Maria's fog with an edge like a razor. Tatum grunted in confirmation.

Raped? Maria's stomach clenched around a black ball, and a curtain of darkness closed around her. The three discussed her as if she wasn't there. Feeling as though both in and outside of her body, she wished she were anywhere else. Instead of with these two men she didn't trust and a girl she barely knew. Yet, she was strangely comforted by the sound of Lizzy's voice when she spoke.

"This is awful!" Lizzy put her hand to her mouth and scrunched up her face. "What's on her? That terrible smell?"

"Are your brothers still in town?" Father Mac asked Lizzy.

Lizzy dropped her hand. "No sir! My brothers left town 'fore the parade ended. They was all loaded up with goodies from my store, which they ran in and stole while drippin' rose petals from some long stems they was clutchin' in their grubby paws."

The priest didn't sound convinced. "They were surely rude acting towards the Rose Queen during the parade."

"Yes sir," Lizzy replied. "My brothers are some rude and unruly sons of bitches." Through the car door Maria saw Lizzy's hand again fly up to her mouth. "Sorry Father, but that's the God's honest truth."

Tatum stood tall in his sheriff's stance, thumbs in his belt loops. "We'll be questioning you further, young lady. Right now we've got to get Miss Styles home to her parents."

Lizzy nodded. "Sure thing. Ya just come on by the store and I'm happy ta talk ta ya. But I know nothin' 'bout who coulda done such a thing ta Maria." Lizzy held out the box of ice cream, now dripping out the bottom corners. "I brought this fer ya, seein' as you were too busy with the parade ta come fer a free cone."

Father Mac glanced at the box and gestured towards the rectory. "There's a refrigerator in the kitchen. Thank you. Just be sure to lock the rectory door when you leave."

The priest closed the car door firmly while Tatum circled around to the driver's side. Maria sank into the seat, sore from head to foot. As they pulled away, leaving Lizzy staring after the car, Maria carefully lowered the scratchy blanket on one side to see a purple bruise swelling on her arm. There was a raw feeling down below and in her belly. Fear welled up, so she stared out the window at the remnants of the parade. Candy wrappers were scattered in the grass at the side of the street. Someone had stuck a little flag in a Coke bottle on top of a mailbox. She closed her eyes. She did not want to face her horrified parents.

Clyde Brown sat in his usual chair in his usual place with his ear cocked to his Philco. One of the few townspeople to miss the spectacle of the parade, he was ready for his own big event, the midday news:

Mass murders of scientists and other intellectuals are occuring in Poland since the Germans have taken the country. Meanwhile in the Soviet Union, Stalin finally reacted to the June twenty-second German invasion by declaring a "scorched earth" policy.

"Son-of-a-bitch," Clyde grumbled. "Sounds like they're about to destroy everythin' and everybody over there."

Meanwhile, Clyde was having his own war right there on Harmony Hill. When he'd failed to cut back on his drinking as asked, Rose had informed him she was moving him up to the mansion in a plan to lock him in a room to sober up. Angry as she was, he figured she'd enjoy watching him practically shake the walls down for lack of a drink. Well, they'd see how far that would go.

He wasn't stupid. Yesterday, he'd talked her into letting him stay at their farm until after all the holiday fuss. Even though she demanded that he not touch a drop if she let him stay, he'd put one over on her, pulling out a dusty bottle he had tucked away on a beam in the haymow. His Rose had raised holy hell when she found him dead to the world in his easy chair with the nearly empty bottle on the table. She'd even gone so far as to throw a glass of ice cold water in his face. That was a hell of a way to wake up.

Clyde set his nearly empty glass next to the Philco and stood from his chair to look out the window. "Oh, my God, the cows are out. Hungry critters, been bellowin' outside my door all durin' the parade." He watched the herd moving past. "Damn! Headed right towards the mansion's front lawn ta sponge off the neighbor's green grass."

He sat down in thought. Then stood again to look. This time he could see that Rose and the boy were herding the cows. Apparently, they were letting the cattle go. There was Benny, not much help, always scared as a rabbit when the cows busted out.

That boy of his. What was he going to do with him? Sometimes he spied on Jubal with O'Mara's girl, Polly, as they met at the Packard. Hot on the likes of a Catholic. He shook his head. The boy wasn't thinking straight. He'd also noticed Jubal spending all his time down at Avery's, not fixing their own fences. They needed to fix some fencing for more pasture because forty cows weren't going to be lasting long on Lady Lamont's five-acre lawn. Maybe Eugene, next door, could give Jubal a hand. No, wait. Rose had mentioned that Eugene was going away to school to join the Tuskegee Airmen. Smart kid.

This gave him an idea—maybe he'd just clear out of town too.

He reached for his glass and finished it in one gulp. "Damn. Slick as a trout."

Rose had no idea what it was like to face the shakes. Sure, she'd watched him try to go cold turkey in the past. But she hadn't *lived* it. It was pure hell. He'd rather be shot. Yet when Rose made up her mind, she was more stubborn than a year-old heifer on a lead rope for the first time. In the beginning, to ease the ill effects, Rose planned to give him small amounts of liquor during his waking hours and then taper it off. He looked over at his Philco. He hated to leave it but it was too large to lug over to Lady Lamont's. Seeing as the July Fourth holiday had passed and the big parade was over, he'd reached the end of his negotiated extra stay.

A short time later, Clyde left his favorite corner carrying a small yellow suitcase with a single change of clothes. He licked his lips, for now setting aside his idea to leave town. A promised drink, even if a small one, was just too strong an urge. He sighed. Besides, maybe this time he could really do it. Sober up, with Rose's help. He did love his Rose. And it was clear Jubal needed him on the farm, but the boy would never speak up directly. The kid mostly just stayed out of his way, and it pained him how they could never be close.

Since Jubal's last date with Polly in the spring, he'd been mulling over her dream of a big Catholic family. Watching his own small family struggle with money, and trying to keep up the farm with only a little help from Benny, Jubal wondered how people managed with many mouths to feed. Besides, he would never convert to Catholicism and he knew that her parents would never approve of such a marriage. He had no intention of telling Polly that they might be first cousins as a reason they shouldn't have kids together. He was having a hard time admitting it even to himself. After their first, brief attempt at making love, he wanted no part in getting her pregnant. From now on, their cuddling would have limits.

He watched their cattle grazing on the mansion's lawn, grateful to Lady Lamont for offering up the rich grass to their skinny cows. He was glad, also, to have changed out of his fancy seersucker suit and back into his usual barn clothes. Before long, Polly came from her house to stand at the edge of the lawn.

She wore the same outfit she'd had on in the parade, the short skirt paired with the terry cloth v-neck top. Seeing her beauty, he practically forgot all of his thoughts only moments earlier of controlling his behavior. She smiled from the edge of the lawn and he smiled back while anticipating taking her in his arms and getting lost in her kisses.

"Jubal, I want to talk to you," she called.

"Sure thing!" He left the cattle munching contentedly and crossed the lawn to greet her.

She reached for his arm and asked, "Do we have a date later tonight at Benny's car?"

"We sure do."

"Good." She patted his arm.

They stood silent. It had been so long since they were together, Jubal felt at a loss for what to say.

"Well . . . I guess I'll see you then," Polly said. She took a couple steps back to look him up and down. "You look good. All that hard outdoor work suits you."

"Thanks. And you look clean and cool. I mean . . . pretty."

She laughed. "See you tonight, Jubal." With that she walked off towards the O'Mara's well-kept house.

Soon Jubal heard voices coming from the second story of one of the mansion's stone turrets. He looked up through the blue sky and saw on the very top that Lady Lamont and Lizzy were looking down at the grazing cattle.

He waved up at them. "Hello, Lady Lamont! I hope you don't mind our cattle on your lawn."

"No, dear. I love seeing them. I only wish I had a bigger lawn." Lady Lamont was smoking from her cigarette holder and spoke with her deep gravelly voice. "You and Benny come in for a late lunch that my Eugene and your mother have been preparing."

Jubal glanced at the cows going after the grass like it was the best feed ever. "I don't think these cows are going anywhere. Thanks, we'll do that."

Lizzy bent over the stone edge and called down, "Hey, Jubal! Ya goin' ta the dance later tanight at the grange? After I finish cleanin' up over at the store where them parade folks made a heck of a mess, I'm goin'."

He shrugged. "I can't, I've got a date with Polly. Anyway, I'd have to walk."

"Shoot. I'm walkin'. Lots of folks is walkin'. It ain't that far from your house . . . only five miles or so."

Lady Lamont corrected her. "It's *not* that far." The two women backed away from the edge out of sight, but he heard the heiress say,

"Around me and customers at the store, you've got to learn to use better English."

Lizzy answered her benefactress. "I know. I'm tryin' but it ain't— It's *not* that easy."

"You'll learn, my dear. I'll teach you, and you keep trying."

He chuckled. If Lady Lamont could actually change Lizzy's backwoods twang, it would be quite the miracle. He left the cows and went to retrieve Benny from the barn where he was sweeping the manger. They washed up in the Browns' kitchen and walked over to the mansion, circling around to the back. Jubal pushed open the massive door and the two entered a short hallway that led to a kitchen nook where his mother was seated at an oak table.

He was surprised to see his dad, who rarely left his drinking corner, come and sit down next to his ma. Benny plunked his big frame heavily in a chair and Jubal pulled up a seat next to his uncle.

"Why hello, Jubal," his ma said. She smoothed her hair with her silver bracelets clinking. "I didn't know you'd be joining us. How nice."

"Lady Lamont just invited us," Jubal said. He raised an eyebrow at his dad. His father nodded but his clenched jaw indicated that he was out of sorts.

Just then Lizzy came breezing in and slid into a chair, informing the group that Lady Lamont chose not to eat, preferring to stay in the turret with her cup of tea and her nose in an art book.

"All she does is paint and read . . . when she's not teachin' me 'bout business that is," Lizzy plucked an egg sandwich from the silver tray. "Dang, I'm hungry. Servin' those cones all mornin' . . . Thought fer sure I'd never get the sticky layer of ice cream off my arm. But I sure liked seein' all them happy faces, 'specially the kids lickin' cones, and everyone was buyin' stuff at the store."

"That was a nice thing you did for the town," his ma said. "It's good to have the Hayesville store bustling again."

Eugene passed an assortment of sandwiches and a pitcher of iced tea to Clyde who passed it around the table.

Lizzy munched on her egg sandwich. "This is mighty good, Eugene. Nice ta sit and eat some decent food—not like tryin' ta pick meat off a squirrel's leg."

Everyone laughed.

"Ya know," she said, leaning forward intently, "what ain't so funny— Er, *isn't* so funny, was seein' Maria Styles after the parade bein' lugged outta the rectory dazed and wrapped in a blanket."

There was a collective gasp around the table. Jubal was all ears. Even his dad stopped chewing and squinted at Lizzy.

She nodded. "Yup, someone beat her up real bad. Her face looked like she'd been drugged through a briar patch."

"Goodness!" Rose exclaimed. "Who would ever do that to Maria Styles and at the rectory of all places? Such a nice girl from a good family."

"It weren't my brothers," Lizzy said quickly. "They left town 'fore the parade ended, havin' stuffed themselves with ice cream and candy from my store."

"Well, who on earth?" Eugene looked stunned at the news. "Right here in our quiet little town." He set his sandwich down, seeming to have lost his appetite.

Thinking of his own mother's story of how she got pregnant, Jubal said, "It's not as quiet as you think."

Jubal felt he knew who the prime suspect might be, but couldn't say. Maria had made him promise secrecy. From what his ma had told him about that night at the abandoned house when someone had slipped her the *mickey*, how she felt after, he figured Maria would be blaming herself for whatever stirred the guy up. He wanted to go right then and beat the crap out of this Freddie Coleman. Guilt washed over him. Should he have said something to someone? Could he have done something to stop this before it happened?

Lizzy shook her head, "That girl's gonna have miles ta go 'fore she'll ever be the same again."

"Miles ta go," Benny said, rocking in his chair as he picked up on the sudden tension at the table.

Jubal put a hand on his uncle to calm him. Outside the window, Jubal could see their team, Dick and Dan, along with Trueboy, grazing for spears of grass up in the old run-out pasture that rose from the back of the mansion. The pasture extended for acres and acres towards the woods and grew mostly clumps of juniper, patches of reindeer moss, and sapling trees. He thought of how Maria, Eugene, Polly, and he used to play with Trueboy, who was gentle as a kitten. Trueboy's only use now on the farm was to pull the hay fork or the dump rake.

Suddenly he had an idea. Maybe Trueboy could somehow be a comfort. He decided to visit Maria and see if she'd like the horse to keep down at Avery's for a while.

His dad jumped up abruptly from the table. "Goddammit, Rose! I need a drink! Ya promised."

Rose glared. "Sit for a minute, Clyde! The world doesn't revolve around your problem."

Clyde scowled and sat down. He wrapped a trembling hand around his empty glass, furiously tapping his index finger. For a moment Jubal hated his father for thinking of himself when his friend Maria was hurting.

"The town needs to take action about Maria," his mother said firmly. "The selectboard should hold a hearing with Tatum and get to the bottom of this crime."

"Heck yeah," Lizzy agreed.

Rose continued, "I won't allow this to be swept under the rug. Lady Lamont is a member of the board and I'm sure she'll agree. Maybe she can contact the Styles family to get their feelings on the matter."

Jubal nodded. "That's certainly something that should happen."

Everyone was quiet for a few minutes, with only the sound of eating and clinks of plateware.

"On another subject," his ma finally said, "we need to make plans for a fence so our cattle can have fresh pasture after tonight's milking."

Clyde complained to no one and everyone, "Goddamn, I can't stand this. Ya've no idea what I'm feelin'."

It dawned then on Jubal that his dad was at the mansion to sober up. Though he doubted it would work, his ma was brave for trying.

"Shoot," Lizzy turned on Clyde. "Ya think ya're the only sap to run outta liquor? Ya should see Big Daddy on a tear when the still come up empty and no furs ta trade in town fer brewin' supplies. Make ya run fer the hills—him as ornery as a bear wakin' up after hibernatin'."

Eugene grinned and looked down at the table as Clyde pursed his lips in a sulk. Jubal had to hand it to Lizzy for putting his father in his place.

"Benny and Eugene," his ma said, "can you two work with Jubal on that fence along Harmony Hill this afternoon so we can have pasture for the cows tonight?" She quickly added, "Lizzy and I'll clean up."

"Sure thing," Eugene said, jumping up. "I'd love to get out of house chores."

Rose turned to Lizzy. "And I'll give you a ride to the store after we finish here and I get Clyde settled."

"Thanks kindly, Miz Brown," Lizzy stood and gathered up the plates closest to her seat.

Outside, Jubal checked the mansion lawn and saw the whole herd resting and chewing their cuds as if they'd just eaten a big Thanksgiving dinner. With Benny and Eugene's help, he got the cows up and drove them to the barnyard so they could get water. Afterwards, he backed the truck up to a pile of fencing supplies. Benny and Eugene began loading while he searched for gloves to handle the barbed wire.

He hurried through the house until he found two pairs of gloves on his bureau sandwiched in next to his glass bank full of cash. Seeing his bank reminded him how someday he'd buy something very special—maybe a well-bred bull with a fine pedigree, a car he could call his own, or maybe something fancy for the girl of his choice. That girl wouldn't be Polly. She already had everything she ever wanted. He found a third pair of gloves in the entryway and headed back out to the truck. Eugene and Benny were waiting by the back bumper, with Eugene being out of his element and Benny generally quiet around strangers. The two brightened as he approached.

"All set you guys," he said, handing them each a pair of gloves. "Let's get this done. I need to get to the chores and wash up for my date tonight."

Benny perked up. "With Polly? She's pretty."

"That's right, Benny, she is," he answered.

The previous winter's storms had totally flattened the fence alongside the road. In the field, the grasses had now matured, it being the beginning of July. The grazing would be poor, but it was better than nothing.

He sent Benny ahead to pull the barbed wire free of an entanglement of tall grass and weeds. His uncle was a good sport to take the hardest job. He and Eugene followed to drive in new posts where needed. Eugene did well setting the posts and had plenty of power to make them stand sturdy. They stretched the three-strand wire fence between the posts, pulling the wire taught and stapling it as they went.

"Driving these posts is like ringing the bell with a hammer at the fair," Eugene commented.

"Well, something like that," Jubal said, glancing at his friend who was confidently swinging the maul. "You're doing that better than I could. Say, I heard you're going to join the Tuskegee Airmen."

Eugene straightened and wiped his brow. "Yup. To be honest, I'm a little nervous about leaving home."

"Aw, you'll be fine," Jubal said.

Eugene nodded. "Going to have to be."

As they spoke, Benny, working down the fencerow ahead, was singing to himself as he sometimes did. He liked the Big Band music that played on Clyde's radio and had an amazing memory for lyrics.

Eugene paused his work, leaning on the handle of the maul. "Gee, that's awful what happened to Maria. She hadn't spent much time off of Avery's farm. Then this happens."

It was torment for Jubal to not be able to share what he knew with his friend. "It's terrible."

Eugene lifted the maul and swung another blow, hitting a six-inch post dead on.

Jubal grabbed the rusty wire that Benny had uncovered and ran it to the next post in line. He pulled the wire tight and stapled it, losing himself in the job at hand. He couldn't have had better help as the three of them finished the fence before night chores. He realized in just that short time working with Eugene that the guy would indeed succeed at whatever he had a mind to do.

Thinking of Maria again, Jubal sighed. If the attack was as serious as it sounded, he wasn't sure what might happen to her now. It was so unfair—proof that maybe his dad was right when he often declared, "There ain't no God."

Chapter Eighteen

After lunch at Lady Lamont's, Lizzy returned to the store where it was considerably quieter than it had been that morning with the ice cream frenzy. She grabbed a broom and began sweeping up the tracked-in dirt and napkins carelessly dropped on the floor. Her thoughts returned to the rectory, to Maria's split lip and bruised face. The scene troubled Lizzy—she could picture and practically feel the horrid event. Her brothers had certainly tried such things some nights when she was younger up on LaFlam Mountain, and she learned to have a good aim to kick them where it counted.

When she finished sweeping, she walked the store aisles checking items that needed restocking. Almost everything did, in particular the hamburger and hot-dog buns. She brought out a large quantity of buns in a pasteboard box from the storeroom. Bending over the box to open it in the aisle, she jumped to attention as a hand rubbed her butt. She turned to face a guy wearing a fancy tan suit.

"Sorry," he said with a laugh. "Couldn't resist your cute ass sticking out like that."

"Look buddy," she warned, backing up, "no one touches Lizzy LaFlam 'less they're invited! And ya ain't invited!" She motioned towards the door. "If ya know what's good fer ya, step away from me!"

"You're cute when you're mad," the guy said. He took a step closer. "Tell you what—I'd like to take you to the dance tonight."

She sized up the jerk, the way he stood in a cocky way as if he owned the place. "Already got my own plans fer the dance and ya ain't in them." She'd not seen this guy around town, and he looked to be twice her age.

"Aw, too bad." He pretended to look sad. "We could have lots of fun in my Ford coupe with the top down, breeze fluttering through your shiny, black hair. We could have a real pow wow!"

"Yeah, well, I ain't wantin' ta hear yer dumb, nasty remarks! Get away from me." She gathered some packages of rolls out of the box and put them on the shelf. The guy didn't move. "On second thought, why don't ya leave my store!"

"Your store? You aren't old enough to own a store." He took another step closer. "Now why are you so standoffish?"

She stared him down. He had a nose just like a pig. With his closeness, a sweet smell turned her stomach. She had a jolt of recognition—it was the same smell that was on Maria. She thought wildly if there was something in the store that she could use as a weapon, felt the Big Daddy in her rising up. She'd fix him but good.

A knowing grin spread slowly across the guy's bronze face.

She pointed towards the door. "Leave! If ya don't, I'll holler fer my clerk just out back. He'll make ya wish ya'd left when asked." She hoped he would buy her lie.

Still smiling, he backed away and sauntered down the aisle, laughing over his shoulder. "See you, Pocahontas."

As the creep left the store, she knew she should tell the sheriff. The sick, sweet smell was unmistakable. She'd read stories where criminals sometimes came back to the scene of the crime. This guy hadn't even left town and maybe he'd try to hurt another girl, especially if he was going to the dance. With parade duties over, Tatum might be in his office across the street. Peering out of the street-side window to make sure there was no sign of the guy, she ran from the store.

When she entered the sheriff's office, Tatum was tipped back in his chair reading a magazine, feet up on his desk. She plunged right in.

"Sheriff, I know who attacked and prob'ly raped Maria. He just left my store, maybe headin' towards the rectory."

Tatum glanced up casually. "Yeah? You think so? What'd he look like?"

"He was dressed slick, like from a city or somethin'. Had a pug nose and was smellin' like a bouquet of lilacs."

He took his feet off the desk and laughed. "That's Freddie Coleman, swim instructor at CYO camp. He ain't the guilty one."

"Well, can ya go ta the rectory and question him?"

Tatum shrugged. "Why? He's a friend of Father Mac's. He wouldn't do a thing like that." His expression turned sour. "Here's what I think. Your hoodlum brothers are guilty as hell. Soon as we get a posse together, we're going after 'em."

"I already explained why it ain't my brothers! They left 'fore the parade ended!" She was exasperated that Tatum didn't see he was on the wrong trail.

"Well, maybe, but your brothers acted plenty nasty to Maria."

"They didn't ever touch her! Anyway, ya know as well as I that no fool's goin' ta Laflam mountain. Big Daddy'll blast yer posse ta bits."

Tatum stood from his chair with his hand on his holster. "I'd like to see your sorry backwoods reject of a father try to blast me."

"Sheriff, I get the idea yer protectin' this Freddie Coleman. What I wanna know is why. What tie does that sleaze have to Father Mac?"

He sat down again. "As I said, they're old friends."

"Yer at CYO camp most of the week. Does this perfumed, tan-suit character have somethin' against Maria?"

Tatum looked down at the floor. "Nope. Nothin'."

She noted his ears turning red. "So ya never saw 'em together. No arguments?"

"Ah . . . nope." He crossed a foot over one knee and picked up his magazine. "You can run along now, young lady. I'll come on over to the store in a bit and ask you some more questions about your no-good brothers."

Lizzy leaned over and pulled down the top of his magazine. "Sheriff, I don't mean no disrespect, but I'm feelin' that yer fillin' me fulla shit!"

"Watch your mouth or you'll be behind bars!" He yanked the magazine away.

"I'm gonna get ta the bottom of this crime. Just remember I've a friend with authority over ya."

His eyes widened.

"Oh yes," she nodded. "And she holds the purse strings on this town. She'll back me all the way!" She turned to leave and paused at the door. "Question this Coleman character, will ya?"

Speechless, his mouth fell open. Lizzy knew she'd just spent a chunk of her popularity in town by pushing herself to the very limit in confronting the law.

※

On their way to and from the barn each night, Jubal went first and Benny followed faithfully always to do the same detail: shoveling the gutters, sweeping the manger and alleyways, and feeding the hay. As a kid, Jubal thought of Benny as a giant; he was well over six feet with huge shoulders, a broad, muscular chest, and arms as big as hams. He had unbelievable strength to do his routine with ease. But he never understood how to milk a cow, so Jubal always had to be with him during chore time.

When they left the barn that evening after the parade, the air was warm with a southern breeze that likely promised a storm. Jubal was in high spirits due to his upcoming date with Polly. With her cute figure and flirting, she'd fired his romantic notions earlier at the edge of Lady Lamont's lawn. It wasn't hard, then, to imagine her kisses and he was eager to meet her at the Packard. He studied the sky as he walked towards the house with Benny scuffing along close behind him.

"Hmm, Benny . . . I think we're going to get a storm, maybe a real soaker. That could help the pastures grow some grass for the horses and cattle."

In spite of his size and strength, Benny had his worries. "Do ya think it will be bad, Jubal, like . . . like the Devil movin' furniture . . . a lotta booms and a monster in the sky breathin' fire?"

"Probably not that bad, Benny, and you'll be protected in the house."

"Yeah, but all alone." Benny glanced up towards the mansion as he trudged along. "Clyde ain't no help. He just sits there. Rose is workin' late. And—" Benny's voice rose in pitch, "Ya said ya ain't goin' ta be here. I'm gonna be scared, Jubal!"

"Benny, it's okay. Take a deep breath like Ma told you."

His uncle sucked in a big gulp of air.

"That's right. Now breathe it out. That's good."

Once they'd washed up, Jubal pulled together some food from the fridge that his ma had left for them. They sat down to a cold meal of roast beef, mashed potatoes, and raw carrots. Despite Jubal's reassurances, Benny started shaking.

"Benny, look . . . after we eat, you go up and get ready for bed. I'll come read to you before I leave on my date."

His uncle stopped trembling. "I like it when Rose and ya read to me."

Jubal wished he hadn't mentioned the storm because now he would have to spend time reading to calm Benny for the night. After dinner he pulled up a chair next to Benny's bed and opened *A Tale of Peter Rabbit,* by Beatrix Potter. Benny held the white sheet close under his chin as he listened to his favorite tale. Jubal didn't read long before his uncle was sound asleep.

Even so, it was nearly eight o'clock before he could meet Polly. When he left the house, he spied her seated in the passenger side of the Packard and she didn't look happy.

"Where have you been?" she asked with a sidelong glance as he opened the car door. She sat rigidly with her arms crossed.

He didn't answer but got in the car. Since midday, she'd put on a white summer jacket with bright red trim and red buttons to match, along with a nice skirt. He could tell she had also added her mail-order falsies, which looked rather silly with her chest sticking out much farther than her normal figure. He wished she could see that her own breasts were perfect just as they were.

"Wow . . . sexy!" he exclaimed. "Nice jacket!"

"I didn't know as you'd get to see it," she sniffed, "since you're so late. Where have you been?"

"Helping Benny feel okay about being left home alone." He rolled down his window to let in a bit of the evening's cool air.

"Well, while you were sweet-talking your dummy uncle, we were losing time for our date." She moved closer to her door and looked out the window.

He couldn't believe her insult to Benny. "Polly, how rude! Don't you dare call Benny what you just did!" He faced her. "You understand?"

"I'm sorry," she pouted.

"Benny can't help who he is," he explained. "Despite what folks in town think, he's a good guy."

"Well, I was just mad you were late because I was hoping you'd take us to the dance."

Her request surprised him. He was pretty sure she knew he hadn't yet taken his driver's test. As he sat behind the wheel, it dawned on him that perhaps her plan all along was to simply get a ride to the dance. He tried to think sensibly.

"Gosh, that's five miles up the road. I can't do that. Benny's car isn't registered." He recalled, "It was just this spring you were scared out of your mind the last time we drove through town."

"You were fooling around then, but this ride has a purpose." She smiled prettily, her lips painted red like her jacket buttons. Then she puckered up and motioned for him to lean over and kiss her. Instead, he frowned.

"Yeah, right. Explain that to Tatum," he muttered.

Though he remained disgusted with her for her heartless comment about Benny, she was cute regardless of her mood. He knew the reasons why he had no future with Polly, but being with her always broke down all the barriers. He sat puzzled over what to do.

"Jubal, you're making too big a deal over the fact you can't be on the road. Just drive slowly and park away from the crowd." She slid over and cuddled into him, lifting his arm over her shoulder while tilting her head to kiss his neck. "Come on, let's do it. Dancing is fun. We could waltz. . . ." She ran one hand across his chest and squeezed his hand with her other.

His whole body jumped to attention at her caress. He wanted more of her affection and to run his hands up under her jacket to feel her softness. "Well, gee, I hope I don't get caught." He started Benny's car.

"Just take it easy and you won't," she said, smiling happily.

Jubal headed out onto Harmony Hill, driving cautiously with Polly still cuddled at his side. She bumped his leg from time to time to make him slow down.

"Uncle Tatum's out here somewhere," she warned. "He'd love to catch you speeding."

"I guess, and this baby blue Packard is like no other in town."

A couple miles north of Avery's place, they came upon Lizzy walking with long strides, no doubt on her way to the dance. She had a flashlight, likely to be used on her way home, sticking out of her jacket pocket.

"That's Lizzy LaFlam," he said. "Let's give her a ride."

Polly slid abruptly from his side. "You aren't stopping for *her*!"

"Of course I am. No reason not to."

Polly looked down at the floorboard in a grump. "At supper my dad said that Lizzy LaFlam ruined his soda fountain business today by giving away all that free ice cream. He'd planned on a big crowd for the parade, but almost no one showed up."

Jubal laughed. "This town has never seen a Lizzy LaFlam." As he brought the car to a stop, he looked in the rearview mirror to see Lizzy running towards the Packard.

Polly huffed, "Well, I can't stand her! Dad said she's blazed a trail of excitement up and down Main Street, especially with the men. How disgusting!"

Lizzy opened the rear door and climbed in, seeming short of breath.

"What luck ta get a ride! I'm late ta the dance after stoppin' up at the mansion. I wanted ta boast ta Lady Lamont 'bout our earnin's during the parade. Hope I ain't— I'm *not* breakin' up a love nest between ya two? But I 'preciate ya pullin' over."

"Not at all," Jubal said. "Glad to stop for a gal who's the talk of the town. We're headed to the dance too."

Polly remained mum.

Jubal pulled the car back onto the road. "So you had a good day down at the store?"

"I guess!" Lizzy said. "Bert said it was the best he's ever seen."

Polly spoke up. "My dad said that you're costing him plenty."

Without missing a beat, Lizzy retorted, "And he's costin' me, chargin' five dollars a day ta travel by stage, carryin' the store's money pouch ta the Rutland Bank."

"You expect the stage to do the trip for nothing?" Polly blurted.

"Well, no," Lizzy said. "But when he's got people and stuff goin' ta Rutland anyway, five dollars seems a little steep."

As the girls bickered back and forth, Jubal stayed quiet. He sure was glad when they arrived at the dance. He found a spot across the street away from all the other parked cars for an easy exit. They would have to walk a short distance to the dance floor. When he stopped, Polly scrambled out, slammed her door, and then ran on ahead.

Watching her run towards the lights of the grange, Jubal commented, "Well, I got her to the dance. Now we won't see her for the rest of the night. I just hope I don't get caught with this car. I'm leaving early for home."

"I surely hope ya don't get caught," Lizzy agreed, "but I'd chance a ride with ya if ya don't mind. I wanna get back ta town at a decent hour."

"Happy to. We can share a jail cell together." He rolled up his window and opened his door.

Lizzy laughed heartily, following him. "Wouldn't that make Big Daddy proud!"

When the two of them entered the grange dance, they saw that the holiday event had drawn a big crowd. There was hardly anywhere to stand in the packed room. Polly was off to the side chatting with some of her friends. She didn't even look their way. With nothing better to do, Jubal wondered if he dared to try dancing. It would be a first attempt.

He held out his hand to Lizzy, "Let's try this."

Lizzy backed away. "No way. I never danced before."

"Neither have I," he said. He shoved his hand in his pocket.

The two of them stood watching the other dancers spin around the room.

"But . . . that makes two of us," he said, flashing Lizzy a hopeful grin. "Two of us to fumble through the steps. Come on . . . what do you say?" He extended his hand.

"Okay, let's make fools of ourselves." Lizzy took his hand in hers.

As he walked her out onto the dance floor, he noticed her pretty floral skirt. It wasn't one that he recognized of his mother's. Lady Lamont must have taken her shopping. The Backcountry Fiddlers were playing an easy, flowing waltz. He copied how the others danced and held Lizzy at arm's length, one hand on her shoulder, the other at her hip as their footwork slid across the floor. The "Tennessee Waltz" was the next selection and Lizzy slipped her right hand around his waist, her skirt twirling as they turned.

The square dances were more difficult; however, they were one inexperienced couple in the round of four, with the other folks giving them plenty of encouragement. The allemande right and allemande left movements were easy to learn, as was the circle left and circle right. After a few tries, they were getting the knack of simple square dancing and he was surprised to find that he was having a good time.

It wasn't long, though, before he saw that Polly had joined up with Freddie Coleman in a group of four dancing couples. He felt he should warn Polly about Freddie, but she already knew the guy from CYO camp. Besides, he was unable to do a thing about it being stuck in his own group of four couples. Polly probably wouldn't listen to him anyway, given the mood she was in. He glanced their way again as he and Lizzy crossed with the opposing couple in a do-si-do. Polly was smiling up at Freddie, her face glowing when Freddie, looking like a rooster who had just selected his hen, took her hand. Jubal sighed as the song came to an end. No doubt Freddie would give Polly a ride home.

"Penny fer yer thoughts?"

Lizzy's voice startled him. He'd almost forgotten she was by his side.

"Oh nothing," he said. He didn't want Lizzy to see he was jealous. He had an urge to get out of there. "What do you say we dance a couple more? And then we can head back to town?"

"Sure thing. If ya don't mind my big feet trompin' all over yers a bit more."

He laughed. "I think your shoes are the ones with my footprints on them."

The next dance started and though Jubal was distracted by listening to the caller and executing the steps, he couldn't shake his bad feeling about Polly and Freddie. He couldn't believe she would just drop him for a slick guy like that.

Chapter Nineteen

A steady rain was falling when Lizzy left the dance hall. She was damp all over by the time she settled into the front seat of the Packard. As Jubal pulled out of the parking spot, she hoped the short trip would go smoothly. Entering the main highway leading to town, they saw a constable on the lookout for speeding drivers. Lizzy held her breath as they passed but Jubal, who didn't seem to talk much while in a tense situation, was driving reasonably. In a short while, they drew closer to home. It looked like they would make it to Main Street without incident.

Especially in her new position in charge of the IGA store, Lizzy didn't want to be caught with Jubal driving illegally. She was building a solid reputation in town after living most of her life next to lawlessness. It was only recently that she'd been freed of living as an outcast.

Suddenly a siren screamed out of nowhere and red lights flashed, bouncing off the rearview mirror. Up ahead, a second set of red lights filled the road—Tatum's checkpoint for those leaving the dance.

Jubal's face, illuminated by the dashboard light, was drawn tight as a fiddle string. When they reached Avery's forty-acre cornfield, she sensed something was coming when Jubal glanced towards the field. She realized desperation had stamped out his common sense.

"Ain't ya stoppin'?" In a flash, she saw what he realized was an escape plan. They were close enough to the police cars to see a guy in rain gear standing by the vehicles. The rain was now coming down in sheets. "What crazy thoughts do ya have?"

Approaching the flashing lights, he said, "Hang to your seat; we'll hit plenty hard on the corn land below the road!"

He swerved. In the turn, the tires squawked before leaving the pavement. The blue Packard flew airborne. Then it landed with a jarring thud, perfectly aligned in the knee-high corn rows. Jubal gripped the wheel as they traveled several car lengths into the black of night.

"Damn Jubal, ya're a crazy bastard! Ya're in big trouble now, runnin' from the law! Besides ruinin' over Avery's corn!"

He swiftly shut everything down—no lights, no engine.

"We're far enough from the road in this rain so they can't see or hear a thing," he told her. "The corn will come right back up if I stay between the rows. I cultivated this corn twice. I can drive it in my sleep."

"Why did ya never bother to get yer license? Ya're sixteen ain't ya? And how come this big fancy car has no registration? Geez, we'll have hell ta pay!"

Jubal spoke in the pitch black. "Calm down, Lizzy. Look—they're giving up."

In the rearview, they saw the flashing red lights stopped at the edge of the road, coming no further. Apparently Tatum didn't have the guts or desire in the pounding rain to walk out some distance into the field. He had easier victims to catch like the townsfolk weaving home from the dance.

With the danger seeming to have passed, Lizzy turned on Jubal. "I can't believe yer gumption! It was risky takin' a ride with ya, but I never thought my night would tip up on its end! What comes next?"

He shrugged.

"I can just see the headline in the paper," she huffed. "'Lizzy LaFlam spends the night in a goddamned cornfield with local lawbreaker, Jubal Brown!' I'm gettin' out and walkin' the rest a' the way home!"

"No you're not! I need you here to help me out of this mess. Can you take your flashlight and crawl to the back seat? Roll down the window and reach out low to the ground so you can shine your light on the corn row. I'll stay off the corn, but they won't see us."

Lizzy pressed the door handle to get out. "I don't think so. Ya got yerself into this mess and I got a fresh reputation ta uphold." She preferred to get soaked to the bone rather than end up in a jail cell.

"Please Lizzy?" he pleaded. "I know I got you into this and for that I'm sorry. But I need your help. My ma can't afford for me to get in trouble."

She knew the Browns were hard up for cash, and Rose had been very generous to her. She let go of the handle. "Okay, Mister Hotshot. Let's get ya outta this pickle."

He started the car crawling along in low gear while she hung her arm down low with the flashlight outside next to the door. In the downpour, her shirt sleeve was quickly soaked.

"Holy jumped up! I feel like Al Capone's sidekick. All I lack is a machine gun!"

Jubal chuckled. "Hang on, we're almost at the end of the row at the hedge."

"But this door is pressin' on my armpit and cuttin' off my blood flow. And fer yer information, my arm feels like I'm washin' in the LaFlam stream. We might make it home, but I'll sacrifice my arm ta the Corn Gods."

"Look!" he said. "We're at the end of the row." He sped up the car. "I want to get out of here before we get stuck in the mud." As he turned the wheel, the Packard bumped over the uneven ground. "Roll up your window and then go to the other side and shine your light on the corn. This will keep me away from the hedgerow."

"Okay, Bossman."

"In a minute we'll be out of here, going up Harmony Hill."

"Ya promise?"

BANG! The impact jolted Jubal up out of his seat and Lizzy hit the floor in back.

"Oh my god!" Lizzy picked herself up and leaned over the front seat. "Jubal, what in hell did ya just hit?"

He sat motionless with both hands on the steering wheel, staring straight ahead.

"What, ya lost yer tongue or somethin'?"

"I forgot about the AKL stone."

"An AK . . . what?" She tried to see up ahead through the windshield, but couldn't make out a thing in the rainy darkness.

"Avery Ketchum Lives—a marker stone we put there this spring."

"Thanks ta Avery," Lizzy grumbled. "Stopped us villains dead in our tracks. Jubal, back up. I want outta here. It's pourin' like a busted water hose. Be a quagmire a' mud 'fore long."

Jubal put the Packard in reverse and with spinning tires, they kept going right onto Harmony Hill. "We're parking this rig on the barn floor," he declared over the rain drumming on the roof.

"Go for it!"

Once on the gravel road, Jubal floored the car, while Lizzy hung to the back of the front seat. In seconds, they were at the double doors of the high drive over the cow barn. Lizzy knew what had to be done and was out of the car before he said, "Pull open those doors."

The torrential downpour instantly soaked her, but she tugged the doors open and the Packard climbed the ramp up into the barn.

Jubal jumped out. "Ha! Just like Clem Gochy in his bootlegging days! Lizzy, hand me your light!" Walking up to the front of the car, he bent down. "Damn, that bumper's bent something awful—practically rubbing on the tire, and the fender looks like someone took a post maul to it."

Lizzy drew alongside and inspected the damage. "That stone sure did a number!"

Jubal groaned, standing up to run his hand through his hair. "I can't have Benny see this!"

"Well, just consider yerself lucky ya ain't behind bars this very minute."

"I forgot all about that stone. It was on my side away from your light."

She shivered and lifted her sopping jacket from her shoulders. "No use cryin' over a bent fender. Let's go. I feel like a drowned rat."

They climbed down to the stable with help from the light and she peered outside, looking skyward.

"The rain's slowin'. My time ta dash home. Can I borrow yer jacket? I'm freezin' in mine. Ya can collect it next time yer at the store, or I'll bring it when I come ta wash my clothes."

"Of course," Jubal unzipped his jacket and handed it to her.

She gave him her coat and he held the soggy cloth at arm's length while she slipped his on.

"Nice and warm," she said. She turned up the collar and wrapped her arms together.

He stood looking at her for a long moment.

"What? Ya need somethin' else? Maybe help ya rob a bank?"

"No, my outlaw days are hopefully over. But hey . . . you were a great help."

He held out her jacket and she wadded it up, tucking it under her arm.

"Thanks fer the ride," she said. "I dare say I never had one like it." She laughed. "Though, I might think twice next time ya offer me a lift."

He nodded. Then she walked out of the barn into the wet summer night, shining her light. Though she'd not care to repeat it any time soon, she'd actually had fun on the wild chase. She had no idea how late it was and didn't much care. Suddenly tired, she looking forward to getting home to her room behind the store. However, she felt no reason to complain. Life was sending her one surprising adventure after another.

Polly's scheme to get a ride with Jubal and later dump him had worked like a charm. And now she was determined to have a good time. Her argument with Lizzy had given her the perfect excuse to leave him behind with his hick friend. Besides, her mother Trudy had recently begged her to cut her romance with Jubal, considering him a lowly farm kid who wore his hair like a girl.

One night when Polly was home from camp, her mom complained, "He's nice but looks and smells like a young urchin bringing us our milk every morning straight from the cow barn."

Polly had been unable to pick up her family's milk as per usual since she'd been away. So Jubal had left it on the back steps of their house, taking back the empty quart can from the day before. When Trudy had greeted him at the door, she'd nearly gagged at his farm smell, hating it so much that she now bought a second can for the next morning's milk.

Meanwhile, Father Mac had been trying to convince Polly to start dating a Catholic boy. So Polly now had her eye on Freddie Coleman. Who better to choose than the guy closest to the church priest? That ought to score her some points. She thought of Freddie as a real stud, but she never got to be near him because Mother Superior had assigned older staff members to be his assistant swim instructors. Polly was stuck helping kids with crafts, like clay picture frames held together with glued popsicle sticks. She hated it. Even worse, her free time and nights were spent in the nurse's quarters comforting homesick kids who had the sniffles.

That morning before the parade, word passed quickly among Hayesville's teenage girls that Freddie Coleman had arrived in his snappy '36 Ford convertible. Polly hoped that he hadn't gotten a date for the night. If he was at the grange dance solo, this was her chance to ditch Jubal and take up with a more promising guy—one who could provide for her in the future and let her live the high life, giving her a house full of good-looking children.

Inside the grange, she noticed a group of girls her age hanging on the sidelines ready and willing to dance if asked. She quickly summed up her competition and judged that she, herself, was without a doubt the classiest looking gal there. Her "knock 'em dead" white jacket with red trim paired with a flowing gingham skirt made her look real spiffy. To add to her glamour, she'd applied plenty of makeup to look much older than she was.

Sadly though, she didn't have a "knock 'em dead" figure like some of the other girls. But she more than made up for it with the clothes that she wore, especially compared to the drab colors she saw—mostly gray, brown, or navy blue skirts and blouses offered in the Montgomery Ward catalogue. Her outfit came straight from Fifth Avenue in New York City, far superior to what the locals could buy—quality that she guessed Freddie Coleman would recognize. Besides, she showed off her own secret up front. She hoped she looked like the real deal in wearing her large mail-order boobs. She was very satisfied also with her new shingle hairdo. Approaching the dance floor, she knew she was shining like a diamond in a bucket of coal.

When the Backcountry Fiddlers stopped after playing a waltz, she walked onto the floor and positioned herself perfectly just as the gal that Freddie was dancing with left for the sidelines. He couldn't miss her and he didn't.

"Hi there, gorgeous. How about being my partner for the next dance?" His smile showed a row of perfect white teeth.

"Sure, why not? I'm available." She had long practiced her repertoire of smiles in front of her dresser mirror and knew exactly how to give it her all for a potential suitor. Of course she poured it on for Freddie.

He looked her up and down. "Well, my goodness, where have you been keeping yourself? I never expected to find such a knockout in a hick town like Hayesville."

"I could say the same about you," she said. "I've noticed you at CYO camp."

"You're at camp?" He raised his eyebrows. "I must be blind not to have noticed you."

"Yeah, well," she shrugged. "I've been stuck in the craft cabin and sleeping nights in the nurse's quarters, trying to keep the kids happy. I'll be there all season."

"Really? So sorry I've missed you. We'll just have to make up for lost time."

"Kinda hard to do that at CYO camp."

Freddie laughed and Polly liked the sound. Just then, the band began the next song, a medium-paced number. All the dancers sprang to action.

He closed his arms around her, guiding her gently around the floor. He was a good dancer.

"Are you from town?" He spoke close to her ear.

As she felt his breath warm on her neck, excitement ran up her spine. "Yeah, I grew up here, but I plan to split for the big time as soon as I'm out of school. Oh, I might go to Wellesley or Bryn Mawr, some high-class girls' college. Of course, I could always fall for a guy with potential and just have a good time."

"I like the sound of a good time," he said, firmly grabbing her by the waist to sweep her off her feet as they circled the floor.

A couple of songs later, she was breathless. Obviously she'd been right that he was a great catch. She relaxed into his arms, pressed against his broad chest and becoming a bit dizzy with her nose buried in the smell of his cologne.

As they spun around, she noticed Jubal and Lizzy on the floor. They were taking baby steps to the "Tennessee Waltz," looking like two stick figures walking on ice. She hid her smile, turning her face into Freddie's suit jacket.

Soon she and Freddie joined a square dance set of three other couples and Polly was having the time of her life. She watched Jubal and Lizzy out of the corner of her eye as they stumbled through the various dance calls. After the square dancing came more waltzes where she could snuggle into Freddie's arms. Before long, he slid his hand down over her butt. A little surprised he would do this in public, she put her hand over his and moved it to her lower back.

He whispered, "Don't you love this?"

She lifted her head from his chest and smiled up at him. "This night is the most fun I've ever had."

He held her away at arm's length. "For real?"

"Truly," she said, sighing as he pulled her close again.

They danced every number until someone yelled, "Rain!"

Freddie stopped abruptly, letting go of her. "Damn. I've got to put my top up on my car right away." He left her standing on the floor as he ran outside.

She followed, holding her skirt with one hand so she could run. "Hey! Can I help?" she called.

"Sure!" he yelled over his shoulder as he made a beeline for his convertible.

The rain dampened Polly's face and hair, and she worried that the moisture would turn her new hairdo into a frizz. They reached the Ford and stood on either side to unsnap the convertible canvas and pull it with the frame into position, connecting the cover at the top of the windshield. The task required strength and she did her best to keep up with Freddie, but was careful not to break a nail, since she'd manicured them just right when getting ready for the night.

Suddenly the skies opened up in a downpour. Her beautiful jacket was wet before she could jump into the car under cover. However, even inside, she discovered the roof canvas was brittle and had leaks in a number of places. Water was dripping down her neck and down her cleavage into her bra. Her classy outfit absorbed it all. A leak directly over the back of her seat ran down the leather, soon causing her to sit in water.

"My car's getting all wet," Freddie groaned. "I've nothing to soak up the water."

He looked around for something he could use as a rag. He studied her. "Uh, maybe your jacket would work?"

"My beautiful jacket?" She shook her head and pulled the front of the coat tightly closed.

"It's already wet. Why not? It'll dry when you get home." He started yanking at her jacket front.

"Well, okay!" She gave in when he already had the jacket nearly off her shoulders. She took it off and gave it reluctantly to him.

She thought of Jubal and Lizzy leaving together in the Packard and wondered if she'd made a terrible mistake. At the very least they'd left with a solid roof over their heads.

Freddie fussed over the rain as it leaked into the car, furiously sopping up the water and wringing out her garment like a washrag. Eventually, he tossed her jacket at her and they took off for home. She sat totally soaked and freezing from the breeze that whistled through the cracks in the roof. Her light cotton blouse clung to her skin such that she worried it might now be a bit see-through. Her bra straps tightened since the spongy falsies had taken on water and were now sagging towards her lap. She discretely tried to cinch up her bra to hold herself together, but to no avail—the adjusters on the straps had reached their limit. Giving up, she held her wrung-out jacket in one hand, with the other hand pressed to her breastbone to lift her fake boobs back into place.

She glanced over at Freddie to see if he noticed her dilemma, but he ignored her. The windshield was a wash of water and the blades were barely able to keep up.

Entering the outskirts of Hayesville, they met Tatum's police car and the deputy's vehicle with lights flashing. They were stopped by the side of the road next to Avery Ketchum's cornfield. Tatum and the deputy stood in rain gear motioning for them to move on.

Polly spoke up. "I live up on Harmony Hill. The left turn is coming right up."

Freddie pressed the brakes. "I suppose you expect me to take you to your door. I'm goddamned soaked and needing to get back to the rectory."

"Well, I'm not walking with it raining like this and it's pitch black."

"Yeah, I guess." He made the turn and stomped on the gas. "This is what I get for having a few dances!" He stopped the car at her drive and gunned the gas impatiently with the clutch to the floor. "See you at camp."

"Sorry, to put you out of your way!" She hastily exited the wet interior of the car. "And thanks for ruining my nice jacket!" she said, slamming the door.

As soon as she was out, he sped off, the convertible throwing mud from the back tires, spattering her skirt and shoes. She walked up her driveway with the rain having slowed to a drizzle and realized that she had just been in the company of the greatest jerk imaginable. She hoped to never see him again, not even at camp. All she had to show now for her high hopes was her ruined jacket in one hand and her soggy fake glamour held in place with the other.

Chapter Twenty

Having parked the Packard in the haymow and after saying goodbye to Lizzy, Jubal rushed to the house. There his dad sat in his drinking corner dead to the world. Jubal was not surprised his father was home from the mansion—he'd likely manipulated his ma into allowing him to spend the night at the farm, rather than the planned lock-in at Lady Lamont's. His ma lacked the energy to fight when his dad got ugly during dry-outs. And somehow she seemed to be clueless about the hidden stash of booze his father kept in the haymow. He suspected his dad had been on a binge ever since lunchtime. Another wasted effort. And with the usual Red Sox game having long passed, Clyde had missed everything.

However, Jubal had no time to waste. Tatum might be arriving at any minute. He hustled upstairs, undressed, and jumped into bed. He could hear Benny in the next room snoring away and figured his ma must be close by at Lady Lamont's. Every so often she would stay the night, preferring to be away from the stress of the farm and wishing to be ready to begin her work day as soon as Lady Lamont was up.

He lay awake, thinking over the day and night just past. The buggy drive in the parade was history. At least he'd prevented, with Maria's help, the Morgans from taking off with the carriage. At the thought of Maria's violent attack, his stomach clenched. He never imagined such an awful thing would happen to his friend and he worried about how she might be feeling. And that wasn't the only unexpected event that had turned his day upside down.

Instead of the romantic date he'd been looking forward to, Polly had split, no longer his girl. And Benny's Packard sat with a smashed fender and bent bumper, hidden in the barn, needing repairs. Not to mention that Jubal was now a fugitive from the law.

It was a good thing he'd avoided being caught at the roadblock. Surprisingly, however, he'd enjoyed the adventure through the cornfield, and even what little dancing he'd done with Lizzy. Getting to know her, she was bold and funny—a real character.

Sleepless with worrying how he'd get Benny's car fixed, he sat upright when red lights flashed across his bedroom ceiling. Soon, there was banging at the door. Of course, his dad wouldn't answer. Jubal ran to the bathroom and wrapped himself in a towel over his underwear. He answered the door and Tatum stepped in without being invited.

"Seen Benny?" Tatum peered from the entry to the kitchen.

Even though Jubal was tall at six feet, he had to look up at the sheriff. "Benny's in bed!"

"Bullshit!" Tatum walked into the kitchen. "I want to see Benny."

Jubal wished he'd put on some pants and shoes. He had hoped the towel would make Tatum uncomfortable while also adding proof that he'd been in bed. Tatum seemed not to notice.

"I told you, Benny's in bed," Jubal said. "He goes to bed early every single night. Just leave him alone."

Tatum glared. "I told you, I want to see your no-good, brainless uncle. That's an order."

"Alright, alright. Just a minute."

Jubal dashed upstairs. First he stopped into his room to put on some clothes. He hated to wake Benny up, knowing his uncle might get scared as he did with any upset of his routine. But Jubal didn't wish to draw attention in a tiff with the law. For this last part, he felt bad—his trip through the cornfield was the reason Tatum was looking to question Benny.

"Benny. Benny! Wake up!" He shook Benny's shoulder.

Benny sat up, rubbing his eyes and raking his fingers through his red hair so that it stuck up on top of his head. "Jubal, that's you?"

"Tatum's downstairs. He wants to see you."

"Me!" Leaving his bed, Benny had on only undershorts. "I . . . I ain't done nothin'. Jubal, he ain't takin' me away? Is he, Jubal?"

There was no time to risk getting Benny into some clothes, as his uncle did most things slowly. Tatum might get tired of waiting and rush up the stairs.

"Just follow me, Benny. I'm looking out for you. Remember?"

"Looking out" was a phrase Jubal used on Benny when he was sensing danger. Jubal knew Benny thought of him as his protector.

"Yes, Jubal." Benny hit the stairs, heavy-footed. "Where's Rose? Rose talks nice ta Tatum."

"Ma's at Lady Lamont's." Jubal, too, wished his ma were home because Benny was right. His mother could always charm Tatum—it had worked in the past when Benny caused trouble.

The only light in the kitchen was on, hanging over the table. Tatum was leaning against the sink and his head barely cleared the low ceiling. Apparently, while Jubal had been upstairs, Constable Stubby Shangraw had arrived as backup. A stout guy, Stubby was also the school's janitor and probably had never fired a gun while on police duty. Tatum was obviously uneasy about confronting Benny who was known around town to turn into a rampaging bull when angry or scared.

Tatum pushed off from the sink. "Benny, what the hell were you doin', drivin' like a goddamned maniac?" Handcuffs dangled from the sheriff's hand. "You ain't got a license to drive. So guess what? I'm taking you in."

Jubal stepped between the two big men. "Benny hasn't done anything. He's been in bed. You aren't taking him anywhere." He spread his arms to hold both men apart, feeling like a referee before a ten-round fight. There was a bad history between the two—previous scuffles in town when Benny was out of control.

"Think about it—is Benny's Packard in the yard?" Jubal said.

Stubby responded in a high squeaky voice. "It wan't in the yard when I drove in."

Jubal quickly put in, "Someone must have stolen it!"

"Is that right boy?" Tatum said, fingering the cuffs. He remained just two feet from Benny with Stubby standing close by.

Jubal held his position. He could see the sheriff was itching for an arrest to put on the books, likely having found no one to harass after the dance.

"Jubal!" Benny spoke up. "Someone stole my blue car? Who took my car?"

Tatum pushed Jubal to the side.

Benny slouched in his undershorts, his hands trembling slightly. "Leave me alone. You ain't . . . ain't takin' . . ."

Tatum lunged for Benny with the cuffs extended, but Benny put out his hands and shoved the sheriff backwards. Tatum let out a soft "oof" as his lower back hit the sink's edge.

Stubby Shangraw drew his pistol, whereupon Jubal dove at him, pushing Stubby's hand to lower the weapon which fired into the floor. Stubby dropped the gun and backed into a corner, showing no further willingness to take on Benny. With the gun report ringing in his ears, Jubal again rushed to get between Tatum and Benny.

Benny was now in full panic mode. He lurched around Jubal and went at Tatum. It was like the clash of two Titans fighting for the right to rule the earth, except Tatum spent most of his days in his sheriff's car or driving Father Mac around, probably drinking coffee and eating candy bars. Meanwhile, Benny worked daily at the end of a manure shovel, wheeling cow slop up a steep ramp and dumping it. He'd been doing this and other farm labor for years. He tossed hundred-pound grain bags as if they were powder puffs.

The two men shoved each other, their weight causing the farmhouse floor to creak and shake. Benny, having a basic animal instinct to go for the throat, easily handled Tatum. He pushed the sheriff backward and shoved his head down into the broad sink. Tatum tried to yell for help but Benny's hand held his jaw shut so that he only blew a *sheee* out the side of his mouth, sounding like a leak in an over-inflated tire. Face up under the water spout, Tatum's eyes bulged in fear. With a stroke of the handle, Benny pumped a gush of water onto Tatum's face. The sheriff began blowing and sucking water through his nose.

Jubal let Benny continue with the water dowsing until he saw Tatum gasping for breath in earnest. Fearing the sheriff might drown, he shouted, "BENNY stop! I'm here, looking out for you!"

At the familiar phrase, Benny let go of the pump handle and the water deluge stopped. Tatum sucked in a huge breath before doubling over and spitting water on the floor.

Suddenly, a blast blew a hole through the wall above the sink. Plaster dust flew into the air. Benny let go of Tatum and lunged to the other side of the table with his fingers in his ears. Tatum hit the floor and Stubby ducked. Through the dust, Clyde leaned against the wooden icebox reloading his double-barrel twelve-gauge. The gun clicked into place. He weaved, ready for a second volley, eyes bloodshot, face red.

"What in hell's goin' on here?" Clyde bellowed.

Tatum stood slowly and wiped his dusty, water-streaked face on his sleeve. "Clyde! You crazy fool shootin' off a gun in your own kitchen!" He drew a wheezing breath. "And you've got a . . . a goddamned monster livin' with you!"

Clyde hugged the icebox in order to stand straight. "Whatcha doin' here, sheriff?"

"I'm takin' Benny in for resistin' arrest." Tatum jerked his thumb at Benny who had moved to be with Jubal.

"Arrest for what?" Clyde sniffed while resting the heft of his weapon on the edge of the icebox. "You ain't takin' Benny!"

"Clyde, you're in deep shit, firing a weapon at me!"

Jubal's dad looked down at his gun on the icebox as if considering for the first time what he had done. He lowered his weapon, leaned it in the corner of the kitchen, and backed into the next room.

Tatum called out, "Your brother-in-law needs to cool his butt in a jail cell for a few days—teach him a lesson!"

Standing by his Philco, Clyde waved Tatum off with both hands in disgust before sinking into his drinking chair.

Partially behind Jubal, Benny whispered, " I . . . I ain't done nothin' wrong!"

"Well, you just almost killed Tatum," Jubal whispered back. He wanted to side with Benny, but there was no way Tatum would let his uncle off the hook now. He realized, also, that it might be convenient for Benny to be out of the barn for a short while until he could figure out what to do with the Packard.

He said quietly, "Benny, just go with the sheriff for now. The jail is safe. No one can hurt you there. You don't want to fight with Tatum anymore, right? Go with him. Ma will be in to see you in the morning."

"No one will hurt me there?" Benny sounded dubious.

"That's right. Do what Tatum says."

Tatum blustered, "Huh, Rose ain't gonna talk me out of it. Benny's goin' to sit in jail and think about what he's done."

Jubal glared at Tatum. The guy had no sense of how to handle Benny.

Benny started crying and wringing his hands. "But . . . I ain't done nothin' wrong! 'til Tatum come! He scared me."

It was hard for Jubal to let Benny go, especially seeing his uncle captive and leaving in handcuffs. He knew his Ma would be furious when she found out the whole truth, and he couldn't get past blaming the whole mess on Polly with her wish to be chauffeured to the dance.

The next morning Jubal hadn't slept much from aching over Benny in jail and the smashed car. He was still kicking himself for allowing Polly to bamboozle him. It had been poor judgement to drive her to the dance, pure and simple.

He got up early to do chores by himself. The cows were crowded at the gate, hungry from lousy grass and wanting to be fed some grain. Iris, a typical Ayrshire being reddish mahogany with white spots, had long pointed horns. She was the leader of the herd, the "boss cow." As he approached, she snorted and threw her head in anger, bellowing by the gate. The other cows simply followed with heads down, accepting their half-starved condition, but not Iris.

Benny was afraid of her, knowing what she could do to him if he was ever caught in an open pasture. No human, especially lumbering Benny, could outrun Iris.

However, she and Jubal had come to an understanding. She'd been whacked a few times with the maple stick he always carried. She respected him as the herdsman and she let him milk her with no problem.

When he flipped the lights on in the barn and the cows entered, their Ayrshire bull acted up like he always did, blasting a roar that would have scared the bravest, but that was his normal greeting. Jubal hated him.

The forty cows gave a piddling amount of milk, barely two forty-quart cans. The pasture that he, Eugene, and Benny had just fixed for them was far from good, all overgrown with juniper, leaving few spaces for grass to grow. He had planned to turn them out into new grazing that day on a small field they had recently finished haying, but, of course, the first order of business was to attend to Benny in jail, as well as his damaged car. All through milking, Jubal also thought about Maria and Polly.

Since Polly was home from CYO camp, he knew she'd have to come for the morning's milk. She was the only O'Mara kid, and her folks had never set foot on the Clyde Brown farm. One thing he'd learned about Andrew O'Mara was that the pharmacist believed in Ayrshire milk. The breed produced the smallest milkfat particle of any dairy cow, and Andrew often recommended the superior digestibility of Ayrshire milk for babies with colic or adults who, like himself, had a touchy stomach. Therefore, Jubal knew Polly's dad would demand fresh Ayrshire milk for his breakfast.

While Polly was at camp, he'd been taking the milk to the O'Mara's. Trudy O'Mara, usually dressed in a lavender robe decorated with sequins, acted out of her mind with thanks. However, he'd seen her wrinkle her nose when he passed her the milk. He could guess what she thought, him smelling like a barn and loving her daughter, imagining him as a future son-in-law. Shortly, she began buying a second quart can so he could simply leave the milk on the back step. There was always a dime placed under the empty container.

But Andrew O'Mara had never once met him at the door. Polly said her dad liked to read his *Wall Street Journal*, checking on his investments daily. It was clear Polly's family stood a few rungs up the ladder from his and regardless of what he did, he'd never measure up.

Since Polly seemed to have dumped him, no way would he bring the milk over the path to their place. Like it or not, she was going to have to come to his farm that morning. Maybe the O'Maras had money, but the Browns had the Ayrshire milk.

He hefted the two nearly-filled forty-quart cans into the cold water of the McCormick Cooler and the compressor motor started its low hum. He was cleaning up in the milk room when he heard the door creak open. Polly stood in a short-sleeved summer dress that showed her slim arms, slender waist, and skinny legs. Her blue, Irish eyes had the same cool, distant look that she'd had when storming off at the dance. She handed him the quart milk can.

He reached for a white enamel dipper. After stirring the milk, he filled the aluminum can, dipper by dipper. The only sounds were the splashing milk and the cooler's hum. On past mornings, they had laughed, visited, and made their date plans, but this morning, neither of them said a word. When he finished, he placed the cover on the can and handed the milk to her.

"So, you made it home from the dance," he said.

"Yes." She tossed her head. "After you ruined the night by giving that hick a ride."

"*That hick* happens to be Lizzy LaFlam and she's a friend of mine," he said. It surprised him to claim the former mountain girl as his friend.

Polly pouted. "A friend . . . I see. And I'll bet you had fun with her in Benny's Packard!"

"Look," he said, meeting Polly's eyes, "let's stop this! My night happened to be miserable."

She scowled. "Oh you have no idea. *My* night was dreadful. I'm sure worse than yours."

Her selfish reply irritated him. "Well, both of our nights were not as bad as Maria's. I hope you are going to see how she is today before you leave for camp?"

She stepped back in surprise and puffed her cheeks—a habit she had when faced with something she didn't like. "Why me?"

"She's your friend, isn't she?"

"Yeah, but Father Mac is really mad at her. It's awful she quit and threw those roses." She shrugged. "She has to do penance."

It was his turn to scowl. Apparently Polly was more concerned with her standing in the church than with Maria's having been attacked. "And so now you've ditched her? A great friend you are!"

She shifted the milk can's weight. "I wouldn't know what to say."

"Forget it!" He picked up a broom and began sweeping.

Polly continued to stand holding the milk can.

He stopped and leaned on the broom with one hand. "You know what?" he said. "I am going to see Maria and loan her Trueboy to ride until we need him."

She twisted her face in disgust. "Oh, you're a big hero! You expect that plug will save the day? If I was in her place, that's just what I'd want! God, an old horse!" She turned to go.

"Aren't you a spoiled brat! Maria likes horses and Trueboy might be just what she needs right now!"

"Good luck!" She tossed the dime on the concrete floor. The coin clinked and rolled as the door slammed behind her.

As she stormed off, an emptiness fell over him. When had the distance between them grown so large? Last time they'd been together they'd been talking marriage and making out in the Packard. He picked up the dime and returned to his chores.

Though he wanted to see Maria soon, first he needed help with a plan to fix Benny's Packard. His ma was the only one who could even begin to right the situation. She knew how to weave her way around the law and best of all keep it a secret. No one needed to know about the big problem parked on the haymow floor.

Before Jubal left the milk room to go eat breakfast, the sheriff's Ford cruiser pulled into the yard. It was decked out with a siren on the fender and enough red lights to stop a freight train. As Tatum got out and strode towards the barn, Jubal tensed, wondering what he would say if Tatum started questioning him.

When the sheriff came through the milk room door, he wasted no time. "Ya seen Benny's Packard?"

"Been busy with chores." Jubal frowned. "Of course, with no help from Benny."

"Benny's right where he should be." Tatum rubbed his neck where there appeared to be red marks from Benny's hands.

Jubal swallowed at the sight of the damage that his uncle could easily do to a guy and hoped his ma could get Benny out of this. "Come into the house," he said, motioning. "I need some breakfast."

The sheriff followed him out of the milk room, and Jubal relaxed, realizing Tatum hadn't come to the farm to question him in particular.

As he entered the house with Tatum in tow, his ma sat at the kitchen table drinking coffee with her back turned. His dad was seated facing them and his glazed eyes widened on seeing the sheriff again. His ma turned at their sound. She looked to not be her cheery self, but judging from her calm reaction on seeing Tatum, she apparently hadn't heard what had taken place the night before or even noticed the hole lacking plaster above the sink. Understandable, since the kitchen plaster had already given way in a number of places, showing the lath.

"Say, where's Benny?" she asked. "He's not with you?"

"Uh . . . Tatum arrested him last night." Jubal stepped back to watch the fireworks.

"What!" His ma leapt to her feet. "On what grounds?"

Tatum paled. "Resistin' arrest."

"Arrest? For what?" She narrowed her eyes. "You just love the thought of getting my brother behind bars, don't you? God . . . man . . ." She plunked back in her chair. "Don't you have anything else to do?"

"Rose," Tatum pleaded, "your brother damn near killed me!" Tatum stretched his neck and turned his head to the side. "See the marks?"

His dad mumbled, "Too bad Benny didn't finish the job."

Jubal put in quickly, "Benny was in bed when Tatum came."

"He was not. I saw him drivin' his Packard like a maniac," Tatum said. "Least, I thought it was Benny." He turned to Jubal. "Unless it was you?"

Clyde pounded the table, rattling the dishes. "My boy was in bed! He wan't out drivin' no goddamned car!" His dad pushed back his chair and wove his way to the next room, snapping on the Philco as he sat down. Strains of a country tune drifted into the kitchen.

"My dad's right, I was in bed," Jubal agreed.

Tatum rubbed his chin. "Well, I'll admit, the car ain't nowhere to be seen—ain't in the yard this mornin'; wasn't in the yard last night."

His ma looked puzzled, gripping her coffee cup with both hands. "Not in the yard? The Packard's always parked in the same place."

"Your son says it was stolen," Tatum said.

She looked over at Jubal. "Stolen! Who'd take our car?"

"I have no idea," Jubal shrugged.

"That's two crimes in our town yesterday. What's going on?" She looked sternly at Tatum. "And what are you doing about it? Arresting Benny, who's innocent!"

She stood from the table and walked over to Tatum where she gathered his shirt collar firmly in both hands. Tatum's face turned beet red. Jubal wondered whether it was from anger or the closeness of the woman for whom the sheriff had once had thoughts of love. His ma leaned in until her face was inches from Tatum's.

"You get Benny back here. Immediately!" She released the sheriff's shirt.

"I can't." Tatum put up his hands. "I've already pressed charges."

"Then drop them!" Her voice rose. Though she was inches shorter than Tatum, to Jubal, his ma in the moment seemed miles taller. "You hear me?"

"Now Rose, ya ain't understandin'. Benny almost killed me! I've got Stubby as a witness! I've got the marks on my neck."

She turned to Jubal. "Jubal, were you a witness?"

"Yeah, as I said, Benny was asleep until Tatum told me to get him." He curled his toes in his shoes, aware how easily he could get caught in a snare. He didn't want to lie to his ma, but for sure, the missing Packard was on Tatum's unanswered list. Best to say as little as possible. He was also grateful that Tatum had not brought up his father's shotgun blast.

"Rose, listen," Tatum explained. "Benny's car ain't here, but I know it landed in a bunch of Avery Ketchum's corn. I saw the Packard fly through the air and hit the dirt while I was standin' at the roadblock. Someone drivin' like a runaway gangster in the pourin' rain." He scratched his head. "Least, I think so. But strangely, this mornin' there ain't no tracks and there ain't no car. Just four wheel dents in the ground where the big car landed."

"Then someone left town in a stolen Packard," his ma said. "Tear up your paperwork. Benny comes home!"

Tatum edged towards the door. "Rose, just come down to the lock-up. I'll be there all mornin'. But this afternoon, I'm leavin' with Father Mac and drivin' to CYO camp, so we'd best get this settled."

After Tatum's departure, his ma said, "Jubal, take a seat."

Jubal did as directed. He knew his ma could read between the lines of a tight situation and likely suspected he wasn't telling the whole story. He wasn't looking forward to spilling the beans about his misdeeds.

"Okay, let's have it," she said. "What went on last night?"

He flopped his head in his arms on the table, hiding his face. He felt her hand on his shoulder.

She gave him a firm squeeze. "Tell me, Jubal."

He sniffed and sat up, fighting to keep his eyes from tearing up. "So much has happened. . . ." He spoke haltingly, telling her nearly all, including Lizzy as a passenger, while holding back on details of his dates with Polly in the Packard. As he spoke, a look of disbelief gradually overcame his mother's face.

"Damn, Jubal! Driving through Avery's corn, wrecked the Packard's fender and bumper! And you with no license!" She sank into a chair and held her head, her fingers buried in her hair. The bangles on her arm rang in a cascade as they slid down to her elbow. She dropped her hands. "I thought all along that— Well, you of all people! And you involved Lizzy in your reckless actions. This doesn't sound like the Jubal I know!"

He tried to explain. "Lizzy didn't urge me on. She just took my offer for a ride is all. It was Polly. She wanted to go to the dance in the worst way! She practically made me."

"What made her think you could take Benny's car?" His ma folded her arms and fixed him with a "tell me the truth and no nonsense" look.

He sighed. "Well, we . . ."

"For goodness' sake, Jubal. Out with it."

He searched for an explanation that made sense. "It just . . . seemed the obvious thing to do."

His mother rang out a sharp laugh. "Good Lord in Heaven! Obvious to break the law?"

"I know! I know. But Polly was so demanding! She's changed."

"Changed from what?"

"From before." He wanted desperately to clam up and not tell the rest. But he'd been taught to respect his ma and never lie.

His mother raised her eyebrows, waiting.

"She's changed her feelings towards me," he admitted. He didn't like the direction the conversation was taking. "She knew all along she was going to dump me at the dance."

His mother nodded. "Did she have cause to end seeing you? Such as something going wrong with your dates at the Packard?"

Dates at the Packard. Jubal's throat tightened, "Hum." She knew more than he realized.

"Jubal," his mother spoke softly. "Did Polly have cause to worry?"

"Worry? Oh! No!" he blurted, feeling the heat rise to his face. "Well, she thought maybe."

"She thought what, maybe?"

"That she could be in, you know, trouble. But I told her that she shouldn't worry." There, he had said it.

"So you and Polly have been having sex in Benny's car?"

"No!" Gosh, it sounded awful when his ma said it. "Only a little."

"A *little* sex? God help us!" She leaned across the table. "Don't you know? There's no such thing as being just a *little* pregnant!"

"Ma relax! Polly isn't pregnant, and she won't ever be with me again. It's over!"

His mother sat back. "Sounds like she was doing you a favor in stopping before it was too late."

"Ma, believe me, she had no cause." He wished he could flee the kitchen to his room.

"Okay, so maybe she left you for other reasons. Another guy, her folks, or the church? I know it's painful, but I can't help you with that part."

"She's chasing after Freddie Coleman, the swim instructor at camp!" As he said this, his eyes welled up.

"Oh, really? What kind of guy is this Freddie Coleman?"

Jubal thought of Freddie in his tan suit, his slick smile. "He's a jerk, twice her age." He wanted to tell his ma more, but didn't dare break his promise to Maria.

His ma got up from the table and poured herself the remainder of the coffee. She sat again, taking a sip. As if reading his mind, she said, "Well, enough about Polly. My heart aches for Maria. Poor girl. If she's been beaten and, as Lady Lamont told me, likely raped, you can't imagine how serious that is."

He stood and went to the window. "If it's true, and I believe Lizzy and Lady Lamont, it sounded pretty terrible." He saw Dick and Dan off in the pasture, with Trueboy not far from them, and he thought back to the spring at Avery's farm. "Maria is special. She's confident and smart. She seems stronger than some of the other girls I know from school." He turned to see if his ma agreed.

She smiled. "She sure is. Though, to be honest, I'm worried folks may just want to cover up her tragedy."

"Well, I want to do what I can for her," he said. He looked out at the horses and his plan to bring Trueboy to Maria seemed more urgent.

"I'm glad you want to help. She'll need her friends," his ma said. She came to stand beside him at the window. "We'll figure out the Packard somehow. And you'll get over losing Polly with time. But Maria? I'm afraid her emotional problems will linger."

Her eyes wandered towards his father in the next room, now slumped asleep in his chair. His dad had passed out so early in the day, right after breakfast. Suddenly everything seemed like such a mess.

"My two favorite men are in trouble," his ma sighed.

Through the panes of glass, the morning sun slanted a narrow shaft of light that shone upon her face and Jubal noticed small lines at the edges of her eyes. She looked worn out. He knew he shouldn't be adding to her burdens and resolved to do better.

She straightened with a determined look. "But I can't give up on your dad. I've got to get Benny out of jail. And, I don't ever want you on the wrong side of the law again."

"I promise," he nodded. "And Polly can't pull a number like that on me anymore. She's history!"

Chapter Twenty-One

It was midmorning when Rose started their truck to go fetch Benny home from jail. She wanted to get there before Tatum took Father Mac back to CYO camp. She didn't want her brother in a cell one minute longer than necessary. Hardly roadworthy, the old pickup's engine smoked like a smudge pot. She headed down Harmony Hill in second gear with the brake pedal close to the floorboard. Bad brakes were nothing new. Someday, maybe, she hoped they could do better than the old truck.

The Hayesville jail was in a wooden building that appeared to have been thrown together in a rush. During the early 1900s, with heavy logging and the Civilian Conservation Corps nearby, workers came into town for wild nights, so a place was needed to keep the troublemakers. The structure possessed a sagging roofline and doors that didn't easily open and close. Townsfolk laughed that a cat could slip through the place not breaking its stride.

This wasn't the first time Benny's short fuse had landed him in trouble. There was the time that young Billy Sanders had teased him. Benny caught Billy by the nape of the neck, picked him up, and carried the kid kicking and hollering into the IGA store. Inside the store, Benny ducked Billy's head down into the pickle barrel. Afterwards, Billy's folks threatened to sue the Browns on behalf of their son who reportedly spit up brine for hours. To settle the matter, Rose had given the Sanders family a fifty-dollar check.

In most of these incidents, she would arrive on the scene and pay the damages, bypassing any charges. However, this wouldn't happen without her first spending time with Tatum behind closed doors, tearing open his weak spot. She knew just how to prod his memory of that awful summer of '24, when she was raped and his sister was killed in a fire.

Pulling up to the curb, she saw Tatum on the porch in front of the lock-up. Her anger flared as she walked up the sidewalk.

"Where are the keys, Tatum?" she called out. "I want my brother out of there this very minute!"

"Rose, take it easy!" he said. "Remember, you're talkin' to the law."

She ignored him and headed for the door, intent on reaching the jail cell.

He moved to block her way. "Whoa, Benny ain't goin' nowhere. Resistin' arrest is a serious charge. Never mind he assaulted an officer. Damn near drowned me."

She stopped on the porch. "And what a phony charge it all is! Benny would have been fine if you hadn't gotten him out of bed and scared him half to death." She again tried to access the door but he stood firmly in her path.

"Rose, someone was drivin' that Packard like a crazy bastard and it's my duty to find out who."

"So the car was stolen. It sits all the time by the barn with the keys in it, in full view from the road. It was easy to steal." She finally pushed Tatum to the side with her hip and shoulder and slipped through the door. His footsteps followed behind on the wood floor as she strode into his office.

"By god now," he said. "I saw that car leave the road and tear into Avery's cornfield!"

She turned to face him. "And?"

Tatum scratched his head. "Well, I dunno. I looked across the field to the hedgerow—no car. 'Course it rained like a bastard, likely rubbin' out the tracks, but the car?"

"Well, you'll just have to solve that mystery." She stuck out her hand. "Let's have the keys."

Tatum shook his head. "No ma'am, that I cannot do."

In response, she crossed to his desk, hoping he'd left the keys lying out in the open. They weren't anywhere in sight. She looked for a hook on the wall above the desk, but all that hung there was a ten-pointer deer rack. A picture beside the trophy showed Tatum claiming that he had bagged the biggest buck ever taken in Hayesville county. Suddenly she heard a low, anxious moan and metal rattling from the next room. She whirled on Tatum.

"You have it in for Benny! You always have. And I won't stand for it!" She wanted in the worst way to shove him, but knew that would be grounds for assaulting an officer. "Now, my advice to you is to stop making up reasons to arrest my brother! You know he wasn't in that car last night. He can't even drive it, to say nothing about having the ability to make it vanish into thin air from a cornfield!"

"But he near killed me!"

"You had no cause to go after him. You roust him out of bed in the middle of the night—you don't think he's going to react?"

"I've never seen anythin' like it. I was dealin' with a keg of dynamite."

"Why don't you deal with something *important* for a change?"

He gave her a blank look, "Like what?"

"You know very well what I'm talking about. Maria Styles."

His swagger returned. "I'll have you know, the LaFlam boys are the prime suspects. Did you see how they took after Maria durin' the parade?"

"I wasn't there."

"Well, see?" Tatum strolled over to stand so close that he towered above her. "Looks like I know more about it than you."

Standing head to head in their mutual anger, the electricity between them fairly snapped. Her stomach lurched at the memory of him that night in the old abandoned house, handing her the drink that held the *mickey*.

Benny moaned again.

"I'm warning you, Tatum O'Mara—you'd better start getting your act together. Elections are coming up in March. And I just happen to have connections in this town, to more important people than that poor excuse for a priest. And I just happen to have personal knowledge of how low *you* can sink."

He shifted to break their closeness. "Gosh, Rose! No need to get so ugly about this."

"Why of course not, Sheriff." She stuck out her hand again. "Now—give me the key to Benny's cell."

His shoulders drooped. She had him right where she wanted him.

He crossed to his desk and opened a drawer. "Rose it just ain't right, comin' in here and freein' a guilty man. You're makin' me look like a goddamn fool." He tossed her the keys.

They clinked as she caught them. "Looking the fool is nothing new for you," she said. "There's so much history between us, Tatum, it's hard to think anything more of you."

He stood slack-jawed. Then he recovered his composure. "I'd like to know what you mean by that?"

The way he stood, lanky and jutting out his square chin, she recalled just briefly how he tried to follow her dance steps when they were young. She turned her back on him and walked into the next room. Benny's face was pressed against the bars with dust marks on his brow and cheeks.

"Rose! Ya came!" Benny said, pulling back from the bars. "I knew ya would."

"Of course, Benny. You're my special guy. Now I've got clean clothes and shoes for you in the truck. Good grief, they took you in your undershorts." She glared at Tatum. "Tatum will let you use the washroom to clean your face and hands. Let's get you dressed."

Polly had no intention of telling a soul, especially her mom, about her disastrous Saturday night with Freddie Coleman. She also didn't show her mother the ruined jacket that Freddie used as a rag. The next morning the red trim had bled dye onto the white, and after it dried, the coat had shrunk to about two sizes too small. The once flashy jacket now had sleeves halfway up her arms. She buried it in her lingerie drawer, along with her falsies. Her mother would never find them—if she did, it would bring on a bushel of questions concerning the night before. Questions that Polly didn't care to answer.

Her mother had always been overprotective. It was clear her mom did not want her to end up pregnant, especially by someone who didn't live up to her standards, such as "the boy next door," and in particular, Jubal. While Polly understood and even shared her mother's concerns, she was growing tired of the constant prying.

One time, after Polly discovered that her birth date and the date of her parents' marriage didn't cover a span of nine months, she had asked her mother about it. In a moment of truth telling, her mom confirmed she'd had a shotgun wedding. The confession revealed that prenuptial sex had definitely occurred. Apparently, at the time, her dad was studying at Saint Augustine's Catholic Seminary in order to become a priest. Her mother told her, "I saw him as quite the catch."

"Does that mean *I* can have sex if the right guy comes along?" Still young, Polly had seen her mother's behavior as terribly flawed.

"Oh no! I made a poor choice in judgment," her mom admitted. "I did it because I wanted him to like me, to *love* me. But I don't think to this day that your father has forgiven me for leading him to a forced marriage."

Considering her mother's resulting opinion about shenanigans with boys, not to mention the budding relationship with Jubal, Polly wasn't surprised when, in early spring, her parents had brought up the idea of her being a counselor at CYO camp. Her mother had urged her dad as a leader at St. Anne's church to use his influence in placing his daughter in a position on the CYO staff.

Polly's camp duties were not at all how she wanted to spend her summer. Other girls in her class were doing much more exciting activities. But it was no use protesting once her mother made up her mind. So, while Polly handed tissues to sniveling children, she pictured how her friends might be sunning themselves on the shores of Lake Champlain or going out on dates.

After Polly stashed the jacket and falsies, she decided to tell her mom how she and Jubal had gone their separate ways the previous evening.

Her mother lit up on hearing the news. "Dear, I am so relieved! I worried about you two." She stood by the stove cooking Sunday breakfast in her robe. "I'm sure, then, that you will be excited to return to camp today." She flipped a neat, round pancake onto a plate and handed it to Polly. "I bet you miss the kids."

Polly forced a smile. "Sure. It will be fun." She carried the plate to the table.

Though Polly was expected back at camp that afternoon, unfortunately her father couldn't bring her due to an out-of-town commitment. He was to give a talk to the Knights of Columbus in Burlington. Consequently, her mother had made arrangements for her to go with Father Mac and Tatum.

"Polly will gladly walk to the rectory," her mother told them. "There's no need to pick her up at our house."

Polly was furious. Why on earth had her mom made this arrangement where she'd have to walk by the men at the IGA store? Obviously her mother had no idea what it was like to hear their crude talk. The bench sitters were a bunch of riffraff, feeding on the slightest tidbit of gossip. They'd ribbed Polly more than once.

When she left the house with her small carrying case of camp clothes, she was ruffled. She did not want to return to camp, especially to face Freddie. And her stomach felt touchy as she recalled the tiff with Jubal. She was not looking forward to the long, hot walk ahead, but she kept quiet. She'd just walk to the rectory and take her chances with the old codgers gathered outside the store.

The Sunday afternoon was clear following the downpour the night before, and the rain had given her surroundings a fresh look. Today, she wore no makeup. For the approval of Mother Superior, she had put on a drab, gray skirt that hung below the knee, a white blouse, and white cotton socks with sneakers. It was also important to look as plain as possible for the bunch she was about to pass at the store. She did, however, have on a pair of large-lens white sunglasses that looked the part of class that some movie star might wear.

At the start of her walk, she passed the Brown Farm where it seemed quiet with nothing going on, but she knew better. By this time of day, Clyde would be dead drunk and probably Jubal would be inside the house with the newly acclaimed star in town, Lizzy Hick-Flam. Since it was Sunday, the store would be closed and Lizzy wouldn't have anything better to do than go to Jubal's house. What an opportunity for some afternoon smooching. Maybe they'd be practicing what they learned the night before—waltzing around the room or even keeping time to the recent hit, "Chattanooga Choo Choo," listening on Clyde's Philco. Polly was sure that Lizzy would be wiggling her butt and pressing her ample boobs to Jubal's chest, and he with his tongue hanging out like a hound dog, all excited over his armload. What a scene!

Oh yes. She knew the real thoughts, the night before, of Jubal Brown when he said, "I have no reason not to give Lizzy a ride." Baloney. Him acting as if he could take it or leave it, not caring that much for Lizzy. What a fake! Polly could see how he practically jumped out of his pants when approaching the talk of the town. He couldn't wait to get Lizzy in the car and give her a ride.

But that had given Polly a reason to dump him, which she'd planned on anyway. Good riddance! She bet next winter there would be proof of what she was sure was happening at the Brown's place this very minute. About the time the snow was two feet deep, Lizzy would be carrying a great big pumpkin, no longer the heroine she currently was, while Jubal would be in his barn wallowing in cow poop and regretting his little jack o'lantern that was about to arrive. Polly laughed as she left the Brown farm behind.

She continued along with her carrying case in her grip, thankful that she was smart enough to leave the farmer boy who was poor as dirt. She realized Freddie Coleman was a mistake, but before long she'd find a guy with promise who would propel her to the top.

The entrance to Jazz Crow's junkyard came up on her right as she descended the hill. Jazz was her father's arch enemy. For years, her dad had tried in vain to get rid of the god-awful mess that Jazz had piled up for all to see. Her dad couldn't look out his beautiful bay window onto Harmony Hill, but what acres of junk cars stared him in the face. To make matters worse, Jazz always packed the town meeting with his friends, causing her dad to be powerless in his motion to rid the town of junk cars. The vote always failed. Jazz was like the little mafia man in town, controlling his power levers out of his junkyard office.

Further on, Polly saw that Miss Curry was sitting out on her front step, her white hair aglow in the sun.

"Hello, Miss Curry. What a beautiful afternoon."

"Yes, Polly, it is. However, at the moment I'm terribly troubled, having just heard the news about our poor Maria."

"Yes, how awful!" Polly said. "We must pray and rally around her." She decided it was a good time to throw in a couple of white lies for the benefit of the sweet old lady. "Jubal and I are doing all we can for her. I just visited her before I left to meet my ride to CYO camp. She's clearly in shock."

Miss Curry stood and came to the edge of the sidewalk. "Oh, I know you're a wonderful help. That's good of you, dear."

Enjoying the compliment, Polly set down her grip for a moment. Though she hadn't brought much, as most of her clothes were already at camp, the case was growing heavy.

Miss Curry beamed. "You were one of my favorite students when I taught catechism. You never missed a class."

Polly smiled. "Thanks for saying that, Miss Curry." She picked up her case again and looked down the street. "Uh, I need to go or I'll miss my ride."

"Well, you run right along then. I'm waiting for Avery. He's taking me for a Sunday afternoon drive."

"How nice. I hope you have fun, Miss Curry."

"Oh, I'm sure I will," Miss Curry said, waving goodbye.

Polly started off in the direction of the rectory, waving back at Miss Curry with her free hand. As she walked on, she thought back to catechism class where she'd always made sure to sit at the front of the room. Every time the subject of premarital sex had come up, Miss Curry crossed her legs and sat up straighter than a poker. At the time, Polly thought the woman had a problem, perhaps bladder control issues causing her to sit so rigidly.

She tried to imagine having a date with Avery Ketchum—a picture sprang to mind of the old folks making out, looking like two dried prunes snuggled cheek to cheek. She laughed out loud, though the image was rather disturbing.

God, she did not want to get old. It looked like absolutely no fun at all. Of course, she was soon to be in the prime of her life, with babies and motherhood, and a gorgeous house to decorate—all on the horizon. She was sure she had the gift to make her home look amazing, just like the pictures she saw in *Ladies Home Journal* and *Better Homes and Gardens,* both sold at her father's store. But her beautiful house would not be in a podunk town like Hayesville. She'd watched how those in town treated her mother like an outsider, even after all these years—a "flatlander." At least her father had the church and the store to give him status amongst the locals. The appealing thing about Freddie had been the idea that maybe he could whisk her away from nowheresville.

Thinking of Freddie brought her back to the night before. First had been the dreamy dancing with his firm arm around her. He had such a handsome face and he was dressed head and shoulders above the rest of the hayseeds in town. But then in the car he had completely changed, all ugly and yanking at her jacket, even as she said no. She thought of Maria and what she must have experienced when attacked. Maybe she really should have gone to see her old friend. But she quickly shrugged it off—there simply wasn't time. She had to get back to camp.

As she neared the Hayesville IGA, she fumed that she did not want or need her mother's help in running her life. She could handle this bunch of guys herself. She just had to act calm and look them square in the eye. The group of six men were all in bib overalls and worn leather work shoes. It was Clem Gochy who spoke first.

"Well, now, here's a young lady that's leavin' town with her suitcase."

"Yes," Polly sniffed, glad to hide behind her large sunglasses. "I'm headed to CYO camp for the week."

Charlie Jones stepped from the crowd. "I heard tell Freddie Coleman teaches swimmin' at that camp. He's a bastard, the one that nearly kilt our Rose Queen. How dare he have his way with her and leave her fer dead!"

Polly felt a chill. "Do . . . do you know that for sure?" Goodness, maybe more than just her jacket had been in danger in that car.

Clem chimed in. "He's the likely one. And the son-of-a-bitch hung 'round flirtin' with Lizzy after like nothin' happened. Even tried ta take her ta the grange dance."

Several of the men shook their heads. "That's right! Lizzy'll tell ya. She's workin' in the store right now."

If Lizzy was in the store, then the afternoon love-o-rama between Lizzy and Jubal was only fantasy. Polly wasn't sure if she was disappointed or glad.

Charlie continued, "Yessiree, Lizzy said that Coleman fella stinks to high heaven like a perfume bottle spilt all over him, with the evidence lingerin' on poor Maria."

So, Lizzy was spreading word that Freddie was the guilty one who attacked Maria, as shown by the trail of his lilac cologne. Polly knew all about it since she had her nose buried in the overwhelming vapors while on the dance floor. It was strong stuff.

She tried to walk by the guys when Oscar Smith came over to stand in her way. His mess of gray hair stuck out from under his old fedora.

"Say," Oscar said. "I was at the grange dance and saw a fancy gal step up ta this Coleman character, pushin' fer a dance. Would ya know who that mighta been?"

"No. I wasn't there, Mister Smith." Was he messing with her? Had her looks changed that much? Maybe it was the sunglasses and no falsies.

Oscar peered closely at her face. "Well, that gal was sure a stranger ta me. Built like a brick backhouse with two round bricks outta place."

Everyone laughed.

Polly sidestepped from the guy's sour breath and whiskers that stuck out like a porcupine.

Clem scolded Oscar. "Now, old man, let the young lady pass." He turned to Polly. "Well it sure wan't you." He pointed. "Look at ya. Skinny as a rail, built like a lean racehorse that I'll bet can run a fast quarter-mile."

Polly pushed through those standing around her. "I guess I'll accept that as a compliment, Mister Gochy. See you guys." She hurried away.

Clem called out, "Stay away from that Coleman character. We don't want another one of our Hayesville gals wiped up off the floor."

Polly didn't answer, but she'd come to the same conclusion. Freddie Coleman was bad news.

Polly's trip to CYO camp was the height of boresville with Father Tee-hee Smiles talking to Tatum about church ledgers and other stuff she didn't care to understand. Of course, they totally ignored her as if she wasn't even in the car. She squeezed as tightly as possible next to the door in the back seat, at times wishing it would fly open and she could escape. She dreamed up a little fantasy. Once free, she'd stand at the side of the road in her movie star sunglasses and stick out her thumb to hitch a ride that would take her all the way to Burlington. There she would visit her friend Gertrude at her camp on Lake Champlain. Wouldn't her friend be surprised!

Her daydream was interrupted by Father Mac and Tatum talking about some gal named Mary Lou. They mentioned her "foredeck," "aft deck," and "outrigger." It sounded dirty, like they were discussing weird women's underwear or something. Apparently Mary Lou lived by the ocean. At the thought of water, Polly drifted back into her fantasy about Lake Champlain, but she took notice when the two men brought up Freddie and his leaky convertible roof. Father Mac shared that Freddie had apparently picked up this unbelievably sexy chick at the dance who worked at the CYO camp. He was talking about her! It was odd to hear a priest say, "sexy chick." Polly glanced sideways at Father Mac, noting how his pale face and red lips floated above his white priest's collar. She knew as a good Catholic girl that she was supposed to view him with respect, but in all honesty, the Father was kind of a drip, especially as he giggled about Freddie's date.

"Who was she?" the priest asked.

Polly turned her face to the window, afraid her embarrassment would give her away.

"That Coleman must be blind," Tatum said over the back seat. "Hey, maybe it's Mother Superior!" They both laughed at that.

As the conversation turned back to church business, Polly stared out at the passing scenery, amazed that her presence at the dance would stir up such talk. She breathed in the air from her open window only to get a whiff of manure as they passed field after field, some with tractors but most with horses pulling hay equipment like Jubal used. The thought of Jubal suddenly made her sad for her loss. There would be no more snuggling in his arms, or kisses. Now she felt stupid in casting him off. He was a nice, fun guy she'd always known. But she'd treated him as if there was a bushel of eligible guys just like him.

Yet . . . the life of a farmer's wife and the stink of the farm—it just wasn't what she wanted.

As they rolled past the agricultural activity, she grew sleepy with the ride to camp seeming to take forever. Dozing off, she lapsed into a dream about a boat ride with Jubal on the reservoir. She'd made him a lunch of egg salad sandwiches and lemonade, along with slices of three-layered chocolate cake that she'd baked special for him. It was just the two of them relaxing on a beautiful, sunny day.

In the boat she did not push herself on him, but was irresistible in her new bathing suit, a feminine pattern of small blue flowers on a cream background. The latest swimsuit top had a lot of extra padding to help her figure, while showing just enough to tease. Jubal noticed, melting at the sight of her clear skin in the afternoon light. Then he leaned over with a kiss and told her how beautiful she looked.

She awoke when Father Mac jostled her as he took off his suit coat and stretched out. It had become very warm in the car even with the windows rolled down. In minutes, the priest was dead to the world, sprawled across most of the back seat. His right hand flopped next to her with his white shirt sleeve unbuttoned and rolled up to reveal a tattoo of a boat with *Connelly's Mary Lou* in red beneath it. Maybe that was the gal they were just talking about, being a boat not a woman! Seeing the design and lettering on a priest struck Polly again as strange.

Father Mac was friends with this Coleman character. She wondered if Freddie really was the one who raped and beat up Maria. Everyone on the street seemed to think so, and if it were true, she could be moving right into a trap. She'd told Freddie that she was staying at the infirmary in the nurse's cabin. No doubt he would come calling. And then what would she do? As for her size and strength to defend herself compared to Maria, well, there was no comparison. Maria had the fight and determination of an American eagle, while she was a bony little hummingbird that Freddie could crush to bits with one hand. Her stomach collapsed inward to her backbone at the thought.

While the big car motored along, Polly grew terrified of her upcoming weeks at CYO camp. How could she have been so stupid as to have thrown herself at this dangerous no-count guy? Without a doubt, she'd end up like a skinned rabbit with no guts.

Chapter Twenty-Two

July 7, 1941: Clyde was spending his first full day locked in a room at the mansion with only reading material and his Philco. He'd insisted, if he was going to suffer, that the radio was worth lugging up to Lady Lamont's. Once Rose had dealt with Tatum to retrieve Benny, she'd come home and dealt with him—she blew her top about the liquor from the haymow and decided that to cure him once and for all of his love for the bottle, it would take a stronger method. Now he was in captivity with no further chance to talk her out of it. At intervals, Rose brought him small shots of whiskey to calm his nerves and ease the terrible transition to sobriety.

He'd immediately plugged his radio into a wall socket to track the world news, especially the latest horrors concerning Hitler.

Ponary, Lithuania: Reports are growing of mass murders of Jews and Poles. Sources say the killings are being carried out by platoons consisting mainly of Lithuanian volunteers.

"Well," he mused, "much as I hate this torture I'm endurin' thanks ta Rose, at least I can read my book without lookin' down the barrel of a gun." He listened to the report some more. "It just ain't right." He shook his head, scowling.

Impatient for his next drink, as stings of craving pulsed through him, Clyde looked out the only window, resting his elbows on the deep sill. The room was stone cold and the morning sun gave little relief from the dampness. Down on his farm below, he could see Jubal mowing the field of hay in back of the barn. The Belgian team stepped right along pulling the mower, and he guessed the crop must be light. Heavy hay yields were only common back when Lady Lamont's folks owned the farm. He knew he'd sucked the life right out of the soil, harvesting his hay crop year after year. He'd never given anything back to the land. But he wasn't going to focus on his failings.

Jubal had stirred his anger. Urging his ma to cut his own dad off at the knees! Clyde glared at the mowing activity off in the distance. Now he was locked up in a goddamned dungeon suffering a dry out. It came down to this: his boy had turned against him.

With nothing better to do, he watched the mowing for over an hour. When the field was nearly finished, he saw their old truck enter, traveling over the swaths of newly cut hay. Rose got out and spoke to Jubal. After she drove away, Jubal finished what was left and drove the team out of the field to the farmyard. He watched his son unhitch and water the horses and then take them on to the horse barn. After which, Benny and Jubal got into the waiting truck and it proceeded to the mansion.

The shakes were scampering up his arms and down his legs. His fingers had the dancing heebie-jeebies. "Goddammit! Rose better be comin' with my next drink, or else there will be hell to pay. If I could get out of this one-room prison, I'd sneak down ta Lady Lamont's liquor cabinet and fix myself up with a bottle. But Rose holds the key." He heard voices coming up the stairway. It was Rose and Benny. He put his ear to the door.

Rose spoke her instructions to her brother simply and clearly. "Now Benny, you sit right here in this chair, and I'll leave the key in the lock. Do not turn the key and let Clyde out unless there's a fire or an emergency."

"Where are ya goin'?" Benny protested. "Ya leavin' me here all alone?"

"You're going to be all right. Eugene's working downstairs in the shop and Lady Lamont is in her art room. I'm taking Jubal to get parts for the hay loader. We should be back by noon. Here are the comic books you like."

"Well . . ." There was a flutter of pages turning. "Okay, I guess."

Clyde banged on the locked door. "For chrissake! Rose, I need my drink!"

"Coming right up. I'll give you what's left in this bottle."

The key turned and she opened the door to pass him a bottle of bourbon. He tipped it up and inspected it in the light from the window. It was almost empty, barely enough to wet his lips.

His wife smiled brightly. "I'll have more for you at lunchtime," she said. She shut the door firmly and locked it.

As her footsteps retreated, he drained every pathetic drop, put the bottle down by his foot, and sent it skidding.

"Ya comin' right back, Rose?" Benny asked. His wooden chair squeaked.

Clyde could picture Benny jiggling in his nervous way.

"Yes, by noon," Rose said. "It won't be long." Her steps tapped down the stairs.

Clyde lingered close by the door, hungering for more bourbon. "That miserly woman. She ain't realizin' I need more so as I don't feel so sick!"

Initially, he'd gone along with the scheme in order to please Rose, thinking maybe it was time to fly straight. But he really had no desire to be dried out, what with the world and the farm both going to hell. Why would he want to face all that? No need. Things would fall apart with him drunk or sober. And drunk, as far as he was concerned, was a lot less painful.

He rapped softly on the door. "Hey Benny . . . Benny, will ya do me a favor?" His voice was almost a whisper, necessary to gain Benny's trust.

"Whaddya want, Clyde?"

"Turn that key, will ya?"

"I ain't 'sposed ta." Benny said in his flat tone. "There ain't no fire."

"I know, but I've gotta go or I'll piss my pants."

"Ya want me ta git ya another pair of pants? Rose will pass 'em ta ya when she comes."

"No, Benny!" He silently clenched his fists in the air and rolled his eyes. He lowered his voice again. "Listen . . . just turn the goddamned key! I'm dyin' Benny. I'm *dyin'*!"

"Rose said nothin' 'bout turnin' the key if ya were dyin'. She said I was ta open the door only if there was a fire or an ee–mergency. Dyin' ain't no fire and dyin' ain't no ee–mergency."

Clyde was not surprised by his inability to budge some understanding from Benny. Several moments passed as he paced the floor until his shaking grew so bad he thought for sure that he *was* going to die. No one would miss him if he did. He sat on the edge of the bed, bent over at the waist and hugging himself. He was on the verge of puking, his gut in a knot. His eyeballs felt on fire. He pictured the clear, shining bottles in Lady Lamont's liquor cabinet. Somehow he had to escape.

He staggered, still in a bent position, to sit by the door. "Benny, are ya awake?"

"Yup. Whaddya want, Clyde?"

"I wanna read ta ya."

Benny was silent. Then he let out a big sigh. "Clyde, ya ain't never read ta me before. Rose and Jubal do, but ya ain't never."

"I know, I know. But ya'll like this poem I found. Turn that old key, come through the door, and then ya can lock it and hold the key so I can't get out. I'll read ya this funny poem."

"But . . . Rose'll be mad."

"She'll never know. Ya can climb into a warm bed, all comfortable, and ya can hold the key while I read."

"That sounds nice." More silence. "I guess I could do that. If ya think Rose won't be mad."

"If she finds out, she'll be happy. She'd want ya to be warm, Benny. This old house is cold as an icebox."

Benny's chair scraped the floor and heavy footsteps came towards the door. Clyde stood and wavered, lightheaded. He retrieved his book from the bedside table and stepped back to the door just as the key turned.

Once in the room, Benny gave him a doubtful look. He fumbled to lock the door behind him, keeping the three-inch skeleton key in hand.

"Now, Benny, take off yer shoes and crawl in bed. I'll cover ya so ya'll be nice and warm."

"Okay." Benny crossed the room and sat on the edge of the bed to untie his shoes.

As he stood at the bedside, Clyde ignored his raw stomach and called on his patience for the minutes it took Benny to finish the task. Finally Benny climbed in and Clyde pulled the patchwork quilt over him.

"See? Nice, huh?"

Benny nodded, holding out his fisted hand. "I have the key."

"I know." Clyde was tickled with himself as he drew up a chair next to the bed. "Now, listen to this poem." He cleared his throat and began:

"'The Raggedy Man,' by James Whitcomb Riley:

O the Raggedy Man! He works fer Pa;
An' he's the goodest man ever you saw!
He comes to our house every day,
An' waters the horses, and feeds 'em hay;
An' he opens the shed—an' we all ist laugh
When he drives out our little old wobble-ly calf;
An' nen—ef our hired girl says he can—
He milks the cow fer 'Lizabuth Ann . . ."

Benny chuckled, "That's funny what yer readin'."

"Thought ya'd like it." Clyde continued.

"Ain't he a' awful good Raggedy Man?
Raggedy! Raggedy! Raggedy Man!"

Soon Benny's eyes closed and his next breath was a low snore. In minutes, the key dropped to the floor and Clyde snatched it up. Triumphant to have outfoxed Benny, he carefully emptied the clothes from his small yellow suitcase onto the floor without making a sound. With the empty case in one hand, he tiptoed to the door to insert the key. The lock turned and he was free.

Sneaking down the stairs, he could hear Eugene clattering around in the shop. A right turn led to the parlor and the liquor cabinet. Through the glass front he saw several bottles—gin, brandy, and bourbon. He yanked open the cherrywood doors and reached for a bourbon that appeared to have been opened. After pulling the stopper, he gulped a number of swallows and felt the familiar burning in his throat. An instant warmth spread through his body, dulling the sharp edges. He stoppered the bottle and stuck it in his suitcase, along with a few more unopened selections. He hated stealing from Lady Lamont, but without cash, he had no choice.

He exited the mansion with the suitcase and headed towards the milk room at his farm. There he sat on a metal can, taking occasional sips from the open bottle as he plotted his next move. It had become clear he would need to get out of Hayesville to live life as he wished. Rose would never give in to let him sit contentedly in his chair. And Jubal now carrying the load of the farmwork, day in and day out, was bound to keep at his mother to do something about his no-good dad. Rose and the boy would return shortly, so he needed a plan quick. He took another sip. Suddenly his son's bank full of cash came to mind.

He located the wooden mallet used to lift milk can covers and carried it into the house. The bank was on the bureau in its usual spot in Jubal's room, revealing through the glass the green wealth of Jubal's having turned his silver change into dollar bills. He picked the bank up and placed it on the bedside stand where he swung the mallet in a powerful blow to smash it. The booze he'd guzzled caused him to miss the bank, as well as the bed stand, with the mallet arcing down to give him a wicked blow to his knee. He howled in pain as he fell to the floor.

He rubbed his knee, wondering if some devil from Hell was looking out to punish him for stealing the bank which represented years of his son's hard work. But he was not a man to believe in God or saints and sinners. Yet, perhaps he was simply getting the message that the glass bank itself should be saved to return to Jubal someday. It would be up to him, in his leisure hours, to figure a way to retrieve the cash without destroying the bank. He liked the thought of such a challenge to pull dollar bills through the glass slot.

His knee pain was fading so he scrambled up off the floor to sit on the edge of Jubal's bed. Opening his case, he found that the rectangular glass bank fit snugly next to the full bottles of liquor and the opened one. To protect his precious cargo, he crumpled up sections of the *Hayesville Weekly,* which he'd found on Jubal's bed stand, stuffing the wadded-up paper between bottles to guard against breakage. He then left the farm, heading towards the village.

As he limped down Harmony Hill in the morning air, he felt for the first time in years a free man, fortified with some top-shelf liquor and a stash of money that would keep him going for weeks. His sense of well-being, though, was the result of Jubal's penny-wise nature, and this gave him the gift of guilt that he hoped wouldn't keep on giving, spoiling his future days. The mere thought prompted a need for a drink. He hid behind a stone wall at the edge of the road, opened his suitcase, and reached for the bottle. Removing the cap, he took several gulps. It felt good to rest his sore knee. He raised his pant leg and inspected the damage, finding a bruise. A small price to pay for freedom. After putting the whiskey bottle, now considerably emptier, back into his case, he stretched out for a snooze, the sun and drink melting him into total relaxation.

He was awoken by a rattle and clank on the road. He sat up to see black belches of smoke coming from his farm truck as it crawled up Harmony Hill. Cursing, he dropped flat to the ground behind the wall. As the truck passed, the springs creaked and the engine blew another dark cloud in his direction. When the engine noise finally faded, he left his hiding place and hightailed it towards town, stopping at the Hayesville store to inquire about a ride to Troy, New York, a place where he figured he could easily hide and not be found.

Oscar Smith and Charlie Jones were in their usual places on the bench just outside the store entrance. Oscar, the more talkative of the two, spoke first.

"Well, well, Clyde Brown. I thought ya'd be dead by now from livin' the high life up on Harmony Hill."

"Huh, it ain't no high life when yer wife cuts yer supply." Clyde took a seat on the bench. "Fellas, I need a ride ta Troy. I'm gettin' outta this hell hole."

Oscar raised his eyebrow and looked over at Charlie.

"What's in Troy?" Charlie asked.

"Oh, I'll get a room at a boardin' house, take in a picture show, stuff like that."

Oscar added, "And do a little drinkin'?"

"Well, yeah. But first I've got ta get ta Troy." Clyde held tightly to his yellow suitcase on his lap.

"Get a ride with Doc Small," Oscar said. "The Doc pulled inta town 'bout an hour ago. He's parked at the rectory—old Plymouth, New York plates."

Charlie leaned forward. "Whatcha got in that suitcase that yer holdin' so tight? Pot of gold or somethin'?"

Clyde gripped his possession. "Suit of clothes. Shavin' kit."

Oscar laughed and thumped Charlie on the knee.

Charlie grinned. "Clyde, you're a lyin' son-of-a-bitch. Ya probably just robbed Lady Lamont. Ya ain't doin' all ya say without some booze and a fist full of cash."

Without a word further, Clyde stood to go. He didn't need to answer to the two ragged men. As he carried his case down Main Street towards the rectory, the two guys roared with laughter. Clyde couldn't wait to get to Doc Small and the New York car. He was already craving his next drink, one he'd share for his ride if he had to. Once in Troy, he could do what he liked, answering to no one, especially clowns like Charlie and Oscar. Hopefully after passing some time there, living the free life, he could forget that he was just a lowdown thief who'd robbed his only son, as well as his wife's employer.

In minutes he'd made arrangements with Doc Small, a like-minded guy in his love for the bottle. Before long, he was settled in Doc's car and leaving town for good. As he and Doc passed the bottle between them, he had high hopes for his next chapter.

Chapter Twenty-Three

As soon as Jubal came home with his ma from their errand to buy hay loader parts, his uncle ran out from the mansion with the news.

"Clyde left!" Benny said, coming up to the truck.

"What?" Rose rolled down her window all the way and stuck her head out. "Benny, how did he get out? Where did he go?"

Benny threw up his hands. "I dunno. Clyde said I could hold on ta the key, and it musta dropped!" He paced beside the truck, obviously quite upset.

Inside the truck cab, Jubal exchanged a puzzled glance with his ma.

"He'll have to come back eventually," Jubal said. "He's got no money." He left the truck and walked over to his uncle, putting a hand on Benny's shoulder to ease his pacing. "Benny, it's okay. Let's go to the house for a bite to eat. What do you say?"

"Oh, oh, I dropped the key. I'm awful sorry, Rose," Benny moaned.

"Don't worry, Benny," she sighed, opening the driver's side door which gave a rusty squeak. "It's up to Clyde at this point what he does. Apparently he thinks he doesn't need us."

His mother headed over to Lady Lamont's to see if she could piece together what happened, and Jubal went to the house with Benny to fix him a sandwich and some milk. He had a hard time believing his dad had actually taken off.

After lunch, Jubal spent the afternoon working on the hay loader. He tried not to think about his dad, shrugging it off as a problem he couldn't solve. However, as he worked, he was forming a plan to avoid Benny discovering the smashed Packard. He'd keep his uncle from going up to the mow to throw down hay, instead doing the task himself. He knew Benny would give him no argument because years back a hobo had appeared from the shadows, having spent the night in the hay. The guy spooked Benny who scrambled down the ladder almost falling to the floor. Ever after, Benny had a lingering fear of the dark places in the mow. Though Jubal wasn't sure how he'd scrape together enough money to fix Benny's car, his ma had promised she'd work on a repair solution that night. Hopefully she'd still be able to help now that his dad had skipped town.

Satisfied to have a plan, Jubal worked with greater ease, replacing broken slats and tacking new rope in place on the bed chain that fed the hay onto the wagon. Before long, he was drenched with sweat from the muggy July heat. In need of a dry shirt, he went to his room. Right away, he missed his glass bank that would have been on the bureau in his line of sight. He whirled to see the wooden mallet on his bed and pages of the *Hayesville Weekly* scattered beside it.

"Damn, my bank!" he yelled. He flopped onto his bed next to the evidence in disbelief. "Dad stole my bank!"

He lay for some time while stunned at the stark reality. His dad knew how much the bank meant to him, and yet had taken it, probably for his booze. That's how far his father had fallen into his mental trap. But the deed was done. It wasn't fair— like many things in life, such as finding a dead cow, or rained-on hay, or facing dismal milk prices. Life was full of trouble and his dad was just such a problem. Now his dad had walked right out of their lives. Jubal got up from his bed, pulled on his clean shirt, and left for the barn where the cows were waiting.

As promised, Rose went that evening with her son to the haymow to inspect Benny's car. She ran a flashlight over the Packard's front end.

Even though Jubal had told her what he'd done, she was surprised by the damage from one rock.

"Jubal, my gosh!" She stood back, taking in the state of her brother's beloved car. It was going to cost considerable cash unless she could work a deal. "The only one I know that can help us is Jazz Crow," she declared.

Jubal stood beside her, his fingers tracing the car's silver door handle. "Won't Jazz talk?"

"Not if I tell him not to." She bent to touch the exaggerated curve of the bumper. "Jazz is an outlaw who doesn't mind keeping secrets for people he likes."

"I guess we don't have much choice," Jubal said.

She'd do what she could to get Jubal out of this fix. She didn't want Benny, who was already feeling bad that he'd let Clyde escape, to see what Jubal had done to the car. It was better to let Benny think the car had been stolen.

"I know we can trust Jazz." She turned to leave the mow. "Let's go talk to him now—he works late."

They both climbed into the old truck and as they rode along, she thought about how to present the problem to the junkyard owner.

"Jazz would love to put one over on Tatum," she told Jubal. "He can hide the car while fixing it. When it's done, he can park it somewhere in town, its sudden reappearance adding to its mystery."

Slumped in the passenger seat, Jubal nodded. She looked sideways at her son. Though she was not happy about the car or his behavior that had caused the damage, the poor kid had been hit with a lot lately.

When they reached the junkyard, Jazz's German shepherd, Babe, sat on the other side of the fence ready for her night duty. Not far from the dog, Jazz, in his greasy coveralls and cap, was getting ready to close. He looked up when hearing their vehicle and met them under the yard light.

With a friendly smile, he leaned on the truck door. "Hey, it's Rose Brown and Jubal. Been ages. What've ya folks been up ta?"

She turned off the engine. "Hello, Jazz. I'm wondering if you've heard about Benny's Packard?"

"Yeah. That's a bum deal. Sorry it was stolen." He signaled to Babe and the dog dropped obediently at his feet.

"Well, it wasn't . . . stolen, that is." Rose looked pointedly into the older man's gray eyes, willing him to take their side. "It's on our barn floor. It, uh, needs some work."

"No foolin'! Didn't think that car ever got drove." Jazz stepped back and removed his cap to scratch his thick, graying hair. "What kinda work?"

"Oh, not much," she said. "Just a new fender and maybe a bumper. Want to see it?"

Jazz raised a pair of eyebrows that reminded Rose of two wooly caterpillars. "That right? Now then, seems I heard a little bird tell me there was a bit of a chase 'round with that car the night it was *stolen*. This wouldn't have anything ta do with that?"

"Just maybe," she replied. She wasn't going to share more unless absolutely necessary.

Jazz leaned in the window, looking across the seat at Jubal who kept a poker face. After another long scratch of his head, Jazz seemed to come to a decision. He put his cap back on his head.

"Well sure, why not. But just so's ya know, I ain't got no '36 Packard on the lot. I'd have ta order parts."

"That's fine." Rose said quickly. "Jump in and I'll take you up to the car."

"I was 'bout ta go home, but I guess I can come." Jazz reached down to scratch Babe between the ears. "Ya know, when I leave, my girl here keeps an eye on things." He opened the passenger door and Jubal slid to the middle. Once settled, Jazz remarked, "Gosh, Jubal, I ain't seen ya since ya stopped pedalin' papers."

"I know," Jubal nodded. "I don't have much time to stop for a visit."

"Well, yer alright," Jazz said, chuckling. "I had ta work hard growin' up too. It ain't hurt me none."

In minutes, the three were in the haymow inspecting the car. Jazz's thick eyebrows dipped as he took in the damage. "My God, Rose, this'll cost ya!"

She wasn't surprised. "How much?"

He shrugged. "Don't really know. As I said, ain't got a '36 Packard in the yard."

Confident she'd work out a way that Jazz could get the job done, she said, "Order the fender and bumper."

"Let's see . . ." Jazz stood in thought. "Well now, Sean O'Grady deals in new stuff."

Rose shook her head. She couldn't risk another guy in the area knowing about this.

Jazz lifted his brows. "Or . . . maybe Sean O'Grady ain't ta know 'bout this?"

Rose nodded. "You're getting the idea."

Jazz turned to Jubal. "Son, ya crashed up this here car?"

"Yeah. Kind of dumb, huh?"

"Ya mean Hayesville's big shot sheriff don't know 'bout this?"

Jubal had a hangdog expression. "Nope."

"God, boy!" Jazz laughed heartily. "I heard this car disappeared in Avery's cornfield the other night without a trace."

"Having cultivated for Avery twice, I knew how to avoid damaging his corn," Jubal explained.

Jazz gave Rose a knowing look. "Yer boy has ta be one helluva driver ta pull that off."

"Well, we were lucky to have had a cloudburst to smooth over the tire tracks," she said.

Jazz was into the details. "Tatum reported no lights and no damaged corn. He's sure wonderin' whatever happened to this here car. How'd ya not trample the corn with no lights?"

"With a flashlight low to the ground," Jubal said. "I followed the row in the pouring rain—"

Rose nudged Jubal before he mentioned Lizzy. The girl wouldn't appreciate being involved in the story of the missing car. Changing direction, she asked, "So you think you can fix it soon, Jazz?"

Jazz bent to look again at the crashed front end. "I won't lie to ya. It's gonna cost a lot ta get this back in shape. How 'bout ya send yer boy down for a couple hours nights after chores and supper? Say 'round seven. He can work off the cost."

Jazz's offer was reasonable, generous even. Yet, she worried about adding extra work to Jubal's day. He already had quite a load, and with school starting up at the end of the summer, another job was a lot to manage. But they didn't have the money to buy costly parts and pay Jazz for all the labor.

She turned to Jubal. "What do you think?"

"Sure, I can do that," Jubal agreed.

Jazz continued with his plan. "For fixin' the car, I'll keep it hid. My guys'll keep it quiet. We don't take kindly ta Tatum and his lot. 'Sides, I'm up for reelection at March town meetin' and needin' all the votes I can get. This way I got a few from Harmony Hill I can count on."

Rose saw no need to mention that she was, at the moment, minus one husband, and thus one vote. "Sure, Jazz. You can count on us."

Jazz grinned. "Way ta go!" He paused. "And would ya work on Hammer fer a vote as well?"

"I'll see what I can do," she said. "But Clyde's brother is an odd one. I can't promise Hammer won't do just as he likes." She stuck out her hand. "Do we have a deal?"

"Fair 'nough." Jazz shook her hand with his own oil-stained one. He walked to the door of the mow and looked out. "Far past supper now." He returned to the Packard and reached for the door's silver handle. "Just 'bout the right time ta sneak this here car down the hill in the dark," he said, climbing in. He fired up the engine, backed the car out of the mow, and proceeded down the hill.

Rose watched, with Jubal at her side, until the red tail lights swung in the turn to the junkyard.

"Boy, I'm relieved to have that car gone from the mow," Jubal commented.

"Right. Now Tatum won't find it if he comes calling," she said.

"That, too. But more because I won't have to keep Benny out of the mow."

"No, I suppose you won't."

They walked together towards the house. She was relieved to have Jazz on their side fixing the Packard in trade for Jubal's work. At least she could cross one problem off her list. Her next task was to fix a late dinner for Jubal and Benny. Then she thought of Clyde. With the Philco still up at Lady Lamont's, the house would be quieter than usual. However, with all the upset of the past few days having felt like a few weeks, quiet was okay. At least for tonight.

As mealtimes came and went, Jubal sat with his ma and Benny around the table where they all tried their best to ignore his dad's empty place. But when he finally revealed the theft of his savings bank, he'd never seen his ma so angry. Even so, she said she would not chase around to try and find Clyde who showed no willingness to be cured. If he didn't come home by his own free will, she predicted he would spend the rest of his days a hopeless drunk and possibly homeless. Figuring she was probably right, Jubal, for the time being, set aside any hope of his dad's return.

Instead, he thought often about the welfare of Maria, making occasional visits to see Lizzy down at the store to discuss the situation. Lizzy had tried to visit Maria, but Maria was keeping to herself, usually in her room with the curtains drawn. And Avery had reported that when he did see Maria about the farm, she was in a stupor.

Jubal had witnessed Maria's deadened state himself only a couple of days after the parade. The Monday they'd gone to Rutland for hay loader parts, his ma had stopped at the Hayesville IGA on the way home to pick up some Rheingold, figuring small amounts of the beer would keep Clyde from getting the shakes too badly while he dried out at Lady Lamont's. Earlier that day, she'd rationed to his dad the last bottle of booze found in their house.

While Jubal had waited for his ma in front of the store, he'd been excited to see Maria in her folks' car when Kathleen Styles pulled up next to the truck. But Maria had looked awful. She wouldn't even talk to him. The image of her pale face and how she had turned away left him terribly worried.

Lizzy agreed that it might help Maria to emerge from her fog if he were to bring Trueboy to the Styles' home. So one day, he set aside time before night chores to finally go and see Maria. In preparation, he asked Benny to bring Trueboy in from the pasture and give him a good brushing.

"I'll go up to the mow to throw down hay for tonight. Then I'm leaving," he told Benny.

"Yes Jubal. I'll get Trueboy 'n brush him fer ya."

After taking care of the hay, Jubal went to the house for a quick sandwich and a change of clothes that didn't reek of the barn. Not that Maria would care, but her mother might. In his bedroom, he glanced sorrowfully where his bank had been. Now he owned nothing except for the clothes he wore and his old rusty bike. His savings gone, he could think of no solution to regain his loss. Maybe Polly was right—he'd never amount to anything. Thinking of Polly reminded him that he also no longer had a girlfriend. At least he still had his ma, who cared a great deal for him, and of course they both looked out for Benny. Then there was Lizzy who seemed to orbit his life in a puzzling way. He enjoyed her company. She often made him laugh, and he supposed she could now be counted as a friend.

His attempt to help Maria was a stab in the dark. He wasn't expecting her to welcome his visit. In fact, he'd be lucky if she would see him at all. Out in the yard, Benny held Trueboy by his halter while feeding him a fistful of hay.

"Good job with the brushing, Benny. Don't think I've ever seen him look this good." He reached for Trueboy's halter. "Can you please go to the barn and get the cattle sprayer so we can drive away the horse flies? And we'll need his bridle."

While waiting for Benny to return, Jubal let go of Trueboy's halter as the horse reached down to nibble the grass growing next to the barn's foundation. He knew Trueboy would stay by his side, remaining always gentle and calm—just the right companion for Maria who likely felt she was living in a world that was no longer safe.

When Benny returned, Trueboy stood still to let the oily mist from the pump sprayer float down over him. Once the horse was covered with the sharp odor that flies avoided, Jubal made the change from halter to bridle and led Trueboy to the back of the truck. He stepped up on the bumper and jumped on Trueboy's broad back. Then he turned and waved to Benny who was already headed back towards the barn.

The late afternoon was hot without a cloud in the sky, and Jubal enjoyed the easy sway of the big horse plodding down Harmony Hill. But shortly he was overcome with doubt. He'd never been to the Styles' home and he didn't know Maria's mother, Kathleen, very well. Maria was their only kid brought up in a protective Catholic household. Again, he wondered what Maria hadn't told him about what had gone on at CYO camp. It was hard for him to figure how his friend had fallen prey to a guy like Freddie Coleman.

When Jubal rounded a curve after riding for about a half-mile, the gravel road passed Avery's AKL stone. He frowned at the hulking object that had done in Benny's car. Avery was a crazy old guy in some ways, but it was what he liked about him. And in spite of the trouble the stone had caused him, Jubal knew he had no one to blame but himself.

He rode into the driveway that ran along in front of Avery's cornfield and ended next to a spacious garden beside the tenant house where Maria lived. From a distance, he saw Kathleen scuffing the soil with a hoe. She didn't look up, though she must have heard them coming. Jubal pulled back on the reins as Trueboy drew near the porch. They were now only some feet away, but Kathleen still didn't react.

"Hello, Mrs. Styles," he called. Trueboy's ears turned at the sound of his voice.

Kathleen stood, holding the hoe with one hand. Her hair was pulled back in a tight bun and she wore a full-length dress with a flower-print apron. As he sat on Trueboy, she turned his way, but offered no welcoming smile. Her blue eyes were striking, similar to Maria's.

"You want somethin'?" she finally asked. She leaned the hoe against a garden stake and rubbed the soil from her hands. She obviously wasn't happy to see him.

"I'm Jubal Brown. A friend of Maria's."

"Yes, I've seen you."

Her high cheekbones gave her a severe look.

"Is Maria home?" he asked.

She looked up at the second story of the house and back at him. "She's ailin'."

He ran his hand over Trueboy's neck. "I wanted her to see this big boy. We used to ride him as kids. He's a great horse." He glanced up and happened to see the edge of an upstairs curtain move.

Kathleen walked over and patted Trueboy's forehead. "He's a nice fella."

"He really likes treats," Jubal said. "He'd maybe like a carrot . . . if they're big enough." He looked towards the garden.

Kathleen went to the garden where she pulled a half-grown carrot and wiped it free of dirt. Trueboy let out a low, rumbling whinny. She broke off the top and held the carrot out on her flat palm until the horse wrapped his lips around the treat.

As Trueboy crunched, Jubal saw the second-story curtain move again. The horse nudged Kathleen for another carrot, and she actually smiled while stepping back to pull one more from her garden plot.

The front door opened and Maria slipped through, coming out to stand on the porch. She was wearing a man's dress shirt with the tails hanging over the pockets of her jeans, her black hair still uncombed. The bruises he'd seen on her face at the IGA were now a sickly yellow. She didn't look at him, only at Trueboy. She came down the steps, holding her arms wide. Trueboy lowered his head and she buried her face in his neck and mane. The only sign that she was crying was a slight shaking of her shoulders.

Surprised, Jubal slid down off the horse and backed away. He turned to Kathleen, not knowing what to do. "Can I pull a couple more carrots?"

Kathleen nodded and sat on the porch.

Jubal took his time getting the carrots while Maria kept her face buried in Trueboy's neck, her fingers wrapped in his silver mane. The horse appeared to have caused her misery to burst like a broken water pipe. He fed Trueboy the treat and sat down on the steps to wait.

After a few minutes, Maria pulled away and he went to her. "Take him for a ride," he offered. He locked his hands. "Here's a boost."

Without a word, she placed her foot in the cup of his fingers, sliding easily up onto the horse's back. She bent forward to cling with her arms on either side of Trueboy's neck while wrapping her long legs around his belly. The horse turned and headed down the driveway. Jubal sat again on the steps, keeping a careful distance from Kathleen who watched her daughter as the horse trod alongside the cornfield.

"No one understands," Kathleen said. "Only the good Lord knows."

"I'm sorry," he replied.

"She's taken to your horse," she said.

Maria was now sitting up tall, having picked up the reins.

"She can keep him here," he said, "if she'll ride him to the farm day after tomorrow. The weather looks clear, so I'll mow some hay. Maybe, when she comes, she could lead him on our hayfork? The last hay I cut got ruined in a downpour." He stopped, not meaning to share his poor timing in drying hay.

Kathleen made no remark about his loss of hay. "Yes, I think she'd like to keep the horse for a spell. And I'll send them up to help with the hayin'. You walkin' home?"

Jubal nodded. "Looks that way." He stood to go and Kathleen stood as well, brushing her hands on her skirt.

"Well, best get back to my gardenin'," she said.

As he walked the gravel drive, Maria was now headed back to the house. She avoided looking at him, but she seemed peaceful as she sat up on the big horse.

"Good boy," she murmured, patting Trueboy.

As Jubal continued on, he felt lighter. The two, horse and girl, were a good match. As hard as it had been to risk intruding on Maria's pain, what he'd just done was worth it. When Maria showed up to help with the haying, he'd be curious to see what other positive changes might have come over her.

Maria's torment eased some while riding Trueboy as he clopped along at a slow walk. She felt safe in a world all her own, the horse being a mountain of strength beneath her. It gave her something else to think about besides her attack.

Most details of the rectory after the parade lay hidden beyond a black wall, a dividing line she was unable to cross. Yet fragments of images struck her—flashing on and off, terrifying. They appeared at odd moments, gripping her entirely. She'd gasp for air, feeling a chokehold on her neck. Sometimes it was hands pawing at her. The memory of the smell was the worst of all, a flowery stench that turned her stomach even in recall. Was it cologne or some kind of liquor? Then there was the sweat, slick under the weight of her attacker. Last came nasty words no innocent girl should ever hear.

All of it made her want to scream. She tried to see the face of her attacker, but could not. Her dad was in a rage to beat the hell out of the guy. If she could picture the guy, she had a hope of landing him behind bars, locked up tight. She suspected it was Freddie, but then again, Lizzy's two brothers had been awful, calling her "Queenie."

But the face never came. How long had she been knocked out? Sometimes anger boiled up, but mostly she wanted nothing more than to stay numb and hidden.

When she'd left the house on Trueboy, her ma told her how Jubal said she could keep the horse as long as she helped with the hay. It would be hard, but going up to the Brown farm was maybe something she could manage.

Riding beyond Avery's, she headed up a logging road towards Hayesville Mountain—a place where her dad and Ned sometimes cut firewood.

She had no plans. When her fear got bad, she had often imagined riding on a cloud in a wide blue sky, but she didn't have to today because she was on Trueboy.

They were about to pass a pile of stacked wood that had yet to be brought down to the farm. A gray squirrel sat on top of the pile with an acorn between its paws. Even though it was only mid-summer, it was already storing food for the long winter ahead, or maybe taking the nut to a litter of young. Seeing horse and rider, the squirrel dove between chunks of wood, flicking its tail as a warning. They continued to climb on the path with trees leafed out in green creating a canopy over the trail.

They came upon an opening where there was once an old homestead. Only the foundation remained and a tree growing nearby was loaded with early summer apples. She stopped Trueboy in the shady, dark woods to watch a doe nibbling on early drops. The deer's half-grown fawn had most of its white spots and was unaware of being watched. When the doe caught scent of them, she wagged her white tail, stamped her hoof, and darted into the woods with the little one following. Had Maria been a poacher, the doe could have been shot, dropped in her tracks. But now the whitetail lived to see another day. Maria thought how if she'd had a chance to run like a deer on that horrible day, things would have been different.

She rode Trueboy over to the tree where the horse was eager to sample a few soft apples that had dropped to the ground. After Maria pulled him away, they continued on until reaching a breathless view looking down over Avery's farm—his big cornfield with rows and rows of dark green leaves growing under the midday sun. Avery was walking towards the barn. Her ma was, as usual, working in their garden. The picture was almost complete with Ned pushing the lawn mower and her dad in the yard fixing the rake. She, of course, was not in the scene today. Tears filled her eyes. She'd always been a part of that picture. Instead, her life had changed into an echoing darkness she could not understand.

The sun dimmed as a cool breeze blew in a few clouds from the west, causing Maria to shiver and turn Trueboy for home. She continued to keep a lookout for wildlife while going down the mountain. She spotted a robin tending her young in a nest of grass and twigs tucked back on a low branch, and shortly after, a garter snake slid across the path and under a rock. Approaching the yard, she heard the clank of her dad's tools as he worked in the shop. He must have seen her coming since he appeared and stood waiting.

"How's it goin' on that fella?" he said, as she rode up to him.

She rubbed Trueboy's neck. "It's good."

Her dad looked down at Trueboy's hooves. Maria had noted when going out for her ride that they were overgrown and chipped.

"Poor fellow seems a little neglected," she said.

Her dad looked the horse over with an expert eye. "I can make this big guy feel a lot better if I trimmed them feet and put shoes on him," her dad said. "Guessin' the Browns ain't got much cash fer a farrier, seein' as I trimmed their team back in the spring. No matter. Got a few shoes in the shop I can adjust ta fit."

"Would you do that?"

He nodded. "Looks he could use a feed of oats and a bit of our good pasture grass too, get some weight on him."

Her dad always knew the best thing that could make a critter feel better. But lately, he hadn't known what to do to fix her pain. The sorrowful way he looked at her across the table during meals made her heart ache even more. But his offer to shoe and care for Jubal's horse reached her.

Her dad took hold of Trueboy's bridle. "We'll get ya fixed up big fella," he said, stroking the horse's white blaze. He glanced up. "Things'll get better."

"Yeah, I hope so."

He turned away and she watched his stiff stride as he made his way back to the shop. Though a man of few words, his emotions ran deep.

Later that evening after supper, Maria lay in bed burrowed under her covers. This time, instead of fighting back tears and imagining her clouds, she planned where to go riding the next day. She was happy Trueboy's hooves were getting shod, as promised by her dad, because she knew all sorts of wooded trails they could explore, just the two of them.

Before long she was riding Trueboy home from Jubal's after a day of haying and helping him with his chores. Jubal had encouraged her to take Trueboy home again on loan. In just a short time, she'd grown to love the horse who always whinnied when she approached his stall with a generous feed of oats.

While working at the Brown farm, she could forget for a while how her attacker had stolen her purity and innocence. Equally important, he'd destroyed her confidence. Sometimes her feelings of guilt and worthlessness were so strong that a sharp knife drawn across her wrists seemed the best way out. But only sometimes, because then she would ride out into the woods on Trueboy where the songs of birds and the rhythm of the horse filled her with hope that this horrible thing would someday pass.

The oddest part was that whenever she passed the AKL stone, it frightened her. The glossy shine of the letters jumped out and triggered an unbelievable anxiety. Avery's barn on sunny days was a problem, too, when bright light struck the newly painted surface. One night she dreamed that the whole front of the barn collapsed, crushing her under the timbers. Nightmares came often and in the morning, she'd leave for Jubal's in darkness so she could pass the farmyard and the AKL stone without seeing them clearly.

She found Jubal okay to work around. Drawn to him still, she felt he was a trusted friend, but all the romantic thoughts she'd had for him were gone, wilted like flowers. Doing farm work with Jubal made life seem once more predictable, almost normal, though that didn't last. She didn't talk to him much. He likely knew the details of what had happened. God, she'd been raped. Surely there were whispers passed around Hayesville, breaking open her innermost privacy for all to see. And it was nearly all her fault. She'd put herself in a position to be noticed. First by flirting with Freddie. Then as the awful Rose Queen, dressed up like a model and paraded through Hayesville.

She thought back to her attempt to ask Jubal for help when she needed it and how she hadn't trusted to tell him enough. She also wondered why Tatum hadn't arrested Freddie when the creep literally tore into Cabin Ten. There was a mystery. Something fishy lay between Freddie, Tatum, and Father Mac.

Chapter Twenty-Four

Jubal was just finishing milking when a new Dodge pickup came in the yard. A tall, young guy wearing a fedora and casual clothes got out and walked towards him.

"Hi," the stranger said, extending his hand. "I'm Chuck Dent, your Hayesville County agricultural extension agent."

"My what?" Jubal was struck with fear. Had this agent with the fancy title come to take their farm?

"This is the Brown farm, right?" Chuck said. "Lois Lamont called and asked me to stop by. I'm here to see if you want my help. "

To Jubal's knowledge, this guy was the first to call Lady Lamont "Lois."

Chuck responded to his puzzled look. "Lois is the eyes and ears of the county, directing me to where I'm most needed."

"Oh." Jubal relaxed. "You've come to the right place because Ma and I sure need a lot of help."

"Lois especially wants your folks' farm to keep going. She loves seeing the cows." Chuck seemed amused by this reason.

"I know," Jubal said. "She raves about how peaceful they look while out grazing."

"Lois is a big supporter of area farmers." Chuck glanced towards the barn. "Would you take me to look around a bit?"

"Sure thing."

"Great! I might have a few ideas for you." Chuck turned to the back of his truck. "First, the Hayesville County Farm Bureau owns this battery-operated electric fencer. Lois has offered that I put it up on her front lawn." Chuck pointed to the green metal fencer about the size of a shoebox.

Jubal looked with interest at the unfamiliar object.

"This model has recently come on the market."

"Really, I never knew. . . ." Jubal said.

"The internal works here can transmit an electrical charge onto a connected wire every half second," Chuck explained. "The charge is shown on the fencer by a blinking red light the size of a silver dollar. Here, give me a hand. In a few minutes, I'll show you how it works."

"I'd be glad to." Jubal was curious to see this gadget running. Barbed wire fencing was hard work even with Benny's strength.

Chuck backed his truck to the edge of the Lamont property. With a hammer, they pounded in the stakes. Then they strung the fence wire on white porcelain insulators and connected the wire onto the fencer. From the unit, Chuck attached a copper ground wire and drove in a metal post. In seconds, they saw the red light and heard the *click, click, click* of the portable electric fencer. Chuck even had a wooden handle for the electric gate.

Jubal stood amazed. "What will the fence do to the cows?"

"Oh, nothing," Chuck shrugged. "Once given a light shock, they won't go near it."

"What a help this will be! Now my Uncle Benny won't have to watch the cows when we put them on new grazing."

Chuck put the hammers in the back of his truck. "You can use this for the remainder of the grazing season. I've already demonstrated it on several farms."

"Wow, thanks!" Jubal stood by the truck, wondering what other neat ideas this guy had up his sleeve.

"Show me around and I'll see if I have some more suggestions."

"I can do that," Jubal said.

They walked towards the barnyard and immediately heard the roar of the bull from inside the barn.

"When's the last time you used him?" Chuck asked.

"Well . . ." Jubal hated to tell all of their failings. He already knew he and his ma were lousy dairy farmers. Since his dad changed occupations, they were running on empty and sort of lost. "To be honest, the bull scares me. My dad, he used him late last winter. But my dad's not around now."

"Late winter?" Chuck frowned as the bull bellowed again.

"Yeah, I know that's a problem. In months, the herd will go bone dry, cows won't be pregnant, and we'll be out of business."

"Look, I don't know if you realize this, but Lois thinks you're a great kid, and she wants me to help you change a few things."

"I'm sure there's quite a lot we could do differently." To hear that Lady Lamont thought highly of him made Jubal want to shape up and make more of himself.

They reached the barnyard where the cows were resting in the shade near a cement water tub. Chuck looked them over, commenting that they were thin and in need of some good feed. Jubal agreed. A few cows stood watching the newcomer curiously. A couple of them stretched, shooting a stream of loose, green manure.

"Gosh, all that lawn grass is giving them the runs," Jubal commented.

Chuck laughed. "More like what should be coming from a high-producing cow. Hard, stiff manure tells us the herd isn't making much milk."

"I didn't know that. But I do know that our cows are a bunch of strippers—most don't give quarts but tea cups."

"Tell you what," Chuck said, "you weigh the milk from each cow tonight and tomorrow morning. Then pick six of your poorest producers that aren't carrying a calf. From what you've told me, few in the herd are bred if the last time that bull was used was this past winter."

"I didn't dare set him loose on the cows. No telling what he'd do. I sometimes think if he had a chance he'd kill me. So he never leaves the pen."

"He sounds dangerous. I'm sure you've heard it's not uncommon for dairy farmers to get badly hurt or killed by a bull. My dad was one of the first farmers in our area that went to AI, especially with us kids around."

"What's AI?" Jubal asked.

"Artificial insemination."

Jubal was at a loss to understand.

"We breed the cows without a bull," Chuck explained. "Someday, I'll tell you more about it and perhaps your farm could do AI. But let's focus on what we can do in the short-term." Chuck took a walk around the barn to become familiar with their situation. "Tomorrow morning we'll load up a couple of trucks with that bull and the poor producers you select. Then I'll bring in a gentle, young sire you can run with the herd. I know of a yearling Ayrshire that would fit here just fine."

"What a relief that would be. But . . . we can't pay for another bull."

"He'll be on loan. All you'll have to do is feed him and take good care of him."

The old knot-head roared again, loud enough to rattle the windows. Jubal scowled in the direction of the sound. "It'll be tough loading that jerk."

Chuck smiled. "You'll be surprised how well he'll climb aboard the truck with a couple of cows ahead of him."

Jubal had his doubts on dealing with the bull. As a young kid, he had gone with his dad to help Avery load a nasty Jersey bull, since Chester was sick with the flu. The trucker handled the animal with a staff held high connected to the bull's ring, which rendered the beast powerless by keeping the animal's nose pointed skyward. His dad and Avery were pushing on the bull's butt to get him to climb the ramp when suddenly the trucker lost his footing and fell, landing at the backend of the truck. The momentary freeing of the upward pressure on the staff allowed the bull to lower his head, giving him the strength of his head and neck. The beast whipped his head in several directions, tearing the staff from his nose. In seconds, the bull turned in a roar, charging after Avery and Clyde who hid behind a full wagon of hay. The bull rammed his head and neck under the wagon rack, lifting one side off the ground. Luckily, the two men sprang from behind the wagon before it rolled to dump the hay in the yard.

His dad split for the barn and made it to safety while Avery ran for his house to get his shotgun. The bull continued to roar and push great mounds of loose hay around the yard. Avery fired his weapon from his porch steps, dropping the bull in his tracks. Out of harm's way, high up in the open outside door of the haymow, Jubal and Maria had watched, wide-eyed. Immediately a very angry Avery called the butcher who soon arrived on the scene. In a few days, the Brown household was treated to several pounds of hamburg.

Though this memory was especially vivid, Jubal had to trust Chuck on loading the bull if he was to be free of the beast.

As promised, the next morning Chuck and two cattle trucks pulled in the yard. Jubal had marked six cows that produced almost nothing and from his dad's sloppy records, they didn't appear to be with calf. The first cattle truck backed up to the barn door. Since the barn sat higher than the ground outside, the bull and cows didn't have much of a climb up the ramp onto the truck.

The two truckers were skilled in handling the bull and the first two cows. With the cows out of their stalls, the bull roared after them, running towards the end of the barn. The cattle clambered up the ramp onto the truck with the bull right behind. Immediately, one trucker slammed the truck's rear gate, shutting the ornery beast in with the two cows. Jubal watched the whole process with Chuck from a spot well out of the way.

"See?" Chuck said. "Worked like a charm. That old knot-head was plain pent up to get to some cows."

"I won't be sorry to see him go."

"Don't blame you. Now wait until you see what I've got for you."

The second truck backed to the door and the driver got out and lowered the tailgate to lead a yearling bull off the truck—a beauty that was tall for his age and angular, with a hide soft as velvet. Chuck explained that the animal had been shown many times at the fair so he now handled like a pet kitten—with no horns and without that awful roar.

"The owner wants you to use him for a year and then he'll take him back," Chuck said.

"Wow! I'm still surprised we don't have to buy him." From his father's records, Jubal knew the bull they'd loaded on the truck had proven worthless, costing the farm in being too difficult to handle. Having the use of a gentle yearling that could easily run with the cows would benefit them.

"This farmer has several bulls on loan. He does this because the user grows the bull without a cost to the owner. That way you and the owner can both be winners."

"Sounds reasonable. What's the bull's name?"

"Peaceful Valley Dynamo," Chuck said, taking the halter to lead Dynamo to his new stall. "Run him full-time with your herd and get these cows bred. By next May you'll have a bunch calving. In the meantime, we'll use your beef money to buy two or three heifers that will calve soon."

As they talked, the remaining beef cows were loaded on the second truck. When all were secure, Chuck said, "We have some great weather coming up. Mow a big jag after breakfast. If it stays hot, your hay can go in the barn tomorrow afternoon."

Jubal could see the guy was always thinking ahead. He vowed he'd try to carry out his farm work the same way.

Before Chuck got in his truck, he noted, "I saw a few yearlings at a distance in a field that looks overgrazed. You ought to park a wagon in that pasture with some hay."

The agent's last suggestion made Jubal feel he'd done almost nothing right since he'd shouldered the farm in place of his father. "I'll give them some that I've just mowed," he said.

Chuck left the yard with a wave out the window and Jubal watched the two cattle trucks following. Things were looking up. He spent some time making sure the new bull was settled, admiring the animal that seemed well-bred and in peak condition. Walking to the house for breakfast, he was humming under his breath, only to have his heart sink as Tatum pulled into the yard.

The sheriff parked in a cloud of dust as if in a hurry. He pulled up his gun belt when leaving the car, scanning the property with the importance of a detective hunting for a runaway criminal. "Seen Benny's Packard yet?"

"Nope. Not this morning." Jubal looked over at the barn and then down at his dirty barn clothes. "But then again, I've had no time to cruise the roads looking."

"Well, this whole mystery of your baby blue Packard vanished into thin air ain't gonna get by me. If and when I find it, somebody's gonna be landin' their ass in jail!"

Jubal frowned. "Well, keep working on it. It's got to show up sometime." He turned on his heel, heading for the house. In a few seconds, a car door slammed behind him and the engine started. After Tatum drove off, Jubal let out a sigh.

In the kitchen, he found Benny seated at the table shoveling in cereal like he was filling an empty pit.

"Geez, Benny, can you slow down a little and chew your food?" He playfully tapped his uncle on the arm. "Listen, after you eat, would you get the horses in from the pasture and brush them? I've got to sit down and talk to Ma."

"Sure, Jubal." Benny wiped some milk off his chin with a napkin. "I like brushing the horses."

As his uncle went outside to get the horses, Jubal called out, "Ma?"

"Yes, Jubal? What do you need?" Her voice came from outside at the clothesline.

"Got a minute to talk?" He peered down the empty hall. In moments, she appeared, holding a bundle of clothes.

"Have you heard anything from Dad?"

"Nope." She set her armload down on the table and began folding. "I'll let him make the next move. He'll find out that living away from the comforts of home isn't much fun. You thought you had a big pile of cash, but it won't last him long. When it's gone, he'll return."

"You know, I sort of want him to come back," he said, slumping into a kitchen chair. "But then . . ."

His mother glanced over at him.

"There's a part of me," he continued, "that feels relieved to not have to watch him sitting there," he gestured towards his father's chair in the next room. "Drinking himself stupid every day."

His mother paused in her folding. "Yes, I do know what you mean."

"Oh! Changing the subject," Jubal sat up. "I don't know if you saw, but Tatum was just here."

His mother nodded.

"Looking for the Packard."

She smiled. "Well, he won't find it."

Jubal was happy to see his ma brighten a little over their joke on Tatum. "He can't stand the fact that it's 'vanished into thin air.' Even better, now we've got a handsome new bull. Best in the whole darned county I bet."

July 12, 1941. The days since Clyde had stolen the glass bank were flying by. He had quickly figured out a way to pull the dollar bills through the glass slot without breaking the bank, using a pair of locking obstetrics tweezers he'd borrowed from Doc Small. The surgical tool, with tiny steel teeth, had tremendous gripping power, enabling him to bite into each greenback and pull it with some force through the narrow opening. He emptied the bank of forty-one dollar bills, triumphant that he had done that much for his boy in saving Jubal's bank. He'd now learned just how long he could stay away from Hayesville. He had never had to manage money so carefully in his whole life.

Convincing Doc Small, a hunched little man with a flushed alcoholic's face, to let him hitch a ride to Troy had been easy once the doctor realized Clyde held an unusual amount of cash and a nice quantity of booze. Apparently, both items were in short supply amongst the doctor's usual clients. Doc Small informed him that Hayesville was the exception, however. For the doctor's services, the priest always slipped him a five in cash, leaving no possible money trail.

The road to Troy was nearly new to Clyde. Years had passed since he'd been on Route 7 heading towards the city. They had ridden past the *All Jersey* creamery, a fancy milk business specializing in a product from the best Jersey cows in the area. Avery Ketchum shipped to them and got a premium price for his milk. Every day from his drinking chair, Clyde had watched the *All Jersey* can truck rumble by on the road to Avery's farm. Of course, the Browns could never qualify, having Ayrshires, and couldn't have passed the strict inspection required anyway.

During the car trip, Doc had offered to rent Clyde a room on the third floor of his Victorian home located on Third Street in Troy, not far from the Hudson River. Clyde had gladly accepted. But upon arrival, he discovered Doc's boarding house was shabby and in the run-down part of town.

Doc Small's office was on the first floor and half the downstairs was taken up by a waiting room. Evening office hours were from six to nine, so when Clyde went upstairs to his room, he could see through the double doors an assembly of patients, mostly women, waiting their turn. Their pay for Doc's services included an array of food items: a pie, a dozen eggs, a peck of potatoes, and a frosted cake. One girl with long, greasy hair held what looked like change she'd put together for her visit bunched up in the toe of a sock.

Doc had introduced him to his assistant and house matron, Bessie Black. Bessie ran the remainder of the building as a boarding house, serving two meals a day. She informed Clyde that his room, including breakfast and supper, would cost six dollars a week. Upon entering, he saw that the room was completely furnished and included an RCA Victor victrola and radio. Each day, Clyde was delighted to be able to catch up on his baseball and the national news from WGY. The world news continued to stream events that were not good.

Soviet Union: The German advance continues as tanks roll towards Smolensk after crossing the Dnieper River.

Clyde thought about how he sat in his room drinking *Jim Beam* while some poor bastards were trying to fight off the Germans. He shut off the news to listen to the only phonograph record, *Handel's Messiah*, that someone had left behind.

He placed the record on the turntable and swung the needle arm into place. The music was unfamiliar, but he gave it a listen so as to forget the current state of affairs. He sat back in his chair while the high-class orchestra music relaxed him, even filling him with joy. Soon, though, it was obvious that the record had been damaged. Not far into the recording, a deep male voice began repeating over and over: *the crooked straight and the rough places plain . . . the crooked straight and the rough places plain . . . the crooked straight and the rough places plain.* His joy evaporated with the music sending him into a sour mood. He wondered if the same mystical force at work when he stole the bank was now blaring a message for his benefit, telling him that he must somehow make his crooked ways straight. How could he ever redeem himself, a drunk and a crook? He couldn't see a way to become a straight and honest man.

Besides, he had deeper worries. He was running out of money, in less than a week, with the forty-one dollars disappearing much sooner than thought. After evening calling hours, Doc had been visiting his room and the two had been finishing off a pint of Lady Lamont's *Jim Beam*, a fact that Clyde found hard to accept. After all, he was far from well-heeled.

Come Monday, he was going to have to pay another six dollars for his room and board, plus purchase a few bottles of liquor. By then Jubal's money would be nearly half gone.

On Sunday morning, when he had sobered up and eaten a full breakfast of coffee, gruel, and toast, he went out for a walk to St. Joseph's Cemetery just down the street from Doc's place. He had discovered the ancient cemetery shortly after arriving in Troy. The graveyard was badly neglected and usually empty with no one there to visit their dearly departed, so he came to this quiet place to get away from the stink of Third Street and the constant noise humming just outside the Victorian house.

As he walked down the street, he considered the brown rats he had been seeing in huge numbers nightly roaming the neighborhood in search of food. From his third-story room he'd been watching them storm the street on their way to the Hudson River, bringing to mind the German army advance reported in the news. There were hundreds of the rodents, looking like a dark brown blanket on the move the width and length of two cars.

Doc informed him that the rats were known to attack the homeless who camped out on the sidewalk, clamping their sharp incisors onto exposed fingers and toes until the person awoke screaming in pain and fear. Picturing this, Clyde curled his fingers into protected fists.

In watching the rats from his high vantage point at the boarding house, memories of when he was a boy came flooding back. He had lived with his brother and folks in a shack of a house. His dad worked on and off, when he was sober, as a farmworker.

After the farm rats had scoured the grainfields for food in the fall, they would invade the Brown's impoverished home. He and his brother slept next to a storeroom that held a quantity of squash, dried onions, and corn. The cold night winds caused the creaking of loose clapboards to echo throughout the house, but not loud enough to drown out the sound of rats climbing the stairs, slapping their long tails against the wooden risers to reach the top floor. They'd scurry under his bed to slip beneath the ill-fitted door to the storage room. As they passed, he lay awake in his bed with his feet and hands tucked safely under the blankets, willing the creatures to keep moving towards the food. His worst fear was that they would climb up onto the bed while he was asleep and chew off his ear.

For years, his fear of rats gave him nightmares. He once dreamed that a rat crawled into his open mouth to gnaw on his throat, only to find upon waking that he'd come down with a painful sore throat.

Clyde wandered into the old graveyard, putting the gruesome memories to rest. He looked for a comfortable place to sit and consider how he might manage the upcoming days. Most of the gravestones were dated to indicate the late eighteen hundreds and many had been carved with the theme of angels resting on the stone at the head of the gravesite. He chose a headstone with an image of an angel looking to be in flight hovering over the grave. Curious, he rubbed the engraving to better read the inscription:

Susy Demare Quigley
Born December 8, 1892 Died Jan 10, 1900
Her smile was just a breath away.

He pursed his lips in sorrow—Susy was only eight years old when she died. As he sat, he landed on the ground with a grunt, feeling as if in the body of an old man. Well, he might feel older than his years, but at least he'd made it past eight. He crossed his legs with some difficulty. Then he took a long, grateful swig from his bottle that was blanketed in a paper sack. Alone at last. No one nagging at him. No cows bellowing. He sat listening to the wind blowing through two tall pines that stood like guardians over the dead. The afternoon was balmy and the sun warm.

Soon lying down with his head next to the stone, Clyde imagined that the angelic image could actually swoop down and wrap him in her wings to protect him from life's hard slog. On his back, he looked up at the smiling cherub, feeling comforted even though he was pretty sure he'd soon be homeless. He stared into the eyes of the stone image. There had to be an alternative to sleeping on the sidewalk and being eaten by rats. He mouthed a silent prayer for help.

Miraculously, he heard a horn blow from the distance. He sat up quickly. Perhaps the angel had sent his answer. He should look for an abandoned car to live in, a vehicle to keep the rain off and offer protection. He took another long drink and stretched out upon Susy's grave to sleep the day away.

Chapter Twenty-Five

An early riser, Lizzy had been in the store since six Sunday morning, mopping the floors and dusting the shelves while there were no customers. Bert promised he'd help after church with a huge hardware order that had arrived on Saturday from Burlington. For years, Bert had ignored the hardware section to the point that folks stopped checking with the store for even something as simple as nuts and bolts. Recently, Lady Lamont had encouraged Lizzy to stock basic items commonly used, such as forks, shovels, hammers, mauls, bars, and saws. The markup on such items was high, making them attractive to have on hand, and once stocked in the store, hardware items required minimal attention, yet drew in more buyers.

The brisk store sales had brought on considerable work. Lizzy was always busy—pricing items and stocking shelves, or finding space for new lines such as Bisquick, a popular baking product she had ordered with an introductory offer. She'd found that Lady Lamont was far from a silent partner. Her benefactress visited frequently with guidance, stressing cleanliness and an orderly store, advising that, when possible, shelves should be stocked at off hours. Lizzy tried hard to follow Lady Lamont's advice.

Recently, Lizzy had vigorously cleaned the glass showcase cooler that had been sitting idle for years. Bert was surprised to see it brought back to life and told her that they were starting it up for the first time since his father had passed away. With the cooler running, she could now offer cuts of meats: hamburg, hot dogs, bologna, turkey, liverwurst, cheeses, and sausage. Because she had added the meats, she was also able to do sandwiches, a service that thrilled the nearby folks at lunchtime. Customers sat out on the porch, where she had placed additional chairs for summer, and chatted as they unwrapped wax paper to bite into stacks of meat and cheese, lettuce, tomato, and pickles. The added offering was so popular that she now needed a person just to be in charge of refrigerated items.

She hated to see customers standing to be waited on when Bert was busy behind the meat case, so she always dropped what she was doing to make things run smoothly. However, adding the refrigerated meats had stretched them to the limit. Clem sometimes helped, but he was working more than she wished or he wanted to for his advanced age. She thought of Bernice, but Bernice was reported as saying that she'd never again speak to Lizzy LaFlam for taking over the store.

Agonizing over who to hire to fill the need, Lizzy came up with no suitable prospects. She discussed the matter with Bert after they'd closed one evening. He'd just finished cashing out, but had yet to lock the door. She approached him where he sat with the deposit in hand at the checkout counter.

"Hey," she said, "do ya think Bernice would be interested in workin' and managin' the meat case?"

With a start, Bert set the deposit pouch on the counter and looked up. "Well . . . I don't really know. Do we need extra help that much to bring Bernice back into the business?"

Lizzy leaned against the counter facing Bert. "We *do* need more help. As it is now, we ain't— *aren't* havin' time ta bone out more beef enough ta always have hamburg on hand, or prepare pork and beef roasts fer folks, as well as make lunches. I'm just thinkin' lots more could be done ta give better service than we're doin' now."

"I expect so . . . but Bernice? She, well, how can I say—"

"I know. She hates me," Lizzy said.

Bert's face reddened. "Sorry Lizzy, but that's the truth."

"Then I'm stumped. I just don't know who ta turn ta. Bernice'd be perfect 'cause ya could teach her the ropes." She sighed, feeling defeated.

Bert came around the counter and put his arm over her shoulder in a fatherly manner. "This isn't the end of the world. We'll manage some—"

Before he could finish, the entrance door flew open and Bernice strutted briskly towards the counter. He quickly pulled his arm away.

"I knew it! I knew it!" Bernice said. Her eyes were wide and her dyed red hair shook atop her head.

Watching the woman come towards them, Lizzy was reminded of a setting hen on the run. She hid her smile as Bernice came up to them.

"You! You two are having a love-fest behind my back," Bernice declared. "I've been watching at the door." She shoved Lizzy away from the counter with her right hand and pushed at Bert with her left, separating them. "Bert! Always coming home late for your supper, saying you had 'odds and ends' to tend to at the store. You think I'm a dimwitted woman? I see what is happening here."

After being roughly shoved and hearing Bernice's foolish words, Lizzy ran out of patience. "Well, Bernice, I'm thinkin' Bert ain't wantin' to tend ta ya 'cause ya're like sidlin' up next ta a porcupine!"

Bernice turned, obviously shocked. "Lizzy LaFlam, you're just . . . just trash! I'll have you know," she said, planting both hands on her hips, "there is no *sidling* that goes on in our home, not that it's any of *your* business!"

There was silence as, one by one, each of them dropped their gaze to the floor.

Bernice blushed, having just admitted out loud her lack of wedded romance. She narrowed her eyes. "I had *friends* before you came along. Now no one wants to go with me to my Temperance meetings."

Lizzy blew out a breath. "Well, I 'spect that's 'cause ya aren't no longer givin' out a free ride and lunch ta boot."

"And what is that supposed to mean?" Bernice said.

"Ya bought yer friends," Lizzy said quietly.

Bert took Bernice's arm. "Let's go home, Bernice. Lizzy was just talking to me about giving you a job. She thought of you for running the meat case. And—"

"But Bert told me how it wouldn't work with ya hatin' my guts," Lizzy put in.

Bernice actually bloomed into a smile. "Me? Work here?" she said, changing her tune. "Well, I never thought I could."

"Ya can have a job if ya want one," Lizzy said. "Work a few hours a day 'round noon, 'til ya get the hang of it."

Bernice fluffed her hair and patted it back into place. After a moment, she replied, "I just might like to try this." She looked sternly at Bert. "It would be a good way to keep an eye on you two!"

"Bernice," Lizzy said, growing serious. "Ya should know it's the God's honest truth that Bert has never, ever laid a hand on me 'til ya rushed through that door just now. I was feelin' in the dumps with him tellin' me 'bout ya hatin' me and all. He's like a father ta me. Much like Clem."

"Really?" Bert said.

"Well, I never thought on it much before, but yeah," Lizzy said.

"That's good," Bert said. "I'm glad to hear it."

Bernice looked from one to the other. "Well then, I guess I need to change my attitude if I'm going to work here. Because you run this place now. I hate to admit it—you've been doing a good job, as I've seen. And I . . . well, I need to earn some money for my Temperance calling. As Benjamin Franklin once said, 'God helps those who help themselves.'"

The Sausvilles strolled out of the store arm in arm, leaving Lizzy to lock up and take the deposit pouch to O'Mara's Drugstore.

With the new arrangement, she kept Bert as checkout clerk because of his friendly personality. In addition, he taught Bernice about the use of the electrical equipment and hand tools at the meat counter. Lizzy didn't feel comfortable having Bernice near the cash drawer because, at one time, Clem had warned how old habits were hard to break. Lizzy convinced Clem to keep working part-time with fewer hours, especially when Bernice went off on Temperance missions. Clem seemed to be loving it, delivering orders and keeping the floor swept. It was good for him to have traded his post on the bench outside for work in the store, though in either position, he remained the chief town gossip.

She laughed to herself as she picked up the duster. With Bernice in the store most days, Clem had competition, for there were now two gossips working at the IGA. And if one wanted to learn the latest news in Hayesville, the store was the place to get it. Like the night after the dance when Tatum hauled Benny to jail in his underwear. That was quite the story. Lizzy was sure glad she had high-tailed it out of Jubal's place before the sheriff arrived.

She checked the clock on the wall by the register. Bert would arrive soon and they'd get to unpacking the hardware, so she set about getting that area of the store ready for display.

Having lived all his life in the routine of farm and school, Jubal knew nothing about wrecked cars, auto parts, or what Jazz would expect of him when working at the junkyard. Nevertheless, he'd begun keeping his end of the bargain. He decided to take the farm truck down the hill as he was unlikely to meet other cars. After a long day of chores and then the extra job, he didn't fancy the idea of walking back up to his house in the dark.

On the first night driving down to Jazz's, he noticed how the low sun had turned the sky a pleasing apricot color. All seemed calm and peaceful with the world, but it wasn't. Since the Philco's return from Lady Lamont's, he'd been hearing a worrisome reminder on WGY's broadcasts:

All men aged 21–45 are required to register with their County Selective Service Board. It's the law.

Turning off the truck in the yard, Jubal heard Jazz's clarinet and the *clickety-clack* sound. He followed the noise and entered the large, dimly-lit shed with its low ceiling. Jazz's helper, Slag Perkins, was dancing in and around any number of auto parts stored on the floor. From behind an old desk, Jazz played a lively tune on his clarinet. Jubal wondered if they even saw him entering in such poor lighting. He took a seat on an engine block to watch and wait.

In a few minutes, the music and dancing stopped. Jazz put his clarinet down amongst the papers and tools lying on his desktop. "Look, Slag—our help is here."

"I can try to help," Jubal said from where he sat on the block, "but I really don't know much about cars."

Jazz leaned back in his office chair. "Ain't hard. Slag here will work with ya until ya get the hang of it. Give him a tour around, Slag."

Slag was a slight guy with a Fred Astaire build who carried himself in a nimble sort of way. As they walked outside, Jubal saw that Slag's face was peppered with scars. He assumed it was from hot metal flying off the welder and cutting torch.

Jazz's junkyard was no small place. Shed after shed lay out of sight away from the road next to the river. Junk cars were shoved into stalls and dismantled for their useable parts. Each stall was organized for parts of a particular brand and year, mainly Chevy, Ford, and Plymouth, what Slag called, "the workin' man's cars." Jazz's counterpart, Sean O'Grady, dealt with "the moneyed cars," like Oldsmobile, Cadillac, Lincoln, and, of course, Packard.

What looked like disorganization from the outside was, in fact, a well-oiled business. Jubal soon understood that Jazz was a clever, busy guy, on the phone in his office most of the day, having garage bays for two full-time mechanics and a body shop. Chain-falls were overhead in the main building, used to lift the cars. A truck was constantly on the road to bring in wrecks from all over the region. One of the biggest employers in town, Jazz was no shade-tree mechanic.

Jubal's main job was to shove wrecked cars into their designated bays, using what Slag called a "doodlebug," an old truck cut down to act as a tractor. It had a wide plank bolted to the front with a lot of push power. The cars were torn apart using wrenches and a great deal of cutting with a torch.

Right away, Jubal discovered Slag was a talker full of opinions. The welder made it known that he liked Jubal's ma.

"In my book, Rose Brown is the star of Hayesville, puttin' all them young whoremasters in their places."

On hearing that, Jubal realized certain things in a small town are never forgotten. He also found that Slag was into world affairs and politics. The guy talked in rapid fashion while working over the flame of his torch or the jangle of hoist chains lifting a car off the floor.

"Ya know, Churchill's runnin' England, gettin' his ass kicked by Hitler. He'll have us inta war 'fore long." Slag paused in his work, pointing a tire iron at Jubal as if expecting some reply.

Jubal was clueless when it came to the world news. He was just trying to get enough milk production on the farm so his family could eat. Leaders of distant countries and how they played into a possible war never entered his thoughts.

Slag bent over to dismount a tire from a rim, rattling on. "Churchill and Roosevelt want all countries ta have it their own way. Meanwhile, German soldiers have poured inta Russia. If I lived in Russia, 'bout now I'd be scared ta death with a German breathin' down my neck."

Slag continued as he removed valuable parts—wheels, the axle, springs, and usable fenders—handing them to Jubal to place on a cart for storage.

Jubal felt he should add to the conversation. "I don't follow politics much." He stood holding a rim in his hand.

"Ya better listen, boy. Ya'll be called ta war like my old man. Ya know, I've had ta register fer the County Selective Service. Bastard!

"I did hear about the draft, but I'm only sixteen, working my folks' farm. The age starts at twenty-one."

Slag laid the torch on the disabled engine. "Wouldn't ya know I'm thirty-two, caught right by the throat. Prob'ly shipped off ta Europe where I'll run up against some Nazis and take a bullet ta the head." Slag fired up his torch and the blue flame cut easily through a metal post like a knife through a cloud of smoke. He turned the torch off with a *pop*. "Ya just wait. Time passes real quick. We're ripe fer war."

"My dad says being a farmer, I won't have to go. He always followed the news on his radio."

Slag looked up. "Followed? Yer pa ain't followin' no more?"

"Uh, he still follows what's going on." Jubal hadn't meant to let slip about his runaway dad.

Taking some unneeded smaller pieces of the car to the trash, Jubal could hear the torch blowing its blue flame and Slag's words like a steady percussion. Returning, he noticed a scar in the shape of New Hampshire on Slag's face. As the guy's rant increased, the scar turned red near the northern tip of the state.

"My old man went ta war when I was just a kid—left fer France. Never came home alive." The whole scar on his cheek turned deep red down to the bottom of the state.

Jubal picked up a tire, threw it onto the cart, and nodded.

Slag paused and turned off his torch. "Yup, in a trench while breakin' through the German line. The sons-a-bitches burned him with mustard gas."

"Really?" At the thought, Jubal's skin crawled.

"My old man turned black like raw meat over a hot fire, they said."

Jubal cringed as he picked up another tire. "That's terrible!"

"Was a wicked cold day when we put him in the ground. My ma and us'ens huddled 'round the grave with townsfolk payin' their respects. Jazz stood with us. After, he said ta my Ma, 'Yer boy can help me at the yard if ya like.'"

New Hampshire faded as Slag sniffed. "I was real young when I started fer Jazz. He put food on the table fer my ma and us three kids."

"Jazz did that?" Jubal said. Now Jazz was helping him and his ma. Apparently, his new boss was a guy with a big heart.

"Yup, Jazz is like my dad. My real dad I ain't never had fer most of my life."

Jubal braced himself for another rant against the Germans, but Slag dropped his head to torch the bolts that held the front axle, quiet for the first time all night.

Jubal's first week at the junkyard sped by. With Slag's help, he learned how to use a cutting torch, wrenches of all sorts, and tire irons—skills that might come in handy at the farm in repairing machinery. He did spend a lot of time lugging parts around on carts to their right places, but with Slag's nonstop chatter, the two hours went by in no time.

When closing the place, Jazz would call Babe from the office to do her night patrolling. "Good girl. Ya want a treat, don't ya?" Jazz would say, as he reached for a piece of dried meat from a package stored on a shelf. Each time, Babe opened her mouth, showing her pink tongue, and grabbed the treat to take it outside.

"On duty, she's a hell of a dog," Jazz explained. "That *Beware of Dog* sign at the gate ain't no joke!"

Before Jubal left work, he would take a minute to check out Benny's car. It was well hidden and covered with a canvas in back of one of the sheds. He knew he had to prove himself in his duties for Jazz if the Packard was ever going to be fixed. On his way home, he looked to see if his dad might be at the side of the road. His dad wasn't the type to live the wild life, so Jubal had been keeping an eye out for him on Harmony Hill just in case. It was too late to tell his dad he missed him, and the thought alone would never bring him back.

Being at CYO camp had taken on a new dimension for Polly after the grange dance, having become an all-out effort to avoid Freddie. She made specific plans for each day, claiming special interest in being on nursing duty. This freed up the camp nurse, Dot Stone, to go out and observe the activities of the kids, as well as take longer meals while chatting with members of the staff. Dot remarked that it was nice to have a bit of freedom.

Polly also begged off of her craft responsibilities, satisfied to stay full-time in the nurse's quarters. She even had meals brought to her, causing her to be a willing prisoner.

Concerned, Dot urged Polly to get some sunshine and fresh air. But Polly declined, instead taking Dot's nursing manual down from the shelf above the sick bed and opening it to read. Thankfully, Dot didn't argue.

One day, Mother Superior called Polly to her office and Polly had no idea why. She felt nervous coming before the strict woman as she entered the rustic room and stood in front of the camp's registration counter. A wrought-iron lamp illuminated the gold crucifix that hung on the wall. Taking in the nun's black habit and white-lined veil, Polly thought that Mother Superior had the face of a shriveled winter apple remaining on a lonely tree.

Mother Superior looked up from a book, her crow's feet deepening, and pointed to the chair she had placed in front of her desk. "Come in, Polly. I've been wanting to visit with you. Have a seat."

"Thank you." She eyed the older woman with fear and respect as she sat.

"How is your extra duty at the nurse's station going?"

"Oh, fine." Polly puffed her cheeks and quickly exhaled.

Mother Superior tapped the cover of her book, thinking. "I remember when I was your age. I had a lot of silly fears. Dot Stone has told me you rarely leave the nurse's cabin since returning from Hayesville."

Polly filled up her cheeks and blew her breath out the corner of her mouth. "I like learning about nursing." It was a bold-faced lie and she sensed the older woman knew it.

Mother Superior slid open a desk drawer and pulled out a folded piece of paper. She opened up the paper and looked down, reading it. This fired up Polly's nerves, wondering what it could be.

"You see, Polly," Mother Superior said, folding the paper again, "Father Mac and all of us in Maria's church family are disturbed about the terrible beating and um . . . rape she suffered. I understand you grew up with Maria Styles and have lived all your life in Hayesville. Would you have any light to shed on this matter? Can you help us determine the guilty party in this crime? I'm hearing varying opinions as to who did the deed."

"Mother Superior, I feel awful this happened to Maria. But, I have no idea who might be the guilty one." Polly tried to maintain a blank expression.

The nun looked over her spectacles, seeming to study her reaction. "Of course, you know I want you to tell me the truth. So you have no information at all?"

"No. I . . . no." She didn't want to be dragged into the matter. She couldn't forget how Freddie grabbed at her jacket in the car or how angry he got about the rain leaking through the roof. The guy had a temper. If she squealed on him, she could possibly end up like Maria.

"Polly, you should know that Freddie Coleman has asked several staff members if they know you. He's been trying to find out where you are keeping yourself at mealtimes. Why would Freddie be looking for you?"

"He has? Uh, I don't know."

"I've tried to make sense of the situation, and I've concluded you must have had some sort of contact with Freddie when he was in Hayesville to attend the parade. I'm fairly sure that you had not met with him prior to that day. Now, let's stop dodging my questions. Please explain yourself, young lady!"

"I have nothing to explain." Polly crossed her arms. To spill the beans was more dangerous than anything the old, shriveled apple could dish out.

"Freddie has told me that he never knew you existed. He denies meeting you when in Hayesville." Mother Superior tilted her head and looked squarely at Polly. "Is that a true statement?"

Polly bowed her head, willing herself to keep it together.

"Polly," Mother Superior said, her voice lower. "Are you aware of the details of Miss Styles' attack? Did you see her bruises?"

Polly shook her head, even as her eyes welled up.

The nun persisted. "Maria Styles' virginity was stolen from her in a brutal manner. Her attacker was like a wolf having torn open an innocent lamb."

Polly exhaled a small cry. "I can't say. I just can't say."

"Why not?"

"I'm afraid of what he might do if I tell!" Tears rolled down her cheeks.

"For heaven's sake! Our conversation is confidential." Mother Superior picked up the letter and unfolded it again. "You see, a high authority wants some answers, as well as I, so I would like your full cooperation. I trust you know Mister Andrew O'Mara, chairman of the St. Anne's church council?"

She met the nun's eyes. "He's my dad."

"Right. And no doubt your father would be ashamed of you that you couldn't be more helpful." Mother Superior placed the letter back in the drawer and slammed it shut. "You spend some time thinking through what you know about this matter. I will be summoning you again. Meanwhile, Freddie has been restricted from coming to the dining hall and must remain in his cabin when not teaching swimming lessons. He has agreed to these terms until we get this matter solved. Please resume taking your meals at the dining hall."

Polly got up from her chair feeling weak in the knees. "Thank you, Mother Superior. I'll do as you ask." She left the office dreading the next meeting with the elderly nun.

Chapter Twenty-Six

Another busy week rolled around to Sunday, providing a chance for Lizzy to finally have some free time. She had just left the mansion and a meeting with Lady Lamont who told her that workers would soon be installing a shower out back at the store. Lizzy considered this a luxury beyond luxuries and was in high spirits on her walk to visit the Browns next door. With a bag full of dirty clothes over her shoulder, she met Rose in the laundry room.

"Hello, Miz Brown," she said.

Rose was loading the wringer washer as the open back door let in the summer air. Lizzy noticed Jubal across the way driving his team. He pulled up to the haymow at the front of the barn with a load of hay.

Rose saw her watching Jubal. "Why don't you leave your laundry here and I'll do it," Rose suggested. "You can go help Jubal with that big jag of hay he has to get in this afternoon."

"Miz Brown, what I know 'bout hayin' I could fit in a thimble. Looks ta me like Jubal's climbin' onta a big pile a' itchiness."

Rose laughed. "You could lead Trueboy on the hayfork rope while Maria helps in the mow. You won't even come near the hay." With the washer loaded, now sloshing clothes, Rose looked at her expectantly. "Go ahead. Maria will show you what to do."

"Okay, Miz Brown. Guess I wouldn't mind helpin'," Lizzy agreed, hoping she wouldn't make a fool of herself.

She could skin a squirrel quick as any, but she wasn't too keen on the idea of walking next to the huge workhorse. Still, it might offer a chance to see how Maria was doing. She'd not stopped thinking about Maria's attack, but hadn't known what to do. Even though they went to school together, she didn't know Maria that well, only once helping Maria pick out some clothes for camp at the store. That was as close as the two had ever come to having a conversation. She admired Maria—who was sensible and beautiful in a country way—but to her disappointment, Maria had not written back to the note she'd sent after the clothes buying.

The day was muggy when she walked out of the laundry room. Under the shade of a big maple, Maria was standing with Trueboy, stroking his white blaze.

"Hey Maria," she said, stopping a few feet away.

As Maria turned, shaken from her horse world, Lizzy noticed she had dark circles under her eyes and her coloring was ashen. Her pretty hair was covered with a blue bandana.

"I'm supposed ta help you guys," Lizzy said. "But when it comes ta hayin' I'm 'bout worthless as a toad in a pond with no warts."

"That's a goofy saying." Maria said, breaking into a smile.

"I might well be goofy standin' next ta this giant." She pointed at Trueboy. "What's with the horse, wearing all that contraption?"

Maria looked at Trueboy's harness and back at her, puzzled.

"It looks like Bernice Sausville's underclothes 'fore she puts on her day dress," Lizzy added.

Maria burst out laughing.

"God, what am I sayin'?" Lizzy struck her forehead with the palm of her hand. "Rest assured, I ain't ever seen Bernice Sausville in her drawers. So, what am I supposed ta do while ya guys heave the hay?"

"Seriously?"

"Well, yeah," she said. She figured she could be as strong as the farm girl before her. "I'm ready ta shoulder the load."

"Okay, I'll explain how this all works." But Maria looked doubtful. "See, Trueboy is hooked with two straps, called tugs, to a wooden whiffletree that has a steel loop in the center. The rope, called a hayfork rope, is tied to the loop. When the rope is pulled, it runs through pulleys and is tied to the fork. You can lead Trueboy. As he walks, he lifts the loaded hayfork off the wagon and up through the open doors to the track that runs across the peak of the barn." Maria stopped. "You understand?"

Lizzy nodded. "Sorta." She was busy trying to follow the ropes and pulleys in her mind.

Maria continued. "I'll stand in the barn with the small rope and watch where Benny wants the fork-load of hay. When you hear me yell, stop Trueboy. I'll yank the trip rope to release the load. Jubal will pull the empty fork back to be reloaded. It usually takes a few trips to unload the wagon."

Lizzy was amazed at how well Maria knew the workings of farm machinery.

"Then you can lead Trueboy back from where you started. Keep doing this until the wagon is empty. We'll wait until Jubal and Benny come with another load."

She nodded.

"Trueboy's so smart he'll practically lead you." Maria turned and walked towards the barn.

From where she stood, Lizzy could see Jubal on top of the load opening the large jaws of the hayfork. He jumped on the teeth, driving them their full extent into the hay. Motioning, he gave his command, "Okay, Trueboy." The horse started without Lizzy holding his halter and she jumped to grab his leadline.

"Damn," she muttered. "I should be the one pullin', and instead this big guy leads me." In moments she heard Maria yell from inside the mow.

"Stop!"

Trueboy stopped and turned immediately to go back to the tree, taking the slack out of the lead strap that Lizzy held. "Alright, big boy, have it yer way. It's so hot out here that mosquitoes can't bite! Ya want shade."

No sooner had they reached the shade of the tree, when Jubal yelled, "Okay, Trueboy."

On the next trip, Lizzy was ready and this time walked beside the horse. On command they returned to the tree together. "Well, Trueboy," she said, "with a little more trainin' we're gonna make one helluva team."

It wasn't long before Benny got aboard the empty hay wagon and Jubal drove the team back to the hayfield. Maria came to sit with Lizzy under the maple tree.

For several minutes, they sat quietly at the base of the tree. Maria's head was bent as if she were about to doze off, but she kept her hand on Trueboy's knee. Lizzy pulled a short seed head of grass and slipped it easily from its sheath. She put the soft end in her mouth, enjoying the sweetness. After a long silence, she flicked the seed head onto the lawn.

"What's the deal with Trueboy?" she asked. "Ya get ta keep him fer the rest a' the summer?"

Maria sighed, as if answering was an effort. "I ride him back and forth to Jubal's and keep him nights at Avery's. I help Jubal in trade for getting to go riding."

"I see. So ya like Trueboy?"

"He's gentle, and smart."

"Fer sure," Lizzy nodded. "I didn't have ta do a thing just now. He did all the work."

Maria looked up at Trueboy who stood napping over them, his big head heavy and his eyes closed. "I trust this horse."

"When I used ta live on the mountain, a pack a' dogs was all I trusted. Them dogs and my mimy. Didn't trust no one else."

Maria stood and brushed some of the hayseed from her coveralls. She came around the tree and knelt in front of Lizzy. "Yes, I suppose it was like that for you." She looked towards the field. "Here comes Jubal with the next load."

Lizzy took her chance. "Look, I, uh . . . Sorry 'bout what happened ta . . . well, after the parade, ya know."

Maria stiffened.

"If ya ever wanna talk . . ." Lizzy offered.

Maria lowered her eyes and shook her head. She stood and started towards the barnyard but turned back towards Lizzy. "Um . . . thanks." She headed to meet Jubal and Benny.

Lizzy got to her feet and took Trueboy's leadrope. "Ready for the next round big guy?"

As the day wore on, the weather was looking like a shower soon, so all four of them worked to beat the rain and Lizzy was left alone leading Trueboy. It hadn't been in her plans to spend her free afternoon making friends with a horse, yet in walking with Trueboy back and forth to the tree, she found he was not so scary. He had a comforting horse smell like dust and grass that came from the sweat marks under his harness. By four o'clock that afternoon, the threat of rain had passed and they'd gotten all the hay in the barn. Lizzy was ready to call it a day, feeling she'd about walked her legs off, but she stopped Maria who was about to jump on Trueboy to go home.

"Hey," Lizzy said, "what would ya think 'bout comin' ta my room at the store fer a bite ta eat later?"

Maria paused, stepping back from the horse. "Why would I want to do that?"

"Maybe somethin' fun ta do fer a change?"

"Fun?" Maria said.

"Yeah. How 'bout ya ride Trueboy down ta the store? We could hitch him ta the wagon stored in the back barn and have a spin through town. You could even stay the night. There's a stall there. Then ride from the store ta Jubal's in the mornin'."

For a moment Lizzy thought Maria wouldn't answer as Maria nimbly jumped up on Trueboy's back.

Maria looked down from atop the horse. "You have a wagon he could pull?"

"That's right," she nodded. "Bert said his granddad used it ta haul and sell firewood."

"I can't go like this." Maria swept her free hand to note her work clothes.

Lizzy waved in the direction of Avery's. "Why don't ya go home and clean up? I'll put together a supper lunch and wait fer ya ta come on Trueboy."

"You have a place I can sleep?"

"Sure do. A cot I found ta use fer a friend."

"Okay." Maria made a clucking sound and Trueboy started down the drive.

Lizzy went to pick up her laundry that hung on the clothesline, glad that Maria had accepted her offer. She met Rose in the laundry sweeping water on the floor, encouraging it down the drain.

"Thanks fer doin' my wash, Miz Brown. I been workin' so long, my clothes must be dry. Guess what? Maria's gonna spend the night with me!"

"She is?" Rose looked up in amazement. "How wonderful! But don't be surprised if she doesn't show, my dear. Her folks are very protective of her."

"I see." Lizzy picked up her laundry bag to get her clothes off the line. "Well, I'll hope fer the best."

"That's a good attitude, Lizzy," Rose said.

A couple of hours later, Lizzy waited for Maria outside the store with a bunch of the usual guys that hung out there on summer evenings. Before walking down to the IGA, she'd washed off the grime while enjoying a bath at the Browns' house. Rose laid out a clean change of clothes for her—a pair of sky-blue slacks and a forget-me-not flowered blouse with white frills at the wrists. Lizzy had pinned a blue velvet ribbon to set off her hair.

The guys cleared a seat for her on the bench and gathered around. They asked who was so special that she'd dress up fit for a queen. Clem remarked that she looked like a blooming blue iris at the center of a bouquet of ragweed. The others laughed, looking down at their patched pants and faded shirts.

"Maria Styles is comin' for supper," she said. "We're gonna take a ride with Jubal's workhorse pullin' that old wagon that's stored in the back shed."

Clem Gochy spoke up. "That rig ain't been used fer fifty years, not since I was a kid."

Lizzy assured him, “I checked the wagon out. Looks good as new.”

Clem recalled, “Bert’s granddad took care a’ his things. I ’spect he greased the axles ’fore he put it away. I’ll wager it’s fit enough fer a ride through town.”

In a few minutes, the group had eyes and ears trained on upper Main Street. Since it was past six, doubt crept up on Lizzy. Maybe Rose was right. Maria was not used to such things as spending time with a friend. Or maybe her folks didn’t want her staying overnight with the girl from LaFlam Mountain.

As if reading her mind, Charlie Jones spoke up. “Ya know what I think? The Styles are churched Irish. They ain’t lettin’ their only gal mingle with us country heathens.”

Oscar Smith stood and pointed. “Yer wrong, Charlie. I’ll put my money on our Lizzy above anybody in this town.”

A chorus of “Yeahs” came from the others.

Lizzy felt her color rise. “Thanks fer yer vote. Ya’ll deserve a big kiss, but guess what? Ya ain’t gettin’ one from me!”

The old-timers broke out laughing.

“Shhh!” Lizzy said. “Hear that guys?” She bent over with an ear towards the gravel. “Clip-clop, clip-clop. She’s comin’, soundin’ like a drumstick beatin’ on the road.” She faced the crew. “Those are Trueboy’s hooves big as dinner plates gettin’ louder and comin’ our way.”

The bench sitters joined her in the road. Sure enough, there was Maria on the horse way up Main Street. Lizzy scolded the guys. “Now get back ta yer seats and hold yer tongues! I don’t want ya scarin’ her away.”

The men did as she asked, settling in on the bench.

Clem commented in a low voice, “I ain’t ever seen a girl ridin’ a horse that size in town.”

As Trueboy and Maria drew up to the store, the men stayed quiet, but their eyes were on the big horse with his harness and Maria astride wearing blue jeans and a polo shirt. She balanced a small bag of oats and a grain sack with hay poking out the top. When they reached the porch, she slid off with both sacks still in her arms.

Maria looked uneasily at the gathered men and then at Lizzy. "My dad put this feed together for Trueboy's stay." She pulled a smaller bag from the burlap sack and held it out to Lizzy. "Ma sent along some muffins for our meal tonight and enough for morning."

Lizzy put her nose to the bag and smelled the still-warm treats. "Mmm! Tell yer ma thanks!" She turned and frowned at the stares of the guys. "Don't ya got nothin' better ta do? Leave us girls be!"

Charlie pulled a newspaper out of his back pocket and one guy got up to head for home. The others found some means of looking busy.

"Follow me," Lizzy said to Maria. She led the way in back of the store. "I'll show ya the stall where I swept out a mess of cobwebs and cleaned some sorta bin in the corner ya can use for Trueboy's oats."

"A manger?" Maria asked, amused. As she brought the tall horse into the stall, his back rubbed the top of the door casing, but Trueboy didn't seem bothered. Once inside, Maria poured grain in the manger and put hay in the rack. Trueboy went right for the feed, perfectly at home.

Still holding Maria's bag in one arm, Lizzy pulled open a side door from the horse stall. She ushered Maria into the big room that was hers to call home. Since the space once held bagged feed sold at the store, it was lined from top to bottom with small mesh wire to keep out the rats and mice. Lizzy often felt like she ate and slept in a wire cage.

"Well, this is where I live," Lizzy said. "If ya need 'em, the toilet and wash basin are down the hallway towards the store."

Maria took in the walls and ceiling of the strange room. "Your home is . . . interesting."

Lizzy set Maria's bag on a small shelf by the door. "I feel safe sleepin' here. There's no way anyone can get ta me 'cept through that door, which if I feel spooked nights, I lock it. Just the same, it's lonely, 'specially if I wake up with the heebie-jeebies."

"Lizzy, your funny words. What are heebie-jeebies?"

"Oh, a bad dream, over and over the same nightmare, like Bernice Sausville chasin' me with a big butcher knife. Her crow's nest hair fallin' over her face and goober-eyes buggin' outta her head."

Maria chuckled. “Surely you don’t have dreams like that?”

“I most surely do. Bad enough so I jump outta bed to see as I’ve locked the door.” Lizzy surveyed her living space, proud of the preparations she’d made for her visitor.

First, she’d wiped down her little round table and two ladder-back chairs. Then she’d laid out two settings of old white china that Lady Lamont had given her. She’d placed two cots side by side with a wooden crate on end between the beds to serve as a nightstand. Usually Lizzy slept in an old army sleeping bag of Bert’s, but the cots were covered with pretty quilts that Rose had let her borrow. Not having pillows, she’d bundled up some clean rags in grain sacks. Lastly, she’d picked a bouquet of daisies and red clover and placed them in a coffee cup in the center of the table.

Lizzy waved towards the chairs. “Have a seat. I’ll start some hamburger.” She’d formed hamburger patties out of ground beef from the meat case to cook in the frying pan on her hot plate.

Maria took a seat at the table. “I love daisies,” she said. She touched the white petals.

“Hard ta be in a bad mood with a daisy starin’ ya in the face,” Lizzy commented as she put some butter in the pan.

The girls sat across from each other at the table while the sizzle and smell of burgers filled the room.

“Should we go see the wagon?” Maria asked.

“Fer sure. But we gotta wait ’cause if I leave, we’ll be eatin’ fried bunny burgers.”

“I won’t ask what those are.”

“Well,” Lizzy said, leaning forward in her chair, “bunny burgers are somethin’ like chewin’ on charcoal. They ain’t— They *aren’*t too appetizin’.”

“I suppose not,” Maria said. “One time my ma was visiting a relative out of town and my dad had to cook.” She grimaced. “Pretty much everything on our plates was black.”

Lizzy laughed. Maria was good company, just like she expected. She was no wallflower like some at school, and not girly like Polly O’Mara and her friends.

In a short while, the girls were eating their burgers, along with some potato salad that Lizzy had also taken from the meat case. They drank milk for a beverage, enjoying the homemade muffins for dessert.

When they finished, Maria suggested, "Let's drive to the reservoir tonight and feed these leftover hamburger buns to the ducks."

"So ya seen ducks at the reservoir? I never stopped long enough ta know. Always runnin' by, late fer school, cold as frozen bird turd, wearin' a skimpy nothin' fer clothes."

"Seems that's better now?" Maria looked at the two beds all made up. "Looks like we'll be warm enough tonight."

"I'd say I've moved up the ladder a peg," Lizzy agreed.

After a quick rinse of the dishes in the hand sink, she led Maria to the bay where the wagon was stored. Maria looked over every inch of the long-forgotten farm cart and declared it to be in good condition. As a team, they were able to push the wagon out of the barn. Lizzy stood by as Maria backed Trueboy into the shafts and dealt with the familiar hookup. Maria explained what she was doing. First, the tugs were hooked, followed by sliding the harness holdback straps through the grommets on the underside of each shaft. After Maria snapped the driving reins into Trueboy's bridle, they were ready to go.

Lizzy climbed aboard and Maria followed to sit on the front bench. Maria picked up the reins and Trueboy started off. The old wagon moved easily with a few creaks as the wheels turned on the axles.

"Slicker than a pollywog!" Lizzy exclaimed, grabbing the side of the wagon.

When they came around to the front of the store, all of the men had left except for Clem who waited to see if the girls were indeed able to take a ride.

"Jump aboard, Clem!" Lizzy hollered. "We'll take ya ta the edge of town in style." She whispered to Maria, "He helps me at the store."

"Don't mind if I do, ladies!" Clem hustled towards the wagon. He climbed on to sit at the backend with his legs dangling. "Okay, I guess I got my old bones settled."

Maria urged the horse into a trot with a light tap on his rump with the reins. Lizzy could see there was something about the control of all that physical power that thrilled Maria. A few town residents waved from their porches and Clem returned the greeting. Lizzy figured it must be quite a sight with the big workhorse pulling the antique wagon down Main Street. After they passed the rectory, St. Anne's, the drugstore, the Baptist church, and Sean O'Grady's garage, Maria pulled Trueboy to a walk and turned to Lizzy.

"I don't want to work him too much. He's already had a hard day."

Lizzy nodded. "I guess. Puttin' all that hay in the barn, I swear I walked ta Boston." She turned to speak to Clem. "We're stoppin' right up here at the reservoir, so we'll let ya off at the entrance."

He jumped off when the wagon stopped. "Appreciate the lift, gals. Ya got me halfway home."

They continued on to the dam at the headwaters. Maria climbed down and unsnapped Trueboy's reins so he was free to graze the white clover that grew inches deep at the water's edge.

"Let's sit on that bench," Lizzy suggested, pointing to a wrought-iron seat on a mowed patch of grass a few feet from shore.

As Maria and Lizzy sat side by side on the bench, a flock of ducks suddenly became airborne, lifting off from the inlet that fed the body of water. Reaching the girls, about eight ducks landed in front of them and paddled in circles close to shore. The girls threw hamburger bun pieces to the water's surface. A real gobble-fest followed with the bread hardly having time to get wet. Soon the buns were gone.

"Gee, I wish we had more," Lizzy said.

"So do I." Maria watched the clutch as they swam about. "The last time I was here was with Jubal. They were just little ducklings following their ma. Now they're nearly all grown, ready to face the hard world."

Lizzy saw how quickly the gloom settled over Maria after the excitement of their ride. She tried to cheer her. "There's somethin' 'bout time. Just keeps on marchin' down the road, leavin' the past behind."

"Yeah, but you can't undo some mistakes," Maria said, her expression darkening further.

"I'm thinkin' mistakes can be a way ta learn." With the toe of her sneaker, Lizzy pushed around some smooth pebbles that had washed up onto the grass. She added, "Long as the lesson don't ruin or kill ya—"

"Kill is the perfect word." Maria bent over and picked up one of the stones, slinging it far out across the water, beyond the ducks. The ducks swam in that direction, probably expecting more bread to be floating.

Lizzy knew how when things got tough, the pain could hang on, like a leaf stuck behind a big stone in a creek. She wondered if that was how Maria was feeling.

Maria looked at Trueboy. "That horse will get a bellyache from eating all this clover if we don't get going."

The girls climbed on the wagon and headed back through town.

Lizzy was curious as to what Maria thought of Jubal. "Is it decent workin' up at the Brown farm? Seems like ya've known Jubal forever."

"It's not bad up there," Maria said.

"And Jubal?"

"He's a good guy. Works hard."

Lizzy was quiet, thinking. "He ever have a girlfriend?"

Maria glanced sideways, surprised at her question. "Ever since we were kids he's been crazy over his neighbor, Polly, but I don't know what he sees in her. She and I used to be friends, but she's grown up to be kind of a snob."

"Ya maybe jealous of those two?" Lizzy teased.

Maria smiled. "I'll admit it. But gosh, I wish he'd cut his hair."

"Hair!" Lizzy laughed. "That what's stoppin' ya from romance?"

"Didn't mean it to sound like that. I've known Jubal so long—he's just a friend."

"I see," Lizzy said. "Ya know, Big Daddy and the boys have long hair. I guess I ain't thought on it much. But fer yer interest, at the grange dance, Polly ditched Jubal and chased after Freddie Coleman."

"Freddie Coleman!" Maria's face went white. "She'll learn how stupid that was."

Maria nudged Trueboy to trot the remainder of the way back to the store and Lizzy could tell the conversation was closed. For the rest of the ride, Lizzy chewed herself up—even Freddie's name must feel like a splash of ice water to Maria.

Back at the shed behind the store, Lizzy stood idle as Maria backed the wagon into the stall, unhitched Trueboy, and removed his harness for the night. To help out, she filled a pail with water and handed it to Maria for the horse. It was nearly dark when they returned to the caged room with no lights. Lizzy lit her only candle which sat on the table. A couple of small lights in the hallway showed the way to the wash basin and toilet. After washing up, Lizzy blew out the candle and they made their way to the beds using a flashlight.

Maria undressed in the semi-darkness, putting on a pair of pajamas for bed. Lizzy wore just a t-shirt and panties, and thus the budding friendship produced a moment of shyness until they were both covered up under the quilts.

Maria now seemed up for chatting. "The ride was fun, Lizzy. Thanks for inviting me here with Trueboy. I never knew this room existed."

"Can't believe that ol' wagon worked," Lizzy said. She swept the flashlight around the room. "Havin' company and goin' fer a ride sure beats sittin' 'round in this hound dog cage all by myself."

"It's a good hound dog cage," Maria said.

Tired from haying and the excitement of the day, it wasn't long before Lizzy fell asleep. However, sometime later in the night, she was awakened by a low whimper, a cry nearly hidden except for the nearby cot that shook. Lizzy left her bed and sat on the edge of Maria's cot.

"Hey," Lizzy said quietly. "Why're ya crying?"

"Oh!" Maria sounded startled. "Sorry, I . . ." In the darkness, she sniffed. "Sorry I woke you."

"What's wrong?" Lizzy felt for Maria's hand. It was cold as ice. "Ya can tell me."

"It's . . ." Another sniff. Maria whispered, "I'm wrung out like a dishrag most days."

Lizzy rubbed Maria's hand. "It might help ya some ta talk. It's not good fer a body keepin' bottled up." Lizzy wasn't sure what else to say. "I'm gettin' cold. Would ya let me crawl under the covers with ya? Tell me just as much as ya like 'bout yer troubles."

Maria moved over and the girls faced each other. Lizzy put her arm over Maria who pressed against Lizzy's shoulder and cried a series of wails, reminding Lizzy of a bobcat in the night behind the cabin on the mountain.

When she quieted, Maria pulled away. "This seems strange," she said. "You in my bed."

"Really?" Lizzy was surprised. "Well, it ain't strange fer me. At least ya ain't Clem Gochy and his bony wife, Millie. The three of us slept in the same bed, Millie's pointy elbow jabbin' me in the back all night like Big Daddy's huntin' knife."

Maria drew a shaky breath and coughed a small laugh. "I can't picture that, all three of you."

"Fer almost three years. Clem's like a dad ta me. Fer a time, he got me away from LaFlam Mountain."

"What was it like, living up on that mountain?" Maria rolled onto her back, seeming to relax.

"Awful. I was sleepin' on the floor in the same room with my horny brothers. Big Daddy hollerin' and ragin' most days. My mimy nothing but a ghost of herself." Lizzy felt Maria's fingertips on her cheek.

"I'm truly sorry. I had no idea," Maria said.

"They can't touch me now," Lizzy said.

"Wish I could say that much."

"Why can't ya?"

"It's the shame," Maria said quietly. "Sometimes I feel I'm in a black cave with no matches."

"Freddie Coleman have somethin' ta do with that blackness?" Lizzy asked.

"Everything." Maria's voice was flat.

"Tell me 'bout Freddie," Lizzy whispered. Lizzy wanted to see if her suspicion was correct that Freddie was the one. "He's slimier than cow shit and not hardly as pleasant," she prompted.

"He's way worse than slime," Maria said. "Just because he's friends with a priest doesn't mean he's not the worst kind of evil."

"Ain't that the truth." Lizzy squeezed Maria's hand. "First time I saw that guy come in the store after the parade, I knew he was no good."

Maria rolled so her back was to Lizzy. Her voice was muffled by the covers. "Let's talk about something else. Tell me more about living at Clem and Millie's."

"Sure," Lizzy said. She didn't blame Maria for wanting to change the subject. "Well, Clem in particular liked ta hear me learn my numbers . . ." She rambled on until she heard Maria's breathing grow deep and even. When she was sure Maria was asleep, she got back into her own bed.

The next morning, as Maria was stuffing her things into her overnight sack, Lizzy offered, "Ya know, often Clem has ta deliver a bunch a' groceries 'round town in a pull cart. How about ya comin' with Trueboy Saturday afternoon and we'll use the wagon ta deliver groceries? Then we can have supper here and do somethin' fun. Maybe ya can teach me a game. I don't know a whole lot 'bout games but always wished I did. If ya want ya can think about it—"

"I'll come," Maria said simply.

"Good, we'll look forward ta that. Just remember, time passin' ain't, uh, *isn't* always bad . . . sometimes it makes things better."

Chapter Twenty-Seven

Before Jubal finished the morning's milking, he checked the weather again while Benny was in the mow throwing down hay. He could see heavy dew on the grass through the open barn door. It would be another nice day for haying. Satisfied, he sat on a stool beneath one of the new Ayrshires and waited for the pulsating beat of the machine to do its job. While he waited, he planned out the day's work. Soon he heard Trueboy coming up the farm drive from the village. In minutes, Maria walked into the barn with her flannel shirt over her shoulder. The morning was already growing warm. Her t-shirt showed her flat stomach and Jubal wondered if she'd lost weight. He hoped she'd had fun the night before, thinking it likely so. Lizzy would have seen to it. He was glad that Maria might be making a new friend.

"Good morning," he said, turning around to greet her. "How was your night?"

"Okay." On seeing two full pails of milk, she picked them up and headed for the milk house without another word.

He thought she might have at least stopped to chat but that was not the new Maria, and he supposed he had to get used to her sullen ways. He really didn't care to—he missed the old Maria. His anger at Freddie boiled up, mixing with his own guilt. Somehow he should have prevented what had happened to her. He took off the machine with a firmer tug than usual, causing the cow to lift her head in surprise and sidestep.

"Sorry, girl." He put his hand on her flank to calm her.

Maria returned with the empty pails and set them down with a clank on the cement aisle in back of the cows.

"Guess what?" he said. "We have a jag of hay down in the big field in back of the barn. It'll nearly finish our first cut."

"That's good." She glanced about the barn and spotted a brush on a windowsill that hadn't been touched in years. "Think I'll brush a few cows."

"Go ahead, but notice the horns. They're like nothing you've seen at Avery's."

She nodded and went to an end stall where she drew the brush down a cow's back. The cow dipped, probably never having felt such a sensation.

Jubal watched her. The idea of brushing the cows had never been part of his busy day.

"She likes this," Maria said.

"Yeah, well her horns are readymade spears. These Ayrshires grow horns like no other dairy breed. I wish Dad had cut them off. Of course, now it will never happen."

"Cut off!" Maria stopped and glared. "How awful!"

"That's the normal practice," he said with a shrug.

She continued brushing the cow, collecting wads of dead hair. "Poor thing has never been brushed," she commented. She would not look at him again.

When his cow had finished milking, he removed the machine and stepped to the feed manger. Benny, down from the mow, fed out a portion of Avery's sweet hay. The cows lowered their heads as they munched. Jubal studied the row of long horns pointed forward, lined up like spears at the start of a battle. At this time in the cows' lives, removing the horns would amount to a mammoth bloodbath. It did seem sort of cruel. He decided to drop the idea for the time being.

Before leaving the barn, he asked Maria if she had eaten breakfast. She nodded yes, concentrating on her newfound connection to the cow.

He motioned towards the manger. "When they finish their hay, would you let them out? About eleven, the dew should be off that field and the mowed hay will be ready for raking." He went to leave but turned. "Oh, and let Benny sweep and clean the barn. He likes doing that."

Maria nodded and kept brushing.

He realized she wasn't going to talk to him unless necessary. When he thought about her sadness, he, too, felt miserable—life with its hard knocks was beyond understanding.

He and Benny ate breakfast in silence. Before his ma had left for work, she'd made some biscuits and salt pork gravy for them—not much of a first-class meal. His mood suddenly went down in the dumps. He wasn't looking forward to spending the afternoon putting up lousy hay hardly worth the space it was going to take up in the mow. He thought maybe it would help to take a break from the farm for an hour or so after breakfast. Anticipating Benny's reaction to being left alone with Maria, he tried a positive angle.

"Say Benny, I bet you and Maria are going to enjoy working together this morning."

Benny looked suspiciously across the table. "Why's that?"

"Oh . . . I have an errand to run."

"I ain't ever worked with her alone." Benny scowled.

"No, but that's okay."

"She don't say nothin'." Benny dropped his fork on his plate with a clatter and pouted.

Maria's silence had Jubal on edge, and apparently Benny as well. Benny began jiggling his knee, a nervous habit when he was asked to do something he didn't like.

"Benny, stop it!" Jubal grabbed his uncle's arm.

Benny jumped and let out a yell.

"Gosh, Benny!" Jubal let go and pulled back. "All I did was touch you."

"You pinched!" Benny accused.

"I did not."

"You pinched and it hurt!" Benny looked down at his arm, inspecting for damage.

Jubal sighed. His day was on a downhill skid and had barely even begun. "Sorry. Okay? Look, Maria is really nice. She'll be good to you; I know she will. Would you please go and help her?"

Benny rolled his eyes towards the ceiling and sat frozen that way for so long that Jubal wondered if he was about to erupt in anger. "Benny?"

Benny dropped his gaze and looked over at him.

"If ya say so, Jubal. I'll go work with Maria."

Jubal let out his breath in relief. "Thanks, Benny."

"Uh huh." Benny pushed back from the table and when reaching the entryway, shoved his feet into his barn boots.

After Benny was gone, Jubal went out around the corner of the house and jumped on his bike. The farm had grown to be a noose around his neck. It was unheard of to take time out of his day to bust free of it. He had no idea where he was headed as he flew down Harmony Hill, but he enjoyed the cool breeze from his speed on the bike. He cruised past Jazz's place, slowing as he neared Miss Curry's library. An idea formed, as he peddled, that he might stop by the library to search for reasons why Maria's usual self had flown the coop. He wanted to know when he might expect her to feel better.

But that would be like work, and the precious couple of hours before haying should be just for pleasure. He realized what he really wanted was to see Lizzy. Now that Polly was no longer his girl, there was no reason he couldn't.

He parked his bike outside the store and entered to find Clem Gochy sweeping the floor.

"Jubal Brown! I don't ever remember seein' ya here in broad daylight when there's work ta be done up the hill." Clem stepped to the side as Jubal passed. "I'll bet a certain someone will be happy ta fill yer grocery order."

"I've, uh, come for my jacket. I loaned it to Lizzy, night of the dance." He was surprised how quickly the excuse came, though he'd nearly forgotten she had his coat. But he didn't fool Clem.

"It's a real hot day ta need a jacket." Clem grinned. "She's down back takin' inventory."

Jubal nodded, glad it was Clem on duty and not nosey Bernice Sausville.

He searched the aisles, looking past the canned goods and boxed cereals. Finally he located Lizzy in the baking aisle holding a clipboard and counting bags of sugar. She looked nice in some dark-blue slacks that he guessed had come from his ma. Her light blue t-shirt fit well—tight, but not like the threadbare ones she'd worn in the past. She didn't see him right away, so he paused to further study her. He liked her short, jet-black hair held by a red ribbon. It set off her dark skin. Her mouth was turned up in a hint of a smile.

"Hi Lizzy," he called, continuing down the aisle.

She laid the clipboard on the shelf in front of her. "Oh my gosh, it's Jubal Brown of Harmony Hill! Come ta take me fer another ride through Avery's cornfield?"

"Only if you act as my guide." He tucked his hands in the pockets of his jeans, suddenly aware of how strongly they smelled of cows. If Lizzy noticed, she didn't let on. "Um, I see you're busy," he said.

"Yeah, but I can take a few minutes fer ya." She brightened as if realizing an idea. "Say, yer jacket! Meant ta bring it up ta ya. Is that why ya came? It's out back in my room."

"Ah, the jacket," he nodded. "You know, I didn't think of it until today. Seems with so much going on—"

"Clem!" she hollered. "I'm goin' out back here with Jubal. Give him somethin' I borrowed."

Clem waved from the storefront. Jubal followed Lizzy to the end of the aisle and towards the back door. Soon they reached the shed, which gave off a hot oven smell as Lizzy pushed open the screened door to the wire-caged room.

"Have a seat," Lizzy offered, pointing to her little round table. She went to an old refrigerator that hummed in keeping her food cold. "Want a drink?" She showed him a quart bottle of soda. "Here's yer choice, long as it's root beer."

He chuckled. "Sure."

As he sat, he looked around. Most would be embarrassed to show him such a meager living space, but not Lizzy—she filled in anything she might lack with good humor. In fact, she seemed to operate outside the rules that most girls followed. She was definitely different than Polly. In Lizzy's company, he never knew what she might say or do. It came to him that this was one of the things he liked most about her.

She placed two jelly jars on the table and filled them with soda. When she slid her chair into place, her knees lightly bumped his.

"Sorry, I ain't— I'm not used ta entertainin' company 'round my table. Well, 'cept Maria last night."

"How did that go?"

"I guess fine." Lizzy tipped back her jelly jar for a sip of soda and set her glass down with a sigh. "I'll tell ya, though, it weren't a bucket of laughs. She seems sadder than a lost puppy."

"I know," he said. "She won't talk to me at all and we used to be pretty good friends." The cold root beer with its smokey fizz was a welcome treat. His family didn't spend much money on extras like soda.

"Well, shoot," Lizzy said. "Don't ya see? Ya're a guy. That's not helpin' none." She shook her head. "Whole thing reminds me of my brothers. And I ain't wantin' ta give the creeps even a cross-eyed look."

Jubal coughed his sip of soda. "Thanks a lot! Comparing me to your brothers!"

"Ya're gettin' me wrong," Lizzy said. "What I mean is, maybe 'fore the attack, Maria mighta felt sweet on ya. But now, not even a *nice* guy is welcome near her."

"I have no idea what she must feel like."

"It's not hard to figure out," Lizzy said. "She's scared, mad, confused. Just all jumbled up inside."

He reached for his glass that rested inches from Lizzy's, accidentally bumping her hand. The contact felt strange, yet exciting with only the two of them in the room. "I think I came here for my jacket."

She laughed and took his hand. "Shucks, is that all?"

Without thinking, he squeezed her hand, causing her to be the one to flush. They dropped their hands and pulled back.

He stood to go. "It's nice that the busiest gal in all of Hayesville has given me a few minutes of her time."

Lizzy stood also, picking up the two jelly jars. She carried them over to a small pan that held a few dishes. "Oh it was sure painful havin' ta leave off countin' them sugar bags fer a sip a' root beer with my new pal Jubal," she said. She crossed to a makeshift coat rack fixed to the wire near her bed. "Why don't ya come again when ya can stay awhile and I don't have ta make a grocery order." She threw him his jacket.

Catching his coat, he stepped to the door. "Maybe I'll do that," he smiled. "Sometime soon when I don't have to spend all afternoon putting up some junky hay."

"Now yer jacket will keep ya warm while ya do it," she teased as they walked towards the store. "Good thing ya came ta get it today." She passed him to push open the back door and then let him pass. "I'll look forward ta the next time ya shirk yer chores and come visitin'."

He glanced at her in surprise. "You don't miss a trick. Ha ha."

As Lizzy returned to her inventory, Jubal slung the jacket over his shoulder, remarking to Clem as he passed, "I'm expecting a cold snap to be coming on soon."

Clem laughed. "No cold snap comin' outta that back room that I can see."

As Jubal rode his bike home, he felt lighter. Lizzy had just turned his dumpy day into a morning delight. It was clear that the real Lizzy LaFlam was somebody quite special, much more so than in his dream of the wooden barrel.

※

Freddie Coleman was beside himself. He'd not been able to get a minute alone with Polly O'Mara since returning to CYO camp. And now Mother Superior was restricting him from coming to meals. He guessed he knew why—so the old bag could put up a fence between him and the daughter of St. Anne's big shot. Polly's dad had power over the doings of the church and plenty of bucks besides.

To make matters worse, Freddie had been warned by Father Mac to keep his nose clean. Time needed to pass so the rape of the Rose Queen could blow over. But Father Mac had just offered some hope. Freddie had been giving a swimming lesson at the beach, with several kids in a line kicking water in the shallows, when Father Mac came to stand at the water's edge. The visit was highly unusual. Freddie told the kids to take a break and come on shore. After the kids sat down on their beach towels, he approached the priest.

Father Mac simply handed him a note and left.

> *Hang in there, Buddy. In a few weeks, we'll be nursing a cool one at sunset. Play nice to the O'Mara girl so we can keep our stories straight. The guilt lies with the Indians. Polly has remained mum about you. I can't believe she's the same gal you picked up at the dance. She goes before Mother Superior again tomorrow. The nun wants to know if Polly has ever met you off the camp's grounds. You should go see Polly tonight at the nurse's station and get her to report things our way. I happen to know the nurse will be out.*

Freddie stuffed the note in the pocket of his swim trunks. When the lesson was over and the kids were gone, he went inside his beach house and cracked open a fresh bottle of *Valley of the Moon.* He tipped the bottle for an occasional swallow as he thought the matter over. He and Father Mac and Tatum had to unite as to the guilty ones in the Styles rape: the half-breed brothers of that smart-mouthed gal down at the store. Otherwise, his butt might very well warm a cell at Windsor State Prison. He wasn't about to accept such miserable confinement as his fate. He'd been through enough hell for one life.

Growing up, he didn't have much of a father. When he was just a kid, his real dad had drowned in a fishing boat accident. After his mother had remarried, his stepfather was often on the road as a salesman. To fill the gap, his mother had arranged for Freddie to spend time in the church, thinking it a place of good influence. But the only devotion Freddie had learned was the role of "boy toy" for one of the priests. He never dared to tell his mother what was going on. She had a fiery temper, especially when she got into her wine, and could deliver a smarting backhand to the face that would bruise his cheek. A devout Catholic, she wouldn't allow a single complaint from him about going to catechism or Mass as an altar boy.

Thus, his bravest payback for years of being used was to give an unusual present to the guilty priest—an eight-inch pork sausage. The priest had opened the gift at a party surrounded by other clergy and nuns, creating a mountain of embarrassment. His mother was horrified that Freddie would show such disrespect to a man of the cloth. The incident, being one of a number of ways that Freddie had been acting out, had landed him in a Catholic home for troubled boys. However, he had no regrets. The Holy Father deserved his joke.

He'd had to stay at the boys' home in South Florida much longer than expected. Around the same time, his mother found out that his stepdad had a secret second marriage to a Georgia woman on his sales route. The news gave his mother such a shock that she sliced her wrists with a paring knife. A neighbor found her dead on the kitchen floor. His stepsister, he learned, was taken in by his aunt, but his aunt wanted nothing to do with him.

It was at the boys' home where he met Father Mac who took an interest in his wellbeing. Holding some sway with the directors, Father Mac took him out of the home. Together they rode the Overseas Railroad down the Florida Keys to Key West where the priest had a new position. In those days, it was the Florida land boom—the Keys were popular with rich American tourists and sport fishermen. Further up the Keys, road builders were constructing the Overseas Highway. He and Father Mac enjoyed the ocean and sun by day, and did a little partying at night. It was there he smoked his first Cuban cigar and got a taste for illegal rum. Freddie thought it likely that Father Mac was attracted to his good looks, though thankfully the guy never acted on it. Whatever—it had freed him from his juvenile prison.

During this time, he also met Tatum O'Mara who had come down the Keys for a little adventure after working a shrimp boat in Georgia. Young Tatum, having quite the swagger, joined up with their little crew. At first, Freddie had been jealous of Tatum, but he soon learned that the guy was a buffoon. Before long, Tatum got himself banned from a couple of bars after making indecent passes at wealthy women.

However, due to the friendship with Tatum, Father Mac was eventually asked to replace Father Henry in the Hayesville parish. Since St. Anne's had a responsibility to administer the summer camp on the shores of Lake Champlain, Father Mac had encouraged Freddie to become a certified swimming instructor. This allowed Father Mac to call on him to fill a vacant position at the CYO camp, so that each summer, Freddie was able to travel up to Vermont to spend time with his old friend.

Apparently, now, the nosey old nun at the camp was going to be his undoing. If she questioned Polly, the girl would tell Mother Superior all about how he'd acted the night of the dance, showing him in an unfavorable light. It would cast further suspicion since he'd hit on a young counselor and taken her in his car. Polly would make it sound as though his taking off her jacket was a filthy act, exaggerating like all girls did.

Yet, he knew he had crossed the line with Maria Styles and for that he was kicking himself, even though it had felt like justice in having his way with her. The girl had yanked his chain—coming on to him and then playing him the fool. No gal, no matter how sexy, could get away with that. He was nobody's plaything. Not anymore. Her stupid rant about the germs on her sandwich had him seething that he'd fallen for it. But now that he'd had time to cool out, he knew he'd done a very stupid thing.

He had to be sure that Miss Polly Perfect saw things his way. No doubt she'd bought into the gossip from the girl at the IGA who was spreading his guilt all over town. As evening came on, he admitted, looking at his bottle now half gone, he had no choice but to strike off and give it his best shot.

To clear the way for his visit, Father Mac had given permission to the nurse, Dot Stone, to attend the birthday of her granddaughter, which involved a number of hours of travel. Therefore, Polly was alone on duty, the perfect time for a little visit.

Sometime later, he hid in a spruce grove, looking up at the infirmary cabin. Daylight lingered in July, so he had to wait a long time for the cover of darkness. When night finally fell, he made a beeline up the hill where he could make sure that Polly O'Mara agreed to his innocence.

It had been a long day of doctoring scraped elbows and skinned knees. In the hot, muggy night, Polly felt like a wilted flower as she changed for bed, putting on only a thin cotton nightie with short sleeves. She did not expect more campers since nine o'clock was lights out for kids and staff. In case of a visitor, though, she placed her bathrobe over a chair. Lights were always on at the infirmary for safety or unexpected sickness.

She sat at the table drinking a glass of warm water with Arm & Hammer bicarbonate of soda to calm her nervous stomach. She was to meet with Mother Superior the next morning for more questions about Freddie Coleman, and Maria's attack. Hating the taste, she forced the baking soda down, but it did help to settle her tummy. She was belching gas when a knock occured at the door. Startled, she jumped up to grab the robe, thrusting her arms through the sleeves. To cover her nightie, she reached in vain for the end of the belt, trying to tie the robe's front.

There was another loud knock and a male voice asked, "Can I come in?"

She stumbled towards the door with the cloth tie dragging behind her. "Coming!" she said.

She had no idea who it could be. She had been keeping to herself so much, she'd barely gotten to know any of the other staff. And she was pretty sure Freddie was minding Mother Superior's orders to keep to his beach house. Maybe it was Father Hebert.

But when she opened the door, there Freddie stood, causing her heart to jump in fear. He pushed through the door just as she tried to close it.

"Hey doll. Remember me? Your handsome partner at the grange dance?"

"Of course." She reached again for the robe's tie, knowing she had to get Freddie out of the cabin and quickly.

He bent over to grab the tip of the belt and passed it to her. "Here you go." He openly checked her out from head to toe. "You look different than at the dance."

Along with a whiff of cologne, Polly smelled booze on his breath and noted his flushed face.

Backing up a couple of steps, she said, "It's past lights out." She held the edges of the robe tight. "You shouldn't be here. Mother Superior would—"

"Screw that old bag. Let's you and me have a visit." He stepped further into the room. "It's a warm summer night and it's boring around here."

"All right then, I suppose you may as well have a seat!" She gestured to the little table and sat stiffly in the chair opposite him. "What is it you need?"

He reached over and grabbed her wrist, his hand twice the size of hers. "I was thinking maybe we could do a little more of that slow dancing. What do you say, honey?"

She yanked her arm away. "In case you hadn't noticed, this is not a dance. It's the nurse's cabin."

"No kidding. But we don't need a dance to get close, honey." He wiped his hand on his shorts. "You sure are sweaty."

She looked sternly at him. "I'm nobody's honey. And I don't intend to be. I'm on nursing duty and it's past curfew—"

"Now, sitting here is real nice," he said, looking around. "And since we're going to be social . . ." He jumped up from his chair and crossed to the door.

As he stepped out, Polly couldn't react fast enough to get up from the table and lock the door. Instead, she stayed rooted to the spot with Clem Gochy's warning in her mind: "Stay away from that Coleman character. We don't want another one of our Hayesville gals wiped up off the floor."

Freddie reappeared with a knowing smile and a wine bottle in his hand. "Let's share a little enjoyment tonight, *Valley of the Moon.*"

Polly shook her head firmly. "No thanks."

As he crossed to the table, he walked a slightly crooked line. The guy was definitely drunk.

"Relax a little, honey," he said as he slumped back into the chair. "I hear you've been working way too hard here at camp." He sprawled his legs, getting comfortable.

"What do you want, Freddie? It's past lights out," she repeated.

Freddie took a long slug of the wine. "You're far from the gal I held in my arms at the dance, wearing them fake titties, painted up like a lady of the night."

She'd never heard a guy talk in such a crude way. "You mean the night you ruined my jacket?"

"That frilly thing?" He laughed. "It wasn't worth much."

"What would you know about it? I don't think you have a favorite anything. Except yourself!"

He didn't move from his casual posture, but his eyes were angry. "Well that's quite a smart mouth."

Polly froze, wondering if he would get up to hit her. Instead, he held out the *Valley of the Moon.* She refused the bottle again.

"Look, we need to have a heart to heart," he said, taking another swig. "First things first—when you talk to Mother Superior tomorrow, you're not going to share our little secret about the dance are you?"

Polly shook her head no.

"Good. Now, I'm guessing you know the Rose Queen girl?" he said. "Maria, that's her name, right?"

"I know her only a little from school," she said. She was going to keep the guy in the dark about Maria.

"You should have seen that Queeny coming on to me. She told me a bunch of lies to get my interest—said she was thirty years old, a teacher, and a bunch of other horseshit. Tried to make me out a goddamn fool."

Polly noticed the bottle was almost gone and suddenly saw a chance to get him to talk. She spoke in her sweetest voice. "That's terrible. I bet you were mad. So . . . what did you do about it?"

Legs still sprawled, he studied the label of his bottle.

"I bet you thought of something to get her back," she said.

When he looked up, his eyes were dangerous and Polly felt the bicarbonate of soda rise in the back of her throat. Across the table, she could tell Freddie knew he'd gotten to her.

"You know what I did?" He grinned darkly. "I beat the shit outta Maria Styles! And then fucked her brains out."

Polly's stomach turned. She belched loudly, quickly covering her mouth.

He laughed. "Yup, that's what I did, Polly. That half-breed gal down at the store got the whole thing right. I was the one who beat the Rose Queen black and blue." He leaned forward. "And you know I'll do the same to you if you breathe a word of this, or even one detail about that night after the dance."

As he rose and came around the table, she clutched the robe tightly at her throat. He grabbed her hair and yanked her head back. With his mouth inches from her face, she could again smell the wine mixed with his cologne.

"Do we have an understanding?" He shook her head a little.

"We do," she said. Her head hurt with her hair pulled tight and she expected him to throw her down on the floor and take her to show her a lesson.

But instead, he let go of her hair and turned to pick up his bottle, draining the rest. When finished, he slammed the bottle on the table before leaving the nurse's cabin. No doubt, he'd gotten what he wanted, scaring her witless.

When he was gone, Polly leapt for the door to throw the lock in place. She sat back down at the table for a long while, staring at the empty *Valley of the Moon* bottle. She tried to reason what to do. If he remained free, Freddie would most certainly make good on his threat, probably even if she didn't tell. Maria was proof of that. When her shaking subsided, Polly resolved to make the strongest move possible to save her own neck. She'd tell on the bastard. He didn't think she had it in her, but she did. He needed to be locked up and soon. Then let him try to come and get her.

Although it was nearly ten o'clock, she threw on shorts and a t-shirt in place of her nightie and ran to Mother Superior's room behind the office. She poured out her story, every detail, leaving a pale and shocked Mother Superior to call Tatum up from Hayesville. While they waited for Tatum to arrive, the nun made Polly a cup of tea and the two of them sat in the office below the cross on the wall.

Polly hoped that Tatum would take care of Freddie, but dreaded what might happen if he didn't. If Tatum didn't arrest the guy, and Freddie found out that she'd told, she was a sitting duck. She squeezed her hands together and drew her shoulders up. Mother Superior looked at her kindly.

"Don't worry child. Your uncle will take care of this. Drink your tea."

After what felt like forever, Tatum blasted into the campground with his lights flashing, and Polly sat on pins and needles while he went to Freddie's beach house. Her uncle was not gone long at all. He returned shortly with Freddie cuffed. Once he had Freddie in the cruiser, Tatum came to the office to report that he had found Freddie dead drunk, flat out on the floor.

Polly had no one to talk to upon returning to her nurse's quarters. Even though it was a steamy night, she sat shaking as if it were a sub-zero evening. She forced down another dose of bicarbonate of soda to calm her nerves, swirling the glass to mix the fine grains of white powder. Alternating between a crying spell and a string of burps, she couldn't endure the aftershock of nailing Freddie Coleman.

As a delayed reaction to the scene, she grew hysterical in total disbelief that she'd handled what she now believed Freddie to be—a cold-blooded killer. And if not a killer, for sure a rapist who could have left her a gutless, skinned rabbit.

In the middle of the night, she woke Mother Superior again to use the phone. She rang her folks, asking that they come for her. When they heard her story, they readily agreed to make the trip.

Her dad on the phone was astounded. "So Freddie Coleman confessed to the rape of Maria Styles? How did you get him to tell?"

Polly figured her mom, by this time, would be listening in on the wooden crank phone, as would the operator who handled all incoming calls from her living room switchboard.

"I . . . I'm not exactly sure." Polly looked over at Mother Superior sitting in her nightgown in the office chair, finding comfort in the nun's presence. "He came to my cabin. And he was drinking. He told me—"

"He was in your cabin? And you were drinking?" her mother cut in sharply.

Her dad shushed her mother. "What did he say?" her father asked.

Polly knew very well that her parents would find Freddie's way of stating things highly inappropriate. "Do you want me to tell you his *exact* words?"

"No!" came her mom's quick response.

"Now listen, Polly," her father instructed. "I know what a judge would want. In case Freddie claims to be innocent when he sobers up, I want you to describe exactly the scene prior to his confession to Mother Superior—"

Polly interrupted with a whimper. "But Mother Superior didn't hear his confession."

"No confession?" Her father paused. "Why not?"

"He never saw Mother Superior. He left my cabin and went back to his. He was drunk, I told you."

There was a silence, her father no doubt in thought. "While it's fresh in your mind, Polly, sit down and write exactly what Freddie did while in your cabin and what he told you. Since you were the only witness to his confession, and you are a minor besides, the attorneys will question you very closely."

"Yes, Dad," she agreed.

"You're a brave girl," her father said. "We'll be at camp in an hour and a half."

As Polly carried out her dad's instructions, writing down the details of the evening brought back her anxiety. Even so, she was glad to have a task to occupy her mind. Thinking of what was to come, she dreaded being grilled by lawyers, but she would do whatever it took. Freddie had to stay behind bars.

Chapter Twenty-Eight

It was time for Jubal to take care of an important matter he'd been putting off. He'd turned sixteen in May, and he needed to get his driver's license. His deepening friendship with Lizzy required more trips to town, and riding his bicycle the distance to the store was getting old. So he and his ma arranged a trip to Rutland one Thursday for him to take the test in the old truck.

Before leaving, Jubal went down to Jazz's place and parked next to the gas pump. Slag came to check the oil in the '34 pickup.

Opening one side of the hood, Slag pulled the dipstick. "Holy mackerel," he exclaimed. "Jubal, yer truck's 'bout ta go bone dry—blow an engine sure as hell. Lucky ya came in."

Jubal leaned on the truck's front fender. "Ma and I are dancing on the edge with this old girl." He watched Slag pour motor oil into the filler pipe. "Think she can make it to Rutland and back so I can get my license? A while ago, we made the trip for hay loader parts."

Slag put the filler cap in place. "I sure ain't bettin' my life on it." He shut the hood and latched it.

"Well, we're chancing it this afternoon."

"Yer ma ought ta own a Texas oil well if she plans ta drive this rig much longer," Slag declared. "Ya can tell Jazz I put in four quarts a' oil and five gallons a' gas. Settle up with him."

In the junkyard office, Jubal asked Jazz if he could trade a few hours extra work for the gas and oil.

"Sure thing. It's an important day fer ya, boy," Jazz said. His face was lit up with pride. "Don't let us down!"

Jubal left Jazz's yard in a cloud of black smoke to drive up Harmony Hill where he met his ma. Soon the old truck hummed and hammered along Route 7. Through holes in the floorboard on the passenger side, Jubal looked down to see the highway surface passing in a blur.

Over the motor noise, his ma shared some of her worries for the farm as she drove. "That place of ours is still losing money. Did you know we haven't paid Lady Lamont on the mortgage in years?"

Jubal put in, "And we don't have enough hay in the barn to make it to next spring. What we do have is crap."

His ma nodded. "I'll talk to Chuck from the Extension Service. Maybe he'll have some ideas." She turned the sloppy steering wheel, her hands working to keep the truck on the road around a corner.

"I was thinking," Jubal said, after a period of silence, "that if Maria keeps helping us, we ought to cut off the cows' horns. I don't want her getting hurt."

"Oh, God!" His ma shook her head. "I'm not sure that's a good idea." She slowed when they came into Rutland city.

"But Chuck says to saw them off an inch or so above the hairline and they won't bleed much."

"Well, I know Maria won't help, and Benny sure won't. They love those cows. They'll think we're torturing them."

"What if we try a few horns when we get back?" he suggested. "See how it goes?"

His ma parked in front of the motor vehicle office. As she cut the motor, she sighed. "I won't like it much."

Once inside the office, they took a seat to wait and Jubal reviewed the manual until he was called. He passed the written test with no problem since most of the driving rules were common sense.

But then he had to take the road test. A portly officer, in his fifties and mostly bald, followed Jubal to their rig and they started off. The officer looked nervous when seeing the road through the holes under his feet.

Even so, everything went smoothly until they started climbing a steep hill connecting to Route 7, the road leaving the city.

The officer surprised Jubal when he yelled, "Stop!"

Jubal jammed the pedal clear to the floor but the truck started rolling backwards. The officer slammed his foot on the floorboard hard enough to break more rusty tin. To stop the descent, Jubal floored the gas. When he let out the clutch, the truck chattered and jumped as they lurched forward up the street.

"Jesus, boy," the officer said. "I thought we'd had it! I'll tell ya, some drivers are gonna send me to my grave. But ya pulled that off real dandy. Yup, real dandy."

"Thanks. Sorry for the truck. It's sort of on its last legs."

The officer chuckled. "Ya ain't kidding. Yup, that emergency stop is required to see if ya could handle it."

Jubal continued on, turning through a few more side streets in Rutland. After the road test was complete, the officer told Jubal where to park.

"Yup, real dandy, boy. Real dandy!"

His ma put down her magazine and raised her eyebrows as they entered the office. Jubal nodded, causing her to break into a smile. When the clerk handed him his temporary license, Jubal was relieved to now be legal on the road. Outside, his ma pointed to the driver's side door.

"Take me home, would you son?" she said, beaming.

Behind the wheel, Jubal realized he could now drive around town without having to worry about Tatum O'Mara. Wouldn't Lizzy be disappointed! No more wild chases in the night.

On their drive home, his ma brought up another challenge. "You know, Jubal, I don't like that you're not planning to return to school this fall for your senior year."

"Gosh, Ma. You know it's just me and Benny keeping the farm going. And with my extra work down at Jazz's, I don't see I have a choice."

As he navigated a corner, his ma put her hand on the dash.

"I know," she said. "But if you don't finish . . . I mean, what if you don't want to milk cows your whole life?"

He tried to imagine doing something different from his daily routine up on Harmony Hill. He couldn't picture wearing trousers and a button-down shirt to shuffle papers in a Rutland office. As much as he complained about his lot, he liked the open air of the farm and the physical work.

"I'll be just fine," he said.

"Well, okay." His mother looked out the passenger window. After a few more miles, she said, "Look, I want you to return to school at some point."

"Sure. I will when Dad walks in the door sober." He pressed the gas hard and the motor hammered so loud it sounded as though it could explode.

"Jubal, for heaven's sake, slow down!" His ma threw her hand out to brace herself. "That comment was uncalled for. And don't you, for one second, feel sorry for yourself! Life doesn't owe us a thing."

"Sorry." He slowed the truck. "I shouldn't have said that. I'll try to go back to school by the first of the year. In the meantime, I'm hoping Miss Curry can help me research and write a paper about what happened to Maria. I want to read all about how a person feels after an attack like that."

His ma looked surprised. "Why, whatever for?"

"Well, I . . . uh, want to understand why Maria acts like she does. And I'm thinking school will give me some English credit for the paper."

"I see," his ma nodded. "That's good of you. But, I'm not sure doctors even have that one figured out. I know I sure don't."

"Can't hurt to learn what they do know, right?"

"No, I guess not."

He and his ma drove on in silence. Jubal wondered if bringing up Maria's rape had caused his ma to drift back to that night at the abandoned house. He hadn't meant to upset her. He just wanted to know about Maria. He couldn't stand his friend being in her darkened mood forever.

Driving into the yard, he saw Benny and Maria hard at work on the manure pile. Benny had been dumping on the pile for years and the rotted manure was the color of coal. The two had already spread enough manure so that big chunks the size of softballs covered the landscape, looking like a terrible black scourge had hit their meadows.

After Jubal changed his clothes, he went to check on his helpers who were loading the spreader. It was the kind of repetitive work Benny did well. Of course, using their old, worn-out spreader meant there were breakdowns, but Maria was resourceful, locating spare parts in their makeshift garage.

Opening the back door of the barn, he looked at the manure mounded up next to the plank ramp. They had already made a big dent in the pile on one side of the planking.

"Golly, you two have done a lot," he commented. He figured he should warn them of his plan about the cows. "We've got a couple of hours before chores. I thought this would be a good time for Ma and me to start cutting off a few horns. They're too dangerous to work around."

Maria stopped in her tracks near the spreader. "No!" she said. She came to him so they were standing face to face. "There will be blood!"

Jubal drew himself up, meeting her eyes. "The county agent tells me there won't be much blood."

Maria's hands balled up into fists.

Benny lumbered over to her side. "I love my cows. Please don't hurt my cows."

"If you cut those horns," Maria said, "you'll be killing who they are! They were meant to have them."

"Oh, don't hurt the cows. Please, Jubal!" Benny began ringing his hands and rocking on his feet.

Jubal was surprised when Maria reached over and patted Benny's arm. His uncle dropped his hands to his sides, his shoulders relaxing and his feet coming to rest.

Jubal looked from one to the other. He looked skyward and back at Maria. "Okay," he said in defeat. "We won't saw off the horns. But you mind yourself when around them!"

Maria nodded and returned to the pile with Benny following her.

Later that afternoon, Jubal parked the truck in front of the IGA. Looking in the truck's mirror, he combed his wind-blown hair back into place with his fingers. A couple of bench sitters took an interest in his arrival.

"Well, lookie here," Oscar Smith said, elbowing Charlie Jones. "Jubal Brown, drivin' on his own!"

"I guess I'd best look out now when I'm walkin' home!" Charlie said.

The two men grinned as Jubal walked towards them.

"Geez, guys," Jubal said. "I'm a good driver. Just got my license today!" He pulled it out of his pants pocket and flashed it at the old men.

"I'll be!" Charlie said, leaning forward to squint at the small document. He looked up at Jubal. "No more trips through the cornfield then?"

"I have no idea what you're talking about," Jubal said.

The two men laughed as he passed to open the door of the store.

Oscar winked. "Yer secrets are safe with us, boy!"

Jubal laughed. "Right, you two gossip like a couple of old setting hens."

Loud laughter followed him through the screen door and down the canned goods aisle, fading when he found Lizzy in her makeshift office.

She was bent over the desk with her back to him, her plain, white shirt neatly tucked under the band of a pair of dark blue slacks. He quietly walked up behind her to run his hand up her back, feeling the soft cotton of her blouse. She reacted with lightning speed, whipping around, about to slap his face.

He jumped back.

"Oh, Jubal!" she exclaimed.

"Wow, you're quick! Sorry I scared you," he said.

"Yer lucky I didn't sock ya one. I'm jumpy ever since that Coleman character came sneakin' 'round."

"Any word on that guy?" Jubal asked, sliding into a low wooden chair near the desk.

"Oh my god, ya haven't heard?" Her face was animated. "The low-down snake confessed. Tatum was in here earlier. Said Freddie Coleman's at Windsor State Prison awaitin' his charges.

"That's good news. The mystery is solved."

Lizzy stood against the desk to tell the story. "Imagine! Polly was the one that got Freddie ta confess. Skinny Polly takin' on the biggest muscle man ever ta be in these parts." She shook her head in disbelief. "I would've liked to have seen that."

Jubal was dumbfounded. "Wow. That sure doesn't sound like her."

"I heard tell she had a total breakdown after, callin' and askin' her folks ta bring her home from camp."

"Now *that* sounds like the Polly I know," he said. "I'll hear all about it when she comes for her family's milk."

Lizzy leaned over and brushed his shoulder. "Some hay or somethin'," she said. She leaned back against the desk.

"Ah," Jubal said. "Must've blown in the truck window from the back." He could still feel her touch.

They were quiet for a moment, sharing a longing. Jubal pictured her bed in the room out back where they could go and make out. The office area was open for all in the store to see. But he knew she had work to do, and so did he.

"I wish it was the end of the story with that guy in jail," he said. "But it still leaves Maria walking around like a dark rain cloud ready to burst."

"I know." Lizzy jumped up to sit on top of the papers on her desk. "I ain't seein' as I've helped her much. I've tried havin' her visit. She seems ta like comin' here, but it don't take away her sadness fer the long run."

She leaned forward. "There's more ta the story, ya know. Freddie told the sheriff that Maria had spun a string a' lies 'bout herself." She sat back. "Now why would she do a thing like that?"

"She's not one to lie." He found it hard to believe Maria would do such a thing. Thinking back to his talks with Maria before the attack, he knew she hadn't been telling him all. "That's why she was so worried Freddie would get even . . . not knowing what he might do."

Lizzy looked puzzled. "*When* was she worried he'd get even?"

Jubal hadn't meant to say this last out loud. "Oh," he shrugged. "I just suppose she would have been worried, you know?"

"Huh, well, yeah!" Lizzy said. "That girl must have been sheltered like a baby bird under her mama's wing. I mean, she's smarter than any person I know when it comes ta runnin' a farm machine, but ya don't go puffin' yerself up with tall tales ta a guy like Freddie. Those type a' guys don't need much to set 'em off."

He defended Maria. "Regardless of what Maria told Freddie, my God, it doesn't give him the right to practically kill her."

"Oh, I ain't sayin' that," Lizzy said. "I'd like ta tie him up smothered in bacon grease and leave him up on the mountain with our hound dogs."

"That would serve him right. But what are we going to do? Seems Trueboy has been good for Maria, but she's still miserable. She's only half living most days."

Lizzy nodded. "I wonder if time heals in the head like it does the body?"

Jubal stood from his chair and crossed to stand in front of Lizzy where she sat on the desk. He took both her hands in his. "I don't know," he said quietly. "But I want to stop at Miss Curry's library and hunt for some answers."

Lizzy squeezed his hands. "Ya sure are somethin' special in wanting ta help. Let's figure this thing out. I couldn't help my mimmy . . . but maybe I can help ya find out what ta do 'bout Maria."

Jubal leaned into Lizzy and pulled her towards him. Without hesitation, she slid off the desk, pressing her body to his. Again, he yearned for the two of them to spend some time in her room. He inhaled the scent of her shiny black hair and she exhaled against his neck. Gently, he touched his lips to hers. She opened her mouth for a long, warm kiss until finally they broke apart.

"I'd best get ta my papers," she said, looking out towards the store. She turned back and grinned. "Good thing ole Bernice didn't come stridin' down the aisle just then."

Jubal laughed. "That's for sure." He held her hands. "Guess what? I got my license today! We'll have to go driving some night."

Lizzy let out a hoot. "Fantastic! I'd like that. Though, it's gonna seem kind a' dull compared ta earlier times."

He laughed. "It will be far from dull, I promise." He kissed her again and dropped her hands. "We'll make a plan, but right now I'm overdue at Jazz's place."

"I know," she said. She turned him around to face the door. "Best get goin' 'fore I haul ya back ta my room."

"I could pretend I had an emergency in the barn and I could be late?"

She laughed and gave him a little shove. "Go on now."

As he headed to the front of the store, he turned to see her as she again bent over her paperwork on the desk. He paused in the aisle to take a deep breath, not wanting the bench sitters outside to see him flustered.

When Sunday came around again, Clyde had been in Troy for three weeks. He counted on his fingers. It was July 27th, the last day for which he'd paid his rent, and he was now squeezed between two forces the likes of which he'd never dealt with before. Bessie Black, the house matron, was sick and tired of seeing Doc Small come to her room every night drunk and stumbling into bed.

She had warned Clyde, "You're leaving if this late night drinking doesn't stop."

To have to leave would ruin his plans. He'd hoped to ask for credit for the upcoming week, with no intentions of paying since he'd run out of money.

Doc, on the other hand, had said, "If you stop havin' me up for a nightcap, you're out of here quicker than the blink of an eye."

Bessie and Doc were mean about their demands. On separate occasions, they each had called Clyde a lousy drunk, right to his face. No one had said such a thing to him before, not even Rose. Further, Bessie said he didn't deserve the room in the first place. He took issue with that since he'd paid and had given Doc all the bourbon he wanted. But she had walked away after telling him he'd better watch his step. He concluded that these folks were far from friends, a fact that made him homesick for Rose and Jubal. They at least cared.

As it was, he hadn't been able to find a vacant car suitable in which to set up camp. All the cars down next to the Hudson River were burned out or had all the windows smashed. He saw rats, even in broad daylight, coming and going, nesting in the horsehair-stuffed seats. Even if he did find a car, what would he do about food? He was down to his last three dollars.

Feeling at the end of his rope, he left the house and headed to Susy Quigley's grave to ask her angel at the headstone what he should do. He'd come to realize that Susy's angel was the only friend he'd made since leaving home. Approaching the grave, he fell on his knees and pounded the sod with his fist.

"Angel of stone, please help me. Make way for me ta enter a new life. Lead me on yer wings of righteousness ta my home where I am loved, and I will never again draw a drunkard's breath." Remembering the damaged phonograph record, he added, "If it's not too late fer me ta make straight my crooked path and rough ways." He knelt motionless for some time with his forehead pressed against the short cemetery grass, propped on his elbows, hands on either side of his cheeks. He waited and listened a long while for a response but heard none.

Lifting his head to gaze eye to eye with the angel at the headstone, his sight was blurry and he could no longer see the angelic engraving. His hands had fallen asleep and were prickling with pins and needles after resting so long with his weight on his elbows. He reached up to search for the carved indents in the stone, but the rock was smooth to his deadened hands. What was happening to him? By some miracle had the angel actually left?

Suddenly, he heard church bells in the distance and a joyous laugh overhead. Seen from the underside, a white bird was circling, wings spread to float upon the warm currents of air. Was it a sea gull coming from the Hudson River or was it Susy Quigley's angel? It could be a laughing gull maybe. He thought there was such a bird, but wasn't sure. The white bird flew east.

He sat up, stunned. It was the sign he needed. He knew he must follow Susy's angel and go home. How he would make the trip, he had no idea. He just had to have faith that three dollars would bring him to Hayesville.

After coming to agreement with Maria about the horns, Jubal sold ten more of their poorest producers. He wanted to include Iris, but the bossy cow was giving over forty pounds of milk a day, proving her worth in spite of his wish to be rid of her. Maria showed some excitement when four young Ayrshires with no horns walked off the truck and into the barn. In addition, the three new heifers that arrived after Chuck Dent's first visit had already calved and were doing well. But Jubal was worried about having to feed out their poor quality hay to get through the winter season.

When Jubal brought up the concern, Chuck suggested they feed the higher producers a generous amount of what he called a forage extender. The next time he came, Chuck brought them a sample of citrus pulp. He explained to Jubal that the seeds, peels, and pulp had been dried as an orange juice by-product. The cows loved it. Jubal's ma gave the okay to buy a ton of the feed that came in hundred-pound hemp burlap bags. Jubal had Maria feed a gallon scoop of the citrus product twice a day to the higher producers, and half that amount to the remainder of the herd. It was obvious Maria enjoyed seeing their cows reach for the sweet citrus.

Due to his evenings spent at the junkyard, Jubal sometimes left the barn early in the afternoon for a short break. One afternoon he decided to take a rest in the overstuffed chair in their living room—his dad's former drinking corner. He realized, while he rested, how much he missed his dad.

Years earlier, his father had made time for him, though the days were long with the farmwork being endless. When Jubal was a kid, his dad took him fishing at the reservoir on summer nights. Sometimes his ma would come along, packing them a supper so they could leave right after chores. The Department of Fish and Wildlife had begun stocking the waters with trout. His dad would find out exactly when so that Jubal could have the thrill of catching a few fish, even if they were too small to keep. But their happy family times quickly faded when his dad's drinking took hold. His ma began spending some nights at the mansion and Jubal noticed there was no more laughter from his parents' bedroom next door.

He still couldn't get over the fact that his dad stole his glass bank and the money he'd carefully saved. Yet, even so, he'd catch himself looking down the slope towards the road, hoping to see his father walking home.

In the chair, Jubal found he couldn't sleep, so he turned on the Philco. The news reporter was explaining the U.S. embargo of exports to Japan and how the government was paying the Japanese back for their embargo of U.S. war supplies going to China. It was all rather confusing and seemed very far away. He drifted to thinking about Lizzy.

He usually drove the truck to Jazz's in the evening, but in a new routine now that he had his license, he often borrowed the truck from his ma a bit earlier to go see Lizzy. His spring dream of Lizzy had become real, minus the barrel. They'd gotten more and more comfortable, enjoying physical affection, but he never let it go too far. After Polly, he was cautious. However, Lizzy, never hung up on what was proper, was all for going as far as they liked. Up on the mountain she'd been sprung from raw nature, and to Lizzy, sex was as natural as the wind in the trees. She'd made it clear it would be just fine with her to enjoy each other fully in the privacy of her caged room.

He was satisfied only that he liked being with her, minus making love. Of course he was tempted, especially since the store sold condoms. But guys at school had often joked about "leaky rubbers." And after his talk with his ma about Polly, he knew an unexpected pregnancy would be a nightmare for his future and Lizzy's. He was aware of the girls who had to leave school and the jokes that trailed after them as they went into hiding. He didn't want that to happen to Lizzy. She'd raised her standing from a dirt-poor wild thing to a smart young woman.

Clem was aware of Lizzy's strong feelings for Jubal and warned, "You two are playin' with fire and those who do usually end up gettin' burnt."

Jubal appreciated Clem's remark as welcome fatherly advice. His newfound love affair with Lizzy created an invitation that could lead to disaster with two lives ruined. They were too young to marry and too young to start a family. Plain and simple.

Chapter Twenty-Nine

Working behind the meat counter at the store, Bernice took an order from Mary White, Hayesville's town clerk, for two pounds of fresh hamburg—the best grade, all meat with little fat. Mary, a middle-aged widow with stylish gray hair and faint lines across her forehead, had an abrupt manner, which Bernice took as a demand.

"I'll pick the hamburger up after closing my office at five tonight," Mary said in a business-like tone.

Bernice had been warned by Lizzy to be pleasant to all customers, so she faked a smile and nodded. "Of course, Mary. I'll have your package waiting."

The woman had irritated Bernice ever since high school when Mary had been elected class president and yearbook editor. Especially annoying was that Mary White had also been named "most likely to succeed," while Bernice had never been recognized for a thing.

Before Mary's husband had died unexpectedly of a heart attack, he had worked for years at the New York Stock Exchange, traveling back and forth on the train to the city. Folks whispered that he'd left his wife a tidy sum. No one knew, of course, Mary's actual financial worth, but Mary had freely stated that she'd run for town clerk "just for something to do." Indeed, the job of town clerk was known for meager pay. Thinking always about how to fill the Temperance purse, Bernice had attempted to bring Mary, with her wealth, into the fold. But in an insult, Mary had declared she had no interest.

The absolute limit came for Bernice when Howard Perkins of the *Hayesville Weekly* had featured Mary with a large, flattering picture in honor of her work organizing an annual pancake breakfast to benefit a Catholic charity. To make matters worse, Bert had mentioned how it was a good article and noted that the picture of Mary must have been taken back when she was a "real looker." Bernice was furious hearing his comment. Howard Perkins had never given but minimal coverage of the Temperance League, since he was reported to carry a whiskey flask in the inner pocket of his suit jacket.

While in the store, Mary bought a few snacks displayed at the counter and before leaving, she shared in passing, "I'm putting on a little cookout for the selectmen tonight. It sure has taken the pressure off of our town in needing answers as to the attack of Maria Styles, now with that Coleman fellow confessing and behind bars."

Bernice merely nodded. She had already heard the news from Lizzy and did not want to get into conversation with Mary about the scandal.

Bert, who was sitting behind the cash register reading the paper, commented, "What an awful crime and Maria Styles, such a beautiful girl."

After Mary left, Bernice admitted to herself that she hated Mary White. "Lord forgive me," she whispered, "for harboring such thoughts. *Psalm 141,* verse five, should rule my life: 'Let the righteous smite me; it *shall be* a kindness . . .'"

She sighed. Sometimes it was hard to be a good Christian. As she fed the meat into the grinder, she consoled herself that she was closer to the Lord than Mary White. She turned the crank, watching the hamburger curling like earthworms, dropping onto the waxed paper as the slab of beef disappeared through the grinder's mouth. It was such boring work. All for a woman that acted like she walked on water. "Oh dear, there I go again," Bernice whispered. "I really must think charitable thoughts."

Bert set down his paper and looked her way. "Did you say something, dear?"

Bernice shook her head, pursing her lips. Lizzy still would not trust her to work behind the checkout counter. So Bert got the clean, easy job, while she had to get all covered with grease and fat, which somehow always got on her clothes even though she wore a full apron and rubber gloves.

Mary also got all the breaks with a perfect nose and attractive features. Bernice herself was saddled with a bumpy nose and a sharp chin. Mary had lovely eyes with long lashes, while Bernice knew that her own eyes looked like they were going to bug out of her head. Each morning while getting dressed, as she saw her reflection in an oval antique mirror that had been her grandmother's, she took in her body shape with a critical view. Just as lumpy as her nose. She tried to say a small prayer of thanks that she had a face and a body at all, knowing it was God's will that she was here on this Earth. But she didn't understand why He would give Mary the good looks, or even worse, Lizzy LaFlam. She felt like crying as the crank kept turning.

Over the noise of the grinder, her sharp ears picked up footfalls, or perhaps she sensed a body nearby. She turned just in time to see Jubal Brown pass out the door. She gasped and without looking pushed another slab of beef into the grinder.

"Lord, what is this place coming to?" she said, craning her neck to observe Jubal's tailend as he headed out to the street.

Bert called out, "Bernice! Pay attention or you'll have your fingers clipped off by that grinder!" He started towards her. "That machine is sharp!"

She yanked her fingers free in the nick of time, stopping the grinder and wiping her hands on the edge of her white apron. She went to Bert's side, out of the earshot of customers. "Did you just see that?"

He held her hand up as if to count her fingers. "Heavens, you scared me. You could have been badly hurt!" Seeing that she was okay, he said, "What was so important, that I missed, such that you nearly maimed your hand?"

"Those two are seeing each other too much!" Bernice pointed to the door that Jubal had just exited. "Look at what you've brought to this store! Shameless kids!" Slightly taller than her husband, she frowned down on him. He was too easygoing. "You know that family on LaFlam mountain breeds like rabbits."

"Bernice, for goodness sakes, they're teenagers." He smiled and reached for her waist. "Don't you remember us at their age?"

She stepped out of his reach. "Mind your manners." She glanced around the store, hoping no one saw them. Seeing his disappointed face, she remarked, "My apron . . . it's all covered with blood." She wiped at the fabric as if she could rub the stains away. "You mark my words. In a matter of a few years we'll have little urchins running up and down these aisles."

Bert scowled. "Frankly, I can't wait to hear the hurried feet of children. It would bring some life to this place." He paused, his face softening. "I remember you were so pretty in your flowing dresses, your curls falling around your bare shoulders. Blue eyes and a broad smile just for me."

She traveled in her memory to a young Bert, dapper in his suit, shoes shined on their wedding day. He was so handsome and she'd been full of expectation. But here they were—old and childless. Just hired help in a small-town store. "Stop, Bert. Those were my foolish days when I was misled."

He reached for her and she again stepped out of his grasp.

"Oh, but it was fun to be in love when your trusses hung low," he said. "With your blooming bosom feeling as soft as an angora cat. I was the luckiest guy in town."

Bernice winced. "We were fools."

Bert spilled his frustration. "We were fools to fall for the line that sex is evil. I say affection and love are of God's making."

She didn't know what to say. Her Bible studies had taught her about the sins of the flesh, and who was she to ignore the Lord's word?

"Bernice." He stood with his shoulders slumped. "Can't you see how our happiness has faded? The minute our knot was tied, you hit the road for Temperance and I watched this store slide to bankruptcy."

"Oh, so now you regret our life together?" For the second time in the last hour she felt about to cry.

He stepped closer and reached for her waist. This time she let him succeed in wrapping his arm around her.

"Dear, dear . . . it's never too late." He tightened his grip and kissed her cheek.

As his lips brushed her skin, her old blood rose like the sap of a young spring maple. "Goodness! Like this in broad daylight?"

He laughed, letting go. "I'll be catching you tonight when we're behind closed doors."

"Bert! What's happening to you?"

"I would venture that Lizzy and Jubal have ignited a spark in this place."

For the rest of the afternoon, from behind the cash register, her husband widened his eyes in adoring looks her way. Each time, she would smile in his direction, feeling for the first time in a long while, beautiful. It didn't matter that the stream of flirtations slowed her production of ground beef for the selectmen's dinner. Mary White would have her hamburger when it was good and ready.

It was midafternoon as Jubal, Maria, and Benny were heading to the barn with a full load of hay. Dick and Dan had just pulled the wagon out of the field when, in the distance, Jubal spotted a black two-door Chevy pulling into the yard. It was his uncle, Hammer Brown. Leaving the car, Hammer strutted towards the wagon, wearing dungarees and a white undershirt.

Jubal climbed down from the wagon to drive Iris and the herd back into their pasture away from the water tub so the wagon could pass. Only within the hour had the cows come for water, so for most of the afternoon, he hadn't had to worry about them. Maria was about to drive the team through, after which Jubal would have to shut two gates: one to the barnyard and one to the field they were haying.

Hammer walked right into the middle of the maneuver, acting as if the world rotated on his big bluster. He threw up his arms to stop the wagon.

Jubal quickly waved the handle of his hayfork in an attempt to hurry Iris and the rest of the cows out of the way.

"Hey, Jubal!" Hammer called out. "Ya need help hayin'? I'll bet it's slow goin' with this couple a' lame-brains on the wagon."

Iris whirled around, hearing the loud voice and smelling a stranger.

"WATCH OUT!" Jubal yelled.

In an instant, Iris charged. Hammer froze in his tracks. Iris's horns were lowered and pointed right at him. She hit him in the stomach, lifting him off the ground and dumping him into the water tub. Jubal ran and waved the fork handle at Iris's head, turning her back to the herd. Meanwhile, Hammer, having had the wind knocked out of him, sank to the bottom of the four-foot tub. Jubal reached out to yank Hammer from the water. At the same time, Maria drove the team and load out of the way so that she could shut the gates. She then stood guard with her fork while Jubal attended to his uncle.

On the ground in a fetal position, Hammer coughed and spit water while holding his midsection in pain.

"I'm . . . I'm comin' (*cough*), comin' back (*cough . . . spit*) with my (*wheeze*) gun. I'll shoot that bastardly cow."

Jubal lifted the undershirt and saw that there was only a scrape rising in a red welt. It didn't look serious. "Hammer, can you stand?"

Under his own power, Hammer rose and then grunted with each step towards his car. The black Chevy left the yard in an erratic fashion, as if the vehicle was barely under control. Weaving onto the road, his uncle's car disappeared. Disgusted, Jubal looked over at Maria.

"That was close," she commented.

Benny stood on the wagon, his eyes wide with fright.

"No kidding," Jubal said. "My dad has his demons, but Uncle Hammer is just plain crazy! What did he think, walking into the middle of those cows?"

Maria nodded. "He could have been killed." She turned to Benny. "It's all over, Benny. Hammer is okay."

"Yes, Maria," Benny said. He sat down on the hay in the wagon.

She drove the wagon to the haymow door and Jubal followed.

After the spectacle, the haying process continued with Maria leading Trueboy, Jubal loading the hayfork and controlling the trip rope, and Benny in the mow doing the best he could to not be buried in hay. An efficient team, the three of them loaded all the windrows from the field by late afternoon. Maria hooked Trueboy to the dump rake to clean up the scatterings while Jubal and Benny let in the cows for night milking.

Before leaving for a bite to eat and Jazz's place, Jubal offered his usual way of helping Maria. "You can ride Trueboy home again tonight and I'll see you in the morning."

She smiled slightly. He knew that riding Trueboy was her joy for the day.

Since his ma had the truck for some errands, Jubal didn't mind walking to Jazz's for a change. When he arrived, he was surprised to see Jazz's place crowded with cars. Local guys from town clustered around a wreck in the yard. Jubal came to the edge of the crowd but was unable to get a good look. He heard one guy say the vehicle was totalled. Another commented that the driver was seriously hurt or maybe even killed. Whenever an accident happened in town, word traveled fast and folks gathered to see the damage.

Howard Perkins was there taking notes for the *Hayesville Weekly*, and Jubal recognized Mike Harlow, who nodded hello. Mike Harlow had always given him a generous tip back when he had his paper route. Jubal couldn't help but like the guy. He waved to Mike before leaving the edge of the crowd to report to his work at the garage. He'd seen enough wrecked cars. Anyway, Tatum had arrived and he didn't care to talk to the sheriff if he could avoid it. He was mighty glad Jazz had taken great pains to keep the Packard hidden in a back shed, covering it with canvas.

Tatum was checking over the wreck, reporting his findings in a booming voice: "Bumper's in the shape of a half-moon. Engine's shoved through the body wall onto the front seat. Windshield smashed and the roof buckled. I'd say he hit a tree on Harmony Hill. Killed him." Tatum eyed the crowd, pleased to have their full attention. "Musta been goin' like hell."

Jazz put in his two cents. "I'd say the car set off the road just as you see it but without the tree." Chuckles rippled through the crowd.

Sometime later, Jubal was on his way to bring a muffler to one of the stalls and had to pass the wrecked car again. The crowd had thinned. He nearly dropped the muffler when he saw the black two-door Chevy. Hammer's car.

The vision before him didn't seem real. His dad's brother was dead? He pictured his uncle limping with one hand held against his gut after being grazed by Iris's horns. Had Hammer been hurt worse than he thought? No, he was pretty sure the wound was just a scrape that would have been, at worst, an eventual bruise. Was it anger that drove Hammer's speed then, or booze? It was often hard to tell what was eating the guy who always seemed fired up about something.

Jubal supposed he should feel sad. But the guy was never much of an uncle to him. In truth, Hammer Brown was a miserable brute—loud, pushy, and mean. Still, it was strange—the guy had been running his mouth just hours earlier. And now he was gone. Just like that.

Mike Harlow came to stand next to him. "Sheriff says he hit a tree. That's your uncle, isn't it? You know about this?"

"No, I've been haying all afternoon." Jubal figured it best to keep quiet about Hammer and Iris.

"What about your dad? He must know."

Jubal shrugged. "Don't think my dad's seen Hammer in a while." It wasn't a lie really.

Over by the cruiser, Tatum appeared to be writing his report. "There ain't no insurance," he called to Jazz, who was walking across the junkyard towards his office. "Might as well tear the rig down."

Jazz stopped and rolled his eyes. "No insurance! Well, there's a shocker. Half the folks in the county ain't got no insurance."

Tatum squared his shoulders. "You'll be interested to know that Doc Peters will be givin' me an autopsy report. Whole thing looks suspicious. Hammer had water in his shoes and that warrants an investigation."

Jazz waved Tatum off to continue to his office.

Not wanting to field any questions, Jubal nodded goodbye to Mike and hustled to the shop to help Slag.

"Investigation, my foot!" Slag sneered as he worked on a bent rim. "What's the big sheriff gonna do, cross examine the tree? A lot he knows, tellin' Jazz ta tear the car down. What kinda policeman dismantles the evidence? I tell ya, that Tatum's a sorry excuse fer the law!" *Bang,* went a blow, steel against steel. "Fool even left his sister ta die in a fire. Nicest kid, Kelly was. I schooled with her. Ain't right he's sheriff." Slag's blood pressure must have been climbing since the New Hampshire scar was bright red.

After a few minutes, the granite state faded to pink. "Ya know, I saw that letter yer ma sent when ya was born. She nailed that bastard. I know Tatum 'bout craps his pants every time he sees yer ma comin'. He's thinkin' he's gonna get called fer child support."

Jubal looked down at the floor as Slag reminded him of a fact he wished he could forget.

"What's the matter, boy?" Slag asked. "Wouldn't ya like yer ma goin' ta Tatum 'bout now, sayin', 'We need ta educate my boy who's lookin' ta go ta Harvard. How 'bout forkin' over five grand?'" Slag grinned, causing New Hampshire to inch northward. "I'd like ta see that dipsy Tatum stiff-kneed and white as a bedsheet."

"Slag, you're dreaming," Jubal protested. "I'm not going to Harvard. I'm not going to any college at all."

"Yer wrong, boy. When ya're Tatum's age, ya'll be runnin' this town."

"Doubt it. All I can call my own is a rusty bike and the clothes on my back."

Slag reached for a wrench. "I've watched a lot of kids grow up. Ya're top rate. Just like that Lizzy LaFlam strutted down that mountain, now makin' a name fer herself." He paused. "She's got a spark like no other. If I was younger, oh man, she'd be my gal. She and I could make some grand music together."

At this, Slag busied himself with his work, humming a little tune.

Heat rushed through Jubal on hearing Lizzy's name. It made him uneasy that another guy was dazzled by her. He studied Slag working on the shell of the car. Scarred, pockmarked, and with a good number of years on Lizzy, the guy was a dreamer.

"Lizzy's got a mind of her own. Makes her own choices," Jubal said.

Slag stopped humming. "Ya ain't got yer hooks in her, have ya?"

Jubal didn't answer, instead piling a bunch of parts onto his cart and pushing the cart into motion. Outside the garage, he took a route down the back side to avoid Tatum. He couldn't blame Slag for his crush on Lizzy. It was not as if there was a long line of single girls in town. But Jubal just happened to know how special Lizzy was and that she currently had a fondness for one farm boy from Harmony Hill. He smiled to himself as the heavy cart dipped while he pushed it down the dirt path.

Because of Tatum's investigation into Hammer's death, Jubal decided that Benny should be at his ma's side for the next day or two. After work, he planned to hurry home to tell his mother the whole story. It was likely no one would miss Hammer Brown. Jubal imagined that Hammer's wife, Gloria, would feel she'd been set free.

When they finally dragged the black Chevy into the garage, he rather enjoyed tearing Hammer's car to pieces. He loosened the lug nuts at each wheel, then let the air out of all four tires, busting them free from the rims with a hard rubber mallet. He followed by using the flat end of a tire iron to free the tubes.

Once the tires were off, Slag hoisted the car with the pulley and chains before torching the bumper bolts and removing the smashed radiator. Hooking onto the engine and transmission, Slag cut them free.

Jubal disconnected the generator. The water pump was junk, along with the fan assembly. The transmission had been driven clear into the back seat. That might be junk as well. After they dismounted the rear axle and springs, they saved the back seat. Next, Jubal pushed the remains of the body shell outside with the doodlebug and down into a row of similar wrecks. Days would pass and Hammer's Chevy would be just a memory.

In no time, Jubal's shift was over and he headed home. He was surprised to find that he felt like crying. In the dark, a meadow mouse scurried across the road and into the underbrush.

"Hmph," Jubal huffed as he climbed the hill. "I'm not so different from that critter, just scuttling along day to day, trying to survive one season to the next."

The higher he got up the hill, the warmer the air became, with crickets singing in the fields. He emerged from under the trees to be struck by the number of stars, with a white wash of the Milky Way hanging over the pasture. In the distance, the kitchen light was on in their farmhouse. No doubt his ma was sitting at the table with her evening cup of coffee, having just gotten home from work. He thought of Slag's comment about his ma—how she was brave in sending out the birth announcement to the guys from the party. She had carried on the best she could, now even without his dad. He quickened his pace. Suddenly he wanted to sit with her and have a glass of milk, just his ma and him.

Chapter Thirty

After receiving the message from Susy Quigley's angel: *Go east and head for home*, Clyde hurried back to his room at the boarding house. He knew he'd have to take Route 7 across the border into Vermont, but to travel the highway beyond that was quite another matter. It would be a trip of close to fifty miles to reach Hayesville. He'd never walked that far in his whole life, to say nothing about doing so in the heat of summer. His plan was to leave at about four in the morning so he could travel before the day got too hot.

Needing food for his journey, he went downstairs into the pantry, finding that all was quiet. He located a brown bag and riffled through the cupboards. He chose a loaf of bread, several biscuits, a jar of jam, a can of beans, some utensils, a can opener, and two bars of soap. His little yellow suitcase couldn't hold much more than this. Even though the glass bank took up room, he wouldn't sacrifice the space for anything less cherished. He hoped his efforts in preserving the bank would allow him to rejoin his family and find his way back into their good graces despite all he'd done.

In the hallway, he passed a selection of coats. He would need something warmer than he had for possible cool nights. He selected a nice woolen overcoat and, in case of wet weather, a pair of rubber boots that looked to be about the right size.

He set about packing in his room, but his hands began to tremble. A small shot would have to settle the shakes. He also had to have room in his suitcase for the last two pints of *Jim Beam*, an absolute necessity. Even at that, he'd have to drink moderately to start his own plan to reach sobriety. His yellow suitcase was soon filled to overflowing, making it barely possible to snap the two latches in place. Last, he found a heavy quilt in his closet and rolled it up with the overcoat inside. He tied it in a bundle with the belt of an old bathrobe.

That night while eating with the boarders and Doc's family, he hoped nobody would notice the missing items he'd taken for his trip. He calmed any guilt over his petty theft by telling himself that he'd given Doc more in the cost of liquor than he'd ever received. At the end of his hearty meal of corned-beef hash, cucumber-tomato salad, and apple pie for dessert, he went upstairs for a small swig and stretched out for a rest. He woke around nine o'clock to slide his suitcase, boots, and blanket roll under his bed. He then straightened the covers, pulling the faded spread to nearly reach the floor, making it look like he'd never used it. Shutting off the light, he crawled under the bed and waited. He was through sharing any of his liquor with Doc Small.

In a short while, he heard footsteps climbing the stairs and his door opened. A hand slid over the wall, searching for the switch. He held his breath as light filtered across the floor, reaching him in the darkness.

"So, that low-down snake has gone and left." The closet door squeaked open before slamming. "Took his liquor too! Land sakes, I need a drink!"

The bedroom door banged shut, and Clyde crawled out from under the bed. He slept on top of the covers until the downstairs clock struck four chimes, after which he rose, already dressed, and checked the street below. The dawn was a bare beginning, yet in the faint, gray light, he could make out several rats scurrying down the sidewalk, heading towards the river. He would wait for the sun to climb a bit higher. He sure wasn't going to start his journey facing a rat attack. Yet he felt an urgency to leave as soon as possible. He had to beat the heat and, more importantly, not get caught walking off with items that didn't belong to him. Since he had little means, living an honest life would apparently have to wait until he got home.

Sunrise came now a little after five. Passing through the kitchen one last time for a hardy snack before hitting the road, he saw that Bessie Black had flipped the calendar the night before to August. Where had the time gone? His dreams of a free and easy life in Troy had not come to be. He gripped his suitcase in one hand, the stolen bedroll and coat in the other, and he slung the snitched rubber boots, tied at the laces, over his shoulder. It was time for his next adventure.

The angel had given him a beautiful day with only a few white clouds overhead as he traveled Route 7 eastbound. He made fairly good time by walking a steady pace, with a few stops for a nip to ease the shakes. He wanted to stay, however, as sober as possible in his new mission to walk the straight and narrow. He knew he looked absolutely frightful, red-eyed and sprouting whiskers. Rose had last cut his hair several weeks before he left home, so that it now hung to his shoulders. Appearing as a backwoods hermit, he figured no one would stop to give him a ride. A few cars and trucks passed by, not slowing down in the least. He would just have to walk all the way to Hayesville.

By midday, his feet gave him unbearable pain with each step he took, especially his heels and toes. He just had to stop when he came to a small stream that crossed the road. He limped down the embankment to reach the water where he found a flat rock and gratefully took off his shoes. The condition of his feet was alarming.

His socks for some time had been worn through, and he was regretting that he left Hayesville in such a hurry that all he had was the single pair. Blisters had broken, showing blood and serum that soaked his socks. He stuck his feet in the water, appreciating the coolness on his open sores. There was plenty of time to consider his next move. He had few options. It was too early in the afternoon to set up camp, which would amount to wrapping himself in the overcoat and blanket to sleep beside the road.

An alternate plan would be to dry his feet, wearing no socks, and put on his shoes to sit at the edge of the road on his suitcase. He crawled up the steep slope, dragging his belongings. This caused him to work up quite a sweat in the hottest part of the day. But he was not worried by his situation, having absolute faith in Susy Quigley's angel. For the first hour or so, he stuck out his thumb, which he considered to be begging but he had no choice. It didn't seem to matter—vehicles sped past as if he didn't even exist. The sun continued to bear down on his mop of sweaty hair.

But sometime in the late afternoon, an old car came chugging up the road. It was a four-door Model A Ford loaded with belongings on the roof and tightly packed with passengers. Even though Clyde had given up sticking his thumb out, the car stopped. A back door flew open and he heard the offer, "Get in."

A man and woman sat in front with a girl around ten years old between them. A younger fellow in back was playing his guitar and singing along with his music, while a slight woman they called Sister and her toddler squeezed next to the back door to give Clyde room. Clyde settled in with his suitcase on his lap. With some difficult maneuvering, he was able to remove his shoes, placing his blistered bare feet on the bedroll with a sigh of relief. The little one, sitting on the floor at her ma's feet, turned to rest her head on the edge of the bedroll. All of the passengers appeared skinny and at the edge of starvation.

The driver shared that his name was Pop. "We're the Holy Gospel Singers," Pop said, holding tight to the wheel and speaking into the rearview mirror. "We're appearin' at a tent revival tanight outside a' Shaftsbury, callin' on the Lord ta give us salvation. My boy Caleb is on the guitar. Give our friend a taste of Thomas Dorsey's best."

Everyone, except for the child resting at her mother's feet, belted out the tune. *"Precious Lord, take my hand. Lead me on, let me stand. I am tired, I am weak, I am worn . . ."*

The volume was earsplitting. However, a ride to Shaftsbury was more than Clyde could ever dream of asking. The town was just a few miles from his home on Harmony Hill.

The woman in front, likely Pop's wife, spoke up. "We need food. The babe ain't had a drop a' milk since yesterday."

Pop remarked, "That's certain, Eva. And we need gas. We ain't makin' it ta Shaftsbury on fumes. We'd better start prayin' fer a miracle."

The thought for Clyde to even take a single step on his blistered feet made him wince. He sat looking straight ahead as the trees flew past on either side. The Model A was eating up the miles—miracle miles delivered to him straight from Susy's angel. Finally he said, "I see there's a store and station up ahead. I'll spring fer some gas and a couple quarts a' milk."

As Eva turned from the front seat, her sunken eyes brightened. "My goodness. I told Pop ta stop fer ya, never knowin' if it might be the Lord himself."

Clyde fished in his pocket for two dollars, leaving the third, and reached over the front seat. "Here ya go."

Eva raised the two dollars in her fist. "Hallelujah, thank ya, Jesus!" She turned to Clyde. "God bless ya!"

Caleb strummed a few notes, making up a little song. "I never know'd that the comin' of the Lord would stink like a skunk."

Everyone laughed, even Clyde.

Clyde told them, "When we get some gas pumped, I'll have the fixin's fer near a full meal: beans, biscuits, bread, jelly, and milk." Taking on the role of grand provider was an experience he never expected. "We'll pass the bread between us, share the beans from a can, and polish off our eats with a little Holy water among us older folks."

"Ya never know on sight of a fella what goes on within," Pop remarked. "We'll be takin' part in a real communion meal, celebratin' the blood and body of Christ."

"Do as ya might," Clyde said. "All I know is I'm gettin' mighty hungry."

While waiting for Pop and Eva when they got out at the store, Clyde opened the suitcase perched on his knees. Sister and Caleb eyed him as he worked his hand into the case to bring out the feast's contents one by one. The young girl in the front seat, having smelled food, sat facing backwards to watch Clyde. Soon, he had the can of beans opened and ready with a spoon for all to use.

When Eva returned with the milk, he passed the beans to Sister with a biscuit. She picked up the child at her feet and balanced the little one on her lap, offering small spoonfuls of beans. The child hungrily fisted crumbs of biscuits into her mouth. Clyde was glad he had stolen enough biscuits to share with everyone. Eva passed the bottle of milk to the girl on the seat beside her, who then passed it over the seat to Sister, who offered it to her child whose face was now sticky with food.

Using the top of his suitcase as a work space, Clyde spread jelly on slices of bread. There was enough for everyone to have two slices for an honest to goodness jelly sandwich.

Pop said, "Well, this is mighty fine a' ya, Mister. Strum us a tune, Caleb?"

Praise God from which all blessings flow. . . .

"Now, Mister, can ya pass around the fire a' the Holy Spirit?" Pop asked. "We need a reminder a' the blood our dear Savior shed fer us all."

Blood or no blood, Clyde was beginning to get the jitters and needed a swig of what Pop called the fire of the Holy Spirit. He uncapped the bottle of *Jim Beam* and took a swig, passing it to Sister for a swallow, who passed it on up to Pop over his shoulder while he continued to drive.

Pop choked on his first gulp. "Holy jumped-up, the spirit a' the Lord just slid down my throat and landed in my belly!"

Another round for a slug and by the time it reached Clyde, he made sure the bottle was empty. Before long, Pop parked the car at a roadside pull-off and the music stopped. A calm had fallen over the Holy Gospel Singers, as well as Clyde. They all drifted into a short nap. When they awoke, they visited the woods before they were again on their way.

They arrived in Shaftsbury by early evening, and Clyde asked if he could be dropped off at the Sunrise Jersey Farm. He knew the *All Jersey* milkcan truck would pick up milk at that farm around three o'clock the next morning. He was hoping the driver would take him to Hayesville on the way to his next milk stop at Avery Ketchum's place.

"I'd drive ya ta yer place if we wan't so late," Pop said. "Our rest next ta the road took awhile."

Clyde pulled on his shoes through unbelievable pain. The farm was coming up soon. "Much obliged, but I'll get out right up there at that driveway."

The family thanked him as he climbed out of the Model A accompanied by shouts of "Thank ya, Jesus!"

Though it was a blessing to help the family make it through the day, Clyde was happy to be free of them. He had his faith in Susy's angel and didn't need to complicate his life with other Godly matters.

He hobbled a short distance from the side of the road to bed down for the night. Before going to sleep, he filled the two empty liquor bottles with water that ran from a culvert at the edge of the road. Finding a soft layer of pine needles for a bed, he sat on the ground and pulled off his shoes with a whimper. He then wrapped himself in the warmth of the stolen wool coat and blanket, his feet sticking out the end. As he stretched out, he rested his head on his yellow suitcase and wiggled his bare toes. The cool evening air soothed his blistered feet. He turned his head to the west to witness an inspiring sunset. He had no doubt that Susy's angel would lead him all the way home and on to sobriety.

Throughout the night, he woke to take sips of water to satisfy his thirst. He could feel the first jitters as the alcohol from earlier in the day left his body. He would have to ride it out. Luckily, he was warm enough with the coat and blanket. But it soon became apparent that something was living in the quilt, as he began to itch. The child at his feet resting her head on his blanket must have left him the gift of lice or bed bugs; however, he was too tired to care.

At three in the morning, right on time, he heard the *All Jersey* truck, milk cans rattling in the back, coming down the road on its way to the Sunrise Jersey Farm. He stood waiting in near total darkness at the farm's driveway while the truck approached. His feet were killing him in his shoes. As the truck made a turn, its load sounded like off-key steel drums, reminding Clyde of a tropical music show he once heard on his Philco. The music had made him wish to sit by the ocean with a nice glass of rum, but he'd known that such a fantasy was unlikely to ever happen. The truck slowed.

He saw that Buster White, a guy he once knew in school, was driving. Clyde remembered the guy as a rugged fellow who fit his job—days that consisted of loading and unloading milk cans that weighed near ninety pounds when full. The guy had done this for most of his adult life for the *All Jersey* creamery. Clyde wondered if Buster would remember him after all these years.

When the truck stopped, Clyde said, "Mornin' ta ya, Buster." He realized it must be strange to see someone standing by the roadside like a ghost in the early hours.

Buster stuck his head out his window. "Who the hell are ya?"

"It's Clyde Brown, from up on Harmony Hill."

"Holy thunder! What the hell ya doin' all this way from home?"

"Just travelin'. I wonder if ya'd give me a lift ta Hayesville? Ya can drop me at Jazz Crow's junkyard, so as ya don't have ta go all the way up the hill."

Buster looked doubtful. "Well, I'd give ya a lift, but my passenger side is filled with milk testin' bottles 'n stuff."

"Aw, I know ya pass close by Jazz's on your way to Avery Ketchum's. Maybe in back with the cans?"

"Hmm, I figure that could work. But ya should know them cans make a helluva racket. And I'd have ta shut the doors and lock ya in."

"Anything ta get home." Clyde clutched his case tight by the handle and held the quilt bundle to his chest, boots slung over his shoulders.

Buster looked at the suitcase, the bundle, and the boots. He studied Clyde for a moment.

Clyde shifted his sore feet, wishing he'd found a way to at least shave before leaving the boarding house.

"Where's yer family that could come ta give ya a lift?" Buster asked.

"I ain't sure. I been on holiday and couldn't reach 'em on the telephone." After sharing his stolen provisions with the Holy Gospel Singers, Clyde had felt less like a thief and more like Robin Hood. But now he was lying again.

"Damn." Buster slammed the steering wheel with his hand. "Look, I run on a tight schedule, ya know?"

Clyde set his suitcase on the ground and sat on it to relieve his pain.

Buster narrowed his eyes, reaching his decision. "I'll pick ya up on my way out. But ya gotta mind yerself in back with all them cans. I don't need ta be gettin' in trouble with my boss thinkin' I picked up a hobo." He rolled up his window and the truck rattled off, climbing the drive to the farm.

Clyde took exception to being called a hobo, but he knew he looked the part and it was his own damned fault.

In less than fifteen minutes, Buster returned. He shut off the truck, jumping out to open his back doors. A cargo light blinked on. Clyde could see several rows of cans stacked three high, held in place by cross-chains.

"I'll throw your stuff in and give ya a hoist," Buster declared.

Clyde held to a sidebar, pulling.

Buster pushed on his butt. "Hell," he coughed. "Clyde, where ya been livin'? Keepin' company with a skunk?"

After Clyde heaved himself onto the truck, Buster slammed the doors shut, leaving Clyde in the dark to crawl to the back where he buried his head in the blanket. He wasn't afraid, locked in with a bunch of rattling cans, but the noise caused him to press the blanket against his ears. He didn't dare take off his shoes, fearing his feet were so bad he'd never get the shoes on again. After a long while, the truck stopped and the doors flew open. They were at the edge of the field at Jazz's place.

Clyde gathered his stuff and had no choice but to jump down from the truck. When he landed, the shoes dug into his sores. He let out a mournful cry and went down on his knees.

"Golly, Clyde, what ails ya?" Buster bent to lend him a hand.

"I'll be alright." But Clyde wondered if he really could make it the rest of the way up Harmony Hill to home.

Buster helped him to stand. "When ya get ta the house, I 'spect yer wife'll throw you directly in the bathtub."

"Most likely. Thanks fer the lift. And good to see ya, Buster."

The *All Jersey* truck went on its way, leaving Clyde standing alone by the junkyard. He considered his next move. The sun had just broken the horizon, washing Jazz's place in gold light. Surprisingly, the guard dog, Babe, wasn't barking. With difficulty, Clyde stepped over a low spot in the fence while clutching the suitcase and boots, dragging the blanket and coat along.

He left the overcoat and boots hidden by the side of the road and hobbled out into the field where he found an open shell of a car. The back seat showed a lot of springs, but it would have to do. He sat and gingerly pulled off his shoes. After a few swallows of water from his bottle, he thanked his angel for leading him safely home. He reached into his pocket for the one dollar he had left and opened the suitcase for the bank, slipping the money through the glass slot. He lay back on the ragged car seat and covered himself completely with the blanket, which seemed to now be free of the tiny insects. Or maybe he just hoped that they were gone. Before long, he drifted into an exhausted sleep.

In the days after Hammer's death, Jubal didn't think about his uncle much. As expected, his ma was not greatly moved by the loss either. They shared the view that the accident was unfortunate, but left it at that, since the guy had made little effort to be part of their family. When Hammer had come around, it had mostly been for a favor, money, or to give Jubal's dad a hard time.

Jubal was starting to feel that his father was truly gone for good and this had him feeling down. However, one evening there was a bit of good news. When he arrived at Jazz's, he noticed a wrecked 1936 Packard in the yard with the parts needed to fix Benny's car.

Looking the green Packard over with his now more experienced eye, Jubal noted the car had been rear-ended with such force that it had sprung the frame. He also saw that the right front fender was already missing, so he hurried to the garage. There in the bay was Benny's Packard, brought up from the back shed. The discovery was such a surprise that there was no longer a tired bone in his body.

When Jazz saw Jubal, he started playing "Happy Birthday" on his clarinet and Slag danced around the spaces between the car parts. Jubal stood speechless until Jazz finished his tune.

"It's yer lucky day!" Jazz declared as he laid down his instrument. "Lady Lamont told me at the selectmen's meetin' that ya'd turned sixteen all the way back in May. I figure it's far past time ta celebrate."

"I just saw the '36 Packard in the yard," Jubal said excitedly. "Gee, I never expected—"

"Most of the thanks goes ta Lois. She paid fer me ta get the car, and I agreed ta fix yer Packard as a high priority if I could sell the parts from the rest a' the wreck."

"Does Ma know?"

"Well, it ain't no secret yer ma has more than just a job up there at the mansion. Don't ya suppose the two women are special friends?"

"They sure are," Jubal agreed. Since Lady Lamont had been overlooking their unpaid debt on the farm, he guessed that springing for a wreck to fix the Packard was likely no big deal. He also trusted that she wouldn't share their secret about the car with Tatum.

"Ya already know I ain't fixin' that car fer nothin'," Jazz cautioned. "Yer gonna be working nights fer the next ten years."

Slag joined in. "Ten years! I'm awful glad ta hear that 'cause I need someone ta talk ta 'bout the world goin' ta hell in a hand basket."

Jubal stuttered, "Well . . . I could work . . . for a while, until . . ."

Jazz laughed. "Nah, I'm foolin' ya." He slapped Jubal on the back. "Work fer a bit more this next week. That'll do. Ya've already put in a lotta time down here." He gestured to Benny's Packard, which even had brand new license plates, registered for the first time in a long while. "Why don't ya have a look? Bumper's been straightened, fender painted. Slag can help ya put the car together tonight, and 'fore ya know it, ya can drive 'round town in style. All legal and everythin'."

"Wow, really?" Jubal pictured taking Lizzy out for a drive. Then he remembered. "But what about Tatum? He thinks this car was stolen."

Jazz and Slag exchanged glances.

"Oh, we got that covered," Jazz said confidently.

"How?"

"Tonight, ya're gonna strip every usable part off that '36 wreck: doors, fenders, headlights, grill, bumper, radiator, engine, transmission, wheels, axles, rear seat, dashboard, steering wheel, and column. Put all them parts in my truck. First thing Monday mornin', my man will take the load outta town ta be sold."

Slag added, "I'll torch the rest inta pieces and add them ta the junk pile."

Jazz continued his plan. "After midnight, Slag and I'll park Benny's Packard at the reservoir with the keys in it."

Slag seemed pleased with the scheme. "Tatum'll piss his pants when he finds that car." He danced a few steps around the blue Packard. "I can hear him now, bustin' with authority: 'This warrants an investigation.'"

"It was too bad ya smashed yer uncle's car," Jazz said, "but I must say it's given me the chance ta pull out a few feathers from that sheriff who goes 'round all puffed up like a peacock."

Jubal listened to more of Jazz's plan as they walked out the door. "This'll take way inta the night ta get all this done. But after, go home and get a good night's sleep 'cause in the mornin' Tatum'll go fishin' at the reservoir. He'll blow a gasket when he finds Benny's Packard. No doubt he'll be wheelin' inta yer yard fer answers."

Jubal had to admit, it pleased the heck out of him to see Jazz and Slag play Tatum for a fool.

"The guys have already cleaned up some a' the evidence," Jazz continued. "They threw the paint, newspaper with spray drift, cleaned the sprayer, and buried the old fender."

"That's good thinking," Jubal said.

Jazz nodded. "It ain't no secret I know what's what with every junk car in the area. Tatum's gonna figure I knew somethin'."

After Jazz left for dinner, Slag and Jubal began their long night's work. The newly painted baby-blue fender bolted on easily, as did the front bumper. By ten o'clock, Benny's Packard was complete. Jubal studied the repair that looked as good as new. It was one of his best birthday presents ever.

Tearing down the wrecked green '36 Packard went just as quickly because, by now, he and Slag were a good team. Relaxed while cutting with the torch, Slag mentioned he'd recently worked on a Plymouth with New York plates owned by a guy named Doc Small.

"Doc Small?" Jubal asked. "Hey, the guys down at the store mentioned that car was parked at the rectory a few weeks ago. Does this doctor come to Hayesville often?"

"From time ta time." Slag gave Jubal an odd look. "Why ya askin'?"

"Just curious," Jubal said. He'd learned the car was at the rectory right about the time his dad skipped town.

"Doc told me he comes here ta help out that St. Anne's priest," Slag shared.

"Why does Father Mac call on a guy from out of state? Doc Peters is just down the street."

"Who knows?" Slag turned up his torch, ready to cut through the sprung frame. "Probably it's a Catholic thing. Doc Peters ain't churched."

The situation seemed strange to Jubal. But then again, Father Mac was strange. He did wonder at the coincidence of the car's appearance about when his dad took off. Did his father also know Doc Small? He grabbed a piece of frame from Slag and lugged it to the cart. It didn't matter. Even if he could trace his dad, it's not like he could force him to come home. Walking back to the '36 Packard, he noted that they were almost done tearing it down. He looked forward to seeing what might happen the next morning when Tatum found Benny's car.

Chapter Thirty-One

With August starting off unseasonably hot, Jubal worried about the pastures drying up and amounting to practically nothing. He'd seen a dramatic increase in milk production when feeding both Avery's quality hay and the citrus pulp, but Avery's hay was nearly gone. Jubal knew if he fed his milkers low-grade pasture and his farm's crappy hay, milk production would most certainly drop. The only solution was to go and see Avery to make another deal for better hay. Before going down to the Ketchum farm, he first planned to mow a two-acre piece just down the hill.

After he and Slag had worked on the green Packard late into the night, he expected to see Benny's car coming up the hill first thing that morning with Tatum behind the wheel. When no one came, Jubal jumped in the truck and took a ride down to the reservoir. The cool dawn showed a mist hanging over the water. He drove onto the lawn and sure enough, the baby-blue Packard sat partially hidden by bushes at the far end of the dam. He turned around and drove back to the farm to complete the morning's barn work. He wasn't going to go near Benny's car. If Tatum caught him, the sheriff would accuse him of knowing where the car had been all along.

Jubal had another worry. By now Tatum had no doubt spoken to Hammer's wife about the crash. Most likely she told Tatum how Hammer had gone to look for work that day at his brother Clyde's farm. The sheriff would come calling, one way or another.

Just in case Tatum showed, Jubal told Benny to take breakfast early and stay with his ma for the morning.

Benny was all questions. "Why's that? It's my job ta clean the barn."

"It is," Jubal said. "But this morning you need to be with Ma."

"I'll do as ya say," Benny said, obviously disappointed not to be doing his chores.

"Good for you." Jubal motioned towards the house. "Go on now. Ma's got some nice blueberry muffins all made."

Benny's eyes lit up. "I love blueberry muffins." He started off, but stopped and turned. "I wanna know why I gotta go."

Jubal sighed. "Because Tatum might show up this morning."

"I ain't done nothin' wrong!" Benny's eyes watered.

"That's right; you haven't, so go get a muffin. I bet they are still warm."

Benny seemed to forget his worry. "I bet she's got butter too!"

"I'm sure she does."

As his uncle trudged to the house with blueberries on his mind, Jubal smiled in spite of his concerns. Benny would never understand that the death of Hammer could be twisted to be his fault, even though Benny had stayed on the wagon while Hammer was dumped in the watering tub. Tatum would question the water in Hammer's shoes, knowing that Benny often used water in a fight.

Maria arrived on Trueboy shortly after Benny went to the house. Each morning, Jubal would ask Maria if she had eaten breakfast. She always nodded that she had but he wondered, since she seemed to be getting thin. He told her his plan for the day.

"Could you please bring the team in from the pasture, hay them, and then hook them up to the mower? I'll cut the last of our hay today."

As usual, she didn't answer, but he knew she'd heard him and would do as he asked.

"Oh, and afterwards, would you ride Trueboy out to check on our heifers? If this hot weather keeps up, we might have to start feeding them more than just pasture grass."

This time she at least gave him one word. "Sure."

He went to the house for breakfast, leaving Maria in the barn. His ma was at the stove frying some bacon and eggs for him. Benny was nowhere to be seen, but a plate of crumbs with a table knife showed that his uncle had enjoyed his treat.

"Where's Benny?" Jubal hoped that his uncle hadn't wandered out the back door to the barn again. Benny was good about doing as he was asked, but sometimes he'd forget his instructions.

"He went to his room," his mother said.

"Good. Make sure he stays with you today."

"Why does he need to stay with me?" His ma flipped the eggs with her spatula. "Is there some kind of trouble?"

"Well, I'm not sure," Jubal said, standing at the edge of the counter. "Tatum might be paying us a visit this morning. The Packard's done." He told his ma about Jazz and Slag's plan for Tatum to find the car. She laughed.

"Leave it to Jazz," she said. "But why does this affect Benny?"

"Because of Hammer's being killed the other day. Tatum will find out Hammer was here first. It was a close call—Iris could have gouged Hammer's gut or trampled him, or he could have drowned in the watering tub. In seconds, he could have been a goner."

His ma passed a plate to him. "But Hammer was okay and left the farm right after, didn't he?"

"Yes, but he was driving crazy-like, the car swerving all over. He barely made it out of the yard."

"Benny can't be charged," his ma said, wiping her hands on a towel. "The accident happened away from the farm."

"Yeah, but Tatum would love to connect Benny to Hammer's death—he won't care that Benny was up on the wagon and had nothing to do with Iris charging."

"Let's sit tight and see what happens." His ma poured herself a cup of coffee. "But I agree. It's safer for me to take Benny over to Lady Lamont's this morning."

"I think that's best." Jubal sat down to his breakfast.

After eating, he started the mowing, making a couple of passes around the field. If it didn't rain, he'd have the hay in the barn by the next afternoon. On his third pass, sure enough, Tatum came barreling up Harmony Hill towards the farm in his Ford cruiser. Either Tatum hadn't been fishing that morning or Benny's Packard was hidden too well. Jubal pulled the reins and stopped the horses.

Tatum drove the Ford straight out into the field, leaving tracks across the rows of freshly cut hay.

"I want to see Benny. He around?" Tatum said, stepping out of his car and coming alongside the mower.

"Why?" Jubal tried to seem relaxed, remaining on the mower seat.

Tatum stuck out his jaw. "Because I'm thinkin' he was the cause of Hammer's death."

Jubal adjusted his cap. "I'm looking a ways down the road at the tree that Hammer hit. So, do you think Benny was standing down by that tree for some reason in the middle of the afternoon?"

Tatum crossed his arms. "Your uncle's done stranger things."

"Well, he and Maria and I were bringing hay in that afternoon. We didn't even hear the crash." Jubal got off the mower seat and pointed across the field. "That tree, right there! I suppose you're now accusing Benny of directing traffic?"

Tatum took a step closer. "No, smart ass, but Hammer was soaked. Doc Peters said his lungs showed signs of having been full of water, and I happen to know that dumb uncle of yours loves to try and drown folks." He glared at Jubal. "The doctor also said that Hammer had marks on his gut."

"Not surprising since he hit a tree."

"Those marks weren't from any car wreck. Doc said it looked like he'd been attacked by an animal or somethin'." Tatum hooked his thumbs in his gun belt. "The water's another story. Hammer's wife told me her husband came to your farm before the accident, and I'm here for some answers."

"Look, I'll tell you exactly what happened to Hammer," Jubal said. He knew Tatum wouldn't let up and he just wanted the guy gone so he could finish mowing. "He came here looking for some work just as we were bringing a hay load to the mow through the barnyard. We were surrounded by the herd on their way for water."

Jubal leaned against the mower. "Like an idiot, Hammer walked hollering right into the middle of the cows. A cow we call Iris got upset and charged him, horns just grazing his stomach. She shoved him backwards into our water tub where he darned near drowned, and I pulled him out. When he came up out of the water he was coughing and gagging, and mad as hell. He threatened to shoot our cow."

Tatum huffed, "Well, if that ain't the biggest line of crap I ever heard."

"You asked and I've told you. That's exactly what happened." Jubal stood tall as he eyed Tatum.

"It is like hell!" Tatum's voice rose. "Benny shoved him and held him under water. Admit it! Benny's more dangerous than any cow."

Jubal was furious. "You calling me a liar? My uncle is as nice as a lamb, unless someone riles him up by being mean. I'm telling you Benny sat on the wagon scared to death while Iris went after Hammer."

"Bullshit." Tatum looked towards the house. "I'm gonna question Benny and see if I can't get a better story outta him."

Slag had given Jubal a wild idea. He thought he'd change the subject and put Tatum on his heels. He tipped his cap towards the sheriff.

"Tatum, you're looking at Jubilant Brown. I'm sure you recall how my ma conceived me in the summer of 1924? She was a comely gal, by the name of Rose Ringquest, and I've heard you were sweet on her. Oh, yes. I know the story—how she was at a party at an old house with lots of guys her age. Someone, and most are thinking it was you, slipped her a *mickey*. Then a bunch climbed aboard and took a turn while she was out cold. This ring a bell?"

Tatum tensed. "This has nothin' to do with Hammer."

"Oh, but it does!" Jubal was on a roll, adding a little fiction with the facts. "I've carried out a bunch of interviews and have learned you were the first to have at it with my ma, and nowadays, we'd call that rape. Right, sheriff? Isn't that rape?"

"You don't know what you're talkin' about."

Jubal could see he had Tatum stunned in his tracks. "Don't you see? Since you were the first, you could be my dad."

"You're makin' this stuff up!" Tatum waved him off while heading towards his car. "I'll come back later and find your uncle."

"Wait! Did you know I'm a top student in my class at Hayesville High? I've decided that in a year when I graduate I want to go to Harvard Medical School. I figure this town needs a decent doctor." Jubal was enjoying laying it on thick. In no way was college in his plans, but it sounded good.

"Why do I care what you do after you graduate?"

"One thing's for sure—Harvard is going to cost big bucks. Here's my plan. How about you agree to fork over five grand to help pay my first year at school . . . Dad?" He let the request sink in.

Tatum stood slack-jawed by the cruiser.

"Ma said you brought her a box of candy sometime after that horrible night. I guess that was your peace offering? Seems an admission of guilt to me. Candy doesn't cut it when it comes to paying for what happened to my ma."

"You ain't able to prove any of what you say."

"That's right. It can be hard to prove how a crime occurred. But in my case, I have witnesses to support my view of this matter, such as Mike Harlow? Zig Kreb? There are others. In the case of Hammer, there wasn't a crime and you've got no witnesses to support your side. Because you aren't getting to Benny. And Maria isn't going to talk to you either."

Tatum's hand was on the car's door handle, his forehead furrowed into a scowl. "Regardless, you can forget me forkin' over any money to you, kid. Especially five grand for college."

"Maybe, maybe not." Jubal climbed back up on the mower seat and picked up the reins. "But this is fair warning to you from Jubal Brown. My ma will be checking in with you from time to time, as you know she does. And she may just be asking for some school money. You'll recall her birth announcement?"

Tatum's eyes widened.

Jubal grinned. "Oh yes, I know about that too. In the meantime, we'll agree that Hammer was killed by accident hitting that tree down the road, which is a fact. It doesn't matter what the guy was doing before he took his crazy drive—Hammer was a loose cannon and you know it."

Tatum had his cruiser door open. "All right, the report will say it was a car accident and we'll leave it at that. Hammer was a powder keg." He spit on the ground and then looked up at Jubal on the mower. "Stubborn kid."

"You've got that right. As stubborn as a certain sheriff I know who never gives up on a thing if he thinks he knows what's what. Problem is, he usually doesn't know."

Tatum raised his eyebrows. He seemed about to say something, but then shook his head and got in his cruiser.

Jubal breathed a sigh of relief as Tatum started out of the field. However, the cruiser stopped and backed up.

"Say, kid, you seen that Packard yet?" Tatum asked out his window.

"Well, it wasn't parked next to the barn when I left to come mowing."

Tatum scratched his head. "Whatever happened to that car?" He spun his wheels as he left.

Jubal laughed as he got the horses moving. He made a pass down the field, the cutter bar chattering through the grass. Maria was off in the distance riding Trueboy in from checking on the heifers. After mowing until noon, he went in for lunch. Feeling sleepy, he sat down in the easy chair and turned on his Dad's Philco.

Word has come that 75 percent of people polled think that World War I was a mistake and surely the entrance into another conflict is out of the question.

He turned the dial, hoping for some music or a Red Sox game. He was sick of news about a possible war. Politics were his dad's interest, not his. Getting mostly static, he turned the radio off. Didn't matter, as it was time to head for Avery's place.

As Jubal started up the truck, he thought of his favorite Red Sox player, Ted Williams, who could find the sweet spot on his bat to hit his home runs. The summer of 1941 was exciting with Williams' high batting average and his best-ever offensive season. Jubal then pictured Tatum's dumbfounded expression earlier that day. In comparison, it was plain to see that finding the sweet spot of Tatum's guilt was Jubal's best offensive strategy—just as he'd seen his ma do time and time again.

⁂

Clyde was horribly uncomfortable and sick lying on his makeshift bed in Jazz's junk car. Having long since finished his last drop of water, his dry mouth felt as if stuffed with straw. He looked down at his feet—they were swollen with blisters on his heels, toes purple at the edges and oozing, and the rest of his feet covered in red blotches. Streaks of spasms shot up both legs. The lice or bed bugs were feasting on him in huge numbers, making him feel like a pincushion. He had the shakes so severe that with every breath he took, the rusty springs beneath him squeaked. Too weak to move, he'd messed his pants.

No one was around to come to his rescue. He was about to reach the other side. Death had come knocking.

In the open field, he figured the birds and other scavengers would pick at his remains in the shell of the car. Delirious at times, he could swear he saw a turkey vulture perching on the sill of the car's broken passenger window above him. The bird's beady black eyes, stark against its red head, searched his own sweaty face, as if deciding which of his eyes to feast on first. He would be helpless to fend it off once it decided to take a bite.

When he looked towards his feet, he could see skyward out the other window. The flock had picked up the stink of his festering sores. The big birds circled with their long black wings, riding the air currents and waiting for him to take his last breath.

In these moments he would whisper a faint prayer to Susy Quigley's angel. Could she really have forsaken him after he'd done as she asked?

He'd not planned to get trapped in the car at Jazz's place. After the *All Jersey* creamery truck dropped him off, he had just needed a rest, as well as to ride out his transition to sobriety. He did not want to climb the hill to the farm until he was stone-cold sober. But apparently that idea had been a mistake. His feet were now so swollen and festered that it would be impossible for him to walk anywhere, even if he had the strength to get up. And so he remained bedded down. He thought maybe it was Sunday. He'd heard activity down at the garage, but for some reason, the guard dog, Babe, had not come sniffing around. It was a shame the dog was not on duty, because her alarm bark would have brought him some help.

He consoled himself, as the hours passed, by thinking of Jubal's glass Esso bank. He pictured handing the bank to his boy who would have the one dollar to begin building a new stash of greenbacks. Perhaps, in saving the bank and the dollar bill, he had achieved a point where the crooked in his life had been made straight.

Seeing the dried-up pasture that bordered the road on the way to Avery's, Jubal vowed he would do anything to get more good hay. He parked the truck in the Ketchum farmyard and entered the barn which smelled of the pine sawdust that bedded the cows. Fans blowing fresh air from outside created a pleasant atmosphere as Avery's Jersey cattle munched on the light-green hay spread before them. Jubal found Avery admiring a heifer that had just calved, adding her to the line of forty brown cows who nearly all had full udders ready to milk.

"Well, look who's here," Avery said. "Jubal, I want ya to take a gander at this beauty." He patted the flank of his latest pride and joy. "Ain't this heifer 'bout the most perfect beast ya ever laid eyes on with that udder smacked on tight as fingers in a closed fist?"

"She's a beauty, Avery. You probably have several coming along that look just like her."

"None the quality a' this gal." Avery motioned to two stools next to the back wall. "Let's take a seat so's I can rest my tired stumps."

Jubal sat and tipped his stool back against the wall. "Summer's getting on. How are things? Haven't seen you since the parade."

"Geez, that was quite a day with them horses 'bout ta dump the two-seater," Avery chuckled. "Just been here mindin' the farm. For an old codger I got nothin' ta complain about. How 'bout up at the Brown farm?"

"A little better. Been feeding some citrus pulp. Production's up."

"Ya don't say! Good news. How ya been otherwise?"

Jubal shrugged. "Okay, I guess. Did some mowing today."

"Good day for mowin'." Avery leaned forward, both hands on his knees. He lowered his voice. "Ya know who's not okay? I'd say our friend Maria ain't doin' so well." He sat back and looked around the barn, making sure no one else was listening. "Now, I know what happened ta the girl was plain awful, but it's been a month. Seems maybe some a' the hurt woulda passed by now? She's pretty much lost her tongue." He shook his head. "And her spark too."

"That's what I'm seeing," Jubal nodded. "Her dad ever said much about it?"

"Chester ain't a talker, but he's hurtin' over it, I can tell. Maria's like my own girl. Kills me seein' her actin' hollow-headed like no one's home."

"I know what you mean." Jubal tipped his stool back down and shoved some sawdust around with the toe of his boot, thinking. Finally he commented, "Well, at least she and Trueboy seem to be good friends."

Avery's smile returned. "Lettin' her bring that horse down here was a smart move, boy. Only time I ever see her eyes light up. And it's good ya got her helpin' up at yer place."

"You miss her?" Jubal suddenly felt bad for taking one of Avery's helpers by trading Maria's work for the use of Trueboy.

"'Course I do. But her folks and I decided ta let her do as she might."

"She seems willing to come up to our place every day," Jubal said. "If you need her, say the word. I'd let her borrow Trueboy anyway."

"Oh, I 'spect she knows that," Avery said. "But I'm guessin' it's easier somehow stayin' outta her old routine." He lifted his cap and scratched his head. "Least she's not settin' in her room in the dark like she was."

What Avery was saying about Maria made Jubal even more determined to do some research at the library, but it was time to get to the point of his visit. "Say, Avery . . . would you be willing to part with more of that nice hay like what I took home from you this past spring?"

Avery's sharp eyes studied him. "What do ya have in mind?"

"For another load, how about Maria, Benny, and I give you a hand during corn cutting? I know it's coming soon."

"Well now, that's an offer. But I ain't so sure Maria would help out. For some reason, she doesn't want ta be 'round this place. She's been leavin' here every mornin' in the dark. What's that about?"

"I wish I knew." Jubal wondered what Maria was doing between morning darkness and the time she showed up at his barn when the sun was up. He guessed maybe taking a long ride on Trueboy, but he couldn't be sure. He doubted she would tell him if he were to pry. It was also likely, leaving so early, that she wasn't eating breakfast. His concern deepened.

Avery stood stiffly. "God, my old bones ache." He stretched. "I can sure use yer help. How 'bout two days durin' corn cuttin'? Come fer the hay anytime."

"Thanks, Avery. Give me a holler when you need us."

It was afternoon when he got back in the truck to leave Avery's. As he drove away, he passed the nicely painted barn and the well-kept house. Ned had just mowed the lawn and the maples in the yard already had a few leaves turning yellow. The farm looked pleasant and safe, like a postcard. Why didn't Maria want to be there? It made no sense.

On the way home, he stopped by Miss Curry's library where he found her seated behind her desk. A pile of books lay on the desktop and a small vase held the stems of wintergreen berries.

"Why Jubal, what a surprise," she said. Though the day was warm, she had on a light purple sweater which set off her white hair. Her eyes were lively as she smiled. "I haven't seen you since the parade."

He pulled up a chair and sat. "Summer's been flying by," he said.

"I know what you mean," she said. "Seems just yesterday I was having such a time in that parade. Of course, then it was quite the excitement wondering if those flighty Morgans were going to run with us to the next county."

"Chester and Maria sure saved us that day. Maria has a gift with horses."

"She's a plucky girl." A look of amazement came over Miss Curry's face. "Though, who would ever dare talk to our Holy Father as she did that day?"

"That's Maria. She speaks her mind when she sees reason to. Or, at least she used to, before . . . you know." He couldn't quite bring himself to describe what happened to his friend, especially to Miss Curry.

"Of course. What a horrible crime committed against her. But no one says much about Maria around town. Several have talked, though, about a swim instructor from the Catholic camp. They say he was the guilty one. Is this true? Imagine!" Miss Curry frowned, the wrinkles deepening around her eyes.

"Yeah, the guy's been taken to Windsor prison," Jubal said. "Doesn't seem to have made Maria feel better though. She doesn't talk much when I see her. Seems lost in her own world of pain."

"How awful! That must make you feel bad, being her friend." Miss Curry opened her desk drawer and pulled out a small white porcelain bowl. She slid the bowl across the desk to Jubal. "Would you like a peppermint?"

Jubal helped himself to a candy and popped it in his mouth. The sharp flavor went clear to his nose, making it hard to talk. When the sensation passed, he admitted, "I don't understand it. I don't know what to do for Maria."

Miss Curry nodded. "You know, Jubal, it sounds similar to something I once read. Shell shock, I think they called it. The article described World War I soldiers as keeping to themselves when they came home, sometimes having angry outbursts and bad dreams. They had a terrible time in the war—all that artillery in those muddy trenches. Their buddies died practically on top of them. It's no surprise that afterwards some of them weren't quite right."

Jubal thought of Slag's father having been in World War I, how the body was all burned when it came home.

"Are you okay, Jubal?" Miss Curry asked.

"Yeah." He ran his hand through his hair, focusing back on the matter at hand. "Some of what you describe sounds the same. One day Maria just about took my head off over some cows' horns. And I'll just bet she's having nightmares too."

"Oh dear!" Miss Curry exclaimed. "I expect she should maybe see a doctor, the type that works on the mind."

"That'll never happen. Her folks don't have much money. I think they see her condition as temporary."

"From what I read, this kind of trauma isn't temporary. I heard that Maria was badly hurt and . . . mistreated in the worst way a lady can be." Miss Curry blushed.

"You mean, she could stay like this for a long time?"

"Not exactly like this," Miss Curry reassured him. "But, the shame and fear can linger beneath the surface. It could have a strong effect on the course of her life."

Jubal stood and walked over to a shelf of books, tracing the covers. He turned back to Miss Curry. "I don't want that to happen to her."

"Well, I'm not sure there is much you can do."

"Yes there is. See, that's why I'm here," he said. "I didn't go to school much last spring with all the farm work, and I have another job now at Jazz's junkyard. Until things get better for us, I can't really go back to school this fall."

"Gracious! That's not a good plan. School is important. But I don't see how this ties to Maria."

He told Miss Curry his idea. "What if I come for a couple of hours during the week and read about the workings of the mind? About this 'shell shock,' as you call it. Do you think I could find some information?"

"Ah, I see. You mean to gain some understanding of Maria's condition. Of course, I'll do some searching for you." Miss Curry smiled. "I like to see our young people interested in research."

"I was also thinking maybe I could get some credit for English at school," Jubal said. "You're the perfect one to help me write a paper about my findings. I'd give it the title: *Mystery of the Mind*."

"Sounds promising. It will be quite a research paper. I'll talk to the school principal," Miss Curry agreed.

"That would be great." He approached her desk again. "Just so you know, I do plan to go back to school after the Christmas holiday."

"That's good to hear, Jubal. And don't worry, I'll see what I can do about arranging some English credit." Miss Curry gathered the books on her desk and stood. "Well, I'd best get to putting these away. I'm glad you thought of me to help."

"I knew you'd be a good person to ask," he said. "I have some mowing to get to, but if it's okay, can I look around for a minute?"

"Why sure," she said. She took the books and crossed to a shelf, peering at the numbers on the book jackets.

The small library space included two rooms, one of which held a set of *World Book* encyclopedias and shelves of bound journals. One journal looked promising: *Modern Day Psychology*. He pulled a volume off the shelf and, in a lucky draw, the book mentioned "shell shock" in the table of contents. He noted the volume number and put it back. No use in checking the book out, as he had too many distractions at home. Over by the window between two shelves was a desk and a chair—the perfect spot to sit and read. As soon as he could, he'd begin his study in the quiet of the little library.

Chapter Thirty-Two

It was the last night that Jubal planned to work for Jazz, so he stayed late to finish the Model A he was tearing down. Around ten o'clock, Babe came in wagging her tail for a treat. As usual, she grabbed the dried beef he gave her and ran outside. All that was left to do was to sweep the garage bay and shut the door. As Jubal swept, he felt sad about leaving, having come to really enjoy the work and the company of Jazz and Slag. He would at least stop by to visit them when he could.

Out in the yard some distance away, Babe opened up with ferocious barking. Jubal paused. Something or someone was out there. He went out to check with the shop's flashlight, casting a beam through the cool, foggy night. Droplets of moisture looked like fine white powder on the grass.

On alert while walking almost to the end of the lot, Jubal swept the light slowly over each oval car shell. Some were on blocks and all lacked wheels, looking like bloated cows with no legs and no heads. Babe stood barking out in the field. As Jubal drew closer, he could see she was focused on the back seat of an old car. Hopefully she'd simply cornered a coon or a stray cat. When reaching her, he cautiously shined his light into the car shell.

Covered by a blanket riddled with holes, a body lay in a heap! A pair of bare feet stuck out past the edge of the blanket. Jubal paused the flashlight, taking in the angry, red sores on the heels and toes. Was the person dead or alive? A small yellow suitcase lay on the floorboard next to the seat.

Babe kept barking, jumping up on the rusted running board, her tail waving back and forth.

"Stop it, girl!" Jubal commanded. "Babe, come!"

Obediently she came to his side. Jazz had trained her well. In the car, a foot moved and Babe jumped forward with another bark.

"Babe! Down!" Jubal said. She dropped to the ground. "Good girl. Stay." He called into the car, "Hello? Who are you? Are you okay?"

The blanket quivered. Jubal stepped forward and pulled a corner of the blanket away from the upper torso. He reached out to touch a wrist and jumped back—the body was stone cold. But it had moved. Whoever it was, was alive. He leaned closer, grimacing at the stench. It had to be a tramp.

"Hey, you! Get up and come with me. I'll get you a cup of hot coffee."

There was no answer.

Jubal reached out again and gently shook the body. "Hey! It's cold out here. You'll be dead by morning. Get up!"

Jubal ran the light over the hump towards the exposed feet and drew in a breath. The ankles, barely visible at the blanket's edge, were peppered with tiny red bites. He shook his hand and wiped it on his pants, regretting that he had touched the body. However, he had to get this stranger, apparently in sorry shape, up and moving. He grabbed the blanket with his thumb and forefinger and gave it a yank.

"Oh my God!" Beneath the matted hair and scruffy beard was a thin man that Jubal knew. "Dad!"

His dad lay on the back seat of the old car, covered in sores and loaded with bugs. Jubal tossed the blanket back over his father and ran down the field to the truck.

After gunning it up Harmony Hill, he charged into the house. "Ma! Ma!"

She stumbled out of her bedroom, sleepy in her nightgown. "What's the matter?"

He pointed in the direction of the junkyard. "It's Dad! Dad's down at Jazz's. Almost dead!"

"*Your* dad?" His mother looked confused.

"For God's sake, Ma," Jubal threw up his hands. "Yeah, it's Dad, lying in the back seat of a junk car! Come quick! He won't wake up."

"Oh, my God! Let me get dressed." His ma ran back to her room.

He called after her. "I'm going to grab a bucket of hot water and soap. Can you get a washcloth and some clean clothes? Oh, and I'm going to the barn to get the cow clippers."

She stuck her head out of the bedroom. "Cow clippers?"

"Yeah, he's lousy with bugs. We shouldn't bring him in the house until we rid him of all his hair and clean him up. He stinks to high heaven!"

They hurried to get ready, and then sped down the hill to Jazz's. Pointing the flashlight out her window, his ma spotted Babe sitting on her haunches, guarding the car. Jubal was barely stopped before his ma jumped out.

Leaning in the car, she yanked off the blanket. "Clyde, it's really you! And your yellow suitcase."

He opened his eyes and let out a feeble, "Ah . . ."

His ma went into action. "Go grab his shoulders," she said.

Jubal did as he was told and got into position near his father's head on the opposite side of the car. Babe trotted back and forth as they worked.

"I'll pull on his feet," his ma said. She reached out and then recoiled. "Good Lord! He stinks." She held the light, looking down at her husband's oozing feet. "Uh . . . on second thought, I'll pull from his legs. You push from your end, okay?"

They held their breath as they heaved and pulled. Even though his dad had lost weight, he was heavy. Finally, they got him out of the car onto the ground, only to find that Clyde couldn't stand. They hoisted him up and carried him with Jubal holding his arms and his ma holding his legs, so that Clyde swung between them like a sack of grain. Whining, Babe followed close behind, a couple of times jabbing her nose into Clyde's body. They hefted him onto the tailgate and Jubal climbed up to drag his dad further into the back of the truck.

His ma returned to the car shell to retrieve the yellow suitcase. She lifted it over the side of the truckbed and put it under Clyde's head.

When they reached Jazz's garage, Jubal backed the truck into the empty bay he'd just left, quickly shutting the door behind them. They slid Clyde towards the rear of the truck. Then they pulled off all of his ragged clothes. Jubal sat his dad up naked on the tailgate while his ma held a cup of water to his dad's lips. His dad took a small drink and coughed. He drank a little more. She set the cup down to hold him upright while Jubal gave him a close cut about the head and face with the cow clippers, followed by all body hair.

"If I can help it, no moochers are going to live," Jubal said. He looked down at the pile of hair on the floor. "Suck on the cement, you freeloaders!"

They soon discovered that Clyde had a terrible case of crotch rot. It turned Jubal's stomach, but he forced himself to continue. Between the legs it looked rotten and raw. Jubal figured it must have been sore as his ma gently washed the area, but his dad didn't flinch. They turned him over to see his rear— caked with crap.

"Ugh," his ma said.

Jubal turned his head for some fresh air. "Poor guy!"

His dad's feet also stunk as his mother held up each one to clean it as best she could.

During the procedure, his father was in and out, mumbling when they finally lifted him off of the tailgate and, with some effort, dressed him in clean clothes. All Jubal could make out was something like "crooked straight." He raised his eyebrows and his ma shrugged as they maneuvered his dad into a nearby chair. She then gave his dad a cracker from a package that Jubal had found in Jazz's desk drawer. Who knew when his dad had last eaten?

Jubal swept up the hair and threw it onto the cinders in the garage incinerator. Tiny bugs—similar to ants but smaller—were still crawling on the floor in search of cover. Grabbing the shop hose, he sprayed the floor and the back of the truck, making sure the insects swirled down the drain. He didn't want them living on Babe, or hitching a ride up to their house.

Finally they helped his dad back into the truck, this time in the cab. Slightly revived, Clyde was able to walk some, moaning in pain with each step, now supported by Jubal and his ma on either side. His ma pushed his dad onto the front seat and held him upright while sliding in alongside. Jubal opened the garage door and backed out.

In minutes, they were home. With each holding an arm, they helped Clyde into the house. Jubal carried warm water for a bath while his mother gave his dad some more tap water to drink, along with some dry toast. His dad continued to be in and out, but so far had said nothing that was understandable.

Clyde loved the warm bath, repeatedly saying, "Ah . . . ah." Judging from his appearance, it was probably his first bath since leaving home. It was almost midnight when they finally got Clyde settled for bed. Luckily, Benny slept soundly and was not woken up by all the activity.

His ma emerged from the bedroom with tears in her eyes. "Jubal, I'm so thankful you found him!"

"Me too." He looked through the door at the form under the blankets, still not quite believing his dad was home.

"No one's to know about this," his ma cautioned, "not even Maria or Benny. Your father is staying right in this room until he rallies."

"Not even Benny's to know Dad is home?"

"No, I don't want anyone to see him this way. And we don't yet know if your father might have picked up something contagious. We don't know where he's been. First thing in the morning, I'm going to see Doc Peters about those infected sores on his feet. I expect the doctor will want to give me the new sulfa drug folks are talking about."

Jubal went upstairs to bed, exhausted. Before he could go to sleep, he wondered about the thin line his dad had walked, challenging death itself. It just so happened by chance that Jubal had heard Babe barking. What if he'd left the shop and gone home earlier? His dad would most likely have been dead by morning. Was it just pure luck that he'd stayed late working on the Model A, or was it something else, a mystery that he couldn't quite comprehend? Was there a God that controlled the levers of this life? No matter the answer, Jubal was relieved that his dad was home safe, though he wasn't sure if he'd yet forgiven his father for taking his money.

He hoped his father's drinking was now in the past. Perhaps somewhere out there on the road, his dad had learned his lesson and turned a corner. Time would tell.

Before Jubal drifted off, thoughts of Lizzy snuck in to replace his wonderings about the deeper mysteries of life. Love itself was a mystery beyond many and all he knew so far was that Lizzy made him feel good. He hoped she was the right girl for him. True love seemed to ask of him a blind faith. His bedroom window was open to the night air and a gentle breeze lulled him to a peaceful sleep.

Freddie Coleman sat in his cell at the Windsor State Prison. What a hellhole to end up in. The place was a goddamned dungeon with just barely enough heat, even in summer, to keep a guy alive. His cell was okay during the day, but it was like an icebox at night when the rats had to wrap themselves around the heating pipes to keep warm. If he could ever get out of the place, he'd drive straight from Vermont back to the Florida Keys. It was always warm there. He'd take up with some rich broad and together they'd tip back a few rum runners at sunset. He was done with swimming instruction and done with CYO camp.

Of course, he had ended up at the state prison because the county jail wouldn't take "violent" criminals. What an idiot he'd been to confess to Goldilocks. He'd pegged her for a fraidy-cat, yet she snitched. He realized he should never have told Polly that he'd beaten and screwed Maria Styles. His strategy to scare the crap out of Polly had failed and he was now in serious hot water. But it had been worth it to feel that lying tease, Maria, fall beneath him in the rectory like a lump of clay. She never knew what hit her.

To get himself out of this mess wasn't going to be easy. The court-appointed attorney was a no-mind, advising that he should plead guilty, saying the court would go easy with only a four or five year sentence. Well, he had news for Mister Lawyer! He was changing his plea to innocent. It was his word against a silly, young girl more concerned with her looks than having a brain. What judge was going to believe Polly?

He heard boots pounding off the cement. Maybe he was finally getting something to eat, though the grub here was so bad that it made the CYO dining hall seem like a gourmet restaurant.

⁂

First thing in the morning Jubal checked on his dad before he left for the barn. The living room lamp cast a light through the bedroom door where his ma lay beside his father. She raised an arm to wave good morning but said nothing. His dad didn't stir.

Outside at 4:30 a.m., the weather was cool. It was not yet dawn and Jubal's light showed the leaves heavy with dew. Benny followed him as usual. Soon, Jubal was surprised to hear Trueboy's steady, heavy-hoofed walk coming up the hill. This morning Maria hadn't even waited until it was light out. He knew better than to ask her questions, but his wonder remained at her apparent need to escape Avery's farm before daybreak.

After breakfast, he planned to have Maria and Benny continue with spreading the neverending manure pile. Fields that were well-fertilized paid back in better hay. That was at least something they could improve. Maybe someday he'd have hay that rivaled Avery's.

He also anticipated that on any given morning Tatum might pull into the yard with the Packard. Folks in town had certainly heard about the vanishing Packard and surely Tatum or someone would go fishing soon and find the car hidden by the reservoir. He was surprised it was taking so long, wishing to get the discovery over with so there would be no more reason for the sheriff to bother them. Also, Benny had been pestering him, wanting to know what had happened to his blue car. "Will someone find my car, Jubal?" Every few days his uncle would ask him this, like a needle skipping on a record. Jubal didn't blame him—one small joy in Benny's life had been polishing the old car until every inch of it shone as if brand new.

Since Polly was home from camp, before long, she'd come for her family's milk. Their morning meetings were different now since he had no more interest in her. He remained peeved at her for pressuring him to drive to the dance, but more so for dumping him as soon as they got there. Though he was annoyed with Polly, he sometimes wondered how she might be feeling about him. Did she regret what she did? Did she want him back? Not that it really mattered with Lizzy in the picture.

Later that morning when chores were complete and Maria and Benny were loading the spreader, he saw Polly coming over the path with a milk can in hand. She was wearing a lot of makeup, causing her to look much older than her fifteen years. Adding to her grown-up look was her outfit—black slacks and a sheer, off-white blouse with a large, black bow tied at the neckline. Her expression was serious. He was on his guard, wondering what might be on her mind, thinking she likely had some sort of scheme up her sleeve.

"Where are you headed dressed like a business woman off to see the governor?" he asked.

She puffed her cheeks before sighing. "My dad's taking me to Rutland to talk with our attorney about Freddie Coleman. I'm going to have to testify before a judge eventually."

"Wow! Better you than me." He took the milk can from her. "I guess this must be your payback for a few swings around the dance floor with that jerk."

She pouted, looking down at the ground. "Yeah, and then that awful ride home in Freddie's leaky convertible." A tear ran down her cheek and she wiped it away. "I . . . I have a favor to ask."

He didn't want to let her tears move him. More than likely it was just another one of her tricks. "Whatever it is, I don't have time." He started towards the milk house, glancing back to see her following. She tried to step carefully so as not to get her dress-up shoes wet from the morning dew which still clung to the grass.

"Please," she said. "You've just gotten your license, right?"

"Yup. But I'm not going to be a taxi service." In the milk house, he set down the can and turned to face her. "Last time I gave you a ride, I didn't get much thanks, remember?" He opened the cooler cover and held the dipper to fill the can. "Get Eugene to drive you around in his mother's fancy new Packard."

Her troubled look fell into a deeper scowl, but no words came. Finally, she choked back a sob.

He didn't know whether to feel impatient or sorry for her. Perhaps this was a different Polly than the smug girl who slammed the car door in his face at the grange dance.

"You haven't seen Eugene?" she said.

"Nope. Been busy. Our paths haven't crossed."

"Well, last night he announced that he's leaving."

"Leaving?" He swung the dipper which clanged against the can. "Now?" This was a sudden change that was hard to believe since they still had another year of high school ahead of them.

"Prep school." Polly dabbed at another tear with a corner of her black bow. "I'm going to miss him terribly. So many times he's been my life saver, doing much more for me than most realized . . . mainly my school work," she finished with a small, embarrassed smile.

"Why prep school? I thought he was going to join the Tuskegee Airmen."

"He's been told if he wants to go to flight school, he needs more math and science than Hayesville offers. Prep school starts much earlier than ours."

Jubal closed the cooler cover. "So he's really leaving?" Gosh, now he wished he'd spent more time with Eugene over the summer, gone fishing or something.

"He is. Since he's not allowed to fly for the U.S. Air Force, he's made plans to join the Tuskegee group. He's determined."

"He never had a chance to tell me all this. I've been so busy. . . ."

"Seems you missed your chance. And now, with him leaving, I don't have a ride to catechism on Wednesday nights."

Jubal rolled his eyes. She wasn't going to get a ride out of him that easily. "You'll just have to walk. Your folks seem to think I'm a bad influence." He knew Polly's dad wouldn't be home from work in time to take her, and her mother didn't drive, but he wanted to torment her a little. He wasn't her errand boy.

"Walk!" Her mouth dropped open. "It's getting dark by seven! My dad told me that just lately he sees your truck parked early evenings down at the store. You could at least bring me to the rectory before stopping by to see *her*!"

"*Her*? You mean Lizzy? She has a name."

Polly put her hands on her hips. "Sorry! Didn't mean to offend your new heartthrob."

Jubal could see Polly was jealous and that gave him a bit of satisfaction. Let her feel replaced. He could also see that his not jumping to give her a ride was getting her steamed. Perhaps she was the same old Polly after all.

She tossed her head and sniffed. "Too bad you don't have that baby blue car to wheel around town. I can just picture her cuddled under your right arm and you trying to handle the big car with one hand." She laughed. "Most likely you'd end up in a ditch, distracted by her giant boob pressed into your armpit."

Jubal shoved the full can at her. "Here's your milk. Go home . . . *please*!"

She set the can down with a thud. "Oh, not just yet. There's something else."

Now he was the one getting steamed. "Quick, what is it? I've got a lot to do this morning." He ran some water in the wash sink and began taking the milking machines apart. Maybe if he just ignored her, she would leave.

"Father Mac wants to see you this Wednesday at catechism."

"What?" He had to raise his voice over the sound of the rushing water. "Is this some kind of joke? I barely even know the priest!"

Polly's face deepened in color. "You don't have to yell at me."

He shut the water off. "Why does he need to see me?"

"Father Mac asked around to see who has been the closest to Maria besides her family. The church is worried about her long absence from Mass, and our Holy Father wants to bring Maria back into the fold."

"And so I'm supposed to make that happen?" He threw the teat cups and milk hoses into the wash tub. "How weird! I'm a lowly farm kid that's never darkened the doors of St. Anne's. If you'll recall, I'm one of those heathens."

"Well . . ." Polly puffed her cheeks. "I suppose they all know that. Dad wants to pay you for your trouble and the gas. Fifty cents?"

"Gee, fifty cents, that's generous!" Feeling surprised, he reconsidered. He wanted to be mean to Polly. But apparently Polly's dad and Father Mac thought he was the best person to talk to about helping Maria. It was true—he was spending more time with Maria than anyone else, and with his library research, he'd soon have some science to back up his thoughts. He took a deep breath.

"Okay, tell your dad, yes. I'll meet with Father Mac." He looked up at Polly. "You win again. You got your ride." He hated to honor her request, but if it would be good for Maria in any way, it was worth caving in to Polly's need.

The morning after they found Clyde, Rose had gone immediately down to see Doc Peters. When she told the doctor the shape her husband was in, especially his infected feet, Doc Peters gave her a prescription for the new sulpha drug as she had guessed. He recommended that she give Clyde the five-day supply in case the sores had progressed to a more serious, life-threatening condition. Since then, she'd been with Clyde nearly full-time, his health being a constant concern. However, she now felt it was okay to take a welcome break to go shopping in the village. Indeed, it was pleasant to take a walk on Main Street where she ran into a couple of townsfolk and chatted for a few minutes. She didn't, however, stay away long.

Upon returning, she checked on Clyde as soon as she got in the house. Her husband lay still in the bed under the covers. On hearing her, he rolled and looked her way with sunken eyes, a slight smile on his lips. Shaven of all hair, his head looked like a mere skull covered in bronze flesh, reminding her of a withered pumpkin that had survived the storms of winter.

Tears trickled down his face as his eyes searched hers. Maybe they were tears of regret, of fondness, or of thanksgiving. Of course she didn't know since he didn't say a word to give any hint of his feelings.

She pictured when he was young and healthy, when they were both under the spell of their new love, enjoying the excitement of their nights together in the very same bed—his body covering hers, and her already carrying the unwanted pregnancy. At the time, he'd accepted her completely, even as she was, and he'd claimed her son as if Jubal were his very own. Though the drink had gotten in the way of Clyde being the father Jubal needed, she had no doubt that he loved her son.

Now it was her time to give to him—the road back to his full health would be long. In recent years he'd caused her plenty of pain, more than enough to justify throwing him out of the house for good. But he seemed different. She sensed that he'd come home somehow a changed man. He still reeked due to his sores, but at least he lacked the sour smell of alcohol that she'd endured for many years.

Breaking her moment of reflection, she leaned down and spoke. "Well, Clyde, it's time for you to sit up and have a drink. How about some milk?" She rolled back his covers and checked the makeshift cloth diaper she'd created. "Let's change that thing and clean you up, huh?"

Clyde nodded weakly.

She removed the safety pins at his hips and rolled him to his side, the guy feeling like a bag of bones, seeming much older than his years. She washed him and reapplied lanolin on his raw sores. Then she pulled his feet and legs around to change his bandages. Already, the sores looked less angry. "Now, my dear man, we'll try a cold drink of Ayrshire milk produced right here on Harmony Hill at the Clyde Brown farm."

He mumbled with a smile and his fingers shook when trying to hold the milk.

She put her arm around him and held his hand to steady the glass. He drank quite a few swallows. She wiped his mouth and was about to lay him back down on the bed when he pointed in the direction of the yellow suitcase sitting on the floor near the closet.

She frowned. "If you're hoping for a drink, I can't help you."

He shook his head no. There was something he wanted in his carrying case and, surprisingly, it didn't seem to be bourbon. She and Jubal had been so involved in Clyde's care and other needs that they hadn't yet bothered to open his suitcase.

She left Clyde propped up in bed to retrieve the case. Setting it on the bed next to him, she pressed the two buttons and the latches snapped open. She looked inside the suitcase, amazed. There lay the glass Esso bank.

"Clyde, you saved Jubal's bank!"

He nodded.

"What a nice surprise for Jubal. You even saved a dollar."

Clyde's eyes watered.

She picked up the bank and turned it this way and that, shaking it a little so that the dollar bill rose and settled again. "Jubal will be so happy to see this!"

She sat at the edge of the bed as Clyde's eyes closed. It didn't take but a small effort to exhaust him. He fell asleep immediately. She'd noticed that there seemed to be a problem with his speech, and she wondered whether he might have had a small stroke. He was about the age where she'd heard of such a possibility, and he had certainly been in dire straights.

She watched him for a while, puzzling over how he could have gotten to that car, even saving the bank, of all things. Where had he been and what had befallen him? Even more importantly, what had made him decide to come home? Until he woke in a clearer state of mind, the answers would have to wait.

At first, she'd thought it strange that Jazz's dog hadn't smelled Clyde's scent when he'd snuck into the junkyard to lay in the car. But according to Jubal, apparently Babe wasn't around. Jazz often took Babe home with him on Sundays for a weekly visit to see his daughter and grandchildren. The kids just loved Babe and usually convinced him to leave the dog overnight. Since Jazz had to pick up some cars that Monday, he wasn't able to fetch Babe until Tuesday morning.

Rose counted in her head. That meant that Clyde could have gotten to the junkyard sometime on Sunday, and Babe had not found him until Tuesday night, almost three days later. If he was in bad shape when he crawled into the old car, she wasn't surprised that he'd gone downhill fast with the infection, the bugs, and going cold turkey off the booze. And who knew what had befallen him in the days before his return?

Watching Clyde's chest rise and fall, she felt some of the old stirrings of her long ago feelings for him. Sometimes near losses brought on new beginnings. She hoped that was so for the two of them, for their marriage. The Brown household could use some new beginnings.

Later that afternoon, she sat at the kitchen table with her cup of coffee. Jubal came into the yard, having brought home a load of hay with help from Chester and Ned. Though the trade of help meant more labor for her boy, she knew that the good hay would ease Jubal's worries about milk production. Soon he stomped into the entryway, kicking off his boots.

"How's Dad?" he asked, barely in the door to the kitchen.

She smiled and held out the Esso bank.

He crossed the room and took it from her hands. "Really!" Jubal stood holding the bank, peering in at the dollar bill. His eyes watered. "He almost dies, but he saves my bank." He shook his head and set the bank on the table.

"Yes, I was shocked. No liquor in the suitcase," she told Jubal. "Just this." There was hope that Clyde was possibly reformed for good and Jubal's savings bank would not leave the house again.

Chapter Thirty-Three

Two weeks had flown by since Babe discovered Clyde in the old car shell. While his ma oversaw his dad's recovery, Jubal turned his attention to pasture improvement for the following year. Maria began preparing the soil on a five-acre plot with Dick and Dan pulling a sulky plow followed by the harrows. She had borrowed the tillage equipment from Avery. Benny picked stones with the stoneboat while Trueboy pulled the rig where needed. When the ground was ready, Jubal planned to seed the five acres with a ladino clover and orchardgrass mix, a pasture combination showing a lot of promise. Maria and Benny worked efficiently together so that Jubal's help was not really needed. He saw his chance to finally take his first research trip down to the library. Leaving his helpers focused on their tasks, he started up the truck and drove down the hill to town.

Miss Curry greeted him as he entered the little library and she couldn't wait to share that she'd talked with the principal at school. She and the principal had agreed on a plan that would allow Jubal to graduate the following June. But he would have to attend school again after Christmas vacation, and even at that, she'd learned that he'd have to complete a number of tests.

Jubal stood by her desk, taking in the news. Christmas seemed such a long way off. He wasn't too keen on tests, but he'd do what he had to. "That all sounds fine to me," he said.

"Tell your mother to stop by the school," Miss Curry said. "She'll need to finalize the plan."

"I sure appreciate your help, Miss Curry."

"Of course," she said. "You might not think so, but you show a lot of promise as a smart, young farmer. I've heard talk in town about the way you've been turning things around up at your place." She smiled, obviously proud of him.

He was pleased that folks had taken notice of his accomplishments, mainly more milk production than Clyde Brown's farm had seen in years.

Miss Curry stood from her desk and handed him an armload of books stacked on a nearby book cart. "These should get you off to a good start on your research project."

As he looked through the books at the reading desk, he grew overwhelmed by the quantity written on his subject of interest: World War I shell shock.

He decided that the focus of his paper would be, "The Causes of Trauma." His understanding came slowly, as his limited time didn't allow for deep study. Most of what he discovered didn't exactly apply to Maria, such as the effects of battles and the horrors of war. The descriptions of grizzly deaths and foul conditions in the trenches were troubling to read.

Before long, his attention wandered to Maria's early morning arrivals at their barn in the dark. He puzzled over possible reasons why she didn't want to work at Avery's when the old farmer had always been so kind to her. Seemed she didn't even want to be at the farm where she lived for much more than sleeping. Try as he might, he could make no sense of it. After an hour of study, he closed his books and decided to go to Avery's to see if he might find some answers.

The yard at Avery's was quiet with no one around the barn or fields. At the house, he found Avery and Ned seated around a small table on the back porch, eating sandwiches and drinking iced tea. Avery motioned for him to join them.

"Didn't expect ya." Avery passed a napkin across his mouth.

"Just came from the library and thought I'd stop by." Jubal looked out across the cornfield where a few rows of tied corn bundles lay all the way to the far end. "Looks like you've already cut some corn."

"Yup, Chester's tryin' out the corn binder, workin' my new team."

"New team?" Jubal was surprised. Avery had been so proud of his Morgans.

"Ain't goin' inta corn cuttin' with jumpy horses I can't trust."

"What did you get?"

Avery shoved an opened loaf of bread towards Jubal, motioning for him to make a sandwich. "Pair a' young Belgians. Swapped even with the Morgans and fancy harnesses for a steady team and old, worn-out leather." He slurped his tea. "Ain't crazy 'bout the deal, but at least I got some calm horses. 'Specially when we get goin' on the corn harvest."

Jubal studied the endless rows of uncut green stalks moving in the light breeze. He guessed he was looking at a lot of hard work, but he really didn't know, since corn wasn't often grown in Hayesville as feed for dairy cows. Each tied bundle probably weighed fifty pounds or more. He pictured lifting bundle after bundle. Avery spoke up, seeming to read his mind.

"Gonna be a heap a' work out there, Jubal. Better eat yer veggies!" Avery laughed. "It's good we got yer uncle Benny on fer the harvest. Each bundle's gotta be hefted and placed in the same direction on the wagon fer easy unloadin'."

Jubal thought about whether he could ever grow corn and give his cows a super charge for their production. He picked up the bread loaf and busied himself with some ham and cheese.

"We'll load a jag and feed it green, cut fresh every day since it's gettin' on ta mid-August," Avery said. "Cows love it. Sweet as candy. The ears are startin' ta dent, nearly ready ta cut. If it fits yer time, I could use yer help, and Benny too. Maybe Maria, if she'll come?"

"I would hope she'd help us," Jubal said.

"Confound it, she's still avoidin' this place fer some reason." Avery turned to Ned. "What'd ya do ta her?"

Ned's thin face turned color. "Nothin'!" His hollow chest sank even further. He didn't look to have the strength to harm a soul.

Jubal looked across the yard at the barn, taking in the fresh paint job which caused a vibrant red glow as the sun's rays struck the gloss. He turned to Avery. "It's nice how you painted your barn this spring."

Avery grinned. "Ain't that an eye poppin' red gloss? Same paint Maria used on my AKL stone." He shaded his eyes and looked out towards the stone. Then he looked over at his barn. "Don't ya think a layer a' fresh paint brings life ta this place?"

Jubal finished his sandwich in big bites. "Sure does," he mumbled with his mouth full. He took a gulp of the refreshing iced tea. The sun was hot for an August day.

Jubal got down to the reason for his visit. "Hey, Avery, mind if I walk around your barn and yard for a bit? I want to see if I can discover anything at all that might be spooking Maria."

"Don't know what yer gonna find," Avery said. "But yer welcome ta look."

As Avery and Ned returned to their work after lunch, Jubal walked all around the barn, noting it was newly red on three sides with peeling white paint on the back. He poked around inside the barn where all seemed in perfect order. Then he walked the edge of the field. He glanced at the AKL stone off in the distance. The stone made him chuckle—Avery and his unusual ideas.

He thought back to the day they had split the stone, how Maria had directed them to try the four-horse hitch as if she were a seasoned farmer three times her age. She'd certainly been perfectly at home on the Ketchum farm then.

He found Avery at the edge of the cornfield. "Well, I can't find a thing, and I've got to get back to work myself."

Avery tipped his cap. "Plan on Monday after next. We'll start cuttin' corn full bore. I hope ta get it harvested 'fore first frost."

"Are you giving us more than two hay loads for our help?"

"'Spect so. With all this corn, I can spare the hay."

Jubal figured he'd made a fair request with the time and energy needed to get the whole cornfield cut and into the new silos—more than two days. If bad weather came, it might even take longer.

As Jubal pulled away from Avery's farm in the truck, he stopped in the driveway for one last look. Studying the scene before him, he couldn't help but think of a drama production they'd done in school. The stage set had a beautiful painting of a farmyard with a traditional red barn. Anything but peaceful, the glowing red on Avery's barn nagged at him as something more than just paint with its aggressive energy. If he ever had time to paint his own barn, he figured to choose a color that was less bold.

Determined to make progress on his project, he stopped again at the library on his way home. Miss Curry, sitting at her usual place behind her desk, looked up in surprise.

"Jubal, I didn't expect you back today! But see here . . ." She gestured to more books and periodicals all marked with white slips of paper. "I've found plenty of resources for you."

Jubal looked at the mountain of texts, wondering how he'd ever find time to get through them all. Determined to learn all he could, even if it was hard, he gathered the additional books with a nod of gratitude. He headed for the reading desk where, soon distracted, he sat staring out the window at the white clapboards on the house next door. A mowed strip of grass lay between the two homes and he idly wondered who mowed the grass patch, Miss Curry or her neighbors. Soon, however, he settled into quietness with plenty of natural light filling his space.

After scanning several books, he came across an article: "The Two Giants of Psychiatry: Sigmund Freud (1856–1939) and Carl Jung (1875–)."

He was astonished to find out that Freud believed sexual desire between a child and the parent of the opposite sex was the root cause of most abnormal behavior. Such an idea had never crossed Jubal's mind. He read with fascination that Freud named the condition the Oedipus complex, after Greek mythology's tale of King Oedipus who killed his father and married his own mother. Though disturbing, Freud's Oedipus theory didn't seem to be leading him to any answers about Maria's problems.

He thumbed through the pages to the next section. There he learned that Freud was considered the founder of what was commonly called "couch therapy." A doctor would ask his patients a series of questions while they lay in comfort on a couch with eyes closed or staring at the ceiling. Freud always began the patient's appointed time with the question: "What's on your mind?" In this approach, Freud managed to bring forth answers that would reveal the cause of his patient's troubles. Jubal wrote down the opening question in his notebook, along with a notation that Freud believed "neurosis lay buried within the subconscious." He had to look up the words *neurosis* and *subconscious,* writing those definitions down as well.

Carl Jung followed Freud's theories but went on to develop the Electra complex, a mother–daughter competition for the attention of the father. Jung believed that many women's psychological troubles grew out of this complex. Jubal couldn't connect this idea to Maria's case either, finding both Jung and Freud rather strange men to be thinking of these things.

More useful was Jung's proposal that the subconscious is often the source of bizarre dreams showing symbols of what might be causing mental trauma. A skilled therapist was thought to bring these dream clues to the surface in order to confront the problem.

Jubal again looked out the window as he wondered if part of Maria's attack lay hidden within her subconscious mind. On the surface, she could function; however, he guessed that she could tell only some of what had happened to her, but not all.

According to his research, Jubal discovered that to lessen the trauma, the patient had to dredge up the full memory, no matter how painful, usually drawing upon the five senses. Jung assumed that the conscious and subconscious parts of the mind have to be in harmony for a person to live a normal, happy life. Without awareness of the full trauma memory, certain triggers could stir up the buried pain. For example, a sound such as a loud *bang* could trigger the memory of a combat scene for a war veteran. Likewise, the smell of a certain perfume could cause an adult to remember an incident with a difficult mother. During such flashbacks, the patient might relive the entire experience as if it were happening again in the moment.

Jubal took notes on the paragraph regarding the five senses, wondering if one of the senses might contain a trigger for Maria. He thought maybe he could try to get her to recall her attack. It was a risk, but he certainly didn't want to see her remain stuck for months, even years. When he finally left the library to get back up to the farm for chores, his mind was swimming with psychology terms.

He went back to Miss Curry's the very next day to work his way through more of the books, taking notes on parts that seemed in keeping with what he'd observed in Maria. It occurred to him that he might find some clues at the rectory, the scene of the crime. As luck would have it, the following evening was Wednesday, the night he was to take Polly to catechism.

In anticipation, Jubal hoped that he wouldn't have to carry Polly as a passenger in the junky truck which would confirm for Polly that farm life was only for those who were down and out. Maybe by some miracle the Packard would be found in the morning. Why Tatum hadn't yet shown up with it, he could only guess. He'd even driven out to the reservoir again to see if the Packard was still there. It was. Part of the problem was that it wasn't visible from the road, being backed in behind the bushes. Why hadn't Tatum gone fishing? Or if he had, why hadn't he seen the car? Jubal told himself he would just have to be patient, and if Polly had to ride in the truck, he'd just have to put up with her complaining.

As expected, Polly was at the farm the next night promptly at a few minutes before seven. Jubal, waiting by the truck, saw the look on her face as she approached wearing a pair of sparkling white sneakers. He chuckled.

"Yup! You're getting a first class ride . . . our best." He slid behind the wheel and shut the creaky door.

Once Polly was in the passenger seat, she couldn't get her door to latch. He leaned over and reached across her middle to pull it closed.

She giggled. "For a minute, I thought you were getting fresh."

"Hardly." He sat back up on his side. "I didn't want to lose you and not earn my fifty cents."

The truck let out a bang upon starting and Polly jumped.

"It always does that," he told her.

As they rumbled down Harmony Hill, she suddenly lifted both feet off the floor. "Whoa!" she exclaimed. "Is that the road?" She looked at him in alarm. "This thing has no floorboards! Does it at least have brakes? Or am I supposed to drag my feet to stop it?"

Jubal sighed. "Will you hold the comments? We'll be there soon."

She folded her arms and looked out her window as they turned onto Main Street. In a few minutes they pulled up in front of the rectory. He turned off the truck and studied the New England colonial-style building.

"This should be interesting," he said. "I haven't had a conversation with Father Mac since my paper route." But he'd seen the priest in action at the parade and hadn't much cared for the guy's rage for all to see. Though Maria had made a scene when throwing her bouquet, he felt that Father Mac's reaction was over the top. Maria was only reacting to the kids that spooked the horses.

Polly craned towards the truck's side mirror, smoothing her hair back into place. "Don't worry," she said. "Father Mac will double over backwards to be nice—you're a new face for his catechism class."

"He can be as nice as he wants," Jubal said as they got out. "I won't be joining."

Polly rolled her eyes. "Suit yourself. You'll be warming your toes in the fires of hell at the end of your road."

"That's ridiculous," he retorted. "I don't believe in heaven or hell."

They went bickering to the front door of the rectory with Polly leading the way. As she pushed the door open, Father Mac came out immediately from his study.

"Hello, kids. Polly, I'm so happy you invited your friend." The priest stuck out his hand to Jubal. "It's been a while."

Jubal clasped Father Mac's hand, which was clammy and soft. He let go quickly.

Father Mac, with an exaggerated smile, moved towards the bottom of a flight of stairs. "I'm so pleased you've come early. Polly, we'll bring Jubal up to our meeting room where we can sit and relax."

As they climbed the narrow stairs, Jubal wondered what sway he could possibly have to bring Maria back into the fold as the priest wished. He suspected it was a black mark on St. Anne's that the attack and rape had taken place on church property. It wasn't surprising that Father Mac had been pressured to do all he could to make good on the matter.

As they entered the second-story meeting room, Jubal did a double take. His entire surroundings were red. He stood stunned, taking in the rose-colored, ornate ceiling and the thick, red carpet. The heavy drapes were a deep blood red. Arranged in the back of the room behind rows of folding wooden chairs were two red leather couches—one large and the other a love seat. Illuminated by wall lamps, the intense color scheme flooded him like he'd just walked into a bath of blood. He wanted to retreat back down into the stairway to catch his breath. Instead, he blinked several times, trying to adjust.

He recalled Maria's reaction to his idea to cut the cows' horns. "There will be blood!" she'd said. She must have been raped in this very room—beaten, her Rose Queen gown torn to tatters as Lizzy had described. It hit Jubal—according to Jung's teachings, the color red might be a trigger in Maria's subconscious mind, recalling the violent afternoon when Freddie unleashed his cruelty. He immediately thought of the fresh coat of glossy red on Avery's barn and the AKL stone. No wonder she'd been avoiding the farm, as well as catechism and church.

Father Mac offered the larger couch at right angles to the love seat. "You two kids get comfortable so we can visit." The priest took his place on the smaller couch.

Jubal sank distractedly onto the red couch and Polly settled in primly next to him, crossing her ankles. Her new white sneakers stood out against the dark carpet.

"Jubal, what do you think of our gathering place?" Father Mac said, gesturing around the room. "Quite stately, is it not?"

"It's . . . unusual."

"Unusual?" Father Mac frowned. "I haven't heard that said before."

"I find it . . . sad," Jubal said. Obviously, this man of God didn't seem to have a clue as to how the room, being the scene of a crime, might feel to a friend of Maria's. He couldn't say more.

Father Mac sat up on the edge of his seat. "Sad?"

"Yes." Jubal met the priest's eyes. "It's sad because Maria may never be the same."

Jubal sensed Polly's unease as she uncrossed her feet and shifted in her seat.

"Yes, yes . . . a crime was committed," Father Mac said, the smile gone from his face. "But as terrible as it was, the guilty one has confessed and is behind bars."

Jubal felt a burst of anger. "Father Mac, that doesn't fix Maria's problem. Folks in town seem to think the whole incident is over and done with, but far from it. Maria Styles will carry the memory of that awful afternoon for her whole life."

Father Mac's eyes widened. "Aren't you being overly dramatic?"

"Absolutely not." Jubal was shocked by how little Father Mac understood. Wasn't part of a priest's job to be a comfort in the face of hardship? "Don't you realize? Her personality has completely changed."

He felt Polly's hand on his arm in warning and shook it off as he continued. "Before this, Maria was strong and . . . and confident. She took life on like taking a bull by the horns. Now she's completely depressed and can hardly speak a full sentence. She's not interested in anything but an old workhorse I've loaned her."

Polly spoke up. "Well, I'm sure she'll be fine." She cast Jubal a frown and turned to the priest who sat with a blank expression. "Father Mac, you can see that Jubal cares quite a lot about some of the lost girls in town."

Just then, a stream of young people began entering the room. Father Mac stood and turned to Jubal. "Son, I'll have to take your word concerning Maria. I haven't seen her since that fateful day. It sounds even more important that she return to our church for help and guidance."

"But don't you see?" Jubal said. "This is where it happened."

The priest nodded, but kept an eye on the entering children. "Maria must face her fears. As we learn in Psalm 46:1-3, *God is our refuge in strength, a very present help in trouble.* See what you can do, Jubal, to convince her to come back to St. Anne's. Now, if you will excuse me. . . ." He walked towards his catechism group. "Welcome, welcome," he called.

Totally put off, Jubal took a seat by the door while observing Father Mac. Did the priest feel the least bit sorry for what had happened? He wanted Maria back in his church, but was it just for appearance and not truly for her sake? There was something about this guy that didn't add up. Father Mac gave the impression that he was more into his position than caring for the flock he served.

Father Mac rolled out a lectern and stood behind it to begin his lesson. "First of all, I want to welcome Jubal Brown."

Low mumbles of "hi" spread throughout the room. Jubal heard a few giggles.

The priest stretched his neck beyond his white collar and started:

Hail Mary full of grace, the Lord is with you. Blessed are you among women and blessed is the fruit of your womb, Jesus.

"Now most of us know," Father Mac continued, "that I just repeated the opening lines of the *Hail Mary* or *The Rosary,* named in reverence for the Blessed Virgin Mary. The rose, for Catholics, is a symbol of the mother of Jesus Christ."

Father Mac held up the stem of a live red rose that he pulled from behind the lecturn for all to see. "Since this flower represents the Blessed Virgin, this room adorned in red reminds us that we are in a Godly place. It follows that we honor a young lady each year by naming a Rose Queen."

He held the rose higher. "It is an honor to hold and carry this blessed symbol in the Fourth of July parade."

Jubal knew right where Father Mac was taking them, and he had the feeling this talk was for his benefit.

Father Mac's voice rose in passion. "It was therefore a heresy, a sin, and an affront against our Catholic faith that a bouquet of these beautiful flowers was thrown at the foot of Hayesville's statue during this summer's parade."

Jubal sat disgusted. With no guilt for Maria's experience, the guy was raving about the loss of a bunch of flowers.

Father Mac went on to say that he had a film to show regarding the history of the rose and its importance to Catholicism, dating back to the Greek Old Testament times, the Book of Wisdom 2:8.

Oh boy, how boring! Jubal was tense and ready to split. When the lights went out, Father Mac would never miss him. So that's what he did. He left, taking each step cautiously and quietly down the carpeted stairs. Since the light was on in Father Mac's study, he went in and took a seat.

The room had a desk with a chair, two other easy chairs, a crucifix, and a calendar showing the Virgin Mary with a blazing red sacred heart beneath her flowing blue robe. Her head was covered with a white shawl. Seeming out of place, across the small room in the center of the wall hung a large-framed picture of a boat with all sorts of rigging. The boat had the name *Mary Lou* painted on its bow and must have meant something to the priest for him to have it in his study. So this was *Connelly's Mary Lou,* the tattoo on the priest's arm that Maria had seen. Again, Jubal wondered about this Connelly person.

Only feet away, two diplomas hung in frames. Jubal stepped in for a closer look and read: *The Roman Catholic Theological College at Saint Mary's, Class of 1922*; *The University of Georgia, Class of 1918*—both presented to a "Patrick MacMurray." The two diplomas were impressive. It had taken Father Mac a lot of studying, apparently, to become Hayesville's priest. Jubal compared how he, himself, was currently not even attending school.

His own diploma seemed a distant future. He idly wondered where Father Mac had gone to high school—likely his hometown.

Wherever the guy was from, Jubal was angry that Father Mac was upstairs righteously lecturing on the symbol of the rose and criticizing Maria's behavior. The guy was certainly showing his true colors.

Jubal scanned the little room and noticed a worn black suit jacket hanging from a coat rack. It was so old that it was frayed at the cuffs and along the edges of the front. Curious to find out what he could about the priest, Jubal walked over to the coat. He glanced at the door to be sure no one was looking. He listened carefully for footsteps in the hall. When he was sure no one was around, he reached his hand into each pocket of the coat. There was nothing in them but a bit of lint. Looking at the door again, he picked the coat up off the rack, turning it this way and that. It seemed an expensive brand. Jubal's own seersucker suit had cost his family more than enough. The label inside the lapel read: *Brunswick Clothiers; Brunswick, Georgia.*

Brunswick. It might mean absolutely nothing. But for some reason, Jubal wanted to know where Father Mac came from, the history of his younger years. He wandered around the tiny study a bit more, not quite daring to go as far as opening the desk drawers. Finding nothing else of interest, Jubal left the room to sit on the stairs to wait for Polly. His thoughts wandered back to his own schooling. While he was dedicated to the farm, he did miss going to school a little. His ma's idea that he return in the spring might not be so bad. He could at least participate in some of the fun spring rituals, like getting his yearbook signed by all the other kids. Thinking of the yearbook suddenly gave him an idea.

Brunswick likely had a town library and, if so, it might still hold copies of old yearbooks. He counted back from 1918, the year Father Mac had graduated from college. That would put Father Mac's high school graduation in the spring of 1914; his hunch was that the high school was in Brunswick. The priest's high school yearbook might just provide a few clues about the guy's past. Yearbooks always listed things about students' personalities, the sports they played, activities they enjoyed, and their ambitions. He wondered if Father Mac always had such a jerky smile. For some reason, he just didn't like the guy. He thought about it for a moment—it could be interesting to see what else he could learn. Maybe Miss Curry could write to the Brunswick Library and have the old yearbook sent up to Hayesville on loan if they had one. When he had time, it couldn't hurt to ask Miss Curry.

He glanced up the stairs as he heard Father Mac's voice droning. The documentary film must be over. Polly was sure taking forever. He stood and went to the lone window just in time to see the street lights flicker on. The night was muggy enough for moths to fly into their glow. Up the street, the IGA lights came on as well. He wondered what Lizzy was up to since she'd be closing for the night. He wanted to stop and spend his fifty cents, if Polly had it, on gas for the truck. Bernice would have left for home, and while Bert pumped the gas, Jubal could slip into the store for a moment with Lizzy. He yearned to see her flirty brown eyes, to steal a kiss and feel her body melt into his squeeze. But then there was Polly. He'd have to tell her to stay in the truck.

In moments, Polly came down the stairs. Jubal didn't wish to say goodbye to Father Mac, feeling too angry with the priest's disregard for Maria. He was out the door and in his truck in a flash.

Polly got in and this time was able to slam the door shut. "Well, we sure left this place in a hurry," she commented.

He didn't answer as he started the truck.

"Knowing how you think," she said, "I bet you can't wait to drive up the street and spend my money to see your sweetie pie."

"If I'm not mistaken," he said, "it's your dad's money. And if you're not happy about your ride, you could walk home. You want to walk home?"

She tossed her head. "No."

"Well, all right then. We need gas." He pulled the truck up beside the gas pump at the end of the IGA where they faced the deserted yard in back of the building. "You have the fifty cents?"

"Yes. I'm coming in. I'll pay." She reached for her door handle.

"No you won't." He held out his open hand across the seat. "Give it here."

"No!" She gripped the coin in her fist held tight to her chest.

"Polly, quit messing around." He wiggled his fingers, reaching his hand out further. "Let me have the money your father promised. And you're staying in the truck."

She wouldn't budge, leaning away from his hand.

"Okay, have it your way!" He slammed his door as Polly got out on the other side of the truck. Her taunting laugh followed him until her soft steps caught up.

She tapped him on the shoulder. "I want a *Sugar Daddy*."

"You just want me to be miserable, that's what you want!" Although he could get home on the little gas he did have, his excuse for stopping had just bit the dust. Polly ruled with her money.

His recent interest in Lizzy had left him financially strapped. The fifteen dollars a month allowance from their farm wasn't enough if he was to pay for gas, wear decent clothes, and buy a snack every time he went to his girlfriend's store. Yet he knew his ma couldn't afford to pay him more. No longer having to buy beer and liquor, they had plans to catch up on their back taxes and hopefully make farm payments to Lady Lamont for the first time in several years. The increased production of nearly three cans of milk a day came at a cost, having to buy citrus pulp and extra grain. But he saw hope for better times when they would milk a full barn of forty highly productive cows. He couldn't wait for the day when he could throw a fifty cent piece in Polly's face.

Polly brushed past him and went to the counter, speaking to Bert, "I want fifty cents of gas for Jubal's truck." She looked through the glass display case at the candy and tobacco below the cash register. "And," she pointed, "a *Sugar Daddy*."

Bert returned a broad smile. "So you're paying Jubal's way tonight?" He passed her the caramel candy.

"That's right!" Polly glanced back at Jubal triumphantly. "We just came from catechism class."

Jubal stepped back when hearing her answer. He hoped Lizzy wasn't within earshot.

Polly threw the candy wrapper in a basket at the end of the counter. She ran her tongue over the sweetness of the *Sugar Daddy* while eyeing Jubal and Bert. Jubal knew she was proud that she had him in a position he hated by paying his way and connecting him to the church. She stood with her elbow resting on the counter, appearing to savor the treat.

Lizzy emerged from a grocery aisle and joined them. She looked Polly up and down and then over his way. "Are ya fixin' ta be a Catholic now, Jubal?"

Before he could explain, Bert chimed in, "I must say, Jubal, I'm a little surprised. The Browns have been home Baptists forever."

Polly's cheeks puffed. "You mean the Browns are heathens. Did you know his father Clyde—"

Jubal had heard enough. Now Polly was going to pick on his dad. She was too full of herself. He lunged toward Polly and yanked the *Sugar Daddy* from her hand, throwing it in the wastebasket with a *thunk*. He glared as her eyes went wide. Everyone in the store froze.

"You know what?" he sputtered. "You can walk home!" He turned on his heel, not even daring to look at Lizzy for her reaction. He knew he was being a jerk. But he couldn't help himself. Picking on his family with their misfortunes wouldn't fly with him, especially coming from a spoiled little rich girl.

Outside the store, the night's balmy air was instantly soothing. He checked his anger before turning the truck's door handle, standing for several moments listening to the crickets in the night. He took a deep breath. He had to go back in to explain his reaction, if not for Bert's sake, at least for Lizzy's.

Polly ran out of the IGA and jumped in the truck to rescue her ride. She waited in the cab, looking over at him expectantly. After a moment, he started back towards the store.

"Wait," Polly called. "What are you doing?"

"Be back in a minute," he muttered.

When he pushed open the screen door, he faced a startled Lizzy and Bert. He walked up to them and shrugged his shoulders. "Look, I'm no

Catholic, as you well know. I went to the rectory with Polly on a request from her dad to try and explain to Father Mac about Maria's condition, since she's working at our place."

Lizzy nodded. "I see. And how did that go?"

Jubal rolled his eyes. "Not very well. Seems Father Mac could care less about how Maria is feeling. He wants her back in church of course, but in his lesson tonight he was all into his roses."

Bert raised an eyebrow. "Meaning?

"The guy was lecturing on how the sacred rose was abused in the parade," Jubal said.

Bert shook his head and busied himself with wiping down the counter. "That's just not right," he commented.

"How else do ya expect him ta act?" Lizzy said matter-of-factly. "Everyone knows that Freddie Coleman and Father Mac are buddies. The rose thing is like a fog ta cover the stink that lives behind that tight collar he wears."

Jubal turned to Lizzy. "You think so?"

"Sure. He's no friend a' Maria's. He thinks her throwin' those roses made him look bad in front a' the whole town."

"I suppose," Jubal said. "Guess I expected something different from a guy who's supposed to be all about doing good." He looked towards the door. "Anyway, I'd better go before the Giant Pain of Harmony Hill comes strutting back in here."

Lizzy laughed. "That's okay. Bert and I gotta close up here soon. Enjoy yer ride home with the Giant Pain."

Bert smiled good naturedly from behind the counter. "Aw, you two, don't be so hard on Polly," he chided. "She's just young and can't help she's been spoiled by her folks. She means well."

"She means to drive me out of my mind!" Jubal said.

Lizzy and Bert chuckled as he headed outside to the truck, the screen door swinging closed behind him. Thankfully, Polly was in a brooding pout on the way home and didn't torment him with any more of her comments. As they chugged up the hill, he considered how Polly was likely to be forever a burr in his backside. But not now. She suddenly turned reasonable, showing her good side.

"I appreciate you giving me a ride, Jubal," she said. "You saved me from a scary walk in the dark."

"Uh huh," he said, still peeved at her, and even more so, at Father Mac. The whole night had stunk.

"We'll meet next week for a ride?" she asked, her voice now sweeter than when holding court in the store.

He glanced over at her in the passenger seat where the dim moonlight revealed her cute smile. It brought him back to kissing her in the Packard and he felt that old pull, the hold she used to have on him. But Lizzy was the one now who lit up his days.

"Sorry," he told Polly. "Will probably be busy with Avery's corn."

The smile left her face. "I see," she said.

She looked a bit like a lost child, leaving him feeling bad for treating her the way he had. At the foot of her drive, she got out of the truck, standing with a taller posture, her pluck returning.

"Don't worry about me," she said. "I can figure out my own way. Enjoy your corn . . . and your mountain girl." She slammed the door and turned on her heel, walking up her drive.

Her little display, surprisingly, did not make him mad, but deepened his guilt for being a jerk at the store and for . . . not being the right guy for her? No, he was glad to be a farmer. Maybe it was just that things didn't seem to work out the way he hoped a lot of the time.

It wasn't until he got home that he realized he'd forgotten all about the gas.

Chapter Thirty-Four

Saturday morning after milking, Jubal broke the news to Maria that she and Benny wouldn't be working the new pasture for seeding, but instead he, Benny, and she would be getting a load of hay from Avery's. He didn't want to ask Chester and Ned as he did on the previous load because their time spent loading his hay wasn't part of the deal. Maria was bent over in the feed alley scooping out citrus pulp for the cows.

She shook her head. "Sorry, I can't. Take Benny." She dropped the scoop and walked down the aisle.

Jubal picked up the scoop and finished feeding the herd, emptying the rest of the citrus pulp bag. If he couldn't get Maria to help with the hay, it was certain that she wouldn't work the corn when the time came. And they needed all hands for that.

He folded the citrus bag, tucking it under his arm, and went to her where she stood at the end of the barn looking out a window.

"I can take Benny," he said. "But we can get a load so much faster with your help."

She shook her head again, still gazing out the window.

Drawing on his hunch about the red paint, he tried to reason. "Look, you can ride Trueboy down to the opening by the rock. Come to the barn by the back side."

She drew in a deep breath and exhaled.

"Please?" he asked.

Suddenly she turned and pulled the folded burlap bag out from under his arm. Curious, he followed her to Trueboy's stall and watched her put on his bridle. She led Trueboy outside and jumped up on his back, placing the bag under her thigh to hold it in place as she rode. And with that, she and Trueboy started down Harmony Hill, likely towards Avery's. He wondered what she was up to.

Benny had left the barn minutes earlier, hungry as usual. When Maria disappeared from sight, Jubal went to the house to join his uncle at breakfast. As they dug into their pancakes, he told his ma of his plan to bring home more hay.

"Avery is a good neighbor to us," his ma commented before taking a sip of her coffee.

Jubal then described how Maria had ridden off with the citrus pulp bag.

"Maria does at times act strangely," his ma said. "But she's at least talking more lately."

"Not to me," he said.

His ma looked at him with sympathy. "When she sees me, she'll talk a bit. That's a good sign that she'll do the same with you at some point. She needs time to heal."

He decided not to share yet about the red paint and his plan to get Maria to recall her attack. He was still thinking about the best way to do it, and he didn't want his ma to talk him out of it. He realized he felt worn out from thinking so much about Maria's problem. But Maria likely felt much worse than he did.

After breakfast, Benny went and got Dick and Dan from the pasture to brush them. When Benny was done, Jubal harnessed the team and hooked them to the wagon. Benny sat on the edge of the wagon with his feet dangling. It was a beautiful late summer day when the horses clopped down the hill. Jubal noted that the terrible dry spell was continuing. The grasses at the side of the road were a dull brown and the only plants remaining remotely attractive were clumps of wild asters with purple blossoms. The season would soon fade into fall with a parched landscape, the pastures and fields in serious need of nature's drink. Jubal hoped they would get a few showers so that he could plant his new pasture seeding before fall.

As they neared Avery's, Jubal saw Trueboy standing at the cornfield's opening. Maria was walking around the AKL stone. Dick and Dan pulled the wagon closer until Jubal could see that Maria was spreading the citrus bag over the face of the stone. When the bag covered the AKL letters, she anchored the top and bottom edges of the burlap with large rocks. He stopped the team, watching her cleverness at work once more. If the red letters were indeed a problem, she'd just temporarily solved it. A hopeful sign.

Maria brushed her hands together, which were brown with dirt from handling the rocks.

Benny waved. "Hi Maria!"

She looked over at the wagon.

Jubal motioned towards the wagon rack. "Come and sit."

She jumped up and sat on the edge on the same side of the wagon with Benny, facing the stone.

Jubal pointed. "What's with the bag?" He knew that Avery would wonder when he saw it.

"That awful stone," she said, frowning at it.

"You painted it yourself, right?" he asked.

"Yes, but it's just . . . irritating," she replied.

Jubal saw his opportunity. "Can you tell me why?"

She raised her voice in frustration. "How should I know?"

Benny started jiggling on the hay rack. "Maria's upset!"

"I'm all right," Maria said, smiling weakly at Benny who settled down at her words.

Jubal didn't let up. He wanted to get at what was eating her up inside. If they got it out in the open, then they could do something about it. "Seriously, what's with the stone, Maria?"

She glared at the stone as if willing it to speak.

He prompted her. "Is the stone now in the way of working the field? Or . . . is it all the labor that it took for us to drag it there? Maybe you don't like the way you painted the letters. I mean, they look just fine to me but—"

"The letters! Every time I see them, they just . . . yell at me."

"The letters are yelling," Benny put in. He started rocking back and forth.

"Shhhh," Maria put a hand on Benny's arm. She said in a quieter tone, "There's something about that red . . ."

Jubal nodded. "I'll admit the color is a bit loud."

"It's like fresh blood. It makes me feel I can't breath . . . and my stomach gets queasy."

"It's the same color as the front of the barn, pretty bright when the sun shines."

"Yes," Maria said. "It . . . terrifies me. I don't get it."

Benny looked from one of them to the other, seeming to be aware something important was happening.

Jubal said softly, "Maria, where else have you seen a lot of red?"

She closed her eyes. One of the horses reached down for some grass and Jubal tugged the reins.

In a few moments, Maria's eyes flew wide. "Oh my God. The red room."

Jubal's plan to get her to recall the attack was unfolding practically without him having to do anything. "Where is this red room?"

"At the rectory." Sitting on the wagon bed in the sun, Maria hugged herself as if in a strong chill.

"Tell me what happened in the red room. Can you remember the details?"

She hugged herself tighter and shook her head no.

Jubal stayed quiet, letting her have some time to think.

In the silence, Benny spoke up. "Maria is scared of the red room, Jubal."

"She might be, yes," Jubal said to Benny. "Try to remember just a little bit?" he asked Maria. "It might help—"

""I can't see his face." Maria's voice broke and she swallowed hard. "I've tried. And I just can't." She looked at Jubal, tears welling up. "Do you see? I wasn't . . . present . . . somehow."

Jubal nodded, remembering his mother's words. "It's going to take some time. You know? You got knocked out. And the rest was awful."

She wiped her eyes and nodded.

He wasn't sure what to say next. The hay wagon was hardly a couch, and he was no Freud or Jung, but the connection to the red room was a start. "It's okay," he said, picking up the reins."Let's load that hay."

Maria slid down off the wagon. As she approached Trueboy, the horse perked up his ears in greeting. She climbed up on the burlap-covered stone to jump on the horse's back, and then she rode behind the wagon to the haybarn.

Clyde came out from his bedroom to the kitchen, his ironwood walking stick that Jubal had cut for him thumping the floor with each step. He headed to get some coffee Rose had left on the back of the stove for when he wanted it. What a good woman she was, thoughtful in caring for him during his recovery. She'd started coming home earlier from Lady Lamont's, earlier than in his drinking days when he didn't give a whit for anyone or anything except for how much was left in the bottle. He could see now what a goddamn waste that was for so many years.

Already he was enjoying the fact of feeling more clear-headed, even though he couldn't seem to talk very well. It was okay with him to stay quiet. Since drowning his mind in his drinking corner, he found now that he didn't have much to say. He could put his arm around his wife at night and hear her sweet words in his ear. He would squeeze her. Then they would kiss. What a gift he'd had all along and he'd never appreciated it.

Feeling his good fortune, he hated to admit he'd once held no spiritual belief. He couldn't imagine a god that would allow the unfolding horrors broadcast daily on his Philco. So for most of his life he'd been satisfied that when it was his time to head for the great beyond, he'd ask no questions. Yet, since Susy Quigley's angel had come into his life, he'd been left to wonder. Maybe there was a special spirit out there that cared for him, leading him to better days. There had been moments when he thought Susy's angel had forsaken him, but she hadn't. She'd landed him back where he belonged. That stinking city and all those hungry rats had been his test. He'd learned while living in Troy that he didn't make any friends by sharing the bottle. In addition, the bottle was no friend to him.

He often thought about the Holy Gospel Singers, the fact that they had stopped for him—a lowly bum who had scarcely the shirt on his back. They, themselves, had almost nothing to share, but they did. He remembered clearly the warm feeling from knowing he could give them what little he had. Maybe that's what real happiness was: the act of giving rather than sponging off the milk money for his next drink. He knew one thing for sure. For the first time in years, he was a happy man.

He wanted to help around the house now, more so than he ever had before. He'd tried to sweep the floor but that was a joke. He ended up using the broomstick as a cane to hold himself upright. His big goal was to make it to the barn before winter set in. He wanted to admire the cows that Jubal, with Rose's help, had put together. He understood that the herd was milking to beat all, making three full cans a day. He couldn't believe it. Never in his day did he have cows like that. Jubal was already some kind of farmer. Golly, was he ever proud of his boy.

As for Jubal's true father, that would always be the big question. His only explanation for who his boy turned out to be was that Rose Ringquest had ruled that very first second of creation on that awful night. Born of a ruggedly strong woman, Jubal stood head and shoulders above any of the guys that were at the party. Especially that no-mind Tatum—what a pathetic excuse for a man he was. Clyde thought back to the night he'd shot through the kitchen wall. Damn, he was lucky he hadn't wound up behind bars. But the dipsy sheriff had been gunning to arrest poor Benny. He now felt ashamed he'd been so drunk. He wasn't able to stop Tatum from hauling Benny down to the jail.

As Clyde limped to the stove, he paused at the window. His thoughts of Tatum and Jubal's parentage quieted when off in the distance he noted a trail of dust kicked up by the spreader. Jubal had shared that he planned to disk and plant the new seeding, so Benny and Maria were engaged in the never-ending task of forking manure. With the fertilizer spread on the fields, there was a good chance come next summer they could put up better hay and not have to barter with Avery.

Clyde liked that his boy had been keeping him updated on the daily goings-on of the farm. He was especially interested in the drought while studying the sky out the window—not a single cloud, clear as a bucket of reservoir water. He shook his head and poured the coffee into his cup, taking a sip of the steaming black bitterness. He hoped to one day be strong enough to get back out there and work side by side with Benny and Jubal. The farm was backbreaking work, but if Jubal could do it, Clyde vowed he'd not gripe about it ever again. While he watched the yard, a bunch of pigeons flew into a nearby tree. He pulled up a chair to enjoy his mug of coffee as he saw a robin pull a worm from the grass beside the path to the barn.

In the early morning, the program hosted by the Chanticleer was playing in the background on the barn radio. Jubal was feeding the cows and horses while Maria was milking, and Benny was up in the mow throwing down hay. At the sound of a car in the yard, Jubal went to the door and looked out. Finally! It was Tatum driving Benny's Packard. So much for their peaceful morning chores.

Jubal turned and spoke quietly to Maria who had come from her task to see who had arrived. "When Tatum comes in the barn," he said, "send him directly to the house."

Maria nodded and he hurried for the haymow. It was best that Tatum be sent from the barn so that Benny wouldn't meet up with the sheriff. Nothing good ever came of that.

Not wanting hay dumped on him, he yelled up to the mow, "Hey, Benny, hold up!"

Benny peered over the edge. "Whatcha want, Jubal?"

Jubal climbed the ladder. Reaching the top, he told Benny, "Tatum just brought your stolen car back."

Benny grinned. "Really, my Packard? My blue car!"

"That's right, but we have to keep quiet because Tatum is coming to the barn."

"Oh no." Benny looked worried.

"Let's sit down in the hay where he won't see us." Jubal pulled on Benny's arm and the two of them dropped down to sit. With the chute open, they could look down onto the pile that Benny had thrown below, and they saw some of the manger floor, as well as the backs of a few cows.

In moments, they heard Tatum's deep voice.

"The kid around?"

"Jubal?" Maria asked in a frosty tone.

"Yeah." The sound of Tatum's hard heels rang off the cement in back of the cows.

Jubal moved his line of sight to see cowboy boots on the back aisle walking towards Maria.

"I have the half-brain's car," Tatum announced.

Maria was curt. "*Benny's* car? He has a name."

"Why so ugly this morning, Miss Styles?" Tatum asked.

Benny leaned toward Jubal and whispered, "He's gonna hurt Maria!"

Jubal whispered back, "He wouldn't dare." He looked down the chute as Tatum's boots moved even closer.

"Look, I wanna see the kid."

"Rose is over at the house." Maria's tone was flat but firm.

"I ain't wantin' Rose. It's the kid. He's made a fool outta me."

Maria kept quiet.

Tatum cleared his throat. "Last I saw of that Packard it was flyin' into Avery's cornfield. Weeks later, it shows up at the reservoir this mornin'. Jubal's gotta know somethin' about this."

After a long pause, Maria spoke. "You'd best be on your way. I need to get my milking done and Jubal isn't here. Go see Rose in the house. That's your only choice."

It was the longest sentence Jubal had heard Maria speak in a while.

"Ain't ya hearin' me? I don't need your invitation. Those two, the kid and the half-brain, are hidin' somewhere. I just know it."

Maria maintained her stubborn silence. After a minute or two, Tatum let out a growl of exasperation.

"You can keep mum all you want. But you tell Jubal after he slinks outta hidin' that when I meet up with him, he'll have to do some fast talkin'." The cowboy boots rang on the cement. Then there was silence.

"He's gone," Maria called up to the mow.

Jubal climbed down while Benny got back to forking hay.

"Gosh, you handled that guy well!" Jubal remarked.

As Maria went back to milking, he thought he saw a hint of a smile.

Shortly, he heard the Packard's engine start but resisted going to the door to see what was happening. Before they finished their work, his ma returned to park the Packard by the barn. Entering the stable, she told them she'd driven Tatum back down to town.

"Benny's car runs like a charm," she commented.

"How did it go with Tatum?" Jubal wondered how long he would be under the sheriff's eye regarding the missing car.

His ma looked satisfied. "He's buffaloed. It's the biggest mystery he's ever faced. On the way to town he kept mumbling, 'Crimes have been committed and I'm seein' who done it.'"

Jubal and Maria laughed at her impression of Tatum. After his ma had gone to the house, Jubal went out to the Packard, looking over the repairs that he and Slag had made. It was hard to tell the car had ever been wrecked. Soon, Benny came out to inspect his prized possession. Like a buyer on a used car lot, Benny opened and shut the doors and ran his hands along the finish, examining the Packard inside and out.

"I wanna go fer a ride in my car," Benny said, looking hopeful.

"We can take a short jaunt soon. But right now, we need to finish chores."

"How soon?" Benny asked.

"Before you know it. Come on. Can't leave Maria to do all the work."

"Maria works hard," Benny said as they headed back to the barn.

"That she does," Jubal agreed.

Though Jubal was relieved to see the car back, the Packard wasn't practical for errands like lugging bags of fertilizer or ladino clover and orchardgrass seed. They relied on the old truck or a delivery service for that. They were lucky to have the hundred-pound bags of grain and citrus pulp delivered by an outfit out of Rutland. However, using their junky truck for other farm errands was beginning to be a problem. As Slag had pointed out, the vehicle was on its last legs. As much as Jubal liked the Packard as a one-of-a-kind showpiece around town, he wondered if he should try to convince Benny and his ma to part with the car for a more practical replacement. Really, having the Packard back on the Clyde Brown farm and trying to use it for errands was a little like doing farm work in a tuxedo.

Chapter Thirty-Five

Riding home after a day's work at the Brown farm, Maria felt beaten down. Even Trueboy couldn't lift her spirits. It wasn't the work. She enjoyed that. She adored Benny with his innocence, and Jubal remained her safe person. But the weight of the recent violence in her life was heavy—especially because of Freddie's drunken admission of his terrible deed. Folks in town, and particularly her parents and Avery, seemed to think that Freddie being behind bars brought the whole matter to a close. She knew they thought she should snap back to her old self. Far from it.

Hearing Freddie's name spoken around was like an electric jolt, similar to the kind delivered by Jubal's new fencing. And the *way* Freddie had confessed was a punch in the stomach. Rumor had it, he'd told Polly without a shred of guilt, as if proud of his deed. This caused Maria fear that he might find her to finish her off if he were to go free. One thing she clearly remembered about the attack was his big hand holding her wrists together to pin her arms above her head. The other hand, which had been covering her eyes, was then pressed to her windpipe as she lost her breath. The last thing before everything went black was the weight of his body, his chest further crushing the wind out of her. She had only disjointed memories of what came next.

Freddie haunted her dreams, so she was afraid to sleep. If she did manage to sleep, she would wake with a start, for a moment not knowing where she was. Then she would creep from her bed in the dark before dawn, escaping the horrible visions.

Jubal had meant well in prying out her fear of the color red, but it picked the scab off of her emotional wound. She knew she shouldn't be so crazy-acting over Avery's stone. Thank goodness for the burlap bag.

On this particular day, it all just felt unbearable. Riding along, she barely noticed the late summer robins singing as evening came on. Usually their song was a welcome gladness. It was the times when she was feeling the saddest that a paring knife came to mind. She pictured the blade cutting deep—the satisfaction of bleeding out her misery. Her Catholic faith taught that it would be a mortal sin to take her own life. She would end up in Hell forever. But she didn't see the difference. She was already living in Hell.

She barely spoke at dinner. Her mother passed her the bowl of mashed summer squash and a roll.

"You need to eat more," her ma said.

Maria obediently took a scoop of squash and buttered the roll. But then she just pushed the yellow mush around her plate, taking only a nibble or two of the bread. She looked up to see her father watching her, his lips drawn tight in concern. She wanted to be in a brighter mood for her dad but it was impossible to fake it.

In the middle of the night when her dad and ma were asleep, she went downstairs and pulled the knife that her dad kept sharp from the kitchen drawer, and then went out on the back porch. Under the pale half moon in the cool night air, she already felt like a ghost, being thin in her white nightgown. She studied the small blade she held in her hand, turning it this way and that, pressing it experimentally on her skin at the wrist. Clutching the handle of the knife, she paused and gazed up at the stars, the last night sky she would ever see. Her sadness deepened. She pictured her parents sleeping in their twin beds, and she nearly sobbed aloud but she had to keep quiet. She swallowed and called forth the flat, gray space she occupied most of the time. She just didn't want to live in that grayness anymore.

Trueboy must have heard her or got a whiff of her scent because he started banging his stall with his front hoof as he sometimes did when he was bored or upset. She paused and looked towards the barn. Did the horse sense somehow what she was about to do? Whatever the case, she laid the knife down on the porch railing and went to him.

He greeted her with his low-throated rumble when she entered the horse barn. She slipped a halter over his head, snapped on a lead rope, and took him from his stall for water outside in the yard, taking care to keep her bare feet out of the way of his large hooves. As he drank, she slid her hand over his velvety coat and down all four of his sturdy legs, making sure that he was okay. She stepped back a few feet, and then ran and leapt onto his back, a move that she'd perfected. With her nightgown hiked up, she hugged her bare legs against Trueboy's warm coat of hair.

As they travelled up Harmony Hill, she guided Trueboy with the lead rope. Towards the top of the hill, she pulled him to a stop and sat listening to the night sounds, especially the crickets. She could see the dim lights down on Main Street. There was not a sound coming from the village. While she sat on the back of the big horse, the beautiful night suddenly captured her in a dream. She imagined herself, in the soft, silky fabric of her nightdress, as a true queen. Not a fake queen made up as a symbol to serve the needs of Father Mac or the church.

She lay back along Trueboy's sturdy spine and let her arms fall open across his broad sides. The night sky spread above her like a blanket of lights. She didn't know how long she lay there lost in the twinkling of stars before she felt a warm breath on her ankle. Trueboy sniffed her leg as if wondering what they were doing. She sat up.

"I know, boy, this must seem strange." She patted his neck and he tossed his head up and down, stepping forward with one hoof. "Okay," she said. "Let's go home."

After riding home and stabling Trueboy, she went to the porch to retrieve the knife from the railing. She stood with it cradled in her palm for several minutes, looking about the farm that she loved so dearly. Soon, she went back into the house and slipped the knife in the kitchen drawer.

As much as she wanted relief, she couldn't bear to miss out on more secret rides in the beauty of night. She couldn't bear the thought of leaving Trueboy behind, knowing the horse would miss her company.

As she settled into her cotton sheets, she tried to focus on the good in her situation. Getting to know the Brown family for one. Benny had a special view of every situation, and he'd do anything for her. She really liked Rose and then there was Jubal, ever a steady presence. She'd come to see he was in love with Lizzy. That was okay with her. She was comfortable now with not thinking of him romantically, and Lizzy was becoming her closest friend. As she drifted off to sleep, for once her body relaxed and she smiled. Maybe this night she would have better dreams.

On Sunday morning, a few days after her night ride, Maria was at the Browns' breakfast table. Jubal's dad, being sober, was looking better than he had in a while. Rose had not gone to work, but had stayed home to cook a Sunday feast—sausage, eggs, bacon, and biscuits, all of which Jubal and Benny were digging into heartily. While the food smelled delicious, Maria didn't eat much. She'd had another one of her dreams.

In this dream, Freddie was wearing only his tight swim trunks as he chased her through the CYO campground with a bottle of wine in his hand. Maria looked back as she ran, in fear that he was getting closer. She could see his swimwear bulge and the sight spurred her to run faster. Though she was almost to her cabin, the cabin kept getting farther and farther away, until it was so distant she knew there was no way she would reach it in time. She'd woken in a sweat with Freddie's laughter ringing in her ears.

After her nightmare, she'd quietly made her way out to the horse barn to take Trueboy up the road to her stargazing spot. Under the vastness of the heavens, she felt safe—as if with all that distance, Freddie couldn't touch her. The stars reminded her that earthly suffering mattered little. One day she would leave this world for Heaven, free from remembering and free of shame. Freddie could not follow her to Heaven. The creep had a ticket straight to Hell.

Tired from not enough sleep, she toyed with her food, stabbing the egg white with her fork.

Jubal glanced at her and offered, "After breakfast, I'm taking Benny for a ride in the Packard. Want to come?"

"No," she answered without a moment's thought. She wanted no breaks from the daily routine that kept her busy working. "I'll help Rose clean up and then harness and hitch the horses. There's plenty of spreading left to do." Since the night with the knife and also the connection made at the AKL stone, she'd found, at least, that her words came easier now.

"We're taking a break from spreading," Jubal declared. "Remember? I told you we're helping Avery, starting tomorrow? It's time to cut the corn. I hope you still plan to help."

Maria nodded with a sinking feeling. "As long as I don't have to work in Avery's farmyard. I'll stay in his cornfield handling the bundles."

Clyde looked at her with a puzzled expression but said nothing.

"Fine with me," Jubal replied. He took a bite of sausage and chewed.

She knew he was resigned to her ways. "If we're not spreading today," she said, "I'll just take Trueboy for a ride."

Rose reached for her hand and gently squeezed. "Go with Jubal. Go for a drive in Benny's Packard."

Benny wiped his messy mouth and chin. "Maria, come with Jubal and me in my blue car!"

Benny's excitement broke through her gloom. It was hard to say no to him. "Well, Benny, okay. You win. I'll come in your blue car."

Benny turned to Jubal. "Maria's coming!"

"I'm glad," Jubal said.

Clyde took a sip of his coffee and set down his cup. "It'll be good fer ya, Maria."

Rose left the table and came back to pass Maria several pieces of toast wrapped in waxed paper. "Take this along. You can feed the ducks at the reservoir."

"Thanks. The ducklings must be big now." Maria wasn't surprised Rose had thought of this. Once over lunch, she'd shared with Jubal's ma about her wagon trip with Lizzy and how they'd fed the ducks.

Benny jumped from his chair. His bulk and weight shook the floor, causing the cups and saucers to rattle. "Come on you guys!" he said. In seconds, he was out the door.

Everyone at the table laughed, further brightening Maria's mood. She and Jubal brought their plates to the sink and followed Benny.

The Packard's blue color was vivid in the sunshine. Benny was already sitting tall in the back seat, looking like a celebrity with his chin jutting out. When he saw her approaching, he broke into a grin.

"You, me, and Jubal are buddies!"

Maria opened the front passenger door and sat in the smooth leather seat. "You're my good friend, Benny," she said, turning to him in the back seat. "No one helps more than you."

Benny nodded. "Oh yes, Maria. I like to help."

Jubal started the car and they rolled down Harmony Hill. By the time they passed Jazz's place, Maria turned to see that Benny had flopped over, already snoring. She smiled to herself and stayed quiet as the powerful car rumbled along Main Street. She was hoping Jubal didn't want to ask her more questions about the afternoon of her attack. As they continued towards the center of town, there was Lizzy, walking in their direction with her long, easy strides.

"Let's stop and offer her a ride," she said to Jubal.

Jubal pulled the Packard over to the sidewalk and rolled down his window. "Where are you headed in such a hurry?"

"Oh by gosh!" Lizzy stopped in her tracks. "I'm off ta Lady Lamont's, but it can wait." She looked from one end of the Packard to the other. "I see ya've got Benny's car back." She walked all around the car once. "Wow, it even has plates!"

"We're all legal and ready to give you a ride," Jubal said. "Come to the reservoir to feed the ducks?"

"Who's we?" Lizzy leaned down and peered through Jubal's window.

"Why ya've got a whole crew with ya! Hey Maria . . . Benny. Golly! He's dead ta the world."

Jubal laughed. "Once Benny falls asleep, not much can wake him short of a bad thunderstorm."

Maria patted the front seat. "Get in and we'll take you to the mansion after our ride." The big car had a wide front seat with room for all three.

"Well, and why not!" Lizzy agreed.

Maria got out to allow Lizzy to sit in the center next to Jubal. She slid back in between Lizzy and the passenger door.

Lizzy chuckled as she settled in. "Hope this turns out better than the last ride I had in this car."

Maria took note of how Lizzy immediately snuggled close to Jubal, placing her hand on his knee. Jubal seemed to like it, leaning across Lizzy to snap on the radio. The soft sound of Benny Goodman's dance band filled the car. Maria tried not to stare at the two lovers, instead watching the passing houses out the window. The lawns bordering the street were faded brown from lack of rain and the summer flowers had all gone by. There was a time when she would have liked the courage to slide close to Jubal, but lately the idea of being hugged or kissed by any guy filled her with panic. A fleeting thought came that maybe she could become a nun to live a celibate life. Her mother and father would approve. Since the attack, her parents seemed uneasy about her going anywhere but the Brown farm. The idea of actually being a nun, however, seemed dreadfully obedient and boring. She'd be stifled, a life inside praying all the time.

Lizzy spoke up. "Ya know, Slag came by a while ago as I was leavin' the store. He was test drivin' a car he'd fixed up the night before. Offered me a lift. I turned him down 'cause I had ta see Mary White up the street 'bout her grocery order."

"Slag!" Jubal gave Lizzy a sidelong glance. "You'd ride with him?"

Lizzy shrugged. "Why not? Was real nice a' him ta offer. Lucky I turned him down though." She gave Jubal's knee a squeeze. "Now I can ride with ya in style."

"Oh, sure," Jubal said. "It was great of him."

"Geez! Ya jealous or somethin'?" Lizzy asked.

Jubal looked straight ahead. "'Course not . . . old scar face."

"Jubal, how mean!" Lizzy scolded.

This was a side of Jubal that Maria had never seen before. She wondered at his words. Maybe Lizzy was right—he was jealous of Slag, of all people. To lighten the mood, she put in, "Well, if the car stalls, and you don't want to call on Slag, we can always ride Trueboy."

The trio of friends laughed. In the back seat, Benny didn't stir, still dead to the world as Jubal cruised slowly down Main Street through the heart of the village. They waved at Miss Curry who was walking to Sunday morning Mass. The other churchgoers turned to stare at the Packard idling along.

Soon Jubal drove past the Hiram Hayes statue. Maria averted her eyes as the taunts of Lizzy's brothers rang in her ears and the bouquet of roses broke apart at the foot of the statue with all the boys diving at the flowers. Next came the image of the horrified faces of Father Mac and the church officials in the stands. It was all so vivid, as if the 5th of July all over again. Maria closed her eyes and drew a breath. It was hard to be in town. Suddenly she wished she'd insisted on staying up at the farm.

Near St. Anne's, cars were parked on both sides of the road since a majority of Hayesville Catholics attended Sunday Mass. Seeing them, Maria felt lonely somehow not to be a part of it. So many people were entering the church that she had known for years.

She spoke her thoughts aloud. "Everyone's dressed up for Sunday Mass. . . . I'd sure like to be going."

Then she saw Tatum standing by the road dressed in his black suit, polishing Father Mac's Cadillac. Tatum, who had done nothing though he'd been present when some of the ugliness with Freddie had occurred. Maria didn't like to even look at the useless sheriff. Thankfully, they soon left town, traveling out of sight of Tatum and the activity at the church.

"What were ya sayin', Maria?" Lizzy asked. "Ya'd like ta be goin' ta Mass?"

"I would. But not now." Maria shook her head. "Not with them."

Lizzy looked confused. "Them, meaning . . ."

"Oh, Tatum . . . Father Mac."

"No kidding," Jubal agreed. "Tatum's a thorn in my side. And Father Mac, well, he's . . . well, he's—"

"Exactly," Maria said.

Despite Maria's dislike of the two men, a strong desire arose to hear the words of God spoken aloud by a good priest, a kind priest. Hearing Mass could provide her some comfort so she didn't have to feel alone with her burden.

"Maybe I'd go on . . . a Saturday night?" Maria said. "My ma says Father Hebert has recently started coming from Rutland to give Saturday Mass."

"Good idea! Why don't ya go?" Lizzy smiled encouragingly.

But Maria didn't know if she could do it—step foot in that building, not by herself. She turned to Lizzy, her words pouring out. "I would, if we went together. What if I delivered groceries on Saturdays with Trueboy and then we could go to Mass in the late afternoon?"

Her answer obviously startled Lizzy who took her hand from Jubal's knee and crossed her arms, inhaling deeply. "Wouldn't yer folks gladly bring ya?"

Maria felt defeated. Obviously Lizzy didn't like the idea. "They always go on Sundays," she said.

"Well, can't they change nights?" Lizzy persisted.

"I wouldn't ask. They think Sunday is the Lord's Day."

"I see." Lizzy furrowed her brow. "Gosh. I'd love ta help ya, but I wouldn't know what ta do enterin' the doors of a church, 'specially a Catholic church." She chuckled. "The place would prob'ly fall in."

"I promise it wouldn't hurt?" Maria said.

Jubal cleared his throat. "Well, I don't know about that. I have to say it was pretty painful when I had to go to catechism with Polly."

Maria saw Lizzy elbow Jubal in the side.

"I suspect that's 'cause a' the company ya were keepin'," Lizzy responded. She turned away from Jubal. "Maria, tell me," she said kindly, "why now all of a sudden? Ya never mentioned this before."

"I don't know." Maria thought for a moment. "If things could get back to normal somehow. I mean . . . I always went to Mass until . . . until . . ."

"Until the parade?" Lizzy said.

"Until the parade."

Lizzy nodded. "I understand."

Maria continued, "It's bad enough to go back into that building, but since Father Mac gives the Mass on Sundays . . . seems like he's got it in for me now. Then Ma mentioned Father Hebert, so . . ."

Jubal broke in. "Father Mac's no favorite of mine. Mr. Smiley Moon Face." He made a face in imitation of the priest, causing all three of them to laugh despite the serious topic.

After they quieted, Lizzy looked thoughtful for a time. The radio was now playing "All of Me" by Billie Holiday as they drove through the outskirts of town.

"Okay . . . I'll go ta Mass with ya, Maria," Lizzy said. "Maybe I'll just learn a thing or two. Or maybe they'll throw me out on my butt."

"If they let me into catechism, they won't think twice about you going to church," Jubal said.

Lizzy chuckled. "Ya got a point."

Maria felt happy. Lizzy was truly her friend to agree to join her for Saturday Mass, though she figured Lizzy would have to do some explaining to the diehard Baptists at the store. But Maria knew Lizzy could handle the Sausvilles.

They soon reached the familiar reservoir drive. Jubal pulled onto the mown field of white clover and turned off the engine. He hadn't exaggerated when he said nothing would wake Benny. Despite the sudden quiet and the doors opening and closing, Benny lay snoring in the back seat. They left the windows rolled down to keep him cool.

As they walked across the reservoir lawn, the ducks circled and swooped down across the glassy surface of the water for a graceful landing. They swam towards shore, ripples flowing outward in their wake. A mother mallard led the way, while her clutch of nearly grown young followed.

"They must have seen us park," Maria said, smiling as she sat with Lizzy and Jubal on the bench. She tore the toast into small pieces and threw one to a nearby duckling. It gobbled the feed in seconds.

She handed some toast to Jubal and Lizzy. They tossed it to the ducks paddling around the water. For a time, the three friends sat peacefully together on the bench, enjoying the breeze while they watched the birds feasting. But then they heard the roar of a car engine.

Jubal jumped to his feet and shielded his eyes. "For crying out loud, it's the church's Cadillac."

As the long, black car pulled into view, Maria said, "I guess the ducks aren't the only ones that saw us coming here."

Jubal stood. "It's probably Tatum. You girls stay here and distract him. If Benny wakes up, I want to keep him calm. We don't need any trouble." He walked quickly to the Packard and slid behind the wheel just as the Cadillac came onto the lawn.

The girls waited on the bench, watching the car until it stopped only a couple of feet from the water. Tatum got out and slammed his door. The ducks took off in a flurry of quacking as he walked to the front of the Cadillac and leaned on the fender.

Lizzy muttered, "Part-time sheriff doin' his best ta look like a big shot in his fancy black suit and chauffeur's cap."

"Hey, girls," Tatum called over to them.

"Ain't ya supposed ta be down at the church where yer priest friend is tellin' folks how they should act?" Lizzy said.

Tatum ignored the question and looked pointedly at Maria. "You think you're hot stuff, ridin' in that big car with the Brown kid?"

Maria looked out over the water. She wasn't going to give the nitwit the time of day. But Lizzy had the courage to talk back.

"If ya think so," Lizzy said. "Just like ya're puffed up in yer suit, drivin' a fancy car fer the priest. All ya are is hired help."

Tatum strode to them, his boots sinking into the beach sand. "Ain't none of your business what kind of help I give or who I give it to. And I'd say it's time, Miz LaFlam, you learn to speak with respect to this town's sheriff."

"Huh," Lizzy said. "Right."

Tatum spread his feet apart and hooked his thumbs in his belt. He looked over towards the Packard where Jubal sat motionless behind the wheel. "You two girls are taking a chance ridin' with that guy. Gonna land in some trouble if you keep hanging 'round with him."

Lizzy looked up angrily. "And it ain't yer business who I spend my time with."

Tatum shrugged. "Jubal ever talk about the night he ran that Packard from the law and escaped through Avery Ketchum's cornfield? I ain't proven his wrongdoing yet, but you should know I intend to."

Maria finally spoke up. "Seems most anybody could see that big car sticking up above corn only a couple feet tall."

Tatum narrowed his eyes.

Lizzy barged ahead. "Don't seem like Jubal would drive that nice car that his uncle loves inta a cornfield of all places. He takes care a' what little his family's got."

"You girls are tryin' to protect Jubal. Well it ain't workin'." Tatum looked again across the lawn at the Packard. "I've a good mind to go over and shake a confession outta that kid."

"Wouldn't try it if I were you," Lizzy warned.

"Don't want to see the darlin' of Harmony Hill shaken up a little?" A dark expression came over Tatum. "Maybe even with his teeth knocked out and his nose spoutin' a bit of blood?" He stopped to see if he'd gotten a reaction.

Maria kept a blank expression. Lizzy was equally stone-faced.

Tatum shrugged. "That would sure make him confess." He started towards the Packard.

Lizzy called after him. "Go on over and try. Ya'll find Benny's sleepin' in the back seat. Two of ya in a scuffle, I'm bettin' he'd kill ya."

Tatum stopped in his tracks. "Benny's layin' on the back seat?"

"Sure is," Lizzy said. "If ya went over there, he'd wake up and bound outta that car ta grab ya like a grain sack. He'd pull ya right over ta the water and dunk ya under. In minutes ya'd be pushin' up daisies."

Tatum felt for his weapon. "Damn! Being a church day, I'm not armed." He looked at Lizzy. "That dumb guy is strong as a prize fighter."

"Ya got that right," Lizzy said. "Folks on the bench outside the store claim Benny can pound the hammer and ring the bell at the fair with one arm tied behind his back. And everyone's seen him hoist ice blocks in winter like they was feathered pillows."

Maria could see the sheriff's lights had been turned on. She remembered Jubal telling her, one day while they were milking, how Tatum had been on the short end of a shoving match with Benny in the Browns' kitchen. She admired how Lizzy was getting the better of Tatum.

Lizzy continued, "I'd say ya best forget 'bout the missin' car that's turned back up a mystery. I'm sure Jubal don't want ya suckin' in reservoir water unless ya're up fer drinkin' the whole pond."

Tatum glanced at his watch. "Gotta get back to the church." He started towards the Cadillac, calling over his shoulder, "Don't ya think I'm done with that kid. He's hidin' secrets."

Lizzy shook her head. "Sheriff, ya can bark up a tree like a hound dog on the hot trail of a coon, but that won't do ya no good. Ya're on the losin' end of this."

Tatum cast an angry look in the direction of the Packard as he opened his door.

After he left, Maria exhaled in relief. "I hate when that guy comes calling."

"I guess scarin' that coward is the best way ta take care a' the law," Lizzy said.

"You said more than I'd ever dare." Maria watched the car moving away on the reservoir road. "Though he's a man with a badge under that black suit, I get the sense somehow he might just force himself on me when I least expect it."

"Yah . . . well," Lizzy shrugged. "I'd be ready and bust his family jewels if he came after me." She took Maria's hand. "Or you."

Jubal hollered from the Packard, "Let's get out of here."

"Sure thing," Lizzy said, waving at Jubal. "Maria, I think our little Sunday drive has been rained on. Ready ta go?"

Maria nodded. She could see Benny sit up in the back as they approached the car, his hair tousled.

"Did ya see any ducks? Did I miss the ducks?" he asked out the open window.

After she and Lizzy were settled, Maria turned to look over the seat. "We did see some ducks, Benny, young ones too."

"'til they were scared away by a big hissing gander," Lizzy put in.

Jubal chuckled. "Tatum always reminds me of a peacock, but a goose is fitting."

Benny's face lit up. "Did ya feed 'em the toast?"

Maria smiled. "We did. And we can all take another drive to feed them again soon."

"I'd like that," Benny said. "In my big blue car."

Chapter Thirty-Six

With Monday morning chores done and breakfast eaten, Jubal and Benny were ready to help Avery with his harvest. Maria had agreed to work in the field loading the corn bundles. Jubal remembered Maria's stories of working the very same field in past summers, how she liked the sweet scent of the fluffy hay as it rolled from the side-delivery rake into perfect windrows. And then there was last spring's plowing—freshly turned earth and later, row upon row of pale-green corn sprouting to life. Maria knew every inch of the ground at Avery's as it lay under foot—the generous land had always been a part of her. It was right, Jubal thought, that she would be part of the first corn harvest.

While the crop was still green, it was almost fully matured as indicated by the dent in the kernels. Avery had said that the thinking among some folks was that corn silage should be chopped and in the silo before the first frost. Avery admitted that the thirty acres he had standing, in all likelihood, would not be completed before frost set in, but most of it could be if started early enough. Even so, Jubal could see Avery had no idea of the time they would need because the old farmer had never grown any such amount of corn before. And of course, neither of them could accurately predict when the first frost would come.

Jubal left the yard for Avery's cornfield with Benny in the passenger seat of the farm truck. Maria was to follow shortly on Trueboy. At the farm, Chester and Ned had already readied the teams and had left for the field while Avery sat waiting with his new Belgians hooked to a flatbed wagon. Jubal looked off and saw acres of corn bundles laid down in rows that from a distance looked like dead soldiers lost in battle.

"Gosh, Avery, you've put a lot down," Jubal remarked as he and Benny jumped up on the flatbed of the wagon.

Avery clucked to the horses. "Gotta get this corn in on the double."

"You'll need to hire an army to do this whole field," Jubal said. He wasn't fooling.

"You folks are the army!" Avery joked as the wagon lurched forward.

Once in the field, Jubal started loading bundles, each six to eight feet long and weighing more than fifty pounds. He was already feeling the hemp twine cut into his fingers.

Avery called down from the wagon, "Hey, Maria comin'?"

"She'll be here soon on Trueboy." Jubal flexed his hands. "Ouch. Next load, I've got to get my gloves. I forgot them in the truck. Maria and Benny have tough hands from forking nearly all of our manure pile, but I'm a softie."

Avery grunted. "Ya won't be soft fer long." He drove the wagon ahead down the row.

Jubal and Benny worked to catch up as they picked up and loaded bundles that lay next to the wagon. Avery watched them with shrewd eyes, measuring every move.

"Thinkin' with all this corn down, we's a might shy on help," Avery noted.

Jubal tossed a bundle onto the wagon bed and wiped his brow to stop sweat from running into his eyes. "I won't argue with that, Avery." He threw on the last bundle for a load just as Maria arrived to tie up Trueboy by the rock. "Good, now we've got more help."

Avery shaded his eyes to watch Maria. "What in heck's that bag doin' coverin' my AKL stone?"

Jubal shrugged. "It's Maria's doing, hiding the red letters."

"I see." Avery pushed up the visor of his Blue Seal cap.

It was clear from his tone and expression that he didn't have a clue as to why.

"At some point, I'll explain," Jubal said quietly.

Maria walked to the full wagon and jumped on. She climbed easily to the height, sitting comfortably on corn bundles next to Benny.

Chester and Ned were already unloading their wagon pulled by the Percheron team. Tied with binder twine, the corn bundle stalk-ends were loaded all in the same direction, lying across the wagon rack. At the silo, Chester threw the bundles onto the moving track of a stationary International silage chopper. The stalks were carried into whirling knives and paddles that created a force of air blowing the chopped corn up a pipe into the silo. The machine was powered by a John Deere belt-driven stationary gas engine. The engine, when power was required, belted out a series of loud *pops*—a sound that could be heard some distance from the farm.

The work was nearly continuous with Chester unloading and Ned guiding the bundles into the chopper head. Neither spoke much, it being too hard to hear over the machinery. The two-wagon process ran smoothly with one wagon unloaded and ready to receive the second full load of bundles. Noon dinner was the only break in sight. Jubal was appreciating their seamless teamwork and admired Benny and Maria's uncomplaining labor in heaving the bundles. The corn harvest had to be intense since Avery was eager to beat the weather. In no time, it seemed the Brown crew had put in their two days as payment for the hay, yet the field of thirty acres was only half harvested.

Near night chore time at the end of the second day, the skies were threatening. Reins in hand, Avery sat with a worried look, ready to go for their last load of the day. Jubal felt bad to tell him that they wouldn't be working the corn any longer, having met their side of the bargain. Besides, he had plans to study at the library, and Maria and Benny needed to do their own chores up at his farm.

Avery scowled. "Ya ain't leavin' me high and dry are ya? I mean, we're only half done."

"I'm sorry, but I told Miss Curry I'd go to the library on Thursday," Jubal explained. "And our stable needs attention. Plus, to get a better harvest next year, we need to keep spreading manure."

Avery raised an eyebrow. "The library?"

"Yeah." Jubal's face reddened. "I'm doing a project for school."

Avery had a sour expression. "Even so, how 'bout the three of ya workin' 'til we get this corn finished? I'll give ya a couple extra loads a' hay if ya'll stay. I ain't needin' as much hay with all this corn."

Jubal paused. It was a good offer. He quickly considered how he could balance the work. "We'll be down around ten tomorrow. It'll give time for the bedding of our cows in the morning and for me to stop by and tell Miss Curry of my change in plans." Though the extra work wouldn't be easy, he hated leaving the old guy in the lurch.

Avery relaxed. "It's a deal. Good of ya, boy!"

On Thursday morning, Jubal headed to the library, regretting that he'd agreed on way more corn harvesting than planned. However, he'd have been crazy to turn down the offer. Quality hay acted like a miracle, boosting production by nearly three cans a day. Soon he hoped that they could easily ship five cans, especially if they traded a bunch of their low producers for several fresh cows at the peak of production. Besides, he wanted to get rid of as many cows with horns as possible.

When he stopped by the library, Miss Curry was disappointed that he wasn't staying to do his research, but she seemed satisfied when he told her they'd probably finish the corn harvest soon. Before he headed off to Avery's, he asked her the favor he'd been thinking of ever since being in Father Mac's office the night he went to catechism.

"Miss Curry, would you be willing to write to the library in Brunswick, Georgia, and see if they'd loan out their 1914 Brunswick High School yearbook?"

Miss Curry made a note on a library card and looked up. "What an unusual request." She asked in some surprise, "What information are you after?"

He stood near the doorway, not wanting to track the manure on his barn boots into her neat library. "It was the year Father Mac graduated, maybe from the high school in Brunswick."

"Goodness, sounds a bit nosey," she said. "I'm not sure we should be chasing after gossip on our Holy Father."

"No one has to know. Just the two of us."

"Why are you questioning Father Mac's past?" Miss Curry looked stern.

He wasn't sure how much he should tell her, wanting to keep his suspicions to himself.

"Poking around in other people's business is asking for trouble, Jubal," she cautioned. "Especially a respected Catholic priest."

"I'm not interested in 'poking around' exactly. I'm just wondering where he came from before arriving here." He met Miss Curry's eyes with what he hoped was an innocent expression. "Father Mac is a big part of our town, and he has influence over my friends, Polly and Maria. He wasn't a Vermonter originally. I'm just curious," he said.

Miss Curry hesitated. Then she nodded slightly. "I suppose I could give it a try. After all, it is public information."

Thankfully it hadn't been too hard to talk her into it. "Appreciate it, Miss Curry. I'll see you next week."

As long as he was near the junkyard, Jubal decided to say hello to Jazz and Slag. When he went into the office, they were deep in conversation.

Jazz said, "I heard last night at the Selective Service Board that a list of guys in town was released of those who are up for the draft."

"Selective my ass!" Slag complained. "I'm on the list. That ain't bein' too selective!"

"Selective Service? That means nothing to me," Jubal broke in.

"The Army, boy! The Army!" Slag barked. "Men twenty-one to thirty-five not eligible for deferment are on the list. It's the law!" He continued. "At 32, I'm ripe fer the pickins! Ripe ta be drafted!" The New Hampshire scar was beet red. He raged, "News comin' from my shortwave radio ain't good!"

Jubal stood stock still. Anything he might have said wouldn't help.

"Ya know what the Army means? I'll be jest like my old man." Slag shook his head mournfully. "Sent home in a goddamned wooden box. My dancin' days are over." He slumped and stared at the floor.

"Gee, I'm sorry," Jubal said, "but you haven't even been called up yet."

"Time, boy, time. Time ain't on my side."

Jazz's main man Slag believed he was dead and buried, and he hadn't even been drafted yet. The news certainly put a cloud of gloom over the garage. However, Jubal understood the heavy mood. He sure would hate to leave for parts unknown at this point in his life, especially to fight with a gun. As a kid, he'd fired a weapon only a couple of times, and the charge kicked his shoulder so bad that it hurt for a week. Furthermore, his dad had always been too under the weather to ever give him any serious instruction on the use of the shotgun. He left the junkyard promising Slag and Jazz that he'd return soon for a longer visit.

For the rest of the day, he worked with Benny and Maria at Avery's. They took only a few minutes for lunch. They loaded bundles until dark, aiming to get ahead of the rain. At day's end, the first silo was completely filled and the second only feet from the top. The corn blower had worked flawlessly, filling the silos without a hitch. But they hadn't finished.

That night, Maria left Trueboy in his usual stall at Avery's and rode with Jubal and Benny to do the chores. The three were silent all the way up Harmony Hill—tired beyond words. After chores were finished, Jubal brought Maria home. They said nothing for a while and then Maria surprised him.

"What are we going to do after corn?" she asked.

Her question stopped him at first. Then he remembered that they hadn't yet done a thing for winter's wood. In recent years they'd burned coal due to Clyde's condition.

"We can cut our wood," he said, as he dropped her off in her yard. "There will be time to put up a good pile before cold weather sets in."

She nodded. When she left, she brushed his hand lightly. "See you in the morning."

Her quick touch was unusual. He left the Styles' yard realizing her contact was simple enough, just a gesture for attention. For the moment, it seemed a sign of her returning to normal.

That night, it rained hard. The news from WGY called it a "torrential downpour." By morning the rain had stopped, leaving cool, cloudy weather hanging over Hayesville. The dark skies threatened even more rain with heavy air and clouds that looked like water-filled balloons that could burst at any time.

They were at Avery's by nine where pools rested in the field's dips and divots. The corn bundles lay soaked since Chester had cut the remaining field. To load the dripping bundles, they had to slog through mud that stuck to their boots like wet cement. Each step labored heavy as stones. Mud built inches thick on the wagon wheels and the horses struggled to pull a full load, their hooves slipping on the waterlogged soil. The two teams occasionally fell to their knees, snorting under the effort to gain solid footing.

Avery was concerned for his horses. "After this, we'll put on only half a load."

Just as he spoke, a heavy downpour began and they all ran for cover. At the same time the drive belt powering the blower started to slip at the engine's pulley, sending up a cloud of smoke. Chester ran to shut down the machine, while Ned hightailed it for his room. Jubal, Maria, and Benny huddled in the stable. Water ran from the band of Jubal's Red Sox cap down his forehead to drip off the end of his nose. Maria wrang the water out of her blue bandana. Her hair lay in strings. They looked pathetic, as if they'd just escaped drowning.

Benny stood hunched with his arms hanging. Water dripped off the ends of his fingers and down into his boots. "I'm all wet . . . but I ain't peed my pants."

Maria burst out laughing as she shook droplets of rain from her hair. Benny began laughing too, and Jubal soon joined in. They mopped their faces and arms with the bottoms of their t-shirts.

"Looks like we don't know enough to come in out of the rain," Jubal said.

After Chester and Avery stabled the teams, Avery came to them.

"We might's well get some dry clothes and continue the corn after lunch," he announced.

Chester came to Avery with the news, "The blower pipe's plugged solid."

Avery turned to Jubal. "When ya come back, ya'll have ta climb the silo. I'll bet the silo's full up with a pile blockin' more from comin' in. If so, ya've got ta stay up there and keep it forked from the end of the blower pipe."

Jubal nodded. He would do as asked, but he wasn't too keen on climbing the high, slippery ladder.

After the heavy rain let up, Maria rode Trueboy back up to the Brown farm for lunch while Jubal and Benny drove on ahead in the truck. They were all eager to get out of their wet clothes. The skies cleared shortly after Maria stabled Trueboy. The horse had been soaked as well while standing tied under the tree near the AKL stone. She joined Jubal and Benny in the kitchen. While enjoying some of Rose's chicken salad, the three chatted idly about the weather and the difficulty of the harvest. All too soon, it was time to return to Avery's. This time Maria rode in the truck, sitting in the middle next to Jubal for easier visiting. He was glad that she was relaxing some and again joining in conversation and friendship.

When they arrived at Avery's, Jubal went to the silo and stood looking forty feet up, all the way to the top. He'd have to carry the eight-tine fork while climbing with both hands on the ladder rungs. To solve the problem, he tied the fork around his waist with a string through the handle. Carefully, he inched his way up the narrow ladder with the fork banging against his legs. Every now and then he paused, clinging to the rungs, and once he looked down. The cement was a long way below, causing his heart to beat faster. If he fell to the ground he'd splat like a bug. He imagined, as he resumed his labored climb, Lizzy at his funeral. She'd be wearing a black form-fitting dress and a hat with a black veil over her face to hide her tears. Polly would stand to the side in a new, bright blue jacket, smirking in amusement that he'd met such a foolish end. He shook his head to clear it so he could concentrate. One hand, then another. One step, then another. Finally, he managed to get the fork and himself to the top.

As the green feed blew into the silo, Jubal forked the chopped corn away from the end of the pipe, doing as Avery asked. He built a heap of silage around himself above the pipe outlet. Avery said that the other silo had settled six to eight feet in the matter of a day.

In brief spells of downtime, Jubal looked out through the silo opening. He felt like a watchman in a lighthouse like he'd once seen in pictures of the Eastern Seaboard. In the distance, Maria and Benny handled the corn, slowly dragging their feet through mud. He wished he could help them instead of standing idle up where the birds flew. As he watched his coworkers struggle, he wondered if the punishing job was helping calm the emotions he suspected rose and fell like waves inside Maria. The trauma seemed maybe to have run its course. He hoped so. Yet, in working with her daily, he observed flashes of sadness that appeared and dissolved like the rings in the wake of the ducks on the reservoir.

By late Saturday, they finally finished the corn. Earlier that day, Jubal had sent word that Lizzy and Clem would have to deliver the Saturday afternoon groceries without Trueboy and the wagon, due to the urgency to finish the harvest. However, he had let Lizzy know that Maria, corn finished or not, would be stopping by on Trueboy in time for the six o'clock Mass.

Before they left, Avery came to them. "Ya kids did a whale of a job. Jest fer that, I'm givin' ya three loads a' hay. I'm sure relieved ta have that corn in the silos. We beat the frost."

Surprised by the offer, Jubal felt good to have helped his neighbor. "Thanks, Avery. We sure can use it."

"Well, ya looked out fer my harvest and that makes a pile a' difference in knowin' we're all set fer winter."

After chores in the dim evening light, the sky again looked heavy with clouds, a forecast for rain. Jubal was thankful the drought had ended, but to avoid another drenching he would have to wait for a clear day to bring home the loads of hay they'd earned. Before heading to the house for dinner, he checked the five-acre future pasture to see if the late summer seeding had been successful. He fell to his knees and upon inspection found tiny ladino clover leaves the size of a pinhead, along with slivers of orchardgrass poking through the bare soil. The seeds, as in near magic, had opened themselves to the sun and the rain—a fact that filled him with joy. He'd timed his seeding correctly, hoping now to get sufficient rain until cold weather arrived and the snow covered the tender seedlings until spring.

⁂

Prior to Saturday evening Mass, Lizzy was tied in a knot over her promise to attend church with Maria. She sat in her makeshift office preparing to break the news to Bert that she was leaving early, meaning he would have to close the store at seven. His added responsibility was the easy part. The difficulty came in letting him know that she was going to the Catholic church.

There was an offish relationship between the Catholics and Baptists in town that few talked about but everyone knew existed. Many Catholic families did their grocery shopping in Rutland, seeking out stores owned and operated by Irish proprietors. Few Catholics of any means bought much at the Hayesville IGA. Though Lady Lamont, a Catholic, was a silent partner making the store what it was, not many thought of the IGA as the heiress's business. Instead the store was considered to belong to Lizzy.

In regards to religion, Lizzy had no church background whatsoever. Attending Mass with Maria would signify a shift. Such a move would mean a lot to the Sausvilles as members of the Hayesville Baptist Church. Bert had said he considered her as his own daughter; therefore, her turning to the Catholic church would be an insult. To be sure, Bernice would object to a promising future member of the Temperance League converting to the "other side." To make matters worse, Lizzy knew she'd probably end up attending Mass regularly if Maria felt comfortable with Father Hebert and appreciated staying over Saturday nights at the store.

Around five-thirty, Lizzy looked up Main Street and saw Maria carrying her overnight bag while riding on Trueboy, leaving little time to inform Bert of her plans. It would be best to catch him off guard and the less said, the better. Lizzy went to the clothing section and quickly thumbed through several silk kerchiefs. She chose an amber color as background for a black floral design to blend with her jet-black hair. Since she kept an ongoing list of items taken from the store, she went to the checkout counter where Bert was sitting.

"My takeout list is under the register," she said, pointing. "I wanna add this kerchief marked at fifty cents."

Bert picked up the kerchief, shaking it open and turning it to see. "My goodness. This has been here for years gathering dust." He gave her a questioning look as he handed the kerchief back and slid the takeout list across the counter. "Tell me, why are you suddenly needing a kerchief?"

"Uh, church. The women have ta cover their hair." Lizzy put the scarf on her head and tied it under her chin. "How's it look?"

"Well okay, but sort of strange. Never seen you wearing such a thing. Wait. Did you say church?"

"Yup. Maria's comin' on Trueboy and we're goin' ta six o'clock Mass," she explained. She picked up a pencil and added the item to her list. "Oh, and would ya close at seven? I won't be back in time."

"The *Catholic* church?" Bert's mouth dropped open in shock. "Why Bernice and I have never—"

"Ya've never invited me ta yer church. So now Maria's invited me ta hers." Lizzy slid the list back to Bert. "Early bird gets the worm."

"But you aren't Catholic!"

"I know. I'm nothin', but this might change. If I join ranks, might draw in some a' the faithful ta buy at our store."

"I can't believe this." Bert looked about as puzzled as could be.

She reached across the counter and patted his forearm. "The sky ain't fallin'. Nobody's gonna die over it, Bert. And hopefully, I'll survive."

She left Bert standing dumbfounded and exited out the back of the store to meet Maria and Trueboy. She knew Bernice would have plenty to say on the matter when Bert told her the news. No doubt he was dreading the confrontation with his wife.

It didn't take the girls long to stable Trueboy and stow Maria's overnight bag in Lizzy's room. Maria was unusually chatty as Lizzy walked with her down the sidewalk towards St. Anne's.

"It's exciting to be going to church again. I wonder what the homily will be?" Maria took up Lizzy's arm as they walked. "I think you'll like Father Hebert. He's a neat Holy Father."

"If ya say so," Lizzy replied. Having had little contact with priests, she wasn't sure how this "neat" priest might compare with another sort. "What's a homily? Sounds like somethin' ta go with scrambled eggs."

"Ha! Oh my, Lizzy." Maria was clearly amused. "It's the priest's message."

"Oh. Speakin' of eggs, they got anythin' ta eat at this? Prob'ly should a' had more fer supper." She put her hand on her stomach, which growled as if to prove her empty belly.

Maria shook her head no. "They have communion. That's wine and a wafer. But I'm sorry to say that you can't have any since you aren't a confirmed Catholic that's been to confession."

"Well, geez," Lizzy remarked. "Catholics ain't the sharin' kind? Nothin' ta feed the hungry and all?"

"You're not missing much," Maria said. "The wafer is dry as sawdust."

They passed the Hiram Hayes monument before reaching the rectory. Lizzy was relieved to see that the black Cadillac was gone, indicating they might not have to deal with Tatum. She certainly hoped she and Maria had discouraged Tatum from ever solving the mystery of the disappearing Packard.

Apparently folks liked Father Hebert. Cars were parked on both sides of the street. As they entered the building that had stood in town for hundreds of years, Maria tied a blue kerchief to cover her head and Lizzy followed with her amber one. Once inside, folks didn't take much notice of the two as they might an outsider so Lizzy's nerves settled somewhat. Maria took the lead before they went into the main church when she dipped the tip of her index finger into a container of water by the door and crossed herself.

Maria recited in a whisper, "In the name of the Father, the Son, and the Holy Ghost." Lizzy marveled that a ghost was part of the prayer. She watched Maria and waited for what to do next.

They entered a cool, dimly-lit cavernous space like nothing Lizzy had ever seen. A blue ceiling arched high above the walls. Three white-painted angels looked to be floating on the ceiling as if opened to the sky—what some might think of as a glimpse of heaven. Lizzy noted all kinds of symbols and images around the room, having no idea what they were.

Maria led her towards the front, passing rows of pews on the right and left, their steps echoing off the hard flooring. Lizzy recognized a life-sized statue of the Virgin Mary who wore a dark-blue robe with light-blue edging. Mary's ivory head-covering hid all but her angelic face. In the center of her chest was a big red heart. Behind Mary, a raised display of small candles flickered teardrop flames. Lizzy stared at the idol in awe until, near the front, Maria stopped at a pew, knelt, crossed herself again, and slid in. Lizzy awkwardly side-stepped to follow and settled onto the smooth wooden seat. Maria pulled a low, padded bench into place and knelt, resting her elbows on the pew in front of her. She took a string of beads from her pocket and dangled them from her hand. Lizzy sensed that her friend had moved into her own inner world, communicating with the unseen in private.

Although the church was nearly filled, it remained quiet. Lizzy looked down the row of worshippers to see several of them doing the same as Maria. She looked to the front and studied a huge cross depicting Christ nailed to the wooden timbers. The nails went right through the palms of his hands with his arms stretched wide. More nails were driven through his feet. He wore only what looked to her like a diaper, and his head was slumped as if he had passed out from pain. So it wasn't just Big Daddy that did terrible things, or the likes of Freddie Coleman. Seems somebody had tortured Jesus in his time and she wondered why.

On the raised area below the cross, two young boys dressed in white robes entered from a side door. They held long golden lighters and reached to light candles on either side of the altar. After the candles were ablaze, they exited. Fascinated, Lizzy wondered what was to happen next. There was a hush over the room. Shortly, the two boys returned. One held a porcelain basin with a small white towel, and the other carried a golden cup and a large gold vessel.

In minutes, Andrew O'Mara in a business suit, his short, graying hair combed perfectly into place, entered from a side door in back of the altar. Father Hebert followed. The priest was quite young and wore a wide satin ribbon that flowed down the front of his robe. As the service began, Mister O'Mara opened the massive Bible on the altar, remaining at Father Hebert's side to turn the pages as needed. It was the largest book Lizzy had ever seen, even bigger than the dictionary in the school library.

She didn't understand any of the service with all the spoken words being in another language. Maria leaned over and whispered that it was Latin. At intervals, a male chant echoed from the choir loft in the rear of the church. Maria passed her the *Catholic Missal* which translated from Latin to English all that was being said or sung. It helped as Lizzy followed along.

The missal called for the reading in English of Psalm 27: *"The Lord is my light and my salvation; whom shall I fear? The Lord is the stronghold of my life; of whom shall I be afraid? . . . For he will hide me in his shelter in the day of trouble."*

After his reading, Father Hebert stepped to the podium below the altar. "Welcome, my fellow Catholics. This evening in Psalm 27 we find words of comfort, assuring us that in all our time here on Earth, the Lord will be our shepherd. He is our shelter from the storms that we cannot help but encounter during our life's journey. What a blessing to discover that almighty God is our refuge, that He will remain thus and will always be with us until our final days."

The idea of God as a shelter and a constant support through troubling times was indeed comforting. Lizzy thought perhaps those words were what Maria had come to hear.

The service continued and Lizzy learned from the missal how Father Hebert was preparing the Eucharist for the Holy Communion. First, he purified the altar with burning incense. Great puffs of smoke flowed from a silver pot on a chain that Father Hebert swung, and the musky scent filled the air. A bell rang and more Latin words were chanted. Lizzy read in the missal that the bell signified the changing of the wine and bread into the blood and body of Christ. She looked up just as the priest took a wafer from the vessel and passed it solemnly between his lips. He paused in thought. Then he drank from the wine cup. One of the altar boys quickly wiped the cup with the towel. She considered why the Catholic practice was to pretend to consume the body and blood of a man who had suffered so badly. She was mystified and had plenty of questions for Maria later.

Row by row the congregation silently filed up to the front and knelt at the altar rail. Maria joined them, her hands folded before her as she walked. Some received a token of the Eucharist while others crossed their arms and hands over their chests and received only a blessing. That was the situation with Maria who had whispered before she left her seat that she needed to go to confession and be purified before she could accept Communion.

Confession! Would Maria have to tell Father Hebert the details of how her body had been used resulting in her no longer being a virgin? Lizzy flushed with embarrassment just thinking of how that might feel for her friend. She wondered if Maria was strong enough to follow through with such a confession.

After Mass, Maria waited in the aisle to introduce Lizzy to the priest where he stood at the rear of the church greeting folks as they left. Lizzy watched his easy-going manner while he took time with each individual in a brief chat. She could see he was genuinely interested in the lives of his flock. The girls were the last to leave. Father Hebert beamed.

"Hello, Maria. I've missed you at camp and on Sundays at the eight o'clock Mass when I sometimes assist Father Mac." He briefly held her hand. "Have you been away?"

Maria obviously wasn't expecting the question and paused. "I've been home," she said quietly. In a brighter tone she said, "I'd like you to meet my friend, Lizzy LaFlam."

Father Hebert turned to Lizzy with a kind expression. "Lizzy, I'm pleased to meet you. Welcome to St. Anne's." He took her hand with a warm, firm grip.

"Thanks!" Lizzy pumped the priest's hand up and down. "Uh . . . ya see, this is all new ta me," she said.

He smiled. "If it's your first time attending, it must have seemed strange."

She nodded. "It was kinda weird. But also like turnin' on a light fer the first time. I never knew some guy was upstairs lookin' after me."

Father Hebert chuckled. "Lizzy, I like your interpretation." He turned back to Maria. "I understand that being Rose Queen didn't work out so well for you, Maria. I wasn't in town and I'm afraid I missed the parade."

"I would say no. It did not work out," Maria answered.

"Oh." Father Hebert appeared concerned. "So you have some upset feelings about this?"

Maria looked to Lizzy for support.

"Tell him," Lizzy urged.

"To be honest, Father," Maria said tensely, "it was awful. I did not enjoy being Rose Queen one bit."

Father Hebert frowned. "I'm so sorry to hear this. Let's talk about it sometime. You can come to me and share what happened. I will listen. I won't judge you."

"I'd like that," Maria said, relaxing.

"Why don't you meet me at five next Saturday and we can visit before Mass."

"I can do that," Maria agreed. "I'll come."

They said their goodbyes and left. On the walk back to the store, Lizzy observed that the further away they got from the rectory, the more Maria's mood lightened.

Trying to make conversation, Lizzy commented, "Well, that Mass was interestin' but I gotta say, some parts were puzzlin'. I'm gonna need ya ta fill me in."

"I suppose it being your first time in a church, it would seem that way," Maria said. "How about when we settle into bed tonight, you can ask me questions and I'll tell you about the Catholic faith."

"Sounds like a plan. But—" Lizzy stopped.

Maria paused on the sidewalk and looked at her questioningly. "What? What is it?"

"I have ta say, ain't it a bit odd how Father Hebert weren't ever told the details 'bout what happened ta ya as Rose Queen? I'm thinkin' somebody is makin' up stories or wantin' ta keep secrets."

Maria sighed. "It's not the first time." She looked up at the sky now filled with stars and seemed to weigh out whether to continue. She spoke as if to the heavens. "The hardest part is how everyone in town wants to sweep what happened to me away. To hide it under the rug like unwanted dirt. Even my own folks. Makes it feel it didn't matter, or was my fault somehow."

"I'm sorry," Lizzy said. "Ya should know I ain't forgotten."

Maria's tone grew angry. "It's like with their silence they're saying, 'Keep quiet, Maria! No one wants to hear about that terrible thing.' They want me to smile and be happy and move on."

Lizzy knew Maria's words to be true. That's how the community—except for her and Jubal and Rose—had reacted to Maria's rape. "Ya know ya can talk ta me or Jubal anytime. Ya don't have ta be quiet."

As Maria looked back up at the stars, her chest rose and fell in a deep breath.

Lizzy wanted to ease her sadness. "Father Hebert gives me a good feelin'. His way seems comfortin' like warm, baked bread. I'm guessin' ya can trust him. I think ya should unload yer burden ta him like he's asked."

Maria met Lizzy's eyes. "You're right. I'll tell him."

"That's good," Lizzy said.

They resumed walking.

"You know," Maria said after a few minutes, "it felt good to be back in church, listening to Father Hebert."

Lizzy nodded. "I liked the psalm about the Lord hidin' us in his shelter in the face a' trouble. Sure had my share a' troubles."

"Yes, like me," Maria said. "But as Father Hebert read that, I sat wondering, where was God that afternoon? I mean, I was in His house when Freddie attacked me. If the psalm says the Lord is always there by our side, where was He that day? Why would a kind and decent God just stand by and let Freddie . . . let Freddie . . . take what was mine? It wasn't his to have!"

Lizzy thought for a moment. "That's a true mystery. Maybe God had other things ta attend ta that day? Maybe somebody somewhere was in even more trouble? It must be hard ta always be everywhere at once. Maybe he was way across the sea dealing with that evil guy Hitler folks keep talkin' 'bout at the store."

Maria nodded. "I'm going to ask Father Hebert for some answers, because I realized as I sat praying today that I'm angry at God, just . . . really mad."

"Can't say I blame ya," Lizzy said. She took Maria's hand in hers just as they arrived at the store.

The two walked to the back of the building where Lizzy helped Maria feed and water Trueboy who gave a small whinny from his stall in greeting. Maria walked to the horse and pressed her forehead to his, remaining in the calming position until Lizzy spoke.

"When yer ready," Lizzy said, "I borrowed some ice cream from the store."

"Borrowed? What, are we going to give it back?" Maria teased.

Lizzy stomped her foot in pretend disgust. "Stop! Ya know what I mean."

The two friends walked together to the wire-caged room. They enjoyed their vanilla ice cream and later, lying in comfort under the quilts on their cots, Lizzy peppered Maria with questions about the ceremony at the church. Maria answered patiently and with enthusiasm. They talked deep into the night.

Chapter Thirty-Seven

As far back as Jubal could remember, his family had heated their house with coal. Clyde wasn't one that enjoyed bucking up a pile of wood even when he was able. However, now that Jubal had Maria's help, providing their own wood heat would save money on the expense of coal. He knew little about the tools needed to deal with firewood, but Maria was well aware of the process, having worked with her dad in the woods for several years. It was obvious they would each need an ax, but Maria explained they would also need a one and two-man crosscut saw, wedges to fell trees and split difficult chunks, and a sledge hammer to drive the wedges. Jubal had used wedges to split Avery's rock but had never used them for their intended purpose. Maria gathered the necessary tools, having seen them lying in various places around the Brown farm.

"These saws and axes are dull and need sharpening," Maria told him. "I'm sure my dad would be happy to sharpen them if we, in turn, help Ma dig, sort, and store her potatoes."

Jubal agreed that it sounded like a good trade. He made arrangements for Benny to finish the barn chores. Afterwards, his uncle was to join Rose up at Lady Lamont's while they were away helping Maria's ma, Kathleen. Clyde, overhearing the plan, was in favor of the idea to put up wood for the winter.

"I only wish I could help ya," he said. He pointed to the wooden cane beside his chair. "I'm still stuck limpin' 'round this place."

"It's okay, Dad," Jubal said. Though his father was not able to help much, Jubal was proud of him. He had not touched a drop of liquor since his return and did not seem tempted in the least. His dad had yet to share what had gone on in Troy, as if keeping close some private conviction, but Jubal knew something important had shifted his father's outlook.

After breakfast, he and Maria loaded the saws and axes into the back of the truck. Maria explained that her mother was so particular in dealing with her "patatas" that the process usually ended in a marital spat resulting in her father retreating to the farm's workshop. Jubal hoped his labor would meet the standards of Maria's ma.

Chester was leaving the barn when they arrived in Avery's yard. Jubal shut off the truck and rolled down the window. "Hey Chester—I've got some tools for you to sharpen."

Maria spoke up. "Like you offered, Dad. A trade. Jubal and I will help Ma with her potatoes."

"Decent deal," Chester said, coming to stand at Jubal's window. "Kathleen and I ain't like-minded when it comes ta her patatas."

"We'll do just as she asks," Jubal assured him.

"With Kathleen ya won't have a choice." Chester looked into the back of the pickup and tipped up the two-man crosscut saw. He ran his fingers over some of the teeth. "Looks like someone's been tryin' ta saw cement."

Jubal nodded. "Something like that. I suspect my dad years back maybe ran it through some sap spouts left in maple trees, or nails and wire from old fencing."

"Yup, that'd do it." Chester said. He lifted the two-handled saw from the truck and headed towards the shop.

Jubal followed carrying the single crosscut, while Maria came with the axes. Like everything at Avery Ketchum's, the farm shop was in perfect order. Tools were hung and stowed in assigned places, and there was enough of a variety of them to fix almost anything—a welder, torches, an arch, complete sets of wrenches, a grinding wheel, and a whetstone. Jubal was envious, vowing someday he'd have a similar shop.

Chester looked at the sharpening needed on the assortment of tools they had given him. "Ya brought me plenty ta do. Take me a coupla days between chores. But Kathleen's patatas will take a chunk a' time as well."

Jubal would do what it took to have sharp tools. Regardless of the job, their condition made a difference, especially at the Clyde Brown farm where almost nothing was done with top-notch equipment.

Kathleen must have seen her help arriving because she came immediately to her garden. She carried two unusual tools with five-foot handles and eight-inch tines in the shape of a hook. Jubal sensed that there wasn't going to be any joking around while harvesting her potatoes of about fifteen hilled rows, each around a hundred feet long.

Kathleen did not offer a greeting but instead spelled out the orders. "Maria, ya pull the dead vines and throw them in a heap at the side of the garden."

Maria started the first row. "Pulling vines for Ma is easy," she explained to Jubal. "If you spike potatoes, she gets upset. Right, Ma?"

"Ya, sure do. Want ta sell as many patatas as possible down ta the store. This young man can do the diggin' right if I show him."

Jubal followed Kathleen's instructions carefully while they moved along behind Maria.

"Always strike low at the bottom of the hill and pull." Kathleen demonstrated by sinking the potato hook into the ground. "If ya strike high, ya'll snare patatas."

Sure enough, when Jubal pulled on the handle, uninjured potatoes near the size of oblong baseballs came rolling out. A few more swings of the fork and the digging was complete. They were ready to move on to the next hill down the row. Jubal found the soil to be soft and fluffy. Maria told him that the potatoes had been "hilled" some weeks earlier to form the ridge, an area big enough for the plant to develop its nest of as many as six potatoes.

Once, when he struck too high with the tines, Kathleen warned him, "Spiked patatas ain't good. Injures 'em. They don't keep the winter and I can't sell 'em at the store."

Kathleen's protectiveness of her patatas was understandable. Jubal realized how she must depend on the income and having saleable produce was good reason to be fussy. They worked along steadily until about eleven-thirty when Kathleen stopped to get lunch ready.

"Well, son ya've got the knack," she said before leaving. "When my girl and ya finish, come fer lunch."

As Kathleen walked towards the house, Maria, having cleared all the vines, picked up the hook her ma had used and helped to finish the job. By twelve-thirty she and Jubal had made the patch look like wall-to-wall brown stones drying in the sun and almost none were damaged in the digging.

"Seems you passed the test," Maria said. "Let's go for lunch."

"Good thing," he said. "I'd hate to get on your ma's bad side." He looked over at the house, wondering what a Styles lunch would be like.

As they walked up along the garden, Jubal thought back to weeks earlier when he first came with Trueboy to ask for Maria's help at the farm. Remembering her bruised face, he hoped that Freddie Coleman was miserable locked in his cell at Windsor prison.

In the entryway, he followed Maria's example and took off his shoes, hanging his cap on a hook. He could see no one wore their work shoes in Kathleen's house.

The kitchen was plain and neat. Jubal took note of the cross over the hallway door with dried palms tucked behind it and a Catholic calendar on a cupboard door showing the Virgin Mary with her red sacred heart. The walls were papered in a small yellow print. A low fire in a Glenwood iron cook stove took the dampness off the room, and a hand pump by the sink was their water supply.

Maria's ma was at the counter kneading a quantity of bread dough. She swiped the graying hair from her face with the back of a flour-covered hand.

"Ya kids wash up in the bathroom and I'll serve ya some lunch." She turned their way. "Maria, yer father's takin' his lunch with Avery so come ta the table when ready."

Jubal waited for Maria to go first. Entering their small bathroom, he splashed his face several times with water cupped in both hands and dried his face on a hand towel embroidered with little yellow flowers. With his fingers, he then combed the sweaty hair that hung down to his shoulders up over the top of his head. When he returned to the kitchen, Maria sat waiting. Her freckled face was no longer smudged with dirt and she had wrapped her hair in a bun to pin it in back of her head.

Kathleen served the food but stood to the side, not eating with them. Jubal pulled up a chair and helped himself to a delicious-looking egg salad sandwich on homemade bread. He also took two dill pickles from a jar in the center of the table.

As he munched, Maria suddenly chuckled. He stopped eating and looked down at the front of his shirt to see if some egg salad had fallen on it.

Not seeing any, he looked up. "What's so funny?"

"Oh, nothing . . . it's just you." Maria picked up a sandwich and took a bite, chasing it down with a drink of milk. "Those pink cheeks and long hair, well . . . you could be a girl."

He was taken aback. "I've always had long hair. Sorry if it bothers you." As he ate, he stewed silently in disgust over Maria's comment.

The room remained quiet. He watched Kathleen fold the dough she was kneading. Her quick hand slid over the wooden counter as she placed portions of the dough in three bread pans. When she finished her task, she came to stand at the back of Maria's chair.

"Ya know, kids, we've got ta wait before we move them patatas into the garage ta be graded. They need ta stay outside a bit ta dry in the sun and warm air." She looked across the table at Jubal. "Now, young man, how about ya let Maria cut yer hair that she's been in such a fix about? She's good. Until just recent, she gave her dad his haircuts."

Jubal was amazed that Maria had even noticed his hair and more so that she'd been in a fix about it. Weeks earlier, she wouldn't give him a glance for the time of day, and Lizzy had said it was because he was a guy. Yet Maria had made a remark about his long hair way back in April when they were plowing together, and she had wanted to cut it then. He wondered if he'd like Maria messing with something as personal as his hair.

"I've always tended to my own hair," he said. He'd never been one to care about fashion. Perhaps if he let Maria have her way, it might bring back more of their closeness. It was only hair after all. "Okay, sure. You can hack away."

Maria had a look of victory, poised to pop out of her chair. She seemed excited to trim off a part of him that he'd always thought added to his character.

"Ya washin' it first?" Kathleen asked her daughter.

"I am—thought I'd first rinse out the burrs, bugs, and brambles," Maria said.

Kathleen chuckled.

Was his hair that bad? Jubal wished he'd taken longer to fix it in the bathroom. He realized the two women were having a laugh at his expense and he played along. "I'll have you both know, I washed my hair last month."

Kathleen spoke up. "I know that ain't true. I'm sure ya keep it washed fer that young lady down ta the store."

Jubal laughed. "Well, you got me there."

"I like that gal," Kathleen commented. "That Lizzy was real sharp when I dealt a trade with her and my patatas. And she's been a good friend ta my Maria."

"She heeds her own mind. I admire that," Maria put in as she got up from the table. "Hope there's enough water in the stove's reservoir." She opened the steel cover and flicked the contents with her finger. "There's plenty and it's nice and warm."

After transferring the stove's water to a kettle, Maria carried it across the kitchen. "Follow me and we'll wash that mop of yours."

Jubal was soon standing awkwardly in the small bathroom as Maria wrapped a towel around his neck.

"Bend over and put your head in the sink," she instructed.

His long hair practically filled the wash basin as he leaned down. The warm water felt good as it traveled over the top of his head.

"Gosh, you've got all kinds of stuff living in this crow's nest." Maria chuckled. "I guess mostly hayseed. Wonder it didn't sprout as green grass."

"You exaggerate." His retort was muffled with his face down in the sink.

Firm fingers combed through his hair, making a sudsy lather. Stuck in a totally helpless position, he felt Maria was now able to dominate a guy, though he was harmless. Enjoying her moment, she hummed a tune as her scrubbing fingers felt like a frog on springs. Soon another quantity of suds filled his hair from the bar of sweet-smelling soap. In minutes, she poured water several times over his head and all the soap swirled down the drain. She squeezed his rinsed hair, shaking it free of water.

"Stand up and I'll get your head as dry as I can," she said, reaching for a towel that hung on a hook. She put the towel over his head and rubbed vigorously. Her hands moved quickly, taking the wet towel from his neck and replacing it with the second. She pinned the new towel, covering his shoulders and front.

"Now for the surgery," he said as she picked up the scissors.

She was about to change what he'd taken pride in as his unique image. He was going to look like every other guy in town. As a kid he had liked courageous storybook characters with long hair like *The Three Musketeers* and *Robinson Crusoe.* But those days were long gone and those characters were only fiction.

He supposed Lizzy wouldn't mind. To her credit she'd never complained about his hair. She met people as they were. Still, he wondered if the two girls had plotted together to trim his locks.

Maria paused humming her little tune to reassure him. "A painless surgery. We're turning you into a sharp-looking guy."

She ran a comb through his hair, gently pulling on the snarls. Next, came the snipping sound. He could see from the corner of his eye great lops of blond hair falling down around his shoulders to the floor. "Dang, I'll have to wear a wool cap after this."

"Maybe in cold weather." The clipping continued. Maria's fingers gathered locks at the sides and back of his head. She finished by cutting quantities that covered his face and fell off his forehead. "There, I think I'm about done." She held up a mirror. "How do you like it?"

He stared. His hair now fell in layers above his ears, his eyes more noticeable with an expanse of forehead. "Wow, I sure look different!" He took the mirror from her and held it to one side and then the other. "I guess that's me, though." He handed the mirror back and she set it on the sink's edge.

"You'll be quite the surprise when you visit a certain someone down at the store." Maria removed the towel. "Go and show my ma."

As Maria stayed in the bathroom to sweep up, he glanced back at the pile of hair representing his youthful fantasies gathered into the dustpan.

Kathleen studied him from her spot by the kitchen counter and nodded. "That's more like it. Never did like long hair on a man." In a surprise move, she slid a generous slice of apple pie onto the table and placed a glass of milk in front of it. "Take a seat and help yerself."

"Gee, thanks." He guessed he was one of the few townsfolk to ever darken the door of the Styles' home. To be given a treat was proof that he was accepted. He took a mouthful. "Mmm. This pie's good!"

She nodded as Maria came and sat at the table.

Kathleen again stood behind her daughter's chair. "Well, Maria, this young man is no longer a kid."

"I wish that's all it would take to become a man." He ran his hand over the top of his head. "I must say I feel a little naked."

Maria studied him intently. "You look handsome, dashing even."

Having finished his pie, Jubal pushed back his chair and stood. "Speaking of dashing, is it time to move some potatoes?"

"I'm ready." Kathleen outlined the plan. "We'll put up and bag five pecks fer the girl at the store and put away what's left in separate bins in case she needs some later if they sell."

The afternoon went smoothly. Jubal collected the potatoes outside in a wheelbarrow and brought them in for sorting as desired. Maria understood exactly what her ma wanted for uniformity in the sale of her patatas. Together, she and her ma packaged and weighed in bags, closing them off with twisted wire ties. By four o'clock, they'd completed the job.

Jubal walked with Maria back to the shop to find Chester seated on the frame that held the grindstone. The circular stone spun with a treadle he pumped with his foot and there was a coffee can with a hole dripping water onto the whetstone. Maria's dad held an ax to the stone as the metal shaped to a thin edge. "These axes ain't never been sharpened right, but I'll have yer tools ready tomorrow afternoon."

They left Chester at his work and climbed into the truck. On the way up Harmony Hill they made their plans to bring in the winter's firewood. At the Brown farm, Jubal's family was seated around the kitchen table eating a snack of chocolate cake and milk.

His ma did a double-take when he and Maria walked in. "Why Jubal, we won't know you with short hair! What a surprise!"

He placed his cap on the back of a chair.

Maria looked at Jubal in satisfaction. "Doesn't he finally look the part of a man?" she said.

His ma hesitated. "Turn around, Jubal, let me see."

Jubal turned in a slow circle.

"Well," his ma remarked, "I guess it's all in what you look for." It was clear she was struggling to get used to the difference.

Her comment hung in the air as Maria's face clouded over. Jubal couldn't believe his mother's words. She knew Maria was more sensitive now. His ma looked at him in question and he frowned. Rose caught her mistake and smiled.

"And yet, I will admit, he does look rather nice all grown up," she said. "I guess we can get used to him."

Maria brightened and the tension in the room eased. Having just had Kathleen's pie, Jubal passed on his ma's offer of a slice of cake, but Maria politely took a small piece, likely to appease his ma after having changed his appearance so dramatically.

The Philco from the other room filtered in snippets of voices. Clyde was his old self again, keeping abreast of world affairs. "Big trouble. This is really big trouble."

Benny paused, fork halfway to his mouth. "Who's in trouble?"

"The trouble is far away across the sea, Benny," Rose said quickly.

Benny relaxed and went back to enjoying his cake.

Rose held up a sales catalogue that rested by her plate. "Changing the subject, see what came in the mail? An Ayrshire sale catalogue. Jubal, the sale is a few weeks away on a Saturday—October 18th at the fairgrounds in Rutland."

Jubal reached for the booklet and saw that the Vermont Ayrshire Breeders were holding a consignment sale. Fifty cows were catalogued, mostly bred heifers and promising young producers. He passed the catalogue to Maria. "How much can we spend?" he asked his ma.

"Six hundred should buy three milkers," his ma said. "What we can save and borrow from Lady Lamont should be enough, as long as you don't blow it all on the top of the sale. I asked Chuck Dent about cattle prices. He said an average milk cow has been fetching under two hundred dollars."

Jubal nodded. "Sounds about right. Well, we still need to add more high producers to our herd." He flipped through the pages. "Wanna go, Maria? You could help me pick out some real promising young cows."

"Maybe." She looked through the catalogue. "Sure, I'll go. It would be interesting."

"It's settled then," his ma said. "More quality for the Brown herd!"

In the weeks leading up to the Ayeshire sale, the activities at the farm flowed easily. In a new development, Clyde began limping down to the barn in the mornings with the help of his cane. Proudly, Jubal showed his dad the new cows they'd gotten from Chuck earlier that summer, the manure they'd spread, and the places where they had put up new fencing. He was especially excited to show the new seeding. His dad patted him on the back more than once.

An evening or two a week, Jubal tried to make time for visiting Lizzy down at the store. It was getting harder not to surrender to temptation when they were alone, but he resisted, feeling the need to be careful with their futures.

The days were growing shorter. In what time they had between chores, he and Maria carefully selected hardwood trees along hedgerows that had encroached over the years into the open meadows. He learned a lot about how to fell trees and buck up firewood. He also noticed that Maria continued to talk more. She appeared happier in conversation and the light seemed to return to her blue eyes. By late afternoon each day they'd load their labors into the truck and stack the wood in the cellar of the farmhouse. During the cool days and nights of fall, Jubal burned coal in the furnace, storing the green wood near the heat so as to season it for burning. The clean fragrance of drying cordwood filtered up through the floorboards, giving the house a fresh smell.

On the evening of October 17th, the night before the cattle sale, Jubal went to the living room to be with his dad. Clyde raised his hand in greeting. For Jubal, it was still a little strange not to see liquor or beer within easy reach of his father's chair. His dad motioned towards the Philco.

"Would ya turn that on, son?" his father asked.

The eight-day clock, placed on the shelf over his father's chair had just struck seven. Jubal reached and turned the knob on the radio:

General Hideki has just taken control as Japan's supreme commander. Negotiations with Washington for the lifting of the blockade and embargo of Japan are underway. The demand by the United States that Japan remove all forces from China and Indochina may be an obstacle in reaching an agreement. . . .

Chapter Thirty-Eight

On the way to the Ayrshire sale, Maria and Jubal were headed north in Benny's big car. Maria enjoyed riding in the Packard, but she wondered what the farmers would think when they saw such a fancy rig pull into the Vermont State Fairgrounds. As they traveled, Maria noticed a cluster of cabins for skiers. She pointed them out to Jubal. They imagined how it would be to sail down over the snow while balancing on two long wooden boards with curled-up tips.

"I'd probably fall and break my arm. Or even worse, my neck," Jubal said.

Maria looked up at the peak of a passing mountain. "I bet it would feel like flying." Leaving Hayesville, Maria had felt a momentary lift to see a change of scenery.

Another improvement in her life was meeting with Father Hebert every Saturday before Mass. The young priest showed compassion and understanding for her problem. Yet, she'd been nervous at their first meeting, expecting Father Hebert to confirm her guilt for having triggered Freddie's attack. They were seated in the community room of the rectory with cups of lemonade. Maria still avoided the red room when possible, and she was glad they didn't meet there.

She had barely been able to speak the words as she told him her story. She ended by confessing, "I shouldn't have flirted with Freddie or told those lies about myself. I've sinned. Seems the rape was my punishment." She slouched as she awaited God's condemnation.

"No, Maria, you're mistaken." Father Hebert leaned forward in his folding chair. "God doesn't work that way, punishing people. No matter what you said or did, Freddie Coleman did not have the right to attack you. What you experienced was a criminal assault."

"But . . ." Her eyes watered. "He said dirty things. He put his hands—I was, well . . . I couldn't stop him." She wiped away a tear. "I've been feeling so ashamed."

"Yes, I can imagine that's how it must feel." Father Hebert was solemn. "Maria, sex is meant to be an act of love. It should never be an expression of anger or domination. You did not deserve to be treated like this. No one does."

At his words, her eyes watered again.

The priest continued, "Freddie had no right to lay his hands on you. It is he who has sinned, Maria, not you."

Her chest and throat were tight. She wanted to believe him, but a part of her would not let go of the guilt. She had been careless. She should have been wiser. She'd wanted attention and to feel special. That was the sin. Father Hebert had to see this. He was just being nice. He didn't truly mean it.

In the end, it took her weeks to realize Father Hebert did mean what he said, and for her to take that to heart and come around to liking herself again. The priest was patient. Before seminary, he'd worked with World War I veterans who had come home emotionally paralyzed. He told her about shell shock. This helped her to realize nothing was wrong with her for not bouncing back. The veterans also had nightmares and some had contemplated suicide. Father Hebert helped her to see Freddie as being corrupted.

"It's rare that a person is born bad," Father Hebert told her. "People get damaged along the way. They need saving, but some are hard to save. We all get a reckoning in the end. You can be assured he will get his."

As the Packard cruised along Route 7, Maria suddenly felt the cool morning air on her face when Jubal rolled down his window. She turned to see him next to her, his hand on the wide steering wheel. In addition to his generous loan of Trueboy, which had been a lifesaver, Jubal had been considerate while she moped around his barn for weeks. He'd even taken special pains to discover the trigger of her anxiety at Avery's. Lizzy had also been caring by going to Mass and inviting her for sleepovers. Maria had her dad's quiet support and now the talks with Father Hebert. It was clear that she was not alone in this, though at times it felt that way. More and more the grayness inside of her was dissolving. She looked out her window, once again focusing on the scenery.

They passed several farmhouses surrounded by large outbuildings. Young cattle roamed freely over corn stubble showing that the crop had been fully harvested. She was glad to be done with hefting corn bundles for the year. Her arms had never ached so much in her life. Since it was late autumn, the work horses stood idle in the barnyards with no farming machines to pull.

Though being away from town for the sale was exciting, she'd miss delivering groceries with Trueboy that afternoon, but she knew Clem could handle the gentle horse and deliver at the necessary stops without her help. To pass the time as they traveled towards Rutland, she read aloud to Jubal the breed facts on the inside cover of the sale catalogue.

> *The Ayrshire breed originated in Scotland in the county of Ayr. Known for their abilities to navigate rocky terrain and tolerate cold, the first importation of the breed to the United States was in 1822. Soon after, an Ayrshire registry was established with offices located in Brandon, Vermont.*

"Sounds like the Ayrshire cow has long been a Vermont breed and common in our state," she said.

"They have?" Jubal glanced her way.

"Yeah, it says here that only New York has more registered Ayrshires. Vermont ranks second with over four thousand." She turned the page. "Did you see, Jubal, that Fillmore Farms in Bennington has consigned Lot One?"

"Yeah, I noticed that. She'll probably top the sale since she's close to being the most valuable heifer consigned. She'll be offered after two or three are sold, so as to get the crowd in the mood to bid."

"Do some people bid though they came with no intention of buying?"

"In some cases."

"That seems a shady way to drive up the price."

Jubal shrugged. "Folks just doing business is all."

Maria read Lot One's pedigree. "I wonder if we could buy her? From the picture, she's a beauty."

"No way!" Jubal said. "Look at entries towards the back of the catalogue—more our speed."

Maria turned the pages to the later entries. They were disappointingly ordinary.

Before long, they pulled into the fairgrounds and parked in front of the grandstand. The catalogue gave directions to a shed that would house the cattle to be sold.

"Let's stop here and walk," Jubal suggested.

Maria agreed."The car, huh?"

"Yeah, this car's too showy."

As they walked past beat-up cars and rusty farm trucks parked near a long, low cattle barn, Maria was glad they had parked far from the rest. They continued towards the barn where Maria noted farmers dressed in bib overalls and felt fedora hats. Many smoked pipes and most had craggy, weathered faces from years of working outdoors in all kinds of weather. Some farmers stared at Maria and Jubal who stood out in clean jeans, flannel shirts, and wool jackets. She smiled and nodded at those that spoke in passing, but most frowned and looked away. Folks were there to see their consignment sell or were in need of milkers to add to their herds. Few had a desire to stand around and visit.

The line of groomed cattle was impressive—all fifty of those listed in the catalogue were halter-tied on a pack of clean shavings. Their tails were brushed and washed sparkling white, white as foam on a pail of milk. Their heads were clipped and long body hair shaved—including from the developed udders of the heifers that were soon to calve and the milking animals.

Right away Maria noticed Lot One standing at the beginning of the line. The deep-bodied, broad heifer had a well-attached developing udder. Her mahogany spotted coat shone even in the dull light. The Brown farm didn't have a single animal that could come close to her beauty.

Next to Lot One, a middle-aged gentleman, not the typical farmer type, stood representing his entry. He had a carefully groomed, graying moustache, and he wore a tweed cap, polished shoes, shirt, and tie, along with a buttoned sports jacket that covered the straps of his coveralls. Avery had once told Maria about Fillmore Farms in Bennington. It was owned by the Colgate family—a hobby farm with plenty of money to keep it going. The man talked with a thick accent that was different from her mother's slight Irish brogue. Maria guessed it was Scottish. She crowded with others around the entry and looked at the picture on page one of the catalogue. The heifer's name was Fillmore Mighty Glow.

"Is she going to calve real soon?" she asked the man in the tweed cap.

"Aye. Young lady, might ye be int'rested?" The gentleman stepped towards her.

"Well, of course. But I'm afraid that my friend and I can't buy her."

"Harry MacLean, Fillmore's farm manager." He stuck out his hand for a shake. "Do ye come from 'round here, lass?"

"Yes, I'm Maria Styles." She took his firm but friendly grip. "I live at the Avery Ketchum farm."

"Jerseys! Ketchum has a fine herd."

Jubal stood in the background as she spoke.

"Avery does have a nice herd," she agreed. "However, today we're interested in Ayrshires." She gestured to Jubal. "We want to improve my friend's herd."

The man looked Jubal up and down. "And who, might I ask, are yer folks, young fella?"

"His folks are Clyde and Rose Brown," Maria answered.

"Sure, sure. I ken 'em. A time ago, the Lamont Estate had some outstandin' Ayrshires." He took a pail of wet, gray-colored feed from a worker and offered it to Glow. The heifer dove into the pail.

Maria asked, "What is it that she seems to like so much?"

"Wet beet pulp. Settles well i' her belly, makin' her look more filled out. We use it a lot at the shows."

"Oh, I see." Maria stood rooted to the spot, observing Glow's fine qualities and her gentle disposition. "The cattle at my friend's farm are nothing like this heifer."

Harry MacLean offered Jubal his hand. "Whit's yer name, son?"

"Jubal Brown." Jubal gave a brief handshake. "Hope you aren't thinking we can buy your entry." He put his hands in his pockets. "We're interested in two or three down the line for not a lot of money."

The older farm manager's bushy eyebrows shot up. "Ah, but should'nae ye be wantin' the best?"

"What we want and what we can afford are very different." Jubal backed away.

At this point, Maria realized Jubal might be thinking the guy would laugh at the piddling amount they'd brought to the sale. She knew Jubal wanted to go and pick out lesser stock before the sale began. Yet, she continued to be star-struck by Glow, checking out every inch of the heifer and looking closely at her udder. It was tightly attached, showing that Glow had the potential for a long, productive life.

In moments, at least two other farmers pressed forward to show an interest in Harry MacLean's entry. Maria positioned herself close to the cow, resting her hand on Glow's rump. Harry MacLean was soon back at her side.

"Glow . . . what a pretty name," she commented. "She's so gentle."

"Aye, my daughter works with our wee kine, ye ken."

Maria was having trouble, at times, understanding the man. "Wee . . . kine?"

"Coos," he said, nodding. "The young 'uns."

"Ah, the young cattle," Maria said. "Working them when they're young certainly helps a lot."

"Aye," Mister MacLean said, giving Glow a pat.

Jubal adjusted his cap, impatient to move on. Maria knew she'd already fallen for the most valuable heifer in the barn with no hope that they'd ever own her. Without a word, Jubal picked up his own catalogue and left for the heifers down the line. As she watched him walk past the other potential buyers and cows, she saw him mark a few entries in his booklet with a pencil. Likely he was choosing cows that were common and not a bit better looking than the new members of the herd at home. The only difference would be that they were registered and none of the cows in the Brown barn were.

Maria remained at Lot One's side and while Harry MacLean was attentive to her, he also addressed the questions of other interested farmers. She began to fear that Lot One would sell before her very eyes.

In a little while, Jubal returned, giving her a look of warning. "We need to move on," he whispered. "I've got some cows down the line and I want your opinion on them."

As she went to answer, Harry MacLean stepped in closer. "Well, well young man. I wondered whar ye went off tae. Son, I want ye and this smart lass tae own this coo."

"What?" Jubal's eyes widened as he looked at Harry.

The farm manager repeated, "I want ye folks tae take Glow home."

Maria could not believe her ears. "Mister MacLean . . . we can't." She looked down at the floor. "We just don't have the money."

But Harry MacLean would not back down. "I ken the sales manager. I'll be makin' the arrangements."

"Doesn't she have to be sold to the highest bidder?" Maria asked.

Still wide-eyed, Jubal looked from Maria to the farm manager. It was clear he didn't know how to react.

The ends of Harry's groomed mustache turned upwards as he smiled. "Miss Maria," he tipped his tweed cap. "Might I call ye by name?"

She nodded. "Certainly."

Harry spoke directly to her. "Maria, ye'll be the highest bidder." His voice was firm while making the offer. "The Colgates at Fillmore want tae help young folks int'rested in Ayrshires. We've a mission tae increase breed numbers. But in exchange, ye'll be givin' us her calf—heifer or bull."

"Is . . . is this legal?" Maria asked. It seemed too good to be true, feeling like a shady deal.

"Indeed," Harry said. "I'll write ye a check for the sale amount and ye can pass it on tae the cashier." He rocked back on his heels with a satisfied expression.

"You must really want us to own your heifer," Jubal put in.

"Yes sirree, son. I dae indeed." Harry patted Glow's shoulder and beamed at Maria. "Ye see, I'm impressed by this young lady's int'rest. The Fillmore name'll give ye the best start possible wi' Ayrshires."

Maria looked around to see if anybody might be listening in. "Oh!" she said. She slowly ran her hand over the heifer's back, taking in every detail of the animal. "Thank you so much, Mister MacLean. Glow will have a good home at the Brown farm."

Jubal elbowed Maria, breaking in. "I must say, I have some doubts about this."

Harry pressed his mustache, looking from Jubal to Maria, and back to Jubal. "I wouldna fret 'bout it, son. She's no free by any means. As I said, I'll be lookin' forward tae gettin' her calf."

"We understand," Maria said quickly. "We're grateful for your help." She ignored Jubal's frown. This particular heifer would be important to the future of Jubal's farm and she had a good feeling as Harry walked away. Jubal brooded as they joined the rest of the farmers for the bidding, but Maria was curious to see how the deal would unfold.

The auctioneer banged his gavel and announced that the sale was about to begin. Jubal and Maria found their seats. Harry MacLean was introduced as chairman of the sale and was praised for the fine selection of animals he had assembled. Maria sensed that Jubal, by his sour expression, was not happy about the deal they had entered into.

"Mister MacLean should know what he's doing," she whispered, nudging him. "He's surely going over the top for us."

Jubal groaned. "I guess he is."

The sales ring was slightly higher than the folding chairs placed in rows where the bidders were seated. The auctioneer sat in an elevated box behind a shelf with another fellow who was a pedigree reader.

The sale began with a young cow that looked to be close to calving. She was beautiful, correct in every way. But she only had fair milk records. Maria and Jubal learned right away that the pedigree spokesman exaggerated the best qualities of each entry as he spoke into his microphone.

"Folks, this is a fine example of the cattle we'll see today. She's ready in a few days to put milk in the can. Take your eyes out of the catalogue and forget her past record. Anyone who gives her a chance will get lots of milk from this cow."

Maria and Jubal agreed that the cow was fancy but they weren't sure how well she'd produce. Jubal thought perhaps she'd be better than many of his cows at home.

The auctioneer started her off at two hundred but quickly backed down when a buyer yelled, "Seventy-five!"

"Okay, seventy-five," bellowed the auctioneer. "The first one always sells cheap. One hundred . . . one . . . one. Come on, anyone!"

In the front row next to the ring, Maria could have reached out to touch the entry controlled by a leadsman as he turned the cow for the crowd to see.

Jubal urged, "Maria, let's bid."

Two ring-men scanned the crowd. Maria raised her hand.

"Yes, in the front row." The auctioneer rapped his gavel. "Now, one and a quarter?" He turned to an offside bidder. "Yes! One-fifty in the front row. Yes, yes! One-seventy-five . . . a fancy young cow here, folks." He looked down at Maria. "Sweetheart, I know you want this cow for two hundred."

Maria didn't bid. Money was precious to the Browns and this entry was not that great.

"Anyone for two hundred?" The auctioneer scanned the crowd.

Jubal nudged her. "Go ahead, she's still cheap."

All eyes were on Maria. She nodded.

"Yes! Now how 'bout two and a quarter? Not much for this fancy cow. Two-twenty-five, anyone?" The ring-men looked over the crowd for a bid. The auctioneer raised his gavel—*bang*. "Sold for two hundred to the young lady in the front row! What a deal she's taking home!"

A young kid came to them to sign an invoice for two hundred.

The next entry was a yearling heifer with an outstanding pedigree that had placed first in her class at several local shows. The breeders went wild over her. She sold for nine hundred.

Then Lot One entered the ring. She led like a pet lamb—head high, showing herself on the move with the slightest pressure on the halter. A hush went over the crowd. The atmosphere was charged and the pedigree reader looked about to bust with excitement. His voice rose to a high pitch as he wiped his brow with a handkerchief. The microphone boomed when he introduced Glow:

"What a heifer! Fillmore Mighty Glow. Look, folks, Harry MacLean has given us a chance to own an animal out of the most outstanding Ayrshire herd in these whole United States. You can see the production behind her with conformation that is nearly perfect. Glow is sired by the great Fillmore Jedda out of Alfalfa Farm Ann. Ann was grand champion at the 1937 National Dairy Show. Here's your chance for a valuable ticket to add to your herd."

The auctioneer rattled his gavel. "One thousand, one, one! A hand went up in the crowd, yelling, "Four hundred!"

"Okay. Now, four-fifty on the gal in the front row. Folks, she knows her cattle."

Maria continued to question the deal. Regardless of the price, Mister MacLean had told them to go all the way.

"Five hundred from a bid in the crowd. Now fifty, yes and now six hundred, yes. Six-fifty, yes. Now seven. Seven-fifty." He scanned the crowd. "Yes, eight. Now eight-fifty, fifty. Eight-fifty on the gal who just loves this heifer. Folks, we want her to have this beautiful Glow, but Harry will be shocked to see her sell for that low a price. Remember she's the best!

"Now, nine, nine? Yes, yes! Now fifty, yes! One thousand, one thousand." He looked the crowd over and paused, waiting for a bid.

The moment suspended in silence. The auctioneer ruled. *Bang.* "Sold for nine-fifty. Sweetheart, you've just bought yourself a deal!"

Maria turned to Jubal who sat dazed.

"In an instant, what have we done?" he said. He looked around the crowd. "Who were we bidding against?"

With virtually no money, they'd just bought the most valuable animal at the sale. Maria figured that Rose, who didn't ever like a handout, would be horrified. Then she, herself, had a terrible thought. What if Glow's calf came breech and suffocated while being delivered? Then what would they do with no way to pay?

Maria sighed. "Maybe I oversold myself? But Harry MacLean seems so genuine."

Jubal only grunted in response. She could tell he was not pleased with her. He was probably also thinking that if Glow's calf didn't live, the deal would be a no deal. Maria knew Jubal was willing to pay for what they got, but he wasn't going to travel to southern Vermont to work off the price for Mister MacLean at Fillmore Farms. Despite her sudden doubts, she felt that in buying Glow, Jubal would come around to having no regrets in owning such a beautiful animal.

As the sale progressed, she could see that the winning bidders had to sign receipts like Jubal did for the first cow they'd bought, but he never signed anything for Glow. She sure didn't want word to get out among the farmers that they'd done something crooked.

Near the end of the sale, Jubal asked her to bid on a real common cow for one hundred and fifty. The entry was close to calving and would fit right in with most of Jubal's pathetic herd before the better cows had been added that summer thanks to Chuck Dent. Reluctantly, she raised her hand. After she got the bid, the kid came with the invoice for Jubal to sign.

She was disgusted. "Jubal, we didn't come all the way up here to bring home some swayback. What were you thinking?"

"Good question," he retorted. "What were *you* thinking with us getting the top of the sale? We aren't leaving here until we fix this mess we've agreed to."

The two of them spoke in hushed tones at their seats, heads together.

She was hurt that he thought of her choice of Glow as a "mess."

He stood abruptly. "Let's get away from the crowd and talk this over."

She followed as they walked down an alley between the barns. The noise of the sale faded to a distant buzz.

She grabbed his arm. "Jubal, what's going on with you?"

He shook off her hand. "I don't like this deal we've walked into." He looked back towards the sale. "Doesn't seem right. I bought that cheap cow, that 'swayback' as you call her, in order to save as much money as we can."

She sat down on a feedbox, wishing he could see how Lot One would be just the ticket to turn things around at his farm for the future.

He planted his feet, standing in front of her. "We're paying for Glow outright."

"Oh, right. Sure we are!" Now he was the one being unrealistic. She scowled. "We'll be lucky to have enough money to buy gas on the way home."

"Look," he said, his tone softening. "I want to keep Glow's calf, and not use it for payment."

She perked up. Now he was thinking her way. She added, "If a bull, you can raise him for future use. If a heifer, she and Glow can be a good herd foundation."

"Exactly." He relaxed and sat beside her.

She was thoughtful. "It's a good plan but . . . the money, Jubal. What about the money?"

"I've thought of that," he said. "We'll make part payment today and send the rest next week."

"How? Are you planning to rob a bank or something?"

"I'm going to make it so that Glow is Benny's cow. He'll fall in love with her, I know it. Then I'll ask Jazz to sell Benny's Packard. Jazz has out-of-town connections."

She jumped up. "What?" The whole day was starting to seem like a weird dream. Had Jubal really just said he was going to sell Benny's *big, blue car*? "Benny will die, seeing that car leave. And your ma . . . geez, Jubal!

Just . . . good luck with that! Now I wish I hadn't caused this deal to come about." The last thing she wanted to was to hurt Benny.

Jubal met her eyes with resolve. "Benny will be fine. I know what I'm doing."

They had been away from the auction for a while and the fairgrounds were quiet. The sale must have finished. Since Jubal now had his own deal planned for Glow, Maria had no choice but to go along with him. Maybe Benny would be so excited about the cow that the car would no longer matter. She felt a twinge of excitement as Jubal's plan sank in. Glow was headed for Harmony Hill.

"Let's go check out your new prize heifer," she said.

The two of them walked back to the auction area where many of the farmers extended congratulations for their buying the top of the sale. After the crowd cleared, Harry MacLean came with a check for nine hundred and fifty dollars.

Maria told him the news. "We can't take this. It was very generous of you to pay for Glow, but if it's okay, Jubal will make part payment today and send the rest next week."

Harry stood in surprise. "I thought yer folks didnae have money tae buy her."

"We don't today, but Jubal will send the remaining balance to the sales manager by the end of next week." Her promise scared her a little, but she acted confident. Jubal would have to convince Benny and his mother that selling the car was the right thing to do. It wouldn't be easy. Without the Packard, the only car the family would have to get around in was the old truck that was not long before it ended up in the junkyard's scrap heap. Jubal would have to work more on his plan.

Harry nodded as he folded the check and put it in his pocket. "Ye know it was truly na trouble, but I ken ye wantin' a clean deal." He beamed at Maria again and took her hand in his. "Ye're a sharp young lass. Ye'll be runnin' a successful dairy someday."

As she shook the farm manager's hand, Jubal seemed to relax for the first time since the sale began. He had now righted the situation to his liking. "Well, we need to head for home," she said. "Thank you again, Mister MacLean."

Harry looked at Jubal. "Send the rest of her fee along when ye can. And let us know how Glow fares in the comin' year?"

"We will," Jubal agreed.

Chapter Thirty-Nine

Jubal settled up at the cashier's desk, making arrangements for the purchase of Glow. Then he found a trucker to deliver their new cattle. On the way home, he mulled over the day at the sale. Even with the trouble ahead concerning his ma's acceptance of his plan, he had to appreciate Maria's eagerness to improve the quality of his herd. They no sooner got home to start night chores when the cattle truck pulled in the yard. Everyone, even Clyde, gathered to see the new arrivals led down the truck ramp. After working all day stacking firewood, Benny looked beat, but he intently watched the truck back up near the barn.

Glow was first down the ramp. The contrast between her and the rest of their herd was obvious. Jubal was pleased to see his mother's face light up as the heifer stood before them.

"Wow, she's a beauty!" his ma exclaimed.

"Isn't she?" Maria said. "Perfect in every way."

Jubal turned to his uncle. "Benny, this will be your cow," he said. "She's got no horns so you can brush her and love her all you want without worries of getting hurt. She's calm as a kitten."

"Really?" His tired uncle perked up. "She's gonna be mine?"

"That's right." Jubal said. He led Glow into the barn with Benny following. "We can keep her in the old bull pen until she calves."

"Can I pet her now?" Benny asked.

Jubal laughed. "Just a minute. Let's get her into her pen."

Benny helped to get the pen ready for Glow, bedding it with hay chaff. He then brought her a pail of water while Jubal filled the manger with some of Avery's excellent hay. As Glow dove into the feed and drank from the pail, Benny stroked her.

"We should go back for the next cow," Jubal said. After Benny reluctantly left Glow's pen, Jubal secured the gate so they could return to the yard.

The first cow they had bought for two hundred was unloaded next. As they approached the truck, Maria took the cow's lead rope from the driver.

His ma commented, "Well, what I see so far for six hundred dollars looks darned good!"

Jubal waited to see if Maria would spill his plan, but she said nothing, passing him the cow's rope. He and Benny took the two-hundred-dollar cow to the barn. While Jubal put her in a stall to get used to the place and got her some feed, Benny went back to Glow's pen. Jubal could tell his uncle was already taking to the heifer.

They got back to the truck just in time for Jubal to take the lead rope of the third cow. As he held her, she stumbled down the ramp and jerked his arm. When reaching the ground, Jubal paused to see her weak back, football-sized udder, and crooked legs. He hadn't looked too closely at her during the sale, being preoccupied with the cost of Glow. Maria was right. She was a swayback and an embarrassment.

His ma looked in surprise from the cow to him. "Well, I'm wondering why you bought this one?"

"Because of money, Ma. We, um . . . owe on the first one."

"Oh." His ma closed her mouth, her lips in a stern, thin line as she stared at the swayback.

Jubal waited tensely. His father also studied the third cow, scratching his head. Maria looked like she wished she were anywhere else but in the Browns' yard at that moment.

"How much?" his ma said finally.

"We still owe seven hundred," Jubal said.

"Seven hundred? Jubal, my god," his ma exclaimed. "Whatever were you thinking?"

Maria tried to explain. "She's got a great pedigree. She'll help grow a top-notch herd here."

Rose frowned at Maria. "Right, but we don't have that kind of money."

Jubal spoke up. "Ma, I have a plan." He took a deep breath to tell her, but in that moment his dad, who still didn't have a lot of stamina, spoke up.

"Rose, I'm sure it will get sorted out. But I need to get back to the house to sit down . . . feeling tired."

His ma went quickly to his dad's side.

"Let's get you a snack," she said, taking Clyde's arm. She turned to Jubal. "I will need to hear this plan when I return and it had better be good!"

Relieved as his ma walked away, Jubal handed the swayback's rope to Maria, "Let's get this one in the barn as well."

Maria nodded and followed him to the barn, the last cow plodding along in her wake. After putting the cow in a stall, she came to Jubal's side where he stood outside Glow's pen. Benny was smiling from ear to ear while brushing Glow.

"She sure is a beauty," Jubal said. At least in seeing the cow, he felt it was the right choice to bring her home.

"She's pretty," Benny agreed. "And she's all mine?"

"All yours," Jubal assured him.

While Maria started milking, Jubal fed out the grain and citrus pulp. Next, he climbed the ladder to the mow to get more hay. Before long, the barn door slammed. It was his ma. He would wait for her up in the mow so that Benny, who was down at the other end of the barn, would be far away from the conversation.

"Where's Jubal?" his ma asked Maria.

Soon he heard his mother's bangles when she reached for the ladder to the mow. As she climbed, the clink of her bracelets turned into a warning. He knew he had to be convincing. Their owning the Packard had always been a big deal—a symbol of the luxury they lacked, representing hope that someday they might do well enough to have nicer things.

The dim light and sweet-smelling hay of the mow at the right time with the right person was pleasant, as it had been when he and Polly had snuck up there to make out. At this moment that was not the case. Standing on the high-drive, he leaned against the hay as his ma approached. She stood tall and imposing before him, though she was out of her element up in the mow in her slacks and loafers.

"Just where in the world do you plan to come up with seven hundred dollars?" she asked.

"I can explain," he began.

"Jubal, I stretched plenty to give you six hundred," she said. "Even at that, I had to get permission from Lady Lamont to take an extra three hundred from her account. We're already in debt and now you and Maria have us in over our heads."

"Um . . ." He swallowed. "My plan is to ask Jazz to . . . sell Benny's Packard."

"What? Oh no. No you don't!"

"It's the best way to get the money," he protested.

"That car is Benny's!" His ma looked furious.

"Look, Ma, Benny is going to love that cow. He's already gushing over her."

"I don't care. He loves his car more."

Jubal backed a few steps from his mother. It was time to tell her what he'd been thinking off and on since he'd gotten his license. "Ma, we just don't need that fancy rig sitting in our shabby farmyard. It's useless for our purposes. I look like a big shot driving the Packard around town."

He and his mother stood face to face, each of them firm.

"Fancy or not," she retorted, "we need something we can depend on for a car. Talk about an embarrassment, what about the truck these days? It's ready to rattle apart!"

"I'll fix us up with a more practical rig."

"Oh, you think so?"

He and his ma seldom argued to such a degree.

"Yeah, I know how to fix up cars now after working at Jazz's."

"What a manipulator you are!" She shook her head. "A car for a cow!"

"Ma, we need a better rig. Like you say, our truck is junk. When it dies, we sure can't be using the Packard to carry heavy farm stuff."

"That car was a special gift to me! And then a special gift from me to Benny. I didn't have any plans to sell it!"

"Benny likes to go for a drive in it now and then, yes. But really, is that a reason to keep it? We looked ridiculous at the Rutland sale. Even Maria mentioned it."

His mother was taken aback. "This is a first. You've never complained before."

"Before I was sneaking around driving without my license. Now I see things differently."

Crossing her arms, his ma looked out the open door of the mow and back at him. "What I'd like to know, is what happened at the sale in the first place. Whatever possessed you and Maria to latch on to such an expensive cow?"

He told her about Maria's instant admiration of Glow, and Harry MacLean, and the wishes of Fillmore Farms to help young farmers get a good start. His ma grew less tense as he told her the details, dropping her arms to lean against the hay.

"Hmm, I see," she said. "And this Mister MacLean thought Maria was making a smart choice?"

"He did. He said she was going to be quite the dairy farmer someday."

"I believe he's right," his ma said.

"Look, I know Glow is going to be worth it," Jubal reasoned, "but I didn't want to take Harry MacLean's charity and accept the check. Nine hundred and fifty dollars is a lot, you know?"

"I agree," his mother nodded. "I would rather pay him on the up and up."

"So I bought the 'old swayback' and gave Harry the rest of the $600 that was left." He waited for her reaction, hoping she'd approve of his choice.

To his surprise, his ma chuckled.

"I certainly don't know my dairy cows, Jubal, but wow. Even I can see what a dud that one is!"

"Maria gave me a hard time too. But the swayback is no matter, not when we'll have Glow to populate our herd with quality producers. This way we get to keep her calf."

His ma met his eyes. "I guess you did the right thing. Gosh, I'll miss that Packard though—my only claim to some class."

He could see his mother fighting her emotions.

"I'll miss it too. Plus, all my work with Slag to repair it! That car has some good stories, especially the 'great disappearance in the corn.'"

His ma smiled. "Keeping Tatum dumbfounded was fun entertainment. Okay, well, I guess there is no other way to pay Harry MacLean. But now you'll have to convince Benny."

Jubal nodded. "It won't be easy. But once Benny has fallen for Glow, and it seems he already has, he'll like owning his own cow better than a big car. He can hug, brush, and lead around a cow, as compared to a car he can't even drive. If he needs to polish something, we've plenty of harnesses in the tack room that need attention."

"You'll have to see what you can do. Benny has his own ideas about things. But I'll support you."

"With any luck, I can sell the Packard and get enough to pay for Glow. Jazz told me that the car sold new for eleven hundred. It's in perfect condition with just a few miles on it. If he asks nine or a thousand, it should sell."

"Sounds reasonable," his mother said. "Now what will we drive instead? I don't much like seeing the road at my feet through the floorboards in that truck."

"I noticed Jazz has a '39 Ford woody, two years old, that just came in. It needs a new front end that I can fix. I don't think he'd charge much, especially if I do the work. I've kind of missed working down there."

"That sounds promising," his ma said. She turned and walked to the ladder. "I want to take another look at this Glow heifer—such class as this barn has never seen."

She disappeared down the ladder and Jubal breathed a sigh of relief. One hurdle down to fixing their mess. He heard his ma down below.

"A cow for a car. I never thought a cow could be my idea of class."

Maria responded, "She's quite an animal, Rose. Glow shows a lot of promise like this barn's never seen."

Sunday morning before breakfast, Jubal entered the living room to be with his dad. Clyde sat next to his Philco with his head cocked, listening intently to the bad news coming over the airwaves:

The U.S. waits on the sidelines while daily our closest ally, England, gets pummelled by German bombers. . . .

"Morning, Dad." Jubal took a seat in a straight-back chair near his father. "Doesn't sound good."

His dad talked through a half-closed mouth. "Not good . . . not at all."

Jubal had noticed his dad's changed speech. His father had now gained back most of his weight and was long recovered from the infection that had started in his feet, though he still walked with a limp and his cane. However, Doc Peters had confirmed for his ma that his dad must have had a small stroke during his ordeal while stuck in the old car at the junkyard.

Regardless, Jubal now appreciated that he could talk some with his dad. "Slag says he expects to be called real soon to enlist in the army," he told his father.

"Slag's a good man. Hope he don't get drafted." His father fumbled for the Philco's off switch. "Fixed Doc's car . . . did good work."

"Doc? Do you mean Doc Small's car? Orange New York plates?"

"Yep, Doc Small." His father looked out the window with a far-off gaze. "Man sure liked his drink."

Jubal was curious how his dad knew the out-of-state doctor. "Did you travel with him?"

"Yep . . . some. Rode with him ta the city."

"Where?"

"Down ta Troy. Doc drives 'round these parts and in the Albany area. Calls on women."

"What kind of women? What for?" Jubal wondered why a family doctor would do such a thing.

His father shrugged. "Women trouble, I guess."

"Women trouble? What do you mean, Dad?"

His dad lifted his hand listlessly and dropped it again. "Dunno. Doc never said. But I'm guessing they was women wantin' ta save themselves a boatload a' shame in town, or the expense of a family fer the poor ones."

"I'm not sure I follow you."

His dad turned from the window to him. "Son, the Doc takes their unwanted babies. From inside 'em." His dad pulled a plain white handkerchief from his pocket and blew his nose.

Jubal was shocked by his father's words. "You mean . . . a doctor can do that?" The thought had never occurred to him, not when he and Polly were scared after their almost having sex in the Packard. He sat quietly for a moment. What if his ma had done such a thing with him? He wouldn't be here right now.

"Guess so," his dad said. "After the rounds, Doc brought me ta his house—"

Jubal's ma interrupted, calling them to breakfast. Jubal wanted to stay and hear more about Doc Small and his father's adventures, but his dad stood stiffly and grabbed his cane, saying no more.

As they ate, Jubal thought over what his dad had said about Doc Small. He wasn't surprised the doctor was involved in something shady. When talking with Slag, Jubal had wondered why Father Mac would call on a guy from New York instead of Doc Peters who lived right down the street. He remembered how two days after the parade he was with his ma parked in front of the IGA, and there was Maria looking to be in shock in her folks' car. It was the same day his dad had skipped town. Now he knew that Doc Small had picked up his father in front of the rectory. Had Maria been to see Doc Small? He'd heard from Lizzy that Father Mac had summoned Maria and her mother to the rectory that day.

"Jubal, you look miles away," his ma observed.

He quickly made an excuse. "Oh, just imagining what our herd will be like if Glow has a bull calf."

His mother smiled. She turned to his dad. "Would you like some more coffee, Clyde?"

His father held out his cup while she poured.

Jubal lapsed back into the mysterious thread he was unraveling. That Doc was there at the rectory the same day that Maria was summoned was likely no coincidence. What had Father Mac asked of Maria and her mother? Jubal didn't figure Kathleen would let the Doc do anything bad to Maria. But . . . did Doc Small maybe have a method to make sure there would be no pregnancy resulting from Freddie? Whatever had gone on, it was no wonder that Maria looked terrible that day in her folks' car. Something wasn't right.

On Monday before morning chores, two days after Glow arrived, Jubal and Benny left the house and walked into a world of white. There had been a killing frost, bringing the very end of the growing season. Grasses were bent over from the burden, finally giving up on life above ground. However, Jubal knew that deep in the soil was enough energy in the storehouse of roots for plant life to reappear in the spring.

Jubal turned up his collar and Benny hunched his shoulders as they hurried through the frosty air to check on their new heifer. Jubal opened the barn door and flicked on the lights. As usual the row of forty cows stirred, eagerly waiting to be fed. What was unusual was the low, motherly mooing of a cow who had just given birth. Benny ran in his stumbling manner to Glow's pen.

"Glow has had her calf!" Benny announced. He hung over the gate as Jubal came to watch the wet newborn trying to stand.

In minutes, the wobbly calf stood and found a teat to suck. Yellow milk leaked from Glow's other three teats as she lapped the calf, drying it while it sucked hungrily, its mouth slipping on and off the teat. Her strong tongue lifted the calf's tail, giving Jubal a chance to see the scrotum. A bull! He couldn't wait to tell his parents and Maria. A high-pedigreed bull was the best outcome they could have hoped for. He silently thanked Maria for her wild idea to get Glow.

Benny was captivated. "Glow," he said to the cow, "ya had a baby boy!" He pointed at the calf. "Can we keep him, Jubal?"

"Of course," Jubal said. "If we're lucky, when he grows up he'll sire many more baby calves. Now don't forget the chores still need doing."

Benny nodded and went to get fresh water for Glow, after which he filled her feeder with hay.

Jubal stood watching the bull calf. "Benny, I'd like you to work with this calf. I want him real gentle when he's grown since he'll be our herd sire."

"Oh, I will! I'll be his friend forever."

"When he becomes a big boy, though," Jubal cautioned, "you'll have to leave him to be himself."

Benny looked thoughtfully at the little calf. "I guess a big, strong bull won't be wantin' any friends."

"You've got the idea." Jubal watched the calf continuing to suck for milk. "Say Benny—why don't you name him?"

"It's gotta be a good name, Jubal." Benny's face brightened. "I'll ask Maria when she comes!"

"Good thinking," Jubal said. "I'll bet Maria picks the perfect name." This was his chance to break the bad news to his uncle. "Benny, listen . . . What would you rather have, Glow and her calf, or your blue car?"

Benny returned a fearful glance. Jubal waited.

"Why, I want my . . . my car, and . . . Glow and . . . her calf."

"Well, you can't have all three." As Jubal suspected, Benny wasn't going to make this easy. He gestured to Glow. "See how beautiful this heifer is? She's very well-bred."

Benny slowly looked over the length of Glow as she munched on hay. Her calf folded its front legs to lie down in the bedding to have its first nap. "Yup, she's special," he said.

"Because she's such a great cow, Glow cost us a lot of money," Jubal explained patiently. "Money we don't have. We can't afford to keep a fancy cow and a fancy car. So unfortunately, either Glow and her calf have to go, or the Packard has to go."

Benny stood staring upward, frozen the way he got when he struggled with a tough idea.

"Do you understand?" Jubal asked.

Benny's eyes filled with tears. "But . . . I love my blue car. And . . ." Tears rolled and Benny made no attempt to wipe them away. "I . . . I love Glow. And her new calf."

"Benny, Benny . . ." Jubal reached for his uncle's arm but Benny shrugged him off, retreating a few steps. His hands began to tremble.

"Why do ya want ta take my car?" Benny asked, a hint of anger in his voice.

Jubal sighed. The calf stood unsteadily to again find its mother's teats. As it nursed, Benny turned and became transfixed by the sight, seeming to forget his upset. Jubal pressed on with his plan.

"Look, Benny. In place of the Packard, I can fix up a nice Ford woody that you'll like. We'll still ride around town in style. I'll take out the back seats and sometimes, when we're not hauling farm supplies, we can put in a mattress for you to sleep on. It will be like a bed on wheels."

"Really?" Benny turned from the calf to him. "Will ya read to me in there?"

"Sure thing. You'll see—the Ford woody will be way more fun than the Packard ever was. You could even sleep in there on cool summer nights if you wanted, sort of like camping."

"Gee . . . campin' in a bed on wheels. . . ."

Jubal grabbed his chance. "Do we have a deal, Benny?"

"I think so, Jubal. I really love Glow and her new calf." And with that, Benny turned and picked up a shovel leaning against the wall to continue his chores.

The matter appeared to be settled, so Jubal headed to the feed room. Before long, he heard Trueboy clopping into the barn. Benny ran to tell Maria the news, his big feet thudding down the feed ally. The two quickly went to Glow's pen with Maria smiling happily.

"Oh, he's so cute," she said, peering down at the calf now standing quietly at his mother's side. "All brown with what looks like a little irregular white mark on his forehead."

Benny turned to her. "What should we name him? Pick a name, Maria!"

Maria stood in thought, looking over every inch of the newborn. "That mark in the middle of his forehead looks like a star. What do you think of Star?"

"Yeah, Star!" Benny agreed, smiling.

Jubal joined them. "We could call him Fillmore Star. Look at the sturdy guy, already gaining leg strength."

Benny's expression became serious. "Maria, Star and Glow cost a lotta money. So Jubal says we can't keep the Packard. I told him that was okay."

Maria met Jubal's eyes and he nodded. The deal was done.

"How responsible," she said, patting Benny on the arm. "I'm proud of you for seeing the need."

"Star's a special calf," Benny said. "And I'm gonna have a bed on wheels!"

Maria glanced at Jubal, confused.

"Don't ask," Jubal muttered. The two of them chuckled as all three left the pen to finish their chores.

On her way to get the morning's milk at the Brown Farm, Polly was wearing her new tailored plaid jacket and red leather gloves. It had been quite some time since she'd seen Jubal. To avoid him, she'd been coming late on purpose to collect the milk, so Jubal had been leaving the full can for her on the steps of the dairy. She had refused to ask him for another ride to catechism. He'd acted like a jerk the last time, disrespecting Father Mac and especially threatening to make her walk home in the dark. If he'd only known how absolutely petrified she was of the dark. By yanking the *Sugar Daddy* right out of her hand to throw it in the wastebasket, Jubal had been showing off his power over her in front of Bert and Lizzy. She'd relived that humiliating moment for days. Since then, her dad had been the one to take her to catechism, conducting his church business at the rectory while he waited.

On this particular morning, however, in high spirits she'd come to the farm early. She wanted to meet up with Jubal because she had interesting information to throw his way—information she hoped would make him squirm, causing him to regret his being so miserable towards her. She planned to ease into a conversation real folksy-like and then drop her news when he least expected it.

First-off, she met Jubal in the milk room where he was washing up the milk dishes. She just couldn't wait to spill that she'd heard from Eugene. Jubal perked up at the mention of his old friend. She informed him that Eugene was doing well as a future Tuskegee Airman, passing all the necessary tests with high grades. This achievement gave him the distinction of having a lot of class, along with his mother's money.

"He's coming home for a week's leave at Thanksgiving and I can't wait to see him." She passed Jubal the milk can she'd brought from the day before. "Eugene says I'll hardly recognize him in his crewcut and new suit."

"Really?" Jubal said, setting the can to the side to wash later.

"Yup, and I'll bet his suit is made of silk, worth hundreds." She hoped to make Jubal jealous. He'd never forgiven her for dumping him at the grange dance for Freddie. Any dream she'd had of reigniting the spark between her and Jubal had long since faded now that he was head over heels for the floozy Lizzy LaFlam. She watched Jubal closely as he filled a clean can with fresh milk. His expression didn't change one bit.

"Gosh," Jubal said. "It's been a long time since I've talked with Eugene. Not since we did some pasture fencing together this summer."

"What a summer it was," she said. "So much has changed. Eugene and I will have a lot to catch up on."

Jubal passed her the full can and she set it down with a thunk on the concrete floor. She was not going to leave until she got a rise out of him.

"Maybe Eugene will take me dancing at the Grange on Saturday after Thanksgiving."

He turned away as he continued washing the milk utensils. "How many times did you write Eugene to get any kind of a response?" he asked over his shoulder.

"Well . . . does that matter?" The question annoyed her. It was none of his business how many times she'd written.

"Sure it matters." He faced her. "Knowing Eugene, he wrote you back just to be polite. He's smarter than to get tied up with a fifteen-year-old white girl who spends her free time listening to soap operas." As he returned to the washtub, metal clanked as he scrubbed. "Eugene is all class. No doubt he's dating a Wellesley celebrity or a Black beauty from Tuskegee, Alabama. I've no doubt Eugene's found some gal to match his looks and intelligence."

"Well, if you aren't the biggest ass on Harmony Hill!" Polly hoisted the can angrily, forgetting the weight of it. Her skinny arms hurt with the effort but she kept her poise. "Maybe you don't recognize that about yourself." She held the can with both arms against her chest. "Besides, you forget who my father is. I also come from class."

"Well, excuse me!" Jubal smirked. "Why don't you continue getting your milk late in the morning, and then I won't have to bow to your make-believe class."

She puffed her cheeks. "If you think my class is make-believe, then you just don't know me. Never did. And too bad for you."

Jubal kept his back to her as he ran water in a pail.

Seeing no reaction, she dropped the really big news that she knew would get under his skin. "Well, it's no wonder Lizzy has taken up with Slag. He gives her all the attention she's missing from you."

Jubal stopped work in the washtub and stood motionless. Water soon overflowed the pail.

Even though Jubal had been treating her like dirt, Polly was still fond of him. "Sorry, I . . ." She set the can back down, more gently this time. "I didn't mean to break the news to you in such a fashion. It slipped out."

Jubal remained still and water continued to overflow the pail.

She continued, "Word on the street has it you're spending all your free time at the library working on some paper for school. Meanwhile, Slag's giving Lizzy a bushel of his attention."

In Jubal's silence, she babbled on. "My . . . my dad's only repeating what Bernice told him yesterday when he stopped in to buy some of her hamburger. My dad said Bernice was fuming mad. 'All this store needs,' Bernice said, 'is Slag sniffing around Lizzy like an old hound dog on a hot trail.'"

Jubal shut off the water and turned around with a steely look.

"Well," Polly sniffed, seeing his ugly expression. "What can you expect really? As they say, when the cat's away, the mouse will play."

"Lies!" Jubal exploded. In one motion, he grabbed the full pail of water and threw the entire contents at her.

The water hit her full in the face and went down her neck, cold as ice. It soaked the front of her new plaid jacket. In her shock, she almost laughed aloud. What was it with guys ruining her nice jackets? But then anger took her.

"Oh! Oh! You've crossed the line but good this time, Jubal Brown!"

"You're spreading bold-faced lies!" he sputtered. His face was redder than she'd ever seen it. "Polly O'Mara, you just can't stand to see me happy with another girl."

"Jealous of you? Ha!" She put her hands on her hips, trying to look dignified though she was sopping wet. "Keep dreaming, farmer boy!"

"Awe, take your damn milk can and run on back home." He waved one hand at her.

She stood her place, sweeping her dripping hair up to wring it out.

"Go!" Jubal said. "I don't want to see you or hear your gossip again!" He stormed from the milk room.

Polly bent to pick up the full can one last time, now shivering in her wet wool coat. She'd probably catch pneumonia. It was just too much, how Jubal was acting. She sure was glad Eugene was coming home. At least he understood her. Soon she'd find a way to leave this lame town with a nice man, a man with money. A man who didn't smell like a cow barn. Somehow, some way, she would do it. She smiled to herself. Jubal Brown would be no great loss.

Chapter Forty

Lizzy and Maria were regularly attending Saturday Mass together while also building a sisterly bond. Maria had given Lizzy a rosary, but Lizzy made little sense of it as her thumb and forefinger passed the string of beads one by one through her hands. She did like repeating the prayers with Maria, and she also liked the parables of Jesus and other Bible stories. With a spellbinding performance, Father Hebert delivered the weekly homily of parables, such as the "The Prodigal Son" and "The Lost Sheep."

From the parable of "The Good Samaritan," Lizzy had learned that Christians must pay attention to the needs of all folks, and especially the very poor. That rang bells for her because she'd been poor most of her life. Father Hebert continually reminded his flock, "We are *all* children of God." He made sure to bring their awareness to the work of Catholic charities and other good deeds for the less fortunate.

These stories left Lizzy turning over the stones in her own life. She thought of the bench sitters hanging around outside the store. They had so little—Oscar Smith, Charlie Jones, and even Clem Gochy at times. She bet they might appreciate a special luncheon. It would be her effort in feeding the poor since they had the very least among the folks of Hayesville. As she'd begun to be a believer in Christ, she felt she needed to do her part for Jesus.

In addition to her spiritual learning and her plans for charitable work, Lizzy had another situation to consider. Just recently, Slag Perkins had begun taking his noon break at the store. He appeared to be just loving a chance to visit with her. She found him a good listener when she explained the parables as told by Father Hebert. Slag especially perked up as she shared her idea of preparing a lunch for the bench sitters. Unfortunately, she had no kitchen in which to do so. Only her hot plate.

"I mean," she told Slag, "I could make 'em sandwiches from the deli, but that ain't very special. They can get that any old day. But even if I could only pass out snacks I'd made, that could be a kindness. I know hunger, bein' brought up under Big Daddy's hand and livin' off his fetchins from the mountain."

Slag listened carefully, and the next thing she knew he surprised her by delivering an electric stove he'd rescued from junk.

"I fixed it up," he said as he set the stove up in the open space in the shed. "Now ya can do cookin' jest like regular folks."

Lizzy saw his smile of satisfaction as he worked to make the needed electrical connections. "Wow, Slag, ain't this a surprise!" She ran her hand over the white enameled appliance and looked in the oven when he turned the control to "On." She was amazed when she felt the heat rush out. "Now I can do some bakin' after work."

Slag's New Hampshire scar fired up to pink on his pitted face.

She checked the four burners. "Wow, they all work! Tell ya what—I'll plan a big feast fer a bunch a' the folks 'round here that have next ta nothin'. And I want ya ta come too."

Slag surveyed the area behind the store. "There's lotsa room here. I can lay out some old doors on sawhorses fer tables and we can set on the empty nail kegs I saw kickin' 'round the back room."

Lizzy agreed and planned the big meal for a Sunday afternoon. She promptly asked Bert and Bernice to come, but Bernice declined, saying she'd be busy at church. Rose could not attend either. Apparently the Browns were invited to dine at Lady Lamont's. Slag told her Jazz was going to be at home with his grandchildren. But Lizzy knew Maria would be sure to come. And she hoped Jubal might choose her luncheon over Lady Lamont's.

On the afternoon following the arrival of the stove, Lizzy had an unexpected visit from Jubal who lately hadn't been stopping by as often as he had in summer. She'd been trying not to let it bother her. She knew he had his hands full at the farm and figured he needed credit on his paper for school. She wondered if his surprise visit was because he'd heard the gossip that Slag had been giving her attention.

As she showed Jubal her ideas about setting up the yard out back for her feast, he stopped in his tracks at the shed.

"Well, a stove," he said.

"Ain't it great?" She grinned. "Slag found it in a junk heap and was able ta get it workin' fer me."

"Slag," Jubal said as they continued on. "So it's true."

"What's true?" she asked casually as the two of them stepped into her caged room.

Jubal slumped into a chair at her little table. "I can't believe it. It wasn't just a lie that Polly spilled this morning. That skinny weasel of a welder is crowding in on my territory! And I thought the guy was my friend after working side by side with him."

Lizzy put her hands on her hips. "Fer starters, I ain't *yer territory.* I'm my own gal. And Slag prob'ly don't even know we had somethin' goin' on."

"Oh, he knew," Jubal replied sulkily. "Town gossip flies plenty at Jazz's." He sat bolt upright. "Wait. You said *had.* We had something going on."

"Cool yerself. Didn't mean nothin' by that." She started wiping a few dishes to put them away on a little shelf, preferring to keep her distance from Jubal.

"For God's sake, Lizzy. Next thing I know, you'll have Slag back here to your room and he'll have you on that bed over there. Or . . . he already has."

She threw the dish towel on the counter. "I'll have ya know he hasn't laid a hand on me! Slag's very sweet. I happen ta like him. He's interested when I tell him 'bout the homilies I'm hearin' at Mass."

Jubal's laugh rang out. "Slag and the Catholic church? Come on. He hates it!"

Lizzy didn't want things to get ugly with Jubal. She sighed and took a seat across from him at her little table. "Look, Jubal. Slag used ta be angry at the world but he's changin' fer the better, 'specially when I explain the importance ta help the needy. He admits he never really knew what church could mean ta folks, that folks could truly believe in the spirit of an almighty God. Well, his eyes have opened, just like mine."

Jubal sat shaking his head. "Sounds as though you and Slag have lost yourselves over the church. But he's filling you full of crap. He hasn't changed. Not that fast."

"Yer wrong. I'm beginnin' ta know someone who's kind, and lovable deep down 'neath all that gruffness."

Jubal turned pale as though he'd been shot. "Do you hear yourself?" he said. "He's winning you over. After all I've meant to you."

Lizzy stood and looked down on Jubal with his shorn hair that he'd let Maria cut. "Lately, when ya can tear yerself away from the cows or from Miss Curry's, ya come here fer a steamy night that ends in a fizzle and then ya leave. Sure ya can talk 'bout Freud as some old guy that looks inta heads. That means nothin' ta me."

"But I thought you loved me." Jubal's eyes filled and he turned his head.

"Maybe fer a time, but love needs more than makin' out ta last." She crossed to sit on the edge of her bed, the only other seat in the room. "Besides, ya're inta Maria plain as day. What happens ta us when she's all better?"

Jubal looked down at the floor. "I . . . I don't really know. Maria may never be free of her trauma."

"I'll tell ya what'll happen. She'll be hangin' on our bedpost watchin' us make a family."

"Lizzy! What a thing to say." He sat for a moment with his head in his hands. Then he pushed up from his chair abruptly. "Well, I guess that settles it then. You can have Scar Face. He's no longer a friend of mine."

She stared as Jubal headed for the door. Sometimes he could be so blind. "Well, ain't ya the righteous one blamin' Slag. How is his payin' me mind any different than me sittin' by while ya work up in that barn and in them fields all day with Maria? Then ya disappear, holed up with books ta find what ails her."

Jubal turned from the door.

Lizzy continued, "Maria will stay my pal no matter what, 'cause I'm no fair weather friend. But I've been patient waitin' fer ya. With Slag, I don't need ta wait." She got up from the bed and went back to tidying her little kitchen area. "Ya might's well go. I wanna practice usin' my new stove." She turned to see that for the second time Jubal looked like he was about to cry. Her heart softened. "That was rubbin' it in a little, huh?"

"Cook with your stove all you want," he said. "I'm guessing we're through." The door slammed behind him.

Lizzy sank into her chair, a jumble of feelings. It was likely the last visit she'd have from Jubal. Their romantic summer had come to an end with the cold wind of winter on the doorstep. But it also stirred her to think of Slag possibly keeping her warm in the months to come.

With a bruised heart, Jubal rose early the next morning to attempt some work on his research paper. It was usually a good distraction. He found he enjoyed learning the rules of writing such a technical work, and Miss Curry had been a huge help. The study had not only taught him about the workings of the mind, but he'd learned some things about Benny's disorder and his dad's alcoholism as well.

This morning, however, it was hard to get much writing done. His mind kept wandering. He couldn't believe Lizzy's affections towards him had run dry and she was taking up with Slag. God, the tough-minded grease monkey was almost old enough to be her father. What an unlikely match! Yet, he had to admit he had been ignoring Lizzy in order to get his paper done by Christmas. Polly had played the gossip in telling him about Slag, but Polly was right after all. Now he felt ashamed that he'd doused her with water. She could be so annoying. Still, he couldn't stay angry with her for long, having known her since they were kids. He looked down at his paper. It was time for chores and he'd barely added a paragraph.

After breakfast, he planned to go see Jazz about the Packard, so he busied himself with cleaning out Benny's car, readying it for sale. While cleaning, he paused at the blanket on the rope hanger attached to the back of the front seat. He thought of Polly again—how they had made out under that blanket many times. He chuckled, remembering her false boobs. More so, he remembered her sweet kisses. In that car they'd dreamed and made promises that they would no longer keep. As he folded the blanket, a sadness came over him.

Polly was right about another thing. Eugene would come home to find Hayesville changed from when he'd left it not long ago. Eugene was sure to have grown, having gone off to school, and Jubal wondered if he, himself, was different somehow. Now many guys in town were called to be ready for a possible war—soon they might leave, and if so, it was uncertain how many would come back. Jubal peered over his shoulder and, with no one looking, put his face to the blanket's softness and sniffed. It smelled of leather and hay. No trace of Polly remained. He stashed the blanket in the house, along with the rest of the stuff that had been in the car. Returning to the car, he did his best to clean out the dirt and wisps of hay. Before long, he started the Packard, leaving Maria and Benny working on their woodpile.

There was a cold, gray sky overhead as he traveled down the hill, but the sun came out now and then, enough to melt the frost that coated the fields. He knew he wouldn't be driving such a classy car for some time to come, if ever again. The thought deepened his gloom. In minutes, he parked at the junkyard and went directly to the office where Jazz sat behind his desk talking on the phone. Jubal took his usual seat on an engine block.

Jazz waved as he ended his call. "What's Jubal up ta today?"

"I'm selling Benny's Packard." Jubal figured he might as well get right to the matter at hand.

Jazz blinked. "No kiddin'! Why all of a sudden?"

Jubal told the story about Glow. "To pay off my debt, I need seven hundred from the sale. I'd also like that woody out there in your yard."

Jazz leaned back in his office chair. "Ya know, son, I don't deal in big cars."

Jubal's heart sank. "I know. But I was thinking you maybe knew someone. . . ."

Jazz tapped a pencil on his desktop, considering the request. Jubal waited.

"I dare say there's a guy in Albany who might buy it," Jazz concluded. "Let's go take a good look at this car a' yers."

In the yard, Jazz walked around the car, examining every inch. He lay down on the ground and looked at the undercarriage. Next, he inspected the interior. He came out from behind the wheel. "It's got real low mileage. Ain't a scratch on it. Paint job's holdin'. Guess my guys did a good job!" He laughed. "She'll do."

After that, they walked over to check out the '39 Ford woody.

"Seems all this one needs is front-end parts and she'll make a good rig for ya," Jazz declared.

"If you sell me the parts, I can fix it myself," Jubal said, pleased that Jazz seemed to be leaning the right way on the possible deal.

"I've no doubt ya'll fix 'er up nice, Jubal." Jazz waved towards the office. "Let's go back inside ta my desk. I gotta look inta how the figures work out."

Inside, Jazz opened a big leather ledger with grease on the cover. He looked over his inventory. "Yeah, looks as though I can do that," he said rechecking the figures on the page. "I ain't makin' much . . . be doin' ya a favor."

"Thanks, Jazz." Jubal reached in his pocket. He held the Packard's keys closed in his fist, remembering now the last ride down to the reservoir. Except for Tatum showing up, it had been a nice time with Lizzy, Maria, and Benny—riding in style and laughing. He took a deep breath.

"Second thoughts?" Jazz raised an eyebrow. "Don't blame ya. She's a sweet ride."

Jubal reached over and dropped the keys into Jazz's outstretched hand. They jingled as they fell. "My mind's made up."

Jazz closed his hand around the keys and nodded at the doodlebug. "Push that woody inta an empty bay and ya can get right ta work." He picked up the phone to make a call. "If the sale goes, I'll have a check for ya tomorrow or the next day."

Glad that Slag wasn't around, Jubal worked the rest of the day on the front end of the woody. His upset over Lizzy and letting go of the Packard lessened as he removed all the damaged parts: bumper, grill, radiator, fan, water pump, hood, and fenders. On the next afternoon, Jubal found that the wheels and undercarriage luckily showed no damage, so he was able to reassemble the front end easily. Though Slag was in the shop on the second day, the two avoided each other with each focused on their own projects. As he worked, Jubal stewed over how he'd been so sure, initially, that Polly's news was false, believing Lizzy's hugs and kisses for him hadn't cooled. Was he ever wrong. His surprise visit to see Lizzy had showed him that. It was hard to look at Slag the same way since learning the guy had stolen his girl.

The woody was soon good to go. Even though the hood was dark brown and the fenders were black, the contrast in colors wasn't enough to give it a new paint job. Jazz had sold the Packard that morning for close to its purchase price of eleven hundred dollars, making out just fine on the deal. Jubal had seven hundred dollars in his pocket to pay for Glow, and he now had a handy vehicle to use for the farm.

It was late afternoon when Jubal drove up Harmony Hill. The cold, cloudy October sky remained over Hayesville but his gloom had lifted. He'd done the hard thing in selling the Packard. Benny must have heard him coming, for he stood waiting in the yard. He hurried to meet Jubal.

"My new car!" Benny said. "Can I go fer a ride?"

"Sure, get in."

Benny opened the passenger door and stood looking at the inside. "But Jubal, where's my bed?"

Jubal laughed. "Haven't put that in yet, Benny, but I will. Let's go down to see Avery."

After Benny squeezed his big frame into the front seat, Jubal fired the eight-cylinder engine with a push button on the dash. "Hear that?" he said to Benny. "Purrs like a contented cat."

"Makes a nice sound," Benny said, still checking out the interior. He looked down at the floor. "No holes!"

"How about that?" Jubal said, smiling.

After a brief visit with Avery, who remarked that the car was "a right practical rig," they returned home. Benny seemed happy with the trade, but he kept bringing up how he wanted to sleep in the back. Jubal promised he'd find an old mattress up in the attic as soon as he had time.

"First," he told Benny, "I've got to find an address and an envelope. It's time to run to town to mail out the check for the seven-hundred dollar balance on your new cow."

Benny opened the door to get out. "I'm not goin' ta town, Jubal. I wanna go see Glow and Star."

Driving back down the hill, Jubal listened to the engine of the new car and enjoyed the relatively smooth ride. It was close to the feel of the Packard though not quite as luxurious. Still, the suspension of the woody was not nearly as jarring as a ride down the hill in the truck. The best part was that the car fit him. He no longer felt out of place driving a rich person's car. At the same time, he no longer felt down and out as when driving the beat-up old truck.

Parking at the curb outside the post office, he saw Miss Curry scurrying along in her winter coat, wool hat, and rubber boots.

He rolled down his window. "Hey, Miss Curry!" He waved, knowing she wouldn't recognize him in his new car.

She peered in his direction from under her hat. Her face registered surprise. "Why hello, Jubal! Look at this—a different car. No more Packard?"

"That's right," he said, climbing out of the woody. "It was time for a change."

Miss Curry nodded. "Well, it's good timing running into you. The postmaster just called and said I have a package from Brunswick, Georgia."

"No kidding!" Jubal said. He was curious to see if the 1914 yearbook would reveal anything new about Father Mac or his boat. It had taken long enough to get the book, being an unusual request.

Inside, he mailed the check to "Ayrshire Sales" while Miss Curry retrieved her package. Back out on the sidewalk, a stiff wind swept through town, causing him to button up his coat. Miss Curry grabbed her hat with one hand and pulled it down snug.

"It's cold," he said. "Miss Curry, can I offer you a ride?"

"Thanks, I'd like that," she said, shivering. "Winter will be here sooner than we'd like."

Jubal opened the passenger door. "My new chariot," he said with a grand gesture. "Let's get in and see what you've got there in that package."

Miss Curry settled herself in the passenger's seat. "My, this is nice! It suits you better."

"That's what I'm thinking," Jubal said. Now that he'd mailed out the check for Glow, the complications from the cattle sale had been cleaned up to his liking.

Before they started off, he waited for Miss Curry to unwrap the brown paper that held the yearbook. He leaned over to see the dark blue cover with bold, black letters:

Brunswick High School
Class of 1914–The Whalers

Miss Curry slowly turned the pages of the slightly weathered book. Jubal noted the principal's message, staff, student officers, and the class will. After several pages, the graduates were listed alphabetically.

"Let's look for our Father Mac," Miss Curry said. "He was christened as Patrick MacMurray." She flipped a few more pages and stopped.

Stunned, neither of them said a word while staring down at the page.

"How strange," Miss Curry finally said.

"Gee, Patrick MacMurray is not the Father Mac we know," Jubal commented.

The guy in the picture had a thick head of curly hair and alert eyes. His face was square and rugged. Miss Curry adjusted her glasses to study the photo. She read aloud:

Patrick MacMurray
Ambition: The priesthood
Past time: Altar boy
Hobby: Life on a shrimp boat

Miss Curry held the book out to Jubal. He took it from her and combed through each graduate's picture. Soon, he found the familiar guy with the round moon face and weird smile. Underneath, it read:

Joseph Connelly
Ambition: Shrimping
Past time: Sailing the Mary Lou
Hobby: The class joker

He pointed to Connelly's entry. "The Mary Lou—that's Father Mac's boat. The one in the picture on the wall in his rectory study."

"I wasn't aware Father Mac was into boats," Miss Curry said. "But then, he hasn't said much about his past." She shook her head. "His personal life doesn't exactly come up in his homilies."

"But . . . Joseph Connelly?"

Miss Curry's tone was serious. "Right, the name sure doesn't match up."

Jubal flipped the pages back and forth. "Patrick MacMurray . . . Father Mac. That's definitely the name he has now." His mouth dropped open and he looked up at Miss Curry. "Do you suppose he could have assumed the identity of Patrick MacMurray?"

"It sure looks possible," Miss Curry said. "Though, I always thought that kind of thing only happened in murder mystery books." She looked thoughtful. "I remember when he came here several years ago with Tatum. He began as our priest right away, replacing our beloved Father Henry. No one questioned or complained. We figured the church had chosen the best man for the job."

"But why would he pretend to be a priest?" Jubal wondered. "Why move up here to freezing cold Vermont from the South? Why leave behind his boat if he loved it so much?" He handed the book back to Miss Curry.

"I have no idea. But what I do know is that Father Mac"—Miss Curry frowned and looked down at the picture—"*Joseph Connelly*, I mean, has certainly enjoyed status in this town as St. Anne's priest."

"He sure has." They sat in silence, processing the news. Jubal spoke up, "What if this guy was running from something?"

"It's possible." Miss Curry closed the book. "And that could be dangerous, so I have no interest in being the one to expose this Connelly character."

"I agree," Jubal said. "I don't want to deal with it either. It can't be good if a guy is posing as someone else." Then it dawned on him. "I always thought his friendship with Freddie Coleman was odd. Freddie is bad news. And then there's Father Mac and Tatum's relation—"

"Now Jubal, you're jumping to conclusions." Miss Curry pursed her lips. "Maybe there's a good reason for this." Her eyes widened. "Maybe someone was trying to kill Connelly and he had to hide? Like witness protection!"

"Gosh, that isn't a good reason!" Jubal could only imagine who might be stalking a creep like Father Mac. "Miss Curry, I think Andrew O'Mara should know about this. He's the leader of your church. I say we leave it up to him."

Miss Curry nodded in agreement. "That's a good plan." She handed Jubal the yearbook. "You'll need to show him this."

"After I drop you off, I'll go to the drugstore and tell Mister O'Mara about our discovery." He set the evidence on the seat beside him. "There's no point in delaying."

"Oh dear, Andrew will be upset." Miss Curry gathered up the brown paper wrapping as they neared the library. "What is our little town coming to? Who would think such a thing could happen here? First Maria, and now this."

After leaving Miss Curry, Jubal drove the woody back down Main Street and parked to the side of the drugstore. He sat dreading the visit. Andrew O'Mara had never been friendly when Jubal brought milk to their house. A question had troubled Jubal in the past, especially when Mister O'Mara looked sternly over his reading glasses at him while holding the *Wall Street Journal* at the breakfast table. What if Polly's father actually knew all, that Jubal's grubby cowbarn hands had explored every inch of Polly? The man had never even said "hello" or "good morning." Jubal simply handed the milk can to Polly's mom as she squinched up her nose from his barn stink. He suspected the pharmacist had often groaned over Polly's choice of a boyfriend.

To make matters worse, he worried whether Polly had told her dad about the *Sugar Daddy* incident, the reason for having to take his daughter to catechism every week. Or the soaking of Polly's expensive new wool jacket with the bucket of water. Jubal felt a lump of guilt in his stomach. Despite Polly's spiteful behavior the night of the grange dance, he'd acted like a heel towards her. She might never own up to her selfishness in dumping him for another guy after manipulating him for a ride. But he realized he owed her an apology. It was time now, though, to face her father to tell him the bad news about Father Mac—news that would surely knock down Andrew O'Mara's pillars of faith. Jubal ran his hand over the yearbook. The Catholic priest was a fake. No doubt Polly's dad had poured out his sins, whatever they might be, in the confessional booth to Father Mac.

Just as he was about to get out of the woody, Jubal paused. Mister O'Mara might question what an unchurched heathen was doing nosing around the qualifications of an established priest. What could he possibly say when being asked such a question? Yet, this so-called priest had stood by and done nothing to console the near destruction of Maria, instead standing by his good time buddy Freddie Coleman while accusing Maria of disrespectful behavior towards the church. What he was about to report about Father Mac would certainly blow the fraud's cover and destroy the guy's career. Jubal opened his door, grabbing the yearbook. He was glad of it!

He passed through the store's center door, walking by a lunch counter and soda fountain on his left and the pharmacy to his right. The whole place was clean and orderly. Mister O'Mara was behind the counter, wearing a white medical jacket buttoned up to the collar. His hair was parted so perfectly that one could lay a straight edge on it without needing to correct a single stray hair. Jubal stood awkwardly, pretending interest in the over-the-counter medicines that were before him. He picked up a package of *Carter's Little Liver Pills* to read the label.

"Well, what a surprise!" Mister O'Mara said, looking down over the counter. "How can I help you, Jubal? Does your liver need a boost today?"

Jubal was caught off guard when Mister O'Mara actually smiled. "Uh no," he said. He set the *Carter's* bottle down, vowing not to make a fool of himself. "My liver is good." He blushed. "I wanted to loan you this yearbook. It has something in it that will most surely interest you."

"Really? How unusual." Mister O'Mara was suddenly all business. "Why, may I ask?"

Jubal reached up with the yearbook and Mister O'Mara took it. "See for yourself," Jubal said. "When you finish with it, it needs to be returned to Miss Curry so she can send it back to the Brunswick Library in Georgia."

"Georgia?" Mister O'Mara raised his eyebrows. "Just what should I be looking for in this?" He studied the cover. "The Whaler's 1914 yearbook?"

"Yes. That's the year Father Mac graduated."

"Why should that be of interest to me?" Mister O'Mara flipped through a few pages and then set the yearbook down on the counter. "I'm pretty busy at this moment. Is this an urgent matter?"

"I think so," Jubal said. "You of all people should see this book. When you have some free time I suspect you will want to look up Father Mac."

"Well, son, I'm in the middle of filling a prescription. I'll check on it later." Mister O'Mara dumped some pills out of a big glass bottle.

Jubal stared at the yearbook on the counter. The sooner the disguise was ripped from Father Mac, the better. He was uncertain if he should press the matter further.

Mister O'Mara looked down at him. "Is there something else I can help you with, Jubal?"

Jubal shook his head. "No. Check the book out as you wish, Mister O'Mara." He turned to leave, feeling cowardly for not clearly stating the reason for his visit. It was a bit like driving a knife into an unsuspecting guy when his back was turned. Yet Jubal preferred the bomb not be dropped until after he had left the pharmacy.

Andrew O'Mara placed the book on a convenient shelf. "I guess I should thank you. It must be important since I don't recall you ever coming in here in recent years."

"Sorry. I haven't had reason to stop. My ma does most of our errands."

"I see," Mister O'Mara said. "From what I hear, you have your hands full on your farm."

Jubal shrugged. "It's a bit of work, Mister O'Mara. Speaking of which, I should get back to it."

After emerging from the store, Jubal drove the woody to a parking spot down the street, still in view of the pharmacy. He turned off the car and slid down in his seat. No one would know the car yet except for Jazz, Slag, Avery, and Miss Curry. He had some free time before night chores to watch what would happen. He suspected Polly's dad would get curious and check out the book before too long. Jubal felt sorry for him and the other Catholics in Hayesville. They had all trusted that the priest was the real deal. Their devotion was about to be upended.

In the car, Jubal grew chilled and sleepy in the late fall afternoon. Suddenly, the pharmacy door flew open and Andrew O'Mara rushed out to the sidewalk in his white coat. He charged towards the rectory with the yearbook in his hand. From his parking spot, Jubal also had a full view of the rectory, as well as the sheriff's office. He waited and wondered if he might see further action. So far, he was more than satisfied with what he assumed was taking place.

Chapter Forty-One

When Jubal left the pharmacy, Andrew O'Mara resumed filling a large order for the nurse's office at Hayesville School that included cough drops, medical tape, and bandages for sprained ankles. Andrew would make out handsomely on the sale despite the twenty-five percent discount he gave the school. He doubled down on counting the pills. Occasionally he glanced up at the book he'd just placed on the shelf. What could possibly be so urgent that he should drop what he was doing to sit down with the yearbook? Likely nothing. He continued filling the order of five hundred gray pills. Gray pills were used for coughs, chills, and all kinds of aches and pains, a remedy close to a sugar pill. The school nurse used the gray pills for kids with common complaints that were often, she declared, just an excuse to miss class.

Strictness for accuracy required that Andrew count such a big order in groups of ten—a mind-numbing task. As the pills dropped off a counting shelf into a container, he thought about Jubal. He'd heard that with help from Rose Brown and Lady Lamont, Jubal was the one holding their farm together.

Ten, Andrew counted, *ten twice. . . .*

A responsible young fellow, the lad would not have brought the book to him if it were not something he should see. He remembered when the boy was born, the scandal that preceded his birth. That was certainly a time of tragedy, especially the loss of Kelly, Andrew's beloved sister.

He'd never truly forgiven Tatum for the death of Kelly, the details of which remained murky. Of course, the church taught all about forgiveness, yet Andrew had found that forgiveness was the hardest endeavor of the human heart.

He had always realized his brother Tatum could be Jubal's father. He shook his head. Poor kid. It was this knowing that had caused Andrew concern over what had appeared to be an ongoing attraction between Polly and Jubal. But something happened over the summer to put an end to that. Andrew didn't care to know what the incident was. He was just glad to avoid a difficult conversation with Polly about close relatives and the "birds and the bees." Better to leave that sort of education to her catechism class.

Ten . . . twenty . . . thirty.

So far, Jubal was on his way to making more of himself than Tatum ever would. Andrew looked over again at the yearbook on the shelf. There was something important in that book for him to see. Soon he reached three hundred pills. He stopped and jotted the number on a pad. He'd just take a quick break to satisfy Jubal's urgency and check out the book.

Sitting down at his desk, Andrew flipped through the yearbook's pages in puzzlement. Nothing but pictures and descriptions of long-ago graduates from another state far away. Why did any of this matter to him? Strangers, all of them. He almost put the book aside to get back to his task, when suddenly he was unable to believe his own eyes. He pulled his glasses out of his coat pocket, put them on, and bent closer to the book. There must be a mix-up. But there he was. St. Anne's priest—*Joseph Connelly* read the name under the picture.

He sat back in wonderment. There had to be an explanation. Maybe it was simply an error. After all, kids and teachers working on the yearbook were often stretched too far. He had staffed the yearbook at his own alma mater. It was a hectic race to meet the deadline, all the while keeping up with homework, playing sports, and doing chores at home. Even so, surely a mistake such as the wrong name of a *graduating* student would have been caught before the book went to print. His own yearbook advisor,

Miss Allington, had been stern and a perfectionist. Nothing escaped her sharp eyes.

He leafed through the rest of the Brunswick senior class and stopped at a later picture. *Patrick MacMurray*, it read. Father Mac. Though the ambition of the priesthood lined up, the picture did not match the Father Mac he knew. It was unlikely there would be *two* mistakes. He flipped the pages back and forth. Unbelievable. The Brown kid was right. This was big.

He looked up at his incomplete order spread out on the counter. The familiar quick-beat of tension filled his chest. How was he going to focus on his work now? He stood and paced back and forth, his wing-tip shoes tapping on the shiny floor. As a leader in the church, he'd taken it upon himself to find a hurried replacement when Father Henry had fallen ill. He'd made the necessary arrangements to have Tatum and Father Mac come to Hayesville after seeking the bishop's approval. The new priest's appointment had seemed a miraculously smooth transition. Andrew stopped short.

Was it possible that all this time his own brother knew Father Mac was fulfilling the role of a priest under an assumed identity? Another betrayal by his brother in all likelihood. Then Andrew nearly wilted recalling a stretch of time when complaining of his shotgun marriage to his wife, Trudy. In the confessional booth, he'd poured out his frustration to Father Mac and admitted his desire of a tryst with Mary White. Andrew sank back into his chair, his hands covering his face.

His temptation was nearly irresistible when sitting near Mary, practically cheek to cheek, as they went over figures for the town's yearly budget. He would inhale the sweet lemon drop scent of the hard candy she loved to let rest on her pink tongue. At home in the dark, with Trudy asleep beside him, Andrew dreamed of taking Mary in his arms to confess his long-held desire to make love. But adultery was wrong. He'd made his bed in having premarital sex with Polly's mother. So over and over, he'd asked Father Mac forgiveness for such sinful lust as he felt for Mary. All along he'd been confessing to a stranger, to Joseph Connelly, a *shrimper* for God's sake.

Probably Connelly, feeling smug in his own deception, had been rolling with laughter on hearing the nitty-gritty failings of his faithful followers. Picturing this, Andrew lifted his head, rage boiling up. He vowed this Joseph Connelly, whoever he was, must leave his position immediately. He would run the guy out of town. And the round-faced liar could take Tatum, his scoundrel brother, with him and good riddance. Andrew jumped from his chair, flailing his fists. He'd love to sock both those jerks.

Soon Andrew stood breathless before the rectory door. He knocked and the housekeeper, Mabel Green, answered.

"Oh it's you, Andrew." Mabel pulled the door wide, her stout figure filling up half the opening. "You know, you hardly need to knock."

Mabel was a slow-moving, easygoing woman. Andrew needed her to quickly do as he asked without a lot of questions. He willed himself to relax. The confrontation would not go well if he was keyed up. Remaining stoic was the way to get things done.

"I need to meet with Father Mac and Tatum immediately," he announced firmly. "Are they available?"

Mabel looked at him curiously. "Yes, I believe they're both upstairs taking a break before dinner."

"Good. I'll return in fifteen minutes, and then I'll want to see them in Father Mac's study."

"Andrew?" Mabel asked, lingering in the doorway. "You seem upset. Are you okay?"

He took a breath. Poker face, he told himself. He gripped the yearbook tightly as though the item were a breakable mirror if dropped.

"Shall I tell Father Mac and the sheriff the reason for your visit?" Mabel asked.

"No, thank you, but I will need to see them both, together." He leaned over and whispered in her ear, "And I need you to call Harold Shangraw, deputy sheriff, over at the school. Tell him to come to the pharmacy on the double."

Mabel stepped back. "You mean Stubby Shangraw?" she exclaimed.

Andrew waved his hand. "Shhh . . . Not so loud."

"Hey, what's that?" Mabel pointed at the yearbook.

"Mabel, please," he said in a low voice. "This is serious, okay?"

She nodded, her eyes on the yearbook. "Sure thing, Andrew."

After Mabel closed the door, Andrew hurried back to the pharmacy. He needed two letters of resignation to present—one for this Joseph Connelly and the second for his brother. He'd keep the documents simple so he could type them quickly. He'd also give the men each one hundred dollars cash to be on their way. He wanted them punished, but not enough to make them homeless. Later on, he would contact the appropriate people to request a stop-payment for their salaries.

Inside the pharmacy, he banged out the two one-line letters of resignation on his typewriter. Then he changed from his white coat into a suit jacket. He shut down the soda fountain and hastily scrawled a sign, "Closed Early Due to Emergency," which he hung on the door. Just then, Shangraw came roaring up the street in his old Plymouth. Outside, Andrew spoke briefly to the deputy, ordering him to remain in his car until he received further instructions.

On return to the rectory, Andrew didn't knock. He pushed open the door where Mabel was waiting in the hallway obviously still wondering about the terrible urgency. Without a word, he strode by her and entered the tiny rectory study. Tatum quickly stood.

"Holy jumped-up! Andrew, what's the meaning of all this flurry?" Tatum grinned at his brother. "One would think there's been a murder or somethin'."

Andrew ignored Tatum and dropped the yearbook on the priest's desk with a thud. He glared at Father Mac and pointed. "Open that book and explain yourself!"

Father Mac glanced at the book's cover and his face turned red.

Tatum looked down at the desk. "An old yearbook. So what?" His grin disappeared.

"It's got to do with your closest friend here." Andrew gestured towards Father Mac. "This guy who's been your *good buddy*! Your jig is up, Tatum!" He was spitting mad as he spoke. "I know all about it now."

"What the hell are you talkin' about, Andrew?" Out of habit, Tatum stuck his thumbs in his holster.

God, Andrew hated when his brother took that stupid sheriff's pose. "This man you dragged up here from your partying days on the Gulf Coast to fill our most holy position at the church is *not* Patrick MacMurray. The yearbook lists him as a *Joseph Connelly*," Andrew said. "Just some . . . some . . . shrimper!"

"Oh for chrissake, Andrew," Tatum said. "You and your damned holier-than-thou crap." He stretched his neck side to side, as if releasing a crick. "Folks in town just love Father Mac, and he does his job. What does a name matter?"

Andrew laughed a short, harsh laugh. He shook his head. "So typical. You think life is a big game. THAT is the problem with you, Tatum. You don't take anything seriously. I've got news for you. A priesthood is holy. This deception is a *sin*. It will not go unpunished by me, or by God." He aimed his glare again at Father Mac. "For either of you!"

Father Mac, now exposed as Joseph Connelly, reached out his hand and slowly pushed the yearbook to the edge of the desk. In seconds the book landed on the floor with a bang as pages fluttered open. Father Mac looked up at Andrew and suddenly grabbed his chest. He opened his mouth and out came an "Aw . . . aw!" like a strangled crow.

Andrew almost laughed. "Nice try. A fake chest pain won't work." He snatched the book off the floor, slapping it back on the desk with a thwack. "I am the leader of this church, Father Mac— I mean, *Joseph*." He glanced down to see the tattoo on Connelly's arm, the shirt sleeve rolled back. "Or shall I call you *Mary Lou*? What's this? In love with some boat?"

Connelly finally sputtered, "Andrew, will . . . will you just take it easy?"

"In this matter, I'll not be easy." Andrew pulled the two letters from a manilla folder and placed them side by side on the desk. "Both of you will need to sign these letters of resignation from your positions, effective immediately!"

Father Mac looked down at the papers in disbelief. "Can't you give us a break? Come on! There must be some leeway. I've served this community—"

"Absolutely not." Andrew stood tall and imposing. "After signing your resignation, you both have one day to pack your bags and load them into the Cadillac. Otherwise, I'm calling for your arrest for fraud." He placed two envelopes each with a hundred dollars next to the letters. "Travel money." He stuck his palm out. "Tatum—give me all that's on your key ring."

Tatum lost his cocky attitude, pleading, "Andrew, geez. I've done a lot of good as sheriff of this town. I'm . . . I'm your brother."

Andrew scowled at Tatum. "Okay, brother, name something good you've done. Just one thing. Besides hassling Jubal's uncle who wouldn't hurt a fly. Oh, and let's see . . . How about failing to ever find out what happened to the Browns' Packard? Here's the best one, not seeing what Freddie Coleman was up to right under your nose at the CYO camp. Instead my teenage daughter, *your niece*, was the one in danger that got him to confess. Yeah, that whole mess ended real well."

"I . . . I was the one who brought Freddie in," Tatum protested.

"Too late. Just like you were too late to help our sister Kelly."

Tatum's eyes widened. From the chair at his desk, Joseph Connelly looked from one brother to the other.

"That's right," Andrew continued. "I put too much trust in my own flesh and blood. I'll be confessing this personal failure to Father Hebert." He looked at Connelly. "*A real priest.* Go ahead," he said, waving at the letters. "Sign them, get your affairs in order, and get out of town."

"Goddammit brother!" Tatum threw the key ring on the desk. "I guess family don't mean a thing to ya!"

"You're quite mistaken," Andrew said evenly. "Family means everything. My church family and my own." He turned to go. "Leave the two signed letters on this desk. Both of you had best be in that Cadillac riding out of Hayesville by sunset tomorrow. If you give me any grief in signing, Stubby is waiting right outside. He'll escort you to the town line with nothing but the shirts on your backs. And if you resist any of my requests, I'll call the Rutland Sheriff's Department. Now, Tatum, hand over your gun."

Tatum hesitated. Andrew curled his fists and took a step towards his brother. Tatum slowly unbuckled the holster and gave it to Andrew who clutched it at his side.

By this time, Joseph Connelly appeared to have gathered his thoughts. Andrew could see by his hangdog expression that the guy realized he was about to lose something he truly benefited from—his corrupt calling.

"Andrew . . . let me have a chance to explain myself," Connelly squeaked. His round face was ashen, paler than usual.

Andrew felt a small amount of pity rise for the trapped cleric. In near disbelief himself over his discovery, he stood back to at least listen to what the fraud had to say. "Go ahead. How is it that you've allowed yourself to commit such a travesty against our beloved church?"

Connelly adjusted his collar and pointed to the picture of the *Mary Lou* hanging in his office. "This was our family boat." His voice fell to a far-off, melancholy tone. "When I was little, my dad had a slip at a small marina on Saint Simons Island. He would take tourists—many who were wealthy, famous executives—out on the *Mary Lou* to fish in and around the barrier islands off the coast of Georgia. When I got old enough to handle ropes and bait, my dad took me with him. The tourists liked me." He smiled at the memory. "They tipped me well."

Connelly looked directly at Andrew. "These were the bigwigs from the railroad industry, the oil industry, you name it. My father had a good business, but things at home were unraveling. My mother was suffering from a deep, ongoing depression and spent days confined to her bedroom. She barely took care of me. In the middle of the day she'd be in bed with the drapes closed, or walking around in her housecoat and slippers. Luckily, I could escape to the boat. My dad did what he could for my mom, taking her to a number of doctors. But nothing helped."

Connelly's eyes grew moist and his mouth turned downward. Andrew reminded himself not to be taken in. It had to be an act—how could he trust what the guy was telling him?

Connelly continued. "After the first world war, the Brunswick shrimping industry was taking off. I was a teenager. My dad helped me refit the

Mary Lou for shrimping. He and I had a few friends down at the docks who were Portuguese—real experts on catching shrimp. Sometimes I went out with them. They had better boats, some with the new otter trawl nets. They taught me everything I knew, so I brought in decent hauls. I was out on the water every day."

Andrew couldn't see what shrimping nets had to do with Connelly's posing as a priest. "Perhaps you're telling this long story hoping for some mercy from me. I assure you, it isn't going to happen. There is no excuse for being an imposter."

Connelly folded his pudgy hands on the desk. "No, but perhaps if you keep listening, it will make my name change more understandable."

"I'm all ears." Andrew crossed his arms, his feet planted wide.

"My dad grew concerned that my whole life was shrimping. He wanted me to have a broader experience, so he connected me with a kindly, older priest. Father Stephens put a Catholic Bible in my hands and tutored me carefully in its lessons. He also convinced me that I should return to Brunswick High School so I could have an education. It was there that I became close with Pat MacMurray.

"Because I was in school on weekdays, Dad had hired Jenny Spear, a gal a few years older than us, to help him with the nets and, when needed, to handle his catch. Still, Pat and I spent every weekend on the *Mary Lou,* even if it remained in the slip.

"When I graduated, I began informal learning about the duties of the priesthood. Father Stephens, in his advanced age, suffered from a painful arthritis, to the point where I did more and more for him—even filling in some of the duties of a priest. He didn't want to report his condition to the bishop for fear of being replaced, so he allowed me to wear a collar on special occasions."

Andrew interrupted. "So that's when you became drunk with power, living the fantasy of a priest."

"Yeah, I'll admit it," Connelly said, nodding. "It felt pretty good to have folks looking up to me. Not many had much respect for a shrimper. But I noticed how they listened to Father Stephen's homilies and gave him their confessions. As I became more focused on the church, Jenny's interest in the shrimping business soon far surpassed mine."

Tatum, who already knew the story, spoke up. "Later on, when we were down in the Keys, I remember you gave the best homilies, manned the confessional booth, baptized babies, even gave the last rights. People loved you."

Andrew turned on his brother, "You *would* think this fakery was okay."

"Christ-almighty, Andrew, you've always been too uptight. Give the guy a break!"

Connelly let out a nervous giggle.

Andrew fixed Connelly with a look of disdain. "I expect right off the bat you performed the Eucharist, the most holy of holies in the high Mass."

"Of course he did," Tatum remarked. "The 'smells and bells' routine. What an act!"

Connelly turned to his friend. "Don't forget, Tatum, for us devout Catholics the Eucharist isn't an act." He looked to Andrew. "To ask your leniency, I need to explain further."

Andrew sat down in the chair opposite the desk, holding Tatum's gun and holster in his lap. Tatum eyed the weapon and slumped against the wall.

"Go ahead," Andrew said.

"Well, the Georgia economy took a dive in the '20s, causing our family considerable hardship. My dad was under a great deal of stress and his health began to decline. Jenny took over most of the boat's business. My dad was having trouble caring for my mom—she was doing very poorly—so we put her in the state hospital." Connelly shivered. "It was a horrible place. A terrible mistake. It crushed my father putting her in there. They said it was a heart attack that killed my dad, but I think it was guilt. Once in the sanatorium, my mother became even more of a shell of herself and died soon after my father."

Connelly grew quiet and no one spoke.

He sighed. "And then, Father Stephens passed not too long after that." He glance at the tattered coat hanging from the coat rack in the corner. "That coat," he said pointing, "I wore it to all three funerals.

"After so much loss, I needed the comfort and routine of the church. Since the church had recently changed bishops, I just kept right on doing what Father Stephens had taught me. My credentials were never checked. I was able to act as a bonafide priest with no questions asked. Meanwhile, Pat MacMurray, now an ordained priest, was spending all of his free time with Jenny on the *Mary Lou*. The inevitable happened. They fell in love. Pat was dedicated to Jenny and found he liked shrimping more than the priesthood. Since he was breaking his celibacy promise, he was eager to shed his former life. My folks were dead. I was alone. So we just traded—names, professions, the whole works, but mainly the credentials.

"Pat and Jenny got a fresh start on the Louisiana Gulf Coast. I left town about the same time to get away from the bad memories."

"But I don't understand how you were never caught in your deception as a priest," Andrew said.

"When Father Stephens was alive, he vouched for me when I helped him out. It was never questioned. After I left Brunswick, I traveled quite a bit around the South. I never stayed long in any one church." Connelly looked intently at Andrew. "In many parishes, a priest is terribly burdened with his responsibilities. A number of them were willing to get a break when my offer came along. So I would serve for a short while, and then I'd leave with some cash in my pockets. Eventually I took a liking to South Florida."

"How clever," Andrew said. "I've just heard the testimony of a makeshift priest. I'm still not impressed." He gestured to the framed diplomas on the wall with Patrick MacMurray's name on them. "These aren't even yours!"

Father Mac glanced at the diplomas with a guilty expression. "Please, let me finish."

"By all means."

"While in Florida, I encountered Freddie Coleman in a Catholic home for troubled boys." Connelly shook his head at the memory. "Boy, was that kid damaged. Feeling sorry for him, I took him under my wing to a new life and a church I was asked to oversee for a short time in Key

West. It was there we met Tatum, and the rest is history. Eventually, I moved north to be St. Anne's full-time priest." He shrugged. "My first permanent position, or so I thought." He looked at Andrew hopefully, gaging how his story had set in.

Andrew thought for several minutes, staring at the man in the white collar to whom he'd poured out his most-secret troubles. After staking his reputation with the Burlington diocese on bringing the supposed Father Mac to Hayesville, he'd now be seen as a fool. Besides, how did he know that the moon-faced imposter wasn't making the whole story up? A low glimmer of anger flared.

"All very interesting. And very sad, I am sure," Andrew said. "But you can forget it if you're looking to me for approval. It took too long for your crookedness to be uncovered. All the while infusing my faith with lies." He stood. "My demand stands. You two guys are out of here. You'd best get to your packing." He turned on his heel.

As Andrew slammed the door, he heard Tatum yell after him: "I hope you burn in hell, brother!"

Andrew stepped into the hall where Mabel was pretending to busy herself with a dustrag. Carefully holding the holster with the gun, he breathed a sigh of relief, yet an emptiness washed over him. Outside, he gave Stubby clear instructions and left for home to make a very difficult call to the bishop.

After several delays by the court-appointed attorney, Freddie Coleman's case was finally set to be heard on October 28, 1941, at the Rutland County Courthouse before Judge Bradley Smathers. Freddie Coleman was charged with assault and battery and the raping of Maria Styles on the fifth of July. Polly O'Mara was ordered to testify on behalf of the prosecution.

When the day arrived, Polly sat in the back seat of her folks' Buick with her hands folded in her lap. It was the day she'd been dreading. Every so often she drew in a deep breath and puffed her cheeks. Her dad drove and her mother was in the passenger seat as the car whizzed along in a steady purr. Few words were spoken.

Finally, Polly couldn't take it. "I'm scared! I can't do this!"

"Of course you can," her father said firmly.

Polly knew her dad was pretty upset about something that had happened at the church recently. She'd heard him and her mom talking late into the night.

Her mother looked back from the front seat. "Honey, I understand. But all you have to do is repeat what you have written down: 'Freddie came to the nurse's station on Wednesday evening, July 23rd, and his confession followed.'"

"Mom! It *wasn't* that simple!" Her parents would never understand what it was like to sit across from that monster, in her nightgown and robe no less, while he leered at her, swigging his wine.

"Well then, you tell me," her mother said. "What are you going to say to the judge?"

Polly hesitated. If the guy was going to get convicted, she had to tell it like it was. "He confessed, 'I beat the shit outta Maria Styles! And then fucked her brains out.'"

The car's right front tire momentarily left the pavement and the Buick rocked as her dad brought the car to a stop.

"My word!" her mother gasped. "How dare you speak so crudely!"

"Well, it was something like that," Polly said. "He's a horrible beast."

Her mother waved a piece of paper over the back seat. "According to your written statement, Polly, Freddie did not say such awful words."

Polly folded her arms. "He did," she said quietly.

Her father turned around with a no-nonsense look. "I will not have my daughter speak such nasty testimony in public. Just follow the notes you took. Tell the judge exactly what Freddie said and stop trying to shock your parents!" Her father put the car in gear and they pulled back onto the road.

As the Buick carried Polly closer and closer to the dreaded confrontation, she put her hands over her stomach, feeling about to be sick. "How come Maria doesn't have to appear?"

"Father Hebert said she would be too traumatized," her mother explained. "Her parents have chosen not to come as well."

"What a lame excuse!"

"Just thank the good Lord it didn't happen to you." Her mother made the sign of the cross.

"Amen," her father agreed.

Polly slouched down in her seat, deliberately goading her parents who hated when she sat in bad posture. But both of them ignored her, staring straight ahead, so she sulked long and hard on their way to Rutland.

Traveling down Merchants Row, they located the courthouse. Polly's insides turned tight as a cork in a bottle on seeing the stately building. She hadn't told her folks all, maintaining her long established behavior that especially her mom shouldn't know all of her business. She didn't mention that Freddie had warned he'd do the same to her as he did to Maria Styles if she squealed. She'd ignored the threat at the time, but now it was taking on real meaning. God, if he ever got free, she'd end up a bag of chicken bones. Yes *chicken!* She had every right to be scared out of her jollies.

Her father and mother walked on either side of her in support while they climbed the courthouse steps and passed between the white columns. They were directed to a small room with a table and chairs to wait for the prosecuting attorney. The little room was elevated above the courtroom where all the action was about to begin. As her folks took seats, Polly chose to stand and look out over the courtroom through a glass window. The central point was the judge's perch—a raised chair and bench placed under a wooden arch. The judge's chair had a clear view of the gallery filled with seating for interested observers. Next to and beneath the judge's chair to his left, separated by a rail, was the witness stand. Before long, Polly would be in that chair getting grilled by the prosecuting and defense attorneys while having to look Freddie in the eye.

She imagined Freddie's cruel stare, his pug-nosed face, and she wished for a dose of bicarbonate of soda. Without a doubt, Freddie would be wanting to ring her neck. What if he jumped from his chair and charged the witness stand? With his power and strength it would be all over in seconds. The indentations of his thumb-marks on her throat would quickly fill with blood as she gasped her last breath. She'd ride home in a coffin.

Just as she was thinking these morbid thoughts, a portly, middle-aged man entered.

"Well, Andrew, this day has finally come," the man said. "It was only with your insistence as well as Lady Lamont's that this case is even still on the docket. The attorney general wouldn't touch it."

Her father shook the guy's hand. "I appreciate your diligence, Attorney Fosterfal. Please meet our daughter, Polly. As the prosecution, Attorney Fosterfal will be the one asking you questions on the stand, Polly."

The attorney put his big hands on his belly and rocked back on his heels. "Polly, I've studied your testimony. It sounds plausible, but you'll have to convince the judge. You're the only witness I will be calling to the stand today. The victim, Maria Styles, has refused to appear. However, your uncle Tatum and the priest have each sent me statements to read. Apparently they are, um . . ." he cleared his throat, "*unable* to appear." He and her father exchanged glances. "The judge has agreed to this allowance for their parts. But since you heard Freddie Coleman's alleged confession, your testimony is key to this case. I expect you've memorized your notes? You must answer my questions crisply, honestly, and with self-assurance."

"I'll do my best," Polly said. Right away, she didn't like the guy. He reeked of cigar smoke and his bulging gut made her think of a big balloon with his belt cutting through and holding the bulge. She imagined one notch tighter and his gut would rupture, blowing ropey intestines all over the room. Due to her touchy stomach, she covered her mouth and burped quietly.

Fosterfal continued. "The defense lawyer was appointed by the court—Attorney Harmon is a real sharp kid known to devour witnesses in cross-examination. So again, Polly, act smart. We have a few minutes to go over your notes. Repeat back to me just as you've written them because you can't take them to the witness stand."

Polly nodded and obediently sat in the chair he indicated.

Her father intervened. "I know the evidence is weak, but in this instance it's a must that justice be served. An awful crime has been committed against one of Hayesville's outstanding young women."

"We'll give it our best," the lawyer assured her father. Fosterfal sat to open his briefcase from which he pulled out a white handkerchief. He mopped a sheen of sweat from his brow. Next pulling some papers from the case, he mindlessly dropped the soiled handkerchief in front of Polly on the table. She stared at it in disgust.

Fosterfal turned to her. "Polly, let's run through the questions I'll be asking for the opening charge."

Polly answered everything accurately with no hesitation. Perhaps being a witness wouldn't be so hard after all. Fosterfal seemed satisfied with her performance, so she was free to watch the courtroom fill up with observers. When it was time, Fosterfal went down to the courtroom and took his seat at the plaintiff's table. Polly remained up in the little room while her parents went to sit in the gallery.

Looking down, Polly saw Freddie Coleman enter in handcuffs, followed by Defense Attorney Harmon. A security guard removed Freddie's cuffs. Then the guard stationed himself near the door from which Freddie had come. As Freddie and his attorney took their seats at the defendant's table, Freddie made eye contact with no one. From a distance, sober and wearing a suit, he didn't seem to be the scoundrel she remembered. He'd lost his tan but was well-shaven, his blond hair cut short.

The bailiff must have directed, "All rise." As those in the courtroom stood, a foggy feeling momentarily came over Polly, but cleared when she saw the judge enter and take his seat. Too nervous to watch anymore, she waited at the little table, wrestling with what she would say when on the stand. Should she play it safe or tell the truth and risk her father's anger? Regardless, whatever she chose would likely cause Freddie to follow through on his threat to turn her into mincemeat if he went free.

Soon there was a knock on the door of the little room. The dreaded moment had arrived. As Polly was escorted downstairs by an older woman in a gray skirt and jacket, the foggy feeling returned. Polly entered the large courtroom with the witness stand looking to be miles away. About to swoon from nerves, she stopped halfway down the aisle. People in the gallery turned to stare. Judge Smathers nodded encouragingly. She continued on, her vision clearing just as she stepped up and took her seat. The stand was directly in front of Freddie who stared down at the table. Sitting next to him, Attorney Harmon narrowed his eyes as if calculating the best way to dice her up. She had to keep her story on track or this Harmon character would make a fool out of her.

When she agreed for the court with her hand on the *Holy Bible*, "to tell the whole truth and nothing but the truth," Freddie suddenly gave her a cold, angry stare. She shivered and felt intense stomach pain, wrapping one arm across her abdomen.

Fosterfal approached the stand and rested his arm casually on the rail, about to begin. The courtroom was so quiet that Polly heard a lone fly thwacking around in the ceiling light above. She looked down at Fosterfal's gold wristwatch nestled in his black arm hairs and watched the secondhand move: tick . . . tick . . . tick. My . . . death . . . by . . . strang . . . u . . . la . . . tion . . . is . . . come . . . ing . . . soon.

After running through Polly's introduction, Fosterfal explained the preliminary details leading to the night of Freddie's supposed confession at the CYO nurse's station. He paced as he spoke. Polly tried not to watch his big belly jiggling like gelatin over the tight belt. Suppressing a burp, her first task was to identify Freddie by pointing him out in the room.

"Now Polly," Fosterfal began, leaning on the rail as if real chummy with her, "explain to the court what happened on the night of July 23rd, 1941."

She took a deep breath. "It was late—time for all the campers to be in bed." The woozy feeling threatened to come back and she puffed her cheeks. "Dot Stone, the camp nurse, had left for her granddaughter's birthday party. Expecting no campers to come for help, I put on my nightie. I . . . I carried my bathrobe to the reception area because it was muggy, and hot."

Fosterfal nodded. "Yes . . . go on."

"So, I sat drinking some bicarbonate of soda to ease my tummy pain like—like I could use right now." A low burp escaped and Polly put her hand to her mouth.

The observers in the gallery chuckled.

Judge Smathers looked at her in pity and rapped his gavel. "I call a short recess for the benefit of the witness."

"Oh." Polly was not expecting this bit of kindness. The white-haired judge was the grandfather type. "Thank you. Your Honor, any tonic water will do."

More laughter bubbled up from below and a stern look from Judge Smathers quieted them. Polly saw her father rush from the room.

Defense Attorney Harmon jumped to his feet. "What kind of show is this? I object!"

Judge Smathers rapped his gavel again. "Overruled."

In a few minutes, her father returned to the courtroom with a bottle of ginger ale and gave it to her mother who brought it to the witness stand. Polly leaned down to her mom and whispered, "I can't continue."

"Oh, honey," her mother said softly, patting her arm. "Just direct your answers to Attorney Fosterfal. Don't even look at Freddie or his attorney."

Polly didn't share with her mother that she found Fosterfal equally revolting. She swallowed several gulps of the soda, releasing a few loud burps in relief. Her mother frowned but the ache in Polly's stomach eased.

"Now relax. You're doing just fine," her mom said before stepping down to return to her seat. Polly saw her dad put his arm around her mom in a comforting way.

As they got back to business, the roiling sea within Polly's stomach was now only occasional waves. The ginger ale was doing its trick.

Judge Smathers asked, "Are you ready to continue, Miss O'Mara?"

"Yes, your Honor." But really, she felt in the corner of round one of a ten-round fight. By round ten, the judge would be calling in the stretcher.

Fosterfal mopped his brow with his handkerchief. "Er, we left off when you were describing your situation at the nurse's station."

"Yes. I was feeling a little nervous about being alone in the cabin at night. Then I heard a knock at the door which surprised me with the campers being in bed. I threw on my robe and when I went to answer, Freddie Coleman stood there asking if he could come in."

"I see. I see. Yes. And what was your response?" Fosterfal asked.

"Well, of course I didn't want him to come in. I informed him it was after curfew, but I must say, he entered with no hesitation. I was trying to close my robe in the front when he reached down and handed me the end of the tie. From the start, he acted overly familiar with me."

"So he came in without your permission," Fosterfal summarized. "What happened next?"

Polly thought of the July 5th grange dance, information that should not leak out in the questioning or she would lose all face.

"Polly, what did he do next?" Fosterfal repeated.

For a moment Polly lost her train of thought. She avoided the temptation to look at Freddie, keeping her eyes trained instead on Fosterfal as her mother had suggested. "Uh . . . wine," Polly finally said. "He grabbed a bottle from outside. As I said, the hour was late and it seemed strange that Freddie had wine at a kids' camp. I'm pretty sure it was against the rules. I tried to make him leave again, but instead he encouraged me to drink." She glanced at her parents who sat in the gallery wide-eyed. "I said no, of course." A look of relief passed over her mom's face.

"I see," Forsterfal said. "Now let me get this straight. Freddie came into your cabin without your permission, saw you were in your nightgown, and tried to make you drink wine? Go on."

Polly badly wanted to gauge Freddie's expression, but willed herself to stay focused. "It was . . . small talk at first. On such a steamy night, the cologne he wore smelled something awful. And his breath reeked of wine. I guessed he'd had plenty from the bottle."

"So, would you say, Miss O'Mara, that Freddie Coleman was drunk?"

Harmon leapt to his feet. "Objection! Leading the witness."

Smathers smacked his gavel. "Overruled. Continue, Miss O'Mara."

"I reminded Freddie it was past time for lights out, but he didn't budge, sprawled out on his chair. The wine was on the table between us, the bottle almost gone. He acted pretty tipsy, so yes, he was drunk."

"She lies!" Freddie burst out.

Polly flinched.

"Silence!" Judge Smathers warned.

Freddie scowled at the floor.

Polly fixed her eyes on the ceiling light where the fly was still thudding around. "He . . . he kept saying it wasn't time to leave because he wanted to have a heart-to-heart with me."

"Did he say why?"

"Not at first. At one point he grabbed my wrist, which hurt, wanting me to dance. Since he wouldn't leave, I began asking him questions about Maria. That's when he told me, 'That half-breed at the store got the whole thing right.'" She took a deep breath. "Then he grabbed my hair."

Her mother gasped as Freddie jumped to his feet.

"A load of horseshit!" Freddie hollered.

Judge Smathers banged his gavel several times. "Mister Coleman, I will not tolerate these outbursts or that language."

Attorney Harmon spoke up. "I'm sorry, your Honor. It won't happen again." Harmon leaned over to Freddie and spoke quietly.

Freddie glowered at Polly in an ugly manner and she was not at all sure he would stay put. She could already feel his fingers around her neck.

"Mister Fosterfal," she said in a low tone, "we need tighter security."

Fosterfal noted Freddie's sour look. "Your Honor, may I approach the bench?"

"You may," Judge Smathers replied.

"This young lady feels unsafe to continue," Fosterfal said.

Judge Smathers banged his gavel. "Court will be in recess until one o'clock."

The two attorneys left for a conference with the judge in his quarters.

Standing out on the court steps for fresh air at the noon hour, Polly regretted not telling the whole truth of that night and especially the reason why she was so afraid of Freddie. She hoped when she returned that the judge would require Freddie to sit in handcuffs. All too soon, she found herself back on the witness stand. She was pleased to see Freddie was indeed wearing the cuffs and that now the security guard stood closer to the defense table. Even so, the awful pain in her belly returned. She took a sip of the warm ginger ale.

Attorney Fosterfal picked up where they'd left off. "Miss O'Mara, do you know who Mister Coleman was referring to when he said . . ." Fosterfal looked down at his notes. "'That half-breed at the store got the whole thing right?'"

"Yes, sir. He was referring to Lizzy LaFlam."

"And who is this Lizzy LaFlam?"

Polly hesitated. She would say as little as possible so as not to show her distaste for the girl that stole her boyfriend. "She's just some girl from school," she shrugged. "She runs the Hayesville IGA."

Fosterfal flipped through the papers in his hand and looked up. "You didn't mention Lizzy LaFlam in your previous written statement, Miss O'Mara, or Mister Coleman's reference to the 'half-breed.' What does this other young lady know about the events of July 5th?"

Oh no, now she'd dragged Lizzy into this. If Freddie didn't strangle her, Lizzy would most certainly drag her behind the grocery delivery wagon by her heels. "I don't think she knows anything. I'm not sure what Freddie meant by that."

"Hmmm." Fosterfal seemed uncertain how to continue. "Is . . . is that all that Mister Coleman said when he . . . as you say . . . grabbed your hair?"

This was Polly's chance to zap them with the incriminating line. All eyes in the room were on her. She spoke up decisively, avoiding the stares of her mother and father. "In his own words, Freddie Coleman told me: 'I beat the shit outta Maria Styles! And then fucked her brains out. And I'll do the same to you if you breathe a word of this.'"

Freddie leapt to his feet, raising his fists held together by the cuffs. "More lies!"

Judge Smathers furiously pounded his gavel. "Sit. Down. Mister Coleman."

The judge turned on Polly, his face no longer that of a kindly grandfather.

"As for you, Miss O'Mara, I am utterly shocked to hear such vulgar language spoken in my courtroom. I simply will not allow it."

Fosterfal sputtered, "This testimony was never reported to me!"

Polly gasped and bent with a hand on her tummy. "I'm sorry, your Honor. I know I told Attorney Fosterfal and my folks differently before. My father doesn't like me to speak that way either. But you asked me to tell the truth, the *whole* truth. Freddie Coleman in his drunken state used those very words to confess the crime he committed against Maria Styles. He scared me to death!"

Attorney Harmon stood. "This young lady's testimony is a travesty!"

Judge Smathers spoke sternly. "I will not allow my courtroom to be lowered to disorder and diabolical language! Attorneys for the prosecution and defense, please step to the bench."

After the conference, Attorney Fosterfal announced, "The prosecution is finished with the witness."

Attorney Harmon rose, "I wish to cross-examine the witness."

Judge Smathers announced, "Permission granted."

On the stand, Polly remained shaken by the judge's reprimand. Embarrassed before the whole court, she now regretted sharing Freddie's exact language. Her parents were likely furious. She braced for Attorney Harmon's questions.

"Miss O'Mara," Harmon began. "You had an upset stomach on the evening of July 23rd as well, correct?"

"Yes," Polly replied.

"Are your stomach issues triggered by nerves?"

"Usually."

"Might I ask, then, why you were so nervous on the evening of July 23rd at the nurse's station so as to need bicarbonate of soda?"

Polly knew she had to be cautious or Harmon would trap her in her own words. "I was all alone. I . . . don't really like the dark. And since the nurse was gone, I wasn't confident I would know what to do if a camper came who was really ill."

"A logical answer," Harmon said, nodding. "But I suspect not entirely truthful. As camp staff, didn't you have backup if you were to need help?"

Polly paused, trying to figure out what he was getting at. "Well . . . at any hour staff at the camp can call on Mother Superior."

"That's right," Harmon said triumphantly. "With Mother Superior nearby, perhaps there was another reason for your nerves? Let's try a little harder." Hands clasped behind his back, Attorney Harmon had the advantage of a powerful tiger playing with its prey before sinking its fangs in.

"I don't know what you mean," Polly said in a small voice. Out of the corner of her eye, she saw Freddie grinning wickedly.

Harmon continued. "Is it possible that you were nervous because you knew Freddie was coming?"

Polly shook her head. "No, sir. I wasn't expecting anyone, which is why I was in my nightgown."

"Was Freddie's coming to you on the night of July 23rd your first encounter with him?" Harmon asked. "Or, is it possible you had already established a relationship with this handsome, talented swim instructor at the Catholic Youth Organization camp?"

"Objection!" Fosterfal called. "Leading the witness, and the description of Mister Coleman is a matter of opinion, extraneous detail."

"Keep to the facts, Attorney Harmon," Judge Smathers instructed.

Polly now knew the attorney was fishing to uncover her bid for Freddie's attention at the grange dance.

"I knew of him, yes," Polly answered. "It's a small camp."

"Oh, come, come. Spill the truth for us all to hear," Harmon said. "Who is the real Polly O'Mara playing dodgeball with the facts?"

Polly puffed her cheeks. "I told you, I knew of Freddie. That's all."

Harmon smiled knowingly. "But isn't it true, Miss O'Mara, that on the night of the July 5th parade, you styled as a hot number in your makeup, flowing trusses, and tight outfit to get Freddie's attention on the dance floor at the grange hall?"

Fosterfal jumped up. "I object to this inappropriate description of my witness."

Judge Smathers said in a monotone, "Overruled. Answer the question, Miss O'Mara."

Polly was trapped. The cat was out of the bag now—Harmon had blown her cover. She had sworn to tell the truth. "I went . . . to the grange dance, yes. But . . . I didn't go intending to dance with Freddie. It just sort of . . . happened."

"I see." Harmon looked satisfied as he stood in front of the rail before her. "Isn't it also a fact that Mister Coleman was kind enough to drive you home after the dance so that you wouldn't get soaked in the rain?"

"He did, yes," Polly answered.

Freddie let out a harsh laugh. Her parents gasped.

Polly stated firmly, "But it didn't take long for me to see the huge mistake I'd made. Before the ride home, Freddie tore my brand new jacket off and used it as a rag to sop up the water in his car! Even though I told him no. He was very angry. I realized he's a jerk and . . . dangerous." She glared at Freddie who continued to grin.

"So then . . . in *fear* of Freddie, back at the camp on July 23rd you purposely let word slip through your friends that Dot Stone, the camp nurse, would be away for the evening?"

Polly was getting peeved as Harmon pelted her with each question. She sniffed. "I had no friends at CYO camp!"

The onlookers chuckled at that, but she didn't let them phase her.

"I did not tell a soul that I would be alone. I barely spoke to any of the camp staff all summer. I knew only the kids."

Harmon nodded. "Still skating around the truth I see. And yet Freddie seemed to somehow know you were alone, since he brought wine. And you put on a skimpy nightie expecting that your robe would be suitable cover for a night visitor?"

Attorney Fosterfal jumped to his feet. "This line of reasoning is preposterous. She already stated it was a hot and muggy evening!"

Judge Smathers warned: “Would the defense please make a logical point to your ramblings?”

“Most definitely, your Honor.” Attorney Harmon looked smugly out over the gallery and then fixed his eye on Polly. “The point is, Miss O’Mara intentionally and successfully gained the attention of Freddie Coleman at the grange dance on July 5th. But he was not the sort of guy she had hoped for, or there was some disagreement between them. So to put an end to her perceived error, she accused Freddie of the crime against Maria Styles, conveniently removing him from the camp staff and potentially from town if he got jail time.”

Before Polly could react, Harmon looked at the clock and suddenly announced, “The defense has finished with the witness.”

Judge Smathers banged his gavel: “Court is adjourned until ten o’clock tomorrow morning.”

It was obvious to Polly that Harmon had timed his last statement so that Judge Smathers would go home with the thought that she had lied for a selfish purpose and that Freddie Coleman was innocent.

The ride home from Rutland was quiet. Polly ached from her botched testimony and she knew her folks were disgusted over her actions.

Finally her father spoke. “Polly, I’m terribly disappointed with this day. The words you shared that Freddie said were . . . disturbing, to say the least. But I realize your mother and I have taught you that honesty usually wins out, so you did what you thought was right. I pushed hard for this case to happen, but if I read the atmosphere at the end of the hearing, we don’t have a case. Attorney Harmon has made sure that Smathers and Fosterfal have been shaken in trusting as fact anything you might say. Why didn’t you tell us about the grange dance?”

Polly started crying. “I’m sorry, Daddy.”

Her mother wasn’t ready to so easily forgive. “Polly, I never knew such a dishonest streak ran through you, and those nasty words will forever ring in my ears.”

Hearing her mother’s judgment, Polly burned with the injustice of it, as well as Harmon’s treatment. All she had done was dance a few dances with a good-looking guy at a public place. Freddie *did* say those terrible things at the nurse's station and he threatened her. By his own confession, he was the one who raped Maria. "Mom, don't act so Simon pure," she retorted. "At least I haven't repeated what *you* did in your teenage years."

"You will not speak ill of your mother," her father declared. "You've done enough for one day."

Her mother crossed her arms and looked out the passenger window. Polly knew she was furious. The fields ticked by with the car's interior choked with uncomfortable silence. Finally her father spoke.

"Look, there's one more angle to try. I believe Lizzy LaFlam would do well on the stand against Harmon."

"Lizzy LaFlam? You can't mean it!" Polly exclaimed. To add further insult to her day, Polly had about had it with Lizzy showing up as better than her.

"I do." Her father said. "The more I think about it, I like the idea. The girl's got pluck."

Polly wasn't surprised by her father's attitude towards Lizzy. Everybody loved Lizzy, admiring the girl's abilities and what she'd accomplished at such a young age in bringing the IGA store back to life. But now there was a persistent rumor that Lizzy had been giving Slag Perkins a lot of attention. Even Polly knew better than that—Slag was a rough character. In contrast, Polly saw Jubal as a first rate guy, though she often fought like fury with him. Slag over Jubal? Lizzy had to be crazy when it came to picking a man. And Polly could only imagine what Harmon would drag up about Lizzy's past to demolish her on the witness stand.

Chapter Forty-Two

Being asked to testify against Freddie Coleman in regards to Maria's case didn't phase Lizzy. She would gladly nail the slimeball. Considering the torment Freddie had caused Maria, not to mention his crude confession to Polly, well, it was past time to bring Mister Pugnose to justice. Time and again, Lizzy had witnessed Maria's struggles in the deep of night as her friend awoke from nightmares when staying over after Mass. Nobody in town could truly understand the damage done. Lizzy was more than ready to set fire to Freddie's defense and whatever lies he might cook up.

For her courthouse appearance, Lizzy dressed professionally in navy blue slacks and a white blouse, pinning her straight, black hair with a red bow. Riding to Rutland in the early morning light, she sat in the back seat of the O'Mara's Buick next to Polly—a test of endurance. Polly whined continually over her belly problems, worrying over what Freddie might do to her now that she'd testified against him. Lizzy felt that the best solution was to castrate the creep. Granted, the solution wasn't practical, but there was a certain joy in imagining what a sharp knife could do. This idea got a laugh out of Polly, but Trudy was a different matter. Polly's prim mother didn't think such talk was funny.

After arriving at the courthouse, they were shown to the upstairs waiting room where Lizzy met with Attorney Fosterfal to review her story. Lizzy could connect the scent on Maria as she was brought out of the rectory to Freddie's cologne when he came to the IGA. And Freddie's questionable character would be shown by his grabbing her butt in the aisle. Put together with Polly's testimony, Fosterfal believed there was enough evidence for a guilty verdict. The session was about to begin, so the O'Maras and the attorney went down to the courtroom to take their places. It was not long before it was time for Lizzy to testify. She followed an older, neatly dressed woman downstairs and when they entered the gallery, Attorney Fosterfal stood.

"I call Lizzy LaFlam to the stand," he announced.

Like Polly had done two days earlier, Lizzy swore an oath on the Bible to tell the truth, a statement she took seriously considering her new dedication to God's work. Fosterfal came to the railing and cleared his throat.

"Now, Miss LaFlam," he said, "please tell the court how you know the defendant, Freddie Coleman."

Lizzy glared down at Freddie seated at the defense table. She had rehearsed her story many times. "Yes, sir. Durin' the July 5th parade, I was offerin' a free ice cream cone fer all who came ta the store. We gave away nearly five gallons a' vanilla ice cream, keepin' it cold with a tub full a' ice chunks. After the festivities was over, I brought some ice cream ta the rectory, seein' as Father Mac and the sheriff had been busy with the parade."

Fosterfal nodded. "Yes, go on."

"When I got ta the rectory, I noticed St. Anne's Cadillac backed up close ta the door. Then I saw Father Mac and the sheriff helpin' the Rose Queen down the stairs. That was Maria, ya know. As they put her inta the back seat, it was clear she was all beat up. Her gown was torn, face a mess, and her lip cut. I held that box a' ice cream meltin' and trinklin' down my hands. I didn't know if what I was seein' was real, like when ya see somethin' ya don't expect, or when ya're in a bad dream."

"Just stick to the facts, Miss LaFlam," Fosterfal instructed.

"Sure thing. Well, that's when I was overtaken by this sickly, sweet smell comin' from Maria. It was enough ta knock over a honey bee dead."

The observers in the gallery chuckled, prompting Judge Smathers to tap his gavel.

Lizzy continued. "Seein' as Father Mac and Tatum had a problem ta deal with, they didn't want the ice cream, so I brought it inside ta the fridge 'fore it was a puddle a' nothin'. Walkin' back ta the store, I was sure shaken up over what I'd seen. Somebody had nearly killed Maria—a lowdown deed ta a gal who wouldn't hurt a fly."

"Facts only," Fosterfal reminded again.

"Back in the store, ta take my mind off Maria, I set ta cleanin' up the mess left after the crowd had stormed the place—"

Attorney Harmon interrupted. "Objection, your Honor! Can the witness get to the point? I see no relevance to this information."

Lizzy gave Harmon a dirty look. "The *point is,* I was bent over cleanin' in the grocery aisle when this stranger—that smug guy sittin' right next ta ya there—came up silently behind me and he felt up my butt."

"My goodness!" Polly's mother exclaimed.

There was a murmur from the gallery.

"That's right," Lizzy looked down at Polly's mom. "I near screamed in surprise. I had the presence a' mind ta tell the jerk ta back off. But he just stood in my face laughin' in his slick, tan suit."

"So, this guy you had never laid eyes on before came into your store and put his hand on your, um, rear end? And you corrected him?" Fosterfal said.

"Yes, sir," Lizzy said.

"Then what happened?"

"That's when it hit me. That sweet smell again, same as was on Maria, now floatin' out from Freddie like a skunk on the run." Lizzy paused, remembering the moment of realization. For emphasis she turned towards Judge Smathers who was listening with rapt attention. "My blood 'bout drained down ta my toes, instantly knowin' Freddie was the creep that had just almost killed Maria Styles."

"Are you *positive* it was the same smell?" Fosterfal asked.

"Damn sure," Lizzy said. She glanced at the judge again. "Sorry, yer Honor. That stink is unmistakable."

"I see," Fosterfal nodded.

Lizzy noticed a sheen had appeared on Fosterfal's brow as her testimony unfolded in the prosecution's favor. "Ya won't believe what came next. Standin' right there in the aisle, Freddie Coleman had the gall ta ask me ta the grange dance that was ta be held that night. When I told him I weren't interested, he turned and walked away with an evil laugh. 'See ya around Pocahontas,' he said. I tell ya, I felt like Satan himself had just paid me a visit."

Harmon leapt to his feet. "Objection!"

Judge Smathers looked down at the court stenographer. "Strike that last line."

"Miss LaFlam," Fosterfal said. "Can you tell the court anything else that might shed light on this case?"

Lizzy nodded. "Over the summer, Maria and I got ta be good friends. We went fer wagon rides over ta the reservoir. Sometimes she stays over with me in my room down ta the store."

"How nice," Harmon spoke up. "Irrelevant."

Judge Smathers glared down at Harmon. "I'll thank you not to speak out of turn, Attorney. Continue, Miss LaFlam."

Harmon looked sour.

"Well, Maria told me how one day at CYO camp Freddie chased her through the woods wearin' nothin' but swim trunks coverin' less a' him than a pair a' worn-out underwear."

"Oh dear!" Trudy commented from the gallery.

"Maria was terrified," Lizzy said. "Feelin' like she was runnin' fer her life. Got ta the safety of her cabin, but Freddie pulled her cabin door right off the buildin'."

"Objection!" Harmon said. "This story is nothing but hearsay."

Judge Smathers sighed. "Sustained. I'm sorry Miss LaFlam, if you weren't a firsthand witness, it's not admissible evidence."

"But Maria ain't here ta tell her—" Lizzy tried.

"The judge is correct, I'm afraid," Fosterfal said. "I have no further questions. Thank you, Miss LaFlam."

It wasn't fair, them not wanting to hear the important details of Freddie's chase, but at least Attorney Fosterfal was done with his questions. Lizzy was glad to leave out the part about going over to the sheriff's office after Freddie's visit. She didn't want any attention on her brothers for being Tatum's main suspects that day. Wild as they were, she was positive her brothers had nothing to do with Maria's rape. No sense in dragging them through the court.

She looked around, wondering where Tatum was and why he wasn't at the hearing in his uniform standing all puffed up like a rooster.

Attorney Harmon stood. "If it would please the court, I'd like to cross-examine the witness."

"Permission granted," Judge Smathers replied.

Lizzy had sized up the defense attorney. He looked sharp, but she was ready for him.

"Miss LaFlam," Harmon began, "did you watch any of the parade that day?"

"Seein' as I was tendin' the store, not much. The little I was able ta poke my nose out the door, I saw a big yellow cat followin' a little kid holdin' an American flag."

"What else did you see?"

"On a break, I spotted Avery Ketchum's Morgan team 'bout ta bust free. Jubal Brown was holdin' the beasts with reins tighter than a banjo string. I had ta get back ta scoopin' ice cream and missed the rest a' the drama. But I was bettin' them nervous horses were gonna tip over the buggy and dump Avery and Miss Curry inta the road."

Attorney Harmon came to the rail and looked up at her intently. "Miss LaFlam, did you see who spooked the horses?"

Lizzy knew her brothers were the cause. They were lawless boys. Folks stepped aside from them when they came to town. But her brothers' actions were a distraction from the matter of Freddie, the real culprit, so she sidestepped Harmon's question.

"I didn't really see," she shrugged. "I saw a mob a' kids down by the statue. I assume it was them."

Harmon frowned. "Let me try this another way. It's well known around town that the Rose Queen threw her bouquet that day, disgracing herself and the church—"

"Objection!" Fosterfal called. "The witness has stated she didn't see anything further. And the judgement about Maria Styles has no place—"

Judge Smathers rapped his gavel hard. "Overruled! Continue, Attorney Harmon."

Harmon looked pleased. "Thank you, your Honor. Miss LaFlam, since you are apparently her friend, I am sure you know why Maria Styles threw those roses. Who, specifically, was taunting her?"

Lizzy hesitated. She knew the accusation against her own flesh and blood would discredit her. But she'd sworn to tell the truth. "My brothers."

Harmon pounced. "Yes! Your brothers who have juvenile records as long as my arm. After spooking the horses and being rude to the Rose Queen, it follows that your brothers then snuck into the rectory after Maria Styles where they beat her up and raped her. Isn't this true, Miss LaFlam?"

Lizzy fixed the attorney with her meanest stare, the one she'd given Big Daddy when he came at her with his hand raised to smack her. "As a big, smart lawyer, ya know perfectly well none a' that's true. Ya're bendin' them facts to suit Freddie Coleman so ya can get the scoundrel off the hook."

"Young lady, I remind you to address Attorney Harmon with respect," Judge Smathers warned.

"Respect?" Lizzy whirled on the judge. "Ya wanna talk 'bout respect? This attorney here is dishin' up lies! Maria's attacker needs ta be brought ta justice! If ya don't lock Freddie Coleman up, he'll be punchin' another girl 'fore long and crawlin' all over her ta get his thrills."

Lizzy heard a gasp from the onlookers. She turned to see Polly looking up from the gallery with her mouth shaped in a round O. Judge Smathers rapped his gavel sharply three times. Lizzy wished he'd stop, as the noise was jangling her nerves.

The older judge looked down at her in exasperation. "What is it with the young women of Hayesville that they speak so indecently in my courtroom? Watch yourself!"

Freddie smirked in his chair.

"Now, Miss LaFlam . . ." Harmon intervened. "It's understandable that you are protecting your family. However, Freddie Coleman's statement to the sheriff explains that Freddie was at the rectory after the parade helping Father Mac to carry water pitchers in from the stands. He says he heard a noise upstairs and came to Maria Styles' rescue. But it was too late. When he helped her to sit up, he left behind the sweet smell of cologne you've noted. He then went to get Father Mac, who got the sheriff." Harmon did an about-face. "I have no further questions for this witness."

Judge Smathers looked wearily down at Fosterfal. "Does the prosecution have any further remarks?"

"No, your Honor," Fosterfal said in a defeated tone.

"You may step down now, Miss LaFlam," Judge Smathers said, looking relieved.

Lizzy took a seat in the gallery not far from the O'Maras. Mister O'Mara turned and gave her a look of sympathy. Polly appeared more tense than ever.

Next, Attorney Fosterfal presented the letters from Father Mac and Tatum. Father Mac's letter first noted Maria's disruptive behavior in throwing the roses at the parade.

"What in heck's that got ta do with bein' raped?" Lizzy muttered. But she was glad the priest, as a supposed witness for the prosecution, made no specific mention of her brothers, only calling the boys at the statue "a group of ruffians." Other than that, the letter simply detailed finding Maria in the rectory. Lizzy noted that nothing was said of the cologne smell on Maria. Lizzy's eyes narrowed. Father Mac had offered no evidence against Freddie. A useless witness.

Tatum's letter was even less helpful. It was quite short, first describing Maria's condition when they found her. Next, the letter mentioned his suspicions of Lizzy's "half-breed" brothers. Lizzy's anger rose. For that, the sheriff had no evidence and a hell of a nerve. He left out the incident at Maria's cabin, a scene, which she knew from Maria, that Tatum had interrupted.

The contents of the two letters stunk like dead fish on the shore of a pond. The priest and the sheriff had been careful to protect their buddy.

After Fosterfal handed the letters to the court stenographer, Freddie was called to the stand for the defense. He was the last to be questioned in the hearing. As Lizzy suspected, Freddie laid out a big pack of lies. He denied ever confessing the rape of Maria Styles to Polly. He did admit to the July 23rd visit to the nurse's station, but only for some headache medication. He was embarrassed to find Polly "prancing around practically in the nude." He had no intention of acting on her obvious invitation. After all, he was a thirty-year-old man, he said, and Polly was a mere child. At this, Lizzy turned to see Polly frown and lean to whisper to her father who nodded solemnly.

Attorney Fosterfal tried in his cross-examination to get Freddie to admit he was drunk since he carried a bottle of wine, but no, the wine acted only as a sedative for Freddie's migraine headache. Freddie was relaxed and confident on the stand, indicating to the casual observer that he was telling the truth.

When Freddie was finished, Judge Smathers announced, "The court will adjourn until one o'clock for a verdict. Will the attorneys please come to my chambers?"

Promptly at one o'clock, Fosterfal and Harmon returned, followed by Freddie. Judge Smathers took his seat and announced from his perch that he was throwing the case out on grounds of insufficient evidence. Since Polly was a minor and not the victim, he explained, her hearsay testimony was of dubious value. Lizzy LaFlam's testimony, while impressive, was also compromised due to her brothers' involvement. However, Freddie Coleman's attorney had agreed in the judge's chambers to certain terms—the defendant was not allowed to return as swimming instructor and lifeguard at the CYO camp. The judge had determined Freddie's character to be questionable, especially in grabbing Lizzy's behind and having wine at a camp for children.

Lizzy was furious as the security guard unlocked Freddie's cuffs. The guy left the courtroom grinning like a cat that just swallowed a country mouse. She and Polly exchanged looks of dismay. Lizzy knew Polly's fears of Freddie's retaliation were tying the girl's gut in a knot. One consolation was that without his summer job and in the face of lingering distrust from folks in town, Freddie would maybe leave Vermont and not return. As for her own worries, Lizzy figured she'd best sleep with a sharp butcher knife under her pillow until there was sufficient proof that Freddie had slithered far from Hayesville like the lowdown snake he truly was.

⁜

Bernice didn't like the fact that Lizzy was serving a special Sunday meal to the riffraff in town. Such charity was more properly the duty of the Temperance League. Still, Bernice couldn't resist checking out the affair. She stood in Lizzy's makeshift office at the store peering through a window to watch the activity out back. She was shocked by what she saw and just had to report her findings to Bert.

It was an unusually warm afternoon for early November, and Bert was sleeping peacefully on his hammock which hung from their front porch. He always waited until the very last minute before winter to take his hammock down, a point that bothered Bernice as it was out of keeping with her fall harvest decorations. Since the hammock was his favorite place to nap, there was no convincing him to take the thing down in September like an ordinary person.

"Bert! Bert, are you awake?" Bernice sat at the edge of the porch railing next to the hammock.

Bert opened one eye. "I'm napping. What do you want?"

"I've just come from next door. Lizzy is now turning our IGA into a low-grade restaurant!"

"Don't worry." Bert waved her off with a flop of his hand. "She won't let things get out of control over there." He closed his eyes.

"Bert, you don't understand!" She tapped him on the shoulder. "That grease-monkey friend of Lizzy's has turned the store's yard into a junk pile.

He's brought over old car seats and he has nail kegs set on tire rims for extra chairs!" Bernice squinted in the direction of the store as laughter trickled across the way. "What on earth would Emily Post think?"

"Who in tarnation is Emily Post?"

"Oh Bert, you're such a clod. You know . . . she's the authority on proper manners and etiquette. She'd faint in her ruffles if she saw what's going on. Charlie Jones, with that awful hat he wears, was talking with a mouthful and slouched over the table. Goodness, he has the worst set of teeth, and the iced tea mixed with roast turkey as he talked . . ." Bernice grimaced. She shook Bert's arm as he dozed off.

He opened his eyes again. "Yeah, Emily Post. Go on," he said.

"Of course, there was Clem with his common-law wife, Millie. She's a pathetic sight. I'm surprised she has enough strength to make it to town. Looked like she had on a bag for a dress, sitting there with that sucked-in face, eyes looking a fright as if she'd just met a ghost in a blind alley. And then Oscar, who can hardly find his mouth with a spoon, drooling like a baby cutting teeth."

Bert was now fully awake. "Well, Jubal was probably there."

"Heavens no! He's disappeared now that Slag Perkins is lurking around."

Bert adjusted his position, rolling onto his side. He plumped up the little pillow he kept on his hammock. "Bernice, let it go . . . just let it go."

"Let it go? Why that girl has lost her head over the real meaning of Christianity. I knew it would be trouble when Lizzy was led to the Catholic church by Maria Styles. Tell me, what is the point of feeding the deadbeats in town in such a fashion? The Lord helps those who help themselves."

"Bernice, do you hear yourself?" Bert rubbed his chin and then his eyes. "You sound about as un-Christian as ever I heard a body."

Bernice paced the porch, her plain black pumps sounding a *"pock, pock"* on the wooden boards. "Respectable work is what's godly. That much is clear. It's . . . it's not even a holiday and Lizzy has freely given out a fancy meal." She stopped by the hammock and leaned down to Bert's ear. "I'll tell you another thing. I say it's time we take charge of our store again and send Lizzy packing back to LaFlam Mountain where she belongs. She can take her grease monkey with her and see what her backwoods father thinks of that."

Bert sat up in shock, nearly falling out of the hammock. "You forget 'our store' belongs to Lois Lamont—not Lizzy. Lady Lamont's money has brought the place up to a high standard. Bernice, we've never had it so good."

Bernice folded her arms. Her husband missed the point most of the time. No matter, she was used to it. "Maybe Lady Lamont holds the purse strings of the store, but I still say we need to put things right."

"I thought you had come around to liking Lizzy. And haven't you noticed how Slag has cleaned himself up? Lizzy's done him a world of wonder." Bert settled back into his hammock on his other side with his back to Bernice. "Slag's found a soft spot in Lizzy's heart."

Bernice sat on the railing again. "Well, I assumed Lizzy would never leave Jubal." She looked over towards the store. "I don't know what's worse—the stink of a cow barn or the smell of an oil-stained mechanic."

Bert turned his head her way. "Can I please get some shut-eye?"

The conversation was over and Bernice knew Bert was right. Nothing was to be done. Lady Lamont now owned the store. Lizzy was her proxy. And Bernice was stuck slicing and grinding meat in the deli. Which reminded Bernice that she needed to get ready for Monday's customers by making up some of her special hamburg. In doing so, she could observe Lizzy's luncheon from a closer vantage point back at the store.

Bernice had been mixing a small portion of pork sausage with the hamburg she prepared and "Bernice Sausville's Blend" had become a popular item. Folks had never tasted hamburger so flavorful, but Bernice tightly held her secret. However, Lizzy had recently commented that they were selling an awful lot of the more expensive sausage. Bernice didn't care that the store was losing money due to her mix, selling it below cost with the secretly-added sausage. Let the lady up in her mansion lose a little. It wouldn't matter. Bernice liked the customers' attention.

Sometimes, though, she wished she and Bert could break free of the store. Another thorn in her side was watching the beer and wine carried out the door. She had often complained to Bert, "My days with the Temperance League have been lost on this town, especially the Catholics. Lord, you should see the wine Trudy O'Mara takes out of the IGA in a week's time. She and Andrew must party every night. If I ran the store, I would put a stop to the sale of liquor."

"Good luck with that!" Bert had said. "The selectmen signed permission for the store to sell spirituous beverages. Besides, the store enjoys a good profit margin on alcohol."

When Bernice returned to the IGA, there were no customers inside. However, loud talking and laughter came from the tattered seats out back arrayed around the makeshift table. She looked through the little window in Lizzy's office. There was Lizzy holding court like a queen, wearing a pretty flowered blouse and neat, black slacks. Maria Styles sat nearby with Clem Gochy on a beige car seat of torn leather. Perched on a nail keg, Slag looked on with a silly grin—the scar on his face was red even from a distance. Lizzy was now cutting up thick pieces of chocolate cake. Bernice's mouth watered, but she was not going to join in.

Behind the meat counter, Bernice broke out a big hunk of cloth-covered sausage. "Profit margins," she mused as she worked, thinking back on what Bert had said. "Lady Lamont sits up there in that big house on the hill, smoking from her cigarette holder and coughing up a storm, telling Lizzy what's what about the business of running a store. Like it or not, we're in cahoots with the Devil."

She could almost hear Bert scolding her: "But remember who signs our paychecks."

Bernice fed a fat chunk of beef into the grinder and mixed the hamburg with a bigger portion than usual of the sausage. "Here's to Harmony Hill's heiress."

Chapter Forty-Three

When Maria heard about the outcome of Freddie's court hearing, her insides twisted up like a hard-wrung dishrag. She'd been forsaken. Her mother was deeply concerned that the guy had been set free, and she said most in town were disgusted over the verdict. Lizzy was furious that her testimony had failed to convince the judge. It was reported, also, that the O'Maras were keeping Polly under close watch, worried about Freddie's threat of retaliation.

Since justice had not been served, more counseling was now needed from Father Hebert for Maria to maintain her belief that regardless of what she'd done, Freddie was in the wrong. Even so, she prayed every night to be forgiven for the lies she had told at camp. She hoped Freddie's miserable weeks locked up in Windsor prison, keeping company with the rats in a cold cell, had at least been a partial punishment for his nasty deed.

Not surprisingly, sleep did not come for Maria on many nights. She feared Freddie would seek her out to finish her off. It was only when she slept at Lizzy's that she felt safe, thanks to the wire-caged room and the long butcher knife that Lizzy had stashed close by her bed. In their cots, the two would talk about anything but the trial—horses, daily events at the store, or the latest homily at Mass. Eventually Lizzy would climb under the blankets of Maria's cot and hug her to a sound sleep.

One morning after Maria dragged herself wearily through the chores, Rose invited her for coffee in the Browns' kitchen. Jubal's ma poured two cups of steaming black coffee, offering Maria fresh milk and a spoonful of sugar. Rose sat down at the table across from her and began to share the details of her rape all those years ago. Maria listened intently. She had heard the rumors and always knew something was amiss with Jubal's birth. Now she knew the full story. She couldn't imagine how Rose had carried on and held her head up after that, especially with all the guys living in town as if nothing had happened. Rose demonstrated a strength that Maria found inspirational.

"You might eventually get to a point," Rose counseled, "where the rape is the least important thing about you. In other words, Maria, you will learn to shape who you are and who you want to be. What Freddie did will no longer hold power over you."

With Rose's words, Maria felt a kinship now, an almost sisterhood with Jubal's ma, who knew firsthand the sense of violation and understood the cause of her devastation. Rose showed a vision that someday Maria could move beyond her fear, anger, and shame.

Maria also daily sent up a prayer for Trueboy—an unbelievable comfort found in a horse. He had carried her through the worst of times, even saved her life the night she'd almost cut her wrists. She often questioned whether he'd sensed that she was about to end it all, banging his hoof as if pleading for her not to leave him. Regardless of whether it was by chance or there was a deep connection driving Trueboy's action, that ride in the middle of the night had been a turning point, giving Maria courage to see another day.

Lastly there was Jubal, a steadfast friend. With Miss Curry's help, he had uncovered the surprise of Father Mac's corrupted name and fake identity. This news had torn the parish in two between the devout and those that weren't so devout. The fact that St. Anne's priest had been a fraud matched Maria's instinct all along that Father Mac was a creep. This was an important consolation, for Maria was struggling to regain trust in herself that she could read a person and make better choices. But until such time as she felt confident again, she found it best to avoid most people. However, in typical fashion, it was not long before Lizzy came up with a plan to try and cheer her up.

"I want ta bring some joy ta this place," Lizzy declared when she broke the news to Maria. "November's so dark and gloomy. And what with possible war comin' and yer attacker gettin' off scott free, seems the bad news drapes over this town like a soggy blanket."

Lizzy then shared that she'd gotten approval from Lady Lamont to hold an IGA store "Appreciation Night" to thank their loyal customers. Lizzy would rent the town hall for the event and everyone would be invited. A short distance down the street from St. Anne's, the town hall was seldom used for any purpose other than for town meeting on the first Tuesday in March. The interior had a stage and seating for about two hundred people. The celebration was to be on Saturday evening, the twenty-second of November.

One night as they lay on the cots in Lizzy's room after Mass, Lizzy excitedly laid out the details. Apple cider and donuts were to be offered as refreshments for the festivities, and the Chanticleer from WGY's morning show would act as MC. He had agreed to bring along a vocalist out of Albany named Betty Sweet to sing a few popular tunes. The night would also feature Slag dancing a variety of numbers with Jazz on the clarinet. A free ticket from the store would be collected at the town hall door for admission and a ticket drawing was to be held during the show. The lucky winner would receive a cartload of groceries featuring Bernice Sausville's popular hamburger blend. Lizzy was including Bernice's hamburger in a wise move to get the difficult woman to support the event.

The amount of planning involved and the size of the event made Maria's head spin. Since the trial, she'd kept to the Browns' barn and the peaceful company of animals unless she was at church or with Lizzy. However, Maria vowed to try her best to get in the spirit so as not to hurt her friend's feelings.

Lady Lamont, apparently, had asked Rose to make all the cider donuts. The store would provide the necessary ingredients such as eggs, flour, sugar, lard, and nutmeg. But Rose would need help.

"Do me a favor, Maria?" Lizzy asked. "Would ya help Rose out with the donuts? We got a lot a' folks already gettin' tickets so we're gonna need a lot. With the Chanticleer hostin' and that singer comin,' I don't believe I've had a single person say no."

Maria agreed, figuring that cooking would be an easy way to support Lizzy's efforts. Yet, Rose was dubious about the donut-making venture.

"This is going to mean a huge amount of donuts. Seriously, a full day's work," Rose sighed one morning when Maria was helping her clean up after breakfast. Jubal and Benny had already headed back out to finish up at the barn.

"Maybe we could get Jubal to help and make it go faster?" Maria suggested.

Rose laughed. "Possibly, but he'd better get cleaned up. We don't want any trace of barn in our cooking."

Maria smiled in response. Maybe Lizzy was right. Now there was a task to keep her mind off things. Not much was happening on the Brown farm with the fields all lying in wait for spring, so once morning chores were done, Maria had lately been at a loss for what to do with herself. Working alongside Rose on the donuts might be a nice way to spend some of her extra time.

Typical of autumn in Vermont, the weather changed abruptly. By mid-November, Harmony Hill had a light dusting of snow overnight—the trees and open meadows were as if sprinkled with powdered sugar. Maria rode in the woody with Rose to pick up the donut ingredients down at the store. The morning sun had melted most of the snow in the yard, but there was still a strip of white in the center of the road as they traveled towards town. Before leaving, Maria had seen how Rose refilled Clyde's coffee cup where he sat in his chair by the Philco. It was a moment of tenderness between the two that Maria had lately observed more and more.

"It's good to see Clyde feeling better these days," Maria commented as they drove.

"Yes." Rose's face softened with a look of affection. "He helps out what little he can. It sure lifts a load of worry for me that he's finally free of the bottle."

Maria considered how Jubal's ma had carried such burdens on her shoulders for many years. Clyde's improved health, along with the farm's doing better on milk production, likely brought Rose some peace of mind.

Nearing the IGA, they saw Bert out in front sweeping snow off the sidewalk.

"Morning ladies." Bert stopped sweeping. "Lizzy has set aside just what you folks are after."

Rose replied as she passed, "It won't be long, Bert, and you'll have to shovel what you sweep today."

"Yeah, don't remind me." Bert tapped the snow off his broom and continued his chore. "A long winter—that's one thing we can depend on."

Inside the store, Lizzy bustled over with a big box of supplies, placing it in Maria's outstretched arms. Maria's arms sagged with the weight.

"Hold on," Lizzy said. "I've got another and a bunch a' empty boxes."

The second armload of ingredients she gave to Rose.

"You're certainly keeping us busy this week, Lizzy," Rose said.

"That's right. Thinkin' ya don't have enough ta do up there on the hill," Lizzy teased.

"Well, I sure hope my donuts live up to the expectation," Rose replied good-naturedly.

"Not ta worry," Lizzy said, grinning. "Folks in town will gobble 'em up like Thanksgivin' turkeys eatin' their last meal."

Maria marveled at how much Lizzy now seemed to enjoy organizing and planning social events for the benefit of others. Her friend had really come into her own since leaving her unfortunate home life just that past spring.

Returning from the store, Maria and Rose lugged the boxes to the kitchen and began unpacking bags of flour and sugar, nutmeg, and lard. Maria arranged it all on the counter while Rose retrieved some more empty boxes for the donuts. Before long, Jubal came in from the barn.

"Hey," Maria called. "How about helping us with this big job of making donuts?"

"Who me?" Jubal glanced back towards the door as if wishing he hadn't come inside.

"Yeah, you don't seem terribly rushed to do anything important," Maria said.

Looking doubtful, Jubal kicked off his barn boots in the entry and slid his feet into some sneakers. "For another one of Lizzy schemes? No thanks."

Maria was surprised. Usually Jubal was willing to help out whenever asked.

Jubal's ma broke in. "Lizzy's just trying to bring us a bit of fun. She means well."

Jubal went to the cupboard and reached for the cookie jar. Munching on a cookie, he turned to them. "Well, you know, since Lizzy and I've gone our separate ways, it's hard for me to get excited over anything she cooks up."

His ma sighed. "I suppose you need to do what feels best, Jubal." She turned to Maria. "I'd say it's about time to fire up the stove to heat the lard."

"Yeah, probably," Maria said. "I'm just about unloaded here." Maria worried that it was going to be hard now with her two best friends in a rift.

After getting the stove going, Rose surveyed the clutter of baking supplies all over the kitchen counter. "Good grief," she sighed. She turned to Jubal. "Are you sure you won't pitch in?"

Jubal reached for another cookie and sat down at the table. "I suppose so," he muttered. He took a bite and chewed before adding, "I guess my not helping you two isn't going to make old Scar Face disappear."

"Jubal!" Maria exclaimed. "Wasn't Slag your friend while you worked at Jazz's? You should know Slag is very nice to Lizzy. I mean, I'm sorry you lost out to him, but—"

Jubal waved her off. "Don't worry about me. Really, I'm over it."

His ma laughed. "It sure doesn't sound that way. It's okay to admit it hurts."

Jubal scowled. "Well, then. It hurts."

"I can bet it does," Maria said.

As Rose tended the fire, metal clanked when she lifted the stove griddles. Maria put on an apron and began by reading Rose's recipe. She then measured out the sugar and flour for a big batch of donuts. Next to her, Jubal stirred the ingredients in a large ceramic bowl. The stove heated up the room in no time, soon causing Maria to wipe sweat from her forehead. Jubal chuckled.

"What?" Maria said.

"You've just wiped some flour in your hair." Jubal grinned as he reached out to brush it off.

Suddenly they heard footsteps in the entry. Lizzy breezed into the kitchen. "Hey folks. Is this the donut capital of Hayesville?" Dressed in jeans and a t-shirt, Lizzy looked ready to work.

At the mixing bowl, Jubal groaned and Maria elbowed him to keep quiet.

Rose looked up from the stove. "Why hello, Lizzy. You're just in time."

"A bunch of us just finished cleanin' the town hall, and so now ta make the donuts," Lizzy said. "We should make at least two hundred so we have enough." She looked over at Jubal. "Hey there, Jubal. Appreciate ya helpin' us out in slingin' donut dough."

"Well, I guess it's better than slinging cow slop in the barn," Jubal said.

"Speaking of which," Rose said quickly, "did you wash up, Jubal?"

"Oh, right. Not yet," he said, and headed to the bathroom.

"Put something on besides those barn clothes," Rose called. She looked at the pot on the stove. "The lard's getting hot now. Seems we're ready. Let's test the batch you've started. Maria, you can roll out the dough." Rose put a donut cutter and spatula on the table. "Jubal can cut the donuts and then slide them into the hot lard. Lizzy, you keep the donuts turned with these tongs, okay? When they're medium brown, place them on that paper on the cool side of the range."

"Rose, ya sound like a real pro," Lizzy said.

"I've made a few donuts at the mansion over the years," Rose explained. "Lady Lamont likes them from time to time with her tea."

When Jubal returned, the team went to work in their assembly line, and soon Maria was staring down at the first donut frying in lard. She closed her eyes and sniffed the sweet, oily scent. "Mmm, smells like Ma's hot cross buns right out of the oven."

"Turn it with the tongs, Lizzy," Rose instructed, "just as it fries brown on the bottom side, so as to deep-fry the other side."

All four watched the first donut turn to the desired brown until Rose announced, "Now take it out, Lizzy, and let's let it cool. We'll taste it to see if we've got the ingredients in the right proportions."

They stood waiting.

Finally Rose said, "Go ahead, Jubal, try the first donut. It should be cool enough."

He took a bite. The donut easily crumbled. "Mmm." He mouthed it as if it were still hot and blew out a puff of air. "It's really good." He then broke pieces for his ma and Maria. As he passed a portion to Lizzy, he looked mischievous.

"You get the one with the dead fly in it," he said.

"Why thanks, Jubal, I could use the extra protein," Lizzy replied without missing a beat. She broke her donut piece apart and looked up. "There's no fly in here!"

Maria burst out a laugh as she set the floured rolling pin on top of another ball of dough. For the remainder of the afternoon, Maria flattened the dough, pushing and pulling the rolling pin in a repetitive rhythm. She was glad Jubal seemed to have set aside his differences with Lizzy, the two even continuing to joke with each other as they worked.

Occasionally, Rose lifted the griddle covers to add more sticks to keep the lard hot. The dry wood crackled in the firebox until the room grew warm, causing Jubal to open a window so that the cold, fresh air brought relief. Pulling the donuts from the lard, Lizzy placed the cooled ones in boxes lined with napkin paper. Soon the cool side of the stove held almost one hundred donuts.

At the end of the day, Maria announced, "This house smells like Rose Brown's donut factory."

All four flopped in chairs to enjoy a drink of iced tea.

"Gosh," Maria said, looking over at the stove. "Fifteen full candy boxes—what a pile of donuts we've turned out."

Lizzy surveyed the kitchen mess with a satisfied expression. "Yup, and look at Jubal all covered with flour. He looks like one big donut."

"Lizzy, you love to exaggerate," Jubal said. He glanced down at his front, which was indeed powdered white. "Time to change out of my baker's clothes and back into the clothes that smell like what I'm used to."

Jubal had agreed to take Maria on the morning after making donuts to pick up a barrel of sweet cider from a Champlain Valley orchard. He still wasn't overly enthused to go out of his way for Lizzy. He finally said yes because it would be an opportunity to take his first long drive in the woody.

Sometimes he missed the Packard, but the woody was proving itself as a practical car. Rolling along Route 7, the car's eight cylinders purred with little effort. The ride was also much smoother than the truck. From time to time, he stole a glance at Maria in the passenger seat. A rosy color had returned to her freckled cheeks, despite her occasional low moods. With all the work on his farm, she was as strong as any guy. She'd grown taller and her black, wavy hair was longer. In spring, she'd struck him as smart but not yet grown up. Now she was, quite simply, a country beauty. What he admired most, though, was that she seemed to have become even stronger on the inside.

Soon they reached the orchard's entrance in Shoreham, and after passing rows and rows of trees now bare of both leaves and apples, they found the warehouse. A big barrel of cider sat waiting on the platform with an invoice for the Hayesville IGA. After loading the barrel in the back of the woody, they started for home.

Maria's ma had packed a lunch for two, so Maria opened a brown paper bag to pass him an egg salad sandwich. He took a bite to find it loaded with mayo, celery, and dill.

"Mmm, this hits the spot," he commented. "I was starving."

Nodding, Maria reached across the front seat. "Here's a bottle of chocolate milk to wash it down."

With one hand on the wheel, he pulled over at a turnout. "Let's take some time so we can enjoy our lunch."

"Good idea. Wouldn't want you to smash up your new rig." Maria settled back as they came to a stop, and started her own sandwich.

For a time, the car was filled with the sound of chewing and wax paper rustling. One thing Jubal liked about Maria was that even if it was quiet between them, it was usually comfortable. Outside the passenger window, he noticed a stream below the turnout, almost hidden by the tangle of bushes along its banks.

Looking out at the woods beyond the stream, he commented, "The young maples and poplars are bare. Always thought this time of year was kind of dreary." He took a drink of his milk.

Maria looked out her window at the small ravine. "It is plain, but still pretty," she said. "Look at that wash of brown and red alongside the water. I always find this is a good time of year to think about things . . . to just . . . rest."

Jubal looked down through the woods and back at Maria's peaceful expression as she stared out at the trees. He'd never thought of November as a special time of year. "Well, anyway, it's a pleasant day for a drive. Even if it is for Lizzy's big shindig. I should have my head examined for helping her out after she dumped me."

Maria turned his way. "It's nice of you. And we get to spend time together." Her face reddened. "You know, without doing chores, or Benny's being around."

He nodded. "Gosh, we're together so much every day, we take each other for granted. Sometimes it feels like we're brother and sister."

"Do you think it will always be that way, like brother and sister?" Her face reddened again.

He paused. "Sometimes I . . . I don't realize how lucky I am. You always being there, a good friend."

She frowned. "Yeah, I'm like an old shoe."

"No . . . not like that," he said quietly. "You'll never be an old shoe to me."

Maria laughed. "Thanks! At least we have that much." She reached for the bag to put her crumpled wax paper in it.

They were on the road again with considerable time passing in silence until they entered Manchester and then continued towards Arlington.

Jubal thought about the coming winter. "Hey," he said. "Are you planning on going back to school after Christmas vacation?" Like him, Maria had taken the fall semester off, still in recovery. Father Hebert had talked with her parents about helping with her home studies if needed.

"Good grief," she grimaced. "School!"

"I have to go back. My ma insists." He smiled encouragingly. "Look, you could come to the farm as usual. We'll do chores and have some breakfast. Afterwards, we could head off to school together."

"I like the together part. At least with you there by my side maybe the other kids won't gawk at the fallen Rose Queen." Maria sighed. "Let me think about it. I'm still not sure if I'm ready to go back."

"Of course," he said. He could see how going back would open her up to more emotions. He turned on the radio and they listened to music all the way to Hayesville. They dropped off the cider at the town hall before traveling up the hill to do night chores.

When they pulled in the yard, Maria spoke up. "We should take a drive again sometime. I enjoyed that." She gathered up the trash from their lunch and held it in her lap.

He parked the woody near the barn and turned to her. Her wavy hair hung loose around her face and he especially noticed her vivid blue eyes. "I agree. We should do it more often," he said.

The two scrambled out of the car to break the moment. Jubal flicked on the barn lights and they went to work in their customary easy rhythm.

Chapter Forty-Four

When morning chores were finished at Jubal's, Maria bundled up in her winter coat, hat, and gloves and rode Trueboy down the hill to help Lizzy at the store. People from town were coming into the IGA in a steady stream for free tickets with Appreciation Night drawing near. They then seemed obliged to buy a few items. Lizzy was quite pleased with the uptick in business. Maria preferred to spend her time stocking shelves away from the hubbub, while Lizzy and Bert attended to customers and last minute details for the approaching event. As best she could, Maria stayed out of Bernice's way—the woman was a shrewd observer and critic of the folks who passed by her deli counter. At day's end, lulled by the sway of the big workhorse, Maria enjoyed her quiet ride home through the cold air. The houses along Main Street looked cozy with smoke spiraling from their chimneys, window lights aglow in the gray twilight.

But one night as Maria prepared to head for home, Lizzy stopped her to ask if she'd help collect tickets at the town hall door.

"Jubal has said he'll also help ta take the tickets," Lizzy explained. "So ya won't be standin' there all alone. I'm gonna be run ragged seein' ta all the refreshments and the stage schedule. Would ya mind?"

Though she'd agreed, Maria was dreading it. She couldn't think of a worse way to spend a couple of hours than making small talk with folks from town. At least Jubal was going to be there at her side.

Her ma, upon hearing the plan, thought it would be good for Maria to be a bit more social. "It's time ya got out more, Maria," her ma remarked. "Ya'll be needin' ta look presentable in a decent outfit. I'll not have my daughter greetin' the whole town in barn clothes," she said.

Maria looked down at her jeans which had spatters of mud on the bottom cuffs. She brushed off bits of hayseed. "My barn clothes are fine," she said. "They're comfortable." The last time she had dressed up fancy before the whole town, she'd been raped. She wondered why her mother couldn't see this. But her ma would not give in.

The next day, her mother carted her off to Rutland where they spent a torturous afternoon in several stores until an outfit was produced that satisfied Kathleen's sensibilities. Back at home as Maria modeled the dearly bought purchases after dinner, her father reassured her that she was lovely in the olive-green slacks, white sweater, and dark-green suit jacket. Maria had absolutely refused to wear a dress, hating to reveal the curves of her body. The worst part was her enhanced bosom showing from the new bra that her ma had insisted they buy. Maria had suffered the IGA bra at CYO camp only because she had to. Otherwise, she preferred her t-shirt method. When she had quit camp, she'd thrown the detested thing away, telling her mother that the strap broke.

She protested her ma in the Rutland store. "But the jacket will cover me." Her raised voice drew the attention of the store clerk behind the counter. Maria whispered, "I don't need the bra."

"I'll not have ya displayed at the door indecently," Kathleen had scolded in a loud voice. "Ya're almost an adult and should dress like one."

The store clerk smirked at the comment. Funny for her, Maria thought sourly as they carried the bag out of the store.

She kept quiet about her gravest fear—what if Freddie came strolling through the town hall door? Seemed no one had thought of that. She'd be like a deer caught in the cross hairs of a rifle.

Since the trial, Lizzy had been assuring her. "Don't ya worry. That creep has long since hightailed it outta Hayesville with his tail 'tween his legs. He knows better than ta show his face 'round here."

But Maria was not convinced.

Her flashbacks and nightmares intensified, with images of Freddie tugging at the door of her cabin, the screw of the eye bending and about to pull out from the wood. In her dreams, she held the handle, pulling back with all her strength. Just as the door broke and he was about to grab her, she'd wake with a start.

On the night of the Appreciation event, she went to Lizzy minutes before it was time to open the town hall doors.

"I—" She was fighting back tears. "I can't take tickets at the door."

Lizzy looked at her in sympathy. "Okay, then." She thought for a moment. "How 'bout ya fill them pitchers over there with cider from the spigot on the barrel? Then ya can fill the cups and place 'em on trays. That way ya'll be outta the way behind the counter."

Maria swallowed and nodded. "Sure, I can do that." Her racing heart slowed in relief.

"Good," Lizzy said. "Ya can do it 'til ya drain the barrel dry. Sorry, gotta run. Lots ta do." Lizzy rushed off.

With the problem solved, Maria took over for Slag who was adjusting the barrel spigot in the proper position. Slag handed over his white apron to cover her nice clothes. Relieved of his cider pouring duty, he offered to join Jubal in taking tickets at the door. This seemed a dubious plan to Maria who suspected there might still be bad feelings between the two guys. After Slag walked off, she quickly found Lizzy to let her know.

"Oh, goodness no," Lizzy said. She looked over at Jubal positioned by the door. "I don't want any hullabaloo breakin' out. This is supposed ta be a special time. I'm gonna get Slag ta help folks find their way ta a seat." She hurried to find Slag.

Willing to do anything for Lizzy, Slag soon took his position near the rows of chairs. Through the wide-open doors to the hall, Maria could see a crowd of people gathered. She shivered, thinking how it would have been to handle that line. She got right to work pouring cider, running the sweet, cinnamon-colored beverage into pitcher after pitcher. The plan was that once people were seated, a serving crew consisting of Bert, Bernice,

Clem, Rose, and Lizzy would pass out the cider and donuts. Soon warm from her activity, Maria took off her suit jacket and laid it on a shelf. She then put the apron on over her white sweater, glad that it covered the results of the new bra. Glancing over at the line, she searched the faces. If Freddie happened to show up, she could duck behind the counter and maybe sneak through the kitchen out the back door.

⁙

Jubal stood at the door of the town hall in the same suit he'd worn during the parade. It was, actually, the only suit he owned. He held a glass gallon jug with a slit in the cover for the tickets while Lizzy announced at the door, "We're seatin' folks with children first and those that have trouble gettin' 'round. So ya folks come on ahead."

Clyde, using his walking stick for support, was first through the door with Benny.

Jubal pointed to a couple of chairs in front of the stage. "Dad, you and Benny can sit in the front row so you can get a good look at the Chanticleer, since you've never seen him in person."

Clyde nodded. "Good deal." They slipped their tickets through the slot.

"You're looking just great all dressed up in your suit," Jubal said as Benny passed.

Benny's eyes were wide. "So many people!" He gave Jubal a worried look. "I think I wanna go home."

"Relax, Benny," Jubal said. "You'll like this. There's going to be singing!"

Benny forced a smile. "If ya say so, Jubal."

As Clyde and Benny moved towards the front of the hall, Jubal was glad his dad was able to come out to a public event without embarrassing himself in drunkenness. Close behind his dad, he met feeble Mister Kreb and his grandson Zig as they slipped their tickets in the slot.

Mister Kreb said, "I pencil-marked my ticket. I'm gonna win that hamburger Bernice Sausville makes."

Jubal smiled. "Good luck."

Zig grinned, showing his bad teeth. As they walked away, Jubal considered once again whether Zig could be his real dad.

While Jubal was pondering the possibility, several folks slipped by but made sure their tickets went in the jar. All Jubal saw was a rush of hands, not knowing who had passed, older folks or those with children.

Next, Henry Quinn hobbled forward on his bowed legs, helped by a family member who didn't look much better off.

"Well, well . . ." Henry squinted his cloudy eyes. His gray hair poked out in all directions from under his hunting cap. "This young man takin' our tickets has growed since bein' our paperboy." He stuffed his free ticket in the jar. "My old man once told me, 'Ya take anythin' that's free even if it's castor oil.'" He laughed just as the crowd pressed forward.

Miss Curry was next, wearing a pretty purple scarf and a black hat with a small red flower. Folks politely gave Miss Curry plenty of space. "My, Jubal, what a night! I must say, you look a little jostled by the crowd." She smiled in amusement, showing fresh pink lipstick.

"No kidding." He looked around the room. So many people he'd known all his life were crowding to get a seat, up front if possible. A loud hum of voices filled the hall and a line still streamed through the door. "I've never seen anything like this!" Though he'd been disappointed to learn that Maria had swapped to a different duty, he could understand now why she had balked.

"By the way," Miss Curry patted his arm. "Your paper on trauma looks very professional all typed up."

"Thanks, Miss Curry," he said.

She was quickly carried forward by the line.

"I'll be in to pick it up," he called, not quite sure if she heard him.

More hands slipped tickets in the slot.

Soon Jazz arrived with his grandchildren and daughter. He carried his clarinet in its case. "Well, Jubal, a little busy tonight. Just so ya know, Slag saved us seats up front since we're performin'." They moved on.

Howard Perkins wasn't far behind. "I'm hoping for a seat up front to get a good report for the paper."

Jubal surveyed the front of the room where folks were milling around. "Go on ahead, but good luck finding an empty chair."

Since Howard was after a story, he didn't care to enter the drawing. "I'll leave that tasty burger to someone who really needs it," he said.

Jubal nodded. His hands held the glass jar steady as folks pushed and shoved the container to find the slot for their tickets.

Avery Ketchum and Ned stepped forward. "Ya lettin' an old man and his sidekick through the door?"

"Sure," Jubal smiled. "Come on ahead."

Avery chuckled as he passed. "With this big line, your job looks harder than dealin' with a kickin' cow."

"That's about right," Jubal said.

Maria's parents were next through the door. As Chester put their two tickets in the jar, Kathleen scanned the room for her daughter.

"What's Maria doin' over there practically hidden by the counter?" She turned to Jubal. "I thought she was goin' ta be doin' the greetin' with ya?"

"She's doing what she likes. And working harder than any of us," Jubal said.

Seeing her folks, Maria came over, wiping her hands on the apron. "Gosh, that cider is so sticky! Dad, Ma . . . when you find a seat, I'll serve you some cider and donuts."

Kathleen eyed Maria's white apron that was splattered with cider. "Seems ya lost yer jacket," she commented.

"Oh, leave her be," Chester said, taking his wife's elbow.

Maria gave Jubal an exasperated look before turning to usher her folks to the rows of chairs.

Mike Harlow and his wife stopped in front of him. "Hey there, Jubal. I'm not old and I can get around still. Have those folks all come in by now? My wife and I are looking for seats."

Jubal held out the jug for the two tickets. "Come ahead. Hope you find some. This place is filling fast."

Mike smiled pleasantly as he took his wife's hand. Of all the guys at the old house the night Jubal's mother was slipped the *mickey,* Mike

Harlow was still the one that Jubal most wished was his real father. But he had a hard time believing Mike had joined in the terrible actions of the others. He sighed. Most of the time he just appreciated Clyde as his dad, especially lately. But seeing so many of the guys streaming past got him wondering all over again.

"Excuse me." Mary White, the town clerk, stood before him. "Are you ready for my ticket?"

Jubal held up the jar. In her wine-colored jacket and straight black skirt, the middle-aged woman was striking all dressed up for the performance.

"Thank you," she said. "Lizzy's event is worthy of a mention in the town report, so I wanted to be sure to come."

The rush of folks was easing some, so Jubal put the jar on a side shelf and announced, "Folks, just slip your tickets in the jug by the door."

After Father Mac's departure, Father Hebert was now the official priest at St. Anne's. When he came to the door, Father Hebert leaned over to Jubal. "Excuse me. I wonder if I might speak with Maria?" he asked.

Jubal pointed to the cider counter and the priest gave a nod of thanks. Maria stopped pouring as Father Hebert approached. Curious as to what the priest wanted, Jubal edged closer so he could overhear the two.

"You look like you have your hands full," Father Hebert was saying.

Maria looked at the jugs and cups scattered around the cider barrel. "I'll never look at cider the same way again."

"I can imagine," Father Hebert said. He looked around the room. "This is quite a gala affair that Lizzy has orchestrated."

Maria nodded. "So many people." As she surveyed the crowd, her face was tense.

"He won't come," Father Hebert said, reading her mind. "He wouldn't dare show up here."

Maria's shoulders relaxed. Jubal knew who she was worried about and scanned the crowd. If Freddie showed up, he wouldn't let the creep get anywhere near her. That would be the easy part. The hard part would be to refrain from socking the guy where it would hurt the most.

Father Hebert tipped his head and asked Maria, "Um, I've been wondering. . . . How come you've missed our weekly meeting? I've been little worried."

Maria brought the heel of her hand to her forehead. "Gosh!" She winced. "I totally forgot. I'm so sorry. I've been helping Lizzy get ready for this Appreciation Night."

"Well, I'm glad nothing was wrong." Father Hebert smiled kindly. "It's good you're helping your friend and keeping busy, Maria. Have a good time tonight. I'll see you next week?"

"Of course. Thank you," she said.

Father Hebert wandered off in the direction of the crowd, while Maria returned to her duty, and Jubal went back to his station. Seemed most everyone had arrived. Jubal was glad Maria planned to keep meeting with the priest, finding support even as she regained her footing.

When nearly everyone was seated, the cider and donut brigade went into action with Jubal's ma, Lizzy, Bert, and the other servers carrying trays of cider and boxes of donuts. As the refreshments were passed hand to hand down the rows, Jubal could hear Bert laughing loudly.

The townsfolk looked happy—jubilant, in fact. Like his full name, Jubal thought. A feeling of pride and belonging warmed him from the inside.

Just then he noticed a few folks remaining outside in the cold November night, standing a few feet from the town hall steps. Since Clem was helping as a server, Millie hung back, looking forlorn as ever as she shivered in her thin coat. Charlie Jones and Oscar Smith were with her, also seeming reluctant to join the crowd. Jubal knew, of all people, Lizzy would want them inside. He stepped out on the landing.

"Hey," he called to them. "Give me your tickets and I'll put them in the jar. The hall is full but I can find you some seats." He turned to take them into the town hall, now cozy from so many gathered together.

But Charlie paused on the steps, looking uncertain. "Uh . . . I seem ta have lost my ticket."

Jubal fished in his pocket and pulled out a few tickets Lizzy had given him earlier. "Here you go." He held out a ticket for Charlie.

"Well ain't that grand," Charlie said, grinning.

Millie and Oscar brightened as the three followed Jubal down the main aisle. After Jubal asked a few folks to slide over to close in the gaps, all three were seated. Soon cups of cider and donuts in paper napkins were passed to them. Later on, when Andrew and Trudy O'Mara came, Jubal could see that the assembly represented a true cross section of people from his town. Just like Lizzy had wanted. It was nearing seven o'clock, the start of the show, when Lady Lamont and Eugene arrived with Polly.

Jubal smiled and shook hands with Eugene. "Welcome home, buddy. Just in time!"

Eugene, in his military posture, bowed slightly. "It's good to be home, Jubal. What do you say we go out and drive in a few fence posts tomorrow while I'm here?"

"Might be tough with the ground half-frozen," Jubal responded.

They both laughed. Lady Lamont cleared her throat.

"Yes, dear," she said to Eugene in her husky voice. "I'm glad to have you back, even if for a little while." She took off her fur wrap and handed it to Jubal. "Would you mind putting this in the coatroom, Jubal? Lizzy has insisted that I extend a welcome to all and introduce the Chanticleer. I expect the radio personality is waiting backstage for me to start the show." As the heiress walked to the front of the hall, heads turned her way.

Jubal stood holding Lady Lamont's wrap and noted that Polly was looking quite nice all decked out in an amber tailored suit with her perfectly-styled hair. She wobbled slightly on high-heeled shoes. As Polly had hoped, she appeared to have snagged Eugene for what looked like a date.

Polly slipped her arm through Eugene's, giving the guy a flirty look that Jubal knew well. "Shall we find our seats, Eugene?" She looked back at Jubal. "We've talked a lot, Eugene and I. He's all caught up on Hayesville's crazy summer."

"I leave for a few months and all hell breaks loose," Eugene said. He put his hand over Polly's.

"Well, things are settling down, finally," Jubal said. "Hopefully for the better. Your being here is icing on the cake." He slapped Eugene lightly on the shoulder. "We'll have to go for a ride in my new woody. I'll fill you in on my side of things. But for now, I think Lizzy has saved you all some seats. Yes, even you, Polly."

Polly stuck out her tongue at him good-naturedly.

Jubal led them to the front of the hall where Lizzy stood. Lizzy scanned the rows and asked a few folks to slide over one chair, creating two seats together for Polly and Eugene. When Jubal returned to the door, a few stragglers came in with tickets in hand. He was about to close the doors when he was surprised to see two of Lizzy's three brothers arrive. Though it was November, neither wore shoes, but rather cutout tire treads held to their feet by rawhide. Their long, black hair was tangled but looked recently washed and their clothes were clean. Remembering how they disrupted the parade with their rudeness, Jubal's first reaction was to stop them from entering.

He waved his hands. "Sorry, you guys are too late. We're filled to capacity." As he blocked the doorway, they fished in their pockets and held their tickets high. The oldest glared at Jubal with a steely look of determination.

"Sister give us tickets. Said we could come."

"Oh." Jubal quickly thought. "You guys wait right here for a minute." He turned from the door, leaving the brothers on the steps, to see Clem coming down the aisle between the chairs.

Jubal hurried to Clem who was now near the back row. "Hey," he said in a low tone. "Lizzy's brothers are here. I wasn't going to let them in but they have tickets." He gestured towards the door.

Clem looked sharply in the direction of the entrance. "So they are." He narrowed his eyes. "I'll take care a' the little bastards."

Clem strolled stiffly over to Lizzy's kin. "Well, well . . . look at ya fellas."

The older one held the tickets out. "Sister give us tickets," he repeated, looking a bit sheepish.

"Did she now?" Clem took the tickets and held them up to the light. He looked back at Lizzy's brothers who shifted their feet. After a dramatic pause, Clem said, "All right. Ya can sit in the back of the hall." He leaned down close to the younger brother. "But if I hear one peep outta ya—one hoot or catcall—I'll have your rear ends booted from this here town hall back up ta LaFlam mountain with one swift kick. Ya understand?"

The brothers nodded. Since all the seats were full, Clem placed two folding chairs for them at the end of the last row, and they quietly took their seats. Lizzy must have seen, for she suddenly appeared with two cups of cider and two donuts.

"Ya both gonna watch yerselves?" she asked brightly, handing them the treats.

The boys nodded again.

A cloud passed over Lizzy's face. "Hey . . . my mimy, how's she doin'?"

The older brother fixed her with a glum stare. "Good 'nough. Big Daddy's been tannin' our hides instead, leavin' her be mostly."

"Well . . ." Lizzy paused. "I'm sure sorry for ya."

The two were silent, resigned to their fate.

"Tell Mimy— I miss her, would ya?"

"Yup, I'll tell her," the older one said.

"Well . . . take care," Lizzy said.

As she turned to resume her duties, Jubal saw that Lizzy's eyes were moist. He sighed and went to close the town hall doors, thinking how not many folks had it easy. He hadn't considered how Lizzy might miss her family. Crazy as they were, family was family.

As the program began, Jubal found two chairs in the coatroom and brought them out to sit next to Maria. She'd taken off her apron and laid it aside. Their jobs for the night were complete. Jubal glanced at her in surprise seeing her new outfit. She now wore a nice suit jacket, the green setting off her dark hair.

"You're looking extra special. Where have you been keeping yourself?"

"Under protective cover," she muttered.

"Well, you don't have to worry about me," he said. "I've apparently lost my knack with girls." He chuckled.

"Oh, I doubt it," she smiled. Lady Lamont took the stage and began the welcome and introduction.

The night's entertainment was a huge success. The Chanticleer, a portly man, told jokes and short stories, bringing on a chorus of laughter. Jubal saw that Maria laughed especially when the crowd was asked, "Why did the little boy bring hay to bed with him?" Silence followed. "To feed his nightmare." Though the joke was corny, the crowd laughed heartily at the punch line.

Betty Sweet played the guitar and sang a string of love songs, including "You Made Me Love You" and "I'll Be With You in Apple Blossom Time."

Hearing the tunes sung in Betty's country twang put Jubal in the mood for romance. He saw several guys slide their arms across their sweethearts' shoulders. He glanced over at Maria and was struck by her beauty as she listened to the music. Her hands were folded in her lap. He felt an impulse to do the same as those other guys and put his arm around Maria. But from what he knew of Maria's troubles, he wasn't about to test the moment. Sitting so close together, it suddenly felt strangely awkward between them. He kept his hands to himself. If the time should ever come, he'd have to let her make the first move.

Later on in the evening at the close of Betty Sweet's performance, she encouraged a sing-along to one of the most popular songs of the time, "You Are My Sunshine." The walls and rafters of the old town hall were filled with singing unlike any heard in a long time. Nearly two hundred in harmony felt as though the old building was being raised from its foundation: *You are my sunshine, my only sunshine, you make me happy when skies are gray. You'll never know dear, how much I love you. Please don't take my sunshine away.*

Though he wasn't much of a singer, Jubal chimed in and Maria joined too. He saw that the light in her eyes returned as she sang, a reminder of earlier that spring when she was full of energy, flashing her confident smile with a face full of freckles.

When the song ended, he checked on the LaFlam boys in the two folding chairs in back. They were behaving perfectly, though they appeared to be eating the last of the donuts and drinking several cups of cider, probably draining the barrel dry.

Jazz ended the program by playing the clarinet with Slag who was, for a change, dressed in slacks and a handsome red shirt. Slag tap-danced through several routines. Though Jubal often thought of Slag only as a shadetree mechanic, he had to admit the guy had real talent. The crowd agreed, clapping enthusiastically for Slag and his *clickety-clack* dancing shoes.

Before the evening closed, Lady Lamont asked Eugene to come up on stage to draw the winning name in the raffle. Everyone hung to their seats. Fumbling through tickets with his hand in the jar, Eugene pulled one out and read the name: "*Mary White!*" There was a collective gasp throughout the crowd. Bernice was heard saying, "Oh, she wins everything!"

The town clerk bounced to her feet and moved quickly to the stage. Shedding her normal serious composure, she faced the crowd and blew several kisses. "Thank you, Lady Lamont, Lizzy, and the IGA country store."

After Mary sat down and the commotion quieted, all eyes were on Slag, who for some reason had come back on stage all by himself.

"Next week as some of ya now know," he announced, "I'm headed ta Fort Bragg ta be trained fer the army. So as I'll have someone ta come home ta, I've asked Lizzy LaFlam ta marry me."

Jubal was more than taken aback to see his former love run up on stage. She jumped to hug Slag. Then she turned to the audience. "I just 'bout fell off my chair, but I said 'yes.' I'm the luckiest gal in town! Tomorrow after evenin' Mass, Father Hebert's gonna marry us!"

Everyone stood and wildly clapped, with a few loud whistles mostly coming from her brothers in the back. Jubal hesitated as the news sank in, until Maria elbowed him and he found himself joining. As he clapped, what felt like a small knot in his chest untied, and he opened his mouth and hooted along with the rest. Maria turned to him and smiled.

As the clapping and whistling and hooting continued, Jubal felt something slide next to his hip and forearm. Surprised and welcoming, he bent his elbow back and took Maria's hand in a firm grip.

Epilogue

December 7, 1941

Jubal had just begun evening chores when his father met him in the milk room. Leaning on his walking stick, his dad stood pale and shaken.

"We've been attacked!" Clyde weaved near a faint and leaned back against the milk cooler. "Son—"

"Attacked . . ." Jubal found it hard to form the questions. "When . . . where?"

"Pearl Harbor, Hawaii. Ships at the dock were bombed." His dad had warned of this for months, due to his close attention to the world news, and now it had happened.

Jubal felt suddenly vulnerable. Did this mean Hayesville could be invaded? He finished the chores as if in a daze. His dad, who seemed to need a distraction, limped around pushing hay in reach of the cows with a broom.

Around the supper table that evening, his family sat speechless and glum, with Benny occasionally rocking and moaning in fear. A few times, Rose put her hand on Benny's arm, her bangles clinking.

"They're far away, Benny," she said.

Later that night, the news on WGY drew Jubal and his family close around the Philco for any additional information. They were stunned to learn of the casualties. They also learned that not a single person, not even the U.S. government, knew of the planned attack.

The next day President Roosevelt gave a speech to Congress and the nation:

"Yesterday, December 7, 1941—a date which will live in infamy—the United States of America was suddenly and deliberately attacked by naval and air forces of the Empire of Japan. . . . I regret to tell you that very many American lives have been lost."

In response to the aggression, the announcement was made that day, the eighth of December: The United States was declaring war on Japan. Four days later, on December 11, 1941, Adolf Hitler's Germany declared war on the United States. The rapid-fire news shook all in town to the core. People down at the store wondered aloud what it meant for Slag, Eugene, and the other guys from Hayesville. Lizzy was much quieter than usual.

The selectboard met and in full agreement voted to form a Civil Defense Committee with a mission to keep Hayesville safe from attack by watching for enemy aircraft. The turret at Lady Lamont's mansion was designated as a watchtower, since it was the highest habitable point in town. News reports coming through the Philco described the country as seeming to unite with political and religious differences set aside in order to support the war effort.

Yet even with a war on, life on the farm required Jubal's ongoing attention. Before long, the short days of December were winding down to the end of the year.

One morning, a few days before Christmas, the wind blew in a blinding snowstorm. Jubal and Benny had slept soundly, unaware of the weather. When Jubal descended the stairs, he found his mother and father already seated at the kitchen table, drinking their coffee. The single, bare bulb hanging above the table cast a glow over the room. His folks had been unable to sleep through the banging of loose shutters outside their bedroom.

After breakfast, Jubal looked out the kitchen window through the faint dawn light at the whirling snow. "Geez. Even with Benny and me shoveling and the horses plowing, it will take most of the morning to get the milk truck up here in this storm."

His ma set down her cup. "Oh dear, I hope the truck can make it. If not, the creamery will have to be satisfied with two-day-old milk."

"Best get started," Jubal muttered. He motioned to Benny.

They went to pull on their jackets and boots while his folks returned to war talk at the breakfast table. When Jubal opened the door, the wind blew a cloud of snow into the entry.

His ma looked up in surprise. "Close that door, for goodness sake!" she called.

As he and Benny hustled out, he closed the door quickly behind them and looked down the drive with concern, for Maria had yet to arrive on Trueboy. Even as he had faith in the horse to carry Maria safely, he was worried about her riding in the near whiteout.

"Can you go to the barn and start chores?" he asked Benny. "I'll wait for Maria. I think I hear her coming." Though he couldn't hear anything but the howl of the wind, he didn't want to worry his uncle.

"Maria's gotta come soon," Benny said, looking worried anyway.

As Jubal walked down Harmony Hill towards Avery's, the dawn light remained obscured by heavy storm clouds. To stay on solid ground he cast his flashlight along the line of fence posts at the road's edge. Gusts of snow blinded him in total whiteness. He was beginning to panic. It was unlike Maria to be so late. In some places the drifts were waist deep and he struggled through the snow. He wondered how they would manage to clear a path for the milk truck.

Suddenly he nearly ran into the massive chest of Trueboy and stopped short. "Oh, here you are!"

Maria's voice was barely audible behind her scarf. "Are you lost or something?" She chuckled. Both she and the horse were blanketed in white.

"It's not funny!" Jubal huddled next to Trueboy's bulk to get out of the wind. "I was worried about you," he said, looking up at Maria.

"Sorry, I know. Dad insisted on winter shoes with cawks for Trueboy. The shoes came in an order yesterday. My dad, up earlier than usual, put them on before I left. He told me he couldn't sleep with this terrible storm going on. He was worried over all this ice we've been having."

"My folks were up early too," Jubal said. "There's plenty of ice beneath this snow, so I'm glad Trueboy has good shoes."

Maria looked around and then pointed. "Hey, I'll ride up close to that post and wire. If you grab my hand, I can help you climb aboard. We'll ride like we did when we were kids."

"I guess we're no longer kids," he said.

She positioned the horse near the post and extended her hand. Jubal scrambled up. The wet horse's back felt warm under his jeans as he slid close to Maria. He put both arms around her midsection. While Trueboy plodded ahead, Jubal held on to Maria tightly. Even as the wind blew, he nudged aside Maria's scarf with his chin and pressed his face against her exposed neck.

She immediately bent forward out of his reach. "Jubal, stop! Your chin is freezing!" She turned, her eyelashes coated in white. "This is serious. We don't want to fall in this awful storm, and we're already late for chores." But the tone of her scolding was light as she squeezed his arm with her mittened hand. He replied by wrapping his arm more snugly around her.

Just loving the moment, Jubal held on to his gal as they climbed the last part of Harmony Hill. Despite a wet seat in a blinding snowstorm, the backbreaking shoveling ahead of him that morning, and a world gone to war, he had faith that things would be okay. The barn lights flickered faintly in the distance through gusts of wind-driven snow.

Acknowledgments

Harmony Hill was truly a pleasure to write, especially as I had the valued input of a number of discerning folks along the way. This novel benefited greatly thanks to my editor, Amabel Síorghlas. She is truly a wordsmith, making for a smooth-reading text, and she had many helpful suggestions for improving point of view, characterization, plot, and setting. As a survivor, Amabel also contributed a woman's perspective on trauma and recovery as it pertains to the characters of Rose and Maria. Special thanks goes to Linda Hall for her artistry in painting the cover of Harmony Hill. In addition, Linda combed through the edited book, offering many insightful suggestions and catching lingering errors. A big "thank you" goes to the following folks who took the time to read and comment on the complete text: Mary Hall, Don Welch, Nancy Martin, Allen Marin, Amanda Legare, Flora Wallman, and Nancy Hill. I also wish to thank my book designer, Doni Hoffman, as well as Rachel Fisher at Onion River Press for applying their creative skills and attention to bring my book into print. Last but most noteworthy is my wife, Donna, who is a huge moral support and helped with the accuracy of this novel.

Bibliography

Brown, Sandra L. *Counseling Victims of Violence: A Handbook for Helping Professionals.* Alameda: Hunter House, 2007.

Freud, Sigmund, LL.D. *A General Introduction to Psychoanalysis.* Translated by G. Stanley Hall. New York: Boni and Liveright, 1920.

Jung, Carl G. *The Undiscovered Self.* Translated by R.F.C. Hull. New York: Signet, 2006.

Koehler, Rev. Theodore A. *The Christian Symbolism of the Rose: Our Lady and the Rose.* "Roses and the Arts: A Cultural and Horticultural Engagement." Central State University, May 8, 1986. Wilberforce, OH.

Roosevelt, Franklin D. "Speech by Franklin D. Roosevelt, New York (Transcript)." 1941. Franklin D. Roosevelt Library. Hyde Park, NY. Library of Congress. https://www.loc.gov/resource/afc1986022.afc1986022_ms2201/?st=text.

Turner, William. *The Essentials of United States History: 1912–1941, World War I, the Depression, & the New Deal.* Piscataway: Research & Education Association, 2000.

"World War II: Causes and Timeline." History. A & E Television Networks, LLC. 2021. https://www.history.com/topics/world-war-ii.